8 T166c v.4
ppan, Eva March, 1854-
30.
e Children's hour

W9-CDB-541

REF

R01167 39430

THE CHILDREN'S HOUR

IN FIFTEEN VOLUMES

ILLUSTRATED

VOLUME IV

Sir Galahad (page 54)

Sir Galahad (page 54)

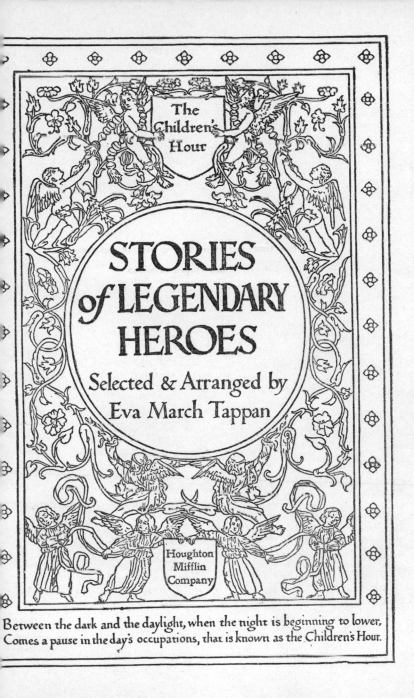

The Children's Hour

STORIES of LEGENDARY HEROES

Selected & Arranged by
Eva March Tappan

Houghton Mifflin Company

Between the dark and the daylight, when the night is beginning to lower,
Comes a pause in the day's occupations, that is known as the Children's Hour.

R0116739430

COPYRIGHT 1907 BY HOUGHTON, MIFFLIN AND COMPANY

ALL RIGHTS RESERVED

NOTE

ALL rights in stories in this volume are reserved by the holders of the copyrights. The publishers and others named in the subjoined list are the proprietors, either in their own right or as agents for the authors, of the stories taken from the works enumerated, of which the ownership is hereby acknowledged. The editor takes this opportunity to thank both authors and publishers for the ready generosity with which they have allowed her to include these stories in "The Children's Hour."

"The Age of Chivalry," by Thomas Bulfinch; published by Lothrop, Lee & Shepard.

"Robin Hood, his Book," by Eva March Tappan; published by Little, Brown & Company.

"The Song of Roland," translated by Isabel Butler; published by Houghton Mifflin Company.

"Gudrun, Beowulf and Roland," by John Gibb; published by T. Fisher Unwin.

"Stories of Charlemagne and the Peers of France," by Alfred J. Church; published by Seeley, Service & Company, Ltd., London.

"Heroes of Eastern Romance," by Alfred J. Church; published by Seeley, Service & Company, Ltd., London.

CONTENTS

PUBLIC LIBRARY   vii

MAY   1987

R01167 39430

TY & COUNTY OF DENVER

CONTENTS

PUBLIC LIBRARY

MAY 1937

TY & COUNTY OF DENVER

ILLUSTRATIONS

TO THE CHILDREN

IF you had landed on the shores of the North Sea fourteen or fifteen centuries ago, the sea guard would have come galloping down to the beach on his horse. He would have shaken his mighty spear and demanded, "Who are you? Where do you come from? Are you false spies come to search out our country? Do you mean peace or war?" If you had shown him that you were friends, he would have said, "Come to the hall where my lord abides. I will guide you, and my men shall watch over your vessel until your return."

Just imagine that you are walking up the road after the sea guard. You wear coats of mail, of course, made of rings closely interwoven. You have spears and bucklers and helmets and swords and battle-axes. They ring and clink and flash in the sunshine, as you march up the rough pathway. At last you come to a long building, where the lord of the land makes his home. As the guard leads you in, you see shields leaning against the walls and spears clustered in the corners. You see a row of stone hearths running up the middle of the hall. On the hearths are blazing fires, where great joints of meat are roasting. Along the sides of the hall are little alcoves, where the thanes, or followers of the lord, sleep. The guard leads you to the farther end of the room, where there is a raised platform, and presents you to his lord. The lord makes sure that you have come as friends, and then he asks you to join in the feasting. Great quantities of meat are eaten, and mighty drinking cups of mead are emptied over and over. Then the gleeman takes his harp and sings of some heroic deeds of old. If there has been a battle not long before, there are treasures to be divided; helmets, banners, horses and trappings, swords, spears, jeweled collars, and heavy rings of silver and of gold. The wife of the lord is present in her golden diadem and her richest robes; and she, too, makes gifts to the men whom her lord most delights to honor.

Such feasts as these were among the greatest pleasures of our ancestors. The men who received the gifts were always those who had been brave in battle, those who had risked their lives to defend their lord or to win treasures for their people. As the years passed, the gleemen began to sing songs of their courageous deeds. By and by, most of the names were forgotten, and the brave acts were all told as if they had been the work of some one hero. They grew bigger and bigger whenever they were sung. If a man had killed a bear, the song was likely to have it that he had overcome a giant. If he had killed a serpent, the serpent was sure to appear in the song as a dragon, then as a fire-breathing dragon; and so the stories increased.

Thus it was that the story of Beowulf grew. When the people who lived about the North Sea came over to England, they still sang the old hero songs. A little while ago, a thousand years or more, some one put these songs together and gave us the poem *Beowulf* as we now have it.

TO THE CHILDREN

Almost every nation has at least one hero of the olden time. The English have Beowulf, Arthur, and Robin Hood; the French have Charlemagne and his knights; the Spanish, the Cid, the Germans, Siegfried; the Scandinavians, Frithiof. Of course, people's notions of what makes a great man have changed a good deal since the early days. When we hear that a man is a hero, we do not ask now, "How many dragons has he killed?" or, "Did he ever dive to the bottom of the ocean to do battle with a sea-monster?" We expect our heroes of to-day to perform quite different exploits from these; but in several respects they and the noblest champions of old are alike; they are fearless in war, gentle in peace, kind to those who are in need of help, faithful to those to whom they owe allegiance, and they are ever sincere, upright, honorable, truthful, and unselfish.

HEROES OF THE BRITISH ISLES

BEOWULF

By John Gibb

THE land of the Danes was without a king. And there was confusion and disorder in all the land. Every one did what was right in his own eyes, for there was none to bear rule.

It happened at this time that there came a single ship to the land from across the waves. The people went on board the ship, and behold, there were no sailors, and no men in armor in the ship. No living thing was to be seen in it, save one little boy lying beside the mast. Around him were laid many precious treasures, rich coats of mail, shields and swords, and gold and precious stones. The men wondered when they saw the child and all the rich treasures which lay around him. But one said, —

"Surely the gods have sent this babe to our kingless land, that he might become our king."

The others hearkened to the voice of him who thus spake, and they made the child king of the Danes, and his name was called Scyld. He grew to man's estate, and became a mighty king, and subdued the peoples under him. All the neighboring peoples across the whale roads obeyed Scyld, the king of the Danes, and paid him tribute. He gave many gifts to his own people, and he was loved by them; and when an heir was born in his hall, all were willing that he should sit upon his father's throne, and that the Scyldings should rule over them forever.

Scyld himself became a very old man, and the time drew near for his departure into the peace of the Lord. Then said he to his comrades before he died, —

"When I am dead, place my body upon a ship, and send me forth on the sea even as I came."

The comrades of Scyld hearkened to the words of their king, and when he died they bore his body to the shore, where the ship was waiting. They laid the old king in the middle of the ship beside the mast, and upon his heart they placed a multitude of precious things. The ship itself they adorned with weapons of war, with coats of mail, and with all that became a warrior's bier. For they said, —

"It is not fitting that he, our king, should now go forth laden with less wealth than when he came to us, a solitary child."

The winds wafted the ship out to sea. It vanished in the distance, and none ever knew whither it bore the body of the king.

After the death of Scyld, his son reigned in his stead.

Now Hrothgar was king of the Danes, and he was of the race of Scyld, the king who came alone in the ship to the land. Hrothgar was brave in battle, and he gained many victories over his enemies. His people loved him, for he often sat upon the gift-throne, and gave away rings and other presents to his people.

Now it came to pass when Hrothgar was an old man, the thought entered into his heart to build a mighty house, in which to sit and drink the mead with his thanes, and where he might set up his gift-throne.

When the work was finished, all men admired it, and it was spoken of in many lands as the greatest palace in all the earth. The king gave to it the name of Heorot or the Stag, because its top was covered with pinnacles as the head of a stag with horns.

In Heorot sat the king upon his gift-throne, and from it he distributed to his heroes the wealth which God had given him. He was willing to give everything, this good king, except land and the lives of men; for these, he said, belonged to no one. Often did he feast with his heroes in Heorot; and in the evenings when it was dark outside, one could hear the noise of those feasting, the glad voice of singing, and the sound of the harp issuing forth from Heorot.

These sounds of mirth reached the ear of Grendel, and he was envious and sore displeased. Now Grendel was a wicked creature, who wandered about among the fens and moors, and dwelt in the dark waters. He was of the race of Cain, and was an enemy of God, and of all men that dwelt upon earth.

It came into the heart of Grendel to silence the voice of mirth and gladness in Heorot, and to turn it into mourning. He went to the hall under cover of the dark night. The heroes were lying in the hall fast asleep, for the feasting was at an end for the night. The fierce monster entered, and he seized thirty of the sleeping thanes and dragged them away with him. In vain did they struggle to escape his loathsome grip. He went away, carrying with him the dead bodies of those whom he had slain. Then was there joy in his evil heart, because of the ruin which he had wrought.

Great was the lamentation when morning came, and it was known what Grendel had done in the night. The old king was sorely afflicted, and sat in sorrow. Next night Grendel returned to the hall, and again carried off thanes to his den; and this he continued to do night after night, until the hall stood empty, for none feasted in it any longer. Yet Grendel never approached the gift-throne where Hrothgar sat; for this the Creator forbade, who wished not that evil should befall the king. But he wandered through the land under cover of the night, and wherever he found one in lone places on the misty moors, he seized him and dragged him to his den. Many a tired warrior and brave young man disappeared, and no one ever saw them again.

For many years Grendel went throughout the land, destroying the great and the lowly, the old and the young, among the Danes. The king and his counselors were filled with grief and perplexity. Often they took counsel together, but they knew not how to deliver the land from this destroyer who walked in the darkness. They went to the temples, and with many words besought the Destroying Spirit to save them. They prayed to the Destroying Spirit, for they were heathen, and they were ignorant of the Lord God their Creator. They knew not how to honor and serve Him.

It came to the ears of Beowulf, in Gotland, what deeds Grendel had done in the land of the Danes, and how he had filled the land with lamentation and mourning.

Now Beowulf was a thane of Hygelac, the king of the Geatas. There was none like unto him for strength and for valor in all the land. And when Beowulf heard of the sorrow of Hrothgar, he said, —

"Make ready for me a good sea-boat. I will go across the swan's path to the help of the noble prince who is in need of me."

The Geatas loved Beowulf, but they did not seek to dissuade him. They knew that he was a strong hero, who had done many mighty deeds, and they said, —

"Of a surety Beowulf will deliver the king of the Danes."

Beowulf then chose fourteen fighting men as his comrades in the adventure. Soon their ship floated on the waves, and the sailors climbed up its sides. The bright armor was taken on board, and the ship was shoved forth from the land.

Wafted by the wind, the ship passed over the waves like a swift bird. On the next morning the sailors looked forth, and behold, steep mountains and white cliffs glittering in the sunlight. They knew that they had reached the land of the Danes, and they guided the ship to the shore. They brought forth their coats of mail from the bottom of the ship, and they clad themselves in armor. They stepped forth upon the sands, and tied their ship to the land.

The warder of the land, whose duty it was to watch the cliffs lest any enemy should approach, saw the mailed warriors come on shore. He tarried not, but rode to the shore to learn who they were. As soon as he met them he spake, saying, —

7

"Make your names known to me quickly, bold men, who have come to this Danish land. I am here to see that none do mischief. Never saw I a form so mighty as that of the earl who leads you. He is not one, I suppose, who stays at home, but one who loves to travel in search of adventures. I must know who you all are, and whence you come, before you leave the shore."

Beowulf answered and said, "We are of the people of the Geatas, and subjects of Hygelac, king of Gotland. My father's name was Ecgtheow, a prince who was well known in many lands. We have come from our own land to render help to the lord of the Danes. For it has come to our ears what things the land is suffering through Grendel, and what he has done in the dark nights."

The warder answered, "If you come as friends to the lord of the Danes, I will be your guide to him. And I will command my comrades to guard your ship, that no one injure it in your absence."

The warder then led the Geatas towards the great hall in which King Hrothgar dwelt. When they saw it they wondered greatly, for never had their eyes seen a palace so splendid before. As soon as they were in sight of it, the warder turned his horse's head, and bade them farewell, saying, —

"May God Almighty guard you. It is time for me to go. I must return to the shore to keep watch against the enemy."

The Geatas laid their shields against the wall of the palace, and they piled their ashen spears together in a sheaf. They entered the hall. Straightway one of

"MAKE YOUR NAMES KNOWN TO ME QUICKLY, BOLD MEN"

BEOWULF

King Hrothgar's warriors, named Wulfgar, came to them and said, —

"Whence come you, men of war, clad in shirts of iron, and with weapons of war in your hands? You are no exiles, but men seeking for adventures."

Beowulf answered, "We are comrades of Hygelac, king of Gotland. My name is Beowulf. I would speak with your King Hrothgar."

Wulfgar went to seek King Hrothgar, and he found the old gray-headed man sitting among his carls. He addressed him, saying, —

"There have come strangers to our land from a far country. They are called Geatas, and their leader is one named Beowulf. He desires to speak with thee. I counsel thee, O King, not to refuse his petition, for he and his followers look like earls in their splendid war-shirts."

Then Hrothgar said, "Has Beowulf come thither? I knew him as a boy, and I have since heard of him oftentimes. Men say that there is the strength of thirty men in the grip of his fist. The holy God has surely sent him to help us against Grendel. Tell him to come quickly into our presence, and say to him that he is right welcome."

Wulfgar reported the words of King Hrothgar to Beowulf and to his companions. He said to them, —

"You may enter the presence of the king clad in your shirts of war, but leave behind here, I pray you, your shields and spears."

The chieftain of the Geatas arose and followed Wulfgar into the presence of the king of the Danes.

9

His followers went along with him, save those he left behind to guard the shields and spears.

The heroes entered the hall of Heorot, where upon a lofty seat sat Hrothgar ready to receive them. Beowulf spake and said, —

"Hail to thee, Hrothgar, king of the Danes! I am the kinsman and the thane of Hygelac, king of the Geatas. The deeds of Grendel became known to me when I was dwelling at home, and wise men counseled me to go to your help. I am strong, and have done many mighty deeds. It was I that destroyed the Jotuns, and who slew the Nicors by night. Alone will I meet this wretch Grendel. I ask this one favor of thee, O King, that thou wilt commit to me and to my companions the task of cleansing Heorot from the foul foe."

Hrothgar answered and said, "Thou hast come as a defense to my land, Beowulf. I am filled with sorrow and shame. Grendel has robbed me of my warriors, and no one dare any more tarry in Heorot after the light of the sun departs. Thou art welcome, since thou hast come to meet the destroyer. Sit down on the benches of the hall, and join in our feasting before thou goest to encounter the enemy."

A bench was cleared in the hall for Beowulf and for his companions, and they sat down and drank the bright ale which was poured out for them from the flagon. A bard raised his voice and sang with a clear voice, and all the warriors rejoiced together, and there was great gladness throughout the hall.

But Hunferth, the son of Ecglaf, who sat at the feet

of King Hrothgar, was displeased. He was grieved that any hero should come to the land boasting that he could do what no one among the Danes could do. He said scornfully to Beowulf, —

"Tell me, art thou the Beowulf whom Breca overcame in a swimming match? I heard the tale. You both ventured out like foolish men among the waves in the days of winter. For seven nights you swam together, but Breca was the stronger. Thou wilt have a worse defeat shouldst thou venture to meet Grendel in the darkness of the night."

Beowulf answered and said, "Hunferth, my friend, thou hast drunken too much beer. Breca never overcame me in swimming, nor did any one. But if thou wouldst hear the tale, thou shalt have it. Breca and I were boys at the time, and we swam out on the wintry sea, with naked swords in our hands to defend ourselves against the sea monsters. For five nights we were together upon the waves, and he could not pass me. The cold north wind blew, and there came a great storm upon the sea, and we were parted. In the darkness there came up from the bottom of the sea one of the monsters that dwell there, and it seized me and dragged me down into the deep waters. The coat of mail which I wore protected me, and I stabbed the wretch with my sword. But a great multitude of other sea monsters set upon me while I was at the bottom of the sea. I stabbed them all with my sword. When it became morning, and the sun rose, they were all washed ashore by the waves, and lay dead upon the sands. My sword had put them to sleep. Never afterwards did they hinder the sailors on their course. Afterwards I continued my journey, although I was wearied, and at length the waves cast me upon the land of the Finns. I never heard that thou didst deeds such as these, Hunferth, nor Breca either. Thou didst slay thy own brothers, I know, for which thou shalt suffer the vengeance of Heaven. Hadst thou been such a hero as thou vauntest thyself, Grendel would not have laid waste the hall of thy lord. But I, a Geat, will soon show what a brave man can do, and all men will sit down cheerfully to the mead benches in this hall when they hear that Grendel is dead."

Hrothgar was well pleased when he heard the bold words of Beowulf, for the shepherd of the Danes put confidence in his promise.

Then entered the hall Waltheow, Hrothgar's queen; and she took the beer cup in her hand, and handed it first to the king, who drank of it joyfully; then she passed it round among the other heroes. She offered it also to Beowulf. He took it from her hand and drank, saying, —

"I came to thy land to do a deed of might in thy hall. To-night I shall surely finish it or end my life."

Hrothgar now rose from his seat to go to rest for the night. All the other Danes rose to go with him. Before he left he addressed Beowulf, saying, —

"Never did I before intrust this royal house to the keeping of a stranger. Guard it well. Be wakeful. Quit thee like a man. Farewell."

There were now none left in Heorot save Beowulf and his companions. Beowulf took off his coat of mail and gave it to his attendant. He gave to him also his sword and his shield, saying to him, —

"I will not meet Grendel with weapons of war, for he knows not how to use them."

He then laid himself down upon a bench, and placed his head upon the bolster. The other Danes did the same.

Meanwhile Grendel was coming up from the misty moors to work ruin. When he reached Heorot he found the doors closed. They were fastened with bars of iron. He tore them open with his great strength, and entered the hall. He pressed forward quickly to the place where the heroes lay. From his eyes there issued forth in the darkness a light like unto fire. He saw the warriors lying asleep, and he laughed in his wicked heart, for he promised himself a feast. He seized the nearest sleeping warrior and tore him to pieces. Bit by bit he devoured his flesh and drank his blood. He then advanced towards Beowulf. The hero was watching him. Raising himself up from his couch, and leaning upon his arm, he seized the hand of Grendel. Never before had Grendel felt a grip so terrible. Fear took hold of him, and he turned to flee. But Beowulf rose to his feet, and held him fast in his grasp of iron. Terrible was the struggle between Grendel and Beowulf. The hall shook with it, the ale was spilt, and all the benches fell. The Geatas awoke from their slumber; they drew their swords and hastened to the help of their lord, but no steel, however sharp, could pierce the hide of Grendel. Presently there was heard a wild yell of pain throughout the hall, and

Grendel fled away, having escaped the grasp of Beowulf; but when the heroes looked, behold, the arm and hand of Grendel were in Beowulf's hand. It was torn from his shoulder. Sore wounded and sick unto death, the evil monster hastened to the dark pool among the fens where he had his dwelling-place.

In the morning the Danish warriors came in crowds to the gift-hall to Heorot, to learn what had happened in the darkness. Right glad they were to hear the tale of the Geatas. Some mounted their horses and followed the traces of Grendel. They rode to the dark pool where he dwelt. The dark waves were disturbed, and colored with blood, and they said one to another, —

"Grendel has breathed out his heathen soul."

They rode back joyfully. Sometimes they ran races. They talked of the brave deed and of Beowulf; and one of the king's thanes, who had a store of such, told stories of great deeds that were wrought by other heroes in olden times.

Then was told to Hrothgar what had taken place, and he went into the hall. He lifted up his eyes towards the high golden roof, and behold, as a trophy of the fight, there hung the arm of Grendel.

The king was glad, and he said to Beowulf, "Thou hast done a deed which all the might and wisdom of man was not able to accomplish. The mother who bore thee may well be proud of thee, Beowulf. Best of men, I love thee as my son. Ask what thou wilt of me, and I will give it. There is nothing I am not willing to give thee."

Beowulf replied, "Willingly have I served thee in

this matter, O King. Would that I had been able to hinder Grendel from going away! But the wretch will not live much longer. Pain will hold him in its deadly grasp until he dies in his den. It is the doom which the pure Creator has appointed for him on account of his crimes."

All looked with wonder upon the hand of Grendel aloft upon the roof. The nails on the fingers were hard as steel. Hunferth, the son of Ecglaf, was silent as he gazed on that hand. By the commandment of the king, Heorot was made ready, for he desired to give a great feast because of the victory of Beowulf. The hall was much shaken and broken, and had it not been for the iron bolts by which it was fastened, it would have fallen when Beowulf and Grendel strove together.

Now were the walls adorned with fair cloth of gold, and with many ornaments. The warriors entered in crowds to the feast, and sat down together on the benches. All gazed on Beowulf, and talked of his mighty deeds. The king brought forth his best gifts, and bestowed them upon the hero. The queen, too, did not forget to reward him. She gave him precious raiment, and she hung around his neck a collar of gold, saying, —

"Receive and wear, dear Beowulf, this collar of gold. Wear this raiment which I give to thee. May all young men follow thy example! Thou shalt be held in honor as long as thou livest for what thou hast done."

The song was sung and the tale was often told within the hall that evening, and the heroes were joyful together.

At length the hall was cleared of the ale benches, and beds and bolsters were spread upon the floor. The heroes desired to spend the night there. They feared Grendel no longer.

But Beowulf did not remain in the hall, because another lodging was made ready for him.

They sank to sleep weary with feasting, and no care or fear kept them awake. But one there paid dearly for his slumber. Grendel's avenger was near. His mother, a wretched woman of the race of Cain, came up from the cold streams in which she dwelt towards Heorot. She burst into the hall among the sleeping Danes. She was in haste, for her heart was less bold than Grendel's, and she wished to escape quickly. She seized that one of the heroes who lay nearest to her, and hastened away with him to the fens. He whom she seized was Æschere, the well-beloved counselor of Hrothgar.

In the morning there was again loud lamentation in Heorot, and in all the dwellings of the Danes, when it was known that Æschere was dead. The old king was greatly troubled in mind, and he sent for Beowulf. And when Beowulf came the king said to him, —

"Sorrow has again fallen upon the Danes. Æschere is dead — he who knew all the secrets of my heart, and who always stood by me in the day of battle."

Beowulf said, "By whom was the deed done, O King?"

Hrothgar answered, "I know who the fiend is, for I have heard men say that often when it was getting dark two forms were seen upon the misty moors. The one

16

was like unto a man, only of larger form — that was
Grendel; the other like unto a wretched woman. She
was his mother, and has done the deed. I know their
home. It is not more than a mile distant. It is in a
dark lake overshadowed by trees. Into that lake the
stag will not plunge, even although the hounds are close
upon it, so fearful and unholy is the place. Thou art
brave and strong, Beowulf; go to the place and seek the
hateful being who has wrought the evil. If thou dost
succeed, rich shall be thy reward."

Beowulf answered the king, and said, "Grieve not,
O wise King. It is better to avenge a friend than to
grieve for him. The end of life comes to us all. But
while we live we must do brave deeds and execute
justice. This is best for those who will come after.
Arise quickly, O King, and let us go and search for
Grendel's mother. I promise thee she shall not escape
me, although she takes refuge in the dark wood or in
the deep waters."

The old king arose from his seat when he heard
the words of Beowulf, and gave thanks to God. He
shouted to his attendants, —

"Bring forth my horse quickly."

Hrothgar's horse was brought forth ready bridled.
He mounted and set out along with Beowulf and a
company of chosen men. They traced the footsteps of
the evil being through the forest walks and across the
dark moor. By a lonely path they found their way to
the lake where the evil ones dwelt. Lying upon a rock
they found the head of Æschere. They sat down and
watched the water. They could see that it was mingled

with blood. And they saw swimming in the water many hideous snakes, and sea-dragons of hideous form. On the rock near were other monsters lying. When these heard the sound of the horns of Hrothgar's men, they darted into the waters. But one of the Geatas took his bow and shot forth an arrow, which struck one of the creatures and wounded it. They dragged it out with a hook, and all looked with wonder on the hideous beast. Beowulf now prepared to explore the waters. He put on his shirt of mail. Upon his head he placed his helmet. In his hand he took the good sword Hrunting. Now Hrunting was the sword of Hunferth, the son of Ecglaf, the same who, drunken with beer, spake proud words to Beowulf. But Hunferth remembered not his former enmity, and lent his sword Hrunting to Beowulf as to a better warrior. When he was armed, Beowulf spake to Hrothgar and said, —

"Wise Prince, I am now ready for my journey. Thou didst promise to be a father unto me, and I beseech thee to protect my thanes should death snatch me away. Send to my Lord Hygelac all the gold and the rich gifts which thou gavest me, that he may know that I found in thee a generous giver."

Having said these words, Beowulf plunged into the water and disappeared among the dark waves. It was long till he found the bottom, so deep did it lie. Soon Grendel's mother discovered that a man had invaded her dark abode. She rushed upon him to destroy him. She took him in her fierce grasp, but the mail-shirt resisted her fingers, and she could not pierce his body. Then she dragged him along to her den. He looked

18

up, and behold, a light as of fire shining above, and he could see the roof and all that was within the den. He grasped his sword, and rushing at the she-wolf, he sought to run her through the body. But the good sword Hrunting could not pierce her skin. Beowulf then grasped her by the shoulder, and sought to overthrow her. And they struggled for life and death within the den. At length Beowulf threw her down, but soon she rose again, and seizing him with a terrible grip, she cast him upon the floor of the den. Then she placed her knee upon his breast, and taking a knife from her bosom she sought to stab him. But the mail-shirt of Beowulf stopped the knife. By the protection of God was he saved, and he threw the fierce woman off, and rose again to his feet.

Beowulf looked round the den, and behold, he saw hanging upon the wall an ancient sword. It was a sword that had belonged to the giants of old — a mighty blade, and strong to smite. He reached forth his hand and seized it, for he thought that he would once more strike for his life. He then smote the woman heavily upon the neck, and it spouted out blood, and she sank dead upon the floor. Beowulf looked at his bloody sword, and at the deed which he had done, and he rejoiced greatly.

After the fight was over Beowulf looked round the cave, and behold, lying in a corner he observed the dead body of Grendel. He went up to it, and with a blow he separated the head from the body, for he wished to bear it to Hrothgar, that he might look upon the head of his enemy. But afterwards the blade of the old sword with which he had conquered his enemy began to melt away. Like ice in heat the blade melted away, for the poisoned blood of Grendel destroyed it. Nothing but the hilt remained in Beowulf's hand.

Meanwhile Hrothgar and his men were gazing earnestly on the water where Beowulf had vanished. They saw blood mingling with the bubbling waters, and they feared, and said one to another, —

"Alas! the water-wolf has destroyed the brave chief. We shall never look on him again."

After long waiting, Hrothgar and his Danes left the place and turned their steps homeward. Hrothgar was sick at heart and very sorrowful. But the Geatas still waited on beside the water, for they were loath to give up hope. After long watching, their eyes were gladdened by the sight of Beowulf swimming as a stout swimmer towards the land. He bore with him the mighty head of Grendel and the hilt of the old sword. His thanes gathered round him rejoicing, and they thanked God for his safety.

Four men took the head of Grendel, and placing it upon a stake, they bore the huge weight along. All went joyfully towards Heorot. And they bore Grendel's head into the hall, where the thanes were sitting drinking the ale. How greatly they all wondered when they saw the fearful sight!

Beowulf approached King Hrothgar and said, "I have brought to thee, O King, a trophy of the fight. It almost cost me my life, but I escaped. God was my protector. It was not with Hrunting that I did the deed, but with this old sword whose hilt is in my hand."

Hrothgar took the hilt of the old sword from the hand of Beowulf to examine it. He saw that there were ancient letters inscribed upon it telling of old strifes. It had belonged to the giants whom God destroyed in the flood.

Hrothgar then addressed Beowulf, saying, "Beowulf, God has given to thee high prosperity. Many winters have taught me wisdom. Refuse not, therefore, to listen to an old man's counsel. There was once a king in this land who was prosperous above all that went before him. But pride lifted him up, and he oppressed the Danes, the companions who sat with him at the board. He gave not rings according to justice, but with greedy soul kept all for himself. He brought disaster upon the land and upon himself. I have told this tale for thy learning. Be thou generous. Let not conscience, the soul's shepherd, sleep within thee, but watch against pride, and against the evil spirit. Now is the day of thy power, but forget not God, the Ruler of glory, and the eternal counsel. For death will soon come to thee, as to all men."

The king then asked Beowulf to go to his seat and join in the feast. It continued until night came, when all retired to rest.

Next morning Beowulf said, "I must now return to my own lord, King Hygelac. Let our ship be made ready."

He restored to Hunferth the sword Hrunting, saying, "It is a right good blade, a friend in battle."

He said not to him that it had failed in the fight with Grendel's mother, for Beowulf was a high-souled chief.

To Hrothgar Beowulf said, "Well hast thou entertained us, O King, and we shall not forget thy goodness. Should it ever come to my ears that thou hast need of my help, I will come quickly, with a thousand thanes behind me."

Hrothgar replied, "Beowulf, thou art mighty in deed and in word. There is none like unto thee among the heroes. None can discourse so wisely, and do such deeds as thou canst. Should sword or poison take away the life of thy Lord Hygelac, the youthful shepherd of the Geatas, they will not easily find a better king than thee."

Hrothgar gave to Beowulf many costly gifts as a reward for the services which he had done to the Danes. He then embraced him, and fell on his neck and kissed him, and they both wept, the old white-haired king and the young hero.

Beowulf then went to his ship, and his men with him. They took on board all the costly gifts of Hrothgar. They spread the sail from the mast, and the ship bounded through the waves, until it reached again the land of the Geatas.

Hygelac was glad to see his kinsman Beowulf return. He and his men were soon sitting at Hygelac's table, for so the king willed it. And the king said, —

"What adventures didst thou meet with, dear Beowulf, in the land of the Danes? It was against my will that thou wentest thither, for I thought it right that the Danes should fight their own battle with Grendel. But I give thanks to God that thou art returned safe and sound."

Beowulf told the king how he slew first Grendel and afterwards Grendel's mother. And all wondered; and there was a great feast, and much rejoicing and singing of songs among the guests. Hygelac's young queen, Hygd, entered the hall, and with her own hand bestowed gifts upon the heroes, and handed to them cups of ale. And Beowulf gave to his King Hygelac of the treasures which Hrothgar had given him. And on Hygd he also bestowed a gift, which he had brought from the land of the Danes, — a rich ornament of gold wrought by a very cunning workman.

It came to pass that after this Beowulf remained at home, by the side of his king and kinsman, Hygelac. But it entered into the mind of Hygelac to invade the land of the Frisians. He was wroth with them, and he desired to carry away much booty from their land. He went thither in many ships; but the people of the land and other peoples went up against him, and there was a great battle. And the Geatas were vanquished, and their King Hygelac was slain. And the enemy stripped him of his armor. But Beowulf they were not able to slay, for he fought his way through their ranks until he reached the water, and he swam back to his own land.

There was weeping and wailing in the land when it was known that King Hygelac was defeated and slain.

When Hygd, the queen of Hygelac, heard that her husband was dead, she said to Beowulf, —

"Be thou king in this land; for my son Heardred is but a child, and cannot rule over this great people."

But Beowulf said, "Not so. It shall never be said that I robbed my lord's son of his crown and his inheritance. But I will stand by him, and guard him, and counsel him, until he grows to man's estate."

This Beowulf did.

After the young king was grown to be a man, and was ruling over the Geatas, he was slain at a banquet by the stroke of a sword by one who bore him hatred.

On the death of King Heardred, Beowulf was chosen king of the Geatas, and for many winters he ruled in the land. Although he fought many battles, and made many wars, yet was his life preserved until he was an aged man.

In the old age of Beowulf there came a great terror in the land. There was an ancient hoard of precious things laid up in a cave near the sea. It had been gathered by those who lived in olden times. Into the cave fled a certain slave who was fleeing from the hand of a cruel master, and he saw the hoard, and knew that the things were precious. He took a cup of gold, curiously carved, in his hand, and he said, " If I return to my master with this in my hand, surely he will be gracious unto me." And he went to his master and gave him the ancient cup, and found grace in his sight.

But there lay beside the ancient hoard a dragon fierce and terrible, and it was the guardian of the hoard. When the dragon knew that the hand of man had been in the ancient hoard which it had so long guarded, it was wroth exceedingly. It issued forth from the cave, and went through the land in the night season. From its mouth there issued streams of fire, and no man could stand before it. Even the houses and cities of men were burned and blasted by its breath.

BEOWULF

The old King Beowulf heard what the dragon was doing to his land and his people. He said, —

"In my youth I fought many fights, and I will go and seek out this monster, and fight with him for my people's sake."

He bade farewell to his men, and went with a few attendants to the cave where he heard dwelt the dragon. He was clad in a coat of mail, and held his sword in his hand. He bore also a shield of iron, that he might withstand the fiery breath of the dragon. But he said to his men, —

"I would not bear sword and shield against this monster if it were possible. Rather would I meet him as I did Grendel of old, with the grip of my hand."

When they drew near the place where the dragon lay, Beowulf said to his followers, —

"Tarry ye here in the wood by the hillside; I will go alone and seek the dragon. I mean to gain the treasure in yonder cave for my people, or to die in the attempt."

The old king then went towards the cave beside the sea, with his shield on his arm, and in his hand the old sword with which he had fought many battles. He saw before him an ancient arch of stone, and issuing from it a stream of water, and the water was hot exceedingly, so that he could not dip his hand in it. He then knew that the dragon was near, and he shouted with a loud voice. The dragon heard his shout, and its rage awoke at the voice of man. It rushed forth from the den to destroy the bold fighter who had come to disturb it. As soon as it saw Beowulf, it vomited forth a stream of burning flame. But he sheltered himself behind his shield, and struck hard blows with his sword. Although he struck often and strongly, he was not able to pierce the thick scales of the monster. And the edge of his sword soon grew blunt with much striking.

Beowulf's men watched the fight from afar. They were hiding in the wood. Fear filled their hearts as they looked upon the fiery monster. One of them, Wiglaf by name, grieved when he saw his master fighting alone against the serpent. He said to the others, —

"When we received many gifts from our lord in the beer hall, we promised to follow him, and to stand by him in the fight. The time is come when our lord hath need of us. Let us go to his help against the fiery dragon, that seems ready to devour him."

Having spoken these words, Wiglaf ran down the hill to the aid of his lord. He shouted to him, —

"Dear Beowulf, strike hard as in the days of thy youth. I will help thee."

But the serpent again came upon them vomiting forth fire, and the shield of Wiglaf was quickly burned up. It was but a wooden shield that the hero bore. Then was he fain to take refuge behind the shield of his lord. The serpent pressed hard upon the two warriors, but Beowulf, mindful of his old deeds, fought mightily with his sword, and kept it off. But at length Naegling, Beowulf's sword, broke in his hand, and he could not longer keep the serpent at a distance. The foul beast drew near to him and clasped him in its horrid coils, so that the blood spouted from the body of the old king. And the fiery breath of the creature burned his hand. But Beowulf yielded not his life. He bethought him of the knife which he bore by his side, and drawing it he plunged its sharp edge into the serpent's belly. It fell dead, and the king was released from its embrace. But Beowulf was sore wounded, and sick unto death. He lay beside the dragon which he had slain, and the wounds which he had received burned as with fire; and he knew that the time had come for him to leave this world.

Wiglaf the thane went to the side of his beloved lord, and he gently bathed him with water, for he was covered with blood. Beowulf looked towards the mouth of the cave from which the dragon came forth, and behold, he saw stone arches strong and mighty, and he knew that they were the work of the giants of old.

Beowulf spake to Wiglaf, and said, "Death is coming near to me, Wiglaf, and had I a son I would now give my armor to him, but no son lives of mine. For fifty winters have I ruled over the Geatas. I have fought the battles of my people, and I have never sworn falsely, nor have I stained my hands in the blood of my kindred. Now I am sorely wounded, and sick unto death. But fain would I look upon the treasure for which I have given my life. Pray, Wiglaf, go quickly into the cave and fetch out some of the precious things, that my eyes may behold them before I die."

Wiglaf obeyed the command of the king, and fetched from the cave bright gold, and precious gems, and ancient cups made in the olden times. On his return he found his lord fainting, and at the point of death. He sprinkled him again with water, and again Beowulf opened his eyes, and he gazed on the beautiful things before him. He said, —

"I give thanks, O Lord of all, King of glory, for this treasure which I have gained for my people in the day of my death. I sorrow not that I have spent my life in the winning of it. Bid my warriors raise a lofty mound on Hrones Ness. Sailors at sea will behold it from afar, and they will call it Beowulf's Mound."

Beowulf then unclasped from his neck a collar of gold and gave it to Wiglaf. He gave to him also his coat of mail and his helmet, and bade him wear them.

"Thou art the last of my race," he said; "for fate has carried away the rest of my kindred, and I go to join them."

These were the last words of Beowulf, king of the Geatas. His spirit left his body and went forth to seek the dwelling-place of the true.

Wiglaf sat beside his lord, and he sought to revive him by sprinkling water upon his face, for he knew not that he was dead.

Then came forth from the wood, where they had been hiding, the unfaithful followers of Beowulf, who did not fight for their lord through fear of the dragon. They came as men ashamed. And Wiglaf reproached them with fierce words. He said to them, —

"The armor which you wear was the gift of the king. He gave it to you when you sat on the ale bench, that you might stand by his side in the day of battle. But he threw it away, for you came not to his help when the mighty beast assailed him. It is better for an earl to die than live the shameful life of a coward."

When it was known among the Geatas that Beowulf their king was dead, there was great sorrow and lam-

entation throughout the land. And men said one to
another, —

"Now cometh a time of trouble and strife, for the
king is dead, and there is no one to rule among us.
Alas! the Franks and Frisians will speedily hear the
tidings, and will greatly rejoice."

Many went out to see the dragon which Beowulf had
slain. It was fifty feet in length, and looked so fearful
that none would have approached it had it been still
living. Beside it lay cups of gold, ancient and precious
swords, and other precious things of ancient times.
Wiglaf spake to those who came, and said to them, —

"These precious things have been won with a great
price, the life of our dear prince, the shepherd of the
people. He, before he died, said many things to me;
and he asked me to say to his warriors to erect a lofty
mound at the place where his body was burned, to keep
alive his name. This he asked as a return for all the
kind deeds which he had done for his people during his
lifetime. Let us make ready to obey his commands."

Wiglaf asked seven thanes of the king to enter again
with him into the cave. One went before him with a
lighted torch. And they carried out what yet remained
of the hoard within the cave.

They pushed the body of the dragon over the cliffs
into the sea. In a wagon they bore away the treasure
of the cave, and the body of the dead King Beowulf was
borne to Hrones Ness.

A mighty funeral pile was there erected, for wood was
brought from many places to build it up. It was hung
round with helmets, with shields, and with coats of mail.

The warriors placed the body of Beowulf in the midst of it, and they kindled the pile with a blazing torch. Then there rose black smoke and bright flame, and the fire roared fiercely. The heavens seemed covered with darkness, and everywhere you might have heard the voice of wailing. At length all was consumed, the fire burned out.

Afterwards a mighty mound was erected on the hill beside the sea. The Geatas buried in it rings of gold and precious things, which they had brought forth from the cave.

Often in after days did the Geatas speak of their King Beowulf, and said, —

"Among the kings of the earth, Beowulf was the greatest lover of glory. He was mild and gentle too, and loved his people."

HEROES OF THE BRITISH ISLES

ARTHUR IS CHOSEN KING AND GETS HIS SWORD EXCALIBUR

By Thomas Malory

IT befell in the days of Uther Pendragon, when he was king of all England, and so reigned, that there was a mighty duke in Cornwall that held war against him long time. And the duke was named the Duke of Tintagil. And so by means King Uther sent for this duke, charging him to bring his wife with him, for she was called a fair lady, and a passing wise, and her name was called Igraine. And the messengers had their answers, and that was this, shortly, that neither he nor his wife would not come at him. Then was the king wonderly wroth. And then the king sent him plain word again, and bade him be ready and stuff him and garnish him, for within forty days he would fetch him out of the biggest castle that he hath. When the duke had this warning, anon he went and furnished and garnished two strong castles of his, of the which the one hight Tintagil and the other castle hight Terrabil. So his wife, Dame Igraine, he put in the castle of Tintagil, and himself he put in the castle of Terrabil, the which had many issues and posterns out. Then in all haste came Uther with a great host, and laid a siege about the castle of Terrabil. And there he

Uther and Igraine.

31

pight many pavilions, and there was great war made on both parties, and much people slain.

But the Duke of Tintagil espied how the king rode from the siege of Terrabil, and therefore that night he issued out of the castle at a postern, for to have distressed the king's host. And so, through his own issue, the duke himself was slain or ever the king came at the castle of Tintagil. Then all the barons by one assent prayed the king of accord between the Lady Igraine and him. The king gave them leave, for fain would he have been accorded with her. So the king put all the trust in Ulfius to entreat between them; so, by the entreat, at the last the king and she met together. Now will we do well, said Ulfius: our king is a lusty knight and wifeless, and my Lady Igraine is a passing fair lady; it were great joy unto us all and it might please the king to make her his queen. Unto that they were all well accorded, and moved it to the king: and anon, like a lusty knight, he assented thereto with good-will, and so in all haste they were married in a morning with great mirth and joy.

Then the time came that the Queen Igraine should bear a child. Then came Merlin unto the king and said, Sir, ye must purvey you for the nourish-
Birth of Arthur. ing of your child. As thou wilt, said the king, be it. Well, said Merlin, I know a lord of yours in this land, that is a passing true man and a faithful, and he shall have the nourishing of your child, and his name is Sir Ector, and he is a lord of fair livelihood in many parts in England and Wales. And this lord, Sir Ector, let him be sent for, for to come and speak with you; and desire him yourself, as he loveth you, that he will put his

own child to nourishing to another woman, and that his wife nourish yours. And when the child is born, let it be delivered unto me at yonder privy postern unchristened. So like as Merlin devised it was done. And when Sir Ector was come, he made affiance to the king for to nourish the child like as the king desired; and there the king granted Sir Ector great rewards. Then when the lady was delivered, the king commanded two knights and two ladies to take the child bound in a cloth of gold, and that ye deliver him to what poor man ye meet at the postern gate of the castle. So the child was delivered unto Merlin, and so he bare it forth unto Sir Ector, and made an holy man to christen him, and named him Arthur: and so Sir Ector's wife nourished him with her own breast.

Then within two years King Uther fell sick of a great malady. And in the meanwhile his enemies usurped upon him, and did a great battle upon his men, and slew many of his people. Sir, said Merlin, ye may not lie so as ye do, for ye must to the field, though ye ride on an horse-litter; for ye shall never have the better of your enemies but if your person be there, and then shall ye have the victory. So it was done as Merlin had devised, and they carried the king forth in a horse-litter with a great host towards his enemies. And at St. Albans there met with the king a great host of the North. And that day Sir Ulfius and Sir Brastias did great deeds of arms, and King Uther's men overcame the Northern battle, and slew many people, and put the remnant to flight. And then the king returned unto London, and made great joy of his victory. And then he fell passing sore sick, so that three days and three nights he was speechless; wherefore all the barons made great sorrow, and asked Merlin what counsel were best. There is none other remedy, said Merlin, but God will have his will. But look ye all barons be before King Uther to-morn, and God and I shall make him to speak. So on the morn all the barons with Merlin came tofore the king: then Merlin said aloud unto King Uther, Sir, shall your son Arthur be king after your days, of this realm, with all the appurtenance? Then Uther Pendragon turned him and said in hearing of them all, I give him God's blessing and mine, and bid him pray for my soul, and righteously and worshipfully that he claim the crown upon forfeiture of my blessing. And therewith he yielded up the ghost. And then was he interred as longed to a king. Wherefore the queen, fair Igraine, made great sorrow, and all the barons. Then stood the realm in great jeopardy long while, for every lord that was mighty of men made him strong, and many wend to have been king.

Then Merlin went to the Archbishop of Canterbury, and counseled him for to send for all the lords of the realm, and all the gentlemen of arms, that they should to London come by Christmas upon pain of cursing: and for this cause — that Jesus, that was born on that night, that He would of his great mercy shew some miracle, as He was come to be king of mankind, for to show some miracle who should be rightwise king of this realm. So the archbishop by the advice of Merlin sent for all the lords and gentlemen of arms, that they should come by Christmas even unto

The Wonder of the Sword.

London. And many of them made them clean of their life, that their prayer might be the more acceptable unto God.

So in the greatest church of London (whether it were Paul's or not, the French book maketh no mention) all the estates were long or day in the church for to pray. And when matins and the first mass was done, there was seen in the churchyard against the high altar a great stone four square, like unto a marble stone, and in the midst thereof was like an anvil of steel a foot on high, and therein stack a fair sword naked by the point, and letters there were written in gold about the sword, that said thus: Whoso pulleth out this sword of this stone and anvil is rightwise king born of all England. Then the people marveled, and told it to the archbishop. I command, said the archbishop, that ye keep you within your church, and pray unto God still; that no man touch the sword till the high mass be all done. So when all masses were done, all the lords went to behold the stone and the sword. And when they saw the scripture, some assayed — such as would have been king. But none might stir the sword nor move it. He is not here, said the archbishop, that shall achieve the sword, but doubt not God will make him known. But this is my counsel, said the archbishop, that we let purvey ten knights, men of good fame, and they to keep this sword. So it was ordained, and then there was made a cry, that every man should assay that would, for to win the sword. And upon New Year's Day the barons let make a justs and a tournament, that all knights that would just or tourney there might play: and all this was ordained for to keep the lords together and the commons, for the archbishop trusted that God would make him known that should win the sword.

So upon New Year's Day when the service was done the barons rode to the field, some to just, and some to Arthur pulls tourney; and so it happened that Sir Ector, out the sword, that had great livelihood about London, rode unto the justs, and with him rode Sir Kay, his son, and young Arthur that was his nourished brother, and Sir Kay was made knight at Allhallowmas afore. So as they rode to the justs-ward Sir Kay had lost his sword, for he had left it at his father's lodging, and so he prayed young Arthur to ride for his sword. I will well, said Arthur, and rode fast after the sword; and when he came home the lady and all were out to see the justing. Then was Arthur wroth, and said to himself, I will ride to the churchyard and take the sword with me that sticketh in the stone, for my brother Sir Kay shall not be without a sword this day.

So when he came to the churchyard Sir Arthur alighted and tied his horse to the stile, and so he went to the tent, and found no knights there, for they were at the justing; and so he handled the sword by the handles, and lightly and fiercely pulled it out of the stone, and took his horse and rode his way till he came to his brother Sir Kay, and delivered him the sword. And as soon as Sir Kay saw the sword he wist well it was the sword of the stone, and so he rode to his father Sir Ector, and said: Sir, lo here is the sword of the stone; wherefore I must be king of this land. When Sir Ector beheld the sword he returned again and came to the church, and there they alighted all three and went into the church, and anon he made Sir Kay to swear upon a book how he came to that sword. Sir, said Sir Kay, by my brother Arthur, for he brought it to me. How gat ye this sword? said Sir Ector to Arthur. Sir, I will tell you: when I came home for my brother's sword, I found nobody at home to deliver me his sword, and so I thought my brother Sir Kay should not be swordless, and so I came hither eagerly and pulled it out of the stone without any pain. Found ye any knights about this sword? said Sir Ector. Nay, said Arthur. Now, said Sir Ector to Arthur, I understand ye must be king of this land. Wherefore I, said Arthur, and for what cause? Sir, said Ector, for God will have it so: for there should never man have drawn out this sword but he that shall be rightwise king of this land. Now let me see whether ye can put the sword there as it was, and pull it out again. That is no mastery, said Arthur: and so he put it into the stone. Therewith Sir Ector assayed to pull out the sword and failed.

Now assay, said Sir Ector to Sir Kay. And anon he pulled at the sword with all his might, but it would not be. Now shall ye assay, said Sir Ector to Arthur. I will well, said Arthur, and pulled it out easily. And therewithal Sir Ector kneeled down to the earth, and Sir Kay. Alas, said Arthur, mine own dear father and brother, why kneel ye to me. Nay, nay, my Lord Arthur, it is not so: I was never your father nor of your blood, but I wote well ye are of an higher blood than I wend ye were. And then Sir Ector told him all, how he was betaken him for to nourish him, and by whose commandment, and by Merlin's deliverance. Then Arthur made great dole when he understood that Sir Ector was not his father. Sir, said Ector unto Arthur, will ye be my good and gracious lord when ye are king? Else were I to blame, said Arthur, for ye are the man in the world that I am most beholding to, and my good lady and mother your wife, that as well as her own hath fostered me and kept. And if ever it be God's will that I be king, as ye say, ye shall desire of me what I may do, and I shall not fail you: God forbid I should fail you. Sir, said Sir Ector, I will ask no more of you but that you will make my son, your foster-brother Sir Kay, seneschal of all your lands. That shall be done, said Arthur, and more by the faith of my body, that never man shall have that office but he, while he and I live. Therewithal they went unto the archbishop, and told him how the sword was achieved, and by whom.

And on Twelfth Day all the barons came thither, and to assay to take the sword who that would assay. But there afore them all there might none take it out but Arthur, wherefore there were many lords wroth, and said it was great shame unto them all and the realm, to be over governed with a boy of no high blood born. And so they fell out at that time that it was put off till Candlemas, and then all the barons should meet there again. But always the ten knights were ordained to watch the sword day and night, and so they set a pavilion over the stone and the sword, and five always watched. So at Candlemas many more great lords came thither for to have won the sword, but there might none prevail. And right as Arthur did at Christmas he did at Candlemas, and pulled out the sword easily; whereof the barons were sore aggrieved, and put it off in delay till the high feast of Easter. And as Arthur sped afore, so did he at Easter; yet there were some of the great lords had indignation that Arthur should be their king, and put it off in a delay till the feast of Pentecost. Then the Archbishop of Canterbury by Merlin's providence let purvey them of the best knights that they might get, and such knights as King Uther Pendragon loved best and most trusted in his days, and such knights were put about Arthur, as Sir Baudwin of Britain, Sir Kay, Sir Ulfius, Sir Brastias. All these, with many other, were always about Arthur, day and night, till the feast of Pentecost.

And at the feast of Pentecost all manner of men assayed to pull at the sword that would assay, but none might prevail but Arthur; and he pulled it out afore all the lords and commons that were *and is chosen king.* there: wherefore all the commons cried at once, We will have Arthur unto our king; we will put him no more in delay, for we all see that it is God's will that he shall be our king, and who that holdeth against it we will slay him. And therewithal they kneeled down all at once, both rich and poor, and cried Arthur mercy, because they had delayed him so long. And Arthur forgave them, and took the sword between both his hands, and offered it upon the altar where the archbishop was, and so was he made knight of the best man that was there. And so anon was the coronation made, and there was he sworn unto his lords and the commons for to be a true king, to stand with true justice from thence forth the days of this life. Also then he made all lords that held of the crown to come in, and to do service as they ought to do. And many complaints were made unto Sir Arthur of great wrongs that were done since the death of King Uther, of many lands that were bereaved lords, knights, ladies, and gentlemen. Wherefore King Arthur made the lands to be given again unto them that owned them. When this was done that the king had stablished all the countries about London, then he let make Sir Kay seneschal of England; and Sir Baudwin of Britain was made constable; and Sir Ulfius was made chamberlain; and Sir Brastias was made warden to wait upon the north from Trent forwards, for it was that time, for the most part, the king's enemies'. But within few years after, Arthur won all the north, Scotland, and all that were under their obeisance. Also Wales, a part of it held against Arthur, but he overcame them all as he did the remnant through the noble prowess of himself and his knights of the Round Table.

Then the king removed into Wales, and let cry a great feast, that it should be holden at Pentecost, after the incoronation of him at the city of Carlion.

Then on a day there came into the court a squire on horseback, leading a knight before him wounded to the death, and told him how there was a knight in the forest had reared up a pavilion by a well, and hath slain my master, a good knight, his name was Miles; wherefore I beseech you that my master may be buried, and that some knight may revenge my master's death. Then the noise was great of that knight's death in the court, and every man said his advice; then came Griflet that was but a squire, and he was but young, of the age of King

Arthur; so he besought the king for all his service that he had done him to give him the order of knighthood.

Thou art full young and tender of age, said Arthur, for to take so high an order on thee. Sir, said Griflet, I beseech you make me knight. Sir, said Merlin, it were great pity to lose Griflet, for he will be a passing good man when he is of age, abiding with you the term of his life. And if he adventure his body with yonder knight at the fountain it is in great peril if ever he come again, for he is one of the best knights of the world, and the strongest man of arms. Well, said King Arthur. So at the desire of Griflet the king made him knight. Now, said Arthur unto Sir Griflet, since I have made you knight, thou must give me a gift. What ye will, said Griflet. Thou shalt promise me by the faith of thy body, when thou hast justed with the knight at the fountain, whether it fall ye be on foot or on horseback, that right so ye shall come again unto me without making any more debate. I will promise you, said Griflet, as you desire.

Then took Griflet his horse in great haste, and dressed his shield, and took a spear in his hand, and so he rode a great wallop till he came to the fountain, and thereby he saw a rich pavilion, and thereby under a cloth stood a fair horse well saddled and bridled, and on a tree a shield of divers colors, and a great spear. Then Griflet smote on the shield with the butt of his spear that the shield fell down to the ground. With that the knight came out of the pavilion and said, Fair knight, why smote ye down my shield? For I will just with you, said Griflet. It is better ye do not, said the knight, for ye are but young, and late made knight, and your might is nothing to mine.

As for that, said Griflet, I will just with you. That is me loath, said the knight, but since I must needs I will dress me thereto: of whence be ye? said the knight. Sir, I am of Arthur's court. So the two knights ran together, that Griflet's spear all to-shivered, and therewithal he smote Griflet through the shield and the left side, and brake the spear, that the truncheon stack in his body, that horse and knight fell down.

When the knight saw him lie so on the ground he alighted, and was passing heavy, for he wend he had slain him, and then he unlaced his helm and gat him wind, and so with the truncheon he set him on his horse and gat him wind, and so betook him to God, and said he had a mighty heart, and if he might live he would prove a passing good knight. And so Sir Griflet rode to the court, where great dole was made for him. But through good leeches he was healed and saved. And the king was passingly wroth for the hurt of Sir Griflet. And so he commanded a privyman of his chamber, that or it be day his best horse and armor, with all that belongeth unto his person, be without the city or to-morrow day. Right so, or to-morrow day, he met with his man and his horse, and so mounted up, and dressed his shield, and took his spear, and bade his chamberlain tarry there till he came again.

And so Arthur rode a soft pace till it was day, and then was he aware of three churls chasing Merlin, and would have slain him. Then the king rode unto them and bade them, Flee churls! Then were they afeard when they saw a knight, and fled. O Merlin, said Arthur, here

Arthur is overcome by the knight at the fountain,

haddest thou been slain, for all thy crafts, had I not been. Nay, said Merlin, not so, for I could save myself and I would, and thou art more near thy death than I am, for thou goest to the deathward, and God be not thy friend. So as they went thus talking they came to the fountain, and the rich pavilion there by it. Then King Arthur was ware where sat a knight armed in a chair. Sir knight, said Arthur, for what cause abidest thou here, that there may no knight ride this way but if he just with thee, said the king: I rede thee leave that custom, said Arthur. This custom, said the knight, have I used and will use maugre who saith nay; and who is grieved with my custom let him amend it that will. I will amend it, said Arthur. I shall defend thee, said the knight.

Anon he took his horse, and dressed his shield, and took a spear, and they met so hard either in other's shields that they all to-shivered their spears. Therewith Arthur anon pulled out his sword. Nay, not so, said the knight, it is fairer that we twain run more together with sharp spears. I will well, said Arthur, and I had any more spears. I have enow, said the knight. So there came a squire, and brought two good spears, and Arthur chose one and he another; so they spurred their horses, and came together with all their mights, that either brake their spears to their hands. Then Arthur set hand on his sword. Nay, said the knight, ye shall do better; ye are a passing good juster as ever I met withal, and once for the love of the high order of knighthood let us just once again. I assent you, said Arthur.

Anon there were brought two great spears, and every

knight gat a spear, and therewith they ran together that Arthur's spear all to-shivered. But the other knight hit him so hard in midst of the shield that horse and man fell to the earth, and therewith Arthur was eager, and pulled out his sword, and said, I will assay thee, Sir knight, on foot, for I have lost the honor on horseback. I will be on horseback, said the knight. Then was Arthur wroth, and dressed his shield towards him with his sword drawn. When the knight saw that, he alight, for him thought no worship to have a knight at such avail, he to be on horseback, and he on foot, and so he alight and dressed his shield unto Arthur. And there began a strong battle with many great strokes, and so hewed with their swords that the cantles flew in the fields, and much blood they bled both, that all the place there as they fought was overbled with blood, and thus they fought long, and rested them; and then they went to the battle again, and so hurtled together like two rams that either fell to the earth. So at the last they smote together, that both their swords met even together. But the sword of the knight smote King Arthur's sword in two pieces, wherefore he was heavy.

Then said the knight unto Arthur, Thou art in my danger whether me list to save thee or slay thee, and but thou yield thee as overcome and recreant thou shalt die. As for death, said King Arthur, welcome be it when it cometh; but to yield me unto thee as recreant I had lever die than to be so shamed. And therewithal the king leapt unto Pellinore, and took him by the middle, and threw him down, and rased off his helmet. When the knight felt that he was adread, for he was a passing

44

big man of might, and anon he brought Arthur under him, and rased off his helm, and would have smitten off his head.

Therewithal came Merlin, and said, Knight, hold thy hand, for and thou slay that knight thou puttest this realm in the greatest damage that ever was but is saved realm; for this knight is a man of more by Merlin. worship than thou wotest of. Why, who is he? said the knight. It is King Arthur. Then would he have slain him for dread of his wrath, and heaved up his sword, and therewith Merlin cast an enchantment to the knight, that he fell to the earth in a great sleep. Then Merlin took up King Arthur, and rode forth on the knight's horse. Alas, said Arthur, what hast thou done, Merlin? hast thou slain this good knight by thy crafts? There lived not so worshipful a knight as he was; I had lever than the stint of my land a year that he were on live. Care ye not, said Merlin, for he is wholer than ye, for he is but on sleep, and will awake within three hours. I told you, said Merlin, what a knight he was; here had ye be slain had I not been. Also there liveth not a bigger knight than he is one, and he shall hereafter do you right good service, and his name is Pellinore, and he shall have two sons that shall be passing good men; save one, they shall have no fellow of prowess and of good living; and their names shall be Percivale of Wales and Lamerake of Wales: and he shall tell you the name of your sister's son that shall be the destruction of all this realm.

Right so the king and he departed, and went until an hermit that was a good man and a great leach. So the hermit searched all his wounds and gave him good salves;

so the king was there three days, and then were his wounds well amended that he might ride and go, and so departed. And as they rode, Arthur said, I have no sword. No force, said Merlin, hereby is a sword that shall be yours and I may. So they rode till they came to a lake, the which was a fair water and broad, and in the midst of the lake Arthur was ware of an arm clothed in white samite, that held a fair sword in that hand. Lo, said Merlin, yonder is that sword that I spake of. With that they saw a damsel going upon the lake: What damsel is that? said Arthur. That is the Lady of the Lake, said Merlin, and within that lake is a rock, and therein is as fair a place as any on earth, and richly beseen, and this damsel will come to you anon, and then speak ye fair to her that she will give you that sword. Anon withal came the damsel unto Arthur and saluted him, and he her again. Damsel, said Arthur, what sword is that, that yonder the arm holdeth above the water? I would it were mine, for I have no sword. Sir Arthur, king, said the damsel, that sword is mine, and if ye will give me a gift when I ask it you, ye shall have it. By my faith, said Arthur, I will give you what gift ye will ask. Well, said the damsel, go ye into yonder barge and row yourself to the sword, and take it and the scabbard with you, and I will ask my gift when I see my time. So Sir Arthur and Merlin alight, and tied their horses to two trees, and so they went into the ship; and when they came to the sword that the hand held, Sir Arthur took it up by the handles, and took it with him. And the arm and the hand went under the water; and so they came unto the land and rode forth.

Arthur gets Excalibur.

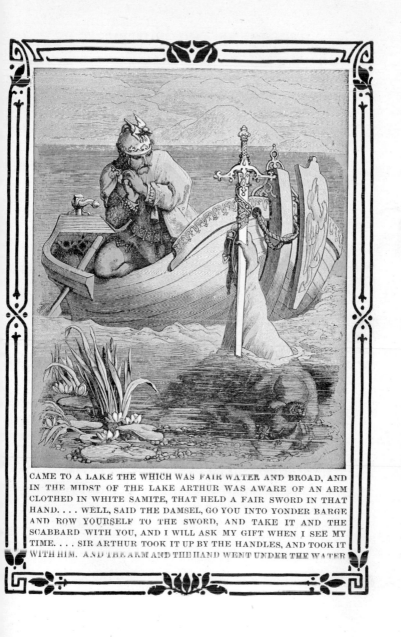

CAME TO A LAKE THE WHICH WAS FAIR WATER AND BROAD, AND
IN THE MIDST OF THE LAKE ARTHUR WAS AWARE OF AN ARM
CLOTHED IN WHITE SAMITE, THAT HELD A FAIR SWORD IN THAT
HAND. . . . WELL, SAID THE DAMSEL, GO YOU INTO YONDER BARGE
AND ROW YOURSELF TO THE SWORD, AND TAKE IT AND THE
SCABBARD WITH YOU, AND I WILL ASK MY GIFT WHEN I SEE MY
TIME. . . . SIR ARTHUR TOOK IT UP BY THE HANDLES, AND TOOK IT
WITH HIM. AND THE ARM AND THE HAND WENT UNDER THE WATER

THE INSTITUTION OF THE QUEST OF THE HOLY GRAIL

By Thomas Malory

AT the vigil of Pentecost, when all the fellowship of the Round Table were comen unto Camelot, and there heard their service, and the tables were set ready to the meat, right so entered into the hall a full fair gentlewoman on horseback, that had ridden full fast, for her horse was all besweat. Then she there alight, and came before the king, and saluted him; and then he said, Damsel, God thee bless! Sir, said she, I pray you say me where Sir Launcelot is? Yonder ye may see him, said the king. Then she went unto Launcelot and said, Sir Launcelot, I salute you on King Pelles' behalf, and I require you come on with me hereby into a forest. Then Sir Launcelot asked her with whom she dwelled? I dwell, said she, with King Pelles. What will ye with me? said Sir Launcelot. Ye shall know, said she, when ye come thither. Well, said he, I will gladly go with you. So Sir Launcelot bade his squire saddle his horse and bring his arms; and in all haste he did his commandment. Then came the queen unto Launcelot and said, Will ye leave us at this high feast? Madam, said the gentlewoman, wit ye well he shall be with you to-morrow by dinner-time. If I wist, said the queen, that he should not be with us here to-morn, he should not go with you by my good-will.

Right so departed Sir Launcelot with the gentlewoman, and rode until that he came into a forest,
Galahad is and into a great valley, where they saw an
knighted by abbey of nuns; and there was a squire ready,
Sir Launcelot. and opened the gates; and so they entered,
and descended off their horses, and there came a fair
fellowship about Sir Launcelot and welcomed him, and
were passing glad of his coming. And then they led
him into the abbess's chamber, and unarmed him,
and right so he was ware upon a bed lying two of his
cousins, Sir Bors and Sir Lionel, and then he waked
them, and when they saw him they made great joy. Sir,
said Sir Bors unto Sir Launcelot, what adventure hath
brought thee hither, for we wend to-morrow to have
found you at Camelot? Truly, said Sir Launcelot, a
gentlewoman brought me hither, but I know not the
cause. In the meanwhile, as they thus stood talking
together, there came twelve nuns which brought with
them Galahad, the which was passing fair and well
made, that unnethe in the world men might not find his
match; and all those ladies wept. Sir, said the ladies,
we bring you here this child, the which we have nourished, and we pray you to make him a knight; for of a
more worthier man's hand may he not receive the order
of knighthood. Sir Launcelot beheld that young squire,
and saw him seemly and demure as a dove, with all manner of good features, that he wend of his age never to
have seen so fair a man of form. Then said Sir Launcelot, Cometh this desire of himself? He and all they
said, Yea. Then shall he, said Sir Launcelot, receive
the high order of knighthood as to-morrow at the rever-

ence of the high feast. That night Sir Launcelot had passing good cheer, and on the morn at the hour of prime, at Galahad's desire, he made him knight, and said, God make him a good man, for beauty faileth you not as any that liveth.

Now, fair sir, said Sir Launcelot, will ye come with me unto the court of King Arthur? Nay, said he, I will not go with you as at this time. Then he departed from them and took his two cousins with him, and so they came unto Camelot by the hour of undern on Whitsun- *The siege perilous and the adventure of the sword.* day. By that time the king and the queen were gone to the minster to hear their service: then the king and the queen were passing glad of Sir Bors and Sir Lionel, and so was all the fellowship. So when the king and all the knights were come from service, the barons espied in the sieges of the Round Table, all about written with gold letters, — Here ought to sit he, and he ought to sit here. And thus they went so long until that they came to the siege perilous, where they found letters newly written of gold, that said: Four hundred winters and fifty-four accomplished after the passion of our Lord Jesu Christ ought this siege to be fulfilled. Then all they said, This is a marvelous thing, and an adventurous. In the name of God, said Sir Launcelot; and then he accounted the term of the writing, from the birth of our Lord unto that day. It seemeth me, said Sir Launcelot, this siege ought to be fulfilled this same day, for this is the feast of Pentecost after the four hundred and four and fifty year; and if it would please all parties, I would none of these letters were seen this day, till he be come that ought to achieve this adventure. Then made they to ordain a cloth of silk for to cover these letters in the siege perilous. Then the king bade haste unto dinner. Sir, said Sir Kay the steward, if ye go now unto your meat, ye shall break your old custom of your court. For ye have not used on this day to sit at your meat or that ye have seen some adventure. Ye say sooth, said the king, but I had so great joy of Sir Launcelot and of his cousins, which be come to the court whole and sound, that I bethought me not of my old custom. So as they stood speaking, in came a squire, and said unto the king, Sir, I bring unto you marvelous tidings. What be they? said the king. Sir, there is here beneath at the river a great stone, which I saw fleet above the water, and therein saw I sticking a sword. The king said, I will see that marvel. So all the knights went with him, and when they came unto the river, they found there a stone fleeting, as it were of red marble, and therein stack a fair and a rich sword, and in the pommel thereof were precious stones, wrought with subtile letters of gold. Then the barons read the letters, which said in this wise: Never shall man take me hence but only he by whose side I ought to hang, and he shall be the best knight of the world. When the king had seen these letters, he said unto Sir Launcelot, Fair sir, this sword ought to be yours, for I am sure ye be the best knight of the world. Then Sir Launcelot answered full soberly: Certes, sir, it is not my sword: also, sir, wit ye well I have no hardiness to set my hand to, for it longed not to hang by my side. Also who that assayeth to take that sword, and faileth of it, he shall receive

50

a wound by that sword, that he shall not be whole long after. And I will that ye wit that this same day will the adventures of the Sancgreal, that is called the holy vessel, begin.

Now, fair nephew, said the king unto Sir Gawaine, assay ye for my love. Sir, he said, save your good grace, I shall not do that. Sir, said the king, assay to take the sword, and at my commandment. Sir, said Gawaine, your commandment I will obey. And therewith he took up the sword by the handles, but he might not stir it. I thank you, said the king to Sir Gawaine. My lord Sir Gawaine, said Sir Launcelot, now wit ye well, this sword shall touch you so sore that ye shall will ye had never set your hand thereto, for the best castle of this realm. Sir, he said, I might not withsay mine uncle's will and commandment. But when the king heard this, he repented it much, and said unto Sir Percivale that he should assay for his love. And he said, Gladly, for to bear Sir Gawaine fellowship. And therewith he set his hand on the sword, and drew it strongly, but he might not move it. Then were there more that durst be so hardy to set their hands thereto. Now may ye go to your dinner, said Sir Kay unto the king, for a marvelous adventure have ye seen.

So the king and all went unto the court, and every knight knew his own place, and set him therein, and young men that were knights served them. So when they were served, and all sieges fulfilled, save only the siege perilous, anon there befell a marvelous adventure, that all the doors and the windows of the place shut by them self. Not for then the hall was not greatly darkened, and therewith they abashed both one and other. Then King Arthur spake first, and said, Fair fellows and lords, we have seen this day marvels, but or night I suppose we shall see greater marvels. In the meanwhile came in a good old man, and an ancient, clothed all in white, and there was no knight knew from whence he came. And with him he brought a young knight, both on foot, in red arms, without sword or shield, save a scabbard hanging by his side. And these words he said, Peace be with you, fair lords. Then the old man said unto Arthur, Sir, I bring here a young knight the which is of king's lineage, and of the kindred of Joseph of Arimathie, whereby the marvels of this court and of strange realms shall be fully accomplished.

The king was right glad of his words, and said unto the good man, Sir, ye be right welcome, and the young knight with you. Then the old man made the young man to unarm him; and he was in a coat of red sendal, and bare a mantle upon his shoulder that was furred with ermine, and put that upon him. And the old knight said unto the young knight, Sir, follow me. And anon he led him unto the siege perilous, where beside sat Sir Launcelot; and the good man lift up the cloth, and found there letters that said thus: This is the siege of Galahad the haut prince. Sir, said the old knight, wit ye well that place is yours. And then he set him down surely in that siege. And then he said to the old man, Sir, ye may now go your way, for well have ye done that ye were commanded to do. And recommend me unto my grandsire King Pelles, and say to him on my behalf, I shall come

Galahad achieves the adventure.

52

and see him as soon as ever I may. So the good man departed, and there met him twenty noble squires, and so took their horses and went their way. Then all the knights of the Round Table marveled them greatly of Sir Galahad, that he durst sit there in that siege perilous, and was so tender of age, and wist not from whence he came, but all only by God, and said, This is he by whom the Sancgreal shall be achieved, for there sat never none but he, but he were mischieved. Then Sir Launcelot beheld his son, and had great joy of him. Then Sir Bors told his fellows, Upon pain of my life this young knight shall come unto great worship.

This noise was great in all the court, so that it came to the queen. Then she had marvel what knight it might be that durst adventure him to sit in the siege perilous. Many said unto the queen, he resembled much unto Sir Launcelot. I may well suppose, said the queen, that he is son of Sir Launcelot and King Pelles' daughter, and his name is Galahad. I would fain see him, said the queen, for he must needs be a noble man, for so is his father; I report me unto all the Round Table. So when the meat was done, that the king and all were risen, the king went unto the siege perilous, and lift up the cloth, and found there the name of Galahad; and then he shewed it unto Sir Gawaine, and said, Fair nephew, now have we among us Sir Galahad the good knight, that shall worship us all, and upon pain of my life he shall achieve the Sancgreal, right so as Sir Launcelot hath done us to understand. Then came King Arthur unto Galahad, and said, Sir, ye be welcome, for ye shall move many good knights to the quest of the Sancgreal, and ye shall achieve that never knights might bring to an end. Then the king took him by the hand, and went down from the palace to shew Galahad the adventures of the stone.

The queen heard thereof, and came after with many ladies, and shewed them the stone where it hoved on the water. Sir, said the king unto Sir Galahad, here is a great marvel as ever I saw, and right good knights have assayed and failed. Sir, said Galahad, that is no marvel, for this adventure is not theirs, but mine, and for the surety of this sword I brought none with me; for here by my side hangeth the scabbard. And anon he laid his hand on the sword, and lightly drew it out of the stone, and put it in the sheath and said unto the king, Now it goeth better than it did aforehand. Sir, said the king, a shield God shall send you.

Now, said the king, I am sure at this quest of the Sancgreal shall all ye of the Round Table depart, and never shall I see you again whole together; therefore I will see you all whole together in the meadow of Camelot, to just and to tourney, that after your death men may speak of it, that such good knights were wholly together such a day. As unto that counsel, and at the king's request, they accorded all, and took on their harness that longed unto justing. But all this moving of the king was for this intent, for to see Galahad proved, for the king deemed he should not lightly come again unto the court after his departing. So were they assembled in the meadow, both more and less. Then Sir Galahad, by the prayer of the king and the queen, did upon him a noble jesserance, and also he did on his

The tournament.

helm, but shield would he take none for no prayer of the king. And then Sir Gawaine and other knights prayed him to take a spear. Right so he did; and the queen was in a tower with all her ladies for to behold that tournament. Then Sir Galahad dressed him in the midst of the meadow, and began to break spears marvelously, that all men had wonder of him, for he there surmounted all other knights, for within a while he had thrown down many good knights of the Round Table save twain, that was Sir Launcelot and Sir Percivale.

And then the king and all estates went home unto Camelot, and so went to evensong to the great minster. And so after upon that to supper, and every knight sat in his own place as they were to-forehand. The vision of the Grail. Then anon they heard cracking and crying of thunder, that them thought the place should all to-drive. In the midst of this blast entered a sunbeam more clearer by seven times than ever they saw day, and all they were alighted of the grace of the Holy Ghost. Then began every knight to behold other, and either saw other by their seeming fairer than ever they saw afore. Not for then there was no knight might speak one word a great while, and so they looked every man on other, as they had been dumb. Then there entered into the hall the holy Grail covered with white samite, but there was none might see it, nor who bare it. And there was all the hall fulfilled with good odors, and every knight had such meats and drinks as he best loved in this world; and when the holy Grail had been borne through the hall, then the holy vessel departed suddenly, that they wist not where it became. Then had they all breath to speak. And then the king yielded thankings unto God of his good grace that he had sent them. Certes, said the king, we ought to thank our Lord Jesu greatly, for that he hath shewed us this day at the reverence of this high feast of Pentecost. Now, said Sir Gawaine, we have been served this day of what meats and drinks we thought on, but one thing beguiled us, we might not see the holy Grail, it was so preciously covered: wherefore I will make here a vow, that to-morn, without longer abiding, I shall labor in the quest of the Sancgreal, that I shall hold me out a twelvemonth and a day, or more if need be, and never shall I return again unto the court till I have seen it more openly than it hath been seen here; and if I may not speed, I shall return again as he that may not be against the will of our Lord Jesu Christ. When they of the Round Table heard Sir Gawaine say so, they rose up the most party, and made such avows as Sir Gawaine had made.

Anon as King Arthur heard this he was greatly displeased, for he wist well that they might not againsay their avows. Alas! said King Arthur unto Sir Gawaine, ye have nigh slain me with the avow and promise that ye have made. For through you ye have bereft me of the fairest fellowship and the truest of knighthood that ever were seen together in any realm of the world. For when they depart from hence, I am sure they all shall never meet more in this world, for they shall die many in the quest. And so it forethinketh me a little, for I have loved them as well as my life, wherefore it shall grieve me right sore the departition of this fellowship. For I have had an old custom to have them in my fellowship.

And therewith the tears filled in his eyes. And then he said, Gawaine, Gawaine, ye have set me in great sorrow. For I have great doubt that my true fellowship shall never meet here more again. Ah, said Sir Launcelot, comfort yourself, for it shall be unto us as a great honor, and much more than if we died in any other places, for of death we be sure. Ah Launcelot, said the king, the great love that I have had unto you all the days of my life maketh me to say such doleful words; for never Christian king had never so many worthy men at this table as I have had this day at the Round Table, and that is my great sorrow. When the queen, ladies, and gentlewomen wist these tidings, they had such sorrow and heaviness that there might no tongue tell it, for those knights had holden them in honor and charity. But among all other Queen Guenever made great sorrow. I marvel, said she, my lord would suffer them to depart from him. Thus was all the court troubled, for the love of the departition of those knights. And many of those ladies that loved knights would have gone with their lovers; and so had they done, had not an old knight come among them in religious clothing, and then he spake all on high and said, Fair lords which have sworn in the quest of the Sancgreal, thus sendeth you Nacien the hermit word, that none in this quest lead lady nor gentlewoman with him, for it is not to do in so high a service as they labor in, for I warn you plain, he that is not clean of his sins he shall not see the mysteries of our Lord Jesu Christ; and for this cause they left these ladies and gentlewomen. And then they went to rest them. And in the honor of the highness of Galahad he was led into King Arthur's chamber, and there rested in his own bed.

And as soon as it was day the king arose, for he had no rest of all that night for sorrow. Then he went unto Gawaine and to Sir Launcelot, that were arisen for to hear mass. And then the king again said, Ah Gawaine, Gawaine, ye have betrayed me. For never shall my court be amended by you, but ye will never be sorry for me, as I am for you. And therewith the tears began to run down by his visage. And therewith the king said, Ah knight, Sir Launcelot, I require thee thou counsel me, for I would that this quest were undone, and it might be. Sir, said Sir Launcelot, ye saw yesterday so many worthy knights that then were sworn, that they may not leave it in no manner of wise. That wot I well, said the king; but it shall so heavy me at their departing, that I wot well there shall no manner of joy remedy me. And then the king and the queen went unto the minster. So anon Launcelot and Gawaine commanded their men to bring their arms. And when they all were armed, save their shields and their helms, then they came to their fellowship, which all were ready in the same wise for to go to the minster to hear their service.

Then after the service was done, the king would wit how many had taken the quest of the holy Grail, and to account them he prayed them all. Then found they by tale an hundred and fifty, and all were knights of the Round Table. And then they put on their helms and departed, and recommended them all wholly unto the queen, and there was weeping and great sorrow. Then the queen departed

The departure of the knights.

58

into her chamber, so that no man should perceive her great sorrows. When Sir Launcelot missed the queen he went into her chamber, and when she saw him she cried aloud, Oh, Sir Launcelot, ye have betrayed me and put me to death, for to leave thus my lord. Ah, madam, said Sir Launcelot, I pray you be not displeased, for I shall come again as soon as I may with my worship. Alas, said she, that ever I saw you! but He that suffered death upon the cross for all mankind, be to your good conduct and safety, and all the whole fellowship. Right so departed Sir Launcelot, and found his fellowship that abode his coming. And so they mounted upon their horses, and rode through the streets of Camelot, and there was weeping of the rich and poor, and the king turned away, and might not speak for weeping. So within a while they came to a city and a castle that hight Vagon: there they entered into the castle, and the lord of that castle was an old man that hight Vagon, and he was a good man of his living, and set open the gates, and made them all the good cheer that he might. And so on the morrow they were all accorded that they should depart every each from other. And then they departed on the morrow with weeping and mourning cheer, and every knight took the way that him best liked.

SIR BORS AND SIR LIONEL

By Thomas Malory

WHEN Bors was departed from Camelot, he met with a religious man riding on an ass, and Sir Bors saluted him. Anon the good man knew him, that he was one of the knights errant that was in the quest of the Sancgreal. What are ye? said the good man. Sir, said he, I am a knight that fain would be counseled in the quest of the Sancgreal: for he shall have much earthly worship that may bring it to an end. Certes, said the good man, that is sooth, for he shall be the best knight of the world, and the fairest of all the fellowship. But wit you well, there shall none attain it but by cleanness, that is, pure confession. So rode they together till that they came to an hermitage. And there he prayed Bors to dwell all that night with him: and so he alight, and put away his armor, and prayed him that he might be confessed; and so they went into the chapel, and there he was clean confessed: and they eat bread, and drank water, together. Now, said the good man, I pray thee that thou eat none other, till that thou sit at the table where the Sancgreal shall be. Sir, said he, I agree me thereto; but how wit ye that I shall sit there? Yes, said the good man, that know I, but there shall be but few of your fellows with you. All is welcome, said Sir Bors, that God sendeth me. Also, said the good man, instead of a shirt, and in sign of

The religious man and the scarlet coat.

chastisement, ye shall wear a garment; thereof I pray
you do off all your clothes and your shirt, and so he did.
And then he took him a scarlet coat, so that should be
instead of his shirt, till he had fulfilled the quest of the
Sancgreal. Then he armed him, and took his leave, and
so departed. So by evensong, by adventure he came to
a strong tower, and an high, and there was he lodged
gladly.

Upon the morn, as soon as the day appeared, Bors
departed from thence, and so rode into a forest unto
the hour of midday, and there befell him a *Bors meets
with his
brother Lionel
bound on a
horse, and
with a gentle-
woman in
distress.*
marvelous adventure. So he met at the departing of the two ways two knights, that led
Lionel his brother all naked, bounden upon
a strong hackney, and his hands bounden tofore his breast: and every each of them held
in his hand thorns, wherewith they went beating him so
sore that the blood trailed down more than in an hundred places of his body, so that he was all blood tofore
and behind, but he said never a word, as he which was
great of heart; he suffered all that ever they did to him
as though he had felt none anguish. Anon Sir Bors
dressed him to rescue him that was his brother: and so
he looked upon the other side of him, and saw a knight
which brought a fair gentlewoman, and would have set
her in the thickest place of the forest, for to have been
the more surer out of the way from them that sought
him. And she, which was nothing assured, cried with
an high voice, Saint Mary, succor your maid!

And anon she espied where Sir Bors came riding.
And when she came nigh him, she deemed him a knight

of the Round Table, whereof she hoped to have some comfort; and then she conjured him, by the faith that he owed unto Him in whose service thou art entered in, and for the faith ye owe unto the high order of knighthood, and for the noble King Arthur's sake, that I suppose that made thee knight, that thou help me, and suffer me not to be shamed of this knight!

When Bors heard her say thus, he had so much sorrow there he nist not what to do. For if I let my brother be in adventure he must be slain, and that would I not for all the earth. And if I help not the maid, she is shamed forever, and also she shall lose her honor, the which she shall never get again. Then lift he up his eyes, and said weeping, Fair sweet Lord Jesu Christ, whose liege man I am, keep Lionel my brother, that these knights slay him not; and for pity of you, and for Mary's sake, I shall succor this maid.

Then dressed he him unto the knight the which had the gentlewoman, and then he cried, Sir knight, let your hand off that maiden, or ye be but dead. And then he set down the maiden and was armed at all pieces, save he lacked his spear. Then he dressed his shield, and drew out his sword, and Bors smote him so hard that it went through his shield and haberjon on the left shoulder; and through great strength he beat him down to the earth; and at the pulling out of Bors' spear there he swooned.

He rescues the gentlewoman.

Then came Bors to the maid, and said, How seemeth it you? Of this knight ye be delivered at this time. Now Sir, said she, I pray you lead me there as this knight had me. — So shall I do gladly: and took the horse of the wounded knight, and set the gentlewoman upon him, and so brought her as she desired. Sir knight, said she, ye have better sped than ye weened, for if ye had not saved me, five hundred men should have died for it. — What knight was he that had you in the forest? — By my faith, said she, he is my cousin. So wot I never with what craft the fiend enchafed him, for yesterday he took me from my father privily; for I nor none of my father's men mistrusted him not. And if he had shamed me, he should have died for the sin, and his body shamed and dishonored forever. Thus as she stood talking with him, there came twelve knights seeking after her, and anon she told them all how Bors had delivered her; then they made great joy, and besought him to come to her father, a great lord, and he should be right welcome. Truly, said Bors, that may not be at this time, for I have a great adventure to do in this country. So he commended them unto God, and departed. Then Sir Bors rode after Lionel his brother by the trace of their horses. Thus he rode seeking a great while.

And then he rode all that day, and harbored with an old lady. And on the morn he rode to a castle in a valley, and there he met with a yeoman _Sir Lionel is_ going a great pace toward a forest. Say me, _wroth with_ said Sir Bors, canst thou tell me of any _Sir Bors,_ adventure? Sir, said he, here shall be under this castle a great and a marvelous tournament. Of what folks shall it be? said Sir Bors. The Earl of Plains (said he) shall be on the one party, and the lady's nephew of Hervin on the other party. Then Bors thought to be there, if he might meet with his brother Sir Lionel, or any other of his fellowship which were in the quest of the Sancgreal. And then he turned to an hermitage that was in the entry of the forest. And when he was come thither, he found there Sir Lionel his brother, which sat all armed at the entry of the chapel door, for to abide there harbor till on the morn that the tournament shall be. And when Sir Bors saw him he had great joy of him, that was it marvel to tell of his joy. And then he alight off his horse and said, Fair sweet brother, when came ye hither? Anon as Sir Lionel saw him he said, Ah Bors, ye may not make none avaunt, but, as for you, I might have been slain; when ye saw two knights leading me away, beating me, ye left me to succor a gentlewoman, and suffered me in peril of death: for never erst ne did no brother to another so great an untruth. And for that misdeed now I ensure you but death, for well have ye deserved it; therefore keep thee from henceforward, and that shall ye find as soon as I am armed. When Sir Bors understood his brother's wrath, he kneeled down to the earth, and cried him mercy, holding up both his hands, and prayed him to forgive him his evil will. Nay, said Lionel, that shall never be, and I may have the higher hand, that I make mine avow to God: thou shalt have death for it, for it were pity ye lived any longer.

Right so he went in, and took his harness, and mounted upon his horse, and came tofore him and said, Bors, keep thee from me, for I shall do to thee as I would to a felon or a traitor, for ye be the untruest knight that ever came out of so worthy an house as was King Bors de Ganis, which was our

and tries to slay him.

64

father; therefore start upon thy horse, and so shall ye be most at your advantage. And but if ye will, I will run upon thee there as ye stand upon foot, and so the shame shall be mine and the harm yours; but of that shame reck I nought. When Sir Bors saw that he must fight with his brother or else to die, he nist not what to do. Then his heart counseled him not thereto, inasmuch as Lionel was born or he, wherefore he ought to bear him reverence; yet kneeled he down afore Lionel's horse feet, and said, Fair sweet brother, have mercy upon me and slay me not, and have in remembrance the great love which ought to be between us twain. What Sir Bors said to Lionel he recked not, for the fiend had brought him in such a will that he should slay him. Then when Lionel saw he would none other, and that he would not have risen to give him battle, he rushed over him, so that he smote Bors with his horse feet upward to the earth, and hurt him so sore that he swooned of distress, the which he felt in himself to have died without confession. So when Lionel saw this, he alight off his horse, to have smitten off his head. And so he took him by the helm, and would have rent it from his head.

Then came the hermit running unto him, which was a good man and of great age, and well had he heard all the words that were between them, and so fell down upon Sir Bors. Then he said to Lionel, Ah, gentle knight, have mercy upon me and on thy brother, for if thou slay him thou shalt be dead of sin, and that were sorrowful; for he is one of the worthiest knights of the world, and of the best condi-

The hermit interfering is slain.

trons. So God me help, said Lionel, Sir priest, but if ye flee from him I shall slay you, and he shall never the sooner be quit. Certes, said the good man, I had lever ye slay me than him, for my death shall not be great harm, not half so much as of his. Well, said Lionel, I am agreed; and set his hand to his sword, and smote him so hard that his head went backward. Not for

Sir Colgrevance comes to the rescue, that he restrained him of his evil will, but took his brother by the helm, and unlaced it to have stricken off his head, and had slain him without fail, but so it happed, Colgrevance, a fellow of the Round Table, came at that time thither, as our Lord's will was. And when he saw the good man slain, he marveled much what it might be. And then he beheld Lionel would have slain his brother, and knew Sir Bors which he loved right well. Then start he down and took Lionel by the shoulders, and drew him strongly aback from Bors, and said, Lionel, will ye slay your brother, the worthiest knight of the world one? and that should no good man suffer. Why, said Sir Lionel, will ye let me? therefore if ye intermit you in this, I shall slay you, and him after. Why, said Colgrevance, is this sooth, that ye will slay him? Slay him will I, said he, who so say the contrary; for he hath done so much against me that he hath well deserved it; and so ran upon him, and would have smitten him through the head; and Sir Colgrevance ran betwixt them and said, And ye be so hardy to do so more, we two shall meddle together. When Lionel understood his words, he took his shield afore him, and asked him what he was; and he told him, Colgrevance, one of his fellows.

Then Lionel defied him, and gave him a great stroke through the helm. Then he drew his sword, for he was a passing good knight, and defended him right manfully. So long endured the battle that Sir Bors rose up all anguishly, and beheld Sir Colgrevance, the good knight, fight with his brother for his quarrel. Then was he full sorry and heavy, and thought, if Colgrevance slew him that was his brother, he should never have joy, and if his brother slew Colgrevance the shame should ever be his. Then would he have risen to have departed them, but he had not so much might to stand on foot: so he abode him so long till Colgrevance had the worse, for Sir Lionel was of great chivalry and right hardy, for he had pierced the hauberk and the helm, that he abode but death. For he had lost much of his blood, that it was marvel that he might stand upright. Then beheld he Sir Bors, which sat dressing him upward, and said, Ah Bors, why come ye not to cast me out of peril of death, wherein I have put me to succor you, which were right now nigh the death? Certes, said Lionel, that shall not avail you, for none of you shall bear other's warrant, but that ye shall die both of my hand. When Bors heard that, he did so much he rose and put on his helm. Then perceived he first the hermit priest which was slain, then made he a marvelous sorrow upon him.

Then oft Colgrevance cried upon Sir Bors, Why will ye let me die here for your sake? if it please you that I die for you the death, it will please me the but is slain better for to save a worthy man. With that also word Sir Lionel smote off the helm from his head. Then

Colgrevance saw that he might not escape; then he said, Fair sweet Jesu, that I have misdone have mercy upon my soul; for such sorrow that my heart suffereth for goodness, and for alms-deed that I would have done here, be to me aligement of penance unto my soul's health. At these words Lionel smote him so sore that he bare him to the earth. So when he had slain Colgrevance, he ran upon his brother as a fiendly man, and gave him such a stroke that he made him stoop; and he, that was full of humility, prayed him, for God's love to leave this battle: For and it befell, fair brother, that I slew you, or ye me, we should be dead of that sin. Never God me help but if I have on you mercy, and I may have the better hand. Then drew Bors his sword, all weeping, and said, Fair brother, God knoweth mine intent. Ah, fair brother, ye have done full evil this day to slay such an holy priest, the which never trespassed. Also ye have slain a gentle knight, and one of our fellows. And well wot ye that I am not afeard of you greatly, but I dread the wrath of God; and this is an unkindly war, therefore God shew miracle upon us both. Now God have mercy upon me, though I defend my life against my brother. With that Bors lift up his hand, and would have smitten his brother.

And then he heard a voice that said, Flee, Bors, and touch him not, or else thou shalt slay him. Right so *Sir Bors is* alight a cloud betwixt them in likeness of a *miraculously* fire, and a marvelous flame, that both their *saved.* two shields burnt. Then were they sore afraid, that they fell both to the earth, and lay there a great while in a swoon. And when they came to themselves, Bors saw that his brother had no harm; then he held up both his hands, for he dread God had taken vengeance upon him. With that he heard a voice say, Bors, go hence and bear thy brother no longer fellowship, but take thy way anon right to the sea, for Sir Percivale abideth thee there. Then he said to his brother, Fair sweet brother, forgive me, for God's love, all that I have trespassed unto you. Then he answered, God forgive it thee, and I do gladly.

So Sir Bors departed from him, and rode the next way to the sea.

LAUNCELOT AND ELAINE

By Thomas Malory

I

HOW SIR LAUNCELOT CAME TO ASTOLAT

SO after the quest of the Sancgreal was fulfilled, and all knights that were left on live were come again unto the Round Table, as the book of the Sancgreal maketh mention, then was there great joy in the court, and in especial King Arthur and Queen Guenever made great joy of the remnant that were come home, and passing glad was the king and the queen of Sir Launcelot and of Sir Bors. For they had been passing long away in the quest of the Sancgreal. Then, as the book saith, Sir Launcelot began to resort unto Queen Guenever again, and forgat the promise and the perfection that he made in the quest. For, as the book saith, had not Sir Launcelot been in his privy thoughts and in his mind so set inwardly to the queen, as he was in seeming outward to God, there had no knight passed him in the quest of the Sancgreal: but ever his thoughts were privily on the queen, and so they loved together more hotter than they did toforehand, that many in the court spake of it, and in especial Sir Agravaine, Sir Gawaine's brother, for he was ever open mouthed.

Thus it passed forth till our Lady day, Assumption.

LAUNCELOT AND ELAINE

Within a fifteen days of that feast the king let cry a great justs and a tournament that should be at that day at Camelot, that is Winchester. And the king let cry that he and the king of Scots would just against all that would come against them. And when this cry was made, thither came many knights. So there came thither the king of Northgalis, and King Anguish of Ireland, and the king with the hundred knights, and Sir Galahalt the haut prince, and the king of Northumberland, and many other noble dukes and earls of divers countries. So King Arthur made him ready to depart to these justs, and would have had the queen with him: but at that time she would not, she said, for she was sick and might not ride at that time. That me repenteth, said the king, for this seven year ye saw not such a fellowship together, except at Whitsuntide, when Galahad departed from the court. Truly, said the queen to the king, ye must hold me excused, I may not be there, and that me repenteth. And many deemed the queen would not be there because of Sir Launcelot du Lake, for Sir Launcelot would not ride with the king: for he said that he was not whole of the wound the which Sir Mador had given him. Wherefore the king was heavy and passing wroth, and so he departed towards Winchester with his fellowship. And so by the way the king lodged in a town called Astolat, that is now in English called Gilford, and there the king lay in the castle.

So when the king was departed, the queen called Sir Launcelot unto her, and said, Sir Launcelot, ye are greatly to blame, thus to hold you behind my lord: what

The king proclaims a tournament at Camelot.

71

trow ye, what will your enemies and mine say and deem ? nought else but see how Sir Launcelot holdeth him ever behind the king, and so doth the queen, for that they would be together; and thus will they say, said the queen to Sir Launcelot, have ye no doubt thereof. Madam, said Sir Launcelot, I allow your wit, it is of late come sin ye were wise; and therefore, madam, as at this time, I will be ruled by your counsel, and this night I will take my rest, and to-morrow by time will take my way toward Winchester. But wit you well, said Sir Launcelot to the queen, that at that justs I will be against the king and all his fellowship. Ye may there do as ye list, said the queen, but by my counsel ye shall not be against your king and your fellowship, for therein be full many hardy knights of your blood, as ye wot well enough, it needeth not to rehearse them. Madam, said Sir Launcelot, I pray you that ye be not displeased with me, for I will take the adventure that God will send me.

And so upon the morn early Sir Launcelot heard mass, and brake his fast, and so took his leave of the queen, and departed. And then he rode so much until he came to Astolat, that is Gilford; and there it happed him in the eventide he came to an old baron's place, that hight Sir Bernard of Astolat. And as Sir Launcelot entered into his lodging, King Arthur espied him as he did walk in a garden beside the castle, how he took his lodging, and knew him full well. It is well, said King Arthur unto the knights that were with him in that garden beside the castle, I have now espied one knight that will play his play at the justs to the which we be gone

Sir Launcelot, on his way to Camelot, comes to Astolat.

72

toward; I undertake he will do marvels. Who is that, we pray you tell us, said many knights, that were there at that time. Ye shall not wit for me, said the king, at this time. And so the king smiled, and went to his lodging. So when Sir Launcelot was in his lodging, and unarmed him in his chamber, the old baron and hermit came unto him, making his reverence, and welcomed him in the best manner; but the old knight knew not Sir Launcelot. Fair sir, said Sir Launcelot to his host, I would pray you to lend me a shield that were not openly known, for mine is well known. Sir, said his host, ye shall have your desire, for me seemeth ye be one of the likeliest knights of the world, and therefore I shall shew you friendship. Sir, wit you well I have two sons which were but late made knights, and the eldest hight Sir Tirre, and he was hurt that same day that he was made knight, that he may not ride, and his shield ye shall have, for that is not known, I dare say, but here and in no place else. And my youngest son hight Sir Lavaine, and if it please you he shall ride with you unto that justs, and he is of his age strong and wight. For much my heart giveth unto you that ye should be a noble knight, therefore, I pray you tell me your name, said Sir Bernard. As for that, said Sir Launcelot, ye must hold me excused as at this time, and if God give me grace to speed well at the justs I shall come again and tell you. But I pray you, said Sir Launcelot, in any wise let me have your son Sir Lavaine with me, and that I may have his brother's shield. Also this shall be done, said Sir Bernard.

This old baron had a daughter that time that was

called that time the fair maid of Astolat. And ever she beheld Sir Launcelot wonderfully. And, as the book *Elaine begs him to wear her token at the justs.* saith, she cast such a love unto Sir Launcelot that she could never withdraw her love, wherefore she died; and her name was Elaine le Blank. So thus as she came to and fro, she was so hot in her love that she besought Sir Launcelot to wear upon him at the justs a token of hers. Fair damsel, said Sir Launcelot, and if I grant you that, ye may say I do more for your love than ever I did for lady or damsel. Then he remembered him that he would go to the justs disguised, and for because he had never afore that time borne no manner of token of no damsel; then he bethought him that he would bear one of her, that none of his blood thereby might know him. And then he said, Fair maiden, I will grant you to wear a token of yours upon my helmet, and therefore what it is shew it me. Sir, she said, it is a red sleeve of mine, of scarlet well embroidered with great pearls. And so she brought it him. So Sir Launcelot received it and said, Never did I erst so much for no damsel. And then Sir Launcelot betook the fair maiden his shield in keeping, and prayed her to keep that until that he came again. And so that night he had merry rest and great cheer. Forever the damsel Elaine was about Sir Launcelot, all the while she might be suffered.

II

THE TOURNAMENT

So upon a day on the morn, King Arthur and all his knights departed; for their king had tarried there three days to abide his noble knights. And so when the king was riden, Sir Launcelot and Sir Lavaine made them ready for to ride; and either of them had white shields, and the red sleeve Sir Launcelot let carry with him. And so they took their leave at Sir Bernard the old baron, and at his daughter the fair maiden of Astolat. And then they rode so long till they came to Camelot, that time called Winchester. And there was great press of kings, dukes, earls, and barons, and many noble knights. But there Sir Launcelot was lodged privily, by the means of Sir Lavaine, with a rich burg that no man in that town was ware what they were. And so they sojourned there till our Lady day, Assumption, as the great feast should be. So then trumpets blew unto the field, and King Arthur was set on high upon a scaffold, to behold who did best. But, as the French book saith, King Arthur would not suffer Sir Gawaine to go from him, for never had Sir Gawaine the better and Sir Launcelot were in the field; and many times was Sir Gawaine rebuked when Launcelot came into any justs disguised.

Then some of the kings, as King Anguish of Ireland and the king of Scotland, were that time turned upon the side of King Arthur. And then on the other party was the king of Northgalis, and the king with the hundred knights, and the king of Northumberland, and Sir Galahalt the haut prince. But these three kings and this duke were passing weak to hold against King Arthur's party: for with him were the noblest knights of the world. So then they withdrew them either party from other, and every man made him

Of the two parties.

75

ready in his best manner to do what he might. Then Sir Launcelot made him ready, and put the red sleeve upon his head, and fastened it fast; and so Sir Launcelot and Sir Lavaine departed out of Winchester privily, and rode until a little leaved wood, behind the party that held against King Arthur's party, and there they held them still till the parties smote together.

And then came in the king of Scots and the king of Ireland on Arthur's party: and against them came the king of Northumberland and the king with the hundred knights; and the king with the hundred knights smote down King Anguish of Ireland. Then Sir Palamides, that was on Arthur's party, encountered with Sir Galahalt, and either of them smote down other, and either party halp their lords on horseback again. So there began a strong assail upon both parties. And then there came in Sir Brandiles, Sir Sagramor le Desirous, Sir Dodinas le Savage, Sir Kay le Seneschal, Sir Griflet le Fise de Dieu, Sir Mordred, Sir Meliot de Logris, Sir Ozanna le Cure Hardy, Sir Safere, Sir Epinogris, and Sir Galleron of Galway. All these fifteen knights were knights of the Round Table. So these with more others came in together, and beat on back the king of Northumberland, and the king of North Wales. When Sir Launcelot saw this, as he hoved in a little leaved wood, then he said unto Sir Lavaine, See yonder is a company of good knights, and they hold them together as boars that were chafed with dogs. That is truth, said Sir Lavaine.

Now, said Sir Launcelot, and ye will help me a little, ye shall see yonder fellowship which chaseth now these

King Arthur's is the stronger.

men in our side, that they shall go as fast backward as they went forward. Sir, spare not, said Sir Lavaine, for I shall do what I may. Then Sir Launcelot and Sir Lavaine came in at the thickest of the press, and there Sir Launcelot smote down Sir Brandiles, Sir Sagramor, Sir Dodinas, Sir Kay, Sir Griflet, and all this he did with one spear. And Sir Lavaine smote down Sir Lucan le Buttelere, and Sir Bedivere. And then Sir Launcelot gat another spear, and there he smote down Sir Agravaine, Sir Gaheris, and Sir Mordred, and Sir Moliot de Logis. And Sir Lavaine smote down Ozanna le Cure Hardy: and then Sir Launcelot drew his sword, and there he smote on the right hand and on the left hand, and by great force he unhorsed Sir Safere, Sir Epinogris, and Sir Galleron. And then the knights of the Round Table withdrew them aback, after they had gotten their horses as well as they might. O mercy, said Sir Gawaine, what knight is yonder, that doth so marvelous deeds of arms in that field? I wot what he is, said King Arthur. But as at this time I will not name him. Sir, said Sir Gawaine, I would say it were Sir Launcelot, by his riding and his buffets that I see him deal: but ever me seemeth it should not be he, for that he beareth the red sleeve upon his head, for I wist him never bear token, at no justs, of lady nor gentlewoman. Let him be, said King Arthur, he will be better known and do more or ever he depart. Then the party that were against King Arthur were well comforted, and then they held them together, that beforehand were sore rebuked.

Then Sir Bors, Sir Ector de Maris, and Sir Lionel

called unto them the knights of their blood, as Sir Blamor de Ganis, Sir Bleoberis, Sir Aliduke,
He is sore
wounded by
Sir Bors, Sir Galihud, Sir Galihodin, Sir Bellangere
le Beuse; so these nine knights of Sir Launce-
lot's kin thrust in mightily, for they were all noble
knights. And they, of great hate and despite that they
had unto him, thought to rebuke that noble knight Sir
Launcelot and Sir Lavaine, for they knew them not.
And so they came hurtling together, and smote down
many knights of Northgalis and of Northumberland.
And when Sir Launcelot saw them fare so, he gat a
spear in his hand, and there encountered with him all
at once Sir Bors, Sir Ector, and Sir Lionel, and all they
three smote him at once with their spears. And with
force of themselves they smote Sir Launcelot's horse
to the earth. And by misfortune Sir Bors smote Sir
Launcelot through the shield into the side, and the spear
brake, and the head left still in his side.

When Sir Lavaine saw his master lie on the ground,
he ran to the king of Scots, and smote him to the earth,
but with the and by great force he took his horse and
help of Sir brought him to Sir Launcelot, and maugre
Lavaine he
gains the day. them all he made him to mount upon that
horse. And then Launcelot gat a spear in his hand,
and there he smote Sir Bors horse and man to the
earth; in the same wise he served Sir Ector and Sir
Lionel, and Sir Lavaine smote down Sir Blamor de
Ganis. And then Sir Launcelot drew his sword, for he
felt himself so sore and hurt that he wend there to have
had his death. And then he smote Sir Bleoberis such
a buffet on the helmet that he fell down to the earth in

a swoon. And in the same wise he served Sir Aliduke and Sir Galihud. And Sir Lavaine smote down Sir Bellangere, that was the son of Alisander le Orphelin. And by this was Sir Bors horsed, and then he came with Sir Ector and Sir Lionel, and all they three smote with swords upon Sir Launcelot's helmet. And when he felt their buffets, and his wound the which was so grievous, then he thought to do what he might while he might endure; and then he gave Sir Bors such a buffet that he made him bow his head passing low, and therewithal he raised off his helm, and might have slain him, and so pulled him down. And in the same wise he served Sir Ector and Sir Lionel. For, as the book saith, he might have slain them, but when he saw their visages his heart might not serve him thereto, but left them there.

And then afterward he hurled in the thickest press of them all, and did there the marvelousest deeds of arms that ever man saw or heard speak of; and ever Sir Lavaine the good knight with him. And there Sir Launcelot with his sword smote and pulled down, as the French book maketh mention, more than thirty knights, and the most party were of the Round Table. And Sir Lavaine did full well that day, for he smote down ten knights of the Round Table.

Mercy, said Sir Gawaine to Arthur, I marvel what knight that he is with the red sleeve. Sir, said King Arthur, he will be known or he depart. And then the king blew unto lodging, and the prize was given by heralds unto the knight with the white shield, that bare the red sleeve. Then came the king with the hundred knights, the king of Northgalis, and the king of North-umberland, and Sir Galahalt the haut prince, and said unto Sir Launcelot, Fair knight, God thee bless, for much have ye done this day for us; therefore we pray you that ye will come with us, that ye may receive the honor and the prize as ye have worshipfully deserved it. My fair lords, said Sir Launcelot, wit you well, if I have deserved thank I have sore bought it, and that me repenteth, for I am like never to escape with my life; therefore, fair lords, I pray you that ye will suffer me to depart where me liketh, for I am sore hurt. I take none force of none honor, for I had lever to repose me than to be lord of all the world.

And therewithal he groaned piteously, and rode a great wallop away-ward from them, until he came under a wood's side; and when he saw that he was *Sir Launcelot being in peril of death* from the field nigh a mile, that he was sure he might not be seen, then he said with an high voice, O gentle knight Sir Lavaine, help me that this truncheon were out of my side, for it sticketh so sore that it nigh slayeth me. O mine own lord, said Sir Lavaine, I would fain do that might please you, but I dread me sore, and I draw out the truncheon, that ye shall be in peril of death. I charge you, said Sir Launcelot, as ye love me draw it out. And there-withal he descended from his horse, and right so did Sir Lavaine, and forewith Sir Lavaine drew the truncheon out of his side. And he gave a great shriek, and a marvelous grisly groan, and his blood brast out nigh a pint at once, that at last he sank down, and so swooned pale and deadly. Alas, said Sir Lavaine, what shall I do? And then he turned Sir Launcelot into the wind, but so he lay there nigh half an hour as he had been dead.

And so at the last Sir Launcelot cast up his eyes, and said, O Lavaine, help me that I were on my horse, for here is fast by within this two mile a gentle hermit, that sometime was a full noble knight and a great lord of possessions: and for great goodness he hath taken him to willful poverty, and forsaken many lands, and his name is Sir Baudewin of Brittany, and he is a full noble surgeon, and a good leech. Now let see, help me up that I were there. For ever my heart giveth me that I shall never die of my cousin-german's hands. And then with great pain Sir Lavaine halp him upon his horse; and then they rode a great wallop together, and ever Sir Launcelot bled that it ran down to the earth. And so by fortune they came to that hermitage, which was under a wood, and a great cliff on the other side, and a fair water running under it. And then Sir Lavaine beat on the gate with the butt of his spear, and cried fast, Let in for Jesu's sake. And there came a fair child to them, and asked them what they would? Fair son, said Sir Lavaine, go and pray thy lord the hermit for God's sake to let in here a knight that is full sore wounded, and this day tell thy lord that I saw him do more deeds of arms than ever I heard say that any man did. So the child went in lightly, and then he brought the hermit, the which was a passing good man. So when Sir Lavaine saw him, he prayed him for God's sake of succor. What knight is he? said the hermit; is he of the house of King Arthur or not? I wot not, said Sir Lavaine, what is he, nor what is his

is brought by Sir Lavaine to a hermit-age.

81

name, but well I wot I saw him do marvelously this day, as of deeds of arms. On whose party was he? said the hermit. Sir, said Sir Lavaine, he was this day against King Arthur, and there he wan the prize of all the knights of the Round Table. I have seen the day, said the hermit, I would have loved him the worse because he was against my lord King Arthur, for sometime I was one of the fellowship of the Round Table, but I thank God now I am otherwise disposed. But where is he? let me see him. Then Sir Lavaine brought the hermit to him.

And when the hermit beheld him as he sat leaning upon his saddle-bow, ever bleeding piteously, and ever the knight hermit thought that he should know him, but he could not bring him to knowledge, because he was so pale for bleeding, What knight are ye? said the hermit, and where were ye born? My fair lord, said Sir Launcelot, I am a stranger, and a knight adventurous that laboreth throughout many realms for to win worship. Then the hermit advised him better, and saw by a wound on his cheek that he was Sir Launcelot. Alas, said the hermit, mine own lord, why hide you your name from me: forsooth I ought to know you of right, for ye are the most noblest knight of the world; for well I know you for Sir Launcelot. Sir, said he, sith ye know me, help me and ye may, for God's sake; for I would be out of this pain at once, either to death or to life. Have ye no doubt, said the hermit, ye shall live and fare right well. And so the hermit called to him two of his servants, and so he and his servants bare him into the hermitage, and lightly unarmed him and laid him in his bed. And then anon the hermit stanched his blood, and made him to

drink good wine, so that Sir Launcelot was well refreshed, and knew himself. For in those days it was not
the guise of hermits as is nowadays. For there were none
hermits in those days but that they had been men of
worship and of prowess, and those hermits held great
household, and refreshed people that were in distress.

III

HOW LAUNCELOT WAS HEALED OF HIS WOUND

Now turn we unto King Arthur, and leave we Sir
Launcelot in the hermitage. So when the kings were
come together on both parties, and the great Sir Gawaine
feast should be holden, King Arthur asked seeks for the
the king of Northgalis and their fellowship knight of the
red sleeve.
where was that knight that bare the red sleeve:—
Bring him before me, that he may have his laud and
honor and the prize, as it is right. Then spake Sir
Galahalt the haut prince and the king with the hundred knights: We suppose that knight is mischieved,
and that he is never like to see you, nor none of us all,
and that is the greatest pity that ever we wist of any
knight. Alas, said Arthur, how may this be? is he so
hurt? What is his name? said King Arthur. Truly,
said they all, we know not his name, nor from whence
he came, nor whither he would. Alas, said the king,
these be to me the worst tidings that came to me this
seven year: for I would not for all the lands I hold, to
know and wit it were so that that noble knight were slain.
Know ye him? said they all. As for that, said Arthur,
whether I know him or know him not, ye shall not know

for me what man he is, but Almighty Jesu send me good tidings of him. And so said they all. By my head, said Sir Gawaine, if it be so, that the good knight be so sore hurt, it is great damage and pity to all this land, for he is one of the noblest knights that ever I saw in a field handle a spear or a sword. And if he may be found I shall find him, for I am sure he is not far from this town. Bear you well, said King Arthur, and ye may find him, unless that he be in such a plight that he may not hold himself. Jesu defend, said Sir Gawaine, but wit I shall what he is, and I may find him. Right so, Sir Gawaine took a squire with him, upon hackneys, and rode all about Camelot within six or seven miles. But so he came again, and could hear no word of him.

Then within two days King Arthur and all the fellowship returned unto London again. And so as they rode by the way, it happed Sir Gawaine at Astolat to lodge with Sir Bernard, there as was Sir Launcelot lodged. And so as Sir Gawaine was in his chamber to repose him, Sir Bernard the old baron came unto him, and his daughter Elaine, for to cheer him, and to ask him what tidings, and who did best at that tournament of Winchester. Truly, said Sir Gawaine, there were two knights that bare two white shields; but the one of them bare a red sleeve upon his head, and certainly he was one of the best knights that ever I saw just in field. For I dare say, said Sir Gawain, that one knight with the red sleeve smote down forty valiant knights of the Round Table, and his fellow did right well and worshipfully. Now blessed be God, said the fair maiden of Astolat, that that knight sped so well,

Sir Gawaine comes to Astolat,

for he is the man in the world that I first loved, and truly he shall be the last that ever I shall love. Now fair maid, said Sir Gawaine, is that good knight your love? Certainly, sir, said she, wit ye well he is my love. Then know ye his name, said Sir Gawaine. Nay, truly, said the damsel, I know not his name, nor from whence he cometh; but to say that I love him, I promise you and God that I love him. How had ye knowledge of him first? said Sir Gawaine.

Then she told him as ye have heard tofore, and how her father betook him her brother to do him service, and how her father lent him her brother Sir Tirre's shield, — And here with me he left his own shield. For what cause did he so? said Sir Gawaine. For this cause, said the damsel, *and recognizes Sir Launcelot's shield.* for his shield was too well known among many noble knights. Ah, fair damsel, said Sir Gawaine, please it you let me have a sight of that shield. Sir, said she, it is in my chamber covered with a case, and if ye will come with me, ye shall see it. Not so, said Sir Bernard till his daughter, let send for it. So when the shield was come, Sir Gawaine took off the case: and when he beheld that shield, he knew anon that it was Sir Launcelot's shield, and his own arms. Ah, mercy, said Sir Gawaine, now is my heart more heavier than ever it was tofore. Why? said Elaine. For I have great cause, said Sir Gawaine: is that knight that owneth this shield your love? Yea truly, said she, my love he is, God would I were his love. Truly, said Sir Gawaine, fair damsel, ye have right, for, and he be your love, ye love the most honorable knight of the world, and the man of most worship.

So me thought ever, said the damsel, for never, or that time, for no knight that ever I saw loved I never none erst. God grant, said Sir Gawaine, that either of you may rejoice other, but that is in a great adventure.

But truly, said Sir Gawaine unto the damsel, ye may say ye have a fair grace, for why, I have known that noble knight this four and twenty year, and never or that day I nor none other knight, I dare make it good, saw nor heard say that ever he bare token or sign of no lady, gentlewoman, nor maiden, at no justs nor tournament. And therefore, fair maiden, said Sir Gawaine, ye are much beholden to him to give him thanks. But I dread me, said Sir Gawaine, that ye shall never see him in this world, and that is great pity that ever was of earthly knight. Alas, said she, how may this be? Is he slain? I say not so, said Sir Gawaine, but wit ye well, he is grievously wounded, by all manner of signs, and by men's sight more likely to be dead then to be on live; and wit ye well he is the noble knight Sir Launcelot, for by this shield I know him. Alas, said the fair maiden of Astolat, how may this be, and what was his hurt? Truly, said Sir Gawaine, the man in the world that loved him best hurt him so; and I dare say, said Sir Gawaine, and that knight that hurt him knew the very certainty that he had hurt Sir Launcelot, it would be the most sorrow that ever came to his heart. Now, fair father, said then Elaine, I require you give me leave to ride and to seek him, or else I wot well I shall go out of my mind, for I shall never stint till that I find him and my brother Sir Lavaine. Do as it liketh you, said her father, for me right sore repenteth of the hurt of that noble knight.

Right so the maid made her ready, and before Sir Gawaine making great dole.

Then on the morn Sir Gawaine came to King Arthur, and told him how he had found Sir Launcelot's shield in the keeping of the fair maiden of Astolat. All that knew I aforehand, said King Arthur, and that caused me I would not suffer you to have ado at the great justs: for I espied, said King Arthur, when he came in till his lodging, full late in the evening in Astolat. But marvel have I, said Arthur, that ever he would bear any sign of any damsel: for, or now, I never heard say nor knew that ever he bare any token of none earthly woman. By my head, said Sir Gawaine, the fair maiden of Astolat loveth him marvelously well; what it meaneth I cannot say; and she is ridden after to seek him. So the king and all came to London, and there Sir Gawaine openly disclosed to all the court that it was Sir Launcelot that justed best. And so leave we them there, and speak we of Sir Launcelot, that lay in great peril.

So as fair Elaine came to Winchester, she sought there all about, and by fortune Sir Lavaine was ridden to play him, to enchafe his horse. And anon as Elaine saw him she knew him, and then she cried on loud until him. And when he heard her, anon he came to her; and then she asked her brother, How did my lord, Sir Launcelot? Who told you, sister, that my lord's name was Sir Launcelot? Then she told him how Sir Gawaine by his shield knew him. So they rode together till that they came to the hermitage, and anon she alight. So Sir Lavaine brought her in to Sir Launcelot. And when she saw

Elaine finds Sir Launcelot at the hermitage,

87

him lie so sick and pale in his bed, she might not speak, but suddenly she fell to the earth down suddenly in a swoon, and there she lay a great while. And when she was relieved she sighed, and said, My lord Sir Launcelot, alas, why be ye in this plight? and then she swooned again. And then Sir Launcelot prayed Sir Lavaine to take her up, — And bring her to me. And when she came to herself, Sir Launcelot kissed her, and said, Fair maiden, why fare ye thus? Ye put me to pain; wherefore make ye no more such cheer, for, and ye be come to comfort me, ye be right welcome, and of this little hurt that I have, I shall be right hastily whole, by the grace of God. But I marvel, said Sir Launcelot, who told you my name. Then the fair maiden told him all, how Sir Gawaine was lodged with her father, — And there by your shield he discovered your name. Alas, said Sir Launcelot, that me repenteth, that my name is known, for I am sure it will turn unto anger. And then Sir Launcelot compassed in his mind that Sir Gawaine would tell Queen Guenever how he bare the red sleeve, and for whom, that he wist well would turn unto great anger.

So this maiden, Elaine, never went from Sir Launcelot, but watched him day and night, and did such attendance to him that the French book saith there was never woman did more kindlier for man than she. Then Sir Launcelot prayed Sir Lavaine to make espies in Winchester for Sir Bors if he came there, and told him by what tokens he should know him, by a wound in his forehead: For well I am sure, said Sir Launcelot, that Sir Bors will seek me, for he is the same good knight that hurt me.

and watches him night and day.

LAUNCELOT AND ELAINE

Now turn we unto Sir Bors de Ganis, that came unto Winchester to seek after his cousin, Sir Launcelot; and so when he came to Winchester, anon there were men that Sir Lavaine had made to lie in a watch for such a man; and anon Sir Lavaine had warning; and then Sir Lavaine came to Winchester, and found Sir Bors, and there he told him what he was, and with whom he was, and what was his name. Now, fair knight, said Sir Bors, I require you that ye will bring me to my lord Sir Launcelot. Sir, said Sir Lavaine, take your horse, and within this hour ye shall see him. And so they departed, and came to the hermitage.

Sir Bors finds his cousin, Sir Launcelot,

And when Sir Bors saw Sir Launcelot lie in his bed, pale and discolored, anon Sir Bors lost his countenance, and for kindness and pity he might not speak, but wept tenderly a great while. And then when he might speak he said thus: O my lord Sir Launcelot, God you bless, and send you hasty recovery; and full heavy am I of my misfortune and of mine unhappiness, for now I may call myself unhappy, and I dread me that God is greatly displeased with me, that he would suffer me to have such a shame for to hurt you, that are all our leader and all our worship, and therefore I call myself unhappy. Alas, that ever such a caitiff knight as I am should have power by unhappiness to hurt the most noblest knight of the world. Where I so shamefully set upon you and overcharged you, and where ye might have slain me, ye saved me, and so did not I: for I, and your blood, did to you our uttrance. I marvel, said Sir Bors, that my heart or my blood would

and begs for his forgiveness.

serve me, wherefore my lord Sir Launcelot, I ask your mercy. Fair cousin, said Sir Launcelot, ye be right welcome, and wit ye well, overmuch ye say for to please me, the which pleaseth me not; for why? I have the same sought, for I would with pride have overcome you all, and there in my pride I was near slain, and that was in mine own default, for I might have given you warning of my being there. And then had I had no hurt; for it is an old said saw, there is hard battle there as kin and friends do battle either against other; there may be no mercy, but mortal war. Therefore, fair cousin, said Sir Launcelot, let this speech overpass, and all shall be welcome that God sendeth; and let us leave off this matter, and let us speak of some rejoicing: for this that is done may not be undone, and let us find a remedy how soon that I may be whole.

Then Sir Bors leaned upon his bed's side, and told Sir Launcelot how the queen was passing wroth with him, because he ware the red sleeve at the great justs. And there Sir Bors told him all how Sir Gawaine discovered it by your shield that ye left with the fair maiden of Astolat. Then is the queen wroth, said Sir Launcelot, and therefore am I right heavy, for I deserved no wrath, for all that I did was because that I would not be known. Right so excused I you, said Sir Bors, but all was in vain, for she said more largely to me than I to you now. But is this she, said Sir Bors, that is so busy about you, that men call the fair maiden of Astolat? She it is, said Sir Launcelot, that by no means I cannot put from me. Why should ye put her from you? said Sir Bors, she is a passing fair damsel, and a well beseen and well taught;

and God would, fair cousin, said Sir Bors, that ye could love her, but as to that I may not, nor I dare not, counsel you. But I see well, said Sir Bors, by her diligence about you, that she loveth you entirely. That me repenteth, said Sir Launcelot. Sir, said Sir Bors, she is not the first that hath lost her pain upon you, and that is the more pity. And so they talked of many more things. And so within three days or four, Sir Launcelot was big and strong again. So then they made them ready to depart from the hermit.

IV

LAUNCELOT LEAVES THE HERMIT

And so upon a morn they took their horses, and Elaine le Blank with them; and when they came to Astolat, there they were well lodged, and had great cheer of Sir Bernard the old baron, and of Sir Tirre his son. And so upon the morn, when Sir Launcelot should depart, fair Elaine brought her father with her, and Sir Tirre and Sir Lavaine, and thus she said: —

My lord Sir Launcelot, now I see ye will depart, now, fair knight and courteous knight, have mercy upon me, and suffer me not to die for thy love. What would ye that I did? said Sir Launcelot. I would have you to my husband, said Elaine. Fair damsel, I thank you, said Sir Launcelot, but truly, said he, I cast me never to be wedded man. Then, fair knight, said she, will ye be my love? Jesu defend me, said Sir Launcelot, for then I rewarded to your father and your brother full evil for their

Elaine in vain prays Sir Launcelot for his love.

great goodness. Alas, said she, then must I die for your love. Ye shall not so, said Sir Launcelot, for wit ye well, fair maiden, I might have been married and I had would, but I never applied me to be married yet. But because, fair damsel, that ye love me, as ye say ye do, I will, for your good-will and kindness, shew you some goodness, and that is this; that wheresoever ye will beset your heart upon some good knight that will wed you, I shall give you together a thousand pound yearly, to you and to your heirs. Thus much will I give you, fair maiden, for your kindness, and always while I live to be your own knight. Of all this, said the maiden, I will none, for, but if ye will wed me, or else be my lover, wit you well, Sir Launcelot, my good days are done. Fair damsel, said Sir Launcelot, of these two things ye must pardon me. Then she shrieked shrilly, and fell down in a swoon; and then women bare her into her chamber, and there she made overmuch sorrow.

And then Sir Launcelot would depart; and there he asked Sir Lavaine what he would do. What should I do, said Sir Lavaine, but follow you, but if ye drive me from you, or command me to go from you? Then came Sir Bernard to Sir Launcelot, and said to him, I cannot see but that my daughter Elaine will die for your sake. I may not do withal, said Sir Launcelot, for that me sore repenteth; for I report me to yourself that my proffer is fair, and me repenteth, said Sir Launcelot, that she loveth me as she doth: I was never the causer of it, for I report me to your son, I early nor late proffered her bounty nor fair behests: and as for me, said Sir Launcelot, I dare do all that a good knight should do, that she is a true maiden, both for deed and for will; and I am right heavy of her distress, for she is a full fair maiden, good, and gentle, and well taught. Father, said Sir Lavaine, I dare make good she is pure and good as my lord Sir Launcelot hath said; but she doth as I do, for since I first saw my lord Sir Launcelot I could never depart from him, nor nought I will and I may follow him.

Then Sir Launcelot took his leave, and so they departed, and came unto Winchester. And when Arthur wist that Sir Launcelot was come, whole and sound, the king made great joy of him, and so did Sir Gawaine, and all the knights of the Round Table except Sir Agravaine and Sir Mordred. Also Queen Guenever was wood wroth with Sir Launcelot and would by no means speak with him, but estranged herself from him, and Sir Launcelot made all the means that he might to speak with the queen, but it would not be.

Sir Launcelot returns to Winchester.

Now speak we of the fair maiden of Astolat, that made such sorrow day and night, that she never slept, eat, nor drank; and ever she made her complaint unto Sir Launcelot. So when she had thus endured a ten days, that she feebled so that she must needs pass out of this world, then she shrived her clean, and received her Creator. And ever she complained still upon Sir Launcelot. Then her ghostly father bade her leave such thoughts. Then she said, Why should I leave such thoughts? am I not an earthly woman? and all the while the breath is in my body I may complain me, for my belief is I do none

Elaine makes such sorrow that she dies.

93

offense though I love an earthly man, and I take God to my record I never loved none but Sir Launcelot du Lake, nor never shall; and a pure maiden I am for him and for all other. And since it is the sufferance of God that I shall die for the love of so noble a knight, I beseech the High Father of heaven to have mercy upon my soul, and upon mine innumerable pains that I suffered may be allegiance of part of my sins. For sweet Lord Jesu, said the fair maiden, I take thee to record, on thee I was never great offender against thy laws, but that I loved this noble knight Sir Launcelot out of measure, and of myself, good Lord, I might not withstand the fervent love wherefore I have my death. And then she called her father Sir Bernard, and her brother Sir Tirre, and heartily she prayed her father that her brother might write a letter like as she did endite it; and so her father granted her. And when the letter was written word by word like as she devised, then she prayed her father that she might be watched until she were dead, — And while my body is hot, let this letter be put in my right hand, and my hand bound fast with the letter until that I be cold, and let me be put in a fair bed, with all the richest clothes that I have about me, and so let my bed, and all my richest clothes, be laid with me in a chariot unto the next place where Thames is, and there let me be put within a barget, and but one man with me, such as ye trust to steer me thither, and that my barget be covered with black samite, over and over. Thus, father, I beseech you, let it be done. So her father granted it her faithfully, all things should be done like as she had devised. Then her father and her brother made great dole, for, when this was done, anon she died. And so when she was dead, the corpse, and the bed, all was led the next way unto Thames, and there a man, and the corpse, and all, were put into Thames, and so the man steered the barget unto Westminster, and there he rowed a great while to and fro or any espied it.

So by fortune King Arthur and the Queen Guenever were speaking together at a window; and so as they looked into Thames, they espied this black barget, and had marvel what it meant. Then the king called Sir Kay, and shewed it him.

Her body comes to Westminster.

Sir, said Sir Kay, wit you well there is some new tidings. Go thither, said the king to Sir Kay, and take with you Sir Brandiles and Agravaine, and bring me ready word what is there. Then these three knights departed, and came to the barget, and went in; and there they found the fairest corpse lying in a rich bed, and a poor man sitting in the barget's end, and no word would he speak. So these three knights returned unto the king again, and told him what they found. That fair corpse will I see, said the king. And so then the king took the queen by the hand and went thither. Then the king made the barget to be holden fast; and then the king and the queen entered, with certain knights with them. And there he saw the fairest woman lie in a rich bed, covered unto her middle with many rich clothes, and all was of cloth of gold, and she lay as though she had smiled.

Then the queen espied a letter in her right hand, and told it to the king. Then the king took it, and said, Now I am sure this letter will tell what she was, and why she is come hither. Then the king and the queen went out of the barget, and so commanded a certain man to wait upon the barget. And so when the king was come within his chamber, he called many knights about him, and said that he would wit openly what was written within that letter. Then the king brake it, and made a clerk to read it; and this was the intent of the letter: — Most noble knight, Sir Launcelot, now hath death made us two at debate for your love; I was your lover, that men called the fair maiden of Astolat; therefore unto all ladies I make my moan; yet pray for my soul, and bury me at the least, and offer ye my masspenny. This is my last request. And a clean maiden I died, I take God to witness. Pray for my soul, Sir Launcelot, as thou art peerless. — This was all the substance in the letter. And when it was read, the king, the queen, and all the knights wept for pity of the doleful complaints.

Then was Sir Launcelot sent for. And when he was come, King Arthur made the letter to be read to him; *Sir Launcelot mourns at her death,* and when Sir Launcelot heard it word by word, he said, My lord Arthur, wit ye well I am right heavy of the death of this fair damsel. God knoweth I was never causer of her death by my willing, and that will I report me to her own brother; here he is, Sir Lavaine. I will not say nay, said Sir Launcelot, but that she was both fair and good, and much I was beholden unto her, but she loved me out of measure. Ye might have shewed her, said the queen, some bounty and gentleness, that might have preserved her life. Madam, said Sir Launcelot, she would none other way be answered, but that she would be my wife,

or else my love, and of these two I would not grant her;
but I proffered her, for her good love that she shewed
me, a thousand pound yearly to her and to her heirs,
and to wed any manner knight that she could find best
to love in her heart. For, madam, said Sir Launcelot,
I love not to be constrained to love; for love must arise
of the heart, and not by no constraint. That is truth,
said the king and many knights: love is free in himself,
and never will be bounden; for where he is bounden he
loseth himself.

Then said the king unto Sir Launcelot, It will be your
worship that ye oversee that she be interred worshipfully. Sir, said Sir Launcelot, that shall be *and causes
her to be*
done as I can best devise. And so many *buried worshipfully.*
knights went thither to behold that fair
maiden. And so upon the morn she was interred richly,
and Sir Launcelot offered her mass-penny, and all the
knights of the Round Table that were there at that
time offered with Sir Launcelot. And then the poor
man went again with the barget. Then the queen
sent for Sir Launcelot, and prayed him of mercy, for
why she had been wroth with him causeless. This
is not the first time, said Sir Launcelot, that ye have
been displeased with me causeless; but, madam, ever
I must suffer you, but what sorrow I endure I take
no force. So this passed on all that winter, with all
manner of hunting and hawking, and justs and tourneys
were many betwixt many great lords; and ever in all
places Sir Lavaine gat great worship, so that he was
nobly renowned among many knights of the Round
Table.

THE DEATH OF KING ARTHUR

By Thomas Malory

A S Sir Mordred was ruler of all England, he did so make letters as though that they came from beyond the sea, and the letters specified that King Arthur was slain in battle with Sir Launcelot. Wherefore Sir Mordred made a Parliament, and called the lords together, and there he made them to choose him king, and so was he crowned at Canterbury, and held a feast there fifteen days, and afterward he drew him unto Winchester, and there he took the Queen Guenever, and said plainly, that he would wed her which was his uncle's wife, and his father's wife. And so he made ready for the feast, and a day prefixed that they should be wedded; wherefore Queen Guenever was passing heavy. But she durst not discover her heart, but spake fair, and agreed to Sir Mordred's will. Then she desired of Sir Mordred for to go to London, to buy all manner of things that longed unto the wedding. And because of her fair speech Sir Mordred trusted her well enough, and gave her leave to go. And so when she came to London, she took the tower of London, and suddenly, in all haste possible, she stuffed it with all manner of victual, and well garnished it with men, and so kept it. Then when Sir Mordred wist and understood how he was beguiled, he was passing wroth out of measure. And a short tale for to make, he went and laid a mighty siege about the tower of London, and made many great assaults thereat, and threw many great engines unto them, and shot great guns. But all might not prevail Sir Mordred, for Queen Guenever would never, for fair speech nor for foul, would never trust to come in his hands again.

And then came the Bishop of Canterbury, the which was a noble clerk and an holy man, and thus he said to Sir Mordred: Sir, what will ye do, will ye first displease God, and sithen shame your- self and all knighthood? Is not King Arthur your uncle, no further but your mother's brother, and are ye not his son, therefore how may ye wed your father's wife? Sir, said the noble clerk, leave this opin- ion, or else I shall curse you with book, and bell, and candle. Do thou thy worst, said Sir Mordred, wit thou well I shall defy thee. Sir, said the bishop, and wit you well I shall not fear me to do that me ought to do. Also where ye noise where my lord Arthur is slain, and that is not so, and therefore ye will make a foul work in this land. Peace, thou false priest, said Sir Mordred, for, and thou chafe me any more, I shall make strike off thy head. So the bishop departed, and did the curse in the most orgulous wise that might be done. And then Sir Mordred sought the Bishop of Canterbury for to have slain him. Then the bishop fled, and took part of his goods with him, and went nigh unto Glastonbury, and there he was as priest hermit in a chapel, and lived in poverty and in holy prayers; for well he understood that mischievous war was at hand.

The bishop curses Sir Mordred.

Then Sir Mordred sought on Queen Guenever by letters and sondes, and by fair means and foul means, for to have her to come out of the tower of London; but all this availed not, for she answered him shortly, openly and privily, that she had lever slay herself than to be married with him. Then came word to Sir Mordred that King Arthur had raised the siege from Sir Launcelot, and he was coming homeward with a great host, to be avenged upon Sir Mordred. Wherefore Sir Mordred made write writs to all the barony of this land, and much people drew to him. For then was the common voice among them, that with Arthur was none other life but war and strife, and with Sir Mordred was great joy and bliss. Thus was Sir Arthur depraved and evil said of. And many there were that King Arthur had made up of nought, and given them lands, might not then say of him a good word.

Lo ye, all Englishmen, see ye not what a mischief here was, for he that was the most king and knight of the world, and most loved the fellowship of noble knights, and by him they were all upholden, now might not we Englishmen hold us content with him. Lo, thus was the old custom and usage of this land. And also men say, that we of this land have not yet lost nor forgotten that custom and usage. Alas, this is a great default of us Englishmen, for there may no thing please us no term. And so fared the people at that time; they were better pleased with Sir Mordred than they were with King Arthur, and much people drew unto Sir Mordred, and said they would abide with him for better and for worse. And so Sir Mordred drew with a great host to Dover, for there he heard say that Sir Arthur would arrive, and so he thought to beat his own father from his lands. And the most party of all England held with Sir Mordred, the people were so new fangle.

And so as Sir Mordred was at Dover with his host, there came King Arthur with a great navy of ships, galleys, and carracks. And there was Sir Mordred ready awaiting upon his landage, to let his own father to land upon the land that he was king over. Then there was launching of great boats and small, and full of noble men of arms, and there was much slaughter of gentle knights, and many a full bold baron was laid full low on both parties. But King Arthur was so courageous, that there might no manner of knights let him to land, and his knights fiercely followed him. And so they landed, maugre Sir Mordred and all his power, and put Sir Mordred aback, that he fled and all his people. So when this battle was done, King Arthur let bury his people that were dead, and then was the noble knight Sir Gawaine found in a great boat lying more than half dead. When Sir Arthur wist that Sir Gawaine was laid so low, he went unto him, and there the king made sorrow out of measure, and took Sir Gawaine in his arms, and thrice he there swooned. And when he awaked he said, Alas, Sir Gawaine, my sister's son, here now thou liest, the man in the world that I loved most, and now is my joy gone: for now, my nephew Sir Gawaine, I will discover me unto your person; in Sir Launcelot and you I most had my joy, and mine affiance, and now have I lost my joy of you both, wherefore all mine earthly joy is gone from me. Mine uncle King

King Arthur lands at Dover, and Sir Gawaino is mortally wounded.

Arthur, said Sir Gawaine, wit you well, my death-day is come, and all is through mine own hastiness and willfulness, for I am smitten upon the old wound the which Sir Launcelot gave me, on the which I feel well I must die; and had Sir Launcelot been with you as he was, this unhappy war had never begun, and of all this am I causer, for Sir Launcelot and his blood through their prowess held all your cankered enemies in subjection and danger: and now, said Sir Gawaine, ye shall miss Sir Launcelot. But, alas, I would not accord with him, and therefore, said Sir Gawaine, I pray you, fair uncle, that I may have paper, pen, and ink, that I may write to Sir Launcelot a schedule with mine own hands.

And then when paper and ink was brought, then Gawaine was set up weakly by King Arthur, for he was shriven a little tofore, and then he wrote thus, as the French book maketh mention, — Unto Sir Launcelot, flower of all noble knights that ever I heard of, or saw by my days, I Sir Gawaine, King Lot's son, of Orkney, sister's son unto the noble King Arthur, send thee greeting, and let thee have knowledge, that the tenth day of May I was smitten upon the old wound that thou gavest me afore the city of Benwick, and through the same wound that thou gavest me I am come to my death-day. And I will that all the world wit that I, Sir Gawaine, knight of the Round Table, sought my death, and not through thy deserving, but it was mine own seeking; wherefore I beseech thee, Sir Launcelot, to return again unto this realm, and see my tomb, and pray some prayer, more or less, for my soul. And this

Before his death Sir Gawaine writes a schedule to Sir Launcelot.

102

same day that I wrote this schedule, I was hurt to the death in the same wound, the which I had of thy hand, Sir Launcelot. For of a more nobler man might I not be slain. Also, Sir Launcelot, for all the love that ever was betwixt us, make no tarrying, but come over the sea in all haste, that thou mayest with thy noble knights rescue that noble king that made thee knight, that is my lord Arthur; for he is full straitly bestad with a false traitor, that is my half brother, Sir Mordred, and he hath let crown him king, and would have wedded my lady Queen Guenever, and so had he done, had she not put herself in the tower of London. And so the tenth day of May last past, my lord Arthur and we all landed upon them at Dover, and there we put that false traitor Sir Mordred to flight, and there it misfortuned me to be stricken upon thy stroke, and at the date of this letter was written but two hours and an half afore my death, written with mine own hand, and so subscribed with part of my heart's blood. And I require thee, most famous knight of the world, that thou wilt see my tomb. — And then Sir Gawaine wept, and King Arthur wept, and then they swooned both. And when they awaked both, the king made Sir Gawaine to receive his Saviour. And then Sir Gawaine prayed the king to send for Sir Launcelot, and to cherish him above all other knights. And so at the hour of noon, Sir Gawaine yielded up the spirit. And then the king let inter him in a chapel within Dover castle; and there yet all men may see the skull of him, and the same wound is seen that Sir Launcelot gave him in battle.

Then was it told King Arthur that Sir Mordred had

pitched a new field upon Barham Down. And upon the
morn the king rode thither to him, and there
The battle
of Barham was a great battle betwixt them, and much
Down.
people were slain on both parties. But at
the last Sir Arthur's party stood best, and Sir Mordred
and his party fled unto Canterbury. And then the king
let search all the towns for his knights that were slain,
and interred them; and salved them with soft salves that
so sore were wounded. Then much people drew unto
King Arthur. And then they said that Sir Mordred
warred upon King Arthur with wrong. And then King
Arthur drew him with his host down by the seaside, west-
ward toward Salisbury, and there was a day assigned
between King Arthur and Sir Mordred, and they should
meet upon a down beside Salisbury, and not far from
the seaside, and this day was assigned on Monday
after Trinity Sunday, whereof King Arthur was passing glad, that he might be avenged upon Sir Mordred.
Then Sir Mordred araised much people about London,
for they of Kent, Southsex, and Surrey, Estsex, and
Southfolk, and of Norfolk, held the most party with Sir
Mordred, and many a full noble knight drew unto
Sir Mordred and to the king; but they that loved Sir
Launcelot drew unto Sir Mordred.

So upon Trinity Sunday at night King Arthur dreamed
a wonderful dream, and that was this, that him seemed
he sat upon a chaflet in a chair, and the chair
King
Arthur's was fast to a wheel, and thereupon sat King
dream.
Arthur in the richest cloth of gold that might
be made: and the king thought there was under him, far
from him, an hideous deep black water, and therein were

all manner of serpents, and worms, and wild beasts, foul and horrible: and suddenly the king thought the wheel turned up so down, and he fell among the serpents, and every beast took him by a limb. And then the king cried as he lay in his bed and slept, Help! And then knights, squires, and yeomen awaked the king; and then he was so amazed that he wist not where he was. And then he fell on slumbering again, not sleeping nor thoroughly waking. So the king seemed verily that there came Sir Gawaine unto him, with a number of fair ladies with him. And when King Arthur saw him, then he said, Welcome, my sister's son, I wend thou hadst been dead, and now I see thee on live, much am I beholding unto Almighty Jesu. Oh, fair nephew, and my sister's son, what be these ladies that hither be come with you? Sir, said Sir Gawaine, all these be ladies for whom I have foughten when I was man living: and all these are those that I did battle for in righteous quarrel. And God hath given them that grace at their great prayer, because I did battle for them, that they should bring me hither unto you, thus much had God given me leave, for to warn you of your death; for and ye fight as to-morn with Sir Mordred, as ye both have assigned, doubt ye not ye must be slain, and the most part of your people on both parties. And for the great grace and goodness that Almighty Jesu hath unto you, and for pity of you and many more other good men there shall be slain, God hath sent me to you, of his special grace, to give you warning, that in no wise ye do battle as to-morn, but that ye take a treaty for a month day; and proffer you largely, so as to-morn to be put in a delay. For within a month shall come Sir Launcelot, with all his noble knights, and rescue you worshipfully, and slay Sir Mordred and all that ever will hold with him. Then Sir Gawaine and all the ladies vanished.

And anon the king called upon his knights, squires, and yeomen, and charged them wightly to fetch his noble lords and wise bishops unto him. And when they were come, the king told them his vision, what Sir Gawaine had told him, and warned him that if he fought on the morn he should be slain. Then the king commanded Sir Lucan de Butlere, and his brother Sir Bedivere, with two bishops with them, and charged them in any wise and they might take a treaty for a month day with Sir Mordred; — And spare not, proffer him lands and goods, as much as ye think best. So then they departed, and came to Sir Mordred, where he had a grim host of an hundred thousand men. And there they entreated Sir Mordred long time, and at the last Sir Mordred was agreed for to have Cornwall and Kent, by King Arthur's days: — after, all England, after the days of King Arthur.

A truce is proposed.

Then were they condescended that King Arthur and Sir Mordred should meet betwixt both their hosts, and every each of them should bring fourteen persons. And they came with this word unto King Arthur. Then said he, I am glad that this is done. And so he went into the field. And when Arthur should depart, he warned all his host that and they see any sword drawn, Look ye come on fiercely, and slay that traitor Sir Mordred, for I in no wise trust him. In like wise Sir Mordred warned his

At the conference an adder causes the battle to begin.

106

host that, — And ye see any sword drawn, look that ye come on fiercely, and so slay all that ever before you standeth: for in no wise I will not trust for this treaty: for I know well my father will be avenged upon me. And so they met as their pointment was, and so they were agreed and accorded thoroughly: and wine was fetched, and they drank. Right so came an adder out of a little heath bush, and it stung a knight on the foot. And when the knight felt him stungen, he looked down and saw the adder, and then he drew his sword to slay the adder, and thought of none other harm. And when the host on both parties saw that sword drawn, then they blew beames, trumpets, and horns, and shouted grimly. And so both hosts dressed them together.

And King Arthur took his horse, and said, Alas this unhappy day, and so rode to his party: and Sir Mordred in likewise. And never was there seen a more dolefuller battle in no Christian land. The battle. For there was but rushing and riding, foining and striking, and many a grim word was there spoken either to other, and many a deadly stroke. But ever King Arthur rode throughout the battle of Sir Mordred many times, and did full nobly as a noble king should: and at all times he fainted never. And Sir Mordred that day put him in devoir, and in great peril. And thus they fought all the long day, and never stinted, till the noble knights were laid to the cold ground; and ever they fought still, till it was near night, and by that time was there an hundred thousand laid dead upon the down. Then was Arthur wroth out of measure, when he saw his people so slain from him. Then the king looked about him, and then was he ware of all his host, and of all his good knights, were left no more on live but two knights, that was Sir Lucan de Butlere, and his brother Sir Bedivere: and they full were sore wounded. Jesu mercy, said the king, where are all my noble knights becomen. Alas that ever I should see this doleful day. For now, said Arthur, I am come to mine end. But would to God that I wist where were that traitor Sir Mordred, that hath caused all this mischief.

Then was King Arthur ware where Sir Mordred leaned upon his sword among a great heap of dead men. Now give me my spear, said Arthur unto Sir Lucan, for yonder I have espied the traitor that all this woe hath wrought. Sir, let him be, said Sir Lucan, for he is unhappy: and if ye pass this unhappy day, ye shall be right well revenged upon him. Good lord, remember ye of your night's dream, and what the spirit of Sir Gawaine told you this night; yet God of his great goodness hath preserved you hitherto. Therefore, for God's sake, my lord, leave off by this. For blessed be God ye have won the field: for here we be three on live, and with Sir Mordred is none on live. And if ye leave off now, this wicked day of destiny is past. Tide me death, betide me life, saith the king, now I see him yonder alone; he shall never escape mine hands, for at a better avail shall I never have him. God speed you well, said Sir Bedivere. Then the king gat his spear in both his hands, and ran toward Sir Mordred, crying, Traitor, now is thy death-day come. And when Sir Mordred heard Sir Arthur, he ran until him with his

King Arthur slays Sir Mordred, and is wounded to the death by him.

sword drawn in his hand. And then King Arthur
smote Sir Mordred under the shield, with a foin of his
spear throughout the body more than a fathom. And
when Sir Mordred felt that he had his death's wound,
he thrust himself, with the might that he had, up to the
bur of King Arthur's spear. And right so he smote
his father Arthur with his sword holden in both his
hands, on the side of the head, that the sword pierced
the helmet and the brain-pan, and therewithal Sir
Mordred fell stark dead to the earth. And the noble
Arthur fell in a swoon to the earth, and there he swooned
ofttimes.

And Sir Lucan de Butlere and Sir Bedivere ofttimes
heaved him up, and so weakly they led him betwixt
them both to a little chapel not far from the
seaside. And when the king was there, he
thought him well eased. Then heard they
people cry in the field. Now go thou, Sir
Lucan, said the king, and do me to wit
what betokens that noise in the field. So Sir Lucan
departed, for he was grievously wounded in many
places. And so as he went, he saw and hearkened by
the moonlight, how the pillers and robbers were come
into the field to pill and to rob many a full noble knight
of brooches and beads, of many a good ring, and of
many a rich jewel; and who that were not dead all out,
there they slew them for their harness and their riches.
When Sir Lucan understood this work, he came to the
king as soon as he might, and told him all what he had
heard and seen. Therefore by mine advice, said Sir
Lucan, it is best that we bring you to some town. I

Sir Lucan and Sir Bedivere carry King Arthur to a chapel.

would it were so, said the king, but I may not stand, my head werches so. Ah, Sir Launcelot, said King Arthur, this day have I sore missed thee. Alas, that ever I was against thee, for now have I my death, whereof Sir Gawaine me warned in my dream. Then Sir Lucan took up the king the one part, and Sir Bedivere the other part, and in the lifting, the king swooned, and Sir Lucan fell in a swoon with the lift, and therewith the noble knight's heart brast. And when King Arthur came to himself again, he beheld Sir Lucan how he lay foaming at the mouth. Alas, said the king, this is unto me a full heavy sight to see this noble duke so die for my sake, for he would have holpen me that had more need of help than I. Alas, he would not complain him, his heart was so set to help me. Now Jesu, have mercy upon his soul. Then Sir Bedivere wept for the death of his brother.

Leave this mourning and weeping, said the king, for all this will not avail me: for, wit thou well, and I might *Sir Bedivere and the sword Excalibur.* live myself the death of Sir Lucan would grieve me evermore; but my time hieth fast, said the king. Therefore, said Arthur, take thou Excalibur, my good sword, and go with it to yonder waterside; when thou comest there, I charge thee throw my sword in that water, and come again, and tell me what thou there seest. My lord, said Bedivere, your commandment shall be done, and lightly bring you word again. So Sir Bedivere departed, and by the way he beheld that noble sword, that the pommel and haft were all of precious stones, and then he said to himself, If I throw this rich sword in the water, thereof shall never come good, but harm and loss. And then Sir Bedivere hid Excalibur under a tree. And as soon as he might he came again unto the king, and said he had been at the water, and had thrown the sword into the water. What saw thou there? said the king. Sir, he said, I saw nothing but waves and winds. That is untruly said of thee, said the king, therefore go thou lightly again, and do my command as thou art to me lief and dear; spare not, but throw it in. Then Sir Bedivere returned again, and took the sword in his hand; and then him thought sin and shame to throw away that noble sword; and so eft he hid the sword, and returned again, and told to the king that he had been at the water, and done his commandment. What saw thou there? said the king. Sir, he said, I saw nothing but the waters wap and the waves wan. Ah traitor, untrue, said King Arthur, now hast thou betrayed me twice. Who would have wend that thou that hast been to me so lief and dear, and thou art named a noble knight, and would betray me for the riches of the sword. But now go again lightly, for thy long tarrying putteth me in great jeopardy of my life, for I have taken cold. And but if thou do now as I bid thee, if ever I may see thee, I shall slay thee with mine own hands, for thou wouldest for my rich sword see me dead.

Then Sir Bedivere departed, and went to the sword, and lightly took it up, and went to the waterside, and there he bound the girdle about the hilts, and then he threw the sword as far into the water as he might, and there came an arm and an hand above the water, and met it, and caught it, and so shook it thrice and brandished, and then vanished away the hand with the sword in the water. So Sir Bedivere came again to the king and told him what he saw. Alas, said the king, help me hence, for I dread me I have tarried over long.

Then Sir Bedivere took the king upon his back, and so went with him to that waterside. And when they were at the waterside, even fast by the bank hoved a little barge, with many fair ladies in it, and among them all was a queen; and all they had black hoods, and all they wept and shrieked when they saw King Arthur. Now put me into the barge, said the king: and so he did softly. And there received him three queens with great mourning; and so they set him down, and in one of their laps King Arthur laid his head, and then that queen said, Ah, dear brother, why have ye tarried so long from me? Alas, this wound on your head hath caught over much cold. And so then they rowed from the land; and Sir Bedivere beheld all those ladies go from him. Then Sir Bedivere cried, Ah, my lord Arthur, what shall become of me now ye go from me, and leave me here alone among mine enemies. Comfort thyself, said the king, and do as well as thou mayest, for in me is no trust for to trust in. For I will into the vale of Avilion, to heal me of my grievous wound. And if thou hear never more of me, pray for my soul. But ever the queens and the ladies wept and shrieked, that it was pity to hear. And as soon as Sir Bedivere had lost the sight of the barge, he wept and wailed, and so took the forest; and so he went all that night, and in the morning he was ware betwixt two holts hoar of a chapel and an hermitage.

Sir Bedivere places Arthur in a barge which bears him from the land.

112

THERE RECEIVED HIM THREE QUEENS WITH GREAT MOURNING

Then was Sir Bedivere glad, and thither he went; and when he came into the chapel, he saw where lay an hermit groveling on all four, there fast by a King Arthur's tomb was new graven. When the hermit saw tomb.
Sir Bedivere, he knew him well, for he was but a little before Bishop of Canterbury, that Sir Mordred banished. Sir, said Sir Bedivere, what man is there interred that ye pray so fast for? Fair son, said the hermit, I wot not verily, but by deeming. But this night, at midnight, here came a number of ladies, and brought hither a dead corpse, and prayed me to bury him; and here they offered an hundred tapers, and gave me an hundred besants. Alas, said Sir Bedivere, that was my lord King Arthur, that here lieth buried in this chapel! Then Sir Bedivere swooned, and when he awoke he prayed the hermit he might abide with him still there, to live with fasting and prayers. For from hence will I never go, said Sir Bedivere, by my will, but all the days of my life here to pray for my lord Arthur. Ye are welcome to me, said the hermit, for I know you better than ye ween that I do. Ye are the bold Bedivere, and the full noble duke Sir Lucan de Butlere was your brother. Then Sir Bedivere told the hermit all as ye have heard tofore. So there bode Sir Bedivere with the hermit, that was tofore Bishop of Canterbury; and there Sir Bedivere put upon him poor clothes, and served the hermit full lowly in fasting and in prayers.

Thus of Arthur I find never more written in books that he authorized, nor more of the certainty of his death heard I never tell, but thus was he led away in a ship wherein were three queens; that one was King Arthur's sister, Queen Morgan le Fay; the other was the queen of Northgalis; the third was the queen of the Waste Lands. Also there was Nimue, the chief Lady of the lake, that had wedded Pelleas the good knight; and this lady had done much for King Arthur; for she would never suffer Sir Pelleas to be in no place where he should be in danger of his life, and so he lived to the uttermost of his days with her in great rest. More of the death of King Arthur could I never find, but that ladies brought him to his burials; and such one was buried there, that the hermit bare witness that some time was Bishop of Canterbury, but yet the hermit knew not in certain that he was verily the body of King Arthur; — for this tale Sir Bedivere, knight of the Round Table, made it to be written.

Yet some men yet say in many parts of England that King Arthur is not dead, but had by the will of our Lord Jesu in another place. And men say that he shall come again, and he shall win the holy cross. I will not say it shall be so, but rather I will say, here in this world he changed his life. But many men say that there is written upon his tomb this verse,

Hic iacet Arthurus Rex quondam Rexque futurus.

OWAIN AND THE LADY OF THE FOUNTAIN

By Thomas Bulfinch

KING ARTHUR was at Caerleon upon Usk; and one day he sat in his chamber, and with him were Owain the son of Urien, and Kynon the son of Clydno, and Kay the son of Kyner, and Guenever and her hand-maidens at needlework by the window. In the centre of the chamber King Arthur sat upon a seat of green rushes, over which was spread a covering of flame-colored satin, and a cushion of red satin was under his elbow.

Then Arthur spoke. "If I thought you would not disparage me," said he, "I would sleep while I wait for my repast; and you can entertain one another with relating tales, and can obtain a flagon of mead and some meat from Kay." And the king went to sleep. And Kynon the son of Clydno asked Kay for that which Arthur had promised them. "I too will have the good tale which he promised me," said Kay. "Nay," answered Kynon; "fairer will it be for thee to fulfill Arthur's behest in the first place, and then we will tell thee the best tale that we know." So Kay went to the kitchen and to the mead-cellar, and returned, bearing a flagon of mead, and a golden goblet, and a handful of skewers, upon which were broiled collops of meat. Then they ate the collops, and began to drink the mead. "Now," said Kay, "it is time for you to give me my story." "Kynon," said Owain, "do thou pay to Kay the tale that is his due." "I will do so," answered Kynon.

"I was the only son of my mother and father, and I was exceedingly aspiring, and my daring was very great. I thought there was no enterprise in the world too mighty for me; and after I had achieved all the adventures that were in my own country, I equipped myself, and set forth to journey through deserts and distant regions. And at length it chanced that I came to the fairest valley in the world, wherein were trees all of equal growth; and a river ran through the valley, and a path was by the side of the river. And I followed the path until midday, and continued my journey along the remainder of the valley until the evening; and at the extremity of a plain I came to a large and lustrous castle, at the foot of which was a torrent. And I approached the castle, and there I beheld two youths with yellow curling hair, each with a frontlet of gold upon his head, and clad in a garment of yellow satin; and they had gold clasps upon their insteps. In the hand of each of them was an ivory bow, strung with the sinews of the stag, and their arrows and their shafts were of the bone of the whale, and were winged with peacocks' feathers. The shafts also had golden heads. And they had daggers with blades of gold, and with hilts of the bone of the whale. And they were shooting at a mark.

"And a little way from them I saw a man in the prime of life, with his beard newly shorn, clad in a robe and mantle of yellow satin, and round the top of his mantle was a band of gold lace. On his feet were shoes of variegated leather, fastened by two bosses of gold. When I saw him I went towards him and saluted him; and such was his courtesy, that he no sooner received my greeting than he returned it. And he went with me towards the castle. Now there were no dwellers in the castle, except those who were in one hall. And there I saw four and twenty damsels, embroidering satin at a window. And this I tell thee, Kay, that the least fair of them was fairer than the fairest maid thou didst ever behold in the island of Britain; and the least lovely of them was more lovely than Guenever, the wife of Arthur, when she appeared loveliest, at the feast of Easter. They rose up at my coming, and six of them took my horse, and divested me of my armor; and six others took my arms, and washed them in a vessel till they were perfectly bright. And the third six spread cloths upon the tables, and prepared meat. And the fourth six took off my soiled garments, and placed others upon me, namely, an undervest and a doublet of fine linen, and a robe and a surcoat, and a mantle of yellow satin, with a broad gold band upon the mantle. And they placed cushions both beneath and around me, with coverings of red linen. And I sat down. Now the six maidens who had taken my horse unharnessed him as well as if they had been the best squires in the island of Britain.

"Then behold they brought bowls of silver, wherein was water to wash, and towels of linen, some green and some white; and I washed. And in a little while the man sat down at the table. And I sat next to him, and below me sat all the maidens, except those who waited on us. And the table was of silver, and the cloths upon the table were of linen. And no vessel was served upon the table that was not either of gold or of silver or of buffalo-horn. And our meat was brought to us. And verily, Kay, I saw there every sort of meat and every sort of liquor that I ever saw elsewhere; but the meat and the liquor were better served there than I ever saw them in any other place.

"Until the repast was half over, neither the man nor any one of the damsels spoke a single word to me; but when the man perceived that it would be more agreeable for me to converse than to eat any more, he began to inquire of me who I was. Then I told the man who I was, and what was the cause of my journey, and said that I was seeking whether any one was superior to me, or whether I could gain the mastery over all. The man looked upon me, and he smiled and said, 'If I did not fear to do thee a mischief, I would show thee that which thou seekest.' Then I desired him to speak freely. And he said: 'Sleep here to-night, and in the morning arise early, and take the road upwards through the valley, until thou reachest the wood. A little way within the wood thou wilt come to a large sheltered glade, with a mound in the centre. And thou wilt see a black man of great stature on the top of the mound. He has but one foot, and one eye in the middle of his forehead. He is the wood-ward of that wood. And thou wilt see a thousand wild animals grazing around him. Inquire of him the way out of the glade, and he will reply to thee briefly, and will point out the road by which thou shalt find that which thou art in quest of.'

"And long seemed that night to me. And the next morning I arose and equipped myself, and mounted my horse, and proceeded straight through the valley to the wood, and at length I arrived at the glade. And the black man was there, sitting upon the top of the mound; and I was three times more astonished at the number of wild animals that I beheld, than the man had said I should be. Then I inquired of him the way, and he asked me roughly whither I would go And when I had told him who I was, and what I sought, 'Take,' said he, 'that path that leads toward the head of the glade, and there thou wilt find an open space like to a large valley, and in the midst of it a tall tree. Under this tree is a fountain, and by the side of the fountain a marble slab, and on the marble slab a silver bowl, attached by a chain of silver, that it may not be carried away. Take the bowl, and throw a bowlful of water on the slab. And if thou dost not find trouble in that adventure, thou needest not seek it during the rest of thy life.'

"So I journeyed on until I reached the summit of the steep. And there I found everything as the black man had described it to me. And I went up to the tree, and beneath it I saw the fountain, and by its side the marble slab, and the silver bowl fastened by the chain. Then I took the bowl, and cast a bowlful of water upon the slab. And immediately I heard a mighty peal of thunder, so that heaven and earth seemed to tremble with its fury. And after the thunder came a shower; and of a truth I tell thee, Kay, that it was such a shower as neither man nor beast could endure and live. I turned my horse's flank toward the shower, and placed the beak of my shield over his head and neck, while I held the upper part of it over my own neck. And thus I withstood the shower. And presently the sky became clear, and with that, behold, the birds lighted upon the tree and sang. And truly, Kay, I never heard any melody equal to that, either before or since. And when I was most charmed with listening to the birds, lo! a chiding voice was heard of one approaching me, and saying, 'O knight, what has brought thee hither? What evil have I done to thee, that thou shouldst act towards me and my possessions as thou hast this day? Dost thou not know that the shower to-day has left in my dominions neither man nor beast alive that was exposed to it?' And thereupon, behold, a knight on a black horse appeared, clothed in jet-black velvet, and with a tabard of black linen about him. And we charged each other, and, as the onset was furious, it was not long before I was overthrown. Then the knight passed the shaft of his lance through the bridle-rein of my horse, and rode off with the two horses, leaving me where I was. And he did not even bestow so much notice upon me as to imprison me, nor did he despoil me of my arms. So I returned along the road by which I had come. And when I reached the glade where the black man was, I confess to thee, Kay, it is a marvel that I did not melt down into a liquid pool, through the shame I felt at the black man's derision. And that night I came to the same castle where I had spent the night preceding. And I was more agreeably enter-

tained that night than I had been the night before.
And I conversed freely with the inmates of the castle;
and none of them alluded to my expedition to the
fountain, neither did I mention it to any. And I remained there that night. When I arose on the morrow
I found ready saddled a dark bay palfrey, with nostrils
as red as scarlet. And after putting on my armor, and
leaving there my blessing, I returned to my own court.
And that horse I still possess, and he is in the stable
yonder. And I declare that I would not part with him
for the best palfrey in the island of Britain.

"Now, of a truth, Kay, no man ever before confessed
to an adventure so much to his own discredit; and
verily it seems strange to me that neither before nor
since have I heard of any person who knew of this adventure, and that the subject of it should exist within
King Arthur's dominions without any other person
lighting upon it."

"Now," quoth Owain, "would it not be well to go and
endeavor to discover that place?"

"By the hand of my friend," said Kay, "often dost
thou utter that with thy tongue which thou wouldest not
make good with thy deeds."

"In very truth," said Guenever, "it were better thou
wert hanged, Kay, than to use such uncourteous speech
towards a man like Owain."

"By the hand of my friend, good lady," said Kay,
"thy praise of Owain is not greater than mine."

With that Arthur awoke, and asked if he had not been
sleeping a little.

"Yes, lord," answered Owain, "thou hast slept awhile."

"Is it time for us to go to meat?"

"It is, lord," said Owain.

Then the horn for washing was sounded, and the king and all his household sat down to eat. And when the meal was ended, Owain withdrew to his lodging, and made ready his horse and his arms.

On the morrow with the dawn of day he put on his armor, and mounted his charger, and traveled through distant lands, and over desert mountains. And at length he arrived at the valley which Kynon had described to him, and he was certain that it was the same that he sought. And journeying along the valley, by the side of the river, he followed its course till he came to the plain, and within sight of the castle. When he approached the castle, he saw the youths shooting with their bows, in the place where Kynon had seen them, and the yellow man, to whom the castle belonged, standing hard by. And no sooner had Owain saluted the yellow man, than he was saluted by him in return.

And he went forward towards the castle, and there he saw the chamber; and when he had entered the chamber, he beheld the maidens working at satin embroidery, in chains of gold. And their beauty and their comeliness seemed to Owain far greater than Kynon had represented to him. And they arose to wait upon Owain, as they had done to Kynon. And the meal which they set before him gave even more satisfaction to Owain than it had done to Kynon.

About the middle of the repast the yellow man asked Owain the object of his journey. And Owain made it known to him, and said, "I am in quest of the knight who guards the fountain." Upon this the yellow man smiled, and said that he was as loath to point out that adventure to him as he had been to Kynon. However, he described the whole to Owain, and they retired to rest.

The next morning Owain found his horse made ready for him by the damsels, and he set forward and came to the glade where the black man was. And the stature of the black man seemed more wonderful to Owain than it had done to Kynon; and Owain asked of him his road, and he showed it to him. And Owain followed the road till he came to the green tree; and he beheld the fountain, and the slab beside the fountain, and the bowl upon it. And Owain took the bowl and threw a bowlful of water upon the slab. And, lo! the thunder was heard, and after the thunder came the shower, more violent than Kynon had described, and after the shower the sky became bright. And immediately the birds came and settled upon the tree and sang. And when their song was most pleasing to Owain, he beheld a knight coming towards him through the valley; and he prepared to receive him, and encountered him violently. Having broken both their lances, they drew their swords and fought blade to blade. Then Owain struck the knight a blow through his helmet, headpiece, and visor, and through the skin, and the flesh, and the bone, until it wounded the very brain. Then the black knight felt that he had received a mortal wound, upon which he turned his horse's head and fled. And Owain pursued him, and followed close upon him, although he was not near enough to strike him with his sword. Then Owain descried a vast and resplendent castle; and they came to the castle gate. And the black knight was allowed to enter, and the portcullis was let fall upon Owain; and it struck his horse behind the saddle, and cut him in two, and carried away the rowels of the spurs that were upon Owain's heels. And the portcullis descended to the floor. And the rowels of the spurs and part of the horse were without, and Owain with the other part of the horse remained between the two gates, and the inner gate was closed, so that Owain could not go thence; and Owain was in a perplexing situation. And while he was in this state, he could see through an aperture in the gate a street facing him, with a row of houses on each side. And he beheld a maiden, with yellow, curling hair, and a frontlet of gold upon her head; and she was clad in a dress of yellow satin, and on her feet were shoes of variegated leather. And she approached the gate, and desired that it should be opened. "Heaven knows, lady," said Owain, "it is no more possible for me to open to thee from hence, than it is for thee to set me free." And he told her his name, and who he was. "Truly," said the damsel, "it is very sad that thou canst not be released; and every woman ought to succor thee, for I know there is no one more faithful in the service of ladies than thou. Therefore," quoth she, "whatever is in my power to do for thy release, I will do it. Take this ring, and put it on thy finger, with the stone inside thy hand, and close thy hand upon the stone. And as long as thou concealest it, it will conceal thee. When they come forth to fetch thee, they will be much grieved that they cannot find thee. And I will await thee on the horse-block yonder, and thou wilt be able to see me, though I cannot see thee. Therefore come and place thy hand upon my shoulder, that I may know that thou art near me. And by the way that I go hence, do thou accompany me."

Then the maiden went away from Owain, and he did all that she had told him. And the people of the castle came to seek Owain to put him to death; and when they found nothing but the half of his horse, they were sorely grieved.

And Owain vanished from among them, and went to the maiden, and placed his hand upon her shoulder; whereupon she set off, and Owain followed her, until they came to the door of a large and beautiful chamber, and the maiden opened it, and they went in. And Owain looked around the chamber, and behold there was not a single nail in it that was not painted with gorgeous colors, and there was not a single panel that had not sundry images in gold portrayed upon it.

The maiden kindled a fire, and took water in a silver bowl, and gave Owain water to wash. Then she placed before him a silver table, inlaid with gold; upon which was a cloth of yellow linen, and she brought him food. And, of a truth, Owain never saw any kind of meat that was not there in abundance, but it was better cooked there than he had ever found it in any other place. And there was not one vessel from which he was served that was not of gold or of silver. And Owain ate and drank until late in the afternoon, when, lo! they heard a mighty clamor in the castle, and Owain asked the maiden what it was. "They are administering extreme unction," said she, "to the nobleman who owns the castle." And she prepared a couch for Owain which was meet for Arthur himself, and Owain went to sleep.

And a little after daybreak he heard an exceeding loud clamor and wailing, and he asked the maiden what was the cause of it. "They are bearing to the church the body of the nobleman who owned the castle."

And Owain rose up, and clothed himself, and opened a window of the chamber, and looked towards the castle; and he could see neither the bounds nor the extent of the hosts that filled the streets. And they were fully armed; and a vast number of women were with them, both on horseback and on foot, and all the ecclesiastics in the city singing. In the midst of the throng he beheld the bier, over which was a veil of white linen; and wax tapers were burning beside and around it; and none that supported the bier was lower in rank than a powerful baron.

Never did Owain see an assemblage so gorgeous with silk and satin. And following the train, he beheld a lady with yellow hair falling over her shoulders, and stained with blood; and about her a dress of yellow satin, which was torn. Upon her feet were shoes of variegated leather. And it was a marvel that the ends of her fingers were not bruised from the violence with which she smote her hands together. Truly she would have been the fairest lady Owain ever saw had she been in her usual guise. And her cry was louder than the shout of the men or the clamor of the trumpets. No sooner had he beheld the lady than he became inflamed with her love, so that it took entire possession of him.

Then he inquired of the maiden who the lady was. "Heaven knows," replied the maiden, "she is the fairest, and the most chaste, and the most liberal, and the most noble of women. She is my mistress, and she is called the Countess of the Fountain, the wife of him whom thou didst slay yesterday." "Verily," said Owain, "she is the woman that I love best." "Verily," said the maiden, "she shall also love thee, not a little."

Then the maiden prepared a repast for Owain, and truly he thought he had never before so good a meal, nor was he ever so well served. Then she left him, and went towards the castle. When she came there she found nothing but mourning and sorrow; and the countess in her chamber could not bear the sight of any one through grief. Luned, for that was the name of the maiden, saluted her, but the countess answered her not. And the maiden bent down towards her, and said, "What aileth thee that thou answerest no one to-day?" "Luned," said the countess, "what change hath befallen thee that thou hast not come to visit me in my grief? It was wrong in thee, and I so sorely afflicted." "Truly," said Luned, "I thought thy good sense was greater than I find it to be. Is it well for thee to mourn after that good man, or for anything else that thou canst not have?" "I declare to Heaven," said the countess, "that in the whole world there is not a man equal to him." "Not so," said Luned, "for an ugly man would be as good as, or better than he." "I declare to Heaven," said the countess, "that were it not repugnant to me to put to death one whom I have brought up I would have thee executed for making such a comparison to me. As it is, I will banish thee." "I am glad," said Luned, "that thou hast no other cause to do so than that I would have been of service to thee, where thou didst not know what was to thine advantage. Henceforth evil betide whichever of us shall make the first advance towards reconciliation to the other, whether I should seek an invitation from thee, or thou of thine own accord shouldst send to invite me."

With that Luned went forth; and the countess arose and followed her to the door of the chamber, and began coughing loudly. And when Luned looked back the countess beckoned to her, and she returned to the countess. "In truth," said the countess, "evil is thy disposition; but if thou knowest what is to my advantage, declare it to me." "I will do so," said she.

"Thou knowest that, except by warfare and arms, it is impossible for thee to preserve thy possessions; delay not, therefore, to seek some one who can defend them." "And how can I do that?" said the countess. "I will tell thee," said Luned; "unless thou canst defend the fountain, thou canst not maintain thy dominions; and no one can defend the fountain except it be a knight of Arthur's household. I will go to Arthur's court, and ill betide me if I return not thence with a warrior who can guard the fountain as well as, or even better, than he who defended it formerly." "That will be hard to perform," said the countess. "Go, however, and make proof of that which thou hast promised."

Luned set out under the pretense of going to Arthur's court; but she went back to the mansion where she had left Owain, and she tarried there as long as it might have taken her to travel to the court of King Arthur and back. And at the end of that time she appareled herself, and went to visit the countess. And the countess was much rejoiced when she saw her, and inquired what news she brought from the court. "I bring thee the best of news," said Luned, "for I have compassed the object of my mission. When willt thou that I should present to thee the chieftain who has come with me thither?" "Bring him here to visit me to-morrow," said the countess, "and I will cause the town to be assembled by that time."

And Luned returned home. And the next day, at noon, Owain arrayed himself in a coat and a surcoat, and a mantle of yellow satin, upon which was a broad band of gold lace; and on his feet were high shoes of variegated leather, which were fastened by golden clasps, in the form of lions. And they proceeded to the chamber of the countess.

Right glad was the countess of their coming. And she gazed steadfastly upon Owain, and said, "Luned, this knight has not the look of a traveler." "What harm is there in that, lady?" said Luned. "I am certain," said the countess, "that no other man than this chased the soul from the body of my lord." "So much the better for thee, lady," said Luned; "for had he not been stronger than thy lord, he could not have deprived him of life. There is no remedy for that which is past, be it as it may." "Go back to thine abode," said the countess, "and I will take counsel."

The next day the countess caused all her subjects to assemble, and showed them that her earldom was left defenseless, and that it could not be protected but with horse and arms, and military skill. "Therefore," said she, "this is what I offer for your choice: either let one of you take me, or give your consent for me to take a husband from elsewhere, to defend my dominions."

So they came to the determination that it was better that she should have permission to marry some one from elsewhere; and thereupon she sent for the bishops and archbishops, to celebrate her nuptials with Owain. And the men of the earldom did Owain homage.

And Owain defended the fountain with lance and sword. And this is the manner in which he defended it. Whensoever a knight came there, he overthrew him, and sold him for his full worth. And what he thus gained he divided among his barons and his knights, and no man in the whole world could be more beloved than he was by his subjects. And it was thus for the space of three years.

_____

It befell that, as Gawain went forth one day with King Arthur, he perceived him to be very sad and sorrowful. And Gawain was much grieved to see Arthur in this state, and he questioned him, saying, "O my lord, what has befallen thee?" "In sooth, Gawain," said Arthur, "I am grieved concerning Owain, whom I have lost these three years; and I shall certainly die if the fourth year pass without my seeing him. Now I am sure that it is through the tale which Kynon, the son of Clydno, related, that I have lost Owain." "There is no need for thee," said Gawain, "to summon to arms thy whole dominions on this account, for thou thyself, and the men of thy household, will be able to avenge Owain if he be slain, or to set him free if he be in prison; and, if alive, to bring him back with thee." And it was settled according to what Gawain had said.

Then Arthur and the men of his household prepared to go and seek Owain. And Kynon, the son of Clydno, acted as their guide. And Arthur came to the castle where Kynon had been before. And when he came there, the youths were shooting in the same place, and the yellow man was standing hard by. When the yellow man saw Arthur, he greeted him, and invited him to the castle. And Arthur accepted his invitation, and they entered the castle together. And great as was the number of his retinue, their presence was scarcely observed in the castle, so vast was its extent. And the maidens rose up to wait on them. And the service of the maidens appeared to them all to excel any attendance they had ever met with; and even the pages, who had charge of the horses, were no worse served that night than Arthur himself would have been in his own palace.

The next morning Arthur set out thence, with Kynon for his guide, and came to the place where the black man was. And the stature of the black man was more surprising to Arthur than it had been represented to him. And they came to the top of the wooded steep, and traversed the valley, till they reached the green tree, where they saw the fountain and the bowl and the slab. And upon that Kay came to Arthur, and spoke to him. "My lord," said he, "I know the meaning of all this, and my request is that thou wilt permit me to throw the water on the slab, and to receive the first adventure that may befall." And Arthur gave him leave.

Then Kay threw a bowlful of water upon the slab, and immediately there came the thunder, and after the thunder the shower. And such a thunderstorm they had never known before. After the shower had ceased, the sky became clear, and on looking at the tree, they beheld it completely leafless. Then the birds descended upon the tree. And the song of the birds was far sweeter than any strain they had ever heard before. Then they beheld a knight, on a coal-black horse, clothed in black satin, coming rapidly towards them. And Kay met him and encountered him, and it was not long before Kay was overthrown. And the knight withdrew. And Arthur and his host encamped for the night.

And when they arose in the morning, they perceived the signal of combat upon the lance of the knight. Then, one by one, all the household of Arthur went forth to combat the knight, until there was not one that was not overthrown by him, except Arthur and Gawain. And Arthur armed himself to encounter the knight. "O my lord," said Gawain, "permit me to fight with him first." And Arthur permitted him. And he went forth to meet the knight, having over himself and his horse a satin robe of honor, which had been sent him by the daughter of the Earl of Rhangyr, and in this dress he was not known by any of the host. And they charged each other, and fought all that day until the evening. And neither of them was able to unhorse the other. And so it was the next day; they broke their lances in the shock, but neither of them could obtain the mastery.

KING ARTHUR

And the third day they fought with exceeding strong lances. And they were incensed with rage, and fought furiously, even until noon. And they gave each other such a shock, that the girths of their horses were broken, so that they fell over their horses' cruppers to the ground. And they rose up speedily and drew their swords, and resumed the combat. And all they that witnessed their encounter felt assured that they had never before seen two men so valiant or so powerful. And had it been midnight, it would have been light, from the fire that flashed from their weapons. And the knight gave Gawain a blow that turned his helmet from off his face, so that the knight saw that it was Gawain. Then Owain said, "My lord Gawain, I did not know thee for my cousin, owing to the robe of honor that enveloped thee; take my sword and my arms." Said Gawain, "Thou, Owain, art the victor; take thou my sword." And with that Arthur saw that they were conversing, and advanced toward them. "My lord Arthur," said Gawain, "here is Owain, who has vanquished me, and will not take my arms." "My lord," said Owain, "it is he that has vanquished me, and he will not take my sword." "Give me your swords," said Arthur, "and then neither of you has vanquished the other." Then Owain put his arms round Arthur's neck, and they embraced. And all the host hurried forward, to see Owain, and to embrace him. And there was nigh being a loss of life, so great was the press.

And they retired that night, and the next day Arthur prepared to depart. "My lord," said Owain, "this is not well of thee. For I have been absent from thee these

three years; and during all that time, up to this very day,
I have been preparing a banquet for thee, knowing that
thou wouldst come to seek me. Tarry with me, therefore, until thou and thy attendants have recovered the
fatigues of the journey, and have been anointed."

And they all proceeded to the castle of the Countess
of the Fountain, and the banquet which had been three
years preparing was consumed in three months. Never
had they a more delicious or agreeable banquet. And
Arthur prepared to depart. Then he sent an embassy
to the countess to beseech her to permit Owain to go
with him for the space of three months, that he might
show him to the nobles and the fair dames of the island
of Britain. And the countess gave her consent, although
it was very painful to her. So Owain came with Arthur
to the island of Britain. And when he was once more
amongst his kindred and friends, he remained three
years, instead of three months, with them.

THE ADVENTURE OF THE LION

And as Owain one day sat at meat, in the city of
Caerleon upon Usk, behold a damsel entered the hall,
upon a bay horse, with a curling mane, and covered with
foam; and the bridle, and as much as was seen of the
saddle, were of gold. And the damsel was arrayed in a
dress of yellow satin. And she came up to Owain, and
took the ring from off his hand. "Thus," said she,
"shall be treated the deceiver, the traitor, the faithless,
the disgraced, and the beardless." And she turned her
horse's head, and departed.

Then his adventure came to Owain's remembrance, and he was sorrowful. And having finished eating, he went to his own abode, and made preparations that night. And the next day he arose, but did not go to the court, nor did he return to the Countess of the Fountain, but wandered to the distant parts of the earth and to uncultivated mountains. And he remained there until all his apparel was worn out and his body was wasted away, and his hair was grown long. And he went about with the wild beasts, and fed with them, until they became familiar with him. But at length he became so weak that he could no longer bear them company. Then he descended from the mountains to the valley, and came to a park, that was the fairest in the world, and belonged to a charitable lady.

One day the lady and her attendants went forth to walk by a lake that was in the middle of the park. And they saw the form of a man lying as if dead. And they were terrified. Nevertheless they went near him, and touched him, and they saw that there was life in him. And the lady returned to the castle, and took a flask full of precious ointment and gave it to one of her maidens. "Go with this," said she, "and take with thee yonder horse, and clothing, and place them near the man we saw just now; and anoint him with this balsam near his heart; and if there is life in him he will revive, through the efficiency of this balsam. Then watch what he will do."

And the maiden departed from her, and went and poured of the balsam upon Owain, and left the horse and the garments hard by, and went a little way off and hid herself to watch him. In a short time she saw him begin to move; and he rose up and looked at his person, and became ashamed of the unseemliness of his appearance. Then he perceived the horse and the garments that were near him. And he clothed himself, and with difficulty mounted the horse. Then the damsel discovered herself to him, and saluted him. And he and the maiden proceeded to the castle, and the maiden conducted him to a pleasant chamber, and kindled a fire, and left him.

And he stayed at the castle three months, till he was restored to his former guise, and became even more comely than he had ever been before. And Owain rendered signal service to the lady in a controversy with a powerful neighbor, so that he made ample requital to her for her hospitality; and he took his departure.

And as he journeyed he heard a loud yelling in a wood. And it was repeated a second and a third time. And Owain went towards the spot, and beheld a huge craggy mound, in the middle of the wood, on the side of which was a gray rock. And there was a cleft in the rock, and a serpent was within the cleft. And near the rock stood a black lion, and every time the lion sought to go thence the serpent darted towards him to attack him. And Owain unsheathed his sword, and drew near to the rock; and as the serpent sprung out he struck him with his sword and cut him in two. And he dried his sword, and went on his way as before. But behold the lion followed him, and played about him, as though it had been a greyhound that he had reared.

They proceeded thus throughout the day, until the

136

evening. And when it was time for Owain to take his rest he dismounted, and turned his horse loose in a flat and wooded meadow. And he struck fire, and when the fire was kindled the lion brought him fuel enough to last for three nights. And the lion disappeared. And presently the lion returned, bearing a fine large roebuck. And he threw it down before Owain, who went towards the fire with it.

And Owain took the roebuck and skinned it, and placed collops of its flesh upon skewers round the fire. The rest of the buck he gave to the lion to devour. While he was so employed he heard a deep groan near him, and a second, and a third. And the place whence the groans proceeded was a cave in the rock; and Owain went near, and called out to know who it was that groaned so piteously. And a voice answered, "I am Luned, the handmaiden of the Countess of the Fountain." "And what dost thou here?" said he. "I am imprisoned," said she, "on account of the knight who came from Arthur's court and married the countess. And he staid a short time with her, but he afterwards departed for the court of Arthur, and has not returned since. And two of the countess's pages traduced him, and called him a deceiver. And because I said I would vouch for it he would come before long and maintain his cause against both of them, they imprisoned me in this cave, and said that I should be put to death unless he came to deliver me by a certain day; and that is no further off than to-morrow, and I have no one to send to seek him for me. His name is Owain, the son of Urien." "And art thou certain that if that knight knew all this he would come to thy rescue?" "I am most certain of it," said she.

When the collops were cooked, Owain divided them into two parts, between himself and the maiden, and then Owain laid himself down to sleep; and never did sentinel keep stricter watch over his lord than the lion that night over Owain.

And the next day there came two pages with a great troop of attendants to take Luned from her cell, and put her to death. And Owain asked them what charge they had against her. And they told him of the compact that was between them; as the maiden had done the night before. "And," said they, "Owain has failed her, therefore we are taking her to be burnt." "Truly," said Owain, "he is a good knight, and if he knew that the maiden was in such peril, I marvel that he came not to her rescue. But if you will accept me in his stead, I will do battle with you." "We will," said the youths.

And they attacked Owain, and he was hard beset by them. And with that, the lion came to Owain's assistance, and they two got the better of the young men. And they said to him, "Chieftain, it was not agreed that we should fight save with thyself alone, and it is harder for us to contend with yonder animal than with thee." And Owain put the lion in the place where Luned had been imprisoned, and blocked up the door with stones. And he went to fight with the young men as before. But Owain had not his usual strength, and the two youths pressed hard upon him. And the lion roared incessantly at seeing Owain in trouble. And he burst through the wall, until he found his way out, and rushed upon the young men and instantly slew them. So Luned was saved from being burned.

Then Owain returned with Luned to the castle of the Lady of the Fountain. And when he went thence, he took the countess with him to Arthur's court, and she was his wife as long as she lived.

PWYLL AND THE GAME OF BADGER IN THE BAG

By Thomas Bulfinch

ONCE upon a time Pwyll was at Narberth, his chief palace, where a feast had been prepared for him, and with him was a great host of men. And after the first meal Pwyll arose to walk; and he went to the top of a mound that was above the palace, and was called Gorsedd Arberth. "Lord," said one of the court, "it is peculiar to the mound that whosoever sits upon it cannot go thence without either receiving wounds or blows, or else seeing a wonder." "I fear not to receive wounds or blows," said Pwyll; "but as to the wonder, gladly would I see it. I will therefore go and sit upon the mound."

And upon the mound he sat. And while he sat there, they saw a lady, on a pure white horse of large size, with a garment of shining gold around her, coming along the highway that led from the mound. "My men," said Pwyll, "is there any among you who knows yonder lady?" "There is not, lord," said they. "Go one of you and meet her, that we may know who she is." And one of them arose, and as he came upon the road to meet her, she passed by; and he followed as fast as he could, being on foot, and the greater was his speed, the farther was she from him. And when he saw that it profited him nothing to follow her, he returned to Pwyll, and said unto him, "Lord, it is idle for any one in the world to follow her on foot." "Verily," said Pwyll, "go unto the palace, and take the fleetest horse that thou seest, and go after her."

And he took a horse and went forward. And he came to an open, level plain, and put spurs to his horse; and the more he urged his horse, the farther was she from him. And he returned to the palace where Pwyll was, and said, "Lord, it will avail nothing for any one to follow yonder lady. I know of no horse in these realms swifter than this, and it availed me not to pursue her." "Of a truth," said Pwyll, "there must be some illusion here; let us go towards the palace." So to the palace they went, and spent the day.

And the next day they amused themselves until it was time to go to meat. And when meat was ended, Pwyll said, "Where are the hosts that went yesterday to the top of the mound?" "Behold, lord, we are here," said they. "Let us go," said he, "to the mound, and sit there. And do thou," said he to the page who tended his horse, "saddle my horse well, and hasten with him to the road, and bring also my spurs with thee." And the youth did thus. And they went and sat upon the mound; and ere they had been there but a short time, they beheld the lady coming by the same road, and in the same manner, and at the same pace. "Young man," said Pwyll, "I see the lady coming; give me my horse." And before he had mounted his horse she passed him. And he turned after her and followed her. And he let his horse go bounding playfully, and thought that he should soon come up with her. But he came no nearer to her than at first. Then he urged his horse to his utmost speed, yet he found that it availed not. Then said Pwyll, "O maiden, for the sake of him whom thou best lovest, stay for me." "I will stay gladly," said she; "and it were better for thy horse hadst thou asked it long since." So the maiden stopped; and she threw back that part of her headdress which covered her face. Then he thought that the beauty of all the maidens and all the ladies that he had ever seen was as nothing compared to her beauty. "Lady," he said, "wilt thou tell me aught concerning thy purpose?" "I will tell thee," said she; "my chief quest was to see thee." "Truly," said Pwyll, "this is to me the most pleasing quest on which thou couldst have come; and wilt thou tell me who thou art?" "I will tell thee, lord," said she. "I am Rhiannon, the daughter of Heveydd, and they sought to give me to a husband against my will. But no husband would I have, and that because of my love for thee; neither will I yet have one, unless thou reject me; and hither have I come to hear thy answer." "By Heaven," said Pwyll, "behold this is my answer. If I might choose among all the ladies and damsels in the world, thee would I choose." "Verily," said she, "if thou art thus minded, make a pledge to meet me ere I am given to another." "The sooner I may do so, the more pleasing will it be to me," said Pwyll; "and wheresoever thou wilt, there will I meet with thee." "I will that thou meet me this day twelve-month at the palace of Heveydd." "Gladly," said he, "will I keep this tryst." So they parted, and he went

back to his hosts, and to them of his household. And
whatsoever questions they asked him respecting the
damsel, he always turned the discourse upon other
matters.

And when a year from that time was gone, he caused
a hundred knights to equip themselves, and to go with
him to the palace of Heveydd. And he came to the
palace, and there was great joy concerning him, with
much concourse of people, and great rejoicing, and vast
preparations for his coming. And the whole court was
placed under his orders.

And the hall was garnished, and they went to meat,
and thus did they sit: Heveydd was on one side of
Pwyll, and Rhiannon on the other; and all the rest
according to their rank. And they ate and feasted, and
talked one with another. And at the beginning of the
carousal after the meat, there entered a tall, auburn-
haired youth, of royal bearing, clothed in a garment of
satin. And when he came into the hall, he saluted
Pwyll and his companions. "The greeting of Heaven
be unto thee," said Pwyll; "come thou and sit down."
"Nay," said he, "a suitor am I, and I will do my errand." "Do so, willingly," said Pwyll. "Lord," said
he, "my errand is unto thee, and it is to crave a boon
of thee that I come." "What boon soever thou mayest
ask of me, so far as I am able, thou shalt have." "Ah!"
said Rhiannon, "wherefore didst thou give that answer?" "Has he not given it before the presence of
these nobles?" asked the youth. "My soul," said Pwyll,
"what is the boon thou askest?" "The lady whom
best I love is to be thy bride this night; I come to ask

her of thee, with the feast and the banquet that are in this place." And Pwyll was silent, because of the promise which he had given. "Be silent as long as thou wilt," said Rhiannon; "never did man make worse use of his wits than thou hast done." "Lady," said he, "I knew not who he was." "Behold, this is the man to whom they would have given me against my will," said she; "and he is Gawl, the son of Clud, a man of great power and wealth, and because of the word thou hast spoken, bestow me upon him, lest shame befall thee." "Lady," said he, "I understand not thy answer; never can I do as thou sayest." "Bestow me upon him," said she, "and I will cause that I shall never be his." "By what means will that be?" asked Pwyll. Then she told him the thought that was in her mind. And they talked long together. Then Gawl said, "Lord, it is meet that I have an answer to my request." "As much of that thou hast asked as it is in my power to give, thou shalt have," replied Pwyll. "My soul," said Rhiannon unto Gawl, "as for the feast and the banquet that are here, I have bestowed them upon the men of Dyved, and the household and the warriors that are with us. These can I not suffer to be given to any. In a year from to-night, a banquet shall be prepared for thee in this palace, that I may become thy bride."

So Gawl went forth to his possessions, and Pwyll went also back to Dyved. And they both spent that year until it was the time for the feast at the palace of Heveydd. Then Gawl, the son of Clud, set out to the feast that was prepared for him; and he came to the palace, and was received there with rejoicing. Pwyll,

also, the chief of Dyved, came to the orchard with a
hundred knights, as Rhiannon had commanded him.
And Pwyll was clad in coarse and ragged garments, and
wore large, clumsy old shoes upon his feet. And when
he knew that the carousal after the meat had begun, he
went toward the hall; and when he came into the hall
he saluted Gawl, the son of Clud, and his company, both
men and women. "Heaven prosper thee," said Gawl,
"and friendly greeting be unto thee!" "Lord," said
he, "may Heaven reward thee! I have an errand unto
thee." "Welcome be thine errand, and if thou ask of
me that which is right, thou shalt have it gladly." "It
is fitting," answered he; "I crave but from want, and
the boon I ask is to have this small bag that thou seest
filled with meat." "A request within reason is this,"
said he, "and gladly shalt thou have it. Bring him
food." A great number of attendants arose and began
to fill the bag; but for all they put into it, it was no fuller
than at first. "My soul," said Gawl, "will thy bag ever
be full?" "It will not, I declare to Heaven," said he,
"for all that may be put into it, unless one possessed of
lands, and domains, and treasure, shall arise and tread
down with both his feet the food that is within the bag,
and shall say, 'Enough has been put therein.'" Then
said Rhiannon unto Gawl, the son of Clud, "Rise up
quickly." "I will willingly arise," said he. So he rose up,
and put his two feet into the bag. And Pwyll turned up
the sides of the bag, so that Gawl was over his head in it.
And he shut it up quickly, and slipped a knot upon the
thongs, and blew his horn. And thereupon, behold, his
knights came down upon the palace. And they seized

all the host that had come with Gawl, and cast them into his own prison. And Pwyll threw off his rags, and his old shoes, and his tattered array. And as they came in every one of Pwyll's knights struck a blow upon the bag, and asked, "What is here?" "A badger," said they. And in this manner they played, each of them striking the bag, either with his foot or with a staff. And thus played they with the bag. And then was the game of Badger in the Bag first played.

"Lord," said the man in the bag, "if thou wouldst but hear me, I merit not to be slain in a bag." Said Heveydd, "Lord, he speaks truth; it were fitting that thou listen to him, for he deserves not this." "Verily," said Pwyll, "I will do thy counsel concerning him." "Behold, this is my counsel then," said Rhiannon. "Thou art now in a position in which it behooves thee to satisfy suitors and minstrels. Let him give unto them in thy stead, and take a pledge from him that he will never seek to revenge that which has been done to him. And this will be punishment enough." "I will do this gladly," said the man in the bag. "And gladly will I accept it," said Pwyll, "since it is the counsel of Heveydd and Rhiannon. Seek thyself sureties." "We will be for him," said Heveydd, "until his men be free to answer for him." And upon this he was let out of the bag, and his liegemen were liberated. "Verily, lord," said Gawl, "I am greatly hurt, and I have many bruises. With thy leave I will go forth. I will leave nobles in my stead to answer for me in all that thou shalt require." "Willingly," said Pwyll, "mayest thou do thus." So Gawl went to his own possessions.

PWYLL AND THE GAME OF BADGER

And the hall was set in order for Pwyll and the men of his host, and for them also of the palace, and they went to the tables and sat down. And as they had sat at that time twelve-month, so sat they that night. And they ate and feasted, and spent the night in mirth and tranquillity. And the time came that they should sleep and Pwyll and Rhiannon went to their chamber.

And next morning at break of day, "My lord," said Rhiannon, "arise and begin to give thy gifts unto the minstrels. Refuse no one to-day that may claim thy bounty." "Thus shall it be gladly," said Pwyll, "both to-day and every day while the feast shall last." So Pwyll arose, and he caused silence to be proclaimed, and desired all the suitors and minstrels to show and to point out what gifts they desired. And this being done, the feast went on, and he denied no one while it lasted. And when the feast was ended, Pwyll said unto Heveydd, "My lord, with thy permission I will set out for Dyvod to-morrow." "Certainly," said Heveydd; "may Heaven prosper thee! Fix also a time when Rhiannon shall follow thee." "By Heaven," said Pwyll, "we will go hence together." "Willest thou this, lord?" said Heveydd. "Yes, lord," answered Pwyll.

And the next day they set forward towards Dyved, and journeyed to the palace of Narberth, where a feast was made ready for them. And there came to them great numbers of the chief men and the most noble ladies of the land, and of these there were none to whom Rhiannon did not give some rich gift, either a bracelet, or a ring, or a precious stone. And they ruled the land prosperously that year and the next.

MANAWYDDAN AND THE SEVEN ENCHANTED CANTREVS

By Thomas Bulfinch

PWYLL and Rhiannon had a son, whom they named Pryderi. And when he was grown up, Pwyll, his father, died. And Pryderi married Kicva, the daughter of Gwynn Gloy.

Now Manawyddan returned from the war in Ireland, and he found that his cousin had seized all his possessions, and much grief and heaviness came upon him. "Alas! woe is me!" he exclaimed; "there is none save myself without a home and a resting-place." "Lord," said Pryderi, "be not so sorrowful. Thy cousin is king of the Island of the Mighty, and though he has done thee wrong, thou hast never been a claimant of land or possessions." "Yea," answered he, "but although this man is my cousin, it grieveth me to see any one in the place of my brother Bendigeid Vran; neither can I be happy in the same dwelling with him." "Wilt thou follow the counsel of another?" said Pryderi. "I stand in need of counsel," he answered, "and what may that counsel be?" "Seven cantrevs belong unto me," said Pryderi, "wherein Rhiannon, my mother, dwells. I will bestow her upon thee, and the seven cantrevs with her; and though thou hadst no possessions but those cantrevs only, thou couldst not have any fairer than they.

Do thou and Rhiannon enjoy them; and if thou desire any possessions thou wilt not despise these." "I do not, chieftain," said he. "Heaven reward thee for thy friendship! I will go with thee to seek Rhiannon, and to look at thy possessions." "Thou wilt do well," he answered; "and I believe thou didst never hear a lady discourse better than she, and when she was in her prime, none was ever fairer. Even now her aspect is not uncomely."

They set forth, and, however long the journey, they came at last to Dyved; and a feast was prepared for them by Rhiannon and Kicva. Then began Manawyddan and Rhiannon to sit and to talk together; and his mind and his thoughts became warmed towards her, and he thought in his heart he had never beheld any lady more fulfilled of grace and beauty than she. "Pryderi," said he, "I will that it be as thou didst say." "What saying was that?" asked Rhiannon. "Lady," said Pryderi, "I did offer thee as a wife to Manawyddan, the son of Llyr." "By that will I gladly abide," said Rhiannon. "Right glad am I also," said Manawyddan; "may Heaven reward him who hath shown unto me friendship so perfect as this."

And before the feast was over she became his bride. Said Pryderi, "Tarry ye here the rest of the feast, and I will go into England to tender my homage unto Caswallawn, the son of Beli." "Lord," said Rhiannon, "Caswallawn is in Kent; thou mayest therefore tarry at the feast, and wait until he shall be nearer." "We will wait," he answered. So they finished the feast. And they began to make the circuit of Dyved, and to hunt, and to take their pleasure. And as they went through the country, they had never seen lands more pleasant to live in, nor better hunting-grounds, nor greater plenty of honey and fish. And such was the friendship between these four, that they would not be parted from each other by night nor by day.

And in the midst of all this he went to Caswallawn at Oxford, and tendered his homage; and honorable was his reception there, and highly was he praised for offering his homage.

And after his return Pryderi and Manawyddan feasted and took their ease and pleasure. And they began a feast at Narberth, for it was the chief palace. And when they had ended the first meal, while those who served them ate, they arose and went forth, and proceeded to the Gorsedd, that is, the Mound of Narberth, and their retinue with them. And as they sat thus, behold a peal of thunder, and with the violence of the thunder-storm, lo! there came a fall of mist, so thick that not one of them could see the other. And after the mist it became light all around. And when they looked towards the place where they were wont to see cattle and herds and dwellings, they saw nothing now, neither house, nor beast, nor smoke, nor fire, nor man, nor dwelling, but the buildings of the court empty, and desert, and uninhabited, without either man or beast within them. And truly all their companions were lost to them, without their knowing aught of what had befallen them, save those four only.

"In the name of Heaven," said Manawyddan, "where are they of the court, and all my host beside? Let us go and see."

So they came to the castle, and saw no man; and into the hall, and to the sleeping-place, and there was none; and in the mead-cellar and in the kitchen there was naught but desolation. Then they began to go through the land, and all the possessions that they had; and they visited the houses and dwellings, and found nothing but wild beasts. And when they had consumed their feast and all their provisions, they fed upon the prey they killed in hunting, and the honey of the wild swarms.

And one morning Pryderi and Manawyddan rose up to hunt, and they ranged their dogs and went forth. And some of the dogs ran before them, and came to a bush which was near at hand; but as soon as they were come to the bush, they hastily drew back, and returned to the men, their hair bristling up greatly. "Let us go near to the bush," said Pryderi, "and see what is in it." And as they came near, behold, a wild boar of a pure white color rose up from the bush. Then the dogs, being set on by the men, rushed towards him; but he left the bush, and fell back a little way from the men, and made a stand against the dogs, without retreating from them, until the men had come near. And when the men came up, he fell back a second time, and betook him to flight. Then they pursued the boar until they beheld a vast and lofty castle, all newly built, in a place where they had never before seen either stone or building. And the boar ran swiftly into the castle, and the dogs after him. Now when the boar and the dogs had gone into the castle, the men began to wonder at finding a castle in a place where they had never seen any building whatsoever. And from the top of the Gorsedd they looked and listened for the dogs. But so long as they were there, they heard not one of the dogs, nor aught concerning them.

"Lord," said Pryderi, "I will go into the castle to get tidings of the dogs." "Truly," he replied, "thou wouldst be unwise to go into this castle, which thou hast never seen till now. If thou wouldst follow my counsel, thou wouldst not enter therein. Whosoever has cast a spell over this land, has caused this castle to be here." "Of a truth," answered Pryderi, "I cannot thus give up my dogs." And for all the counsel that Manawyddan gave him, yet to the castle he went.

When he came within the castle neither man, nor beast, nor boar, nor dogs, nor house, nor dwelling, saw he within it. But in the centre of the castle floor he beheld a fountain with marble-work around it, and on the margin of the fountain a golden bowl upon a marble slab, and chains hanging from the air, to which he saw no end.

And he was greatly pleased with the beauty of the gold, and with the rich workmanship of the bowl; and he went up to the bowl, and laid hold of it. And when he had taken hold of it his hands stuck to the bowl, and his feet to the slab on which the bowl was placed; and all his joyousness forsook him, so that he could not utter a word. And thus he stood.

And Manawyddan waited for him till near the close of the day. And late in the evening, being certain that he should have no tidings of Pryderi or the dogs, he went back to the palace. And as he entered Rhiannon looked at him. "Where," said she, "are thy companion and thy dogs?" "Behold," he answered, "the adventure that has befallen me." And he related it all unto her. "An evil companion hast thou been," said Rhiannon, "and a good companion hast thou lost." And with that word she went out, and proceeded towards the castle, according to the direction which he gave her. The gate of the castle she found open. She was nothing daunted, and she went in. And as she went in she perceived Pryderi laying hold of the bowl, and she went towards him. "O my lord," said she, "what dost thou here?" And she took hold of the bowl with him; and as she did so her hands also became fast to the bowl, and her feet to the slab, and she was not able to utter a word. And with that, as it became night, lo! there came thunder upon them, and a fall of mist; and thereupon the castle vanished, and they with it.

When Kicva, the daughter of Glynn Gloy, saw that there was no one in the palace but herself and Manawyddan, she sorrowed so that she cared not whether she lived or died. And Manawyddan saw this. "Thou art in the wrong," said he, "if through fear of me thou grievest thus. I call Heaven to witness that thou hast never seen friendship more pure than that which I will bear thee, as long as Heaven will that thou shouldst be thus. I declare to thee that, were I in the dawn of youth, I would keep my faith unto Pryderi, and unto thee also will I keep it. Be there no fear upon thee, therefore." "Heaven reward thee!" she said; "and that is what I deemed of thee." And the damsel thereupon took courage, and was glad.

"Truly, lady," said Manawyddan, "it is not fitting

for us to stay here; we have lost our dogs, and cannot get food. Let us go into England; it is easier for us to find support there." "Gladly, lord," said she, "we will do so." And they set forth together to England.

"Lord," said she, "what craft wilt thou follow? Take up one that is seemly." "None other will I take," answered he, "but that of making shoes." "Lord," said she, "such a craft becomes not a man so nobly born as thou." "By that, however, will I abide," said he. "I know nothing thereof," said Kicva. "But I know," answered Manawyddan, "and I will teach thee to stitch. We will not attempt to dress the leather, but we will buy it ready dressed, and will make the shoes from it."

So they went into England, and went as far as Hereford; and they betook themselves to making shoes. And he began by buying the best cordwain that could be had in town, and none other would he buy. And he associated himself with the best goldsmith in the town, and caused him to make clasps for the shoes, and to gild the clasps; and he marked how it was done until he learned the method. And therefore is he called one of the three makers of gold shoes. And when they could be had from him, not a shoe nor hose was bought from any of the cordwainers in the town. But when the cordwainers perceived that their gains were failing (for as Manawyddan shaped the work so Kicva stitched it), they came together and took counsel, and agreed that they would slay them. And he had warning thereof, and it was told him how the cordwainers had agreed to slay him.

154

"Lord," said Kicva, "wherefore should this be borne from these boors?" "Nay," said he, "we will go back unto Dyved." So towards Dyved they set forth.

Now Manawyddan, when he set out to return to Dyved, took with him a burden of wheat. And he proceeded towards Narberth, and there he dwelt. And never was he better pleased than when he saw Narberth again, and the lands where he had been wont to hunt with Pryderi and with Rhiannon. And he accustomed himself to fish and to hunt the deer in their covert. And then he began to prepare some ground, and he sowed a croft, and a second, and a third. And no wheat in the world ever sprung up better. And the three crofts prospered with perfect growth, and no man ever saw fairer wheat than it.

And thus passed the seasons of the year until the harvest came. And he went to look at one of his crofts, and, behold, it was ripe. "I will reap this to-morrow," said he. And that night he went back to Narberth, and on the morrow, in the gray dawn, he went to reap the croft; and when he came there he found nothing but the bare straw. Every one of the ears of the wheat was cut off from the stalk, and all the ears carried entirely away, and nothing but the straw left. And at this he marveled greatly.

Then he went to look at another croft, and, behold, that also was ripe. "Verily," said he, "this will I reap to-morrow." And on the morrow he came with the intent to reap it; and when he came there he found nothing but the bare straw. "O gracious Heaven!" he exclaimed, "I know that whosoever has begun my ruin is completing it, and has also destroyed the country with me."

Then he went to look at the third croft; and when he came there, finer wheat had there never been seen, and this also was ripe. "Evil betide me," said he, "if I watch not here to-night. Whoever carried off the other corn will come in like manner to take this, and I will know who it is." And he told Kicva all that had befallen. "Verily," said she, "what thinkest thou to do?" "I will watch the croft to-night," said he. And he went to watch the croft.

And at midnight he heard something stirring among the wheat; and he looked, and behold, the mightiest host of mice in the world, which could neither be numbered nor measured. And he knew not what it was until the mice had made their way into the croft, and each of them climbing up the straw, and bending it down with its weight, had cut off one of the ears of wheat, and had carried it away, leaving there the stalk; and he saw not a single straw there that had not a mouse to it. And they all took their way, carrying the ears with them.

In wrath and anger did he rush upon the mice; but he could no more come up with them than if they had been gnats or birds of the air, except one only, which, though it was but sluggish, went so fast that a man on foot could scarce overtake it. And after this one he went, and he caught it, and put it in his glove, and tied up the opening of the glove with a string, and kept it with him, and returned to the palace. Then he came to the hall where Kicva was, and he lighted a fire, and hung the glove by the string upon a peg. "What hast thou there, lord?"

said Kicva. "A thief," said he, "that I found robbing me." "What kind of thief may it be, lord, that thou couldst put into thy glove?" said she. Then he told her how the mice came to the last of the fields in his sight. "And one of them was less nimble than the rest, and is now in my glove; to-morrow I will hang it." "My lord," said she, "this is marvelous; but yet it would be unseemly for a man of dignity like thee to be hanging such a reptile as this." "Woe betide me," said he, "if I would not hang them all, could I catch them, and such as I have I will hang." "Verily, lord," said she, "there is no reason that I should succor this reptile, except to prevent discredit unto thee. Do therefore, lord, as thou wilt."

Then he went to the Mound of Narberth, taking the mouse with him. And he set up two forks on the highest part of the mound. And while he was doing this, behold, he saw a scholar coming towards him, in old and poor and tattered garments. And it was now seven years since he had seen in that place either man or beast except those four persons who had remained together until two of them were lost.

"My lord," said the scholar, "good-day to thee." "Heaven prosper thee, and my greeting be unto thee! And whence dost thou come, scholar?" asked he. "I come, lord, from singing in England; and wherefore dost thou inquire?" "Because for the last seven years," answered he, "I have seen no man here save four secluded persons, and thyself this moment." "Truly, lord," said he, "I go through this land unto mine own. And what work art thou upon, lord?" "I am hanging a thief that I caught robbing me," said he. "What manner of thief is that?" asked the scholar. "I see a creature in thy hand like unto a mouse, and ill does it become a man of rank equal to thine to touch a reptile such as this. Let it go forth free." "I will not let it go free, by Heaven," said he; "I caught it robbing me, and the doom of a thief will I inflict upon it, and I will hang it." "Lord," said he, "rather than see a man of rank equal to thine at such a work as this, I would give thee a pound, which I have received as alms, to let the reptile go forth free." "I will not let it go free," said he, "neither will I sell it." "As thou wilt, lord," he answered; "I care naught." And the scholar went his way.

And as he was placing the cross-beam upon the two forks, behold, a priest came towards him, upon a horse covered with trappings. "Good-day to thee, lord," said he. "Heaven prosper thee!" said Manawyddan; "thy blessing." "The blessing of Heaven be upon thee. And what, lord, art thou doing?" "I am hanging a thief that I caught robbing me," said he. "What manner of thief, lord?" asked he. "A creature," he answered, "in form of a mouse. It has been robbing me, and I am inflicting upon it the doom of a thief." "Lord," said he, "rather than see thee touch this reptile, I would purchase its freedom." "By my confession to Heaven, neither will I sell it nor set it free." "It is true, lord, that it is worth nothing to buy; but rather than see thee defile thyself by touching such a reptile as this, I will give thee three pounds to let it go." "I will not, by Heaven," said he, "take any price for it. As it ought, so shall it be hanged." And the priest went his way.

Then he noosed the string around the mouse's **neck,**

and as he was about to draw it up, behold, he saw a bishop's retinue, with his sumpter-horses and his attendants. And the bishop himself came towards him. And he stayed his work. "Lord Bishop," said he, "thy blessing." "Heaven's blessing be unto thee!" said he. "What work art thou upon?" "Hanging a thief that I caught robbing me," said he. "Is not that a mouse that I see in thy hand?" "Yes," answered he, "and she has robbed me." "Ah," said he, "since I have come at the doom of this reptile, I will ransom it of thee. I will give thee seven pounds for it, and that rather than see a man of rank equal to thine destroying so vile a reptile as this. Let it loose, and thou shalt have the money." "I declare to Heaven that I will not let it loose." "If thou wilt not loose it for this, I will give thee four and twenty pounds of ready money to set it free." "I will not set it free, by Heaven, for as much again," said he. "If thou wilt not set it free for this, I will give thee all the horses that thou seest in this plain, and the seven loads of baggage, and the seven horses that they are upon." "By Heaven, I will not," he replied. "Since for this thou wilt not set it free, do so at what price soever thou wilt." "I will that Rhiannon and Pryderi be free," said he. "That thou shalt have," he answered. "Not yet will I loose the mouse, by Heaven." "What then wouldst thou?" "That the charm and the illusion be removed from the seven cantrevs of Dyved." "This shalt thou have also; set therefore the mouse free." "I will not set it free, by Heaven," said he, "till I know who the mouse may be." "She is my wife." "Wherefore came she to me?" "To despoil thee," he answered. "I am Lloyd, the son of Kilwed, and I cast the charm over the seven cantrevs of Dyved. And it was to avenge Gawl, the son of Clud, from the friendship that I had towards him, that I cast the charm. And upon Pryderi did I avenge Gawl, the son of Clud, for the game of Badger in the Bag, that Pwyll, the son of Auwyn, played upon him. And when it was known that thou wast come to dwell in the land, my household came and besought me to transform them into mice, that they might destroy thy corn. And they went the first and the second night, and destroyed thy two crops. And the third night came unto me my wife and the ladies of the court, and besought me to transform them. And I transformed them. Now she is not in her usual health. And had she been in her usual health, thou wouldst not have been able to overtake her; but since this has taken place, and she has been caught, I will restore to thee Pryderi and Rhiannon, and I will take the charm and illusion from off Dyved. Set her therefore free." "I will not set her free yet." "What wilt thou more?" he asked. "I will that there be no more charm upon the seven cantrevs of Dyved, and that none shall be put upon it henceforth; moreover, that vengeance be never taken for this, either upon Pryderi or Rhiannon, or upon me." "All this shalt thou have. And truly thou hast done wisely in asking this. Upon thy head would have lit all this trouble." "Yea," said he, "for fear thereof was it that I required this." "Set now my wife at liberty." "I will not," said he, "until I see Pryderi and Rhiannon with me free." "Behold, here they come," he answered.

THE SEVEN ENCHANTED CANTREVS

And thereupon behold Pryderi and Rhiannon. And he rose up to meet them, and greeted them, and sat down beside them. "Ah, chieftain, set now my wife at liberty," said the bishop. "Hast thou not received all thou didst ask?" "I will release her, gladly," said he. And thereupon he set her free.

Then he struck her with a magic wand, and she was changed back into a young woman, the fairest ever seen.

"Look round upon thy land," said he, "and thou wilt see it all tilled and peopled as it was in its best estate." And he rose up and looked forth. And when he looked he saw all the lands tilled, and full of herds and dwellings.

ROBIN HOOD AND THE SORROW-
FUL KNIGHT

Adapted by W. C. Hazlitt

I

ROBIN stood in Barnsdale, and leaned against a
tree. By his side were John, Scathlock, and
Much. Presently unto Robin spake John thus: —
"Master, an ye would give us the word that we might
dine, it were well."

"Nay," quoth Robin, "thereto I have no lust, until I
see some baron bold or other guest unbekenned, or
some squire or some knight that may pay worthily for
his cheer. Take your bows in your hands, good fellows, and leave me here; and walk up to the Sayles, and
so on to the Watling Street. Abide there until ye become aware of any that may lighten the cost of our
meal."

They went to the Sayles and to the Watling Street;
and they looked east and they looked west; and no
manner of man might they espy. Yet at the last, as
they cast their eyes down a byway in Barnsdale, they
perceived where a knight came riding along. Heavy
was his bearing and little his pride; one foot was in the
stirrup, and the other out. His hood hung over his
eyes, and his garb was simple enough: a sorrier man,

162

"TRULY I HAVE EXPECTED THEE THESE TWO HOURS"

forsooth, never rode in the merry woods on a summer's day.

The yeomen approached him full courteously, and Little John, because he knew that he was of knightly degree, bending his knee at the saddlebows, welcomed him to the forest side. "My master," quoth he, "hath waited dinner for you these three hours past."

"Who is your master?" the knight demanded.

"His name, sir, is Robin Hood."

"He is a good yeoman," the stranger returned, "whom-of I have heard much commendation. Albeit my purpose was to have dined to-day at Blithe or Doncaster, yet I consent with you three to go unto your master."

Then they went all together, and as he rode along the tears stole from his eyes, and coursed down his cheeks. They brought him to the place where their master tarried, who unto him said, as he doffed his headgear, and beseemingly knelt: "Welcome art thou to me, sir knight! Truly I have expected thee these two hours."

"God thee save, good Robin," quoth the knight, "and all thy comrades so gallant and free!"

They sat to their dinner, and numbles of the deer, and waterfowl, and pheasant, with wine and bread in plenty, they had; and Robin bade the knight eat and drink and spare not.

"Gramercy, Robin," said his guest, "such a fair meal have I not seen these three weeks. If ever I come again this way, I trust to give thee as good."

"I am not so nice in the order of my diet," cried Robin. "But since it was never the manner for a yeoman

163

to pay for a knight's cheer, thou wilt clear the score, wilt thou not, ere thou goest hence?"

"I have nought in my purse," the stranger answered and said, "that I can proffer for shame."

"Tell me truth, sir," quoth Robin, "how much hast thou, all told?"

"Ten shilling and no more," said the other.

"An' so it be," said Robin, "not one penny do I touch, and an thou needest more for thy occasions, I shall freely lend it thee."

Little John searched the knight's mail, and found indeed that he had sooth spoken; and thereupon Robin commanded them to bring wine of the best, and bade the knight drink to his content.

"Tell me now, knight," he presently said, "and I shall keep thy counsel right well: wert thou made a knight *malgré* thyself, or one of yeomanry? Hast thou been an unthrifty husband of thy substance, or an usurer?"

"None of these, by my faith, Robin, have I been," he protested, "for, God is my witness, an hundred winter herebefore my ancestors knights have been. I am called Sir Richard at the Lee. Within this two or three year, my neighbors well know that I could spend four hundred pound by the year. Now have I no goods save my children and my wife, till God amend my estate."

"How hast thou lost thy riches, then?" Robin demanded.

"By my not overwise kindness. I had a son forsooth, Robin, that should have been my heir, and when as he had but twenty winters, jousted he with the best, and for that he slew on a time a knight of Lancashire; I was fain to lay my estate to pledge to save his life. To the Abbot of St. Mary's at York, Robin, my lands are in gage, and are forfeit, alas! unless so be the money be repaid within a short day. And whereas I have it not, I go to seek grace; and so, farewell, for the time draweth nigh."

"What is the sum?" Robin asked.

"Four hundred pound," said he.

"What, then, wilt thou do, put-case thou losest thy inheritance?"

"I shall cross the salt sea, Robin, and go to the Holy land, where Christ our Saviour was quick and dead, and to the Mount of Calvary." And the tears once more started to his eyes.

"Hast thou no friends?"

"Whenso I was rich of estate, Robin, yea, verily, had I store; but now they shun me, and know me not."

"Pass the wine round," said Robin; "the knight drinks not. Well, and hast thou neither any one who would be thy surety?"

"By Him that died on a tree, none, save, maybe, Peter, Paul, and John."

"Cease thy jesting, knight, for by Him that made me, and shope both sun and moon," said Robin, "nought set I by such warrantise."

"None other have I," quoth he, "unless it be Our Dear Lady, that never yet failed me in my need."

"In faith, thou couldest have no better an one. John, go to my coffers, and tell truly four hundred pounds."

And John went, as he was bidden, and Scathlock with him, and they brought the money to Robin, eighteen score pounds and upwards.

Then Much spake grudgingly, whenas he saw so large a treasure about to go to Sir Richard at the Lee; but John chid him, saying it was a good almsdeed to help so gentle a knight; and withal he prayed Robin, if it were not meet to offer his guest a new livery, that he might appear before the lord abbot as became his condition.

"For ye have scarlet and green, master," said John. "There is many a merchant in England that hath not so rich a store."

And when Robin gave leave, he took his bow, and measured three ells of each color, and at every ell he leapt.

"What devil's-kin draper is this?" muttered Much.

"He may give him all the better measure," cried Scathlock, laughing, "since it costeth him so little."

But John marked them not; and he prevailed on Robin, who was nothing loath, to find him a new gray courser, and a new saddle.

"What dost thou give the knight thyself, John?" Robin inquired.

"Even a pair of gilt spurs, master," he answering said, "that he may pray for all this company."

"To-morrow," said Sir Richard at the Lee, " I must be at St. Mary's to redeem my lands, or they go from me forever. When shall be my day, Robin?"

"This day twelvemonth in this place," the yeoman replied; "and I lend thee John to keep thee company to

York as thy servant, and to aid thee to his power, because it were shame that a knight should go unattended."

The knight set out from Barnsdale, blessing Robin Hood and his men for the best friends that could to him have befallen; and with John at his side pricked forward on his way to the abbey of Our Blessed Lady, merrier in heart than he had weened evermore to be; for in his mail he carried the freedom of his fair lands and his children's heritage.

II

The lord abbot sat in high state at St. Mary's at York, and with him were the high cellarer and the chief justiciary of England and the sheriff of Yorkshire, that were partakers, all of them, in the venture whereby on failure of his day Sir Richard at the Lee, that gentle knight, lost his lands at Utersdale for aye.

The high abbot remembered them all, who were there present, how this day twelvemonth the knight of Utersdale had borrowed of him four hundred pound, and laid his lands in pledge; and that if he came not soon to redeem them, he should suffer disherison.

"It is full early," said the prior; "the day has much to run. I had liever lay down a hundred pound than take away too lightly the knight's belongings. He is maybe beyond sea, and cannot reach England in just time. I wis he may be suffering great hardship; and it were sore pity to deal too strictly with him, and too sternly use our power."

"Thou art ever in my beard," quoth the high abbot.

"He is dead or hanged, doubtless," said the high

cellarer, "and we shall have anon four hundred pounds more to spend by the year."

"He will not come yet, I dare well undertake," said the chief justiciary.

Meanwhile, Sir Richard at the Lee and Little John had ridden well, until they came to the abbey of Our Lady at York, and ere they drew within sight of the gates, that gentle knight threw off his upper habit, and clothed himself in poor weeds, and Little John in like manner; and when they knocked at the gates, the porter opened to them, and showed them how the lord abbot, with many more of high degree, were at their meat.

They descended from their horses, and the porter said: "Lead them into the stable, where they may have whereof to eat, and rest, till ye have for them again need."

"Nay," quoth Little John, "they go not thither by my counsel." And whileas the knight, whose valet for the nonce he was at this time, was brought into the hall, John stayed behind with the horses and the mail wherein the money lay, that they had carried therewithal.

The knight went forth into the hall, where they sat at table, and kneeled down, and in lowly wise saluted the high abbot and all there assembled.

"Sir abbot," said the knight, "I am here to keep my day."

"Thou hast brought with thee the four hundred pound, hast thou not?"

"Not one penny," quoth the knight.

"Thou art a shrewd debtor," cried the abbot. "Sir

168

justice, it is well; I drink to thee! — What doest thou here, then, sirrah, that thou art before me without the money?"

"I am here, sir abbot, to pray your good lordship of a longer day," he said, and yet knelt.

"The time has come and gone, and thy lands have passed from thee," said the high abbot.

The knight besought the chief justiciary, and likewise the sheriff, and once again the high abbot, that he would lend a merciful ear unto him, and unto the lord abbot: "I will be thy true servant, my lord," quoth he, "till I have well gotten the four hundred pound," and to him still denying: "But I have my land again, full dearly it shall be bought. It is good, lords, to assay a friend, ere a man have of him need."

The lord abbot looked upon that gentle knight full angerly, and bade him quit the hall, calling him a false knight. But he shewed the lord abbot that he spake not truly, for he had never been other than true; and then he rose to his feet, and to the lord abbot he said: "To suffer a knight to kneel so long is scant courtesy. I have been in many a tourney and many a fight, and have ever stood in the front."

"Sir abbot," said the chief justiciary, "what wilt thou give over and above, that the knight may sign a release? Else dare I to swear that never shall ye hold your land in quiet."

"An hundred pound more I will give," said the high abbot.

"Give him two," said the chief justiciary.

"Forbear your reckonings, my lords," said the knight

more firmly. "Not one, nor two hundred, nor a thousand should serve; I will not have, for heir to my lands, abbot, justice, or friar."

They all sat marveling what he might signify, and conferred together. But the knight started to the door of the hall, and returned straightway, bearing in both his hands a bag; to the board where they sat he advanced, and loosening the cords, he shook out four hundred pound.

"Here is the gold, sir abbot," he cried, "that thou diddest lend to me on my lands. Haddest thou been more courteous, thou mightest have had something to boot."

They had all laid down their knives and spoons, and ate and drank no more.

"Sir abbot, and all the others that I see," said the knight, "ye have your money again, agree among you, as ye may; and since my day I have kept, I shall take back my land, whatever ye may do."

He marched straight out of the hall, a proud and jocund man, and found Little John in the court awaiting him; and they took horse and went their way; and whenso they had lost sight of York, they donned again their gayer raiment, and proceeded on their road together, until John took leave of that gentle knight to go unto Nottingham, and Sir Richard at the Lee drew not rein until he came to his own gates at his house in Utersdale in the forest.

"Welcome, my lord," said his wife, "albeit lost is all our good."

"Nay, madam," he replied, "not so; be of better

cheer, and pray for Robin Hood, that his soul may enter into bliss; for without his bounty we had been beggars for a certainty. As I went by the way, madam, I met that excellent yeoman, and he lent unto me the money, wherewith I have freed our lands."

III

The day was at hand when the knight of Utersdale was under covenant to render himself in Barnsdale, and restore to Robin the four hundred pound that so happily redeemed his lands from pawn.

Robin stood in the forest, and with him were John, Scathlock, and Much the Miller's son.

"Shall we go to our nunchion, master?" asked John, for it was mid-day.

"Nay," said Robin; "I doubt that Our Lady is wroth with me, that she sendeth me not my money."

"Have no fear," John replied; "the sun has some way to go ere it set, and I dare answer for the knight, that he is trusty and true."

"Take thy bow in thy hand, John," quoth his master, "and let Scathlock and Much bear thee company, and go up to the Watling Street. Thou mayest by chance alight on some one, be he a messenger from Our Lady or a man that can make us mirth, or a needy yeoman that I might bestead."

Not well pleased was John to go longer fasting; yet he girt on his sword, and they all sallied forth to do as their master had commanded them, and presently they descried a right royal equipage, as it came by the way.

171

Two black monks went before, each on a fair palfrey, and after them followed seven sumpter-mules well-laden, and men-at-arms fifty and two. No bishop rode more proudly in progress.

"I lay my life," cried John, plucking up his heart again, "that these holy men have brought us our pay. Make ready your bows, my brethren, and fear not. There are but three of us, all told; yet our master will give us a sorry welcome, an we bring not these guests to dine with him this day."

"Stay, churlish monks," John cried, "or you are dead. Full wroth ye have made our master, that stays fasting for you."

"Who is your master?" demanded the foremost monk.

"Robin Hood."

"He is a strong thief, whom-of heard I ever yet no good."

"He is a yeoman of the forest," said John, "and he has bidden you both to dine with him yonder where he lies."

But Much let fly a bolt at one of those holy men, and he fell to the earth; and of those fifty men and two that were set as a guard over the sumpters, all, save a little page and one other, fled out of view.

They led the other monk, that was truly the high cellarer of St. Mary's at York, to the lodge-door, and Robin did off his hood, but the cellarer lacked the like courtesy.

"He is a churl," said John.

"No matter," said Robin. "How many had he with him?"

" Fifty-two and another monk, that we left on the ground."

" Let the horn sound," said Robin, " that we may have company befitting, put-case they should return."

The high cellarer, after he had washed, sat to dinner, and drank of the best, and Robin and John served him right dutifully, till, when all was done, Robin shewed him how he had lent, it was a twelvemonth, a little money to Sir Richard at the Lee, so that he might acquit himself of a debt to St. Mary's. The high cellarer sware that he wist nought of such a matter; but Robin held that because he was an officer of the abbey, he must be the messenger sent to keep the day, and for that he was so true to the time he yielded him great thanks. The high cellarer made a vow, that he had but twenty marks in his mail.

" If it be so," quoth Robin, " thou mayest even keep them, and I will lend thee more an need be."

John spread his mantle on the ground, and out of the cellarer's coffers he took eight hundred pieces and more. " The abbey," said he, " hath doubled our venture."

" Monk," said Robin, in high glee, " Our Lady is the truest woman whom-of I ever heard tell. An I had searched all England through, I could not have placed my money to more profitable usance. Fill of the best wine, John; let the cellarer drink ere he go."

But the cellarer said " Nay," and put spurs to his palfrey, as to go.

" Whither are ye bound, sir?" asked Robin.

" To certain manors in this country," he answered, " whereas our reeves do us wrong."

"Greet well your abbot from me," said Robin, "and your prior also, and pray them well every day to send us such a guest."

IV

In the meantime the knight of Utersdale came not, and seemed like to break his day. But about three hours after noon, as Robin and John and certain others yet lingered on the scene, rode Sir Richard at the Lee in sight, attended by his following; and as he drew near, he alighted from his palfrey and bent his knee to Robin.

"God save thee, good Robin Hood, and all this company," quoth he.

"Rise, gentle knight," quoth Robin; "right welcome art thou to me. And, I pray you, what taketh thee so late to the greenwood?"

"It was my duty, good Robin," he answered; "but I shall tell you, that I was kept at a wrestling, whereby I passed, namely, at Wentbridge, and holp a poor yeoman, whom they would have wronged else."

"'Fore God, thereof give thee thanks, knight; he that aids poor yeomen is my friend."

"Have here, Robin," proceeded the knight, "four hundred pound that I borrowed, and twenty marks for the courtesy."

"Nay," Robin answered; "Our Lady by her cellarer hath already satisfied me; and if I should take it twice, it were a shame indeed. But truly, knight, thou art welcome; and what import these bows and arrows, so fair and fine, that thou hast brought thee-with?"

"A poor gift to thee, Robin."

174

Robin took them in good part, and then he told the knight all the story about the high cellarer; and over their supper well they laughed.

"And hast thou gotten thy lands securely back into thy hands?" the yeoman demanded.

"Ay, at length; but the abbey labored shrewdly to dispossess me, and sent messengers to London to make suit to our king thereupon; and the high cellarer himself was to have gone thither to moot farther therein, and was only by thee stayed from his purpose."

"He let me understand differently," quoth Robin, "and he was a false monk. What was the wrestling at Wentbridge, knight, whereat thou didst so courteously intervene?"

The knight showed how there was published a wrestling for a prize to the winner of a pair of gloves, a gold ring, and a pipe of wine, and how a stranger yeoman won it; but they denied him his right, and would have slain him forsooth, had he, the knight and his retinue, not ridden into the throng, and for the sake of Robin Hood defended that yeoman, and caused to be delivered unto him the trophies of the day. "And I gave him," added he, "five marks for his wine, that it might be broached, drink who would."

Robin was right glad; and because the knight was not rich, and had spent of his substance not a little in coming thither so accompanied, and in furnishing a hundred bows and the like number of sheaves of arrows, all of the best, his heart opened, and he said to John, as the knight made ready to go before the gloaming: "Fetch me four hundred pound of the cellarer's treasure that he left behind."

Then when John had brought the money, he turned to Sir Richard at the Lee, and said: "Thou wilt keep thy four hundred pound, knight, and four hundred other I count out to thee for thy bows and thy arrows; and if thou ever standest in requirement of more, let me have thy news. But my counsel to thee is, for the time to come be a better husband of thy store."

So they parted for awhile, Sir Richard at the Lee and Robin Hood; and Robin holp him to mount his palfrey, and bade him heartily well to fare.

ROBIN HOOD AND THE BUTCHER

By Eva March Tappan

"THANK you kindly, sir," said the little old woman
to Robin Hood. "It's more than once that you've
helped me, when the cow went dry and the pig died.
It's better than a pig that you've been to me many and
many a time, sir. And then there's the good brown
cloth that you gave me for a cloak, sir. There isn't
another woman in town that has so fine a cloak. You'd
know it came from over the sea by the feel of it; and
there's folk in the town that has felt of it, too, and it was
the sheriff's wife, it was. She came up, tossing her
head with all the feathers on it, and followed me in
through the door of the church to mass, and —"

"Did you go in through the door ahead of the sheriff's
wife?" interrupted Robin, with a merry twinkle in his
eye.

"Truly, I did, sir. I said to myself, said I, 'Now I'm
naught but a poor little old woman, and I live in a hut
with a thatched roof, and she lives in a stone house; but
when the great folk give me such a fine cloak as this, it's
but the reverence that's due to them to take it into the
church before the rain might come to wet it.'"

"And so you went ahead of the sheriff's wife!"

"I did that, and I felt the sheriff's wife a-feeling of it
when she went through the door. You're good to me,

177

indeed, sir. Will you come into the cottage, and let me make you an oaten cake?"

Robin went into the cottage, and sat down on a wooden stool. The little old woman bustled about, and stirred up the oaten meal and spread it out thin on the board, and set it up before the fire to bake. Then she pulled forward the iron crane, and on the hook she hung a little iron pot full of the nicest porridge that ever was made. Very soon the porridge began to bubble, and the oaten cake was brown as a berry.

"No, no, thank you humbly, sir," said she, "but I'll not sit down, sir. I'll stand by your stool and serve you. It's a proud woman that I am to have you sit at my table, and eat my oaten cake, and drink my porridge." So she poured more and more of the porridge into the wooden bowl, and put piece after piece of the oaten cake on the table beside it.

By and by Robin pushed the stool back from the table.

"So you walk into the church before the sheriff's wife," said he, "and you won't sit down at the table with a simple bowman like me that the sheriff thinks is only fit to be hanged."

"It's a humble little old woman that I am," she answered, "but it's the poor folk that know the real gentlefolk like you, sir. The sheriff's wife is naught but the wife of the sheriff."

"It's time for me to be going," said Robin. "Have you a bit of meat for your dinner?"

"It's oaten cake and porridge that I'll be having for my dinner," answered the little old woman simply.

178

ROBIN HOOD AND THE BUTCHER

"There's the butcher down the road," said Robin, shading his eyes, for the sun was coming up over the trees. "He's on his way to Nottingham, and we'll lighten his cart for him; or should you rather have a bit of lightfoot?"

The little old woman began to tremble.

"Don't you, sir," she pleaded, "and don't you be taking it amiss, but I'm afeard by week-days and afeard by Sundays when I think of you. Won't you get the king's pardon, sir, and then I'll know you'll not be hanged on the gallows-tree?"

But Robin had gone down the road, and he called to the butcher:—

"Hoot, man, have you a juicy slice of mutton that's fit to go under the finest cloak in Nottingham?"

"Indeed, I have, and it's on its way to the wife of the sheriff," called the butcher.

Robin looked closely at the man and asked slyly:—

"Have you maybe a good bit of lightfoot hidden away in that cart of yours?" Then the butcher laughed and Robin laughed.

"It's all the fault of the little woman at home," said the butcher. "She said that she worrited by day and worrited by night, and she sent me off to get the king's pardon. The best of women have a bit of foolishness in them."

"And the better they are, the bigger it is," declared Robin gravely, "but it might be that a woman would give good advice. Here's the little old woman in the cottage yonder, she's been telling me to get the king's pardon; and when a woman wears a cloak like hers, a man must hearken well to what she says. I 'll tell you what we 'll do. I 'll try being a butcher for a day. How much is your meat worth?"

"It might be one mark," answered the butcher.

"That 's one, and the use of the horse is two, and the cart, three; and, oh, the frock and the cap. I 'll borrow it all, and I 'll give you four broad marks of gold. Do you take my good green cloak and my hunting-horn and my hat with the feather and bide with the little old woman till I come back. The sheriff shan't be hungering for his meat either. The best slice goes to the little old woman, but the next best goes to the wife of the sheriff, and I 'll carry it to her myself."

"There 's more than one that would grieve if you should fall into trouble," said the butcher.

"And why should one butcher fall into trouble more than another?" queried Robin lightly. "It might be that I 'd bring the sheriff back with me. It 's often enough that he 's sought me to come to him."

Robin put on the long white butcher's frock and the little round cap, and into the cap he stuck a red rosebud, and then he set off for Nottingham.

"Good-by, good-by," he cried to the little old woman; but she only threw her apron over her face and crept into the house.

"Hold, here 's the whip," called the butcher.

"Never a whip do I use for my beasts," cried Robin over his shoulder.

The good horse looked back at Robin. Then she switched her tail and winked her left ear at him, and they set off in the wildest gallop that ever carried a butcher's cart up the road to Nottingham. One wheel went over a log, and one went over a rock, and the pieces of meat bounded up into the air like hailstones that had struck a roof. The mutton hammered the beef, and the pork pounded the chicken, and again the good horse switched her tail and winked her left ear and galloped on to Nottingham. She dashed through the brook, she scrambled up the hill, she almost rolled down the hill, and the cart was now on one side of the road and now on the other. The ducks called "Quack, quack!" The little dogs ran out to bark at the ducks, and scampered back with their tails between their legs. The cats sat on the fences ready to spit at the dogs, but the cats, too, ran for their lives without ever saying "Pst!" The rooster strutted across the road, and the hens fluttered after him; but they had no time to go back again, for the butcher's cart was upon them. The people in the cottages put their heads out of the windows; but there was nothing to see except a great cloud of dust whirling up the road, so they crossed themselves and bolted the doors; for perhaps the fiend himself was in that cloud of dust, they whispered to one another fearfully. And still the good horse switched her tail and winked her left ear and galloped on to Nottingham.

The keeper of the town gates flung them wide open, and in came Robin, in his long white frock and white cap with the red rosebud in it. Every piece of meat lay still in its place, and the good horse arched her neck and went proudly up the street with the great white cart till she stood in the square in front of the sheriff's house.

"Meat to sell, good meat to sell," cried Robin. The

wife of the sheriff opened the door and came out on the steps.

"How much is your nice, juicy mutton?" asked she.

"A penny a pound," quoth Robin.

"Give me four pounds," said the sheriff's wife quickly, for good mutton was full threepence a pound.

"Here's a pound weight," cried Robin, and in one hand he caught up a stone as big as his head while in the other he held the nice, juicy piece of mutton. "Here's a forequarter, that's one pound; and here's another forequarter, that's two pounds. Here's a hindquarter, that's three; and here's the other hindquarter, that's four."

Then the sheriff's wife ran into the house as fast as she could run to get the sheriff to carry in the meat, for she had no mind to lose such a bargain as that. The sheriff came out and made sure of the two forequarters and the two hindquarters, all for fourpence.

Robin went on calling, "Meat to sell, good meat to sell;" and again the sheriff's wife came out on the steps and asked:—

"How much is your good, tender beef?" and Robin answered:—

"A penny a pound, but I'm to have my own dinner of it."

The sheriff sat behind the shutters, and he whispered to his wife:—

"Ask him to dinner. I've thought of something."

"Will you come to dinner with us?" asked the sheriff's wife. "I'll buy your beef for a penny, and give you a dinner from it."

"Ay, that will I gladly," answered Robin heartily.

ROBIN HOOD AND THE BUTCHER

"Come when the sun is on the noon mark in the square," said she; and the sheriff whispered to her from behind the shutter:—

"I know him, I know him. It takes a wise man to be a sheriff, and I can tell who he is."

The other butchers had been gazing with their mouths and their eyes wide open, and one whispered to another:—

"The man's on a wager; he's no butcher."

"Yes, he is," said the other softly; "but the poor fellow's mad."

"Let's get him away," said the first, "before the sheriff cheats him out of every penny."

"We'll ask him to dine with us," suggested a third. "We'll find where he lives, and when the sheriff is taking his nap, we'll carry him home." So one of them went up to Robin and said:—

"We be all butchers together, sir, and we've come to ask you to eat dinner with us at the little inn beside the oak-tree."

"Thank you kindly," responded Robin. "He's no true man who'll deny one of his own trade. Shall we dine one hour before the sun is on the noon mark in the square?"

"Yes," answered they; and an hour before the sun was on the noon mark in the square, they all went away to the inn. They called for ale and beer and black pudding; but soon Robin began to call, and he called for fish and fowl and veal and marrow pasties and beef and cheese-cakes and tansy-cake and syllabub and jelly and junket and meat and sack. Never in all their lives had the butchers eaten such a dinner.

"However shall we pay the reckoning?" they began to whisper, but Robin kept on calling; and now there came in so many bottles of the inn-keeper's best wine that the good butchers soon forgot all about the reckoning, and they did not even notice when Robin slipped out of the door and left them all sitting around the table.

"Here's a five-pound note for the dinner," he said to the innkeeper, and the innkeeper said: —

"Will you kindly come again, sir?"

"That will I," replied Robin. "Never a day will I sell meat in Nottingham that I do not have a dinner at your own good inn."

It was almost noon by the mark in the square when Robin walked boldly up to the sheriff's front door.

"Come in, come in," called the sheriff. "There's always a welcome for good true men like you."

"I'm grateful for your courtesy," said Robin. "When a man's but a simple butcher, he's humbly thankful for a great man's kindness."

"Oho!" roared the sheriff. "It's a witty fellow that you are. There's no man that likes a good jest better than myself."

"Truly, Master Sheriff," said Robin gravely, "if I'm not a butcher, what am I then? Must not a poor man have some trade?"

"Oh, I know well who you are," cried the sheriff, "and there's no man in Nottingham that would be more welcome to my house."

Then in came the sheriff's wife. She wore a blue silk gown that dragged behind her an ell or more. She had beads about her neck and rings on her fingers and a feather in her hair; and it was all to do honor to Robin, for the sheriff had said to her: —

"Put on your best blue silk gown, and beads around your neck and rings on your fingers and a feather in your hair. I know who he is. His father owned the wide lands to the west of us, and he had the best herd of horned beasts in all Yorkshire. Bring out the oldest wine from the north side of the cellar. The son's naught but a prodigal, and it won't be my fault if those wide lands and that herd of horned beasts are n't my own before I'm a day older. We'll give him wine till his head turns, and then I'll say, 'Have you any horned beasts to sell?' and I'll say, 'Have you any good land to sell?' and I'll get his fine herd of cattle, and I'll get his land, I will, and it'll cost me little save the wine that he'll drink."

"It 's a pity to waste the best wine," said the sheriff's wife; "and I think, if I 'd only held on a bit, I might have had the mutton for twopence instead of four."

"We 'll try to make it up on the land," said the sheriff.

All three sat down to the table. There was the roast beef, and there was not very much besides, for the sheriff's wife had thought: —

"What is the use of wasting a good dinner on a man who 'll drink so much wine that he 'll not know whether he 's had anything to eat or not?"

Robin had some black bread and a piece of roast beef. It was not the best piece either, for the sheriff thought: —

"He 'll be but a beggar in an hour from now, and it won't take so much good wine to turn his head if he 's had little to eat."

Very soon the wine was brought in. Each of them had a wooden cup with a silver rim, and the sheriff filled the cups again and again.

"He's drunk twice as much as I," said the sheriff to himself in great delight, for he did not know that Robin had poured two glasses out of every three down upon the rushes under the table. Pretty soon the sheriff's wife touched her husband's foot, and he began: —

"And so you're playing at being a butcher?"

"Yes," said Robin, rather sleepily.

"You sell good meat, but have you by chance any horned beasts to sell?" The sheriff's wife gave a nod and a smile that meant: —

"How well he is doing it!" and Robin answered gravely: —

"Yes, Master Sheriff, I have horned beasts; it might be two or three hundred of them."

"I'm not buying cattle, but young men like you often need a bit of money; and if you are anxious to sell, I might take them, just to help you along."

The sheriff's wife nodded a deeper nod and smiled a wider smile than before, and the sheriff went on boldly: —

"Perhaps you have a little land that you want to get rid of? Of course you could buy it back again some day, but I'll take it of you now, if you will. It isn't every man that would do it, but I'm always ready to oblige a friend in need."

The sheriff's wife nodded till one of her feathers fell off, and when she left the table to fasten it on again, she smiled so loud that Robin asked: —

"What was that?"

"Oh, only the cackling of the hens under the window," answered the sheriff. "And now," said he, "you want the money right away; young folk are always in a hurry; and if you'll take me in your butcher's cart, we'll go and see the horned beasts and the bit of land."

Then the sheriff and Robin climbed up into the cart. Again the good horse switched her tail and winked her left ear, and again she galloped away over logs and rocks and brooks, uphill and downhill.

"But this is the road to the forest," cried the sheriff, in alarm.

"It's the nearest way to my herd of horned beasts," said Robin.

The sheriff was badly frightened, for he thought: "Surely, the fellow's mad;" but he could call upon no one for help, for the gates were fastened, and the doors were bolted, and the shutters of every house that they passed were closed tight. Every man that lived on the road had crossed himself and crept into bed when he heard the wild galloping, for he had thought, "One may escape the fiend once, but not twice."

The sheriff trembled, and clung to the seat to keep from falling out of the cart. Then they turned into the forest road, and now the sheriff trembled so that he shook the cart.

"The saints preserve us from Robin Hood," cried he. "Are you sure that your horned beasts are here?" Just then a herd of deer flashed by.

"Those are my horned beasts," said the wild young butcher, "and all around us is the good free land; and if

187

you'll have it, I'll give you as good a title to it as my father gave to me."

"He's surely mad," moaned the sheriff; and as they came to a little cottage, he called out: —

"Help, help! Save me from the madman!"

It was the little old woman's cottage. She came running to the door, and when she saw the sheriff, she, too, set up a screaming and a screeching: —

"Oh, Master Robin, Master Robin! The sheriff's got him, the sheriff's got him, and he'll be hanged on the gallows-tree. Oh, oh, oh!"

The real butcher man sat in a corner of the little old woman's cottage, and now he put his head out of the window and blew a long, long blast on Robin's horn. There was a sound of tramping through the woods, and in a minute Little John and his merry company were with them.

"What is your will, Master?" asked they.

"I think it is the sheriff that wants to see you," said Robin soberly.

The sheriff was whiter than the butcher's frock. He had fallen down on his knees, and was shaking more than he had shaken when the cart jolted over the logs and over the rocks. Not a word said Robin's men, but every one of them slowly fitted an arrow to his bow and aimed it at the sheriff.

"Master, shall we shoot?" asked they.

"I'm afraid you might hit him," answered Robin.

"We'll just send him home with a present for his wife. It's she that likes good mutton, and we'll send her a fourpenny bit." Then a forequarter of mutton was tied upon the sheriff's right shoulder and another forequarter upon his left shoulder.

"Take a hindquarter in each hand," bade Robin, "and go you straight home to your wife."

So the sheriff went stumbling and staggering under the weight up the long road to the gates of Nottingham. He did not dare to drop his burden, for Robin had said: —

"It's not fitting for a great man like the sheriff to journey over the land alone, and we'll give him a goodly band of followers, four and twenty of the best bowmen in the country;" and whenever the sheriff stopped a minute to rest, an arrow would whiz by his ear, and Robin would call out: —

"It's not courtesy to keep a great lady waiting for a little fourpenny gift like that."

SCANDINAVIAN AND DANISH
HEROES

THE STORY OF FRITHIOF

By Julia Goddard

I

IN a cottage overshadowed by wide-spreading oaks, and surrounded by a garden in which bloomed the sweetest flowers of summer, lived an aged peasant named Hilding.

Two children might be seen playing about the garden from sunrise to sunset, but they were not old Hilding's children. The handsome boy was the son of the Thane, Thorsten Vikingsson; the little girl, with dovelike eyes and silken tresses, was the daughter of good King Belé.

Together the little ones played through the long pleasant days in their foster-father's garden, or wandered through the woods, or climbed the hills that sheltered them from the northern winds. The boy would seek treasures from the birds' nests for his fair companion, not even fearing to rob the mountain eagle, so that he might bring the spoil to Ingebjorg. He would also take her far out on the blue sea in his little boat, and Ingebjorg never felt afraid as long as Frithiof was with her.

As Frithiof grew older, he became a great hunter, and once he slew without weapons a fierce bear, which he brought home in triumph and laid at Ingebjorg's feet.

During the winter evenings, they sat by the blazing logs on the hearth, and Hilding told them wonderful stories of Asgard and all its glories, of Odin the king of the gods, and of the beautiful Friga.

But Frithiof thought she could not be half so beautiful as Ingebjorg. And once he said so to her, and it pleased her exceedingly. And he said, moreover, that when he was a man, Ingebjorg should be his wife. This also she was glad to hear, for she loved Frithiof better than any one in the world.

But Old Hilding told them not to talk nonsense, for Ingebjorg was a king's daughter, and Frithiof but the son of a Thane.

II

In a room of his palace stood King Belé. He was leaning on his sword, musing over all that was past, and thinking of the future. He was an old man, and he felt that his strength was failing him.

With him was his faithful friend Thorsten Vikingsson. They had grown up to manhood together, they had fought in many a battle side by side. They had been companions at many a feast and revel; and now, when old age had fallen upon them, they drew closer to one another, feeling that the hand of death was raised to summon them into another world.

"The end of life is near," said the king; "the shadow of death is cast upon me. No longer do I care for all that men call pleasure. The chase hath lost its charm, the helmet sits heavy upon my brow, and the mead hath lost its flavor. I would that my sons were here so that I might give them my blessing."

Then the servants summoned to King Belé's presence his two sons, Helgi and Halfdan. Dark was the countenance of Helgi, and there was blood upon his hands, for he had just been assisting at the mid-day sacrifice. But the face of Halfdan was bright as the early morning, and he was as light and joyous as his brother was dark and gloomy.

Frithiof also came, for the Thane Thorsten Vikingsson desired to see him, that he too might bless his son when King Belé blessed the royal princes.

And the two old friends spoke words of wisdom to their children, and prayed that the gods might be with them in peace and war, in joy and sorrow, and grant them a long life and a glorious death.

And when their counsels and prayers were ended, King Belé said, "And now, O sons, I bid you remember, in that day when death shall claim me and my faithful friend, that ye lay our bones side by side near the shore of the great ocean."

III

In due time, King Belé died, and Helgi and Halfdan shared his kingdom between them.

Thorsten Vikingsson died also, and Frithiof became lord of his ancestral home of Framnäs.

Much treasures did that home contain, three of them of magic power.

The first was the sword of Angurvadel. Blood-red

it shone in time of war, and woe to him who contended with its owner on the battlefield.

Next was an arm-ring of pure gold, made by the god Völund, and given by him to one of Thorsten Vikingsson's forefathers. Once it was stolen and carried to England by the Viking Soté, but Thorsten and his friend King Belé pursued the robber. Over the sea they sailed after the Viking, and landed at a lonely place where the rocks reared up their sharp points and made the coast dangerous.

There were deep caverns which the waters filled when the tide was up, so lone and dark that men were almost afraid to go into them.

But Thorsten Vikingsson and the king his master were not daunted. Hither had they come after the pirate, and here it was that he had last been heard of; and they searched along the shore and in the caves, and peered into every hole and cranny, until their eyes grew strained and heavy, but no Viking Soté was to be seen.

They had almost given up hope of finding him, when, looking through a chink that had hitherto escaped their notice, a fearful sight was seen by the valiant Thane.

Within a mighty vault, forming a still cold tomb, there lay a vessel all complete, with masts and spars and anchor; and on the deck there sat a grim skeleton clad in a robe of flame, and on his skinless arm glittered the golden arm-ring wrought by Völund. The figure held in his left hand a blood-stained sword, from which he was trying to scour away the stains.

"It is my arm-ring," said Thorsten Vikingsson; "it is the spirit of the Viking Soté."

And forthwith he forced his way into the tomb, and, after a deadly conflict with the spectre, regained his treasure.

And the two friends sailed home in triumph.

The third great thing that Frithiof inherited was the dragon-ship Ellide, which his forefathers had won in the following manner: —

One of them, a rough, rude Viking, with a tender heart, was out at sea, and on a wreck that was fast sinking saw an old man with green locks sitting disconsolately.

The good-natured Viking picked him up, took him home, gave him of the best of food and of sparkling mead, and would have lodged him in his house; but the green-haired man said he could not tarry, for he had many miles to sail that night.

"But when the sun comes up in the east," added the stranger, "look for a thank-gift on the wild sea-shore."

And behold, as morning dawned, the Viking saw a goodly vessel making gallant headway. As she drew near the land with streamer flying and broad sails flapping in the wind, the Viking saw that there was no soul on board of her; and yet, without steersman to guide her, the vessel avoided the shoals and held her way straight to the spot where he was standing.

Her prow was a dragon's head, a dragon's tail formed her stern, and dragon's wings bore her along swifter than an eagle before the storm.

The green-haired stranger was a sea-god, and the dragon-ship Ellide was his thank-gift.

Thus Frithiof, though only the son of a Thane, had treasures that might have been coveted by kings and princes. He sat in his father's halls, surrounded by his companions; upon his right was seated his bosom friend Bjorn, and twelve bold champions clad in steel were ranged around the board. And they drank in silence to the memory of Thorsten Vikingsson.

But suddenly the harps struck up, and the skalds poured forth their songs in honor of the dead Thane.

And Frithiof's eyes filled with tears as he listened to his father's praises.

IV

In spite of Frithiof's wealth, Helgi and Halfdan looked with disdain upon the son of their father's friend; and when Frithiof asked to have Ingebjorg for his wife, Helgi scornfully answered, " My sister shall not wed the son of a Thane. If you like to be our serf, we will make room for you among our servants."

Then went Frithiof away in wrath.

There was another suitor for the hand of Ingebjorg, good old King Ring, who, having lost his wife, thought that the Lily of the North would make a tender mother to his little son.

And he sent to Helgi and Halfdan to ask for Ingebjorg in marriage, but the brothers treated him as they had treated Frithiof; and the old king was roused, and he swore he would revenge himself.

Helgi and Halfdan were afraid when they found that Ring was really making ready for war. They began to get their army into order, and placed Ingebjorg for safety in the temple of Balder, and in their distress they even sent to Frithiof to ask him to come and help them.

They chose wisely in the messenger they sent to plead for them, for it was none other than old Hilding, who had been so kind to Frithiof in his childhood.

Frithiof was playing at chess with Bjorn when Hilding arrived. He pretended not to hear the message, and went on with his game.

"Shall the pawn save the king?" he asked of Bjorn.

And after a time he added: "There is no other way to save the queen." Which showed that he had been all the time occupied with Hilding's errand.

Therefore he returned with the old peasant, and contrived to see Ingebjorg in the temple of Balder, and found that she still loved him as much as he loved her, and did not wish to marry any one else.

And again he asked Helgi and Halfdan if they were willing that Ingebjorg should be his wife.

And again the brothers said, Nay, with scorn, and told him that he had profaned the temple of Balder by speaking to Ingebjorg within its walls.

"For such a misdeed," said Helgi, "death or banishment is the doom, and thou art in our power. Nevertheless, we are willing, as we wish to make thee useful to us, to forego the penalty. Thou shalt therefore sail forth to the distant Orkney Isles, and compel Jarl Angantyr to pay the tribute that he owes us."

Frithiof would have refused to go, but Ingebjorg persuaded him to undertake the mission; for she was afraid of her brothers, and knew that Frithiof would be safer on the wild seas than in their hands.

At last Frithiof consented, and he took leave of Ingebjorg, and placed the golden bracelet that Völund had made upon her arm, praying her to keep it for his sake.

And then he sailed away over the heaving waters, and Ingebjorg mourned that her lover was gone.

V

Over the sea. It was calm enough when Frithiof started; the storm-winds were asleep, and the waters heaved gently as though they would fain help speed the dragon-ship peacefully on her way.

But King Helgi standing on a rock repented that he had suffered the noble Frithiof to escape his malice; and as he watched the good ship Ellide riding over the sea, he prayed loudly to the ocean fiends that they would trouble the waters and raise a fierce tempest to swallow up Frithiof and the dragon-ship.

All at once, the sparkling sea turned leaden gray, and the billows began to roll, the skies grew dark, and the howl of the driving wind was answered by a sullen roar from the depths beneath. Suddenly, a blinding flash of lightning played around the vessel, and as it vanished the pealing thunder burst from the clouds. The raging sea foamed, and seethed, and tossed the vessel like a feather upon its angry waves, and deeper sounded the thunder, and more fiercely flashed the lightning round the masts.

Wilder, wilder, wilder, grew the storm. Alas, for Frithiof!

"Ho! take the tiller in hand," shouted Frithiof to Bjorn, "and I will mount to the topmost mast and look out for danger."

And when he looked out, he saw the storm-fiends riding on a whale. One was in form like to a great white bear, the other like unto a terrible eagle.

"Now help me, O gift of the sea-god! Help me, my gallant Ellide!" cried Frithiof.

And the dragon-ship heard her master's voice, and with her keel she smote the whale; so he died, and sank to the bottom of the sea, leaving the storm-fiends tossing upon the waves.

"Ho, spears and lances, help me in my need!" shouted Frithiof, as he took aim at the monsters.

And he transfixed the shrieking storm-fiends, and left them entangled in the huge coils of seaweed which the storm had uprooted.

"Ho, ho!" laughed rugged Bjorn, "they are trapped in their own nets."

And so they were; and they were so much taken up with trying to free themselves from the seaweed and from Frithiof's long darts, that they were unable to give any heed to the storm, which therefore went down, and Frithiof and his crew sailed on, and reached the Orkney Isles in safety.

"Here comes Frithiof," said the Viking Atlé. "I know him by his dragon-ship."

And forthwith the Viking rose and went forth; he had heard of the strength of Frithiof, and wished to match himself against him.

He did not wait to see whether Frithiof came in

enmity or friendship. Fighting was the first thing he thought of, and what he most cared for.

However, the Viking had the worst of it in the battle.

"There is witchcraft in thy sword," said he to Frithiof.

So Frithiof threw his sword aside, and they wrestled together, unarmed, until Atlé was brought to the ground.

Then spake Frithiof: "And if I had my sword thou wouldst not long be a living man."

"Fetch it, then," replied Atlé. "I swear by the gods that I will not move until thou dost return."

So Frithiof fetched his sword, but when he saw the conquered Viking still upon the ground, he could not bring himself to slay so honorable a man.

"Thou art too true and brave to die," said Frithiof. "Rise, let us be friends."

And the two combatants went hand in hand to the banquet hall of Angantyr, Jarl of the Orkney Islands.

A splendid hall it was, and a rare company of heroes was there; and all listened eagerly as Frithiof told his story, and wherefore he had come.

"I never paid tribute to King Belé, though he was an old friend of mine," said the Jarl, as Frithiof ended his speech, "nor will I to his sons. If they want aught of me, let them come and take it."

"It was by no choice of my own that I came upon such an errand," returned Frithiof, "and I shall be well content to carry back your answer."

"Take also this purse of gold in token of friendship," continued the Jarl, "and remain with us, for I knew thy father."

Thus Frithiof and the Jarl became good friends, and Frithiof consented to stay for a while in the Orkney Islands; but after a time he ordered out his good ship Ellide, and set sail for his native land.

VI

But fearful things had come to pass since he had left his home! Framnäs, the dwelling of his fathers, was a heap of ruins, and the land was waste and desolate.

And as he stood upon the well-loved spot, striving to find some traces of the past, his faithful hound bounded forth to greet him, and licked his master's hand. And then his favorite steed drew near, and thrust his nose into Frithiof's hand, hoping to find therein a piece of bread, as in the days of old. His favorite falcon perched upon his shoulder, and this was Frithiof's welcome to the home of his ancestors.

There had been a fierce battle, for King Ring with his army had come against Helgi and Halfdan, and the country had been laid waste, and many warriors slain.

And when all chance of withstanding him was at an end, the brothers, rather than lose their kingdom, had consented that Ingebjorg should be the wife of Ring.

Ingebjorg was married! Frithiof's heart was full of deep sorrow, and he turned his steps towards the temple of Balder, hoping that at the altar of the god he might meet with consolation.

In the temple he found King Helgi, and the sorrow that was weighing down Frithiof's heart gave place to hatred and revenge.

Caring nothing for the sacred place, he rushed madly forward. "Here, take thy tribute," said he, and he threw the purse that Jarl Angantyr had given him with such force against the face of the king that Helgi fell down senseless on the steps of the altar.

Next, seeing his arm-ring on the arm of the statue, for Helgi had taken it from Ingebjorg and placed it there, he tried to tear it off, and, lo! the image tottered and fell upon the fire that was burning with sweet perfumes before it.

Scarcely had it touched the fire when it was ablaze, and the flames spreading rapidly on every side, the whole temple was soon a smouldering heap of ruins.

Then Frithiof sought his ship. He vowed that he would lead a Viking's life, and leave forever a land where he had suffered so much sorrow. And he put out to sea.

But no sooner were his sails spread than he saw ten vessels in chase of him, and on the deck of one stood Helgi, who had been rescued from the burning temple, and had come in chase of him.

Yet Frithiof was rescued from the danger as if by miracle; for one by one the ships sank down as though some water giant had stretched out his strong arm, and dragged them below, and Helgi only saved himself by swimming ashore.

Loud laughed Bjorn.

"I bored holes in them last night," said he; "it is a rare ending to Helgi's fleet."

"And now," said Frithiof, "I will forever lead a Viking's life. I care not for aught upon the land. The sea shall be my home. And I will seek climes far away from here."

So he steered the good ship Ellide southward, and among the isles of Greece strove to forget the memories of bygone days.

VII

In and out of the sunny islands that lay like bosses of emerald on a silver shield sailed Frithiof, and on the deck of the dragon-ship he rested through the summer nights, looking up at the moon, and wondering what she could tell him of his northern land.

Sometimes he dreamed of his home as it was before the war-time. Sometimes he dreamed of the days when he and Ingebjorg roamed through the fields and woods together, or listened to old Hilding's stories by the blazing hearth; and then he would wake up with a start and stroke his faithful hound, who was ever near him, saying, "Thou alone knowest no change; to thee all is alike, so long as thy master is with thee."

One night, however, as Frithiof was musing on the deck of his vessel, gazing into the cloudless sky, a vision of the past rose up before him: old familiar faces crowded round him, and in their midst he marked one, best beloved of all, pale, sad, with sorrowful eyes; and her lips moved, and he seemed to hear her say, "I am very sad without thee, Frithiof."

Then a great longing came upon Frithiof to see Ingebjorg once more. He would go northward, even to the country of King Ring; he must see Ingebjorg. What did he care for danger? He must go.

To the cold, dark north.

Yet he dared not go openly, for King Ring looked upon him as an enemy, and would seize him at once, and if he did not kill him would shut him up in prison, so that either way he would not see the beautiful queen.

Frithiof therefore disguised himself as an old man, and, wrapped in bearskins, presented himself at the palace.

The old king sat upon his throne, and at his side was Ingebjorg the Fair, looking like spring by the side of fading autumn.

As the strangely dressed figure passed along, the courtiers jeered, and Frithiof, thrown off his guard, angrily seized one of them, and twirled him round with but little effort.

"Ho!" said the king, "thou art a strong old man, O stranger! Whence art thou?"

"I was reared in anguish and want," returned Frithiof; "sorrow has filled a bitter cup for me, and I have almost drunk it to the dregs. Once I rode upon a dragon, but now it lies dead upon the seashore, and I am left in my old age to burn salt upon the strand."

"Thou art not old," answered the wise king; "thy voice is clear, and thy grasp is strong. Throw off thy rude disguise, that we may know our guest."

Then Frithiof threw aside his bearskin, and appeared clad in a mantle of blue embroidered velvet, and his hair fell like a golden wave upon his shoulder.

Ring did not know him, but Ingebjorg did; and when she handed the goblet for him to drink, her color went and came "like to the northern light on a field of snow."

"O STRANGER! WHENCE ART THOU?"

THE STORY OF FRITHIOF

And Frithiof stayed at the court until the year came round again, and spring once more put forth its early blossoms.

One day a gay hunting train went forth, but old King Ring, not being strong, as in former years, lay down to rest upon the mossy turf beneath some arching pines, whilst the hunters rode on.

Then Frithiof drew near, and in his heart wild thoughts arose. One blow of his sword, and Ingebjorg was free to be his wife.

But as he looked upon the sleeping king, there came a whisper from a better voice, "It is cowardly to strike a sleeping foe."

And Frithiof shuddered, for he was too brave a man to commit murder.

"Sleep on, old man," he muttered gently to himself.

But Ring's sleep was over. He started up. "O Frithiof, why hast thou come hither to steal an old man's bride?"

"I came not hither for so dark a purpose," answered Frithiof; "I came but to look on the face of my loved Ingebjorg once more."

"I know it," replied the king; "I have tried thee, I have proved thee, and true as tried steel hast thou passed through the furnace. Stay with us yet a little longer, the old man soon will be gathered to his fathers, then shall his kingdom and his wife be thine."

But Frithiof replied that he had already remained too long, and that on the morrow he must depart.

Yet he went not; for death had visited the palace, and old King Ring was stretched upon his bier, whilst the bards around sang of his wisdom.

Then arose a cry among the people, "We must choose a king!"

And Frithiof raised aloft upon his shield the little son of Ring.

"Here is your king," he said, "the son of wise old Ring."

The blue-eyed child laughed and clapped his hands as he beheld the glittering helmets and glancing spears of the warriors. Then tired of his high place, he sprang down into the midst of them.

Loud uprose the shout, "The child shall be our king, and the Jarl Frithiof regent. Hail to the young king of the Northmen!"

VIII

But Frithiof in the hour of his good fortune did not forget that he had offended the gods. He must make atonement to Balder for having caused the ruin of his temple. He must turn his steps once more homeward.

Home! Home! And on his father's grave he sank down with a softened heart, and grieved over the passion and revenge that had swayed his deeds. And as he mourned, the voices of unseen spirits answered him, and whispered that he was forgiven.

And to his wondering eyes a vision was vouchsafed, and the temple of Balder appeared before him, rebuilt in more than its ancient splendor, and deep peace sank into the soul of Frithiof.

"Rise up, rise up, Frithiof, and journey onward."

The words came clear as a command to Frithiof, and he obeyed them. He rose up, and journeyed to the place where he had left the temple a heap of blackened ruins.

And, lo! the vision that had appeared to him was accomplished, for there stood the beautiful building, stately and fair to look upon. So beautiful, that, as he gazed, his thoughts were of Valhalla.

He entered, and the white-robed, silver-bearded priest welcomed the long absent Viking, and told him that Helgi was dead, and Halfdan reigned alone.

"And know, O Frithiof," said the aged man, "that Balder is better pleased when the heart grows soft and injuries are forgiven, than with the most costly sacrifices. Lay aside forever all thoughts of hatred and revenge, and stretch out to Halfdan the hand of friendship."

Joy had softened all Frithiof's feelings of anger, and, advancing to Halfdan, who was standing near the altar, he spoke out manfully.

"Halfdan," he said, "let us forget the years that have gone by. Let all past evil and injury be buried in the grave. Henceforth let us be as brothers, and once more I ask thee, give me Ingebjorg to be my wife."

And Halfdan made answer, "Thou shalt be my brother."

And as he spoke, an inner door flew open, and a sweet chorus of youthful voices was heard. A band of maidens issued forth, and at their head walked Ingebjorg, fairer than ever.

Then Halfdan, leading her to Frithiof, placed her hand within that of the Viking.

"Behold thy wife," said Halfdan. "Well hast thou won her. May the gods attend upon your bridal."

So Ingebjorg became the wife of Frithiof at last.

Thus steps of sorrow had but led them to a height of happiness that poets love to sing. Paths thick with thorns had blossomed into roses, and wreaths of everlasting flowers had crowned the winter snows. And midst the lights and shadows of the old Northland, their lives flowed on like to two united streams that roll through quiet pastures to the ocean of eternity.

HAVELOK

By George W. Cox and E. H. Jones

THERE was once a king of England named Athelwold. Earl, baron, thane, knight, and bondsman,
all loved him; for he set on high the wise and the just
man, and put down the spoiler and the robber. At that
time a man might carry gold about with him, as much
as fifty pounds, and not fear loss. Chapmen and mer-
chants bought and sold at their ease without danger of
plunder. But it was bad for the evil person and for
such as wrought shame, for they had to lurk and hide
away from the king's wrath; yet was it unavailing, for
he searched out the evil-doer and punished him, where-
ever he might be. The fatherless and the widow found
a sure friend in the king; he turned not away from the
complaint of the helpless, but avenged them against the
oppressor, were he never so strong. Kind was he to
the poor, neither at any time thought he the fine bread
upon his own table too good to give to the hungry.

But a death-sickness fell on King Athelwold, and
when he knew that his end was near he was greatly
troubled, for he had one little daughter of tender age,
named Goldborough, and he grieved to leave her.

"O my little daughter, heir to all the land, yet so young
thou canst not walk upon it; so helpless that thou canst
not tell thy wants, and yet had need to give command-

ment like a queen! For myself I would not care, being
old and not afraid to die. But I had hoped to live till
thou should'st be of age to wield the kingdom; to see
thee ride on horseback through the land, and round
about a thousand knights to do thy bidding. Alas,
my little child, what will become of thee when I am
gone?"

Then King Athelwold summoned his earls and barons,
from Roxborough to Dover, to come and take counsel
with him as he lay a-dying on his bed at Winchester.
And when they all wept sore at seeing the king so near
his end, he said, "Weep not, good friends, for since I am
brought to death's door your tears can in nowise deliver
me; but rather give me your counsel. My little daughter
that after me shall be your queen; tell me in whose charge
I may safely leave both her and England till she be
grown of age to rule?"

And with one accord they answered him, "In the
charge of Earl Godrich of Cornwall, for he is a right
wise and a just man, and held in fear of all the land.
Let him be ruler till our queen be grown."

Then the king sent for a fair linen cloth, and thereon
having laid the mass-book and the chalice and the paton,
he made Earl Godrich swear upon the holy bread and
wine to be a true and faithful guardian of his child,
without blame or reproach, tenderly to entreat her, and
justly to govern the realm till she should be twenty winters old; then to seek out the best, the bravest, and the
strongest man as husband for her and deliver up the
kingdom to her hand. And when Earl Godrich had so
sworn, the king shrived him clean of all his sins. Then

having received his Saviour he folded his hands, saying, "Domine, in manus tuas;" and so died.

There was sorrow and mourning among all the people for the death of good King Athelwold. Many the mass that was sung for him and the psalter that was said for his soul's rest. The bells tolled and the priests sang, and the people wept; and they gave him a kingly burial.

Then Earl Godrich began to govern the kingdom; and all the nobles and all the churls, both free and thrall, came and did allegiance to him. He set in all the castles strong knights in whom he could trust, and appointed justices and sheriffs and peace-sergeants in all the shires. So he ruled the country with a firm hand, and not a single wight dare disobey his word, for all England feared him. Thus, as the years went on, the earl waxed wonderly strong and very rich.

Goldborough, the king's daughter, throve and grew up the fairest woman in all the land, and she was wise in all manner of wisdom that is good and to be desired. But when the time drew on that Earl Godrich should give up the kingdom to her, he began to think within himself, — "Shall I, that have ruled so long, give up the kingdom to a girl, and let her be queen and lady over me? And to what end? All these strong earls and barons, governed by a weaker hand than mine, would throw off the yoke and split up England into little baronies, evermore fighting betwixt themselves for mastery. There would cease to be a kingdom, and so there would cease to be a queen. She cannot rule it, and she shall not have it. Besides, I have a son. Him will I teach to rule and make him king."

So the earl let his oath go for nothing, and went to Winchester where the maiden was, and fetched her away and carried her off to Dover to a castle that is by the seashore. Therein he shut her up and dressed her in poor clothes, and fed her on scanty fare; neither would he let any of her friends come near her.

Now there was in Denmark a certain king called Birkabeyn, who had three children, two daughters and a son. And Birkabeyn fell sick, and knowing that death had stricken him, he called for Godard, whom he thought his truest friend, and said, "Godard, here I commend my children to thee. Care for them, I pray thee, and bring them up as befits the children of a king. When the boy is grown and can bear a helm upon his head and wield a spear, I charge thee make him king of Denmark. Till then hold my estate and royalty in charge for him." And Godard swore to guard the children zealously, and to give up the kingdom to the boy. Then Birkabeyn died and was buried. But no sooner was the king laid in his grave than Godard despised his oath; for he took the children, Havelok, and his two little sisters, Swanborough and Helfled, and shut them up in a castle with barely clothes to cover them. And Havelok, the eldest, was scarce three years old.

One day Godard came to see the children, and found them all crying for hunger and cold; and he said angrily, "How now! What is all this crying about?" The boy Havelok answered him, "We are very hungry, for we get scarce anything to eat. Is there no more corn, that men cannot make bread and give us? We are very hungry." But his little sisters only sate shivering with

the cold, and sobbing, for they were too young to be
able to speak. The cruel Godard cared not. He went
to where the little girls sate, and drew his knife, and took
them up one after another and cut their throats. Havelok, seeing this sorry sight, was terribly afraid, and fell
down on his knees begging Godard to spare his life.
So earnestly he pleaded that Godard was fain to listen:
and listening he looked upon the knife, red with the
children's blood; and when he saw the still, dead faces
of the little ones he had slain, and looked upon their
brother's tearful face praying for life, his cruel courage
failed him quite. He laid down the knife. He would
that Havelok were dead, but feared to slay him for the
silence that would come. So the boy pleaded on; and
Godard stared at him as though his wits were gone; then
turned upon his heel and came out from the castle.
"Yet," he thought, "if I should let him go, one day he
may wreak me mischief and perchance seize the crown.
But if he dies, my children will be lords of Denmark
after me." Then Godard sent for a fisherman whose
name was Grim, and he said, "Grim, thou wottest well
thou art my thrall. Do now my bidding, and to-morrow
I shall make thee free and give thee gold and land.
Take this child with thee to-night when thou goest a-
fishing, and at moonrise cast him in the sea, with a good
anchor fast about his neck to keep him down. To-day
I am thy master and the sin is mine. To-morrow thou
art free."

Then Grim took up the child and bound him fast,
and having thrust a gag of clouts into his mouth so that
he could not speak, he put him in a bag and took him on

his back and carried him home. When Grim got home his dame took the bag from off his shoulders and cast it down upon the ground within doors; and Grim told her of his errand. Now as it drew to midnight he said, "Rise up, dame, and blow up the fire to light a candle, and get me my clothes, for I must be stirring." But when the woman came into the room where Havelok lay, she saw a bright light round the boy's head, as it had been a sunbeam, and she called to her husband to come and see. And when he came they both marveled at the light and what it might mean, for it was very bright and shining. Then they unbound Havelok and took away the gag, and turning down his shirt they found a king-mark fair and plain upon his right shoulder. "God help us, dame," said Grim, "but this is surely the heir of Denmark, son of Birkabeyn our king! Ay, and he shall be king in spite of Godard." Then Grim fell down at the boy's feet and did him obeisance, and said "Forgive me, my king, for that I knew thee not. We are thy thralls, and henceforth will feed and clothe thee till thou art grown a man and can bear shield and spear. Then deal thou kindly by me and mine, as I shall deal to thee. But fear not Godard. He shall never know, and I shall be a bondsman still, for I will never be free till thou, my king, shall set me free."

Then was Havelok very glad, and he sat up and begged for bread. And they hasted and fetched bread and cheese and butter and milk; and for very hunger the boy ate up the whole loaf, for he was well-nigh famished. And after he had eaten, Grim made a fair bed and undressed Havelok and laid him down to rest, saying, "Sleep, my son; sleep fast and sound and have no care, for nought shall harm thee."

On the morrow Grim went to Godard, and telling him he had drowned the boy, asked for his reward. But Godard bade him go home and remain a thrall, and be thankful that he was not hanged for so wicked a deed. After awhile Grim, beginning to fear that both himself and Havelok might be slain, sold all his goods, his corn, and cattle, and fowls, and made ready his little ship, tarring and pitching it till not a seam nor a crack could be found, and setting a good mast and sail therein. Then with his wife, his three sons, his two daughters, and Havelok, he entered into the ship and sailed away from Denmark; and a strong north wind arose and drove the vessel to England, and carried it up the Humber so far as Lindesay, where it grounded on the sands. Grim got out of the boat with his wife and children and Havelok, and then drew it ashore.

On the shore he built a house of earth and dwelt therein, and from that time the place was called Grimsby, after Grim.

Grim did not want for food, for he was a good fisherman both with net and hook, and he would go out in his boat and catch all manner of fish — sturgeons, turbot, salmon, cod, herrings, mackerel, flounders, plaice, lampreys, and thornback, and he never came home empty-handed. He had four panniers made for himself and his sons, and in these they used to carry the fish to Lincoln, to sell them, coming home laden with meat and meal, and simnel cakes, and hemp and rope to make new nets and lines. Thus they lived for twelve years.

But Havelok saw that Grim worked very hard, and being now grown a strong lad, he bethought him "I eat more than Grim and all his five children together, and yet do nothing to earn the bread. I will no longer be idle, for it is a shame for a man not to work." So he got Grim to let him have a pannier like the rest, and next day took out a great heaped basket of fish, and sold them well, bringing home silver money for them. After that he never stopped at home idle. But soon there arose a great dearth, and corn grew so dear that they could not take fish enough to buy bread for all. Then Havelok, since he needed so much to eat, determined that he would no longer be a burden to the fisherman. So Grim made him a coat of a piece of an old sail, and Havelok set off to Lincoln barefoot to seek for work.

It so befell that Earl Godrich's cook, Bertram, wanted a scullion, and took Havelok into his service. There was plenty to eat and plenty to do. Havelok drew water and chopped wood, and brought turves to make fires, and carried heavy tubs and dishes, but was always merry and blythe. Little children loved to play with him; and grown knights and nobles would stop to talk and laugh with him, although he wore nothing but rags of old sail-cloth which scarcely covered his great limbs, and all admired how fair and strong a man God had made him. The cook liked Havelok so much that he bought him span-new clothes, with shoes and hosen; and when Havelok put them on, no man in the kingdom seemed his peer for strength and beauty. He was the tallest man in Lincoln, and the strongest in England.

Earl Godrich assembled a Parliament in Lincoln,

and afterward held games. Strong men and youths came to try for mastery at the game of putting the stone. It was a mighty stone, the weight of an heifer. He was a stalwart man who could lift it to his knee, and few could stir it from the ground. So they strove together, and he who put the stone an inch farther than the rest was to be made champion. But Havelok, though he had never seen the like before, took up the heavy stone, and put it full twelve foot beyond the rest, and after that none would contend with him. Now this matter being greatly talked about, it came to the ears of Earl Godrich, who bethought him, — "Did not Athelwold bid me marry his daughter to the strongest man alive? In truth, I will marry her to this cook's scullion. That will abase her pride; and when she is wedded to a thrall she will be powerless to injure me. That will be better than shutting her up; better than killing her." So he sent and brought Goldborough to Lincoln, and set the bells a-ringing, and pretended great joy, for he said, "Goldborough, I am going to spouse thee to the fairest and stalwartest man living." But Goldborough answered she would never wed with any but a king. "Ay, ay, my girl; and so thou wouldst be queen and lady over me? But thy father made me swear to give thee to the strongest man in England, and that is Havelok, the cook's scullion; so lief or loth to-morrow thou shalt wed." Then the earl sent for Havelok and said, "Master, wilt wive?" "Not I," said Havelok; "for I cannot feed nor clothe a wife. I have neither stick nor stem — no house, no cloth, no victuals. The very clothes I wear do not belong to me, but to Bertram the cook, as I do." "So much the better," said the earl; "but thou shalt either wive with her that I shall bring thee, or else hang upon a tree. So choose." Then Havelok said he would sooner wive. Earl Godrich went back to Goldborough and threatened her with burning on a stake unless she yielded to his bidding. So, thinking it God's will, the maid consented. And on the morrow they were wed by the Archbishop of York, who had come down to the Parliament, and the earl told money out upon the mass-book for her dower.

Now after he was wed, Havelok wist not what to do, for he saw how greatly Earl Godrich hated him. He thought he would go and see Grim. When he got to Grimsby he found that Grim was dead, but his children welcomed Havelok and begged him bring his wife thither, since they had gold and silver and cattle. And when Goldborough came, they made a feast, sparing neither flesh nor fowl, wine nor ale. And Grim's sons and daughters served Havelok and Goldborough.

Sorrowfully Goldborough lay down at night, for her heart was heavy at thinking she had wedded a thrall. But as she fretted she saw a light, very bright like a blaze of fire, which came out of Havelok's mouth. And she thought "Of a truth but he must be nobly born." Then she looked on his shoulder, and saw the king-mark, like a fair cross of red gold, and at the same time she heard an angel say, —

"Goldborough, leave sorrowing, for Havelok is a king's son, and shall be king of England and of Denmark, and thou queen."

Then was Goldborough glad, and kissed Havelok,

who, straightway waking, said, "I have seen a strange dream. I dreamed I was on a high hill, whence I could see all Denmark; and I thought as I looked that it was all mine. Then I was taken up and carried over the salt sea to England, and methought I took all the country and shut it within my hand." And Goldborough said, "What a good dream is this! Rejoice, for it betokeneth that thou shalt be king of England and of Denmark. Take now my counsel and get Grim's sons to go with thee to Denmark."

In the morning Havelok went to the church and prayed God speed him in his undertaking. Then he came home and found Grim's three sons just going off a-fishing. Their names were Robert the Red, William Wendut, and Hugh Raven. He told them who he was, how Godard had slain his sisters, and delivered him over to Grim to be drowned, and how Grim had fled with him to England. Then Havelok asked them to go with him to Denmark, promising to make them rich men. To this they gladly agreed, and having got ready their ship and victualed it, they set sail with Havelok and his wife for Denmark. The place of their landing was hard by the castle of a Danish earl named Ubbe, who had been a faithful friend to King Birkabeyn. Havelok went to Earl Ubbe, with a gold ring for a present, asking leave to buy and sell goods from town to town in that part of the country. Ubbe, beholding the tall, broad-shouldered, thick-chested man, so strong and cleanly made, thought him more fit for a knight than for a peddler. He bade Havelok bring his wife and come and eat with him at his table. So Havelok went to fetch Goldborough, and

Robert the Red and William Wendut led her between them till they came to the castle, where Ubbe, with a great company of knights, welcomed them gladly. Havelok stood a head taller than any of the knights, and when they sat at table Ubbe's wife ate with him, and Goldborough with Ubbe. It was a great feast, and after the feast Ubbe sent Havelok and his friends to Bernard Brown, bidding him take care of them till next day. So Bernard received the guests and gave them a rich supper.

Now in the night there came sixty-one thieves to Bernard's house. Each had a drawn sword and a long knife, and they called to Bernard to undo the door. He started up and armed himself, and told them to go away. But the thieves defied him, and with a great boulder-stone brake down the door. Then Havelok, hearing the din, rose up, and seizing the bar of the door stood on the threshold and threw the door wide open, saying, "Come in, I am ready for you!" First came three against him with their swords, but Havelok slew these with the door bar at a single blow; the fourth man's crown he brake; he smote the fifth upon the shoulders, the sixth athwart the neck, and the seventh on the breast; so they fell dead. Then the rest drew back and began to fling their swords like darts at Havelok, till they had wounded him in twenty places. For all that, in a little while he killed a score of the thieves. Then Hugh Raven, waking up, called Robert and William Wendut. One seized a staff, each of the others a piece of timber big as his thigh, and Bernard his axe, and all three ran out to help Havelok. So well Havelok and his fellows laid about them, breaking ribs and arms and shanks, and cracking crowns, that not a thief of all the sixty-one was left alive. Next morning, when Ubbe rode past and saw the sixty-one dead bodies, and heard what Havelok had done, he sent and brought both him and Goldborough to his own castle, and fetched a leech to tend his wounds, and would not hear of his going away ; for, said he, "This man is better than a thousand knights."

Now that same night, after he had gone to bed, Ubbe awoke about midnight and saw a great light shining from the chamber where Havelok and Goldborough lay. He went softly to the door and peeped in to see what it meant. They were lying fast asleep, and the light was streaming from Havelok's mouth. Ubbe went and called his knights, and they also came in and saw this marvel. It was brighter than a hundred burning tapers; bright enough to choose money by. Havelok lay on his left side with his back towards them, uncovered to the waist; and they saw the king-mark on his right shoulder sparkle like shining gold and carbuncle. Then knew they that it was King Birkabeyn's son, and seeing how like he was to his father, they wept for joy. Thereupon Havelok awoke, and all fell down and did him homage, saying he should be their king. On the morrow Ubbe sent far and wide and gathered together earl and baron, dreng [servant] and thane, clerk, knight and burgess, and told them all the treason of Godard, and how Havelok had been nurtured and brought up by Grim in England. Then he showed them their king, and the people shouted for joy at having so fair and strong a man to rule them. And first Ubbe sware

fealty to Havelok, and after him the others both great
and small. And the sheriffs and constables and all that
held castles in town or burg came out and promised to
be faithful to him. Then Ubbe drew his sword and
dubbed Havelok a knight, and set a crown upon his
head and made him king. And at the crowning they
held merry sports, — jousting with sharp spears, tilting
at the shield, wrestling, and putting the stone. There
were harpers and pipers and gleemen with their ta-
bours; and for forty days a feast was held with rich
meats in plenty and the wine flowed like water. And
first the king made Robert and William Wendut and
Hugh Raven all barons, and gave them land and fee.
Then when the feast was done, he set out with a thousand
knights and five thousand sergeants to seek for Godard.
Godard was a-hunting with a great company of men,
and Robert riding on a good steed found him and bade
him come to the king. Godard smote him and set on
his knights to fight with Robert and the king's men.
They fought till ten of Godard's men were slain; the
rest began to flee. "Turn again, O knights!" cried
Godard; "I have fed you and shall feed you yet. Forsake me not in such a plight." So they turned about
and fought again. But the king's men slew every
one of them, and took Godard and bound him and
brought him to Havelok. Then King Havelok summoned all his nobles to sit in judgment and say
what should be done to such a traitor. And they
said, "Let him be dragged to the gallows at the
mare's tail, and hanged by the heels in fetters, with
this writing over him, 'This is he that reft the king

out from the land, and the life from the king's sisters.'"
So Godard suffered his doom, and none pitied him.

Then Havelok gave his sceptre into Earl Ubbe's
hand to rule Denmark on his behalf, and after that took
ship and came to Grimsby, where he built a priory for
black monks to pray evermore for the peace of Grim's
soul. But when Earl Godrich understood that Havelok
and his wife were come to England, he gathered together
a great army to Lincoln on the 17th of March, and came
to Grimsby to do battle with Havelok and his knights.
It was a great battle, wherein more than a thousand
knights were slain. The field was covered with pools
of blood. Hugh Raven and his brothers, Robert and
William, did valiantly and slew many earls; but terrible
was Earl Godrich to the Danes, for his sword was swift
and deadly as the levin fork. Havelok came to him
and minding him of the oath he sware to Athelwold
that Goldborough should be queen, bade him yield the
land. But Godrich defied him, and running forward
with his heavy sword cut Havelok's shield in two. Then
Havelok smote him to the earth with a blow upon the
helm; but Godrich arose and wounded him upon the
shoulder, and Havelok, smarting with the cut, ran upon
his enemy and hewed off his right hand. Then he took
Earl Godrich and bound him and sent him to the queen.
And when the English knew that Goldborough was the
heir of Athelwold, they laid by their swords and came
and asked pardon of the queen. And with one accord
they took Earl Godrich and bound him to a stake and
burned him to ashes, for the great outrage he had done.

Then all the English nobles came and sware fealty to

Havelok, and crowned him king in London. Of Grim's two daughters, Havelok wedded Gunild, the elder, to Earl Reyner of Chester; and Levive, the younger, fair as a new rose blossom opening to the sun, he married to Bertram, the cook, whom he made Earl of Cornwall in the room of Godrich.

Sixty years reigned Havelok and Goldborough in England, and they had fifteen children, who all became kings and queens. All the world spake of the great love that was betwixt them twain. Apart, neither knew joy or happiness. They grew never weary one of the other, for their love was ever new; and not a word of anger passed between them all their lives.

HEROES OF FRANCE

HOW RALPH THE CHARCOAL-BURNER ENTERTAINED KING CHARLES, AND AFTERWARDS WENT TO COURT

By Alfred J. Church

ON the feast of St. Thomas, which is four days before Yule, King Charles rode out of the city of Paris with a great company of princes and nobles. As they rode across the moor, a great tempest from the east fell upon them. So fierce was the wind and so heavy the rain, that they were scattered over the country; nor could they tell, the day being well-nigh as dark as night, whither they were going. Of what befell the rest of the company, there is no need to tell; this tale concerns King Charles only.

As he rode in sore plight, not knowing where he might find shelter, he was aware of a churl, who was leading a mare carrying two great panniers. "Now tell me your name," said the king. "They call me Ralph the Charcoal-burner," said the man. "I live in these parts, — my house is seven miles hence, — and I earn my bread with no little toil, selling coals to such as need them." "Friend," said the king, "I mean you no ill, for I judge you to be an honest man." "Judge as you will," answered Ralph, "I care not." "I am in sore need of a friend," said the king; "for both my horse and I are ready to perish, the storm is so fierce. Tell me then where I can find shelter." "Shelter!" said Ralph, "I know of none, save in my own cottage, and that is far hence in the forest. But to that you are welcome, if you care to come with me."

The king was right glad to hear these words. "That is well," said he; "God reward you for your goodness." "Nay," answered the churl, "keep your thanks till they have been earned. As yet you have had from me nothing, neither fire, nor meat, nor dinner, nor resting-place. To-morrow when you go you can thank me, if you be so minded, with better reason. To praise first, and, maybe, to blame afterwards — that is contrary to sense." "So shall it be," said the king. So they went their way, talking as they went.

When they were come to the house, Ralph called with a loud voice to his wife, "Are you within, dame? Come out, open the door without delay. My guest and I are shivering with cold; such evil weather I have never seen." The good wife, when she heard her master's voice, made all haste to the door, knowing that he was a man of a hasty temper. "You are welcome home," said she to Ralph; and to the stranger, "You are welcome also." "Kindle a great fire," said Ralph, "and take two capons of the best, that we may have good cheer;" and he took the king by the hand, and would have him go before him into the house. But the king stood back by the door, and would have the charcoal-burner pass in before him. "That is but poor courtesy," said the man, and took him by the neck and pushed him in.

When they had warmed themselves awhile by the

fire, which was blazing in right royal fashion, Ralph cried to his wife, "Let us have supper, Gillian, as quickly as may be, and of the best, for we have had a toilsome day, and may well have a merry night. Never have I suffered worse weather or been so near to losing my way as when I met with this stranger here."

In no long time, when they had washed themselves, the supper was ready. "Now, friend," said Ralph, "take the dame by the hand, and lead her to the board." And when the king held back, he cried, "Now this is the second time," and smote him suddenly under the ear with his right hand, so strongly that he staggered half across the chamber, and fell to the ground. When the king rose, and indeed he could scarcely stand, "Now, Gillian," said Ralph, "take him by the hand and go to the table as I bid you." To his guest he said, "Now this is the second time that you have been lacking in courtesy, first by the door, and then at the table. Will you not do as you are bid? Am not I the master of my own house?" The king said to himself, "These are strange doings. Never have I been so dealt with in all my life." Nevertheless, for peace' sake he did as he was bid, and giving his hand to the dame, led her to the table. So they sat, the charcoal-burner on one side of the table, and the king and dame Gillian on the other. Right good cheer they had, fat capons, and bread, and wine of the best. Truly they wanted for nothing.

Said the churl to the king, "Sir, the foresters in this place threaten me much about the deer. They say that I am ever bringing down the fattest of the herd.

They will hale me, they say, to Paris, and bring me before the king, and make complaint against me. Say what they will, why should I not have enough for myself, ay, and to set before a guest? And now, my friend, spare not; there is enough and more." When they had well eaten, Ralph said to his wife, "Now, Gill, send round the cup. I will drink to my friend, and he shall drink to me." So the dame handed the cup, and the two drank to each other. Then, supper being ended, they sat by the fire, and the charcoal-burner told many merry tales. When it grew late, he said to the king, "Tell me now where you live." "I live at Court," said he, "where I have an office with the queen." "And what is your office?" "I am gentleman of the queen's bed-chamber." "And what is your name?" "My name is Wymond; Wymond of the Wardrobe they call me. And now, if you will come to Court, I can doubtless serve you, for I will see that you have a good sale for your fuel." Said Ralph, "I know not where the Court of which you speak may be." But Charles urged him, saying that the king and queen would be in Paris to spend Yuletide together, and that there would be much merry-making, and that without doubt he would sell his fuel to great advantage. "You seem to talk reason," said Ralph; "I will come. And now let us have another cup, and so to bed." So the collier and the dame led him to another chamber, where there was a bed handsomely furnished, and closed in with curtains. When they saw that he was well served and had all that he needed, they bade him good-night, and the king thanked them for their courtesy.

HOW RALPH WENT TO COURT

The next day as soon as it was light, the king rose from the bed and dressed himself without help, for, indeed, he had neither valet nor squire. Then his palfrey was brought to him, which when he had mounted, he called to Ralph, where he lay, for he would take his leave in friendly fashion, as was fitting in one that had had such good cheer. When the churl was roused, he said to the king, "Now tarry awhile till this evil weather be ended." "Nay," answered the king, "I must needs to my work and office; Yuletide is now at hand, and he that is found wanting will be greatly blamed. And now call thy good wife that I may pay her for the shelter and good cheer that I have had." "Nay," cried Ralph, "that shall never be; to think that I should take pay for sheltering one that is of the Court of King Charles!" "So be it," answered the king; "but at least if you will not take pay, come to the Court with a load of fuel as soon as may be; I warrant that if you will do so, you will make good profit of your goods." "That will I," answered Ralph. "I would fain see how coals sell at Court. And now tell me your name once more, lest I forget it."

Then the king rode away, nor had he traveled long when Roland and Oliver, with a thousand men after them, met him. They had come forth to search for him, and right glad were they to find him. So they turned their horses' heads and journeyed back to Paris. When they were near the town, Turpin the Archbishop came forth from the gates to meet them, with a great company of bishops and priests and others, giving thanks to God that their lord the king was come again to Paris. And when they had come to Paris, they went to the Church of

St. Denis, where there was service. And after service they went to the palace, and kept their Yule feast with much mirth and plenty of good things. For one-and-twenty days did they feast. Never had such a Yuletide been kept in the land of France.

The next day, Ralph, having thought much on what he had undertaken, loaded his mare, as he was wont to do, with two panniers full of coals, and made ready to start on his journey to the Court. "This is not of my counsel," said Gillian, his wife; "this journey will not be to your profit. Remember the shrewd blow that you dealt him. Keep from the Court, say I." "Nay, Gill," said the charcoal-burner, "I must have my way. I promised that I would go, and go I will, whether my going be for profit or for harm." So he loaded the panniers and went his way to the Court.

Meanwhile King Charles had not forgotten the matter. He called Roland to him, for, indeed, there was no man whom he trusted more, and said to him, "To-morrow morning take your horse and your harness, and watch well the road by which we went on the day that I was lost, and if you see any one coming this way, whatever his errand may be, bring him with you to this place, and take care that he sees no one before he sees me."

Roland wondered much what the king might mean, for it seemed a strange thing that on the very day of Yuletide, when a man should rest, he should be sent on such an errand. Nevertheless, he took his horse and his harness and rode forth early in the morning, and watched the roads as he had been commanded. For a long time he saw nothing either far or near; but a little past midday he saw the charcoal-burner come driving his mare before him, with two panniers filled with coals. The sight pleased him well; so he rode up to him with all the speed that he could. The man saluted him courteously, and Roland, in his turn, also saluted him. Their greetings ended, he said to the man, "Come now to the king; let nothing hinder you." "Nay," said Ralph, "I am not so foolish. This is a jest, Sir Knight, and it is ill courtesy for a knight to jest with a common man. There be many men better than I that come and go to Paris, and the king has no thought of them, whether it be morning or night. If you are in mind to trick me, I can hold my own, for all that I am ill-clad." "This is but foolishness," said Roland, "the king has straightly commanded that you should be brought to him." "Nay," answered Ralph, "I am on my way, according to promise made to one Wymond, and to him I will go and to none other." "Have done with your Wymond," cried Roland; "I must take you to the king as the king has commanded."

So they wrangled a long time, and still the churl was firmly set that he would go to Wymond and to none other. "And where dwells this Wymond of yours?" said Roland. "He dwells with the queen at Paris, if his tale be true." "If that be so," answered Roland, "seeing that I know well the queen and her ladies, and you are on your way to them, I will trust to your going. Only you must give me a pledge that this is truly your purpose." "Nay," said the charcoal-burner, "I will pledge you no pledge. And as for you, get you out of my way, or it will be the worse for you."

Roland said to himself, "Now this is but folly to dispute any longer with this fellow." And he took his leave of the man full pleasantly. But Ralph liked not such ways; for he thought that this knight that was so gayly clad had him in scorn. "Come hither, Sir Knight, to-morrow when we can be alone together, you and I; surely you shall see how I will deal with you."

Then Roland rode back to the king. By this time mass was ended, and the king had put on his robes. "You are well come, Sir Roland," said he; "have you done my errand?" "Sire," answered Sir Roland, "I went as you gave me commandment, and watched the ways, but saw no man, but one only." "And who was this one?" asked the king. "He," said Roland, "was but a churl that had with him two panniers of coal." "Why did you not bring this said churl to me, as I bid you? It may be you durst not."

Roland saw that the king was wroth, and was not a little glad to go forth from his presence. Going forth he met a porter, "Whither go you, lazy loon?" said he. Said the porter, "There is one at the gate, a churl that has a mare and two panniers of coals, and he clamors to be let in at the gate." "Whom does he want?" said Roland. The porter answered, "He asks for one Wymond." Then Roland said, "Go back to your place, porter, and open the gate and bid him enter. But say that it does not lie within your office to go to this Wymond, but that he must himself seek him."

So the porter went back to the gate and opened it, saying to the charcoal-burner, "Enter, man; but I have no leisure to seek for this Wymond for whom you ask. You must seek him yourself." Said Ralph, "If you will

karolus inpaint magnus Anus 14

CHARLEMAGNE

not seek the man, I must needs do it myself; see you then that no harm come to the mare and the coals, and I will look for Wymond, for certainly it was he that bade me come hither."

So the charcoal-burner went his way through the palace asking for Wymond. There was not one that knew the man, or had so much as heard the name. They seemed to Ralph to lack courtesy; nevertheless he would not cease from his quest, nor was there any one of whom he failed to inquire. After he had passed through many chambers, he came to one that was more splendid than all that he had seen before. It was a great hall finely painted and hung about with tapestries, and there the king sat at dinner in great state. On the table were many dainties, and there was a store of dishes both silver and gold, and many other adornments. "Here is royalty enough," cried Ralph. "If I could only have speech with Wymond, I would away, for this methinks is no place for a simple man." And still he went on. Many sought to put him back, for he seemed to press on in an unmannerly fashion; but he was a stalwart man that gave as much as he took.

At last, after not a little trouble, he came near to the king, where he sat in state at the table. "See," he cried, "that is Wymond, yonder, the man whom I seek. Well do I know him, though, indeed, he is otherwise clad than when I last saw him. Now he is in cloth of gold. Truly he must be some greater man than he said. Alas, that I have been wiled hither. Truly this man has beguiled me." When the king heard this he laughed.

Ralph looked about on the company that sat with the

king, for many worshipful men were there. But when he saw the queen, then he was greatly troubled. "Lady," he said, "I am sorely troubled to see your fine attire, so splendid is it. Now if I can but escape hence this day, nothing in the whole world shall bring me hither again."

And now, dinner being over, the king rose from the table; and he told before the whole company how he had fared with the charcoal-burner. The churl quaked as he heard the tale. And he said, "Would I were on the moor again this very hour, and the king alone, or any one of his knights, be he the bravest and strongest of them all."

Then the lords laughed aloud. Some, however, were angry, and would have had the man hanged. "What is this churl," said they, "that he should so misuse the king?" But Charles would have none of such doings. "He is a stalwart man, and can strike a hard blow. Heaven forbid that I should harm him. Rather will I make him a knight." So he dubbed Ralph the Charcoal-burner a knight, and gave him a revenue of £300 by the year; and "the next fee in France that shall come into my hands, that," said he, "will I give you. But now you must win your spurs." So the king gave him his armor and arms, and sixty squires of good degree to be his company. And Ralph was in after time a very perfect, noble knight, and did good service to the king.

HOW FIERABRAS DEFIED KING CHARLES

By Alfred J. Church

BALAN, who was admiral of the Moors in Spain, had a son, Fierabras by name, who was the most marvelous giant that ever was born of woman. There was no man that could be matched with him for height, and bigness of limb, and strength of body. This Fierabras was king of Alexandria, and ruled the whole land of Babylon from the Red Sea eastwards. Russia also he possessed, and Cologne; he was lord, moreover, of Jerusalem, and had possession of the Sepulchre of our Lord. It happened on a certain day that this man came riding furiously to the camp where King Charles lay with his army, and asked that some one should come forth and fight with him. No man answering him or coming forth, he fell into a great rage and sware by his god Mahomet that he would not depart from the place till he should have done battle with some Christian man; but still no one came forth to him. Then he cried with a very loud and terrible voice, "King of Paris, send out to me your strongest and bravest knight, be he Roland, or Oliver, or Thierry, or Ogier the Dane, that he may fight with me. Nay, and if you will send out against me six or seven of your strongest knights, I swear by my god Mahomet that I will not refuse to fight with them all. But if you will not send out any man, then I will assuredly assail your camp before nightfall this very day, and strike off your head, and lead away Roland and Oliver as prisoners. You have come into this my land without cause, and verily you shall depart without honor."

When he had thus spoken he lay down under a tree, and having tied his horse to one of the boughs, took off his armor. This done, he cried to the king, "Send now Roland or Oliver to fight with me. And if these dare not come alone, then let two others come together with them; and if the four be afraid, let six come. Ten kings have I slain already in single combat; there was not one of them, for all that they were mighty men of valor, that could stand against me."

When King Charles heard these threatenings and challenges, he said to Richard of Normandy, "Who is this knight that speaks so boldly?"

Duke Richard answered, "This, my lord king, is the strongest of all men born of women, and he is persuaded that there is no king in the whole world that is a match for him."

"For all that," said the king, "I will find one of my knights that shall encounter him. But tell me his name."

"His name," answered Duke Richard, "is Fierabras. He is an infidel, and has done much harm to Christian men. For he slew our lord the Pope, and hanged many holy men and women, and to this day he holds possession of the holy Sepulchre of our Lord."

"I am the more firmly resolved," said the king, "hearing what you say, that one of my knights shall meet him."

Thereupon he turned to Roland and said, "I pray you, dear nephew, go forth and meet this Turk in battle."

But Roland answered him, "Not so, fair uncle; why should I do your bidding in this matter? Do you bear in mind what happened but yesterday, when we were so near to being taken by the heathen, how they fell upon us with fifty thousand men, and how we the younger knights bore the burden and brunt of the day and suffered many grievous wounds, so that Oliver my comrade was brought near to death, and indeed, but for your help, we had all perished? And do you remember further how last night, when we were resting in our tents, you, being full of wine, declared stoutly that your old knights would have borne themselves better than we of the younger sort had done? Now it shall be seen how these said old knights shall stand up against this heathen man, for indeed of the younger no one will go forth against him."

When the king heard this, he smote Roland his nephew in the face with his gauntlet so sharply that the blood gushed out abundantly. Thereupon Roland drew his sword and would have smitten his uncle had he not been held by the bystanders. And the king cried, "Now, this is a most monstrous thing for any man, much more a kinsman. Seize him, for he shall die the death for this wickedness." But when the courtiers made as if to lay hands upon him, Roland cried, "Now, if any man touch me, I will cleave his head in two." Nor did any man dare to come near him. But Ogier the Dane said, "Now, Roland, you did ill to threaten your uncle, whom you are bound to honor above all men." "It is true," answered

Roland. "I was greatly provoked; nevertheless I repent of my deed."

The king said to the Peers of France, "I am much troubled in this matter. First, Roland my nephew, that should have been zealous to help me, threatens to slay me, and then there is no man that is willing to do battle with this pagan."

"Take courage, my lord king," said the Duke Naymes, "some one will be found to do you this service." But the king refused to be comforted.

Now Oliver lay sick in bed, for he had been sorely wounded in battle. But when he heard how the king and Roland had fallen out, and how Fierabras had defied the king and his army, and no man had gone forth to meet him, he straightway rose from his bed and began to stretch and try himself to see whether by any means he could bear his armor. In so doing he made his wounds bleed afresh. But when he had bound them again as best he could, he said to Garin his squire, "Come, bring me my arms, for I will go out and meet this pagan." Said Garin the squire, "Now, my lord Oliver, have pity on yourself. You will compass your own death." Oliver answered, "Do my bidding, for this is an occasion of honor that no man should miss." So Oliver put on his armor, Garin helping him. This done, he took his sword, Hautclere by name, which he loved above all things. Then they brought him Ferraunt, his horse, ready saddled and bridled. And Oliver leapt lightly into the saddle without so much as touching it, and put his shield into place, and took a spear very long and sharply pointed. Then he struck his horse with his spurs, and Ferraunt leapt up under him. It was a noble sight to see, so gallant was the knight and so brave the steed.

Oliver rode up to the king's tent and saluted him, saying, "My lord, I have served you faithfully for these three years past without reward or wages. I pray you, therefore, that you give me this day the thing I shall desire of you." The king answered, "Most noble earl, I will do this with a good will. There is not in this land of France a city or town or castle that I will not give you at your desire." But Oliver said, "My lord king, I ask neither towns nor castles, but only this — that you suffer me to do battle with this pagan."

When the other knights heard this, they were not a little shamed that a wounded man should take up the challenge, while they themselves held back. "What is this," they said, "that Oliver, who was hurt well-nigh to death, would now go forth to battle!" As for the king, he said, "Now, Oliver, you have surely lost your wits. You know that you have been sorely wounded, and yet you will run into a worse danger. Go back to your bed and rest; assuredly I will not suffer you to do battle with this pagan."

Then Ganelon, who was afterwards the traitor, rose up in his place and said, "Sir, this is against the custom of France that you should deny Oliver his request." The king was very angry, and said, "Ganelon, you are not well disposed in this matter. If this be as you say, then Oliver shall fight with this pagan, and if he fight, then he can hardly escape death. But mark you this: I swear by my faith that if he be slain or taken in this battle, then not all the gold in the world can save you from a shameful death; ay, and all your house shall perish with you."

"Sir king," said Ganelon, "may God and Our Lady keep me!" but to himself he said secretly, "Now God forbid that Oliver should come back safe. Rather may this pagan smite off his head!" But when King Charles saw that he could not hinder Oliver from doing battle with Fierabras, he said, "Now may God be with you and help you, and bring you back with joy!" and he reached to him his glove, which Oliver took with much pleasantness and humility.

But Reyner, that was father to Oliver, when he saw his son ready to go forth, came to the king, and knelt down at his feet, and cried in sore trouble, "Now, my lord king, have pity on my son and me. He is young and presumptuous, full of pride and ambition, but so sorely wounded that he cannot fight; forbid him, therefore, to go forth." But the king said to Reyner, "What I have given I may not withdraw." Then Oliver stood up and spake with a loud voice, "Sir king and all you lords of France, if I have offended any man in word or deed, I pray him to forgive me." There was not a man but wept to hear these words. The king himself wept, and commended him to the keeping of God.

Oliver rode forth and came to the tree where Fierabras lay at ease and unarmed. The giant did not so much as look at him, but turned away his head, for he despised Oliver as being but little of stature in comparison with himself. Oliver said to him, "Awake, you have called me many times this day; lo! now I have come. And first tell me your name." Fierabras answered him, "I am

Fierabras of Alexandria. It was I that destroyed the city of Rome and slew the Pope, and carried away the holy things. And Jerusalem is mine, and the place where, as you say, your God is buried."

Oliver said, "If these things are true, it is time that you should suffer due punishment for your misdeeds. But enough of talking. Make ready and arm yourself, or else, by the God in whom I believe, I will smite you where you lie!" When Fierabras heard him speak so fiercely, he began to laugh, and said, "You are a bold talker, but first tell me who you are, and of what rank." Oliver answered, "Before night come, pagan, you shall know full well who I am. But now hear this: my lord the king has sent this message by my mouth: 'Renounce Mahomet your god, and all other idols, and believe in the true God that made heaven and earth and all that is therein.' Meanwhile, take your choice of two things: either depart out of this country, taking nothing with you, or stand forth and fight with me."

Fierabras said, "Fellow, you are not able to meet me, even were I without arms. But tell me now thy name and lineage." Oliver answered, "My name is Garin, and I am a poor knight; King Charles has sent me to do battle with you; make ready, therefore, for battle." But Fierabras would not consent. "Now tell me, Sir Garin," said he, "why Roland, or Oliver, or Ogier the Dane, who are all, men say, of high renown, have not come out against me." "They have not come," answered Oliver, "because they think too meanly of you."

This he said with such vehemence that his wounds opened again. When Fierabras saw the blood he said,

"Are you perchance wounded, Sir Garin?" "Not I," answered Oliver; "this blood that you see comes from my horse where I spurred him." But Fierabras saw that the blood was not from the horse, and said: "You speak no truth when you say that you are not hurt. This is no horse's blood, but of your own body that I see. Now drink of this flagon of balm that I took from the city of Jerusalem. When you have drunken you shall be whole in body, and then you shall be fit to defend yourself in battle." But Oliver would have none of it. "This," said he, "is but folly."

Fierabras, seeing that he must needs fight, said to Oliver, "Come now, help me to arm myself." Said Oliver, "Can I trust you?" "Yea," answered Fierabras, "that can you: never have I been traitor to any man, nor ever will." So Oliver armed him; he helped him to don first a suit of leather of Arabia, and after this a coat and habergeon of steel, and an helmet richly garnished with jewels for his head. Was ever such courtesy in this world, Oliver helping this pagan to arm, whom, being unarmed, he might full easily have slain, and the pagan having pity upon Oliver as not being his match in fighting, and all the more when he saw that he had been wounded? Would that there were more of such courtesy between Christian men!

When he was armed, Fierabras took the three swords that he had, Pleasance and Baptism and Grabon, all being of so fine a temper that there was no armor made but they could break through it. The three were made by one of three brothers; another of these three made three more, of which Durendal, the sword of Roland,

246

was the most famous; and yet another brother also made three, of which it suffices to name Hautclere that was the sword of Oliver, and Joyous that was one of the chief treasures of King Charles. On his shield he had the image of his god, Apollyon to wit, to whom when he had commended himself, he yet once again besought Oliver to depart. And when Oliver had again refused, saying that he trusted to prevail by the help of his God, Fierabras said to him, "Now as you are a Christian man, I adjure you by the font wherein you were baptized and by the cross to which your God was nailed, to tell me truly your name and lineage."

Oliver answered, "You could not have adjured me by greater things than this same font and cross; know therefore that I am Oliver, the son of Reyner, close comrade of Roland, and one of the Twelve Peers of France."

Then said Fierabras, "I knew that you were no poor and unknown knight, but a great warrior and a famous, so great was your courage. But you are wounded, and it would be dishonor to me should I overcome you by means of your weakness." But Oliver answered him fiercely, "Enough of these idle words; when we come to fight together you shall see that I am no dead man. Nevertheless, as you are a courteous knight, I will require you once again to forsake Mahomet and your false gods, and submit yourself to be baptized. So shall you have Roland and King Charles for your friends." "Nay," said Fierabras, "but this is folly. Let us address ourselves to battle without more delay."

Then did these two champions lay their spears in rest and make ready to charge. When the men of France saw this, they were in great fear lest some mischance should befall Oliver; as for the king, he hid his face in his mantle, and kneeling before the crucifix embraced it, weeping the while, and crying, "O Lord, I beseech Thee keep Oliver and suffer not the Christian faith to be dishonored by his downfall." Meanwhile the two warriors met in the shock of battle, and that so fiercely that the sparks flew from their spearheads when they smote on the shields, and that the shafts of both were broken. The reins dropped from their hands, and they were both so astonied that they scarce knew where they were. But then coming to themselves, they drew each man his sword. And first Oliver with Hautclere smote Fierabras so fiercely on the helmet that he shore off a great portion of it, and the jewels wherewith it was garnished fell to the ground. Nor was the force of the blow yet spent: it reached the giant's shoulder, but the cuirass which was of stout leather of Cappadocia, stayed it; nevertheless the giant's feet were thrust out of the stirrups, and he came very near to being overthrown. And all the men of France cried with one voice, "Blessed Mary, what a mighty stroke has Oliver dealt to this pagan!" "'T is true," said Roland, "would I were with him this day!" Then Fierabras, in his turn, smote Oliver with his sword Pleasance on the helmet. From the helmet it glanced down and grievously wounded the Christian's horse. Then Oliver was not a little dismayed, and commended himself to God and the Virgin. Which, when Fierabras heard, he said, "I am ill content to have so hurt you. Hardly shall you see the sun set this day, for already you grow faint. But this has befallen you because you are already wounded. Be wise therefore, and leave the battle while there is yet time." But Oliver would have none of such counsel. Therefore they fell to fighting again, and this so fiercely that the armor of the two of them was well-nigh broken to pieces.

When the king saw this, and perceived that Oliver was in no little danger, he was greatly troubled. He prayed aloud, saying, "O Lord God, now keep the valiant Oliver, that he be not slain or taken. Verily, if aught happen to him, I swear by my father's soul that I will burn every monastery and church and altar in the land." But the Duke Naymes rebuked the king, saying, "Speak not thus, Sir King. Rather pray to God that of His goodness He will help Oliver." And the king said, "You are right; I spake foolishly."

Meanwhile the two champions continued to fight fiercely, more fiercely than befitted prudent or experienced warriors. Oliver especially was so carried out of himself that his hand grew numb with the frequency of his blows, and at last his sword flew out of his hand. Straightway he ran to regain it, putting his shield over his head to cover himself from the enemy's blows. But this did not avail him, for Fierabras smote twice on the shield, and so mightily that he brake it into pieces, and the breastplate under it also. And Oliver durst not go forward to take up his sword, for he feared greatly what the giant might do to him. When the men of France saw in what straits he was, they made as if they would arm themselves and go to his help. But this King Charles would not suffer. "Not so," said he; "God can save him and maintain him in the right, and He will do so."

Then the others abode in their place. But now Fierabras began to jeer and scoff at Oliver, "Now I know that you are vanquished, for you dare not put out your hand to take your sword for fear of me; no, you would not stoop to the ground to gain the wealth of the whole world. Now hearken to me: if you will deny your faith and declare that your God is no god, and believe in Mahomet, then I will give you my sister Floripas in marriage, than whom there is no fairer maid upon earth, and we two will conquer France or ever this year shall have passed, and I will make you king of one half of this realm." Oliver answered, "Now God forbid that I should listen to such folly. These your gods are no gods at all, and have no goodness or strength." Fierabras said, "I see that you are firmly set in your mind not to do these things. Now there was never man on earth who has given me such trouble of mind as have you. But now take up your sword; for without it you can have no more strength in battle than a woman." "That will I not do," answered Oliver. "I will not take my sword by your courtesy. My life and death are with God; and I will win my sword by fair fight or not at all."

Thereupon Fierabras came against Oliver, having his sword Pleasance in his hand. Then was Oliver in a great strait; for he had no sword, and his shield was cleft in twain, and his armor grievously broken. But God had mercy upon him, and put it in his head to look about him. And looking he saw the horse of Fierabras, and on the saddle two swords, Baptism and Grabon. Whereupon he made haste and laid hold on the sword Baptism. And when he had possessed himself of it, he said, "King of Alexandria, now the time of reckoning has come. See, I have one of your swords; you must take good care lest it be your destruction." When Fierabras saw what Oliver had done, he changed color and said, "O Baptism, my good sword, what is this? Never did better weapon hang by my side or by the side of any man living upon earth." Then he said to Oliver, "You are, I well know, an honorable knight. Come, now, take your own sword and give to me that which is mine." "Not so," answered Oliver; "I will make no agreement with you, save this: that I will do my best to slay you, and you shall do the same with me."

And when he had said this, Oliver ran at Fierabras as fiercely as a lion that leaps upon its prey. Nor was Fierabras slow to meet him. Indeed, he smote him so stoutly that he brake through his helmet, wounding the knight's head. Seeing this, he cried, "Now you are wounded, Sir Oliver. Never more shall you see King Charles or Roland; so shall I at last have my desire." But Oliver answered, "Be not so proud nor boast overmuch. I have a good confidence that I shall either slay you or conquer you." Then he made a feint to strike the pagan on the head; and Fierabras, raising his shield over high to cover himself from the blow, left his side unguarded, which Oliver, quickly perceiving, drove his sword with all his might into the pagan's side. And the man fell with the blow, so mighty was it, for Oliver dealt it with all his strength that so he might put an end to the fight.

THE BATTLE AT RONCEVALS

By Isabel Butler

THEN Oliver goes up into a high mountain, and looks away to the right, all down a grassy valley, and sees the host of the heathen coming on,

The coming up of the host.

and he called to Roland, his comrade, saying: "From the side of Spain I see a great light coming, thousands of white hauberks and thousands of gleaming helms. They will fall upon our Franks with great wrath. Ganelon the felon has done this treason, and he it was adjudged us to the rear-guard, before the Emperor." "Peace, Oliver." saith Count Roland, "he is my mother's husband; speak thou no ill of him."

Oliver has fared up the mountain, and from the summit thereof he sees all the kingdom of Spain and the great host of the Saracens. Wondrous is the shine of helmets studded with gold, of shields and broidered hauberks, of lances and gonfanons. The battles are without number, and no man may give count thereof, so great is the multitude. Oliver was all astonied at the sight; he got him down the hill as best he might, and came to the Franks, and gave them his tidings.

"I have seen the paynims," said Oliver; "never was so great a multitude seen of living men. Those of the vanguard are upon a hundred thousand, all armed with shields and helmets, and clad in white hauberks; right straight are the shafts of their lances, and bright the points thereof. Such a battle we shall have as was never before seen of man. Ye lords of France, may God give you might! and stand ye firm that we be not overcome." "Foul fall him who flees!" then say the Franks, "for no peril of death will we fail thee."

"Great is the host of the heathen," saith Oliver, "and few is our fellowship. Roland, fair comrade, I pray thee sound thy horn of ivory, that Charles may hear it and return again with all his host." "That were but folly," quoth Roland, "and thereby would I lose all fame in sweet France. Rather will I strike good blows and great with Durendal, that the blade thereof shall be blooded even unto the hilt. Woe worth the paynims that they came into the passes! I pledge thee my faith short life shall be theirs."

Oliver prays Roland to sound his horn.

"Roland, comrade, blow now thy horn of ivory, and Charles shall hear it, and bring hither his army again, and the king and his barons shall succor us." But Roland answers him, saying: "Now God forfend that through me my kinsman be brought to shame, or aught of dishonor befall fair France. But first I will lay on with Durendal, the good sword that is girded here at my side, and thou shalt see the blade thereof all reddened. Woe worth the paynims when they gathered their hosts! I pledge me they shall all be given over to death."

"Roland, comrade, blow thy horn of ivory, that Charles may hear it as he passes the mountains, and I pledge me the Franks will return hither again." But Roland saith: "Now God forfend it be said of any living man that I sounded my horn

The pride of Roland.

for dread of paynims. Nay, that reproach shall never fall upon my kindred. But when I am in the stour I will smite seven hundred blows, or mayhap a thousand, and thou shalt see the blade of Durendal all crimson. The Franks are goodly men, and they will lay on right valiantly, nor shall those of Spain have any surety from death."

Saith Oliver, "I see no shame herein. I have seen the Saracens of Spain; they cover the hills and the valleys, the heaths and the plains. Great are the hosts of this hostile folk, and ours is but a little fellowship." And Roland makes answer: "My desire is the greater thereby. May God and His most holy angels forfend that France should lose aught of worship through me. Liefer had I die than bring dishonor upon me. The emperor loves us for dealing stout blows."

Roland is brave, and Oliver is wise, and both are good men of their hands; once armed and a-horseback, rather would they die than flee the battle. Hardy are the counts and high their speech. The felon paynims ride on in great wrath. Saith Oliver: "Roland, prithee look. They are close upon us, but Charles is afar off. Thou wouldst not deign to sound thy horn of ivory; but were the king here we should suffer no hurt. Look up towards the passes of Aspre and thou shalt see the woeful rear-guard; they who are of it will do no more service henceforth." But Roland answers him: "Speak not so cowardly. Cursed be the heart that turns coward in the breast! Hold we the field, and ours be the buffets and the slaughter."

When Roland sees that the battle is close upon them,

he waxes fiercer than lion or leopard. He calls to the Franks, and he saith to Oliver: "Comrade, friend, say not so. When the emperor left us his Franks, he set apart such a twenty thousand of men that, certes, among them is no coward. For his liege lord a man ought to suffer all hardship, and endure great heat and great cold, and give both his blood and his body. Lay on with thy lance, and I will smite with Durendal, my good sword that the king gave me. If I die here, may he to whom it shall fall, say, 'This was the sword of goodly vassal.'"

Roland is fain for battle.

Nigh at hand is Archbishop Turpin; he now spurs his horse to the crest of a knoll, and speaks to the Franks, and this is his sermon: "Lords, barons, Charles left us here, and it is a man's devoir to die for his king. Now help ye to uphold Christianity. Certes, ye shall have a battle, for here before you are the Saracens. Confess your sins and pray God's mercy, and that your souls may be saved I will absolve you. If ye are slain ye will be holy martyrs, and ye shall have seats in the higher Paradise." The Franks light off their horses and kneel down, and the archbishop blesses them, and for a penance bids them that they lay on with their swords.

The archbishop's sermon.

The Franks get upon their feet, freed and absolved from sin; and the archbishop blesses them in the name of God. Then they mounted their swift horses, and armed themselves after the manner of knights, and made them ready for battle. Count Roland calls to Oliver, saying: "Sir comrade, rightly thou saidst Ganclon hath betrayed us all, and hath received gold and silver and goods therefor; but the emperor will well revenge us. King Marsila hath bought and sold us, but he shall pay for it with the sword."

Roland rides through the passes of Spain on Veillantif, his good horse and swift. He is clad in his harness; right well it becomes him, and as he rides he brandishes his spear, turning its point towards heaven; and to its top is bound a gonfanon of pure white, whereof the golden fringes fall down even unto his hands. Well fashioned is his body, and his face fair and laughing; close behind him rides his comrade; and all the Franks claim him as their champion. Full haughtily he looks on the Saracens, but gently and mildly on the Franks, and he speaks to them courteously, saying: "Lords, barons, ride on softly. The paynims come seeking destruction, and this day we shall have plunder so goodly and great that no king of France hath ever taken any of so great price." At these words the two hosts come together.

Saith Oliver: "I have no mind for more words. Thou wouldst not deign to sound thy horn of ivory, and no help shalt thou get from Charles; naught he knows of our case, nor is the wrong his, the baron. They who are beyond the mountains are no wise to blame. Now ride on with what might ye may. Lords, barons, hold ye the field! And in God's name I pray you bethink you both how to deal good blows and how to take them. And let us not forget the device of our king." At these words all the Franks cried out together, and whosoever may have heard that cry of Montjoy must call to mind valor and worth. Then they rode forward, God! how proudly, spurring their horses

Franks and paynims join battle.

for the more speed, and fell a-smiting — how else should they do? But no whit adread were the Saracens. And lo you, Franks and paynims come together in battle.

The nephew of Marsila, who was called Ælroth, rides before all his host, and foul are his words to our Franks: "Ye Frankish felons, to-day ye shall do battle with us. He who should have been your surety has betrayed you; mad is the king who left you behind in the passes. To-day shall fair France lose her fame, and the right arm of Charles shall be smitten off from his body." When Roland hears this, God! how great is his wrath. He spurs as fast as his horse may run, and with all the might he hath he smites Ælroth, and breaks his shield, and rends apart his hauberk, that he cleaves his breast and breaks the bone, and severs the spine from the back; with his lance he drives out the soul from the body, for so fierce is the blow Ælroth wavers, and with all the force of his lance Roland hurls him from his horse dead, his neck broken in two parts. Yet Roland still chides him, saying, "Out, coward! Charles is not mad, nor loves he treason. He did well and knightly to leave us in the passes. To-day shall France lose naught of her fame. Franks, lay on! Ours is the first blow. Right is with us, and these swine are in the wrong."

The Franks win the first blow.

Among the paynims is a duke, Falsaron by name, who was brother to King Marsila, and held the land of Dathan and Abiram; there is no more shameless felon on all the earth; so wide is his forehead that the space between his eyes measures a full half foot. When he sees his nephew slain, he is full of dole, and he drives through the press as swift as he may, and cries aloud the paynim war cry. Great is his hatred of the Franks. "To-day shall fair France lose her fame!" Oliver hears him and is passing wroth; with his golden spurs he pricks on his horse and rides upon him like a true baron; he breaks the shield, tears asunder the hauberk, and drives his lance into the body up to the flaps of his pennon, and with the might of his blow hurls him dead from the saddle. He looks to earth where lies the felon, and speaks him haughtily: "Coward, naught care I for thy threats. Lay on, Franks; certes, we shall overcome them." And he cries out Montjoy, the war cry of Charles.

A king there is, Corsablis by name; he is of Barbary, a far-off land, and he spoke to the Saracens, saying: "We shall win a fair day on these Franks, for few is their fellowship. And such as be here shall prove themselves of small avail, nor shall one be saved alive for Charles; the day has come whereon they must die." Archbishop Turpin hears him right well, and to no man under heaven has he ever borne such hate; with his spurs of fine gold he pricks on his horse, and rides upon the king with great might, cleaves his shield and rends his hauberk, and thrusts his great lance into his body, and so drives home the blow that sorely the king wavers, and with all the force of his lance Turpin hurls him dead into the path. He looks on the ground where he sees the glutton lie, nor doth he withhold him from speech, but saith: "Coward and heathen, thou hast lied! Charles, my liege lord, is ever our surety, and our Franks have no mind to flee; and we shall have a care that thy comrades go

The slaying of the paynim peers.

not far hence; yea, and a second death must ye suffer. Lay on, ye Franks, let no man forget himself! This first blow is ours, thanks be to God." And he cries out Montjoy, to hold the field.

And Gerin smites Malprimis de Brigal, that his good shield no whit avails him; he shatters the jeweled boss thereof, and half of it falls to earth; he pierces the hauberk to the flesh, and drives his good lance into the body; the paynim falls down in a heap, and his soul is carried away by Satan.

And Gerier, the comrade of Gerin, smites the Emir, and shatters his shield and unmails his hauberk, and thrusts his good lance into his heart; so great is the blow his lance drives through the body, and with all the force of his shaft he throws him to the ground dead. "Ours is a goodly battle," quoth Oliver.

Samson the duke rides upon the Almaçur, and breaks his shield all flowered and set with gold; nor doth his good hauberk give him any surety, but Samson pierces him through heart and liver and lungs, and fells him dead, whether any one grieves for him or no. Saith the archbishop: "That was knightly stricken."

And Anseïs urges on his horse and encounters with Turgis of Tortosa, cleaves his shield below the golden boss, rends asunder his twofold hauberk, and sets the point of his good lance in his body, and thrusts so well that the iron passes sheer through him, that the might of the blow hurls him to the ground dead. "That was the buffet of a man of good prowess," saith Roland.

And Engelier, the Gascon of Bordeaux, spurs his horse, slackens his rein, and encounters with Escremis of Valtierra, breaks and carves the shield from his shoulder, rends apart the ventail of his hauberk, and smites him in his breast between his two collar bones, and with the might of the blow hurls him from the saddle, saying: "Ye are all given over to destruction."

And Oton smites the paynim Esturgant upon the leathern front of his shield, marring all the blue and white thereof, breaks through the sides of his hauberk, and drives his good spear and sharp into his body, and casts him from his swift horse, dead. "Naught may save thee," saith Oliver thereat.

And Berengier rides on Estramaris, shatters his shield, rends asunder his hauberk, and drives his stout lance into his body, and smites him dead amid a thousand Saracens. Of the Twelve Peers ten are now slain, and but two are still living men, to wit, Chernuble and Count Margaris.

Margaris is a right valiant knight, strong and goodly, swift and keen; he spurs his horse and rides on Oliver, breaks his shield below the boss of pure gold, that the lance passed along his side, but by God's help, it did not pierce the body; the shaft grazes him but doth not overthrow him; and Margaris drives on, in that he has no hindrance, and sounds his horn to call his men about him.

Now the battle waxes passing great on both parties. Count Roland spares himself no whit, but smites with his lance as long as the shaft holds, but by fifteen blows it is broken and lost; thereupon he draws out Durendal his good sword, all naked, spurs his horse and rides on Chernuble, breaks his helm whereon the carbuncles blaze, cleaves his mail-coif and the hair of his head that the sword cuts through eyes and face, and the white hauberk of fine mail, and all the body to the fork of the legs, sheer into the saddle of beaten gold, nor did the sword stint till it had entered the horse and cleft the backbone, never staying for joint, that man and horse fell dead upon the thick grass. Thereupon Roland cried: "Coward, woe worth the day thou camest hither! no help shall thou get from Mahound; nor by such swine as thou shall to-day's battle be achieved."

Count Roland rides through the press; in his hand he hath Durendal, right good for hacking and hewing, and doth great damage upon the Saracens. Lo, how he hurls one dead upon another, and the bright blood flows out on the field. All reddened are his hauberk and his arms, and the neck and shoulders of his good horse. Nor doth Oliver hold back from the battle; the Twelve Peers do not shame themselves, and all the Franks smite and slay, that the paynims perish or fall swooning. Then saith the archbishop, "Our barons do passing well," and he cries out Montjoy, the war cry of Charles.

The Franks do passing well.

Oliver drives through the stour; his lance is broken, and naught is left him but the truncheon; yet he smites the paynim Malsaron that his shield patterned with gold and flowers is broken, and his two eyes fly out from his head, and his brains fall at his feet; among seven hundred of his fellows Oliver smites him dead. Then he slew Turgin and Esturgus, and thereby broke his lance that it splintered even unto the pommel. Thereat Roland saith: "Comrade, what dost thou? I have no mind for a staff in so great battle, rather a man hath need of iron and steel. Where is thy sword Halteclere?" "I may not draw it," Oliver answered him. "So keen am I to smite."

But now the lord Oliver hath drawn his good sword, even as his comrade had besought him, and hath shown it to him in knightly wise; and therewith he smites the paynim Justin de Val Ferrée that he severs his head in twain, cuts through his broidered hauberk and his body, through his good saddle set with gold, and severs the backbone of his steed, that man and horse fall dead on the field before him. Then said Roland: "Now I hold you as my brother, and 't is for such buffets the emperor loves us." And on all sides they cry out Montjoy.

Count Gerin rides his horse Sorel, and Gerier, his comrade, rides Passecerf; both slacken rein, and spurring mightily set upon the paynim Timosel; one smites him on the shield, and the other on the hauberk, that both their lances break in his body; and he falls dead in the field. I wot not, nor have I ever heard man say, which of the twain was the more swift. Then Esperveris, son of Borel, died at the hand of Engelier of Bordeaux. And the archbishop slew Siglorel, that enchanter who of old had passed down into hell, led thither by the spells of Jupiter. "Of him we are well rid," quoth Turpin. And Roland answered him: "Yea, the coward is overthrown. Oliver, my brother, such buffets please me right well."

Meantime the battle waxes passing hard, and both Franks and paynims deal such blows that it is wonder to see; here they smite, and there make what defense they may; and many a lance is broken and reddened, and there is great rending of pennons and ensigns. **Many a good Frank** loses his youth, and will never The battle again see wife or mother, or the men of waxes hard. France who await him in the passes. Charles the Great weeps for them, and makes great sorrow; but what avails it? no help shall they get therefrom. An ill turn Ganelon did them the day he sold his own kindred in Saragossa. Thereafter he lost both life and limb therefor; in the council at Aix, he was condemned to hang, and with him upon thirty of his kindred to whom death left no hope.

Dread and sore is the battle. Roland and Oliver lay on valiantly, and the archbishop deals more than a thousand buffets, nor are the Twelve Peers backward, and all the Franks smite as a man. The paynims are slain by hundreds and thousands; whosoever does not flee has no surety from death, but will he, nill he, must take his end. But the Franks lose their goodliest arms; lances adorned with gold, and trenchant spears, and gonfanons red and white and blue, and the blades of their good swords are broken, and thereto they lose many a valiant knight. Never again shall they see father or kindred, or Charles their liege lord, who abides for them in the passes.

Meantime, in France, a wondrous tempest broke forth, a mighty storm of wind and lightning, with rain and hail out of all measure, and bolts of thunder that fell ever and again; and verily therewith came a quaking of the earth that ran through all the land from A wondrous Saint Michael of the Peril, even unto Xanton, tempest. and from Besançon to the port of Guitsand; and there was not a dwelling whose walls were not rent asunder. And at noon fell a shadow of great darkness, nor was there any light save as the heavens opened. They that saw these things were sore afraid, and many a one said: "This is the day of judgment, and the end of the world is at hand." But they were deceived, and knew not whereof they spoke; it was the great mourning for the death of Roland.

Meantime the Franks smote manfully and with good courage, and the paynims were slain by thousands and by multitudes; of a hundred thousand not two may survive. Then said the archbishop: "Our Franks are of good prowess, no man under heaven hath better, it is written in the annals of France that valiant they are for our emperor." And the Franks fare through the field seeking their fellows, and weeping from dole and pity for their kin, in all love and kindness. But even now King Marsila is upon them with his great host.

Of all the paynims only Margaris escapes the battle.

Count Roland is a knight of much worship, so likewise are Oliver and the Twelve Peers, and all the Franks are good warriors. By their great might they have made such slaughter of paynims that, of a hundred thousand, only one hath escaped, Margaris to wit. Blame him not that he fled, for in his body he bore the wounds of four lances. Back he fared in haste towards Spain, and came to Marsila and gave him tidings. . . . And in a loud voice he cried: "Good king of Spain, now ride on with all speed, the Franks are weary and spent with the smiting and slaying of our Saracens; they have lost their lances and spears, and a good half of their men, and those who

THE FRANKS SMOTE MANFULLY AND WITH GOOD COURAGE

yet live are weakened, and the more part of them maimed and bleeding, nor have they more arms wherewith to help themselves."

Marsila comes on down the valley with the mighty host that he has assembled; full twenty battles the king has arrayed. There is a great shining of helmets, set with gold and precious stones, and of shields and of broidered hauberks.

The second paynim host.

Trumpets to the number of seven thousand sound the onset, and the din thereof runs far and wide. Then saith Roland: "Oliver, comrade and brother, Ganelon the felon has sworn our death. The treason is manifest, and great vengeance shall the emperor take therefor. The battle will be sore and great, such a one as was never before fought of man. I will smite with Durendal, my sword, and do thou, comrade, lay on with Halteclere. Through many lands have we carried them, and with them have we conquered many a battle; no ill song must be sung of them."

When the Franks see how great is the multitude of the paynims, that on all sides they cover the field, they call upon Roland, and Oliver, and the Twelve Peers, that they be their defense. Then the archbishop tells them his mind, saying: "Lords, barons, put from you all cowardly thoughts; and in God's name I pray you give not back. Better it were that we die in battle than that men of worship should speak foully of us in their songs. Certain it is we shall straightway take our end, nor shall we from to-day be living men; yet there is a thing I can promise ye, blessed paradise shall be opened to you, and ye shall take your place among the innocent." At his words, the Franks take heart, and every man cries out Montjoy.

Wily and cunning is King Marsila, and he saith to the paynims: "Now set your trust in me; this Roland is Grandonie leads the second battle. of wondrous might, and he who would overcome him must strive his uttermost; in two encounters he will not be vanquished methinks, and if not, we will give him three. Then Charles the king shall lose his glory, and shall see France fall into dishonor. Ten battles shall abide here with me, and the remaining ten shall set upon the Franks." Then to Grandonie he gave a broidered banner, that it might be a sign unto the rest, and gave over to him the commandment.

King Marsila abides on the mountain, and Grandonie comes on down the valley. By three golden nails he has made fast his gonfanon; and he cries aloud: "Now ride on, ye barons!" And for the more goodly noise he bids them sound a thousand trumpets. Say the Franks: "God our Father, what shall we do? Woe worth the day we saw Count Ganelon! he hath sold us by foul treason. Now help us, ye Twelve Peers!" But the first to answer them is the archbishop, saying: "Good knights, this day great honor shall be yours, for God will give you crowns and flowers in Paradise among the glorious; but therein the coward shall not enter." And the Franks make answer: "We will lay on as one man, and though we die we will not betray him." Then they spur on with their golden spurs to smite the miscreant felons.

Among the paynims is a Saracen of Saragossa, lord

he is of half the city, and Climborin, he hight; never will
he flee from any living man. He it was who swore fellowship with Count Ganelon, kissed *Engelier is slain.*
him in all friendship upon the lips, and gave him his
helm and his carbuncle. And he hath sworn to bring the
Great Land to shame, and to strip the emperor of his
crown. He rides his horse whom he calls Barbamusche,
that is swifter than falcon or swallow; and slackening his
rein, he spurs mightily, and rides upon Engelier of Gas-
cony that neither shield nor byrnie may save him, but
he drives the head of his lance into his body, thrusting so
manfully that the point thereof passes through to the
other side, and with all the might of his lance hurls him
in the field dead. Thereafter he cries: "These folk are
good to slay!" But the Franks say: "Alack, that so
good a knight should take his end."

And Count Roland speaks to Oliver, saying: "Sir
comrade, now is Engelier slain, nor have we any knight
of more valor." And the count answers him, saying:
"Now God grant me to avenge him." He pricks on his
horse with spurs of pure gold, and he grasps Halteclere
— already is the blade thereof reddened — and with all
his strength he smites the paynim; he drives the blow
home that the Saracen falls; and the devils carry away
his soul. Then Oliver slew Duke Alphaïen, and cut off
the head of Escababi, and unhorsed seven Arabs, —
never again shall they do battle. Then said Roland:
"Wroth is my comrade, and now at my side he wins
great worship; for such blows Charles holds us the more
dear." And he cried aloud: "To battle, knights, to
battle!"

Hard by is the paynim Valdabrun, that had stood godfather to King Marsila; on the sea he is lord of four

Roland
avenges
Samson.
hundred dromonds, and well honored of all shipmen. He it was who aforetime took Jerusalem by treason, violated the temple of Solomon, and slew the patriarch before the baptismal fonts. And he had sworn fellowship with Ganelon, and had given him a sword and a thousand mangons. He rides a horse called Gramimond, swifter than any falcon; he spurs him well with his sharp spurs, and rides upon Samson the mighty duke, breaks his shield, and rends his hauberk, and drives the flaps of his gonfanon into his body, and with all the force of his lance hurls him from the saddle dead. "Lay on, paynims, for hardily we shall overthrow them!" But the Franks cry: "God, woe worth the good baron!"

When Roland sees that Samson is dead, ye may guess he is sore stricken; he spurs his horse and lets him run as fast as he may; in his hand he holds Durendal, of greater worth than is pure gold, and with all the might he hath, he smites the paynim on the helm set with gold and gems, and cuts through head and hauberk and body, and through the good saddle set with gold and jewels, deep into the back of the horse, and slays both him and his rider, whosoever has dole or joy thereof. Cry the paynims: "That was a woeful blow for us." Then quoth Roland: "No love have I for any one of ye, for yours is the pride and the iniquity."

Among the paynims is an African, Malquiant, son of King Malcud; his armor is all of the beaten gold, and brighter than all the rest it shines to heaven. His horse, which he calls Salt-Perdut, is so swift that he has not his fellow in any four-footed beast. And now Malquiant rode on Anseïs, and smote him full on the shield that its scarlet and blue were hewn away, and he rent the sides of his hauberk, and drave his lance into his body, both point and shaft. Dead is the count and done are his life days. Thereat cry the Franks: "Alack for thee, good baron!"

Through the press rides Turpin the archbishop, — never did another priest say mass who did with his own strength so great deeds of arms, — and he saith to the paynim: "Now may God bring all evil upon thee! for thou hast slain one for whom my heart is sore stricken." Then he set his good horse at a gallop, and smote Malquiant on his shield of Toledo, that he fell dead upon the green grass. *Turpin slays Malquiant.*

Hard by is the paynim Grandonie, son of Capuel, king of Cappadocia; he rides a horse called Marmorie, swifter than any bird that flies; he now slackens rein, and spurring well, thrusts mightily upon Gerin, breaks his crimson shield that it falls from his shoulder, and rends all asunder his hauberk, and thereafter drives all his blue gonfanon into his body that he falls dead beside a great rock. Then he slays Gerier, Gerin's comrade, and Berengier, and Guyon of Saint-Antonie; and thereafter he smote Austor, the mighty duke that held Valence and the land along the Rhône, and felled him dead that the paynims had great joy thereof. But the Franks cry: "How many of ours are stricken."

Roland holds his ruddied sword in his hand; he has heard the Franks make lament, and so great is his sorrow that his heart is nigh to bursting, and he saith to the paynims: "Now may God bring all evil upon thee! Methinks thou shalt pay me dear for him thou hast slain." And he spurs his horse, which springs forward eagerly; and let whoso will pay the price, the two knights join battle.

Grandonie was a man of good prowess, of much valor and hardiness, and amid the way he encounters with Roland, and albeit before that time he had never set eyes upon him, he none the less knew him of a certainty by his look and countenance; and he could not but be sore adread at the sight, and fain would he have fled, but he could not. The count smites him mightily that he rends all his helm down to the nasal, cleaves through nose and mouth and teeth, through the hauberk of fine mail, and all the body, splits the silver sides from off the golden saddle, and cuts deep into the back of the horse, that both he and his rider are slain beyond help. Thereat those of Spain make great lament, but the Franks cry: "That was well stricken of our captain."

Grandonie is smitten down.

Wondrous and fierce is the battle; the Franks lay on in their wrath and their might, that hands and sides and bones fall to earth, and garments are rent off to the very flesh, and the blood runs down to the green grass. The paynims cry: "We may not longer endure. May the curse of Mahound fall upon the Great Land, for its folk have not their fellows for hardiness." And there was not a man but cried out: "Marsila! haste, O King, for we are in sore need of thy help."

Again the paynims give back.

Wondrous and great is the battle. And still the Franks
smite with their burnished lances. There is great dolor
of folk, and many a man is slain and maimed and bleeding, and one lies on another, or on his back, or face down.
The Saracens may not longer endure, but howsoever
unwillingly they must give back. And eagerly the Franks
pursue after them.

Marsila sees the slaughter of his people, and lets sound
his horns and bussynes, and gets to horse with all his
vassal host. In the foremost front rides the
Saracen Abisme, the falsest knight of his
fellowship, all compact of evil and villainy.
He believes not in God the son of Mary; and he is black
as melted pitch. Dearer than all the gold of Galicia he
loves treachery and murder, nor did any man ever see
him laugh or take disport. But he is a good man of arms,
and bold to rashness, wherefore he is well beloved of the
felon King Marsila, and to him it is given to bear the
Dragon, around which the paynims gather. The archbishop hath small love for Abisme, and so soon as he
sees him he is all desirous to smite him, and quietly,
within himself, he saith: "This Saracen seems a mis-
believing felon, I had liefer die than not set upon him to
slay him; never shall I love coward or cowardice."

Whereupon the archbishop begins the battle. He
rides the horse that he won from Grossaille, a king whom
he slew in Denmark; the good steed is swift and keen,
featly fashioned of foot, and flat of leg; short in the thigh
and large of croupe, long of flank and high of back; his
tail is white and yellow his mane, his head is the color of
the fawn, and small are his ears; of all four-footed beasts

none may outstrip him. The archbishop spurs mightily, and will not fail to meet with Abisme and smite him on his shield, a very marvel, set with gems, — topaz and amethysts, and precious crystals, and blazing carbuncles; the gift it was of Galafré the Amiral, who had received it of a devil in Val-Metas. Now Turpin smites it and spares it not, that after his buffet it has not the worth of a doit. And he pierces Abisme through the body, and hurls him dead in the open field. And the Franks say: "That was a good deed of arms; in the hands of our archbishop safe is the crosier."

And Count Roland speaks to Oliver, saying: "Sir comrade, what say ye, is not the archbishop a right good knight, that there is no better under heaven? for well he knows how to smite with lance and spear." "Now let us aid him," the count makes answer. And at these words the Franks go into battle again; great are the blows and grievous the slaughter, and great is the dolor of the Christians.

The Franks are sore smitten.

The Franks have lost much of their arms, yet still there are a good four hundred of naked swords, with which they smite and hew on shining helmets. God, how many a head is cleft in twain; and there is great rending of hauberks and unmailing of byrnies; and they smite off feet and hands and heads. The paynims cry: "These Franks sore mishandle us, whoso doth not defend himself hath no care for his life." King Marsila hears them make lament, and saith in his wrath: "Terra Major, now may Mahound destroy thee, for thy folk hath discomfited mine, and hath destroyed and spoiled me of many cities which Charles of the white beard now

holds; he hath conquered Rome and Apulia and Cala-
bria, Constantinople, and Saxony the wide; liefer had I
die than flee before him. Paynims, now lay on that the
Franks may have no surety. If Roland dies, Charles
loses the life of his body; if he lives, we shall all take our
end."

The felon paynims again smite with their lances upon
shields and bright helmets; so great is the shock of iron
and steel that the flame springs out toward heaven; and
lo, how the blood and the brains run down! Great is the dolor and grief of Roland when Roland's grief.
he sees so many good knights take their end; he calls
to remembrance the land of France, and his uncle,
Charlemagne the good king, and he cannot help but be
heavy.

Yet still he thrust through the press and did not leave
from smiting. In his hand he held Durendal, his good
sword, and rent hauberks, and broke helmets, and
pierced hands and heads and trunks that he threw a
hundred paynims to ground, they who had held themselves for good men of arms.

And on his side the lord Oliver drave forward, smiting
great blows; in his hand he held Halteclere, his good
and trusty sword that had not its fellow under heaven,
save only Durendal, and with it he fought valorously;
all stained he was with blood even to his arms. "God,"
saith Roland, "that is a goodly baron. O gentle count,
all courage and all loyalty, this day our friendship must
have an end, for to-day through great woe we twain must
part. Never again shall we see the emperor; never
again shall there be such lamentation in fair France.

The Frankish folk will pray for us, and in holy churches orisons will be offered; certes, our souls will come into Paradise." Oliver slackens rein and spurs his horse, and in the thick of press comes nigh unto Roland, and one saith unto other: "Comrade, keep near me; so long as death spares me I will not fail thee."

Would ye had seen Roland and Oliver hack and hew with their swords, and the archbishop smite with his lance. We can reckon those that fell by their hands, for the number thereof is written in charter and record; the Geste says more than four thousand. In four encounters all went well with the Franks, but the fifth was sore and grievous to them, for in this all their knights vere slain save only sixty, spared by God's mercy. Before they die they will sell their lives dear.

When Count Roland is ware of the great slaughter of his men, he turns to Oliver, saying: "Sir comrade, as

He would fain blow his horn. God may save thee, see how many a good man of arms lies on the ground; we may well have pity on sweet France, the fair, that must now be desolate of such barons. Ah, king and friend, would thou wert here! Oliver, my brother, what shall we do? How shall we send him tidings?" "Nay, I know not how to seek him," saith Oliver; "but liefer had I die than bring dishonor upon me."

Then saith Roland: "I will sound my horn of ivory, and Charles, as he passes the mountains, will hear it; and I pledge thee my faith the Franks will return again."

But Oliver chideth him. Then saith Oliver: "Therein would be great shame for thee, and dishonor for all thy kindred, a reproach that would last all the days of their life. Thou wouldst not sound it when I bid thee, and now thou shalt not by my counsel. And if thou dost sound it, it will not be hardily, for now both thy arms are stained with blood." "Yea," the count answers him, "I have dealt some goodly blows."

Then saith Roland: "Sore is our battle, I will blow a blast, and Charles the king will hear it." "That would not be knightly," saith Oliver; "when I bid thee, comrade, thou didst disdain it. Had the king been here, we had not suffered this damage; but they who are afar off are free from all reproach. By this my beard, an I see again my sister, Aude the Fair, never shalt thou lie in her arms."

Then saith Roland: "Wherefore art thou wroth with me?" And Oliver answers him, saying: "Comrade, thou thyself art to blame. Wise courage is not madness, and measure is better than rashness. Through thy folly these Franks have come to their death; nevermore shall Charles the king have service at our hands. Hadst thou taken my counsel, my liege lord had been here, and this battle had been ended, and King Marsila had been or taken or slain. Woe worth thy prowess, Roland! Henceforth Charles shall get no help of thee; never till God's Judgment Day shall there be such another man; but thou must die, and France shall be shamed thereby. And this day our loyal fellowship shall have an end; before this evening grievously shall we be parted."

The archbishop, hearing them dispute together, spurs his horse with his spurs of pure gold, and comes unto them, and rebukes them, saying: "Sir Roland, and thou, Sir Oliver, in God's name I pray ye, let be this strife.

Little help shall we now have of thy horn; and yet it were better to sound it; if the king come, he will revenge us, and the paynims shall not go hence rejoicing. Our Franks will light off their horses, and find us dead and maimed, and they will lay us on biers, on the backs of sumpters, and will weep for us with dole and pity; and they will bury us in the courts of churches, that our bones may not be eaten by wolves and swine and dogs." "Sir, thou speakest well and truly," quoth Roland.

And therewith he sets his ivory horn to his lips, grasps it well and blows it with all the might he hath. High The Franks are the hills, and the sound echoes far, and hear the blast. for thirty full leagues they hear it resound. Charles and all his host hear it, and the king saith: "Our men are at battle." But Count Ganelon denies it, saying: "Had any other said so, we had deemed it great falsehood."

With dolor and pain, and in sore torment, Count Roland blows his horn of ivory, that the bright blood springs out of his mouth, and the temples of his brain are broken. Mighty is the blast of the horn, and Charles, passing the mountains, hears it, and Naymes hears it, and all the Franks listen and hear. Then saith the king: "I hear the horn of Roland; never would he sound it, an he were not at battle." But Ganelon answers him, saying: "Battle is there none; thou art old and white and hoary, and thy words are those of a child. Well thou knowest the great pride of Roland; a marvel it is that God hath suffered it thus long. Aforetime he took Noples against thy commandment, and when the Saracens came out of the city and set upon Roland the good knight (he slew them with Durendal his sword); thereafter with water he washed away the blood which stained the meadow, that none might know of what he had done. And for a single hare he will blow his horn all day long; and now he but boasts among his fellows, for there is no folk on earth would dare do him battle. I prithee ride on. Why tarry we? The Great Land still lies far before us."

Count Roland's mouth has burst out a-bleeding, and the temples of his brain are broken. In dolor and pain he sounds his horn of ivory; but Charles hears it and the Franks hear it. Saith the king: "Long drawn is the blast of that horn." "Yea," Naymes answers, "for in sore need is the baron who blows it. Certes, our men are at battle; and he who now dissembles hath betrayed Roland. Take your arms and cry your war cry, and succor the men of your house. Dost thou not hear Roland's call?"

The emperor has commanded that his trumpets be sounded, and now the Franks light down from their horses and arm themselves with hauberks and helms and swords adorned with gold; fair are their shields, and goodly and great their lances, and their gonfanons are scarlet and white and blue. Then all the barons of the host get them to horse, and spur through the passes; and each saith to other: "An we may but see Roland a living man, we will strike good blows at his side." But what avails it? for they have abode too long.

Charles turneth back.

Clear is the evening as was the day, and all their armor glistens in the sun, and there is great shining of hauberks, and helms, and shields painted with flowers, and lances, and gilded gonfanons. The emperor rides on in wrath, and the Franks are full of care and foreboding; and not a man but weeps full sore and hath great fear for Roland. Then the king let take Count Ganelon, and gave him over to the cooks of his household; and he called Besgon their chief, saying: "Guard him well as beseems a felon who hath betrayed my house." Besgon took him, and set a watch about him of a hundred of his fellows of the kitchen, both best and worst. They plucked out the hairs of Ganelon's beard and mustache, and each one dealt him four blows with his fist, and hardily they beat him with rods and staves; then they put about his neck a chain, and bound him even as they would a bear, and in derision they set him upon a sumpter. So they guard him till they return him unto Charles.

Ganelon a prisoner.

High are the hills and great and dark, deep the valleys, and swift the waters. To answer Roland's horn all the trumpets are sounded, both rear and van. The emperor rides on in wrath, and the Franks are full of care and foreboding; there is not a man but weepeth and maketh sore lament, praying to God that he spare Roland until they come unto the field, that at his side they may deal good blows. But what avails it? They have tarried too long, and may not come in time.

Charles the king rides on in great wrath, and over his hauberk is spread his white beard. And all the barons of France spur mightily, not one but is full of wrath and grief that he is not with Roland the captain, who is at battle with the Saracens of Spain. If he be wounded, what hope that one soul be left alive? God, what a

sixty he still hath in his fellowship; no king or captain
ever had better.

Roland looks abroad over hill and heath and sees the
great multitude of the Frankish dead, and he weeps for
them as beseems a gentle knight, saying: "Lords and
barons, now may God have mercy upon you, and grant
Paradise to all your souls, that ye may rest among the
blessed flowers. Man never saw better men of arms
than ye were. Long and well, year in and year out,
have ye served me, and many wide lands
have ye won for the glory of Charles. Was
it to such an end that he nourished you? O
France, fair land, to-day art thou made desolate by
rude slaughter. Ye Frankish barons, I see ye die
through me, yet can I do naught to save or defend you.
May God, who knows no lie, aid you! Oliver, brother,
I must not fail thee; yet I shall die of grief, and I be
not slain by the sword. Sir comrade, let us get us into
battle."

So Count Roland falls a-smiting again. He holds
Durendal in his hand, and lays on right valiantly, that
he cleaves in twain Faldron de Pui, and slays four and
twenty of the most worshipful of the paynims. Never
shall ye see man more desirous to revenge himself. And
even as the hart flies before the hounds, so flee the
heathen from before Roland. "Thou dost rightly," then
said the archbishop; "such valor well beseems a knight
who bears arms and sits a good horse; in battle such a
one should be fell and mighty, or he is not worth four
deniers, and it behooves him to turn monk and get him
into a monastery to pray the livelong day for our sins."

Roland maketh lament.

279

And Roland answered him, saying: "Smite and spare not." And at these words the Franks go into battle again, but great is the slaughter of the Christians.

That man who knows he shall get no mercy defends him savagely in battle. Wherefore the Franks are fierce Marsila as lions. Marsila like a true baron sits his taketh flight. horse Gaignon; he spurs him well and rides on Bevon — lord he was of Beaune and Dijon — and breaks his shield, and rends his hauberk, that without other hurt he smites him dead to ground. And thereafter he slew Ivon and Ivory, and with them Gerard the Old of Roussillon. Now nigh at hand is Count Roland, and he saith to the paynim: "May the Lord God bring thee to mishap! And because thou hast wrongfully slain my comrades thou shalt thyself get a buffet before we twain dispart, and this day thou shalt learn the name of my sword." And therewith he rides upon him like a true baron, and smites off his right hand, and thereafter he takes off the head of Jurfaleu the Fair, the son of King Marsila. Thereat the paynims cry: "Now help us, Mahound! O ye, our gods, revenge us upon Charles! He has sent out against us into our marches men so fierce that, though they die, they will not give back." And one saith to another: "Let us fly." At these words a hundred thousand turn and flee, and let whosoever will, call them, they will not return again.

King Marsila has lost his right hand; and now he throws his shield to earth, and pricks on his horse with his sharp spurs, and with slackened rein, flees away towards Spain. Upon twenty thousand Saracens follow after him, nor is there one among them who is not maimed or hurt of body, and they say one to another: "The nephew of Charles has won the field."

But alack, what avails it? for though Marsila be fled his uncle the caliph yet abides, he who ruled Aferne, Carthage, Garmalie, and Ethiopia, a cursed land; under his lordship he has the black folk, great are their noses and large their ears, *The onset of the caliph.* and they are with him to the number of fifty thousand. And now they come up in pride and wrath, and cry aloud the war cry of the paynims. Then saith Roland: "Now must we needs be slain, and well I know we have but a little space to live; but cursed be he who doth not sell himself right dear. Lay on, lords, with your burnished swords, and debate both life and death; let not sweet France be brought to shame through us. When Charles, my liege lord, shall come into this field, he will see such slaughter of the Saracens, that he shall find fifteen of them dead over against each man of ours, and he will not fail to bless us."

When Roland sees the cursed folk whose skin is blacker than any ink, and who have naught of white about them save their teeth, he saith: "Now I know in very sooth that we shall die this day. Lay on, lords, and yet again I bid thee, smite." "Now foul fall him who lags behind," quoth Oliver. And at this word the Franks haste into the fray.

Now when the paynims see how few are the Franks, they have great pride and joy thereof; and one saith to another: "Certes, the emperor is in the wrong." The caliph bestrides a sorrel horse, *Oliver sore hurt.* he pricks him on with his spurs of gold, and smites

Oliver from behind, amid the back, that he drives the mails of his white hauberk into his body, and his lance passes out through his breast: "Now hast thou got a good buffet," quoth the caliph. "On an ill day Charles the Great left thee in the passes; much wrong hath he done us, yet he shall not boast thereof, for on thee alone have I well revenged us."

Oliver feels that he is wounded unto death; in his hand he holds Halteclere; bright was its blade, and with it he smites the caliph on his golden pointed helmet, that its flowers and gems fall to earth, and he cleaves the head even unto the teeth, and with the force of the blow smote him dead to earth, and said: "Foul fall thee, paynim! *Say not that I am come to my death through Charles;* and neither to thy wife, nor any other dame, shalt thou ever boast in the land from which thou art come, that thou hast taken from me so much as one farthing's worth, or hast done any hurt to me or to others." And thereafter he called to Roland for succor.

Oliver feels that he is wounded unto death; never will he have his fill of vengeance. In the thick of the press he smites valiantly, cleaving lances and embossed shields, and feet and hands and flanks and shoulders. Whosoever saw him thus dismember the Saracens, and hurl one dead upon another, must call to mind true valiance; nor did he forget the war cry of Charles, but loud and clear he cries out Montjoy! And he calls to Roland, his friend and peer: "Sir comrade, come stand thou beside me. In great dolor shall we twain soon be disparted."

Roland looks Oliver in the face, pale it is and livid

and all discolored; the bright blood flows down from amid his body and falls in streams to the ground. "God," saith the count, "now I The comrades disparted. know not what to do. Sir comrade, woe worth thy valor! Never shall the world see again a man of thy might. Alas, fair France, to-day art thou stripped of goodly vassals, and fallen and undone. The emperor will suffer great loss thereby." And so speaking he swoons upon his horse.

Lo, Roland has swooned as he sits his horse, and Oliver is wounded unto death, so much has he bled that his sight is darkened, and he can no longer distinguish any living man whether far off or near at hand; and now, as he meets his comrade, he smites him upon the helm set with gold and gems, and cleaves it down to the nasal, but does not come unto the head. At the blow Roland looks up at him, and asks him full softly and gently: "Comrade, dost thou this wittingly? I am Roland who so loves thee. Never yet hast thou mistrusted me." Then saith Oliver: "Now I hear thee speak, but I cannot see thee; may the Lord God guard thee. I have struck thee, but I pray thy pardon." "Thou hast done me no hurt," Roland answers him; "I pardon thee before God, as here and now." So speaking, each leans forward towards other, and lo, in such friendship they are disparted.

Oliver feels the anguish of death come upon him; his two eyes turn in his head; and his hearing goes from him, and all sight. He lights down from his horse and lies upon the ground, and again and again he confesses his sins; he holds out his clasped hands toward heaven

and prays God that he grant him Paradise, and he
blesses Charles and sweet France, and Roland, his comrade, above all men. Then his heart fails him, and his
head sinks upon his breast, and he lies stretched at all
his length upon the ground. Dead is the count and
gone from hence. Roland weeps for him and is sore
troubled; never on the earth shall ye see a man so
sorrowful.

When Count Roland sees his friend lie prone and
dead, facing the east, gently he begins to lament him:
"Sir comrade, woe worth thy hardiness! We twain
have held together for years and days, never didst thou
me wrong or I thee. Since thou art dead, alack that I
yet live." So speaking, the count swoons as he sits
Veillantif his horse; but his golden spurs hold him firm,
and let him go where he will, he cannot fall.

So soon as Roland comes to his senses, and is restored from his swoon, he is ware of the great slaughter
The coming   about him. Slain are the Franks, he has
of Gualter.   lost them all save only Gualter del Hum
and the archbishop. Gualter has come down from the
mountains, where he fought hardily with those of Spain;
the paynims conquered, and his men are slain, and
howsoever unwillingly, he must perforce flee down into
the valley and call upon Roland for succor. "O gentle
count, brave captain, where art thou? for where thou
art I have no fear. It is I, Gualter, who conquered
Maëlgut, I the nephew of Droön the old, the hoary, I
whom thou wert wont to love for my hardihood. Now
my shield is pierced, and the shaft of my lance is broken,
and my hauberk rent and unmailed; I have the wounds

of eight lances in my body, and I must die, but dear have I sold myself." So he saith, and Roland hears him, and spurs his horse and rides towards him.

"Sir Gualter," then saith Roland, "thou hast, as I know, done battle with the paynims, and thou art a hardy and valiant warrior. A thousand good knights thou didst take with thee, my men they were, and now I would ask them of thee again; give them over to me, for sore is my need." But Gualter makes answer: "Never again shall ye see one of them alive. I left them on the dolorous field. We encountered a great host of Saracens, Turks and Armenians, Persians, and men of Canaan and of Lude, warriors of the best, mounted on swift Arabian horses. And we fought a battle so fierce that never a paynim shall boast thereof, sixty thousand lie dead and bleeding; and we, on our part, lost all our Franks, but vengeance we took therefor with our swords of steel. Rent and torn is my hauberk, and deadly wounds I have in side and flank, and from all my body flows out the bright blood, and takes from me my strength; certes, my time is nigh spent. Thy man am I, and I look to thee as protector. Blame me not, that I fled." "Nay, I blame thee no whit," quoth Count Roland. "But now do thou aid me, so long as thou art a living man."

Full sorrowful is Roland and of great wrath; he falls a-smiting in the thick of the press, and of those of Spain he cast twenty to the ground dead, and Gualter slew six, and the archbishop five. Then say the paynims: "Fierce and fell are these men. Take ye heed, lords, that they go not hence

The three Franks still make stand.

285

alive. He who doth not set upon them is traitor, and recreant he who lets them go hence." Then the hue and cry begins again, and from all sides they close about the three Franks.

Count Roland is a full noble warrior, and a right good knight is Gualter del Hum, the archbishop is of good valor and well tried; not one would leave aught to his fellows, and together, in the thick of the press, they smite the paynims. A thousand Saracens get them to foot, and there are still forty thousand on horseback; yet in sooth they dare not come nigh unto the three, but they hurl upon them lances and spears, arrows and darts and sharp javelins. In the first storm they slew Gualter, and sundered the shield of Turpin of Rheims, broke his helmet and wounded him in his head, and rent and tore his hauberk that he was pierced in the body by four spears; and his horse was slain under him. The archbishop falls; great is the pity thereof.

But so soon as Turpin of Rheims finds himself beaten down to earth with the wounds of four lances in his body, he right speedily gets him afoot again; he looks towards Roland, and hastes to him, and saith: "I am nowise vanquished; no good vassal yields him so long as he is a living man." And he draws Almace, his sword of brown steel, and in the thick of the press he deals well more than a thousand buffets. Afterwards Charles bore witness that Turpin spared himself no whit, for around him they found four hundred dead, some wounded, some cut in twain amid the body, and some whose heads had been smitten off; so saith the Geste and he who was on the field, the valiant Saint Gilles, for whom

God wrought miracles; he it was who wrote the annals of the monastery of Laon. And he who knows not this, knows naught of the matter.

Count Roland fights right nobly, but all his body is a-sweat and burning hot, and in his head he hath great pain and torment, for when he sounded his horn he rent his temples. But he would fain know that Charles were coming, and he takes his horn of ivory, and feebly he sounds it. The emperor stops to listen: "Lords," he saith, "now has great woe come upon us, this day shall we lose Roland my nephew. I wot from the blast of his horn that he is nigh to death. Let him who would reach the field ride fast. Now sound ye all the trumpets of the host." Then they blew sixty thousand, so loud that the mountains resound and the valleys give answer. The paynims hear them and have no will to laugh, but one saith to another: "We shall have ado with Charles anon."

The trumpets of France.

Say the paynims: "The emperor is returning, we hear the trumpets of France; if Charles come hither, we shall suffer sore loss. Yet if Roland live, our war will begin again, and we shall lose Spain our land." Then four hundred armed in their helmets, and of the best of those on the field, gather together, and on Roland they make onset fierce and sore. Now is the count hard bestead.

When Count Roland sees them draw near, he waxes hardy and fierce and terrible; never will he yield as long as he is a living man. He sits his horse Veillantif, and spurs him well with his spurs of fine gold, and rides into the stour upon them all; and at his side is Archbishop

Turpin. And the Saracens say one to another: "Now save yourselves, friends. We have heard the trumpets of France; Charles, the mighty king, is returning."

Count Roland never loved the cowardly, or the proud, or the wicked, or any knight who was not a good vassal, and now he calls to Archbishop Turpin, saying: "Lord, thou art on foot and I am a-horseback, for thy love I would make halt, and together we will take the good and the ill; I will not leave thee for any living man; the blows of Almace and of Durendal shall give back this assault to the paynims." Then saith the archbishop: "A traitor is he who doth not smite; Charles is returning, and well will he revenge us."

"In an evil hour," say the paynims, "were we born; woeful is the day that has dawned for us! We have lost our lords and our peers. Charles the valiant cometh hither again with his great host, we hear the clear trumpets of those of France, and great is the noise of their cry of Montjoy. Count Roland is of such might, he cannot be vanquished by any mortal man. Let us hurl our missiles upon him, and then leave him." Even so they did; and cast upon him many a dart and javelin, and spears and lances and feathered arrows. They broke and rent the shield of Roland, tore open and unmailed his hauberk, but did not pierce his body: but Veillantif was wounded in thirty places, and fell from under the count, dead. Then the paynims flee, and leave him; Count Roland is left alone and on foot.

The paynims flee in anger and wrath, and in all haste they fare toward Spain. Count Roland did not pursue

TAKES HIS HORN OF IVORY, AND FEEBLY HE SOUNDS IT

after them, for he has lost his horse Veillantif, and whether he will or no, is left on foot. He went to the help of Archbishop Turpin, and unlaced his golden helm from his head, and took off his white hauberk of fine mail, and he tore his tunic into strips, and with the pieces bound his great wounds. Then he gathers him in his arms, and lays him down full softly upon the green grass, and gently he beseeches him: "O gracious baron, I pray thy leave. Our comrades whom we so loved are slain, and it is not meet to leave them thus I would go seek and find them, and range them before thee." "Go and return again," quoth the archbishop. "Thank God, this field is thine and mine."

Roland seeketh the Twelve Peers

Roland turns away and fares on alone through the field; he searches the valleys and the hills; and there he found Ivon and Ivory, and Gerin, and Gerier his comrade, and he found Engelier the Gascon, and Berengier, and Oton, and he found Anseïs and Samson, and Gerard the Old of Rousillon. One by one he hath taken up the barons, and hath come with them unto the archbishop, and places them in rank before him. The archbishop cannot help but weep; he raises his hand and gives them benediction, and thereafter saith: "Alas for ye, lords! May God the Glorious receive your souls, and bring them into Paradise among the blessed flowers. And now my own death torments me sore; never again shall I see the great emperor"

and Turpin gives them absolution.

Again Roland turned away to search the field; and when he found Oliver his comrade, he gathered him close against his breast, and as best he might returned again unto the archbishop, and laid his comrade upon a shield beside the others; and the archbishop absolved and blessed him. Then their sorrow and pity broke forth again, and Roland saith: "Oliver, fair comrade, thou wert son of the great Duke Reinier, who held the Marches of Rivier and Genoa; for the breaking of lances or the piercing of shields, for vanquishing and affrighting the proud, for upholding and counseling the good, never in any land was there a better knight."

When Roland sees the peers, and Oliver whom he so loved, lying dead, pity takes him and he begins to weep; and his face is all discolored; so great is his grief he cannot stand upright, but will he, nill he, falls to the ground in a swoon. Saith the archbishop: "Alack for thee, good baron."

When the archbishop sees Roland swoon, he has such dole as he has never known before. He stretches out his hand and takes the horn of ivory, for in Roncevals there is a swift streamlet, and he would go to it to bring of its water to Roland. Slowly and falteringly he sets forth, but so weak he is he cannot walk, his strength has gone from him, too much blood has he lost, and before a man might cross an acre his heart faileth, and he falls forward upon his face, and the anguish of death comes upon him.

The death of the archbishop.

When Count Roland recovers from his swoon, he gets upon his feet with great torment; he looks up and he looks down, and beyond his comrades, on the green grass, he sees that goodly baron, the archbishop, appointed of God in His stead. Turpin saith his *mea culpa*, and looks up, and stretches out his two hands towards heaven, and prays God that he grant him Paradise. And so he dies, the warrior of Charles. Long had he waged strong war against the paynims, both by his mighty battling and his goodly sermons. May God grant him his holy benison.

Count Roland sees the archbishop upon the ground; his bowels have fallen out of his body, and his brains are oozing out of his forehead; Roland takes his fair, white hands and crosses them upon his breast between his two collar bones; and lifting up his voice, he mourns for him, after the manner of the people: "Ah, gentle man, knight of high parentage, now I commend thee to the heavenly Glory; never will there be a man who shall serve Him more willingly; never since the days of the apostles hath there been such a prophet to uphold the law, and win the hearts of men; may thy soul suffer no dole or torment, but may the doors of Paradise be opened to thee."

Now Roland feels that death is near him, and his brains flow out at his ears; he prays to the Lord God for his peers that He will receive them, and he prays to the Angel Gabriel for himself. That he may be free from all reproach, he takes his horn of ivory in the one hand, and Durendal, his sword, in the other, and farther than a cross-bow can cast an arrow, through a cornfield he goeth on towards Spain. At the crest of a hill, beneath two fair trees, are four stairs of marble; there he falls down on the green grass in a swoon, for death is close upon him.

Roland feeleth death near him.

High are the hills and very tall are the trees; the four stones are of shining marble; and there Count Roland swoons upon the green grass. Meantime a Saracen is watching him; he has stained his face and body with blood, and feigning death, he lies still among his fellows; but now he springs to his feet and hastens forward. Fair he was, and strong, and of good courage; and in his pride he breaks out into mighty wrath, and seizes upon Roland, both him and his arms, and he cries: "Now is the nephew of Charles overthrown. This his sword will I carry into Arabia." But at his touch the count recovered his senses.

Roland feels that his sword hath been taken from him; he opens his eyes, and saith: "Certes, thou art not one of our men." He holds his horn of ivory which he never lets out of his grasp, and he smites the Saracen upon the helm which was studded with gold and gems, and he breaks steel and head and bones that his two eyes start out, and he falls down dead at his feet. Then saith Roland: "Coward, what made thee so bold to lay hands upon me, whether right or wrong? No man shall hear it but shall hold thee a fool. Now is my horn of ivory broken in the bell, and its gold and its crystals have fallen."

Now Roland feels that his sight is gone from him. With much striving he gets upon his feet; the color has

He would fain break his sword.

gone from his face; before him lies a brown stone, and in his sorrow and wrath he smites ten blows upon it. The sword grates upon the rock, but neither breaks nor splinters; and the count saith: "Holy Mary, help me now! Ah, Durendal, alas for your goodness! *Now am I near to death, and have no more need of you.* Many a fight in the field have I won with you, many a wide land have I conquered with you, lands now ruled by Charles with the white beard. May the man who would flee before another, never possess you. For many a day have you been held by a right good lord, never will there be such another in France the free."

Roland smote upon the block of hard stone, and the steel grates, but neither breaks nor splinters. And when he sees that he can in nowise break it, he laments, saying: "O Durendal, how fair and bright thou art, in the sunlight how thou flashest and shinest! Charles was once in the valley of Moriane, when God commanded him by one of his angels that he should give thee to a chieftain count; then the great and noble king girded thee upon me; and with thee I won for him Anjou and Bretagne, and I conquered Poitou and Maine for him, and for him I conquered Normandy the free, and Provence, and Acquitaine; and Lombardy, and all of Romagna; and I conquered for him Bavaria, and Flanders, and Bulgaria, and all of Poland; Constantinople which now pays him fealty, and Saxony, where he may work his will. And I conquered for him Wales, and Scotland, and Ireland, and England which he holds as his demesne. Many lands and countries have I won with thee, lands which Charles of the white beard rules. And now am I heavy of heart because of this my sword; rather would I die than that it should fall into the hands of the paynims. Lord God our Father, let not this shame fall upon France."

And again Roland smote upon the brown stone and beyond all telling shattered it; the sword grates, but springs back again into the air, and is neither dinted nor

He calleth to mind his conquests.

broken. And when the count sees he may in nowise break it, he laments, saying: "O Durendal, how fair and holy a thing thou art! In thy golden hilt is many a relic, — a tooth of Saint Peter, and some of the blood of Saint Basil, and hairs from the head of my lord, Saint Denis, and a bit of the raiment of the Virgin Mary. It is not meet that thou fall into the hands of the paynims, only Christians should wield thee. May no coward ever possess thee! Many wide lands have I conquered with thee, lands which Charles of the white beard rules; and thereby is the emperor great and mighty."

Now Roland feels that death has come upon him, and that it creeps down from his head to his heart. In all *He turneth his face towards Spain.* haste he fares under a pine tree, and hath cast himself down upon his face on the green grass. Under him he laid his sword and his horn of ivory; and he turned his face towards the paynim folk, for he would that Charles and all his men should say that the gentle count had died a conqueror. Speedily and full often he confesses his sins, and in atonement he offers his glove to God.

Roland lies on a high peak looking towards Spain; he feels that his time is spent, and with one hand he beats upon his breast: "O God, I have sinned; forgive me through Thy might the wrongs, both great and small, which I have done from the day I was born even to this day on which I was smitten." With his right hand he holds out his glove to God; and lo, the angels of heaven come down to him.

Count Roland lay under the pine tree; he has turned his face towards Spain, and he begins to call many things to remembrance, — all the lands he had won by his valor, and sweet France, and the men of his lineage, and Charles, his liege lord, who had brought him up in his household; and he cannot help but weep. But he would not wholly forget himself, and again he confesses his sins and begs forgiveness of God: "Our Father, who art truth, who raised up Lazarus from the dead, and who defended Daniel from the lions, save Thou my soul from the perils to which it is brought through the sins I wrought in my life days." With his right hand he offers his glove to God, and Saint Gabriel has taken it from his hand. Then his head sinks on his arm, and with clasped hands he hath gone to his end. And God sent him His cherubim, and Saint Michael of the Seas, and with them went Saint Gabriel, and they carried the soul of the count into Paradise.

THE GERMAN HERO

SIEGFRIED

Adapted by M. W. Macdowall

I

SIEGFRIED'S YOUTH

ONCE upon a time there was a noble prince in the Netherlands called Siegfried. His father, Sigmund, was descended from the glorious race of the Wölfungs, who traced their lineage back to Wodan. His mother, Sigelinde, was of equally high birth. They both rejoiced in the early signs of strength and activity displayed by their son, and hoped that when grown to man's estate, his heroic deeds might gain him glory and renown.

The boy, however, soon became aware of his wonderful strength, and showed a haughty, unbending spirit. He would suffer no contradiction: he beat his playfellows black and blue when they displeased him, even those among them who were much bigger than he. The older he grew, the more he was hated by all the other boys, and the more anxious his parents became regarding his future.

At last Sigmund told the queen that he knew of only one way to bring the young rebel under rule, and that was to apprentice him to the smith, Mimer, who lived in the neighboring forest, and who was a strong and wise man, and would teach the boy how to forge the weapons he should one day wield as a warrior. The queen gave her consent, so the father took the necessary steps.

When the smith heard the whole story, he declared himself ready to undertake the task assigned him; for he had a strong belief in the pacifying effects of hard work. Everything went well for a time. One year passed after another, till the prince grew almost to man's estate. But labor in the smithy was irksome to him, and when his comrades set him right, he beat them, threw them down, and, on one occasion, went so far as to drag the best smith among them — Wieland — by the hair to his master's feet.

"This will not do at all," said Mimer; "come here and forge yourself a good sword."

Siegfried was quite ready to do so. He asked for the best iron and the heaviest hammer, which was such a weight that it took both hands to wield it. Mimer drew the strongest bar of iron out of the forge, glowing red, and laid it on the anvil. Siegfried swung the hammer with one hand, as though it had been a plaything; but when it came down upon the iron the blow was like a clap of thunder, the house shook to its foundation, the iron shivered into splinters, and the anvil sank a foot deep into the ground.

"This will never do," said the master, as before; "we must try another plan, my boy, if you are to make yourself a suitable weapon. Go to the charcoal-burner in the pine wood, and fetch me as much of his charcoal as you can carry on your strong shoulders. Meanwhile I shall prepare the best iron to make you a sword, such as never yet was possessed by any warrior."

Siegfried was so pleased to hear this, that picking up the largest axe he could find, he set out into the forest. It was a beautiful spring day. The birds were singing and the grass was studded with violets and forget-me-nots. He plucked a bunch of the flowers, and stuck them in his leather cap, from a half-conscious feeling that they might perhaps bring him good luck. He went on farther and farther, till he reached the middle of a dark pine forest. Not a bird was to be seen; but the gloomy silence was broken by a gurgling, hissing, and roaring, that might easily have affrighted a less daring spirit. He soon found the reason of the noise. A dismal swamp lay before him, in which gigantic toads, snakes, and lind-worms were disporting themselves.

"I never saw so many horrible creatures in my life," said Siegfried; "but I will soon stop their music."

So saying, he picked up dead trees and threw them into the morass, till he had completely covered it; after which, he hastened on to the charcoal-burner's house. Arrived there, he asked the man to give him fire that he might burn the monsters.

"Poor boy," said the charcoal-burner, "I am very sorry for you; but if you go back the way you came, the great dragon will come out of his cave and make but a single mouthful of you. Smith Mimer is a faithless man; he came here before you, and told me that he had roused the worm against you, because you were so unmanageable."

"Have no fear, good man," answered Siegfried; "I shall first slay the worm, and then the smith. But now give me the fire, that I may burn the poisonous brood."

The lad was soon back at the swamp. He set fire to the dry wood with which he had covered it, and let it blaze. The wind was favorable, and fanned the flames to a great fire, so that the creatures were all burnt up in a short space of time. The lad then went round the dismal swamp, and found a small rivulet of hot fat issuing from it. He dipped his finger in it, and found, on withdrawing it, that it was covered with a horn-like skin. "Ah," he thought, "this would be useful in war." He therefore undressed, and bathed his whole body in the liquid fat, so that he was now covered with horn from head to foot, except in one place, between his shoulders, where a leaf had stuck to his skin. This he did not discover until later. He dressed himself again in his leather garments, and walked on, his club resting on his shoulder. Suddenly the dragon darted out upon him from its hiding-place; but three good blows of his club slew the monster. He then went back to the smithy, to take vengeance on the master smith and his comrades. At sight of him, the men fled affrighted into the forest, but the master awaited the youth's arrival. At first Mimer tried the effect of flattering words; but finding they were vain, he took to his sword. Siegfried then dealt him one mighty blow, and had no need to strike again.

Having done this, the lad went into the smithy, and with great patience and care forged himself a sword, whose blade he hardened in the blood of the lind-worm. Then he set out for his father's palace. The king sharply rebuked him for his evil deed in slaying the master smith, who was so good a subject, and so useful to the whole country. And the queen, in her turn, reproached him with many tears, for having stained his hands with innocent blood. Siegfried, sobered by his father's reproof, and softened by his mother's tears, did not try to excuse himself; but, falling at the queen's feet and hiding his face in his hands, he said the sight of her tears cut him to the heart, and for the future he vowed that his deeds should be those of a gentle knight. Then the hearts of the parents were comforted.

From that time forward Siegfried was changed. He listened to the advice of men of understanding, and strove to learn how to act wisely and well. Whenever he felt one of his old fits of passion coming over him, he thought of his mother's tears and his father's reproof, and conquered the evil spirit that threatened to master him. The expectations of the people were great respecting him: they were sure that in him their nation had found a new hero. And then, he was so handsome and graceful, that the women admired him as much for his looks as the men did for his prowess.

II

YOUNG SIEGFRIED SAILS TO ISENLAND

His father and mother were so proud of him that they longed for the day when his name and fame should be hailed with applause in every land.

The king at length deemed that the time was come to give Siegfried and his comrades, and many young nobles of his own and other lands, the sword and armor that marked a warrior. This investiture was in those days a ceremony of great importance, and took the same place in a young man's life as the ceremony of knighthood in later times. The solemn investiture was succeeded by feats of arms and trials of skill. Siegfried was victorious in all, and, at the end of the day, the populace shouted: "Long live young Siegfried, our king; long may he and his worthy father rule over us!"

But he signed to them, and said, " I am not worthy of such high honor. I must first win a kingdom for myself. I will entreat my noble father to allow me to go out into the world, and seek my fortune."

When the warriors were all assembled at the feast in the royal hall, Siegfried did not take his place at the upper end of the table beside his father, but modestly seated himself among the young warriors who had still their names to make. Some of the party began to talk of distant Isenland, the kingdom of the beautiful and warlike Brunhild, who challenged all her wooers to do battle with her, thereby slaying many.

They talked of the land of the Nibelungs, learned in magic; of the Drachenstein, where a flying dragon, of fiendish aspect, had taken up its abode.

Others, again, talked of the lovely princess at Worms on the Rhine, who was carefully guarded by her three brothers and by her uncle, strong Hagen.

"Oh, how pleasant it must be to see such marvels, and to seek out adventures!" cried Siegfried, and approaching his father, he asked his permission to go out and see the world.

The king understood his desire, for he had had an

adventurous youth himself; and promised to let him go, provided his mother gave her consent.

It was pain and grief to the queen to part with her son, but she at last permitted him to go; and one fine morning he set out, dressed in a shining suit of armor, mounted on a swift horse, and bearing the sword which he himself had made. His spirits were high, and his heart full of hope, as is the case with every youth of spirit who goes out into the unknown world to seek his fortune.

He went northwards in the direction of Isenland. On reaching the seashore, he found a vessel ready to start; but the skipper feared a storm, and only set sail at Siegfried's entreaty. After a quick but tempestuous voyage, Siegfried landed, and went up to the palace.

Queen Brunhild received him in the great hall, where many warriors were assembled, each of whom had come determined to woo the lady by great feats of arms.

On the following day the warriors assembled in the lists, where Brunhild joined them before long. She was clad in full armor, and looked as haughty and as beautiful as Freya, when she led the Valkyrs of old to the battles of the heroes.

Siegfried gazed at her in astonishment, she was so much taller and more noble looking than any of the maidens in her train, who were armed equally with herself. He almost wished to join the ranks of the wooers, and win her hand. He raised a stone in sport, and flung it far beyond the lists; then, turning to the queen, took leave of her with all reverence, and returned again to the vessel, saying to himself:—

"I could never love her, she is too like a man. That

maiden must be shy and modest, gentle and kindly, who would gain the heart of a brave warrior so utterly that he would think nothing of spending his heart's blood in her service."

After a quick voyage, he resumed his journey by land, now through rich and well-cultivated plains, and again through desert lands, where wild beasts and robbers had their abode. He had many a hard fight by the way, and slew all manner of giants and monsters. The minstrels sang of his great deeds in cottage and in castle, so that his name became known far and wide.

When he reached the land of the Nibelungs, the kings of that country, Schilbung and Nibelung by name, asked him to divide between them the treasure left them by their father Nibeling, for they could not agree as to what was a fair division. In payment for this service they offered him the good sword Balmung, which was the handiwork of dwarfs, and was tempered in dragon's blood. The hero divided the treasure with the utmost fairness, yet the brothers were not satisfied. They told him that they were sure he was keeping back the most valuable things for himself, and commanded twelve enormous giants to seize him, and confine him in the hollow mountain where the treasure was kept. The hero at once drew Balmung, and began slaying one giant after another. Then the royal magicians chanted their spells, and called up a thick mist; a storm arose, and the mountain trembled under repeated thunder-claps. All in vain. The last of the giants fell, and finally the two brothers were slain; then the mist cleared away, and the sun shone full on the victorious warrior.

When the Nibelung people saw the wonders that had been done, they greeted Siegfried as their king. But even yet his difficulties were not at an end. An avenger had arisen: this was Alberich the dwarf. Well armed with enchanted weapons, he came up against the bold warrior. He was now visible, now invisible, according as he drew the cap of darkness over his helmet, or took it off. After a long struggle, Siegfried overthrew him.

The dwarf was now in his power, but Siegfried could not kill a defenseless foe. Alberich was so touched with this generosity that he swore to be true to his victor: an oath he never broke. After this, no one disputed the hero's right to the land of the Nibelungs. He was recognized as king by the whole people, and also became possessed of all the treasures in the hollow mountain, and of Alberich's cap of darkness by reason of his victory over the dwarf.

When Siegfried had reduced the whole kingdom to order, and appointed proved men to be governors of the provinces, he chose out twelve noble warriors to be his trusty companions. The treasure furnished him with rings and chains of silver and gold with which to enrich his followers. The whole band looked like an assemblage of kings, under the lead of some yet mightier chieftain.

He and his men now set out on their journey homewards, and reached the Netherlands without further adventure. The king and queen were overjoyed to see their son, of whom they had for a long time heard nothing but indistinct rumors. Siegfried remained at home for many days to rest and recover from his weariness. He often passed hours sitting at his mother's feet, as when he was a little boy, and telling her of his hopes and longings. His confidence and trust in her made her very happy. But when he stood before her in all the panoply of war, her heart beat high with pride that she had such a hero for a son.

Pleasant as it was to be at home again, Siegfried could not long be contented with idleness; his soul panted to be out in the battle of life, where alone a man preserves his strength of mind and body. He told his father that he wished to go to Worms, in the Rhine land, and try his fortune with the great warriors of Burgundy.

The king's face clouded when he heard this. "My son," he said, "do not go to Burgundy, for there dwell the boldest warriors in the whole world. No hero has as yet withstood them. There are grim Hagen, strong Ortewin of Metz, and King Gunther, with his brother Gernot. They all unite in guarding the lovely maiden Chriemhild, whom many a brave man has wooed, only to lose his life."

"Ha! That is a good story!" cried bold Siegfried. "These mighty warriors shall yield me their kingdom, and the lovely maid as well, if she be pleasing in my eyes. With my twelve Nibelungs at my back, I have no fears about the fighting."

The king's remonstrances and the queen's entreaties were alike in vain. They were obliged to consent to their son's undertaking this adventure.

SIEGFRIED

III

SIEGFRIED IN BURGUNDY

The lovely maiden Chriemhild, who lived in the land of Burgundy, was the daughter of King Dankrat and his wife, the lady Ute. Her father had long been dead; but his three sons, Gunther, Gernot, and the boy Giselherr, nicknamed "The Child," regarded their beautiful sister as the costliest pearl in their crown. The royal brothers were surrounded by brave warriors, to whom fear was unknown. First among these was grim Hagen of Tronje, unbeautiful of face, and one-eyed, but known and feared, both in the land of the Teuts and in that of the Latins. He enjoyed great honor for another reason, that he was the uncle of the kings. After him came his brother, the marshal Dankwart; Ortewin of Metz; the margraves, Gere and Eckewart; Rumolt, the chief cook; Volker of Alzeyen, the faithful minstrel; Sindolt, the cupbearer; and Hunolt, the steward. These and many other brave men, too numerous to mention, served the kings, and guarded their interests.

Young Chriemhild lived very much alone. She loved to wander about the garden and under the shady trees, and hated all sights and sounds of war. Her brothers once persuaded her to go out hunting with them; but a roe-deer fell dead at her horse's feet, and the sight so distressed her, that she went straight home, and could never be induced to go out hunting again.

One day the queen entered her daughter's room at an

early hour, and seeing her look sad and troubled, she asked what ailed her.

Chriemhild answered: "I dreamed that I had brought up a noble falcon, and had grown very fond of it; but once, when I let it fly up among the cliffs, two eagles attacked and killed it before my very eyes."

"My child," said the mother gravely, "the falcon is some noble warrior, whom you will learn to love with all your heart; and the eagles are two false men, who will seek to compass his death by cunning. May God give you strength and wisdom to turn their plans to naught!"

"Mother!" said Chriemhild, "do not speak to me of men. I fear to go amongst them. If there were no men on the earth, there would be no more wars or bloodshed."

"Who knows?" answered her mother, laughing. "Women often shed more blood, and cut deeper with their tongues, than any man with his sword. But the time will come when you will learn to love some hero, and will become his wife and chief admirer."

"Never," cried the maiden, in a voice of horror. "Mother, you terrify me even more than my dream."

Ute and Chriemhild went down to the garden. They had not been there long when they heard the sound of horses prancing in the court, and horns blowing. The queen went to see what was going on, and soon came back to tell her daughter of the arrival of some strange warriors in shining armor, and mounted on beautiful horses. She asked the girl to come and help her to receive the guests. But Chriemhild refused to do so, and Ute returned to the palace alone. Meanwhile Gunther and his brothers had heard of the coming of the strangers. No one knew who they were, so Hagen was sent for, and he at once recognized Siegfried. He further advised his nephew to receive the hero and his men with all honor, and to enter into friendly alliance with them.

Gunther resolved to follow Hagen's counsel; but Siegfried said that he had come to prove to his own satisfaction whether the Burgundian warriors were as great in battle as he had always heard. He offered them the Nibelung realm and treasure as the prize of victory, and said that for his part he was ready to defend himself against double or threefold the number of his own party, if the kings of Burgundy would venture their kingdom against his. Bold Ortewin and other Burgundian heroes answered that it was not their habit to fight strange warriors for aught else than their armor and horses. And King Gernot came forward and said, —

"Lord Siegfried, we want neither your goods nor your blood; I rather desire to receive you as an honored guest, and become your friend and ally, if you will also be ours." So saying, he held out his hand, which Siegfried clasped in his, as he replied, —

"God be my witness that I will be your faithful friend and ally, and if you ever come to see me, I shall greet you as honored comrades."

The Nibelungs then followed their hosts into the banqueting hall, where many a toast was drunk to the success of the new alliance.

Siegfried enjoyed his stay in the land of roses and vineyards. The days passed happily in hunting or jousting; but a great longing to see fair Chriemhild took

311

possession of him, and grew stronger every day, for he was always hearing of her sweetness, modesty, and gentleness — qualities that had ever pleased him best in women.

Chriemhild had also heard of him; but the only time she had ever seen him was once when curiosity led her to peep out of a high window, when he was jousting in the court below. He seemed to her like the white god Balder, of whose beauty and glory her forefathers had told many a tale. At that very moment he looked up, and she shrank away, fearing lest he had seen her; but he had not. Chriemhild could not understand herself. She hoped that he would stay at Worms — she, who had never before cared who came or went.

An embassy from Daneland and Saxonland arrived at Worms. The kings Lüdegast and Lüdeger declared war against Burgundy, if the kings of Burgundy did not at once pay them tribute, as in olden times.

The tribute was refused, and the Burgundian army was called out. Siegfried and his men joined King Gunther's forces. The armies met. The Danes and Saxons numbered forty thousand; the Burgundian forces were much fewer. Each side fought bravely, but Siegfried's performances were perhaps more wonderful than any other man's. He took King Lüdegast prisoner, and brought him sorely wounded into camp; handed him over to the care of servants, and returned to the battle. The fight raged on for hours. Grim Hagen was always in the front rank, and near him were Volker, Sindolt, and Hunolt. Siegfried fought by their side, always keeping the king of Saxony in sight. At length

he reached Lüdeger, and swung his sword over his head.
Then the Saxon king exclaimed, —

"Ha, Siegfried of the Netherlands, the devil has given
me into your hands. I acknowledge myself your prisoner."

The battle was at an end, and the victors, covered
with glory and laden with booty, set out on their return
to the Rhine. They were received at Worms with great
joy, and Siegfried's name was in every mouth. King
Gunther prepared a feast of victory, which was to take
place some weeks later, so that the wounded warriors
might be well enough to take part in it. Lüdeger and
Lüdegast offered a large ransom for their liberty.
While the Burgundians were debating what sum it
would be proper to demand, Siegfried exclaimed, —

"A king's head is neither to be bought nor ransomed
for gold, silver, or precious stones. It can only be won
in love through well-doing. Let the imprisoned kings
go free, provided they promise Burgundy their help in
war."

When the days of feasting were over, the guests all
took their leave, and the Nibelung hero was about to do
the same. But Gunther, acting on Ortewin's advice,
begged him to tarry a little longer; for the women, and
more especially his sister, Chriemhild, wished to show
him their gratitude. The hero's face lighted up with
pleasure, while he answered that in that case he would
stay. When the king went to the women to tell them
what he wished them to do, he felt at the bottom of his
heart a little fear lest his sister should refuse; but,
though she blushed, she consented to do his will.

At the time appointed, she entered the hall at Lady Ute's side; and as she entered, her eyes and Siegfried's met. She said a few words to him with her usual gentle courtesy, and his heart beat with a feeling he had never known before. No one in the crowd noticed the look that had passed between them except Queen Ute, who rejoiced to see it, for she loved them both. She contrived that the hero should sit next to her daughter at the feast, and that he should afterwards join them in the garden, while the other warriors sat over their wine.

IV

THE DRAGONSTONE

Siegfried returned to his lodging that evening, feeling happier than he had ever done before. Early next morning, he rode out into the wood to hunt; but his thoughts were so full of Chriemhild, that he let the game pass by unheeded. Coming back empty-handed in the afternoon, he found both town and palace in great confusion. Warriors and citizens were shouting and crowding in every open place. Queen Ute was weeping and wringing her hands. Siegfried heard broken fragments of conversation, but no one answered his questions. At length he entered the great hall, where he found Hagen, and asked him the meaning of the disturbance, and whether some dreadful thing had happened.

"That it has," replied Hagen; "it could not be worse: but what is to be, must be, and, as men said in the olden time, 'What the Norns have ordained must needs be best.' Hearken, Siegfried. When we were in the tilt-yard this morning, we were startled by hearing a rushing noise in the air, and the brightness of the sun was darkened as if the wolf Skiöll were devouring it. The thing of terror that approached was a flying dragon, of shape so monstrous that there is none like it in all the realm of Helle. As it flew over our heads, we flung spears at it, but they bounced off its horny skin like reeds. Next moment we heard a cry, and saw that the monster had caught up sweet Chriemhild from her seat in the garden, and was bearing her off through the air so rapidly that both were soon out of sight."

"And none of you went in pursuit!" shouted the Nibelung hero, "cowards that you are!"

"Are you mad?" asked Hagen, unmoved. "Are you a bird, that you can fly through wind and cloud?"

"I shall seek out the monster," said Siegfried quietly; "if I have to wander through the whole world and Helle's realm itself, I shall find the maiden, or — my death."

He hastened away, mounted his horse, and rode by unknown paths, leading he knew not whither. A ferryman set him across the Rhine, and then he wandered about among the bare mountains, but found no trace of the dragon's abode. At length he reached a dark and trackless pine forest. The boughs of the trees hung so low that he had to dismount, and lead his horse by the bridle. As night came on, he threw himself under a tree. utterly exhausted, leaving his steed to graze at will.

At midnight he heard the tramp of a horse's hoofs, and looking up saw a faint red light approaching. The rider was a little dwarf. On his head was a golden crown, the point of which was formed of a shining carbuncle. The hero asked the dwarf to show him the way out of the forest, and the little creature answered that he was glad they had met, for no one knew the forest better than he; adding, that he was the dwarf-king Eugel, who lived in the mountains hard by with his brothers, and thousands more of their race.

"As for you," he continued, "I know that you are Siegfried of the Netherlands. I have often seen you when I have been going about the world with my cap of darkness on. You could never have got out of the wild wood without my help, but would infallibly have found your grave at the Drachenstein, where the terrible giant Kuperan and the great dragon have taken up their abode."

On hearing this, Siegfried shouted aloud for joy, and promised the dwarf a rich reward, even to the whole Nibelung hoard, if he would lead him to the Drachenstein. This Eugel refused to do, fearing for the hero's life; but when Siegfried threatened to slay him, and at the same time seized him by the waist and shook him till his crown fell off, he promised to obey. He replaced his crown, and rode on first through the dark forest. At daybreak they reached their destination.

"Knock at that door," said the little king. "It is there that Kuperan lives. If you are hero enough to slay the giant, I and mine will serve you, for now we are entirely in the power of that monster."

Having thus spoken, he donned his cap of darkness, and vanished.

Siegfried knocked at the door, at first gently, then louder and louder, at the same time shouting to Kupe-

ran to give him the keys of the Drachenstein. Suddenly
the door sprang open, the giant rushed out in a tremendous passion, and asked in a thunderous voice
what Siegfried meant by disturbing his morning's sleep.
With these words he hit out at the warrior with the
pole he had in his hands, which was taller than any
of the treetops, and every blow of which rang like a
castle bell. Siegfried sprang aside to avoid the pole,
and then the battle began. The giant swung his pole
with such good will that trees and rocks came rattling
down, but he never succeeded in touching his agile foe.
At length, holding his weapon in both hands, he brought
it down on the ground with such terrible force that it
clove the earth three fathoms deep. As he stooped to
draw it out, the hero sprang upon him and gave him
three deep wounds. The giant, howling with pain,
slunk into his dwelling, and slammed the door behind
him. Siegfried battered at the iron door, but could not
move it. He sought to force an opening with his good
sword, and succeeded in cutting some holes and crannies.
He peeped into the inner room, and saw the giant binding up his wounds, and then arming himself in a suit of
mail that glistened like the sun when mirrored in the
sea. In another minute Kuperan came forth, and the
combat was renewed. After a long struggle, Siegfried
had the best of it, and the giant begged for his life,
swearing to be a true comrade and helper in the hero's
fight with the dragon, who could not be overcome without his aid. Upon this Siegfried gave Kuperan his hand
in friendship, bound up his wounds, and promised, on
his side, to be his faithful comrade; but, as he entered

the cavern first, the false giant hit him so hard a blow on his helmet that he fell senseless to the ground. Eugel, who was watching all that passed, unseen, came up at the same moment and flung his cap of darkness over the hero. While the monster thought he had vanished through enchantment, and felt about for him outside, Siegfried recovered from his swoon, sprang to his feet, and tearing off the cap of darkness, cut down the giant with the first blow. He once more forgave the traitor, but forced him to go on before.

Faithless Kuperan again tried to murder the hero at the entrance of the Drachenstein, and Siegfried would not have again forgiven him if he had not needed his help to save the maiden. The giant now brought out the key, unlocked the door, and led the hero through many passages into a vaulted chamber, in which a soft twilight reigned. Looking round, Siegfried saw her whom he sought, looking pale and wan, but very beautiful. He called her name, and hastened to her. He even dared to clasp her in his arms; he felt that she returned his kiss, and the consciousness that he was loved made him feel so strong that he could have fought all the powers of hell for her sweet sake. Chriemhild wept bitterly, and entreated him to be gone before the dragon came back; but Siegfried asked for nothing better than to come face to face with the monster, hew him in pieces, and save the princess. The giant now told them that a sword was hidden in the Drachenstein, so fashioned that it could cut through the scales of a dragon. The warrior set out to fetch it, accompanied by Kuperan and Chriemhild. Siegfried saw the hilt of a sword on a ledge of rock just below the edge of the beetling cliff. He stooped to pick it up, and at the same moment the monster seized him, and strove to fling him over. A terrible struggle began, in which the bandages came off the giant's wounds, his blood streamed down, his strength failed him, and Siegfried flung him into the depths below. A loud laugh of joy was heard, and the victor, turning, saw King Eugel, who thanked him heartily for having delivered the dwarfs from their cruel task-master. At his command a number of manikins appeared, bearing food and wine to refresh the brave warrior after his exertions. He was much in need of food, for he had not tasted a mouthful for two days. The dishes Chriemhild placed before him, and the wine she gave him, tasted better than anything he had ever eaten or drunk before.

All at once a rushing sound was heard in the air, and a howl of rage so terrible that all the dwarfs hid themselves in any crannies of the rock that they could find, and the hero and maiden were startled out of their momentary feeling of security. Chriemhild entreated, prayed her lover to conceal himself; but he was a stranger to fear, and refused to fly. The monster approached like a storm-cloud, preceded by flames of fire. It came nearer and nearer, dark, mysterious, gruesome. The mountain trembled, and the little dwarfs, hiding in the fissures of the rock, feared to be crushed to death. At Siegfried's request, Chriemhild withdrew into the vaulted chamber. And now the dragon fell upon the hero, tore away his shield with its claws, and tried to seize him in its great teeth. The warrior knew how to act; he sprang aside, until the fiery breath that issued from the dragon's yawning jaws had cooled. Then he renewed his attack, now on the right, now on the left of the monster, taking care to avoid its claws.

All at once he felt himself encircled by the dragon's tail. He made a marvelous spring, freed himself, and sought to attack the creature in front, where it was undefended by scales. Upon this, the dragon caught him so tight within its curling tail that he could not free himself. In sore distress, he seized his good sword Balmung in both hands, and gave so hard a blow that the rocks trembled; but his object was attained. The tail was cut off, and rolled thundering over the edge of the cliff. A second blow, as hard as the first, divided the monster in two. 'T is true, the jaws still snapped at the hero; but he, with the last effort of his strength, flung the pieces over the cliff. Having done this, he fell back exhausted and half stifled by the poisonous breath with which the dragon had so long surrounded him. When he came to himself he found Chriemhild's arms round him, and the dwarfs busily engaged in burning herbs and sprinkling essences to do away with the baneful effect of the fetid odors with which the place was impregnated.

The dwarfs now led the hero and the maiden into their underground kingdom, where a feast was prepared for them. While they rested, Eugel told them that the dragon had formerly been a man of handsome figure and face, but that a mighty enchantress, whom he had deserted, changed him into a dragon, under which form he was to remain for the rest of his life, unless

NOW ON THE RIGHT, NOW ON THE LEFT OF THE MONSTER

a pure maiden should consent to marry him within six years.

The dwarfs offered the warrior his choice of all their treasures. He took certain things from them, placed them on his horse beside Chriemhild, and, accompanied by Eugel, set out on his return to Worms. When they reached the edge of the wild forest, the dwarf-king looked at him sadly, and said, —

"You must know, bold warrior, that your life will be short, but glorious. You will fall by the envy of your own kindred. But your fame will last through all ages, and your name will be held in honor by the bards of every nation as long as the human race exists on the earth."

Eugel then took leave of him, and returned to his home in the forest. When Siegfried and Chriemhild came down to the banks of the Rhine, the hero took the treasure that the dwarf had given him, and sunk it in the deep waters of the river.

"What is the use of gold to me?" he said. "My life is to be short, but glorious! Hide it in thy bosom, mighty river; may it gild thy waves and make them gleam more brightly in the sunlight! Gold does the devil's work in the hands of the children of men; it sharpens the assassin's dagger to strike some unsuspecting heart — perhaps mine. But as yet I live in the light of day. I will rejoice in my glory, and in my love for the sweetest maiden on the face of the earth."

He then rejoined Chriemhild, and called the ferryman to take them across the Rhine, after which they pursued their way to Worms, and were received there with great rejoicing.

Siegfried took the first opportunity when he found Gunther alone to ask him for his sister's hand, and the king answered, —

"I will give her to you with all my heart, if you will first help me to win a high-born and most heroic woman to be my wife. I mean Brunhild, the proud queen of Isenland, for whose sweet sake many a wooer has already gone to his death."

"I know her well," replied Siegfried, "and have seen how she bears herself in the fray. She fights bravely and well, yet I do not fear but that she will find her masters in you and me. You will do well to prepare for an early start, that we may get back before the end of summer."

Queen Ute and her daughter feared the result of the adventure, but Siegfried told them to be of good courage. He promised to stand by Gunther in life and death — even the proud queen of Isenland would scarcely prove so hard an antagonist as the monster of the Drachenstein. The king proposed to take a thousand warriors in his train, but Siegfried dissuaded him; and when at last they started, the party of adventurers consisted of Gunther, grim Hagen, Dankwart, and himself.

V

THE WOOING OF BRUNHILD

After a favorable voyage they arrived at Isenstein, and rode up to the palace. Servants hastened to meet them and take their armor and horses. Hagen was at first unwilling to give up his horse and armor, but he yielded when Siegfried told him that such was the law and custom at Isenstein. The warriors entered the hall where Brunhild awaited them, clad in her royal robes. She greeted her guests with courtesy, and told the Nibelung hero how glad she was to see him again, as she had been told of his great deeds of valor; adding that she supposed he had come to enter the lists. Siegfried then informed her that he had only come as the comrade of King Gunther, his lord, who desired to try his fortune, and who was well worthy of the high prize of victory.

"This is news to me!" said the queen, "I always thought you were your own man, and owed no allegiance to another."

Then, turning to King Gunther, she told him that she had also heard of his great deeds, and asked him who were the warriors that bore him company. Gunther answered with many thanks for her kind reception, and explained who and what his companions were. Brunhild laughed, and asked whether he intended to fight aided by his three comrades.

"No, I alone am to fight," answered the king; "I alone compete for the great prize."

"Very well," said the lady, "the lists are open; prepare to do your best."

The warriors were led into the castle court, where a wide space was inclosed for the combat. The queen's serving-men surrounded it, well armed. One of these proclaimed in a loud voice: —

"If any nobly-born warrior ventures to play the three fold play with the queen, and gains the victory, she and her kingdom shall be his; but if he is conquered, his head and wealth belong to her."

Four grooms now dragged a great stone into the lists, which the combatants were to "put" (throw). It was as large and heavy as a mill-stone. Three other men brought in the huge broadsword which the maiden was accustomed to fling.

"If the woman can play with such a thing as that," said Hagen, "she is the devil's bride. No son of man can win her!"

"If we only had our weapons," cried Dankwart, "neither the king nor we need lose our lives."

"Be of good courage, King Gunther," said Siegfried; "I will fetch my cap of darkness from the ship, and will help you without any one's seeing that I do so."

He hastened away whilst all eyes were fixed upon the queen, who now entered the court, surrounded by her ladies, and clad in full armor.

"Is it right, noble queen," said Hagen, "that your men should be armed, while we remain defenseless?"

"Bring the warriors their armor," commanded Brunhild. Then turning to Hagen, she continued: "But, for all that, you must lose your lives here. If I conquer Gunther, as I have hitherto conquered all who have entered the lists with me, your heads will fall under the axe of yonder man."

The heroes looked in the direction in which she pointed, and perceived a man clad in blood-red garments standing without the barrier, holding a sharp axe in his hand.

The trial of strength began.

Brunhild went up to the stone, lifted it in both hands, and flung it the length of six fathoms. After which, she leapt forward with one spring as light as a bird, making the point of her foot touch the stone. This feat was greeted with applause. Then came a silence as of death. Gunther advanced. Aided by Siegfried's strength, he lifted the stone, weighed it in one hand, and flung it a full fathom farther than the queen. It was a stronger hand than his that helped him both in this and in the leap that followed, which carried him beyond the stone.

In the first feat of strength, he was thus indisputably the conqueror.

Then Brunhild rose with flashing eyes, and seized the heavy spear with its sharp steel point.

"Now look to yourself, proud king," she cried, and flung the weapon with such force that it crashed through his shield, and would have laid him prostrate had not Siegfried come to his aid by turning the point towards the edge of the shield instead of the centre. Then tearing it out of the broken shield, he turned the weapon so that the blunt end pointed at the queen, and guiding Gunther's hand, Siegfried launched it at her. And immediately Brunhild fell backwards, her chain armor rattling with the force of her fall.

The combat was at an end, the victory won. Brunhild rose. She stood calmly before the people, accepting her fate; but whoever could have read her heart would have seen it full of shame, anger, and a wild thirst for vengeance. The notables of Isenland were summoned to appear at Isenstein within three days, to take the oath of allegiance to Gunther. Brunhild begged the Burgundian warriors to remain her guests during that time. She asked where the Nibelung hero was, and when he stepped forward, and said that he had been busied about the ship and the sailors, she called him a faithless servant for not having been by while his master played so dangerous a game.

A great feast was made in the hall. Many ladies were present, but the queen remained in her own apartment. Gunther's feelings were very mixed. He was ashamed not to have won the victory single-handed, and yet he was pleased at having gained his object. Hagen drained many a cup of wine, and watched the laughing warriors around with a grim look on his stern face. When the heroes of the Rhine were taken to their common chamber, Hagen advised them to see that their weapons were at hand, because he feared the queen was nursing some treacherous plan against them. Bold Siegfried answered that he would at once set out for the land of the Nibelungs and return with an army of good men and true. He made his way to the ship unperceived in the darkness, and set sail for his own kingdom. Arrived there, he went straight to the dwarf Alberich who guarded the treasure, and desired him to call out a thousand well-armed men to go with him to Isenland. His commands were obeyed in an incredibly short time, and he and his troops set out to join his friends. On the third morning, he landed in front of the palace, to the great joy of the Burgundians. The queen, on the other hand, was anxious, not knowing what the arrival of so large a force might mean. But Gunther comforted her by explaining that Siegfried had brought over a band of his Nibelungs to do honor to him — the king.

During the next few days everything was arranged for the proper government of Isenland, and when Brunhild at length took leave of her people and her mother's brother, who had been appointed governor, there was hardly a dry eye to be seen. The queen herself was not happy, for she felt sure she would never see her home again; but Gunther would not let her lose time, being anxious to get back to Worms to celebrate his marriage.

When the travelers arrived in Burgundy, they were received with great joy by every one. The Lady Ute welcomed Brunhild as a daughter, and Chriemhild kissed her, and promised to be a faithful sister to her. So the two maidens stood side by side: the one, grand, beautiful, and mysterious as a starlight night; the other sweet, gentle, and lovely as a May morning. None looking at them could say which was the fairest. But Siegfried had no doubt. He never moved from Chriemhild's side till they reached the castle.

That evening Gunther asked Siegfried and Chriemhild if they were still of the same mind as before, and, finding that they were, announced that he would make preparations for a double wedding on the following day.

Brunhild sat at the feast that evening by Gunther's side, pale and cold as marble, while Chriemhild sat smiling and whispering between her mother and her lover.

"King of Burgundy," said Brunhild, at last, "I cannot understand why you give your sister in marriage to one of your vassals. She ought to be the wife of a great king."

"Say not so," answered Gunther; "Siegfried is as much king as I am. He is king of the Nibelungs, and, after the death of his father Sigmund, the whole Netherlands will belong to him."

"It is a strange story," she said; "he told me himself that he was your man."

"I will explain it all to you another time," replied Gunther. "We 'll say no more about it just now."

The double wedding took place next day. When the ceremony was over, the old queen showed her daughter-in-law all her possessions, and gave up to her all authority in the house.

"Ah, mother Ute," said the young wife, "the Burgundians are rich in wealth and great in power; but they are poor in wisdom and weak in action, otherwise King Gunther never would have come to Isenland."

Without waiting for an answer, she turned and left the room.

The feast was at an end, twilight had long fallen, and the guests all sought their beds. Gunther and his queen went to their private apartments. When he would have followed her into her room, she barred the way, saying:

"This is no place for you; you can find a more fitting room elsewhere in the palace. If I permitted you to enter, I should lose my great strength."

At first he tried entreaties, then threats, and lastly force. They wrestled together, but she very soon mastered him, bound him hand and foot, and left him lying outside the door. He did not sleep much that night.

Next morning, before the household was stirring, the

proud queen loosed her husband's bonds, desired him to hold his peace, and to respect her will in future. Gunther was sad at heart the whole day long; he looked at his wife with a feeling that was almost horror, and often left the feast to walk alone in the garden. Siegfried met him there, and asked what ailed him. When he heard the strange story, he cried, —

"Be comforted, dear comrade; we have conquered this proud woman before, and I think we shall get the better of her again. I will follow you to-night, hidden under my cap of darkness, when you take the queen to her room. Blow out the candles and let me take your place. Then she shall have an opportunity of trying her great strength against me."

"Ah, good comrade," said Gunther, "I fear for your life. We did ill to bring her from Isenland to the sunny banks of the Rhine. She is a demon, as Hagen says, and has her marvelous strength from her friends the devils."

"Well," said Siegfried, "and even if a demon has taken up his abode in her heart, it shall go hard, but we'll get the better of him. I shall be with you to-night in my cap of darkness."

The kings returned to the feast, Siegfried looking as cheerful as ever, while Gunther was bowed down by manifold cares and anxieties. At midnight Gunther led Brunhild to her room, blew out the candles, and immediately Siegfried took his place. The wrestling began, Brunhild pushed him between the wall and a cupboard, and tried to bind him with her girdle. She squeezed his hands till the blood spurted from under his nails. Such a wrestling match was never seen between a man and a maid. He used all his hero-might, and pressed her into a corner of the room with such force, that, shivering and moaning, she entreated him not to kill her, and she would be an obedient wife. No sooner did Siegfried hear this than he slipped softly away, leaving Gunther alone with the queen.

The wedding festivities lasted eight days longer; then the guests took leave of their host, and went home with many rich gifts. Siegfried and his wife also made ready for their departure. The hero refused to take any dowry with his wife, for, in his opinion, the Nibelung treasure was wealth enough.

It was on a beautiful day that the travelers reached the Netherlands. King Sigmund and Queen Sigelinde came out to meet them, and received them with great joy. An assembly of the people was summoned to meet, and after a short speech from the throne, the old king and queen placed their crowns on the heads of Siegfried and Chriemhild. The people shouted, "Long live our young king and queen! May they reign as long and as happily as their forerunners!"

It seemed as if the people's wish were to be realized, for years passed on, and all went well with the royal family. Queen Sigelinde had the great joy of holding a grandson in her arms. The child received the name of Gunther, in honor of his uncle in the distant Rhineland. And King Gunther, who had a son born about the same time, called the infant Siegfried. Not long after this the old queen was taken ill and died. This made a break in their domestic happiness; but still there was peace in the realm, and along its borders.

VI

TREASON AND DEATH

Eight years, or thereabouts, had come and gone, when messengers arrived from Burgundy inviting Siegfried and Chriemhild to a great feast. They accepted the invitation, and Sigmund determined to accompany them to Worms.

Brunhild had said one day to her husband, "King Gunther, why does your brother-in-law Siegfried never come to our court like the other vassals? I should like to see both him and your sister Chriemhild. Pray send, and command their presence at court."

"I told you before," answered Gunther, somewhat nettled, "that my brother-in-law is as mighty a king as I. He rules over the Nibelungs and the Netherlands."

"How strange!" she replied. "You cannot deny that he called himself your man when he was in Isenland."

"Oh! he only said that to help me in my wooing," said Gunther, feeling uncomfortable.

"You only say that," was her answer, "to make your sister seem to have a higher rank. But, however that may be, I should very much like to see them both at our court."

"Very well," he answered kindly, "I will send messengers to invite them to the Midsummer feast, and they will not refuse to come."

He went away, and did as he had said. Brunhild remained alone, plunged in thought.

"There he goes," she muttered. "The man that conquered the once heroic maiden, who thought herself strong enough to brave the battle like the Valkyrs of old. And he, what is he but a weak reed, moved hither and thither by every breath of wind that blows? How much greater Siegfried is! He is a hero, with the world at his feet. But then a vassal! To be sure, none such could dare to raise his eyes to the queen of Isenland. Had he done so, she must have scorned him, and would scorn him to this very hour."

Siegfried and his party came to Worms at the appointed time. There was no end to the feasting, tilting, and minstrelsy. Old Sigmund renewed his youth again, and delighted to talk of old days with the Lady Ute, whom he had known as a child. The young queens were always together, at church, or at the feast, or else in the gallery overlooking the tilt-yard. The only amusement to which Chriemhild did not accompany her sister-in-law was the chase.

One day when they were sitting together in the gallery watching the feats of agility and skill shown by the warriors, she said, in the joy of her heart,—

"Is not my Siegfried glorious among warriors, like a moon among the pale stars of night? He is a royal hero."

"He is well deserving of your praise," replied Brunhild, "but still he must yield the first place to my husband."

"Of a truth," answered Chriemhild, "my brother is a bold warrior, but he does not equal my husband in feats of arms."

"Why," said Brunhild, "did not he win the prize at Isenstein, while Siegfried remained with the ship?"

"Do you mean to accuse the Nibelung hero, the dragon-queller, of cowardice?" cried the young wife indignantly.

"He cannot stand so high as the king of Burgundy," answered Brunhild, "for he is not his own man, but owes fealty to my husband."

"You lie, proud woman!" exclaimed Chriemhild, her face flushing with anger; "you lie most insolently. My brother would never have let me marry a man who was not free. Siegfried owes no man allegiance, neither for Nibelungland nor yet for Netherland. The first kingdom he conquered with his own right hand, the other is his inheritance; and I, his queen, may hold my head as high as you."

"Try it, chatterer! I shall always walk into church before you."

With these words Brunhild left the gallery. Chriemhild felt both hurt and angry. It was the first grief that had ever befallen her, and she could not get over it. She went to her rooms, put on her costliest garments and the jewels that had come out of the Nibelung treasure; then, followed by her ladies and serving-men, she walked to the minster. Brunhild was already there with her train. She would have passed the proud woman silently, but the latter exclaimed: —

"Your husband is my husband's man; so wait here, and let your queen go first."

"Better for you had you held your peace," said Chriemhild. "A paramour go before a king's wife, indeed!"

"Are you mad?" asked Brunhild. "What do you mean?"

"I will tell you what I mean," replied Chriemhild, "when I come out of church," and passing before her enemy she went into the house of God.

The proud queen stood still, weeping, at the entrance door. Shame and anger struggled in her breast, and she could scarcely wait till the end of the service. At length the door opened, and Chriemhild appeared.

"Now," exclaimed Brunhild, "stop, and explain what you meant by your insulting words, you wife of a bondsman."

"Wife of a bondsman?" repeated Chriemhild, as though she had not heard the other words. "Do you recognize the gold ring on my hand, shaped like a serpent?"

"It is mine," said Brunhild. "Now I know who stole it from me."

"Well," continued Chriemhild, "maybe you also remember the silken girdle I wear round my waist, with its gold buckles and precious stones. My husband gained both the ring and the girdle that night, when he, not Gunther, conquered you."

Chriemhild went her way with the air of a hero on the day of his greatest victory. The proud queen remained standing where her sister-in-law had left her, her head bowed with shame. She sent for her husband, and when he came, told him how she had been insulted. And Gunther promised to ask Siegfried if he had any knowledge of what had taken place. He received his brother-in-law in the royal hall, and in the presence of many of his bravest warriors. He told him what had chanced, and immediately the Nibelung hero declared, in all good truth, that he had never spoken of dishonor and of the queen in the same breath; adding that too much weight should not be laid on the words that women spoke in anger. He then offered to clear himself by a solemn oath. But Gunther interrupted him, saying he knew him of old, and that his word was as good as his bond.

"Hearken, then, ye men of Burgundy," said the hero; "you see that I am pronounced innocent of causing the humiliations your queen has endured, and indeed I have always regarded her as a modest woman, and a good wife. And now, dear comrade Gunther, chide your wife as I shall chide mine for what they have this day done, that we may never again be brought to dispeace by their idle chatter."

He then turned and left the hall; but many a Burgundian felt that their queen had suffered a cruel wrong.

Next day Brunhild began to make preparations for her departure to Isenland. The king and his brothers entreated her to stay; but she sat silent and immovable as a stone figure.

"We cannot let you go," cried the king. "We will at any cost expiate my sister's thoughtless speech. What price do you demand?"

She rose, looked round the circle of warriors, and said in a hoarse and hollow voice: —

"Blood!"

The Burgundians started, and stared at each other, none daring to speak. She continued in the same tone: —

"Not all the waters of the Rhine could wash the stain

335

from my honor. The heart's blood of yonder man alone can do it."

The uneasiness of the warriors increased; but Hagen said, —

"Are the bold Burgundians grown weak with age? Have they become children again? I will explain the matter. Our queen demands the heart's blood of Siegfried. Ha! The words seem to terrify you!"

The Burgundians exchanged whispers about Siegfried's strength, how it were certain death to fight with him, and, moreover, that he was innocent of all blame in the matter.

Then grim Hagen turned to Brunhild, and said, "Lady, it was against my advice that Gunther went to woo you in Isenland; but now that you are our queen your honor shall be safe in our hands. I will satisfy your desire."

" But," exclaimed young Giselherr, "it is not the way in Burgundy to return evil for good. Siegfried has always been true to us, and I, at least, will not be false to him."

Hagen tried to persuade Volker, the minstrel, to help him in the work of assassination, for Siegfried was not a man they could attack openly. But Volker refused. Ortwin offered himself in his stead, saying that the mere fact of Siegfried having given the ring and girdle to his wife was an insult to the queen of Burgundy, and must therefore be revenged.

Gunther here broke in passionately, "Such a murder would cast dishonor on all Burgundy, and it is my duty as the king to prevent it."

"Lord of the Rhine," cried Brunhild, rising from her seat, "I give you three days to think of it. After that, I either go to Isenland, or have my revenge." With these words she left the room.

"No weapon can hurt him," said the Margrave Gere, "for he has bathed in dragon's blood, and is only vulnerable in one place, on which a lime leaf fell when he was doing it."

"If he guesses what we are after," added Sindolt, "he and his thousand Nibelungs will conquer the kingdom."

"I will do it by cunning," said grim Hagen.

The king could not make up his mind one way or the other. He would — and would not. And when the warriors separated, nothing was settled. Three days later, when Gunther saw that the queen's mind was fully made up, he consented with a sigh to let his uncle Hagen try his plan.

About this time heralds came from Ludegast and Ludeger to declare war against Burgundy. Siegfried at once promised to help his brothers-in-law to defend the country. The ladies were all busy preparing the jerkins their husbands were to wear. One day when Chriemhild was thus employed, Hagen entered her room. He bade her be of good cheer, because the hero having bathed in dragon's blood was invulnerable.

"Good friend," she answered sadly, "my Siegfried is so bold that he often pushes into the midst of the enemy, and, in such a case, he might easily be wounded in his only vulnerable point."

Hagen begged her to embroider a little cross upon his jerkin to mark the place, so that he might always cover it with his shield. She promised to do so, and immediately worked a little cross with silver thread upon the garment. Her anxiety was needless, for the next day fresh messengers came to say that the kings had changed their minds regarding war, and were now determined to be true to their old alliance. Soon after this, Gunther made preparations for a great hunt to be given in honor of the continued peace. On the morning on which it was to be held, Chriemhild entreated her husband to remain at home. She had had such terrible dreams the night before, that she feared for his life. He laughed at her, and then kissed her, saying that a bad dream would be a foolish reason for keeping away from the hunt.

"Besides that, be comforted, dear wife. What harm can happen to me? I shall be amongst faithful friends and comrades all day long. I shall take Balmung and a sharp spear with me, and I should like to see him who would dare withstand me."

He kissed her again, and hastened away. She ran to the window, and watched him until he disappeared from sight. The morning passed very pleasantly, and then the warriors sat down to their mid-day meal, which was spread out on the grass. There was food in plenty, but the wine ran short. Hagen explained that he had sent the wine on to another place, thinking it was there they should have dined; but he told his friends of a cool spring under a lime tree not far off, and offered to run a race there with Siegfried. The latter laughingly accepted the challenge, adding that he would carry his sword and hunting-tackle, while Hagen went empty-handed, that the race might be more equal. The two warriors ran across the meadow ground towards the linden, and, as they ran, the field flowers tried to stop bold Siegfried, the branches of the trees beckoned him to go back, and the birds in the linden sang sadly as though they would say, "Turn back, noble hero, the traitor is behind you." But Siegfried did not understand the language of the flowers, trees, and birds. He trusted his friend as himself.

"Here we are at last," he cried to the panting Hagen. "Here is the clear spring; see how the water sparkles. Let us rest under the cool shade of the linden, until the king comes up, for he must have the first draught."

He laid aside his sword and other weapons, and threw himself on the flowery grass.

"How dull you look!" he continued to Hagen; "and yet it is such a bright and beautiful day, and we have had such good sport this morning. Ah, here are the others. Come, Gunther, we are waiting for you. You must have the first draught."

Gunther stooped and drank of the fresh, clear water of the spring, then Siegfried followed him, saying, with a laugh,—

"I intend to have a real good drink. But do not fear, noble friends, I shall leave you plenty. This spring is like mankind: one part goes down into the earth, and another comes up into the light of day; but it never ends."

"Very true," said Hagen; "what matters one life more or less?"

The Nibelung hero bent over the well and drank thirstily, and, as he did so, Hagen caught up his spear and plunged it into his back, in the exact spot where Chriemhild had embroidered the silver cross on his jerkin. He did it with such force, that the point of the weapon went through his back and came out at his chest. The wounded man sprang to his feet, and, not finding his sword where he had put it, for it had been removed by one of the conspirators, seized his shield and struck the murderer to the ground. More he could not do. He sank helplessly amongst the flowers, which were dyed red with his blood. The silver stream was also reddened, and all the sky was crimson with the light of the setting sun. It seemed as if nature were blushing for the evil deed that had just been done.

Once more the hero feebly raised his beautiful head, and said, looking round upon the Burgundians, —

"Ye murderous hounds, what harm did I ever do you? Had I known of your treachery, ye had all lain dead at my feet. A devil from hell must have tempted you to do this foul deed. None of you ventured to meet me in open battle, and so you fixed upon Hagen to do the cowardly deed. Your names will be known until the latest times as those of cowardly traitors. And now, King Gunther, dishonored as you are through this ill deed, and weak of will, listen to the words of a dying man. Protect my wife, she is your own sister, protect my poor wife from Hagen."

These were the last words of the royal hero.

The warriors stood silently around him, their hearts filled with sorrow and repentance. Gunther at length said, —

"We will tell the people, who all loved the dead man,

that he was murdered by robbers. Chriemhild will never then hold us to blame."

"Nay," said Hagen, "that may not be. I will not deny what my own cunning and my own hand have done. Our queen has now the expiation that she demanded, and your honor required. Burgundy is safe from all enemies, for no man was ever Siegfried's equal, or ever will be. What do I care for the complaints of a people or for the tears of a woman? Let us make a bier of branches, that the dead warrior may be borne to Worms thereon. Ha! here is Balmung, his good sword; to-day it shall do its old master a last service, and its new master a first."

When the bier was made, the hunting party set out for Worms in very different fashion from that in which they had started in the morning. They did not arrive until late at night. It almost seemed as though the dead hero inspired both warriors and serving-men with terror. None of them would carry him up the staircase. Hagen called them cowardly loons, and raising the body on his shoulders, carried it up, and laid it outside Chriemhild's door. Next morning early the queen got up, and made ready to go to the sanctuary. She called a chamberlain, and he, seeing a dead man, whom he did not recognize in the half-light, lying in the passage, told his mistress. She shrieked aloud, —

"It is Siegfried! Hagen has murdered him at Brunhild's command!"

The servants brought lights, and they saw that she had spoken truth. She threw herself on her husband's body, and with her tears washed his face clear of the blood stains that marred it. There he lay before her, pale, cold, and motionless; never, never again should she hear his voice — never again. The words rhymed in her ears, and seemed to madden her. She would willingly have died with him, and have gone down to the grave; or, as her forefathers believed, have rejoined him in Freya's halls.

Old Sigmund, on hearing the news, uttered no word, but his heart seemed broken. He kissed his son's wounds, as though he hoped thereby to recall him to life. Suddenly he started to his feet, and the old spirit awoke in his heart.

"Murder! Vengeance!" he cried. "Up, Nibelungs, up, and avenge your hero."

He hastened into the court, and the Nibelungs, hearing his words, crowded round him in full armor. The old man received a sword and coat of mail from them, but his trembling hands were too weak to hold them, and next moment he had sunk unconscious on the ground. The Burgundians were awaiting the assault with arms in their hands, and grim Hagen was bringing up new forces to help those already there.

The Nibelungs retired gnashing their teeth.

On the third day after this, the bier was taken to the sanctuary to be blessed by the priest. The populace crowded into the church, that they might give a last look at the dead hero, who had done so much for Burgundy. Chriemhild stood by the uncovered coffin, which was adorned with gold and precious stones. Her eyes were tearless, but all could read her sorrow in her face and bearing. A veiled woman passed close by amongst the crowd. Chriemhild alone recognized her.

"Go, murderess," she cried, "do not approach him, lest the very dead should bear witness against you."

The unknown vanished in the crowd.

The Burgundian warriors now came to view the corpse, as custom demanded. When Hagen came up, the wounds of the dead man opened, and his blood flowed forth in a warm stream, as at the hour of the murder.

"Do not stand there, assassin," said Chriemhild; "do you not see how the dead bears witness against you?"

The bold warrior remained where he was.

"I do not deny what my hand has done. I only acted as I was bound to act by my fealty to my liege lord and his queen."

If Chriemhild had had a sword in her hand, and had been possessed of a man's strength, Hagen had scarcely quitted the sanctuary alive.

Many gifts were made to the poor in honor of the dead hero, who was buried on the fourth day. The grave-chamber was richly decorated, and over it rose a high mound. Chriemhild followed the coffin to its quiet resting-place. There the lid was opened once more at her command. She kissed and wept over the pale face of her husband. Her women at length had to bear her away, for she would have remained there forever. Hagen was standing without, grim and unmoved as ever, and said with his usual fatalism, "What has happened, must needs have happened. The will of the Norns must be done." The queen did not hear him. She did not even see how Gunther, Gernot, and many of the other warriors tried to hide their grief and repentance. Her thoughts were all with the dead.

Sigmund and the Nibelungs prepared to return home. They wanted to take Chriemhild with them, to guard her from the false Burgundians; but she would not leave her husband's grave, and only begged the old king and the Margrave Eckewart to take care of her little son, and bring him up to be like his father. For she said he was an orphan, fatherless, and perhaps motherless. She had only one wish, which she whispered in the old man's ear — the wish for vengeance. Sigmund took leave of none but the Lady Ute, who mourned for Siegfried as if he had been a son of her own, and of Giselher, the youngest of the brothers. Then he set out for the Netherlands.

Time passed on, and it almost seemed as though Chriemhild had grown content, and had become reconciled to her brother. Grim Hagen alone seemed to fill her with horror, and Brunhild she also avoided. She one day told her brother that she wished the Nibelung treasure to be brought up to Worms, as it was her private property. Gunther rejoiced at this proof of her renewed confidence in him, and at once consented to send for it. Alberich delivered the treasure to the messengers without hesitation, and at length it arrived at Worms. The queen made generous gifts to the people, and whenever she found a brave warrior who possessed but few worldly goods, she would provide him with all that was necessary for his calling, and with daily pay besides. So that she gradually became complete mistress of a small army, which grew daily larger, and more powerful.

Hagen warned the kings of this; he told them that the Lady Chriemhild meditated vengeance. He did not care for his own life, he said, but the fair land of Burgundy must not fall into her hands. The only way that he could see of preventing this consummation would be for the kings to take the Nibelung treasure under their own care. The brothers would not consent. Gernot said that enough harm had been done to their sister already without heaping small indignities on her. Once, when his liege lords were absent, Hagen, who had always considered that prevention was better than cure, called his men together, and fell upon the warders who had charge of the Nibelung treasure. He carried off all that remained of it, and sank it in the deep waters of the Rhine. It was of little use that the kings heard of his ill deed on their return; it was of little use that Chriemhild made indignant complaint: the deed was done, and could not be undone.

"If you were not our uncle," said Gunther and Gernot, "this should have cost you your life."

A short time afterwards, Hagen showed his nephews the place in the Rhine where he had hidden the treasure, and made them swear that none of them would betray its hiding-place as long as one of them was alive. Chriemhild was sad and sorrowful as before; she always sat with her mother, and embroidered tapestry in which she depicted the scene of Baldur's death, and showed how he was cruelly slain by his brother Höder, and how Nanna died of a broken heart, and shared her husband's bier. But in Baldur every one recognized the features of her hero, and in Nanna her own; while Höder had the features, garments, and murderous weapon of grim Hagen. She often held the needle suspended in her fingers, and sat watching the picture thoughtfully. When the Lady Ute asked her, on such occasions, "What are you thinking of, my child?" she would answer, "I was thinking of Hagen."

THE SPANISH HERO

RODRIGO AND THE LEPER

Adapted by Robert Southey

RODRIGO forthwith set out upon the road, and took with him twenty knights. And as he went he did great good, and gave alms, feeding the poor and needy. And upon the way they found a leper, struggling in a quagmire, who cried out to them with a loud voice to help him for the love of God; and when Rodrigo heard this, he alighted from his beast and helped him, and placed him upon the beast before him, and carried him with him in this manner to the inn where he took up his lodging that night. At this were his knights little pleased. And when supper was ready he bade his knights take their seats, and he took the leper by the hand, and seated him next himself, and ate with him out of the same dish. The knights were greatly offended at this foul sight, insomuch that they rose up and left the chamber. But Rodrigo ordered a bed to be made ready for himself and for the leper, and they twain slept together. When it was midnight and Rodrigo was fast asleep, the leper breathed against him between his shoulders, and that breath was so strong that it passed through him, even through his breast; and he awoke, being astounded, and felt for the leper by him, and found him not; and he began to call him, but there was no reply. Then he arose in fear, and called for light, and it was brought him; and he looked for the leper and could see nothing; so he returned into the bed, leaving the light burning. And he began to think within himself what had happened, and of that breath which had passed through him, and how the leper was not there. After a while, as he was thus musing, there appeared before him one in white garments, who said unto him, Sleepest thou or wakest thou, Rodrigo? and he answered and said, I do not sleep: but who art thou that bringest with thee such brightness and so sweet an odor? Then said he, I am Saint Lazarus, and know that I was a leper to whom thou didst so much good and so great honor for the love of God; and because thou didst this for his sake hath God now granted thee a great gift; for whensoever that breath which thou hast felt shall come upon thee, whatever thing thou desirest to do, and shalt then begin, that shalt thou accomplish to thy heart's desire, whether it be in battle or aught else, so that thy honor shall go on increasing from day to day; and thou shalt be feared both by Moors and Christians, and thy enemies shall never prevail against thee, and thou shalt die an honorable death in thine own house, and in thy renown, for God hath blessed thee; — therefore go thou on, and evermore persevere in doing good; and with that he disappeared. And Rodrigo arose and prayed to our lady and intercessor St. Mary, that she would pray to her blessed son for him to watch over both his body and soul in all his undertakings; and he continued in prayer till the day broke. Then he proceeded on his way, and performed his pilgrimage, doing much good for the love of God and of St. Mary.

And as he ....
....
....

THE KNIGHTING OF RODRIGO

Adapted by Robert Southey

NOW it came to pass that while the king lay before Coimbra, there came a pilgrim from the land
of Greece on pilgrimage to Santiago; his name was
Estiano, and he was a bishop. And as he was praying
in the church he heard certain of the townsmen and of
the pilgrims saying that Santiago was wont to appear in
battle like a knight, in aid of the Christians. And when
he heard this, it nothing pleased him, and he said unto
them, Friends, call him not a knight, but rather a fisherman. Upon this it pleased God that he should fall
asleep, and in his sleep Santiago appeared to him with
a good and cheerful countenance, holding in his hand a
bunch of keys, and said unto him, Thou thinkest it a
fable that they should call me a knight, and sayest that
I am not so: for this reason am I come unto thee that
thou never more mayest doubt concerning my knighthood; for a knight of Jesus Christ I am, and a helper of
the Christians against the Moors. While he was thus
saying, a horse was brought him the which was exceeding white, and the apostle Santiago mounted upon it,
being well clad in bright and fair armor, after the manner
of a knight. And he said to Estiano, I go to help King
Don Ferrando, who has lain these seven months before
Coimbra, and to-morrow, with these keys which thou

seest, will I open the gates of the city unto him at the hour of tierce, and deliver it into his hand. Having said this, he departed. And the bishop, when he awoke in the morning, called together the clergy and people of Compostella, and told them what he had seen and heard. And as he said, even so did it come to pass; for tidings came, that on that day, and at the hour of tierce, the gates of the city had been opened.

King Don Ferrando then assembled his counts and chief captains, and told them all that the monks of Lorvam had done, in bringing him to besiege the city, and in supplying his army in their time of need: and the counts and chief captains made answer and said, Certes, O king, if the monks had not given us the stores of their monastery, thou couldest not have taken the city at this time. The king then called for the abbot and the brethren, for they were with him in the host, and said the hours to him daily, and mass in St. Andre's, and buried there and in their monastery as many as had died during the siege, either of arrow-wounds or by lances, or of their own infirmities. So they came before him and gave him joy of his conquest; and he said unto them, Take ye now of this city as much as ye desire, since by God's favor and your council I have won it. But they made answer, Thanks be to God and to you, and to your forefathers, we have enough and shall have, if so be that we have your favor and dwell among Christians. Only for the love of God, and for the remedy of your own soul, give us one church with its dwelling-houses within the city, and confirm unto us the gifts made to us in old times by your forefathers, and the good men to whom

God give a happy rest. With that the king turned to his sons and his soldiers, and said, Of a truth, by our Creator, these who desire so little are men of God. I would have given them half the city, and they will have only a single church! Now therefore, since they require but this, on the part of God Almighty let us grant and confirm unto them what they ask, to the honor of God and St. Mamede. And the brethren brought him their charters of King Ramiro, and King Bermudo, and King Alfonso, and of Gonzalo Moniz, who was a knight and married a daughter of King Bermudo, and of other good men. And the king confirmed them, and he bade them make a writing of all which had passed between him and them at the siege of Coimbra; and when they brought him the writing, they brought him also a crown of silver and of gold, which had been King Bermudo's, and which Gonzalo Moniz had given to the monastery in honor of God and St. Mamede. The king saw the crown, how it was set with precious stones, and said to them, To what end bring ye hither this crown? And they said, That you should take it, sire, in return for the good which you have done us. But he answered, Far be it from me that I should take from your monastery what the good men before me have given to it! Take ye back the crown, and take also ten marks of silver, and make with the money a good cross, to remain with you forever. And he who shall befriend you, may God befriend him; but he who shall disturb you or your monastery, may he be cursed by the living God and by his saints. So the king signed the writing which he had commanded to be made, and his sons and chief captains signed it also, and in the writing he enjoined his children and his children's children, as many as should come after him, to honor and protect the monastery of Lorvam; upon his blessing he charged them so to do, because he had found the brethren better than all the other monks in his dominions.

Then King Don Ferrando knighted Rodrigo of Bivar in the great mosque of Coimbra, which he dedicated to St. Mary. And the ceremony was after this manner: the king girded on his sword, and gave him the kiss, but not the blow. To do him more honor the queen gave him his horse, and the Infanta Doña Urraca fastened on his spurs; and from that day forth he was called Ruydiez. Then the king commanded him to knight nine noble squires with his own hand; and he took his sword before the altar, and knighted them. The king then gave Coimbra to the keeping of Don Sisnando, bishop of Iria; a man, who having more hardihood than religion, had by reason of his misdeeds gone over to the Moors, and sorely infested the Christians in Portugal. But during the siege he had come to the king's service, and bestirred himself well against the Moors; and therefore the king took him into his favor, and gave him the city to keep, which he kept, and did much evil to the Moors till the day of his death. And the king departed and went to Compostella, to return thanks to Santiago.

But then Benalfagi, who was the lord of many lands in Estremadura, gathered together a great power of the Moors and built up the walls of Montemor, and from thence waged war against Coimbra, so that they of Coimbra called upon the king for help. And the king came up against the town, and fought against it, and took it. Great honor did Ruydiez win at that siege; for having to protect the foragers, the enemy came out upon him, and thrice in one day was he beset by them; but he, though sorely pressed by them, and in great peril, nevertheless would not send to the camp for succor, but put forth his manhood and defeated them. And from that day the king gave more power into his hands, and made him head over all his household.

Now the men of Leon besought the king that he would repeople Zamora, which had lain desolate since it was destroyed by Almanzor. And he went thither and peopled the city, and gave to it good privileges. And while he was there came messengers from the five kings who were vassals to Ruydiez of Bivar, bringing him their tribute; and they came to him, he being with the king, and called him Cid, which signifieth lord, and would have kissed his hands, but he would not give them his hand till they had kissed the hand of the king. And Ruydiez took the tribute and offered the fifth thereof to the king, in token of his sovereignty; and the king thanked him, but would not receive it; and from that time he ordered that Ruydiez should be called the Cid, because the Moors had so called him.

THE CID IS DRIVEN INTO BANISHMENT

Adapted by Robert Southey

AFTER this King Don Alfonso assembled together all his power and went against the Moors. And the Cid should have gone with him, but he fell sick and perforce therefore abode at home. And while the king was going through Andalusia, having the land at his mercy, a great power of the Moors assembled together on the other side, and entered the land, and besieged the castle of Gormaz, and did much evil. At this time the Cid was gathering strength; and when he heard that the Moors were in the country, laying waste before them, he gathered together what force he could, and went after them; and the Moors, when they heard this, dared not abide his coming, but began to fly. And the Cid followed them to Atienza, and to Ciguenza, and Fita, and Guadalajara, and through the whole land of St. Esteban, as far as Toledo, slaying and burning, and plundering and destroying, and laying hands on all whom he found, so that he brought back seven thousand prisoners, men and women; and he and all his people returned rich and with great honor. But when the king of Toledo heard of the hurt which he had received at the hands of the Cid, he sent to King Don Alfonso to complain thereof, and the king was greatly troubled. And then the Ricos-omes who wished ill to the Cid, had the way open to do him evil with the king, and they said to the king, Sir, Ruydiez hath broken your faith, and the oath and promise which you made to the king of Toledo; and he hath done this for no other reason but that the Moors of Toledo may fall upon us here, and slay both you and us. And the king believed what they said, and was wroth against the Cid, having no love towards him because of the oath which he had pressed upon him at Burgos concerning the death of King Don Sancho, his brother. And he went with all speed to Burgos, and sent from thence to bid the Cid come unto him.

Now my Cid knew the evil disposition of the king towards him, and when he received his bidding, he made answer that he would meet him between Burgos and Bivar. And the king went out from Burgos and came nigh unto Bivar; and the Cid came up to him and would have kissed his hand, but the king withheld it, and said angrily unto him, Ruydiez, quit my land. Then the Cid clapt spurs to the mule upon which he rode, and vaulted into a piece of ground which was his own inheritance, and answered, Sir, I am not in your land, but in my own. And the king replied full wrathfully, Go out of my kingdoms without any delay. And the Cid made answer, Give me then thirty days' time, as is the right of the hidalgos; and the king said he would not, but that if he were not gone in nine days' time he would come and look for him. The counts were well pleased at this; but all the people of the land were sorrowful. And then the king and the Cid parted. And the Cid sent for all his friends and his kinsmen and vassals, and told them how King Don Alfonso had banished him from the land, and asked of them who would follow him into banishment, and who would remain at home. Then Alvar Fañez, who was his cousin-german, came forward and said, Cid, we will all go with you, through desert and through peopled country, and never fail you. In your service will we spend our mules and horses, our wealth and our garments, and ever while we live be unto you loyal friends and vassals. And they all confirmed what Alvar Fañez had said; and the Cid thanked them for their love, and said that there might come a time in which he should guerdon them.

And as he was about to depart he looked back upon his own home, and when he saw his hall deserted, the household chests unfastened, the doors open, no cloaks hanging up, no seats in the porch, no hawks upon the perches, the tears came into his eyes, and he said, My enemies have done this. . . . God be praised for all things. And he turned toward the east and knelt and said, Holy Mary Mother, and all saints, pray to God for me, that he may give me strength to destroy all the pagans, and to win enough from them to requite my friends therewith, and all those who follow and help me. Then he called for Alvar Fañez and said unto him, Cousin, the poor have no part in the wrong which the king hath done us; see now that no wrong be done unto them along our road: and he called for his horse. And then an old woman who was standing at her door said, Go in a lucky minute, and make spoil of whatever you wish. And with this proverb he rode on, saying, Friends, by God's good pleasure we shall return to Castile with great honor and great gain. And as they went out from Bivar they had a crow on their right hand, and when they came to Burgos they had a crow on the left.

My Cid Ruydiez entered Burgos, having sixty streamers in his company. And men and women went forth to see him, and the men of Burgos and the women of Burgos were at their windows, weeping, so great was their sorrow; and they said with one accord, God, how good a vassal if he had but a good lord! and willingly would each have bade him come in, but no one dared so to do; for King Don Alfonso in his anger had sent letters to Burgos, saying that no man should give the Cid a lodging; and that whosoever disobeyed should lose all that he had, and moreover the eyes in his head. Great sorrow had these Christian folk at this, and they hid themselves when he came near them because they did not dare speak to him; and my Cid went to his Posada, and when he came to the door he found it fastened, for fear of the king. And his people called out with a loud voice, but they within made no answer. And the Cid rode up to the door, and took his foot out of the stirrup, and gave it a kick, but the door did not open with it, for it was well secured; a little girl of nine years old then came out of one of the houses and said unto him, O Cid, the king hath forbidden us to receive you. We dare not open our doors to you, for we should lose our houses and all that we have, and the eyes in our head. Cid, our evil would not help you, but God and all his saints be with you. And when she had said this, she returned into the house. And when the Cid knew what the king had done, he turned away from the door and rode up to St. Mary's, and there he alighted and knelt down and prayed with all his heart; and then he mounted again and rode out of the town, and pitched his tent near Arlanzon, upon the Glera, that is to say, upon the sands. My Cid Ruydiez, he who in a happy hour first girt on his sword, took up his lodging upon the sands, because there was none who would receive him within their door. He had a good company round about him, and there he lodged as if he had been among the mountains.

Moreover the king had given orders that no food should be sold them in Burgos, so that they could not buy even a pennyworth. But Martin Antolinez, who was a good Burgalese, he supplied my Cid and all his company with bread and wine abundantly. Campeador, said he to the Cid, to-night we will rest here, and to-morrow we will be gone: I shall be accused for what I have done in serving you, and shall be in the king's displeasure; but following your fortunes, sooner or later, the king will have me for his friend, and if not, I do not care a fig for what I leave behind. Now this Martin Antolinez was nephew unto the Cid, being the son of his brother, Ferrando Diaz. And the Cid said unto him, Martin Antolinez, you are a bold lancier; if I live I will double you your pay. You see I have nothing with me, and yet must provide for my companions. I will take two chests and fill them with sand, and do you go in secret to Rachel and Vidas, and tell them to come hither privately; for I cannot take my treasures with me because of their weight, and will pledge them in their hands. Let them come for the chests at night, that no man may see them. God knows that I do this thing more of necessity than of willfulness; but by God's good help I shall redeem all. Now

Rachel and Vidas were rich Jews, from whom the Cid used to receive money for his spoils. And Martin Antolinez went in quest of them, and he passed through Burgos and entered into the castle; and when he saw them he said, Ah, Rachel and Vidas, my dear friends! now let me speak with ye in secret. And they three went apart. And he said to them, Give me your hands that you will not discover me neither to Moor nor Christian! I will make you rich men forever. The Campeador went for the tribute and he took great wealth, and some of it he has kept for himself. He has two chests full of gold; ye know that the king is in anger against him, and he cannot carry these away with him without their being seen. He will leave them therefore in your hands, and you shall lend him money upon them, swearing with great oaths and upon your faith, that ye will not open them till a year be past. Rachel and Vidas took counsel together and answered, We well knew he got something when he entered the land of the Moors; he who has treasures does not sleep without suspicion; we will take the chests, and place them where they shall not be seen. But tell us with what will the Cid be contented, and what gain will he give us for the year? Martin Antolinez answered like a prudent man, My Cid requires what is reasonable; he will ask but little to leave his treasures in safety. Men come to him from all parts. He must have six hundred marks. And the Jews said, We will advance him so much. Well then, said Martin Antolinez, ye see that the night is advancing; the Cid is in haste, give us the marks. This is not the way of business, said they; we must take first, and then give. Ye say well, replied the Burgalese: come then to the Campeador, and we will help you to bring away the chests, so that neither Moors nor Christians may see us. So they went to horse and rode out together, and they did not cross the bridge but rode through the water that no man might see them, and they came to the tent of the Cid.

Meantime the Cid had taken two chests, which were covered with leather of red and gold, and the nails which fastened down the leather were well gilt; they were ribbed with bands of iron, and each fastened with three locks; they were heavy, and he filled them with sand. And when Rachel and Vidas entered his tent with Martin Antolinez, they kissed his hand; and the Cid smiled and said to them, Ye see that I am going out of the land, because of the king's displeasure; but I shall leave something with ye. And they made answer, Martin Antolinez has covenanted with us, that we shall give you six hundred marks upon these chests and keep them a full year, swearing not to open them till that time be expired, else shall we be perjured. Take the chests, said Martin Antolinez; I will go with you, and bring back the marks, for my Cid must move before cock-crow. So they took the chests, and though they were both strong men they could not raise them from the ground; and they were full glad of the bargain which they had made. And Rachel then went to the Cid and kissed his hand and said, Now, Campeador, you are going from Castile among strange nations, and your gain will be great, even as your fortune is. I kiss your hand, Cid, and have a gift for you, a red skin; it is Moorish and honorable. And the Cid said, It pleases me: give it me if ye have brought it; if not, reckon it upon the chests. And they departed with the chests, and Martin Antolinez and his people helped them, and went with them. And when they had placed the chests in safety, they spread a carpet in the middle of the hall, and laid a sheet upon it, and they threw down upon it three hundred marks of silver. Don Martin counted them, and took them without weighing. The other three hundred they paid in gold. Don Martin had five squires with him, and he loaded them all with the money. And when this was done he said to them, Now Don Rachel and Vidas, you have got the chests, and I who got them for you well deserve a pair of hose. And the Jews said to each other, Let us give him a good gift for this which he has done; and they said to him, We will give you enough for hose and for a rich doublet and a good cloak; you shall have thirty marks. Don Martin thanked them and took the marks, and bidding them both farewell, he departed right joyfully.

When Martin Antolinez came into the Cid's tent he said unto him, I have sped well, Campeador! you have gained six hundred marks, and I thirty. Now then, strike your tent and be gone. The time draws on, and you may be with your lady wife at St. Pedro de Cardeña, before the cock crows. So the tent was struck, and my Cid and his company went to horse at this early hour. And the Cid turned his horse's head toward St. Mary's, and with his right hand he blessed himself on the forehead, and he said, God be praised! help me, St. Mary. I go from Castile because the anger of the king is against me, and I know not whether I shall ever enter it again in all my days. Help me, glorious Virgin, in my goings, both by night and by day. If you do this and my lot be fair, I will send rich and goodly gifts to your altar, and will have a thousand masses sung there. Then with a good heart he gave his horse the reins. And Martin Antolinez said to him, Go ye on; I must back to my wife and tell her what she is to do during my absence. I shall be with you in good time. And back he went to Burgos, and my Cid and his company pricked on. The cocks were crowing amain, and the day began to break, when the good Campeador reached St. Pedro's. The Abbot Don Sisebuto was saying matins, and Doña Ximena and five of her ladies of good lineage were with him, praying to God and St. Peter to help my Cid. And when he called at the gate and they knew his voice, God, what a joyful man was the Abbot Don Sisebuto! Out into the courtyard they went with torches and with tapers, and the abbot gave thanks to God that he now beheld the face of my Cid. And the Cid told him all that had befallen him, and how he was a banished man; and he gave him fifty marks for himself, and a hundred for Doña Ximena and her children. Abbot, said he, I leave two little girls behind me, whom I commend to your care. Take you care of them, and of my wife and of her ladies: when this money be gone, if it be not enough, supply them abundantly; for every mark which you expend upon them I will give the monastery four. And the abbot promised to do this with a right good-will. Then Doña Ximena came up and her daughters with her, each of them borne in arms, and she knelt down on both her knees before her husband, weeping bitterly, and she would have kissed his hand; and she said to him, Lo, now you are banished from the land by mischief-making men, and here am I with your daughters, who are little ones and of tender years, and we and you must be parted, even in your lifetime. For the love of St. Mary, tell me now what we shall do. And the Cid took the children in his arms, and held them to his heart and wept, for he dearly loved them. Please God and St. Mary, said he, I shall yet live to give these my daughters in marriage with my own hands, and to do you service yet, my honored wife, whom I have ever loved, even as my own soul.

A great feast did they make that day in the monastery for the good Campeador, and the bells of St. Pedro's rung merrily. Meantime the tidings had gone through Castile how my Cid was banished from the land, and great was the sorrow of the people. Some left their houses to follow him, others forsook their honorable offices which they held. And that day a hundred and fifteen knights assembled at the bridge of Arlanzon, all in quest of my Cid; and there Martin Antolinez joined them, and they rode on together to St. Pedro's. And when he of Bivar knew what a goodly company were coming to join him, he rejoiced in his own strength, and rode out to meet them and greeted them full courteously; and they kissed his hand, and he said to them, I pray to God that I may one day requite ye well, because ye have forsaken your houses and your heritages for my sake, and I trust that I shall pay ye twofold. Six days of the term allotted were now gone, and three only remained: if after that time he should be found within the king's dominions, neither for gold nor for silver could he then escape. That day they feasted together, and when it was evening the Cid distributed among them all that he had, giving to each man according to what he was; and he told them that they must meet at mass after matins, and depart at that early hour. Before the cock crew they were ready, and the abbot said the mass of the Holy Trinity; and when it was done they left the church and went to horse. And my Cid embraced Doña Ximena and his daughters, and blessed them; and the parting between them was like separating the nail from the quick flesh; and he wept and continued to look round after them. Then Alvar Fañez came up to him and said, Where is your courage, my Cid ? In a good hour were you born of woman. Think of our road now; these sorrows will yet be turned into joy. And the Cid spake again to the abbot, commending his family to his care; — well did the abbot know that he should one day receive good guerdon. And as he took leave of the Cid, Alvar Fañez said to him, Abbot, if you see any who come to follow us, tell them what route we take, and bid them make speed, for they may reach us either in the waste or in the peopled country. And then they loosed the reins and pricked forward.

That night my Cid lay at Spinar de Can, and people flocked to him from all parts, and early on the morrow he set out; Santestevan lay on his left hand, which is a good city, and Ahilon on the right, which belongs to the Moors, and he passed by Alcobiella, which is the boundary of Castile. And he went by the Calzada de Quinea, and crossed the Douro upon rafts. That night, being the eighth, they rested at Figeruela, and more adventurers came to join him. And when my Cid was fast asleep, the Angel Gabriel appeared to him in a vision, and said, Go

on boldly and fear nothing; for everything shall go well
with thee as long as thou livest, and all the things which
thou beginnest, thou shalt bring to good end, and thou
shalt be rich and honorable. And the Cid awoke and
blessed himself; and he crossed his forehead and rose
from his bed, and knelt down and gave thanks to God for
the mercy which he had vouchsafed him, being right joyful because of the vision. Early on the morrow they set
forth; now this was the last day of the nine. And they
went on towards the Sierra de Miedes. Before sunset
the Cid halted and took account of his company; there
were three hundred lances, all with streamers, besides
foot-soldiers. And he said unto them, Now take and eat,
for we must pass this great and wild Sierra, that we may
quit the land of King Alfonso this night. To-morrow he
who seeks us may find us. So they passed the Sierra that
night.

THE CID COMES TO THE AID
OF HIS KING

Adapted by Robert Southey

AT this time it came to pass that Almofalez, a Moor of
Andalusia, rose up with the Castle of Rueda, which
was held for King Don Alfonso. And because he held
prisoner there the brother of Adefir, another Moor, Adefir
sent to the king of Castile, beseeching him to come to
succor him, and recover the castle. And the king sent
the Infante Don Ramiro his cousin, and the Infante Don
Sancho, son to the king of Navarre, and Count Don
Gonzalo Salvadores, and Count Don Nuño Alvarez, and
many other knights with them; and they came to the
castle, and Almofalez said he would not open the gates to
them, but if the king came he would open to him. And
when King Don Alfonso heard this, incontinently he
came to Rueda. And Almofalez besought him to enter to
a feast which he had prepared; howbeit the king would
not go in, neither would his people have permitted him
so to have risked his person. But the Infante Don Sancho entered, and Don Nuño, and Don Gonzalo, and
fifteen other knights; and as soon as they were within the
gate, the Moors threw down great stones upon them and
killed them all. This was the end of the good Count Don
Gonzalo Salvadores, who was so good a knight in battle
that he was called He of the Four Hands. The bodies

were ransomed, seeing that there was no remedy, the castle being so strong; and Don Gonzalo was buried in the monastery of Ona, according as he had appointed in his will; and the Infante Don Sancho with his forefathers, the kings of Navarre, in the royal monastery of Naxara.

Greatly was King Don Alfonso troubled at this villainy, and he sent for the Cid, who was in those parts; and the Cid came to him with a great company. And the king told him the great treason which had been committed, and took the Cid into his favor, and said unto him that he might return with him into Castile. My Cid thanked him for his bounty, but he said he never would accept his favor unless the king granted what he should request; and the king bade him make his demand. And my Cid demanded, that when any hidalgo should be banished, in time to come, he should have the thirty days, which were his right, allowed him, and not nine only, as had been his case; and that neither hidalgo nor citizen should be proceeded against till they had been fairly and lawfully heard; also, that the king should not go against the privileges and charters and good customs of any town or other place, nor impose taxes upon them against their right; and if he did, that it should be lawful for the land to rise against him, till he had amended the misdeed. And to all this the king accorded, and said to my Cid that he should go back into Castile with him; but my Cid said he would not go into Castile till he had won that castle of Rueda, and delivered the villainous Moors thereof into his hands, that he might do justice upon them. So the king thanked him greatly, and returned into Castile, and my Cid remained before the castle of Rueda. And he lay before it so long, and beset it so close, that the food of the Moors failed, and they had no strength to defend themselves; and they would willingly have yielded the castle, so they might have been permitted to leave it and go whither they would; but he would have their bodies, to deliver them up to the king. When they saw that it must be so, great part of them came out, and yielded themselves prisoners; and then my Cid stormed the castle, and took Almofalez and they who held with him, so that none escaped, and he sent him and his accomplices in the treason to the king. And the king was right glad when they were brought before him, and he did great justice upon them, and sent to thank my Cid for having avenged him.

After my Cid had done this good service to king Don Alfonso, he and King Zulema of Zaragoza entered Aragon, slaying, and burning, and plundering before them, and they returned to the castle of Monzon with great booty. Then the Cid went into King Abenalfange's country, and did much mischief there; and he got among the mountains of Moriella, and beat down everything before him, and destroyed the castle of Moriella. And King Zulema sent to bid him build up the ruined castle of Alcala, which is upon Moriella; and the Cid did so. But King Abenalfange being sorely grieved hereat, sent to King Pedro of Aragon, and besought him to come and help him against the Campeador. And the king of Aragon gathered together a great host in his anger, and he and the king of Denia came against my Cid, and they halted that night upon the banks of the Ebro; and King

THE CID AIDS HIS KING

Don Pedro sent letters to the Cid, bidding him leave the castle which he was then edifying. My Cid made answer, that if the king chose to pass that way in peace, he would let him pass, and show him any service in his power. And when the king of Aragon saw that he would not forsake the work, he marched against him, and attacked him. Then was there a brave battle, and many were slain; but my Cid won the day, and King Abenalfange fled, and King Don Pedro was taken prisoner, and many of his counts and knights with him. My Cid returned to Zaragoza with this great honor, taking his prisoners with him; and he set them all freely at liberty, and having tarried in Zaragoza a few days, set forth for Castile, with great riches and full of honors.

Having done all these things in his banishment, my Cid returned to Castile, and the king received him well and gave him the castle of Dueñas, and of Orcejon, and Ybia, and Campo, and Gaña, and Berviesca, and Berlanga, with all their districts. And he gave him privileges with leaden seals appendant, and confirmed with his own hand, that whatever castles, towns, and places he might win from the Moors, or from any one else, should be his own, quit and free forever, both for him and for his descendants. Thus was my Cid received into the king's favor, and he abode with him long time, doing him great services, as his lord.

HOW THE CID MADE A COWARD INTO A BRAVE MAN

Adapted by Robert Southey

AT this time Martin Pelaez the Asturian came with a convoy of laden beasts, carrying provisions to the host of the Cid; and as he passed near the town the Moors sallied out in great numbers against him; but he, though he had few with him, defended the convoy right well, and did great hurt to the Moors, slaying many of them, and drove them into the town. This Martin Pelaez who is here spoken of, did the Cid make a right good knight, of a coward, as ye shall hear. When the Cid first began to lay siege to the city of Valencia, this Martin Pelaez came unto him; he was a knight, a native of Santillana in Asturias, a hidalgo, great of body and strong of limb, a well-made man and of goodly semblance, but withal a right coward at heart, which he had shown in many places when he was among feats of arms. And the Cid was sorry when he came unto him, though he would not let him perceive this; for he knew he was not fit to be of his company. Howbeit he thought that since he was come, he would make him brave, whether he would or not. And when the Cid began to war upon the town, and sent parties against it twice and thrice a day, as ye have heard, for the Cid was alway upon the alert, there was fighting and tourneying every day. One day it fell out that the Cid and his kinsmen and friends and vassals were engaged in a great encounter, and this Martin Pelaez was well armed; and when he saw that the Moors and Christians were at it, he fled and betook himself to his lodging, and there hid himself till the Cid returned to dinner. And the Cid saw what Martin Pelaez did, and when he had conquered the Moors he returned to his lodging to dinner. Now it was the custom of the Cid to eat at a high table, seated on his bench, at the head. And Don Alvar Fañez, and Pero Bermudez, and other precious knights, ate in another part, at high tables, full honorably, and none other knights whatsoever dared take their seats with them, unless they were such as deserved to be there; and the others who were not so approved in arms ate upon *estrados*, at tables with cushions. This was the order in the house of the Cid, and every one knew the place where he was to sit at meat, and every one strove all he could to gain the honor of sitting to eat at the table of Don Alvar Fañez and his companions, by strenuously behaving himself in all feats of arms; and thus the honor of the Cid was advanced. This Martin Pelaez, thinking that none had seen his badness, washed his hands in turn with the other knights, and would have taken his place among them. And the Cid went unto him, and took him by the hand and said, You are not such a one as deserves to sit with these, for they are worth more than you or than me; but I will have you with me: and he seated him with himself at table. And he, for lack of understanding, thought that the Cid did this to honor him above all the others. On the morrow the Cid and his company rode towards

Valencia, and the Moors came out to the tourney; and Martin Pelaez went out well armed, and was among the foremost who charged the Moors, and when he was in among them he turned the reins, and went back to his lodging; and the Cid took heed to all that he did, and saw that though he had done badly he had done better than the first day. And when the Cid had driven the Moors into the town he returned to his lodging, and as he sat down to meat he took this Martin Pelaez by the hand, and seated him with himself, and bade him eat with him in the same dish, for he had deserved more that day than he had the first. And the knight gave heed to that saying, and was abashed; howbeit he did as the Cid commanded him: and after he had dined he went to his lodging and began to think upon what the Cid had said unto him, and perceived that he had seen all the baseness which he had done; and then he understood that for this cause he would not let him sit at board with the other knights who were precious in arms, but had seated him with himself, more to affront him than to do him honor, for there were other knights there better than he, and he did not show them that honor. Then resolved he in his heart to do better than he had done heretofore. Another day the Cid and his company and Martin Pelaez rode toward Valencia, and the Moors came out to the tourney full resolutely, and Martin Pelaez was among the first, and charged them right boldly; and he smote down and slew presently a good knight, and he lost there all the bad fear which he had had, and was that day one of the best knights there: and as long as the tourney lasted there he remained, smiting and slaying

and overthrowing the Moors, till they were driven within
the gates, in such manner that the Moors marveled at
him, and asked where that devil came from, for they
had never seen him before. And the Cid was in a place
where he could see all that was going on, and he gave
good heed to him, and had great pleasure in beholding
him, to see how well he had forgotten the great fear
which he was wont to have. And when the Moors were
shut up within the town, the Cid and all his people
returned to their lodging, and Martin Pelaez full leisurely and quietly went to his lodging also, like a good
knight. And when it was the hour of eating, the Cid
waited for Martin Pelaez; and when he came, and they
had washed, the Cid took him by the hand and said, My
friend, you are not such a one as deserves to sit with me
from henceforth, but sit you here with Don Alvar Fañez,
and with these other good knights, for the good feats
which you have done this day have made you a companion for them; and from that day forward he was
placed in the company of the good. And the history
saith that from that day forward this knight Martin
Pelaez was a right good one, and a right valiant, and a
right precious, in all places where he chanced among
feats of arms, and he lived alway with the Cid, and
served him right well and truly. And the history saith,
that after the Cid had won the city of Valencia, on the
day when they conquered and discomfited the king of
Seville, this Martin Pelaez was so good a one, that setting
aside the body of the Cid himself, there was no such good
knight there, nor one who bore such part, as well in the
battle as in the pursuit. And so great was the mortality

which he made among the Moors that day, that when he returned from the business the sleeves of his mail were clotted with blood, up to the elbow; insomuch that for what he did that day his name is written in this history, that it may never die. And when the Cid saw him come in that guise, he did him great honor, such as he never had done to any knight before that day, and from thenceforward gave him a place in all his actions and in all his secrets, and he was his great friend. In this knight Martin Pelaez was fulfilled the example which saith, that he who betaketh himself to a good tree, hath good shade, and he who serves a good lord winneth good guerdon; for by reason of the good service which he did the Cid, he came to such good state that he was spoken of as ye have heard: for the Cid knew how to make a good knight, as a good groom knows how to make a good horse.

HOW THE CID RULED VALENCIA

Adapted by Robert Southey

ON the following day after the Christians had taken possession of the town, the Cid entered it with a great company, and he ascended the highest tower of the wall and beheld all the city; and the Moors came unto him, and kissed his hand, saying he was welcome. And the Cid did great honor unto them. And then he gave order that all the windows of the towers which looked in upon the town should be closed up, that the Christians might not see what the Moors did in their houses; and the Moors thanked him for this greatly. And he commanded and requested the Christians that they should show great honor to the Moors, and respect them, and greet them when they met: and the Moors thanked the Cid greatly for the honor which the Christians did them, saying that they had never seen so good a man, nor one so honorable, nor one who had his people under such obedience.

Now Abeniaf thought to have the love of the Cid; and calling to mind the wrath with which he had formerly been received, because he had not taken a gift with him, he took now great riches which he had taken from those who sold bread for so great a price during the siege of Valencia, and this he carried to the Cid as a present. Among those who had sold it were some men from the islands of Majorca, and he took from them all that they had. This the Cid knew, and he would not accept his gifts. And the Cid caused proclamation to be made in the town and throughout the whole district thereof, that the honorable men and knights and castellans should assemble together in the garden of Villa Nueva, where the Cid at that time sojourned. And when they were all assembled, he went out unto them, to a place which was made ready with carpets and with mats, and he made them take their seats before him full honorably, and began to speak unto them, saying, I am a man who have never possessed a kingdom, neither I nor any man of my lineage. But the day when I first beheld this city I was well pleased therewith, and coveted it that I might be its lord; and I besought the Lord our God that he would give it me. See now what his power is, for the day when I sat down before Juballa I had no more than four loaves of bread, and now by God's mercy I have won Valencia. And if I administer right and justice here, God will let me enjoy it; but if I do evil, and demean myself proudly and wrongfully, I know that he will take it away. Now then, let every one go to his own lands, and possess them even as he was wont to have and to hold them. He who shall find his field, or his vineyard, or his garden, desert, let him incontinently enter thereon; and he who shall find his husbanded, let him pay him that hath cultivated it the cost of his labor, and of the seed which he hath sown therein, and remain with his heritage, according to the law of the Moors. Moreover, I have given order that they who collect my dues take from you no more than the tenth, because so it is appointed by the custom of the Moors, and it is what ye have been wont to pay. And I have resolved in my heart to hear your complaints two days in the week, on the Monday and the Thursday; but if causes should arise which require haste, come to me when ye will and I will give judgment, for I do not retire with women to sing and to drink, as your lords have done, so that ye could obtain no justice, but will myself see to these things, and watch over ye as friend over his friend, and kinsman over his kinsman. And I will be Cadi and Guazil, and when dispute happens among ye I will decide it. When he had said these things, they all replied that they prayed God to preserve him through long and happy years; and four of the most honorable among them rose and kissed his hands, and the Cid bade them take their seats again.

Then the Cid spake unto them and said, It is told me that Abeniaf hath done much evil, and committed great wrong toward some of ye, in that he hath taken great riches from ye to present them to me, saying, that this he did because ye sold food for a great price during the siege. But I will accept of no such gift; for if I were minded to have your riches, I could take them, and need not ask them neither from him, nor from any other; but thing so unseemly as to take that which is his from any one, without just cause, I will not do. They who have gotten wealth thus, God hath given it them; let them go to Abeniaf, and take back what he hath forced from them, for I will order him to restore the whole. Then he said, Ye see the riches which I took from the messengers who went to Murcia; it is mine by right, for I took it in war because they brake the covenant which they had made, and would have deceived me: nevertheless I will restore it to the uttermost farthing, that nothing thereof shall be lost. And ye shall do homage to me that ye will not withdraw yourselves, but will abide here, and do my bidding in all things, and never depart from the covenant which ye make with me; for I love ye, and am grieved to think of the great evil and misery which ye endured from the great famine, and of the mortality which there was. And if ye had done that before which ye have done now, ye would not have been brought to these sufferings and have bought the *cafiz* of wheat at a thousand *maravedis;* but I trust in God to bring it to one *maravedi.* Be ye now secure in your lands, and till your fields, and rear cattle; for I have given order to my men that they offer ye no wrong, neither enter into the town to buy nor to sell; but that they carry on all their dealings in Alcudia, and this I do that ye may receive no displeasure. Moreover I command them not to take any captive into the town, but if this should be done, lay ye hands on the captive and set him free, without fear, and if any one should resist, kill him and fear not. I myself will not enter your city nor dwell therein, but I will build me a place beside the bridge of Alcantara, where I may go and disport myself at times, and repair when it is needful. When he had said these things he bade them go their way.

Well pleased were the Moors when they departed from him, and they marveled at the greatness of his promises, and they set their hearts at rest, and put away the fear which they had had, thinking all their troubles were over; for in all the promises which the Cid had made unto them, they believed that he spake truth; but he said these things only to quiet them, and to make them come to what he wished, even as came to pass. And when he had done, he sent his Almoxarife, Abdalla Adiz, to the custom house, and made him appoint men to collect the rents of the town for him, which was done accordingly. And when the Cid had given order concerning his own affairs at his pleasure, the Moors would fain have entered again into possession of their heritages as he told them; but they found it all otherwise, for of all the fields which the Christians had husbanded, they would not yield up one; albeit they let them enter upon such as were left waste: some said that the Cid had given them the lands that year, instead of their pay, and other some that they rented them and had paid rent for the year. So the Moors, seeing this, waited till Thursday, when the Cid was to hear complaints, as he had said unto them. When Thursday came all the honorable men went to the garden, but the Cid sent to say unto them that he could not come out that day, because of other causes which he had to determine; and he desired that they would go their way for that time, and come again on the Monday: this was to show his mastery. And when it was Monday they assembled again in the garden, and the Cid came out to them, and took his seat upon the *estrado*, and the Moors made their complaint. And when he had heard them he began to make similitudes, and offer reasons which were not like those which he had spoken the first day; for he said to them, I ask of ye, whether it is well that I should be left without men? or if I were without them, I should be like unto one who hath lost his right arm, or to a bird that hath no wings, or to one who should do battle and hath neither spear nor sword. The first thing which I have to look to is to the well-being of my people, that they may live in wealth and honor, so that they may be able to serve me, and defend my honor: for since it has pleased God to give me the city of Valencia, I will not that there be any other lord here than me. Therefore I say unto you and command you, if you would be well with me, and would that I should show favor unto you, that ye see how to deliver that traitor Abeniaf into my hands. Ye all know the great treason which he committed upon King Yahia, his lord and yours, how he slew him, and the misery which he brought upon you in the siege; and since it is not fitting that a traitor who hath slain his lord should live among you, and that his treason should be confounded with your loyalty, see to the obeyment of my command.

When the honorable Moors heard this, they were dismayed; verily they knew that he spake truth touching the death of the king, but it troubled them that he departed from the promise which he had made; and they made answer that they would take counsel concerning what he had said, and then reply. Then five of the best and most honorable among them withdrew, and went to Abdalla Adiz, and said unto him, Areed us thy reed now the best and truest that thou canst, for thou art of our law, and oughtest to do this: and the reason why we ask counsel of thee is this. The Cid promised us many things, and now behold he says nothing to us of what he said before, but moveth other new reasons, at which great dismay hath seized us. And because thou better knowest his ways, tell us now what is his pleasure, for albeit we might wish to do otherwise; this is not a time wherein anything but what he shall command can be done. When the Almoxarife heard this he made answer, Good men, it is easy to understand what he would have, and to do what should be done. We all know the great treason which Abeniaf committed against ye all in killing your lord the king; for albeit at that time ye felt the burden of the Christians, yet was it nothing so great as after he had killed him, neither did ye suffer such misery. And since God hath brought him who was the cause to this state, see now by all means how ye may deliver him into the hands of the Cid. And fear not, neither take thought for the rest; for though the Cid may do his pleasure in some things, better is it to have him for lord than this traitor who hath brought so much evil upon ye. Moreover the things of this world soon pass away, and my heart tells me that we shall ere long come out of the bondage of the Cid, and of the Christians; for the Cid is well-nigh at the full of his days, and we who remain alive after his death shall then be masters of our city. When the good men heard what he said, they thanked him much, and held themselves to be well advised, and said that they would do willingly what he bade them; and they returned forthwith to the Cid, and said unto him that they would fulfill his commandment. Incontinently did the good men dispeed themselves of the Cid, and they went into the city, and gathered together a great posse of armed men, and went to the place where Abeniaf dwelt; and they assaulted the house and brake the doors, and entered in and laid hands on him, and his son, and all his company, and carried them before the Cid. And the Cid ordered Abeniaf to be cast into prison.

and all those who had taken counsel with him for the death of King Yahia.

When this was done, the Cid said unto the good men, Now that ye have fulfilled my bidding, I hold it good to show favor unto you in that which ye yourselves shall understand to be fitting for me to grant. Say therefore what ye would have, and I will do that which I think behooveth me: but in this manner, that my dwelling-place be within the city of Valencia, in the Alcazar, and that my Christian men have all the fortresses in the city. And when the good men heard this, they were greatly troubled; howbeit they dissembled the sorrow which they resented, and said unto him, Sir Cid, order it as you think good, and we consent thereto. Then said he unto them that he would observe towards them all the uses and customs of their law, and that he would have the power, and be lord of all; and they should till their fields and feed their flocks and herds, and give him his tenth, and he would take no more. When the Moors heard this they were well pleased; and since they were to remain in the town, and in their houses and their inheritances, and with their uses and customs, and that their mosques were to be left them, they held themselves not to be badly off. Then they asked the Cid to let their Guazil be the same as he had first appointed, and that he would give them for their Cadi the Alfaqui Alhagi, and let him appoint whom he would to assist him in distributing justice to the Moors; and thus he himself would be relieved of the wearisomeness of hearing them, save only when any great occasion might befall. This Alhagi was he who made the lamentation for Valencia, as ye have

heard; and when the Cid was peaceably established in
Valencia, he was converted, and the Cid made him a
Christian. And the Cid granted this which they required, and they kissed his hand, and returned into the
town. Nine months did the Cid hold Valencia besieged, and at the end of that time it fell into his power,
and he obtained possession of the walls, as ye have heard.
And one month he was practicing with the Moors that he
might keep them quiet, till Abeniaf was delivered into
his hands; and thus ten months were fulfilled, and they
were fulfilled on Thursday, the last day of June, in the
year of the æra one thousand one hundred and thirty
and one, which was in the year one thousand ninety and
three of the incarnation of our Lord Jesus Christ. And
when the Cid had finished all his dealings with the
Moors, on this day he took horse with all his company in
good array, his banner being carried before him, and
his arms behind; and in this guise, with great rejoicings
he entered the city of Valencia. And he alighted at the
Alcazar, and gave order to lodge all his men round about
it; and he bade them plant his banner upon the highest
tower of the Alcazar. Glad was the Campeador, and
all they who were with him, when they saw his banner
planted in that place. And from that day forth was the
Cid possessed of all the castles and fortresses which were
in the kingdom of Valencia, and established in what
God had given him, and he and all his people rejoiced.

THE MARRIAGE OF THE CID'S TWO DAUGHTERS TO THE IN- FANTES OF CARRION

Adapted by Robert Southey

WHEN the Infantes of Carrion, Diego Gonzalez and Ferrando Gonzalez, saw the noble present which the Cid had sent unto the king, and heard how his riches and power daily increased, and thought what his wealth must needs be when he had given those horses out of the fifth of one battle, and moreover that he was lord of Valencia, they spake one with the other, and agreed, that if the Cid would give them his daughters to wife, they should be well married, and become rich and honorable. And they agreed together that they would talk with the king in private upon this matter. And they went presently to him, and said, Sir, we beseech you of your bounty to help us in a thing which will be to your honor; for we are your vassals, and the richer we are the better able shall we be to serve you. And the king asked of them what it was they would have, and they then told him their desire. And the king thought upon it awhile, and then came to them, and said, Infantes, this thing which you ask lies not in me, but in the Cid; for it is in his power to marry his daughters, and peradventure he will not do it as yet. Nevertheless, that ye may not fail for want of my help, I will send to tell him what ye wish. Then they

kissed his hand for this favor. And the king sent for
Alvar Fañez and Pero Bermudez, and went apart with
them, and praised the Cid, and thanked him for the
good-will which he had to do him service, and said that
he had great desire to see him. Say to him, he said, that
I beseech him to come and meet me, for I would speak
with him concerning something which is to his good and
honor. Diego and Ferrando, the Infantes of Carrion,
have said unto me that they would fain wed with his
daughters, if it seemeth good to him; and methinks this
would be a good marriage. When Alvar Fañez and Pero
Bermudez heard this, they answered the king, and said,
Certain we are, sir, that neither in this, nor in anything
else will the Cid do aught but what you, sir, shall command or advise. When ye have your meeting, ye will
agree concerning it as is best. Then they kissed his
hand, and took their leave.

On the morrow the messengers of the Cid departed
from Valladolid, and took their way towards Valencia;
and when the Cid knew that they were nigh at hand
he went out to meet them, and when he saw them he
waxed joyful; and he embraced them, and asked what
tidings of his Lord Alfonso. And they told him how they
had sped, and how greatly the king loved him; and when
we departed, said they, he bade us beseech you to come
and meet him anywhere where you will appoint, for he
desireth to speak with you, concerning the marriage of
your daughters with the Infantes of Carrion, if it should
please you so to bestow them: now by what the king said,
it seemeth unto us that this marriage pleaseth him. And
when the Cid heard this he became thoughtful, and he

said to them after awhile, What think ye of this marriage? And they answered him, Even as it shall please you. And he said to them, I was banished from my own country, and was dishonored, and with hard labor gained I what I have got; and now I stand in the king's favor, and he asketh of me my daughters for the Infantes of Carrion. They are of high blood and full orgulous, and I have no liking to this match; but if our lord the king adviseth it we can do no otherwise: we will talk of this, and God send it for the best. So they entered Valencia, and the Cid spake with Doña Ximena touching this matter, and when she heard it it did not please her; nevertheless she said, if the king thought it good they could do no otherwise. Then the Cid gave order to write letters to the king, saying, that he would meet the king as he commanded, and whatever the king wished that he would do. And he sealed the letters well, and sent two knights with them. And when the king saw the letters he was well pleased, and sent others to say that the time of their meeting should be three weeks after he received these letters, and the place appointed was upon the Tagus, which is a great river.

Now began they to prepare on both sides for this meeting. He who should relate to you the great preparations, and the great nobleness which were made for the nonce, would have much to recount. Who ever saw in Castile so many a precious mule, and so many a good-going palfrey, and so many great horses, and so many goodly streamers set upon goodly spears, and shields adorned with gold and with silver, and mantles, and skins, and rich sendals of Adria? The king sent great store of food to the banks of the Tagus, where the place of meeting was appointed. Glad were the Infantes of Carrion, and richly did they bedight themselves; some things they paid for, and some they went in debt for: great was their company, and with the king there were many Leonese and Galegos, and Castilians out of number. My Cid the Campeador made no tarriance in Valencia; he made ready for the meeting: there was many a great mule, and many a palfrey, and many a good horse, and many a goodly suit of arms, cloaks, and mantles both of cloth and of peltry; . . . great and little are all clad in colors. Alvar Fañez Minaya, and Pero Bermudez, and Martin Munoz, and Martin Antolinez that worthy Burgalese, and the Bishop Don Hieronymo that good one with the shaven crown, and Alvar Alvarez, and Alvar Salvadores, and Muño Gustios that knight of prowess, and Galind Garcia of Aragon; all these and all the others made ready to go with the Cid. But he bade Alvar Salvadores and Galind Garcia, and all those who were under them, remain and look with heart and soul to the safety of Valencia, and not open the gates of the Alcazar neither by day nor by night, for his wife and daughters were there, in whom he had his heart and soul, and the other ladies with them; he, like a good husband, gave order that not one of them should stir out of the Alcazar till he returned. Then they left Valencia and pricked on more than apace; more than a thousand knights, all ready for war, were in this company. All those great horses that paced so well and were so soft of foot, my Cid won; they were not given to him.

King Don Alfonso arrived first by one day at the place of meeting, and when he heard that the Cid was at hand, he went out with all his honorable men, more than a long league to meet him. When he who was born in a good hour had his eye upon the king, he bade his company halt, and with fifteen of the knights whom he loved best he alighted, and put his hands and his knees to the ground, and took the herbs of the field between his teeth, as if he would have eaten them, weeping for great joy; . . . thus did he know how to humble himself before Alfonso his lord; and in this manner he approached his feet and would have kissed them. And the king drew back and said, The hand, Cid Campeador, not the foot! And the Cid drew nigh upon his knees and besought grace, saying, In this guise grant me your love, so that all present may hear. And the king said that he forgave him, and granted him his love with his heart and soul. And the Cid kissed both his hands, being still upon his knees; and the king embraced him, and gave him the kiss of peace. Well pleased were all they who beheld this, save only Alvar Diez and Garcia Ordoñez, for they did not love the Cid. Then went they all toward the town, the king and the Cid talking together by the way. And the Cid asked the king to eat with him, and the king answered, Not so, for ye are not prepared; we arrived yesterday, and ye but now. Eat you and your company therefore with me, for we have made ready. To-day, Cid Campeador, you are my guest, and to-morrow we will do as pleases you. Now came the Infantes of Carrion up and humbled themselves before the Cid, and he received them well, and they promised to do him service. And the company of the Cid came up, and kissed the king's hand. So they alighted and went to meat; and the king said unto the Cid that he should eat with him at his table; howbeit he would not. And when the king saw that he would not take his seat with him, he ordered a high table to be placed for the Cid and for Count Don Gonzalo, the father of the Infantes of Carrion. All the while that they ate the king could never look enough at the Cid, and he marveled greatly at his beard, that it had grown to such length. And when they had eaten they were merry, and took their pleasure. And on the morrow the king and all they who went with him to this meeting, ate with the Cid; and so well did he prepare for them that all were full joyful, and agreed in one thing, that they had not eaten better for three years. There was not a man there who did not eat upon silver, and the king and the chief persons ate upon dishes and trenchers of gold. And when the Infantes saw this, they had the marriage more at heart than before.

On the morrow as soon as it was day, the Bishop Don Hieronymo sung mass before the king, in the oratory of the Cid; and when it was over, the king said before all who were there assembled, Counts and Infanzones and knights, hear what I shall say unto the Cid. Cid Ruydiez, the reason wherefore I sent for you to this meeting was twofold: first, that I might see you, which I greatly desired; for I love you much because of the many and great services which you have done me, albeit that at one time I was wroth against you and banished you from the land. But you so demeaned yourself that you never did me disservice, but contrariwise, great service both to God and to me and have won Valencia, and enlarged Christendom; wherefore I am bound to show favor unto you and to love you alway. The second reason was that I might ask you for your two daughters, Doña Elvira and Doña Sol, that you would give them in marriage to the Infantes of Carrion, for this methinks would be a fit marriage, and to your honor and good. When the Cid heard this, he was in a manner bound to consent, having them thus demanded from him; and he answered and said, Sir, my daughters are of tender years and if it might please you, they are yet too young for marriage. I do not say this as if the Infantes of Carrion were not worthy to match with them, and with better than they. And the king bade him make no excuse, saying that he should esteem himself well served if he gave his consent. Then the Cid said, Sir, I begat them, and you give them in marriage; both I and they are yours; . . . give them to whom you please, and I am pleased therewith. When the king heard this he was well pleased, and he bade the Infantes kiss the hand of the Cid Campeador, and incontinently they changed swords before the king, and they did homage to him, as sons-in-law to their father-in-law. Then the king turned to the Cid, and said, I thank thee, Ruydiez, that thou hast given me thy daughters for the Infantes of Carrion: and here I give them to the Infantes to be their brides; I give them and not you, and I pray God that it may please him, and that you also may have great joy herein. The Infantes I put into your hands: they will go with you, and I shall return from hence; and I order that three hundred marks of silver be given to them for their marriage, and they and your daughters will all be your children.

Eight days this meeting lasted; the one day they dined with the king, and the other with the Cid. Then was it appointed that on the morrow at sunrise every one should depart to his own home. My Cid then began to give to every one who would take his gifts, many a great mule, and many a good palfrey, and many a rich garment, . . . every one had what he asked, . . . he said no to none. Threescore horses did my Cid give away in gifts; well pleased were all they who went to that meeting. And now they were about to separate, for it was night. The king took the Infantes by the hand, and delivered them into the power of my Cid the Campeador, . . . See here your sons: from this day, Campeador, you will know what to make of them. And the Cid answered, Sir, may it please you, seeing it is you who have made this marriage for my daughters, to appoint some one to whom I may deliver them, and who may give them, as from your hand, to the Infantes. And the king called for Alvar Fañez Minaya, and said, You are sib to the damsels: I command you, when you come to Valencia, to take them with your own hands, and give them to the Infantes, as I should do if that I were there present: and be you the bride's father. Then said the Cid, Sir, you must accept something from me at this meeting. I bring for you twenty palfreys, these that are gayly trapped, and thirty horses fleet of foot, these that are well caparisoned, . . . take them, and I kiss your hand. Greatly have you bound me, said King Don Alfonso; I receive this gift, and God and all saints grant that it may well be requited; if I live, you shall have something from me. Then my Cid sprung up upon his horse Bavieca, and he said, Here I say before my lord the king, that if any will go with me to the wedding, I think they will get something by it! and he besought the king that he would let as many go with him as were so minded; and the king licensed them accordingly. And when they were about to part, the company that went with the Cid was greater than that which returned with the king. And the Cid kissed the king's hand and dispeeded himself with his favor, and the king returned to Castile.

My Cid went his way toward Valencia, and he appointed Pero Bermudez and Muño Gustios, than whom there were no better two in all his household, to keep company with the Infantes of Carrion and be their guard, and he bade them spy out what their conditions were; and this they soon found out. The Count Don Suero Gonzalez went with the Infantes; he was their father's brother, and had been their *Ayo* and bred them up, and badly had he trained them, for he was a man of great words, good of tongue, and of nothing else good; and full scornful and orgulous had he made them, so that the Cid was little pleased with them, and would willingly have broken off the marriage; but he could not, seeing that the king had made it. And when they reached Valencia, the Cid lodged the Infantes in the suburb of Alcudia, where he had formerly lodged himself; and all the company who were come to the marriage were quartered with them. And he went to the Alcazar.

On the morrow the Cid mounted his horse and rode

into Alcudia, and brought the Infantes his sons in-law
from thence with him into the city to the Alcazar, that
they might see their brides Doña Elvira and Doña Sol.
Doña Ximena had her daughters ready to receive them
in full noble garments, for since midnight they had done
nothing but prink and prank themselves. Full richly
was the Alcazar set out that day, with hangings both
above and below, purple and samite, and rich cloth.
The Cid entered between the Infantes, and all that
noble company went in after them; and they went into
the chief hall of the Alcazar, where Doña Ximena was
with her daughters; and when they saw the Cid and the
Infantes, they rose up and welcomed them right well.
And the Cid took his seat upon his bench, with one of
the Infantes on one side of him and one on the other,
and the other honorable men seated themselves on the
estrados, each in the place where he ought to be, and
which belonged to him; and they remained awhile silent.
Then the Cid rose and called for Alvar Fañez and said,
Thou knowest what my lord the king commanded; fulfill
now his bidding; . . . take thy cousins, and deliver
them to the Infantes, for it is the king who gives them
in marriage, and not I. And Alvar Fañez arose and
took the damsels one in each hand, and delivered them
to the Infantes, saying, Diego Gonzalez, and Ferrando
Gonzalez, I deliver unto you these damsels, the daughters of the Cid Campeador, by command of King Don
Alfonso my lord, even as he commanded. Receive you
them as your equal holpmates, as the law of Christ
enjoineth. And the Infantes took each his bride by the
hand, and went to the Cid and kissed his hand; and the

same did they to their mother, Doña Ximena Gomez:
and the Bishop Don Hieronymo espoused them, and
they exchanged rings. When this was done, the Cid
went and seated himself on the *estrado* with the ladies, he
and Doña Ximena in the middle, and beside him he
placed Doña Elvira his eldest daughter, and by her, her
spouse the Infante Diego Gonzalez; and Doña Sol was
seated on the other side, by her mother, and the Infante
Ferrando by her. And when they had solaced themselves awhile, the Cid said that now they would go eat,
and that the marriage should be performed on the morrow; and he besought and commanded the Bishop Don
Hieronymo to perform it in such a manner that no cost
should be spared, but that everything should be done
so completely, that they who came from Castile to this
wedding might alway have something to tell of.

On the morrow they went to the church of St. Mary,
and there the Bishop Don Hieronymo sat awaiting them,
and he blessed them all four at the altar. Who can
tell the great nobleness which the Cid displayed at that
wedding, the feasts and the bull-fights, and the throwing
at the target, and the throwing canes, and how many
joculars were there, and all the sports which are proper
at such weddings? As soon as they came out of church
they took horse and rode to the Glera; three times did the
Cid change his horse that day; seven targets were set up
on the morrow, and before they went to dinner all seven
were broken. Fifteen days did the feasts at this wedding
continue; then all they who had come there to do honor
to the Cid took leave of him and of the Infantes. Who
can tell the great and noble gifts which the Cid gave to

them, both to great and little, each according to his quality, vessels of gold and silver, rich cloth, cloaks, furs, horses, and money beyond all reckoning, so that all were well pleased. And when it was told in Castile with what gifts they who had been to the wedding were returned, many were they who repented that they had not gone there.

THE TRIAL BY SWORDS

Adapted by Robert Southey

NOW King Alfonso misdoubted the Infantes of Carrion that they would not appear at the time appointed, and therefore he said that he would go to Carrion, and the battle should be fought there. And he took with him the counts whom he had appointed alcaldes, and Pero Bermudez and Martin Antolinez and Muño Gustioz went with the Count Don Remond, to whose charge the king had given them. And on the third day after the Cid departed from Toledo the king set forth for Carrion; but it so chanced that he fell sick upon the road, and could not arrive within the three weeks, so that the term was enlarged to five. And when the king's health was restored he proceeded and reached Carrion, and gave order that the combat should be performed, and appointed the day, and named the plain of Carrion for the place thereof. And the Infantes came there with a great company of all their friends and kindred, for their kinsmen were many and powerful; and they all came with one accord, that if before the battle they could find any cause they would kill the knights of the Cid: nevertheless, though they had determined upon this, they dared not put it in effect, because they stood in fear of the king.

And when the night came of which the morrow was appointed for the combat, they on one side and on the other kept vigil in the churches, each in that church to which he had the most devotion. Night is passed away, and the dawn is now breaking; and at daybreak a great multitude was assembled in the field, and many Ricos-omes came there for the pleasure which they would have in seeing this battle, and the king sent and commanded the champions to make ready. Moreover he made the two counts his sons-in-law, Don Anrrich and Don Remond, and the other counts and their people, arm themselves and keep the field, that the kinsmen of the Infantes might not make a tumult there. Who can tell the great dole and sorrow of Count Gonzalo Gonzalez for his sons the Infantes of Carrion, because they had to do battle this day! and in the fullness of his heart he cursed the day and the hour in which he was born, for his heart divined the sorrow which he was to have for his children. Great was the multitude which was assembled from all Spain to behold this battle. And there in the field near the lists the champions of the Cid armed themselves on one side, and the Infantes on the other. And Count Don Remond armed the knights of the Cid, and instructed them how to do their devoir, and Count Garci Ordoñez helped arm the Infantes of Carrion and their uncle Suero Gonzalez, and they sent to ask the king of his favor that he would give command that the swords Colada and Tizona should not be used in that combat. But the king would not, and he answered that each must take the best sword and the best arms that he could, save only that the one should not have more than the other. Greatly were they troubled at this reply, and greatly did they fear those good swords, and repent that they had taken them to the Cortes of

Toledo. And from that hour the Infantes and Suero Gonzalez bewrayed in their countenances that they thought ill of what they had done, and happy men would they have thought themselves if they had not committed that great villainy, and he if he had not counseled it; and gladly would they have given all that they had in Carrion so it could now have been undone.

And the king went to the place where the Infantes were arming, and said unto them, If ye feared these swords ye should have said so in the Cortes of Toledo, for that was the place, and not this; . . . there is now nothing to be done but to defend yourselves stoutly, as ye have need, against those with whom ye have to do. Then went he to the knights of the Cid, whom he found armed; and they kissed his hand and said unto him, Sir, the Cid hath left us in your hand, and we beseech you see that no wrong be done us in this place, where the Infantes of Carrion have their party; and by God's mercy we will do ourselves right upon them. And the king bade them have no fear for that. Then their horses were brought, and they crossed the saddles, and mounted, with their shields hanging from the neck; and they took their spears, each of which had its streamer, and with many good men round about they went to the lists; and on the other side the Infantes and Count Suero Gonzalez came up with a great company of their friends and kinsmen and vassals. And the king said with a loud voice, Hear what I say, Infantes of Carrion! . . . this combat I would have had waged in Toledo, but ye said that ye were not ready to perform it there, and therefore I am come to this which is your native place, and have brought the knights of the Cid with me. They are come here under my safeguard. Let not therefore you nor your kinsmen deceive yourselves, thinking to overpower them by tumult, or in any other way than by fair combat; for whosoever shall begin a tumult, I have given my people orders to cut him in pieces upon the spot, and no inquiry shall be made touching the death of him who shall so have offended. Full sorrowful were the Infantes of Carrion for this command which the king had given. And the king appointed twelve knights who were hidalgos to be true-men and place the combatants in the lists, and show them the bounds at what point they were to win or to be vanquished, and to divide the sun between them. And he went with a wand in his hand, and saw them placed on both sides; then he went out of the lists, and gave command that the people should fall back, and not approach within seven spears' length of the lines of the lists.

Now were the six combatants left alone in the lists, and each of them knew now with whom he had to do battle. And they laced their helmets, and put shield upon the arm, and laid lance in rest. And the knights of my Cid advanced against the Infantes of Carrion, and they on their part against the champions of the Campeador. Each bent down with his face to the saddle-bow, and gave his horse the spur. And they met all six with such a shock, that they who looked on expected to see them all fall dead. Pero Bermudez and Ferrando Gonzalez encountered, and the shield of Pero Bermudez was pierced, but the spear passed through on one side, and hurt him not, and brake in two places; and he sat firm in his seat. One blow he received, but he gave another; he drove his lance through Ferrando's shield, at his breast, so that nothing availed him. Ferrando's breastplate was threefold; two plates the spear went clean through, and drove the third in before it, with the *velmez* and the shirt, into the breast, near his heart; . . . and the girth and the poitrel of his horse burst, and he and the saddle went together over the horse's heels, and the spear in him, and all thought him dead. Howbeit Ferrando Gonzalez rose, and the blood began to run out of his mouth, and Pero Bermudez drew his sword and went against him; but when he saw the sword Tizona over him, before he received a blow from it, he cried out that he confessed himself conquered, and that what Pero Bermudez had said against him was true. And when Pero Bermudez heard this he stood still, and the twelve true-men came up and heard his confession, and pronounced him vanquished. This Ferrando did thinking to save his life; but the wound which he had got was mortal.

Martin Antolinez and Diego Gonzalez brake their lances on each other, and laid hand upon their swords. Martin Antolinez drew forth Colada, the brightness of which flashed over the whole field, for it was a marvelous sword; and in their strife he dealt him a backhanded blow which sheared off the crown of his helmet, and cut away hood and coif, and the hair of his head and the skin also: this stroke he dealt him with the precious Colada. And Diego Gonzalez was sorely dismayed therewith, and though he had his own sword in his hand he could not for very fear make use of it, but he turned his horse and fled; and Martin Antolinez went after him, and dealt him another with the flat part of the sword, for he missed him with the edge; and the Infante began to cry out aloud, Great God, help me and save me from that sword! And he rode away as fast as he could, and Martin Antolinez called out after him, Get out, Don Traitor! and drove him out of the lists, and remained conqueror.

Muño Gustioz and Suero Gonzalez dealt each other such strokes with their spears as it was marvelous to behold. And Suero Gonzalez, being a right hardy knight and a strong, and of great courage, struck the shield of Muño Gustioz and pierced it through and through; but the stroke was given aslant, so that it passed on and touched him not. Muño Gustioz lost his stirrups with that stroke, but he presently recovered them, and dealt him such a stroke in return that it went clean through the midst of the shield, and through all his armor, and came out between his ribs, missing the heart; then laying hand on him he wrenched him out of the saddle, and threw him down as he drew the spear out of his body; and the point of the spear and the haft and the streamer all came out red. Then all the beholders thought that he was stricken to death. And Muño Gustioz turned to smite again. But when Gonzalo Ansures his father saw this, he cried out aloud for great ruth which he had for his son, and said, For God's sake do not strike him again, for he is vanquished. And Muño Gustioz, like a man of good understanding, asked the true-men whether he were to be held as conquered for what his father said, and they said not, unless he confirmed it with his own mouth.

And Muño Gustioz turned again to Suero Gonzalez where he lay wounded, and lifted his spear against him; and Suero Gonzalez cried out, Strike me not, for I am vanquished. And the judges said it was enough, and that the combat was at an end.

Then the king entered the lists, and many good knights and hidalgos with him, and he called the twelve true-men, and asked them if the knights of the Cid had aught more to do to prove their accusation; and they made answer that the knights of the Cid had won the field and done their devoir; and all the hidalgos who were there present made answer, that they said true. And King Don Alfonso lifted up his voice and said, Hear me, all ye who are here present: inasmuch as the knights of the Cid have conquered, they have won the cause; and the twelve true-men made answer, that what the king said was the truth, and all the people said the same. And the king gave command to break up the lists, and gave sentence that the Infantes of Carrion and their uncle, Suero Gonzalez, were notorious traitors, and ordered his seneschal to take their arms and horses. And from that day forth their lineage never held up its head, nor was of any worth in Castile; and they and their uncle fled away, having been thus vanquished and put to shame. And thus it was that Carrion fell to the king after the days of Gonzalo Gonzalez, the father of the Infantes. Great was their shame, and the like or worse betide him who abuseth fair lady, and then leaveth her.

THE CID'S LAST VICTORY

Adapted by Robert Southey

THREE days after the Cid had departed King Bucar came into the port of Valencia, and landed with all his power, which was so great that there is not a man in the world who could give account of the Moors whom he brought. And there came with him thirty and six kings, and one Moorish queen, who was a negress, and she brought with her two hundred horsewomen, all negresses like herself, all having their hair shorn save a tuft on the top, and this was in token that they came as if upon a pilgrimage, and to obtain the remission of their sins; and they were all armed in coats of mail and with Turkish bows. King Bucar ordered his tents to be pitched round about Valencia, and Abenalfarax, who wrote this history in Arabic, saith that there were full fifteen thousand tents; and he bade that Moorish negress with her archers to take their station near the city. And on the morrow they began to attack the city, and they fought against it three days strenuously; and the Moors received great loss, for they came blindly up to the walls and were slain there. And the Christians defended themselves right well; and every time that they went upon the walls, they sounded trumpets and tambours, and made great rejoicings, as the Cid had commanded. This continued for eight days or nine, till the companions of the Cid had

405

made ready everything for their departure, as he had commanded. And King Bucar and his people thought that the Cid dared not come out against them; and they were the more encouraged, and began to think of making bastiles and engines wherewith to combat the city, for certes they weened that the Cid Ruydiez dared not come out against them, seeing that he tarried so long.

All this while the company of the Cid were preparing all things to go into Castile, as he had commanded before his death; and his trusty Gil Diaz did nothing else but labor at this. And the body of the Cid was prepared after this manner: first it was embalmed and anointed as the history hath already recounted, and the virtue of the balsam and myrrh was such that the flesh remained firm and fair, having its natural color, and his countenance as it was wont to be, and the eyes open, and his long beard in order, so that there was not a man who would have thought him dead if he had seen him and not known it. And on the second day after he had departed, Gil Diaz placed the body upon a right noble saddle, and this saddle with the body upon it he put upon a frame; and he dressed the body in a *gambax* of fine sendal, next the skin. And he took two boards and fitted them to the body, one to the breast and the other to the shoulders; these were so hollowed out and fitted that they met at the sides and under the arms, and the hind one came up to the pole, and the other up to the beard; and these boards were fastened into the saddle, so that the body could not move. All this was done by the morning of the twelfth day; and all that day the people of the Cid were busied in making ready their arms, and in loading beasts with all that they

THEN CAME THE BODY OF THE CID WITH AN HUNDRED KNIGHTS

had, so that they left nothing of any price in the whole city of Valencia, save only the empty houses. When it was midnight they took the body of the Cid, fastened to the saddle as it was, and placed it upon his horse Bavieca, and fastened the saddle well; and the body sat so upright and well that it seemed as if he was alive. And it had on painted hose of black and white, so cunningly painted that no man who saw them would have thought but that they were grieves and cuishes, unless he had laid his hand upon them; and they put on it a surcoat of green sendal, having his arms blazoned thereon, and a helmet of parchment, which was cunningly painted that every one might have believed it to be iron; and his shield was hung round his neck, and they placed the sword Tizona in his hand, and they raised his arm, and fastened it up so subtilely that it was a marvel to see how upright he held the sword. And the Bishop Don Hieronymo went on one side of him, and the trusty Gil Diaz on the other, and he led the horse Bavieca, as the Cid had commanded him. And when all this had been made ready, they went out from Valencia at midnight, through the gate of Roseros, which is towards Castile. Pero Bermudez went first with the banner of the Cid, and with him five hundred knights who guarded it, all well appointed. And after these came all the baggage. Then came the body of the Cid, with an hundred knights, all chosen men, and behind them Doña Ximena with all her company, and six hundred knights in the rear. All these went out so silently, and with such a measured pace, that it seemed as if there were only a score. And by the time that they had all gone out it was broad day.

Now Alvar Fañez Minaya had set the host in order, and while the Bishop Don Hieronymo and Gil Diaz led away the body of the Cid, and Doña Ximena, and the baggage, he fell upon the Moors. First he attacked the tents of that Moorish queen the negress, who lay nearest to the city; and this onset was so sudden, that they killed full a hundred and fifty Moors before they had time to take arms or go to horse. But that Moorish negress was so skillful in drawing the Turkish bow, that it was held for a marvel; and it is said that they called her in Arabic *Nugueymat Turya*, which is to say, the Star of the Archers. And she was the first that got on horseback, and with some fifty that were with her, did some hurt to the company of the Cid; but in fine they slew her, and her people fled to the camp. And so great was the uproar and confusion, that few there were who took arms, but instead thereof they turned their backs and fled toward the sea. And when King Bucar and his kings saw this, they were astonished. And it seemed to them that there came against them on the part of the Christians full seventy thousand knights, all as white as snow: and before them a knight of great stature upon a white horse with a bloody cross, who bore in one hand a white banner, and in the other a sword which seemed to be of fire, and he made a great mortality among the Moors who were flying. And King Bucar and the other kings were so greatly dismayed that they never checked the reins till they had ridden into the sea; and the company of the Cid rode after them, smiting and slaying and giving them no respite; and they smote down so many that it was marvelous, for the Moors did not turn their heads to defend

408

themselves. And when they came to the sea, so great
was the press among them to get to the ships, that more
than ten thousand died in the water. And of the six
and thirty kings, twenty and two were slain. And King
Bucar and they who escaped with him hoisted sails
and went their way, and never more turned their heads.
Then Alvar Fañez and his people, when they had discomfited the Moors, spoiled the field, and the spoil
thereof was so great that they could not carry it away.
And they loaded camels and horses with the noblest
things which they found, and went after the bishop Don
Hieronymo and Gil Diaz, who, with the body of the Cid,
and Doña Ximena, and the baggage, had gone on till
they were clear of the host, and then waited for those who
were gone against the Moors. And so great was the spoil
of that day, that there was no end to it: and they took up
gold, and silver, and other precious things as they rode
through the camp, so that the poorest man among the
Christians, horseman or on foot, became rich with what
he won that day.

THE BURIAL OF THE CID

Adapted by Robert Southey

ON the third day after the coming of King Don Alfonso, they would have interred the body of the Cid; but when the king heard what Doña Ximena had said, that while it was so fair and comely it should not be laid in a coffin, he held that what she said was good. And he sent for the ivory chair which had been carried to the Cortes of Toledo, and gave order that it should be placed on the right of the altar of St. Peter; and he laid a cloth of gold upon it, and upon that placed a cushion covered with a right noble *tartari*, and he ordered a graven tabernacle to be made over the chair, richly wrought with azure and gold, having thereon the blazonry of the kings of Castile and Leon, and the king of Navarre, and the Infante of Aragon, and of the Cid Ruydiez the Campeador. And he himself, and the king of Navarre, and the Infante of Aragon, and the Bishop Don Hieronymo, to do honor to the Cid, helped to take his body from between the two boards, in which it had been fastened at Valencia. And when they had taken it out, the body was so firm that it bent not on either side, and the flesh so firm and comely, that it seemed as if he were yet alive. And the king thought that what they purported to do and had thus begun, might full well be effected. And they clad the body in a full noble *tartari*, and in cloth of purple, which the Soldan of Persia had sent him, and put him on hose of the same, and set him in his ivory chair; and in his left hand they placed his sword Tizona in its scabbard, and the strings of his mantle in his right. And in this fashion the body of the Cid remained there ten years and more, till it was taken thence, as the history will relate anon. And when his garments waxed old, other good ones were put on.

King Don Alfonso, and the sons-in-law of the Cid, King Don Ramiro of Navarre, and the Infante Don Sancho of Aragon, with all their companies, and all the other honorable men, abode three weeks in St. Pedro de Cardeña, doing honor to the Cid. And the Bishop Don Hieronymo, and the other bishops who came with King Don Alfonso, said every day their masses, and accompanied the body of the Cid there where it was placed, and sprinkled holy water upon it, and incensed it, as is the custom to do over a grave. And after three weeks they who were there assembled began to break up, and depart to their own houses. And of the company of the Cid, some went with the king of Navarre, and other some with the Infante of Aragon; but the greater number, and the most honorable among them, betook themselves to King Don Alfonso, whose natural subjects they were. And Doña Ximena and her companions abode in San Pedro de Cardeña, and Gil Diaz with her, as the Cid had commanded in his testament. And the Bishop Don Hieronymo, and Alvar Fañez Minaya, and Pero Bermudez, remained there also till they had fulfilled all that the Cid Ruydiez had commanded in his testament to be done.

Gil Diaz did his best endeavor to fulfill all that his
lord the Cid Ruydiez had commanded him, and to serve
Doña Ximena and her companions truly and faithfully; and this he did so well, that she was well pleased
with his faithfulness. And Doña Ximena fulfilled all
that the Cid had commanded her; and every day she
had masses performed for his soul, and appointed many
vigils, and gave great alms for the soul of the Cid and of
his family. And this was the life which she led, doing
good wherever it was needful for the love of God: and
she was alway by the body of the Cid, save only at meal
times and at night; for then they would not permit her
to tarry there, save only when vigils were kept in honor
of him. Moreover Gil Diaz took great delight in tending
the horse Bavieca, so that there were few days in which
he did not lead him to water, and bring him back with
his own hand. And from the day in which the dead
body of the Cid was taken off his back, never man was
suffered to bestride that horse; but he was alway led
when they took him to water, and when they brought
him back. And Gil Diaz thought it fitting that the race
of that good horse should be continued, and he bought
two mares for him, the goodliest that could be found;
and when they were with foal, he saw that they were well
taken care of, and they brought forth the one a male
colt and the other a female; and from these the race of
this good horse was kept up in Castile, so that there were
afterwards many good and precious horses of his race,
and peradventure are at this day. And this good horse
lived two years and a half after the death of his master
the Cid, and then he died also, having lived, according

to the history, full forty years. And Gil Diaz buried him before the gate of the monastery, in the public place, on the right hand; and he planted two elms upon the grave, the one at his head and the other at his feet, and these elms grew and became great trees, and are yet to be seen before the gate of the monastery. And Gil Diaz gave order that when he died they should bury him by that good horse Bavieca, whom he had loved so well.

Four years after the Cid had departed, that noble lady Doña Ximena departed also, she who had been the wife of that noble baron the Cid Ruydiez, the Campeador. At that time Don Garcia Tellez was abbot of the monastery, a right noble monk, and a great hidalgo. And the abbot and Gil Diaz sent for the daughters of the Cid and Doña Ximena to come and honor their mother at her funeral, and to inherit what she had left. Doña Sol, who was the younger, came first, because Aragon is nearer than Navarre, and also because she was a widow; for the Infante Don Sancho, her husband, had departed three years after the death of the Cid, and had left no child. King Don Ramiro soon arrived with the other dame, Queen Doña Elvira his wife, and he brought with him a great company in honor of his wife's mother, and also the Bishop of Pamplona, to do honor to her funeral; and the Infante Don Garcia Ramirez, their son, came with them, being a child of four years old. Moreover, there came friends and kinsmen from all parts. And when they were all assembled they buried the body of Doña Ximena at the feet of the ivory chair on which the Cid was seated; and the Bishop of Pamplona said mass, and the abbot Don Garcia Tellez officiated. And they tarried there seven days, singing many masses, and doing much good for her soul's sake. And in that time the Bishop Don Hieronymo arrived, who abode with King Don Alfonso, and he came to do honor to the body of Doña Ximena; for so soon as he heard that she was departed, he set off, taking long journeys every day. And when the seven days were over, King Don Ramiro and Queen Doña Elvira his wife, and her sister, Doña Sol, set apart rents for the soul of Doña Ximena, and they appointed that Gil Diaz should have them for his life, and that then they should go to the monastery forever: and they ordained certain anniversaries for the souls of the Cid and of Doña Ximena. After this was done they divided between them what Doña Ximena had left, which was a great treasure in gold and in silver, and in costly garments; . . . the one half Queen Doña Elvira took, and Doña Sol the other. And when they had thus divided it, Doña Sol said that all which she had in the world should be for her nephew, the Infante Don Garcia Ramirez, and with the good-will of Queen Elvira his mother she adopted him then to be her son, and she took him with her to Aragon, to the lands which had been given her in dower, and bred him up till he became a young man; and after the death of his father he was made king of Navarre, as may be seen in the book of the chronicles of the kings of Spain. And when all these things were done, they departed each to his own home; and Gil Diaz remained, serving and doing honor to the bodies of his master the Cid and Doña Ximena his mistress.

Now Don Garcia Tellez the abbot, and the trusty

Gil Diaz, were wont every year to make a great festival on the day of the Cid's departure, and on that anniversary they gave food and clothing to the poor, who came from all parts round about. And it came to pass when they made the seventh anniversary, that a great multitude assembled as they were wont to do, and many Moors and Jews came to see the strange manner of the Cid's body. And it was the custom of the abbot Don Garcia Tellez, when they made that anniversary, to make a right noble sermon to the people: and because the multitude which had assembled was so great that the church could not hold them, they went out into the open place before the monastery, and he preached unto them there. And while he was preaching there remained a Jew in the church, who stopped before the body of the Cid, looking at him to see how nobly he was there seated, having his countenance so fair and comely, and his long beard in such goodly order, and his sword Tizona in its scabbard in his left hand, and the strings of his mantle in his right, even in such manner as King Don Alfonso had left him, save only that the garments had been changed, it being now seven years since the body had remained there in that ivory chair. Now there was not a man in the church save this Jew, for all the others were hearing the preachment which the abbot made. And when this Jew perceived that he was alone, he began to think within himself and say, This is the body of that Ruydiez the Cid, whom they say no man in the world ever took by the beard while he lived. . . . I will take him by the beard now, and see what he can do to me. And with that he put forth his hand to pull the

beard of the Cid; . . . but before his hand could reach
it, God, who would not suffer this thing to be done, sent
his spirit into the body, and the Cid let the strings of his
mantle go from his right hand, and laid hand on his
sword Tizona, and drew it a full palm's length out of the
scabbard. And when the Jew saw this, he fell upon his
back for great fear, and began to cry out so loudly, that
all they who were without the church heard him, and the
abbot broke off his preachment and went into the church
to see what it might be. And when they came they found
this Jew lying upon his back before the ivory chair, like
one dead, for he had ceased to cry out, and had swooned
away. And then the abbot Don Garcia Tellez looked
at the body of the Cid, and saw that his right hand was
upon the hilt of the sword, and that he had drawn it out
a full palm's length; and he was greatly amazed. And
he called for holy water, and threw it in the face of the
Jew, and with that the Jew came to himself. Then the
abbot asked him what all this had been, and he told
him the whole truth; and he knelt down upon his knees
before the abbot, and besought him of his mercy that he
would make a Christian of him, because of this great
miracle which he had seen, and baptize him in the name
of Jesus Christ, for he would live and die in his faith,
holding all other to be but error. And the abbot baptized him in the name of the Holy Trinity, and gave him
to name Diego Gil. And all who were there present were
greatly amazed, and they made a great outcry and great
rejoicings to God for this miracle, and for the power
which he had shown through the body of the Cid in this
manner; for it was plain that what the Jew said was

verily and indeed true, because the posture of the Cid
was changed. And from that day forward Diego Gil
remained in the monastery as long as he lived, doing
service to the body of the Cid.

. After that day the body of the Cid remained in the
same posture, for they never took his hand off the sword,
nor changed his garments more, and thus it remained
three years longer, till it had been there ten years in all.
And then the nose began to change color. And when the
abbot Don Garcia Tellez and Gil Diaz saw this, they
weened that it was no longer fitting for the body to
remain in that manner. And three bishops from the
neighboring provinces met there, and with many masses
and vigils, and great honor, they interred the body after
this manner. They dug a vault before the altar, beside
the grave of Doña Ximena, and vaulted it over with a
high arch; and there they placed the body of the Cid,
seated as it was in the ivory chair, and in his garments,
and with the sword in his hand, and they hung up his
shield and his banner upon the walls.

THE PERSIAN HERO

THE CHILDHOOD OF RUSTEM

By Alfred J. Church

THERE was never in the world such a child as
Rustem the son of Zal. He was fed with the milk
of ten nurses; and when he was weaned, his food was
bread and meat, and he ate as much as five men. As for
his strength and stature, they were such as never had
been seen before or will be seen again.

One day he was sleeping in his chamber when he
heard outside his door a great cry that the king's white
elephant had broken its chain and was at liberty, and
that the inhabitants of the palace were in great danger.
In a moment he rushed to seize his grandfather's club,
and prepared to go out. The attendants tried to stop
him. "We dare not incur your father's rage," they said,
"by opening the door. The night is dark; the elephant
has broken his chain; and yet you are going out. What
folly is this!" Rustem was greatly enraged to be so hindered, and struck the man who spoke so terrible a blow
between the head and the nape of the neck, that his head
fell off like a ball with which children play. When he
turned to the others, they soon made way for him. Then
he struck the door with his club, and burst the bolts
and bars with a single blow. This done, he laid the
club upon his shoulder, and hastened after the elephant.
As for his warriors, they were all as afraid of the beast

as a lamb is afraid of a wolf. When the furious beast saw him, it rushed at him, lifting its trunk to strike him. Rustem gave it one blow, for only one was wanted; its legs failed under it and it fell; you had said, so vast was it, that a mountain had fallen. Rustem returned to his chamber and finished his sleep.

The next day Zal, hearing what his son had done, sent for him, and covered him with praises. "My son," he said, "you are yet but a child, and yet there is no one to match you in courage and stature. I have an enterprise for you to conduct. Many years ago my grandfather was sent by the king to take an enchanted fortress which is situated upon Mount Sipend, and was killed by a rock that was thrown upon his head by one of the besieged after he had attacked it in vain for a whole year. After this my father San assembled an army, and marched against the place. But he could never find the way which led to the place. It is, indeed, so well provided that no one need ever leave it to get anything from without. San indeed wandered for years over the deserts looking for the fortress, but was obliged at last to return without having avenged his father's death. Now, my son, it is your turn. Go in disguise; the keepers of the fort will not know you; and when you have made your way into the fortress, destroy the wretches root and branch."

"I will do it," said Rustem.

Zal went on: "Disguise yourself as a camel-driver. Pretend that you are coming in from the desert, and that you have a cargo of salt with you. There is nothing in that country that they value more than salt. Let them once hear that this is what you are bringing, and great and small will welcome you."

Rustem gladly undertook this business. He hid the great club with which he had slain the white elephant in a load of salt, and he chose a number of companions who were as prudent as they were brave. Their arms also were hidden in loads of salt, and so they approached the fortress.

The keeper of the gate saw them from a distance, and ran to the prince, saying, "A caravan with a number of camel-drivers has arrived. If you ask me for what purpose they have come, I should say that, in my opinion, they have salt to sell."

Accordingly the prince sent a messenger to the master of the caravan, to ask him what his packages contained.

Rustem said, "Go back, and tell your master that I have salt in my packages."

The prince, on receiving this message, in great joy ordered the gate to be thrown open, and Rustem with his camels and their drivers, and the packages which they had with them, all entered the fortress. Rustem was courteously greeted by the prince, and greeted him courteously in return. Then he made his way to the bazaar, taking his camel-drivers with him. The people crowded round him, some with clothing, others with gold and silver; all were eager for his merchandise; and there was not a thought of fear or suspicion in the heart of any one of them. When the night came on, Rustem executed his plan of attack. First, he fell upon the prince and leveled him to the ground with a single blow of his club. There was not a chief in the whole fortress that could stand before him. Some he struck down with his club, and some with his sword. When the morning came, there was not a single man of all the defenders of the fortress that was not either dead or disabled.

In the middle of the fortress there was a building of stone, with a gate of iron. Rustem gave a blow of his club to the gate, and it flew open before him. Within there was a great vaulted hall, full of gold pieces and pearls. There never was such a sight in the world.

Rustem sent a message to his father to tell him of his victory, and to ask him what he should do.

Zal wrote back to this effect: "I send you herewith two thousand camels to carry away your booty. Load them with all that is precious, and then burn the place with fire."

This Rustem did. He loaded the camels with precious stones, and gold, and costly swords, chains and girdles, pearls and jewels worthy of a king, and Chinese brocades richly embroidered with figures. This done, he set fire to the fortress, and so departed.

All this Rustem did while he was yet a child.

THE SEVEN ADVENTURES
OF RUSTEM

By Alfred J. Church

KING Keïkobad died, and his son Kaoüs sat upon
his throne. At first he was a moderate and prudent prince; but finding his riches increase, and his armies
grow more and more numerous, he began to believe that
there was no one equal to him in the whole world, and
that he could do what he would. One day as he sat
drinking in one of the chambers of his palace, and boasting after his custom, a Genius, disguised as a minstrel,
came to the king's chamberlain, and desired to be admitted to the royal presence. "I came," he said, "from
the country of the Genii, and I am a sweet singer.
Maybe the king, if he were to hear me, would give me
a post in his court."

The chamberlain went to the king, and said, "There
is a minstrel at the gate; he has a harp in his hand, and
his voice is marvelously sweet."

"Bring him up," said the king.

So they brought him in, and gave him a place among
the musicians, and commanded that he should give them
a trial of his powers. So the minstrel, after playing a
prelude on his harp, sang a song of the land of the Genii.

"There is no land in all the world" — this was the
substance of his song — "like Mazanderan, the land

425

of the Genii. All the year round the rose blooms in its gardens and the hyacinth on its hills. It knows no heat nor cold, only an eternal spring. The nightingales sing in its thicket, and through its valleys wander the deer, and the water of its stream is as the water of roses, delighting the soul with its perfume. Of its treasures there is no end; the whole country is covered with gold and embroidery and jewels. No man can say that he is happy unless he has seen Mazanderan."

When the king heard this song, he immediately conceived the thought of marching against this wonderful country. Turning, therefore, to his warriors, he said: "We are given over to feasting; but the brave must not suffer himself to rest in idleness. I am wealthier and, I doubt not, stronger than all the kings that have gone before me; it becomes me also to surpass them in my achievements. We will conquer the land of Genii."

The warriors of the king were little pleased to hear such talk from his lips. No one ventured to speak, but their hearts were full of trouble and fear, for they had no desire to fight against the Genii.

"We are your subjects, O king," they said, "and will do as you desire." But when they were by themselves, and could speak openly, they said one to another, "What a trouble is this that has come of our prosperous fortune! Unless by good fortune the king forgets in his cups this purpose of his, we and the whole country are lost. Jemshid, whom the Genii and the Peris and the very birds of the air used to obey, never ventured to talk in this fashion of Mazanderan, or to seek war against the Genii; and Feridun, though he was the wisest of kings, and skillful in all magical arts, never cherished such a plan." So they sat, overwhelmed with anxiety.

At last one of them said, "My friends, there is only one way of escaping from this danger. Let us send a swift dromedary to Zal of the white hair, with this message: 'Though your head be covered with dust, do not stay to wash it, but come.' Perhaps Zal will give the king wise advice, and, telling him that this plan of his is nothing but a counsel of Satan, will persuade him to change his purpose. Otherwise we are lost, small and great."

The nobles listened to this advice, and sent a messenger to Zal, mounted on a swift dromedary.

When Zal heard what had happened, he said, —

"The king is self-willed. He has not yet felt either the cold or the heat of the world. He thinks that all men, great and small, tremble at his sword, and it must needs be that he learn better by experience. However, I will go; I will give him the best advice that I can. If he will be persuaded by me, it will be well; but if not, the way is open, and Rustem shall go with his army." All night long he revolved these matters in his heart. The next morning he went his way, and arrived at the court of the king.

The king received him with all honor, bade him sit by his side, and inquired how he had borne the fatigue of his journey, and of the welfare of Rustem, his son. Then Zal spoke, —

"I have heard, my lord, that you are forming plans against the land of the Genii. Will it please you to listen to me? There have been mighty kings before you, but never during all my years, which now are many, has any one of them conceived in his heart such a design as this. This land is inhabited by Genii that are skillful in all magical arts. They can lay such bonds upon men that no one is able to hurt them. No sword is keen enough to cut them through; riches and wisdom and valor are alike powerless against them. I implore you, therefore, not to waste your riches, and the riches of your country and the blood of your warriors, on so hopeless an enterprise."

The king answered, "Doubtless it is true that the kings my predecessors never ventured to entertain such a plan. But am I not superior to them in courage, in power, and wealth? Had they such warriors as you, and Rustem your son? Do not think to turn me from my purpose. I will go against the country of these accursed magicians, and verily I will not leave one single soul alive in it, for they are an evil race. If you do not care to come with me, at least refrain from advising me to sit idle upon my throne."

When Zal heard this answer, he said: "You are the king, and we are your slaves. Whatever you ordain is right and just, and it is only by thy good pleasure that we breathe and move. I have said what was in my heart. All that remains now is to obey, and to pray that the Ruler of the world may prosper your counsels."

When he had thus spoken, Zal took leave of the king, and departed for his own country.

The very next day the king set out with his army for the land of the Genii, and, after marching for several days, pitched his tent at the foot of Mount Asprus, and held a great revel all the night long with his chiefs. The next morning he said, "Choose me two thousand men who will break down the gates of Mazanderan with their clubs. And take care that when you have taken the city you spare neither young nor old, for I will rid the world of these magicians." They did as the king commanded, and in a short space of time the city, which was before the richest and most beautiful in the whole world, was made into a desert.

When the king of Mazanderan heard of these things he called a messenger, and said: "Go to the White Genius and say to him, 'The Persians have come with a great army and are destroying everything. Make haste and help me, or there will be nothing left to preserve.'"

The White Genius said, "Tell the king not to be troubled; I will see to these Persians."

That same night the whole army of King Kaoüs was covered with a wonderful cloud. The sky was dark as pitch, and there fell from it such a terrible storm of hailstones that no one could stand against them. When the next morning came, lo! the king and all that had not fled — for many fled to their own country — or been killed by the hailstones, were blind. Seven days they remained terrified and helpless. On the eighth day they heard the voice, loud as a clap of thunder, of the White Genius.

"King," said he, "you coveted the land of Mazanderan, you entered the city, you slew and took prisoners many of the people; but you did not know what I could do. And now, see, you have your desire. Your lot is of your own contriving."

The White Genius then gave over the king and his

companions to the charge of an army of twelve thousand Genii, and commanded that they should be kept in prison, and have just so much food given them as should keep them alive from day to day. Kaoüs, however, contrived to send by one of his warriors a message to Zal the White-haired, telling him of all the troubles that had come upon him. When Zal heard the news he was cut to the heart, and sent without delay for Rustem. "Rustem," said he, "this is no time for a man to eat and drink and take his pleasure. The king is in the hands of Satan, and we must deliver him. As for me, I am old and feeble; but you are of the age for war. Saddle Raksh, your horse, and set forth without a moment's delay. The White Genius must not escape the punishment of his misdeeds at your hands."

"The way is long," said Rustem; "how shall I go?"

"There are two ways," answered Zal, "and both are difficult and dangerous. The king went by the longer way. The other is by far the shorter, a two weeks' march and no more; but it is full of lions and evil Genii, and it is surrounded by darkness. Still, I would have you go by it. God will be your helper; and difficult as the way may be, it will have an end, and your good horse Raksh will accomplish it. And if it be the will of heaven that you should fall by the hand of the White Genius, who can change the ordering of destiny? Sooner or later we must all depart, and death should be no trouble to him who has filled the earth with his glory."

"My father, I am ready to do your bidding," said Rustem. "Nevertheless, the heroes of old cared not to go of their own accord into the land of death; and it is only he who is weary of life that throws himself in the way of a roaring lion. Still I go, and I ask for no help but from the justice of God. With that on my side I will break the charm of the magicians. The White Genius himself shall not escape me."

Rustem armed himself, and went on his way.

Rustem made such speed that he accomplished two days' journey in one. But at last, finding himself hungry and weary, and seeing that there were herds of wild asses in the plain which he was traversing, he thought that he would catch one of them for his meal, and rest for the night. So pressing his knees into his horse's side, he pursued one of them. There was no escape for the swiftest beast when Rustem was mounted on Raksh, and in a very short time a wild ass was caught with the lasso. Rustem struck a light with a flint stone, and making a fire with brambles and branches of trees, roasted the ass and ate it for his meal. This done he took the bridle from his horse, let him loose to graze upon the plain, and prepared to sleep himself in a bed of rushes. Now in the middle of this bed of rushes was a lion's lair, and at the end of the first watch the lion came back, and was astonished to see lying asleep on the rushes a man as tall as an elephant, with a horse standing near him. The lion said to himself, "I must first tear the horse, and then the rider will be mine whenever I please." So he leaped at Raksh; but the horse darted at him like a flash of fire, and struck him on the head with his fore feet. Then he seized him by the back with his teeth, and battered him to pieces on the earth. When Rustem awoke and saw the dead lion, which indeed was of a monstrous size, he said to Raksh, "Wise beast, who bade you fight with a lion? If you had fallen under his claws, how should I have carried to Mazanderan this cuirass and helmet, this lasso, my bow and my sword?" Then he went to sleep again; but awaking at sunrise, saddled Raksh and went on his way.

He had now to accomplish the most difficult part of his journey, across a waterless desert, so hot that the very birds could not live in it. Horse and rider were both dying of thirst, and Rustem, dismounting, could scarcely struggle along while he supported his steps by his spear. When he had almost given up all hope, he saw a well-nourished ram pass by. "Where," said he to himself, "is the reservoir from which this creature drinks?" Accordingly he followed the ram's footsteps, holding his horse's bridle in one hand and his sword in the other, and the ram led him to a spring. Then Rustem lifted up his eyes to heaven and thanked God for His mercies; afterwards he blessed the ram, saying, "No harm come to thee forever! May the grass of the valleys and the desert be always green for thee, and may the bow of him that would hunt thee be broken, for thou hast saved Rustem; verily, without thee he would have been torn to pieces by the wild beasts of the desert."

After this he caught another wild ass, and roasted him for his meal. Then having bathed in the spring, he lay down to sleep; but before he lay down, he said to Raksh, his horse: "Do not seek quarrel or friendship with any. If an enemy come, run to me; and do not fight either with Genius or lion."

After this he slept; and Raksh now grazed, and now galloped about over the plain.

Now it so happened that there was a great dragon that had its bed in this part of the desert. So mighty a beast was it, that not even a Genius had dared to pass by that way. The dragon was astonished to see a man asleep and a horse by his side, and began to make its way to the horse. Raksh did as he had been bidden, and running towards his master, stamped with his feet upon the ground. Rustem awoke, and seeing nothing when he looked about him — for the dragon meanwhile had disappeared — was not a little angry. He rebuked Raksh, and went to sleep again. Then the dragon came once more out of the darkness, and the horse ran with all speed to his master, tearing up the ground and kicking. A second time the sleeper awoke, but as he saw nothing but darkness round him, he was greatly enraged, and said to his faithful horse, —

"Why do you disturb me? If it wearies you to see me asleep, yet you cannot bring the night to an end. I said that if a lion came to attack you, I would protect you; but I did not tell you to trouble me in this way. Verily, if you make such a noise again, I will cut off your head and go on foot, carrying all my arms and armor with me to Mazanderan."

A third time Rustem slept, and a third time the dragon came. This time Raksh, who did not venture to come near his master, fled over the plain; he was equally afraid of the dragon and of Rustem. Still his love for his master did not suffer him to rest. He neighed and tore up the earth, till Rustem woke up again in a rage. But this time God would not suffer the dragon to hide himself, and Rustem saw him through the darkness, and, drawing his sword, rushed at him.

But first he said, — "Tell me your name; my hand must not tear your soul from your body before I know your name."

The dragon said, — "No man can ever save himself from my claws; I have dwelt in this desert for ages, and the very eagles have not dared to fly across. Tell me then your name, bold man. Unhappy is the mother that bare you."

"I am Rustem, son of Zal of the white hair," said the hero, "and there is nothing on earth that I fear."

Then the dragon threw itself upon Rustem. But the horse Raksh laid back his ears, and began to tear the dragon's back with his teeth, just as a lion might have torn it.

The hero stood astonished for a while; then, drawing his sword, severed the monster's head from his body. Then, having first performed his ablutions, he returned thanks to God, and mounting on Raksh, went his way.

All that day he traveled across the plain, and came at sunset to the land of the magicians. Just as the daylight was disappearing, he spied a delightful spot for his night's encampment. There were trees and grass, and a spring of water. And beside the spring there was a flagon of red wine, and a roast kid, with bread and salt and confectionery neatly arranged. Rustem dismounted, unsaddled his horse, and looked with astonishment at the provisions thus prepared. It was the meal of certain magicians, who had vanished when they saw him approach.

Of this he knew nothing, but sitting down without question, filled a cup with wine, and taking a harp which he found lying by the side of the flagon, sang: —

> "The scourge of the wicked am I,
>   And my days still in battle go by ;
>   Not for me is the red wine that glows
>   In the reveler's cup, nor the rose
>   That blooms in the land of delight ;
>   But with monsters and demons to fight."

The music and the voice of the singer reached the ears of a witch that was in those parts. Forthwith, by her art, she made her face as fair as spring, and, approaching Rustem, asked him how he fared, and sat down by his side. The hero thanked heaven that he had thus found in the desert such good fare and excellent company; for he did not know that the lovely visitor was a witch. He welcomed her, and handed her a cup of wine; but, as he handed it, he named the name of God, and at the sound her color changed, and she became as black as charcoal.

When Rustem saw this, quick as the wind he threw his lasso over her head.

"Confess who you are," he cried; "show yourself in your true shape."

Then the witch was changed into a decrepid, wrinkled old woman. Rustem cut her in halves with a blow of his sword.

The next day he continued his journey with all the speed that he could use, and came to a place where it was utterly dark. Neither sun, nor moon, nor stars could be seen; and all that the hero could do was to let the reins fall on his horse's neck, and ride on as chance might direct.

In time he came to a most delightful country, where the sun was shining brightly, and where the ground was covered with green. Rustem took off his cuirass of leopard skin, and his helmet, and let Raksh find pasture where he could in the fertile fields, and lay down to sleep. When the keeper of the fields saw the horse straying among them and feeding, he was filled with rage; and running up to the hero, dealt him with his stick a great blow upon the feet.

Rustem awoke.

"Son of Satan," said the keeper, "why do you let your horse stray in the corn-fields?"

Rustem leaped upon the man, and without uttering a word good or bad, wrenched his ears from his head.

Now the owner of this fertile country was a young warrior of renown named Aulad. The keeper ran up to him with his ears in his hand, and said, —

"There has come to this place a son of Satan, clad in a cuirass of leopard skin, with an iron helmet. I was going to drive his horse out of the corn-fields, when he leaped upon me, tore my ears from my head without saying a single word, and then lay down to sleep again."

Aulad was about to go hunting with his chiefs; but when he heard the keeper's story he altered his plan, and set out to the place where he heard that Rustem had been seen. Rustem, as soon as he saw him approach, and a great company with him, ran to Raksh, leaped on his

WHEN THE WHITE GENIUS SAW HIM HE RUSHED AT ONCE TO DO
BATTLE WITH HIM. FIRST HE CAUGHT UP FROM THE GROUND A
STONE AS BIG AS A MILLSTONE AND HURLED IT AT HIM. FOR
THE FIRST TIME RUSTEM FELT A THRILL OF FEAR, SO TERRIBLE
WAS HIS ENEMY. GATHERING ALL HIS STRENGTH HE STRUCK

back, and rode forward. Aulad said to him, "Who are you? What are you doing here? Why did you pluck off my keeper's ears and let your horse feed in the cornfields?"

"If you were to hear my name," said Rustem, "it would freeze the blood in your heart."

So saying he drew his sword, and fastening his lasso to the bow of his saddle, rushed as a lion rushes into the midst of a herd of oxen. With every blow of his sword he cut off a warrior's head, till the whole of Aulad's company was either slain or scattered. Aulad himself he did not kill, but throwing his lasso, caught him by the neck, dragged him from his horse, and bound his hands. "Now," said he, "if you will tell me the truth, and, without attempting to deceive, will show me where the White Genius dwells, and will guide me to where King Kaoüs is kept prisoner, then I will make you king of Mazanderan. But if you speak a word of falsehood you die."

"It is well," said Aulad; "I will do what you desire. I will show you where the king is imprisoned. It is four hundred miles from this place; and four hundred miles farther, a difficult and dangerous way, is the dwelling of the White Genius. It is a cavern so deep that no mere man has ever sounded it, and it lies between two mountains. Twelve thousand Genii watch it during the night, for the White Genius is the chief and master of all his tribe. You will find him a terrible enemy, and, for all your strong arms and hands, your keen sword, your lance and your club, you will scarcely be able to conquer him; and when you have conquered him, there will still be much to be done. In the city of the king of Mazanderan there are thousands of warriors, and not a coward among them; and besides these, there are two hundred war-elephants. Were you made of iron, could you venture to deal alone with these sons of Satan?"

Rustem smiled when he heard this, and said, "Come with me, and you will see what a single man, who puts his trust in God, can do. And now show me first the way to the king's prison."

Rustem mounted on Raksh, and rode gayly forward, and Aulad ran in front of him. For a whole day and night he ran, nor ever grew tired, till they reached the foot of Mount Asprus, where King Kaoüs had fallen into the power of the Genii. About midnight they heard a great beating of drums, and saw many fires blaze up.

Rustem said to Aulad, "What mean these fires that are blazing up to right and left of us?"

Aulad answered, "This is the way into Mazanderan. The great Genius Arzeng must be there."

Then Rustem went to sleep; and when he woke in the morning he took his lasso and fastened Aulad to the trunk of a tree. Then hanging his grandfather's club to his saddle-bow, he rode on.

His conflict with Arzeng, the chief of the army of the Genii, was soon finished. As he approached the camp he raised his battle-cry. His shout was loud enough, one would have said, to split the very mountains; and Arzeng when he heard it, rushed out of his tent. Rustem set spurs to his horse, and galloping up to the Genius, caught him by the head, tore it from the body, and threw it into the midst of the army. When the Genii saw it, and caught sight also of the great club, they fled in the wildest confusion, fathers trampling upon their sons in their eagerness to escape. The hero put the whole herd of them to the sword, and then returned as fast as he could to the place where he had left Aulad bound to the tree. He unloosed the knots of the lasso, and bidding him lead the way to the prison-house of the king, set spurs to Raksh, Aulad running in front as before.

When they entered the town, Raksh neighed. His voice was as loud as thunder, and the king heard it, and in a moment understood all that had happened. "That is the voice of Raksh," he said to the Persians that were with him; "our evil days are over. This was the way in which he neighed in King Kobad's time, when he made war on the Scythians."

The Persians said to themselves, "Our poor king has lost his senses, or he is dreaming. There is no help for us." But they had hardly finished speaking when the hero appeared, and did homage to the king. Kaoüs embraced him, and then said: "If you are to help me, you must go before the Genii know of your coming. So soon as the White Genius shall hear of the fall of Arzeng, he will assemble such an army of his fellows as shall make all your pains and labor lost. But you must know that you have great difficulties to overcome. First, you must cross seven mountains, all of them occupied by troops of Genii; then you will see before you a terrible cavern — more terrible, I have heard say, than any other place in the world. The entrance to it is guarded by warrior Genii, and in it dwells the White Genius himself. He is both the terror and the hope of his army. Conquer him, and all will be well. A wise physician tells me that the only remedy for my blindness is to drop into my eyes three drops of the White Genius' blood. Go and conquer, if you would save your king."

Without any delay Rustem set forth, Raksh carrying him like the wind. When he reached the great cavern, he said to Aulad, who had guided him on his way as before, "The time of conflict is come. Show me the way."

Aulad answered, "When the sun shall grow hot, the Genii will go to sleep. That will be your time to conquer them."

Rustem waited till the sun was at its highest, and then went forth to battle. The Genii that were on guard fled at the sound of his voice, and he went on without finding any to resist him till he came to the great cavern of which the king had spoken. It was a terrible place to see, and he stood for a while with his sword in his hand, doubting what he should do. No one would choose such a spot for battle; and as for escaping from it, that was beyond all hope. Long he looked into the darkness, and at last he saw a monstrous shape, which seemed to reach across the whole breadth of the cave. It was the White Genius that was lying asleep. Rustem did not attempt to surprise him in his sleep, but woke him by shouting his battle-cry. When the White Genius saw him, he rushed at once to do battle with him. First he caught up from the ground a stone as big as a millstone and hurled it at him. For the first time Rustem felt a thrill of fear, so terrible was his enemy. Nevertheless, gathering all his strength, he struck at him a great blow with his sword and cut off one of his feet. The monster, though having but one foot, leaped upon him like a wild elephant, and seized him by the breast and arms, hoping to throw him to the ground, and tore from his body great morsels of flesh, so that the whole place was covered with blood. Rustem said to himself, "If I escape to-day I shall live forever;" and the White Genius thought, "Even if I do deliver myself from the claws of this dragon, I shall never see Mazanderan again." Still he did not lose courage, but continued to struggle against the hero with all his might.

So the two fought together, the blood and sweat running from them in great streams. At last Rustem caught the Genius round the body, and, putting out all his strength, hurled him to the ground with such force that his soul was driven out of his body. Then he plunged his poniard into the creature's heart, and tore the liver out of his body. This done he returned to Aulad, whom he had left bound with his lasso, loosed him, and set out for the place where he had left the king. But first Aulad said to him, "I have the marks of your bonds upon me; my body is bruised with the knots of your lasso; I beseech you to respect the promise which you made me of a reward. A hero is bound to keep his word."

Rustem said: "I promised that you should be king of Mazanderan, and king you shall be. But I have much to do before my word can be kept. I have a great battle to fight, in which I may be conquered, and I must rid this country of the magicians with whom it is encumbered. But be sure that, when all is done, I will not fail of the promises which I have made."

So Rustem returned to King Kaoüs, and, dropping

the blood of the White Genius into his eyes, gave him back his sight. Seven days the king and his nobles feasted together, Rustem having the chief place. On the eighth day they set out to clear the country of the accursed race of magicians. When they had done this, the king said, "The guilty have now been punished. Let no others suffer. And now I will send a letter to the king of Mazanderan."

So the king wrote a letter in these words: "You see how God has punished the wrong-doers — how He has brought to naught the Genii and the magicians. Quit then your town, and come here to pay homage and tribute to me. If you will not, then your life shall be as the life of Arzeng and the White Genius."

This letter was carried to the king by a certain chief named Ferbad. When the king had read it, he was greatly troubled. Three days he kept Ferbad as his guest, and then sent back by him this answer: "Shall the water of the sea be equal to wine? Am I one to whom you can say, 'Come down from your throne, and present yourself before me?' Make ready to do battle with me, for verily I will bring upon the land of Persia such destruction that no man shall be able to say what is high and what is low."

Ferbad hastened back to the king of Persia. "The man," he said, "is resolved not to yield." Then the king sent to Rustem. And Rustem said, "Send me with a letter that shall be as keen as a sword and a message like a thunder-cloud." So the king sent for a scribe, who, making the point of his reed as fine as an arrowhead, wrote thus: "These are foolish words, and

442

do not become a man of sense. Put away your arrogance, and be obedient to my words. If you refuse, I will bring such an army against you as shall cover your land from one sea to the other; and the ghost of the White Genius shall call the vultures to feast on your brains."

The king set his seal to this letter, and Rustem departed with it, with his club hanging to his saddle-bow. When the king of Mazanderan heard of his coming, he sent some of his nobles to meet him. When Rustem saw them, he caught a huge tree that was by the wayside in his hands, twisted it with all his might, and tore it up, roots and all. Then he poised it in his hand as if it were a javelin. One of the nobles, the strongest of them all, rode up to him, caught one of his hands, and pressed it with all his might. Rustem only smiled; but when in his turn he caught the noble's hand in his, he crushed all the veins and bones, so that the man fell fainting from his horse.

When the king heard what had been done, he called one of his warriors, Kalahour by name, the strongest man in his dominions, and said to him, "Go and meet this messenger; show him your prowess, and cover his face with shame." So Kalahour rode to meet Rustem, and, taking him by the hand, wrung it with all the strength of an elephant. The hand turned blue with the pain, but the hero did not flinch or give any sign of pain. But when in his turn he wrung the hand of Kalahour, the nails dropped from it as the leaves drop from a tree. Kalahour rode back, his hand hanging down, and said to the king, "It will be better for you to make peace than to fight with this lion, whose strength is such that no man can stand against him. Pay this tribute, and we will make it good to you. Otherwise we are lost."

At this moment Rustem rode up. The king gave him a place at his right hand, and asked him of his welfare. Rustem, for answer, gave him the letter of Keï-Kaoüs. When the king had read the letter, his face became black as thunder. Then he said, "Carry back this answer to your master; 'You are lord of Persia, and I of Mazanderan. Be content; seek not that which is not yours. Otherwise your pride will lead you to your fall.'"

The king would have given Rustem royal gifts, robe of honor, and horses, and gold. But the hero would have none of them, but went away in anger. When he had returned to the king of Persia, he said to him, "Fear nothing, but make ready for battle. As for the warriors of this land of Mazanderan, they are nothing; I count them no better than a grain of dust."

Meanwhile the king of the magicians prepared for war. He gathered an army, horsemen and foot-soldiers and elephants, that covered the face of the earth, and approached the borders of Persia; and, on the other hand, King Kaoüs marshaled his men of war and went out to encounter him. The king himself took his place in the centre of the line of battle, and in front of all stood the great Rustem.

One of the nobles of Mazanderan came out of their line, with a great club in his hands, and approaching the Persian army, cried in a loud voice, "Who is ready to fight with me? He should be one who is able to change water into dust."

None of the Persian nobles answered him, and King Kaoùs said, "Why is it, ye men of war, that your faces are troubled, and your tongues silent before this Genius?"

But still the nobles made no answer. Then Rustem caught the rein of his horse, and, putting the point of his lance over his shoulder, rode up to the king, and said, "Will the king give me permission to fight with this Genius?"

The king said, "The task is worthy of you, for none of the Persians dare to meet this warrior. Go and prosper!"

So Rustem set spurs to Raksh, and rode against the warrior who had challenged the Persians.

"Hear," he said, as soon as he came near, "your name is blotted out of the list of the living; for the moment is come when you shall suffer the recompense of all your misdeeds."

The warrior answered, "Boast not yourself so proudly. My sword makes mothers childless."

When Rustem heard this, he cried with a voice of thunder, "I am Rustem!" and the warrior, who had no desire to fight the champion of the world, turned his back and fled. But Rustem pursued him, and thrust at him with his lance where the belt joins the coat of mail, and pierced him through, for the armor could not turn the point of the great spear. Then he lifted him out of his saddle, and raised him up in the air, as if he were a bird which a man had run through with a spit. This done, he dashed him down dead upon the ground, and all the nobles of Mazanderan stood astonished at the sight.

After this the two armies joined battle. The air grew dark, and the flashing of the swords and clubs flew like the lightning out of a thunder-cloud, and the mountains trembled with the cries of the combatants. Never had any living man seen so fierce a fight before.

For seven days the battle raged, and neither the one side nor the other could claim the victory. On the eighth day King Kaoüs bowed himself before God, taking his crown from his head, and prayed with his face to the ground, saying, "O Lord God, give me, I beseech Thee, the victory over the Genii who fear Thee not."

Then he set his helmet on his head, and put himself at the head of his army. First of all Rustem began the attack, charging the centre of the enemy's army. He directed his course straight to the place where the king of Mazanderan stood, surrounded with his chiefs and a great host of elephants. When the king saw the shine of his lance, he lost courage, and would have fled. But Rustem, with a cry like a lion's roar, charged him, and struck him on the girdle with his spear. The spear pierced the steel, and would have slain the king, but that by his magic art he changed himself, before the eyes of all the Persian army, into a mass of rock. Rustem stood astonished to see such a marvel.

When King Kaoüs came up with his warriors, he said to Rustem, "What is it? What ails you that you tarry here, doing nothing?"

"My lord," answered Rustem, "I charged the king

of Mazanderan, spear in hand; I struck him on the girdle, but when I thought to see him fall from his saddle, he changed himself into a rock before my eyes, and now he feels nothing that I can do."

Then King Kaoüs commanded that they should take up the rock and put it before his throne. But when the strongest men in the army came to handle the rock, or sought to draw it with cords, they could do nothing, it remained immovable. Rustem, however, without any one to help him, lifted it from the earth, and carrying it into the camp, threw it down before the king's tent, and said, "Give up these cowardly tricks and the art of magic, else I will break this rock into pieces."

When the king of Mazanderan heard this, he made himself visible, black as a thunder-cloud, with a helmet of steel upon his head, and a coat of mail upon his breast. Rustem laughed, and caught him by the hand, and brought him before the king.

"See," said he, "this lump of rock, who, for fear of the hatchet, has given himself up to me!"

When Kaoüs looked at him and observed how savage of aspect he was, with the neck and tusks of a wild boar, he saw that he was not worthy to sit upon a throne, and bade the executioner take him away and cut him in pieces. This done, he sent to the enemies' camp, and commanded that all the spoil, the king's throne, and his crown and girdle, the horses and the armor, the swords and jewels, should be gathered together. Then he called up his army, and distributed to them rewards in proportion to what they had done and suffered. After this he spent seven days in prayer, humbling himself before God, and offering up thanksgiving. On the eighth day he seated himself on his throne, and opened his treasures, and gave to all that had need. Thus he spent another seven days. On the fifteenth day, he called for wine and cups of amber and rubies, and sat for seven days on his throne, with the wine-cup in his hand.

He sent for Rustem, and said, "It is of your doing, by your strength and courage, that I have recovered my throne."

Rustem answered, "A man must do his duty. As for the honors that you would give me, I owe them all to Aulad, who has always guided me on the right way. He hopes to be made king of Mazanderan. Let the king, therefore, if it please him, invest him with the crown."

And this the king did.

The next day Kaoüs and his army set out to return to the land of Persia. When he had reached his palace, he seated himself upon his throne, and sending for Rustem, put him at his side.

Rustem said, "My lord, permit me to go back to the old man Zal, my father."

The king commanded that they should bring splendid presents for the hero. The presents were these: A throne of turquoise, adorned with rams' heads; a royal crown set about with jewels; a robe of brocade of gold, such as is worn by the king of kings; a bracelet and a chain of gold; a hundred maidens, with faces fair as the full moon, and girdles of gold; a hundred youths, whose hair was fragrant with musk; a hundred horses, caparisoned with gold and silver; a hundred mules with black hair, with loads of brocade that came from the land of Room and from Persia. After these they brought and laid at the hero's feet a hundred purses filled with gold pieces; a cup of rubies, filled with pure musk; another cup of turquoise, filled with attar of roses; and, last of all, a letter written on pages of silk, in ink made of wine and aloes and amber and the black of lamps. By this letter the king of kings gave anew to Rustem the kingdom of the south. Then Kaoüs blessed him, and said: "May you live as long as men shall see the sun and the moon in heaven! May the great of the earth join themselves to you! May your own soul be full of modesty and tenderness!"

Rustem prostrated himself on the earth, and kissed the throne; and so took his departure.

RUSTEM AND SOHRAB

By Alfred J. Church

ONE day Rustem thought that he would hunt. So he filled his quiver with arrows, and, mounting his horse Raksh, set out for the country which borders on Tartary. As he went he came upon a plain which was covered with herds of wild asses. Rustem smiled to see them, and, pursuing them on his fleet-footed horse, killed many of them, some with his arrows, and some, first catching them with his lasso, with his club. His hunting done, he lighted a great fire of brushwood, brambles, and branches of trees; then taking a young tree to serve him for a spit, ran it through the body of one of the asses, and roasted the flesh at the fire. When it was well done, he tore it joint from joint, ate his full of it, and broke the bones for the marrow. His meal finished, he lay down to sleep, while Raksh grazed on the plain. While he slept, seven Tartar warriors came that way, and saw the tracks of Raksh, who had wandered far away from his master's camping-place. Not long afterwards they came upon him, and made haste to possess themselves of him. First they tried to throw a lasso over him, but when Raksh saw the lasso he rushed at them like a lion, struck two of them dead with two blows of his fore feet, and bit off the head of a third. Thus three of the company were dead, and the brave Raksh was not yet taken.

Nevertheless, the other four entangled him with their lassos, and, so capturing him, took him with them to the town.

When Rustem woke from his sleep, he looked about for his horse, but could find no traces of him. "How can I go," he said to himself, "carrying my quiver and my club, this heavy helmet, this sword, and this coat of mail? The Tartars will say, 'Rustem slept and some one stole his horse,' and I shall be covered with shame."

When he came near to the town of Semengan, the king and his nobles saw that it was Rustem that was approaching. The king went out to meet him, and said: "What has happened? How is it that you came on foot? Tell us how we can serve you. We are all at your bidding."

Rustem saw that they were friends, and answered: "My horse Raksh has escaped from me on this plain, without bit or reins. Find him for me, and I will reward you as is fitting. But if Raksh is not found, I will make many suffer for it."

The king said: "No one will dare to do you a wrong in this matter. Come and be my guest. Let us drive away care with the wine-cup. Anger profits nothing. It is by charming that one brings the serpent out of his hole. As for the horse Raksh, it is not possible that he should be hid, for all the world knows of him. We will look for him, and bring him to you without delay."

So Rustem put away all suspicion out of his mind, and became the guest of the king. So they sat and drank wine together, and the king waited upon him as though he were his slave.

While the hero tarried in the palace, the king's daughter, who had often heard of his prowess and courage, and of the great exploits which he had done, saw him and loved him. She was the most beautiful of maidens. Her eyebrows were arched, the two plaits of her hair like the ropes of a lasso, her lips like rubies, and she was tall as a cypress.

Rustem asked her in marriage of her father, and the king, who was glad to find so noble a husband for her, gladly listened to his suit. So the two — the maiden's name was Tehmina — were married with much rejoicing.

When the time came that Rustem must leave the king's court, — for there were grave matters that called him back to Persia, — he took an onyx bracelet that he wore upon his arm, and gave it to his wife, saying, "If God should give you a daughter, fasten this bracelet under the curls of her hair. But if you should bear a son, let him wear it on his arm, as his father has worn it."

So Rustem departed, taking his horse with him, for the king had found Raksh.

In due time Tehmina bore a son. The infant was as beautiful as the moon. When he was but a month old he had the limbs of a yearling child; at three years he learned exercises of arms; at five he was as bold as a lion; and at ten there was not a man in the whole country that dared wrestle with him. One day he went to his mother, and said, "Tell me who I am. What must I say when they ask me my father's name?"

Tehmina said, "You are the son of Rustem. Never since God made the world has there been such a warrior as he:" and she showed him a letter from Rustem, and three rubies which he had sent for a gift. "But," she said, "King Afrasiab must know nothing of this, for he is the sworn foe of Rustem. He would kill the son because he hates the father. And besides, if your father knew to what strength and stature you are grown, he would send for you, and your mother's heart would break for grief."

Sohrab said — for that was the youth's name: "This is a story that cannot be hid. But listen to what I will do. I will put myself at the head of an innumerable army of Tartars. I will deprive King Kaoüs of his kingdom. I will set Rustem upon his throne; and, this done, I will make war against Afrasiab and possess myself of his throne. Seeing that Rustem is my father and I am his son, I will not suffer that there should be any kings in the world but he and I."

Sohrab, after he had chosen for himself a horse, having the good fortune to find one that was of the breed of Raksh, asked his grandfather to help him. "I would go," he said, "to the land of Persia, and help my father."

The king loaded him with gifts, and sent him away.

Meanwhile it was told to King Afrasiab that Sohrab was gathering an army against the king of Persia. He called his nobles and said: "Listen to me; I have a plan which shall rid us of our enemies. Rustem must not know that Sohrab is his son. The two will meet in battle, and it may be that the young lion will kill the old one. If it be so, one day we will take Sohrab by stratagem and slay him. But if Rustem, on the other hand, should slay his son, then his heart will be eaten away with grief, and we need fear him no more."

Accordingly Afrasiab sent messengers to Sohrab with gifts and this message: "You will do well if you can conquer the land of Persia. I send you for your help such an army as is fitting. Go on, and prosper."

So Sohrab set out with his army. He came in his march to a certain stronghold that was called the White Fort, and was the chief hope of the Persians. The governor of the fort was an old man and very feeble; but in the garrison there was a very brave champion, Hedjir by name, who, when he saw the army of Sohrab approaching, rushed out to meet him. "Come to me," he said, in his pride, "and I will cut your head from your body, and give your flesh to the vultures to eat."

Sohrab smiled to hear such brave words, and charged his enemy. The two met. Hedjir struck Sohrab on the girdle with a spear, but the point did not pierce the armor. But Sohrab, reversing his spear, struck Hedjir with the shaft, and felled him from his saddle; then, leaping from his horse, stood over him, and would have cut his head from his body, but that the vanquished man begged for quarter. Sohrab granted him his life, bound him with cords, and sent him a prisoner to the king.

The old governor of the fort had a daughter, Gurdafurd by name, a very fair maiden, but as strong and brave as any warrior in the land. It troubled her greatly to see the young champion discomfited and bound, and without hesitating a moment she armed herself, hid her long hair under her helmet, and rode forth from the fort to do battle with the Tartars.

She rode in front of the army of the besiegers, and said, "Who is there among you that will come and fight with me?" None of them were willing to accept her challenge; but when Sohrab saw her he said, "Here is another wild ass for my lasso!" and hastily putting on his armor, rode out to meet her. The girl let fly a storm of arrows at him, attacking him first from one side, then from the other; and when Sohrab charged her, threw her bow over her shoulder, put her spear in rest, and galloped to meet him. Sohrab drew his spear back so far that the point was almost level with his body; then, delivering it with all his force, struck Gurdafurd on the girdle, burst the fastenings of her coat of mail, and hurled her from her saddle like a ball struck by a racquet. The girl twisted herself under her saddle, drew a sword from her girdle, and cut Sohrab's spear in half. Then she jumped again into the saddle, but turned to fly, for she had little liking for the conflict. Sohrab slackened the reins of his horse, and, galloping after her at full speed, overtook her, and catching her by the helmet, drew it from her head. Then all her long hair fell down, and the young hero knew that he had been fighting with a girl. "Well!" said he, "if the maidens of Persia fight in this fashion, the men must be notable warriors." He threw his lasso round her waist, and said, "Do not attempt to escape; but tell me, beautiful girl, why did you seek this conflict?"

The girl said, "All the army will laugh at you, if they should see my face and my hair. They will say, 'The brave Sohrab went out to fight a woman.' Let us conceal this adventure. The fort is yours, and all the soldiers in it, and all the treasure, as soon as you shall be pleased to take possession of it."

Sohrab said, "Do not fail of your promise, and do not trust in the strength of your walls. Were they as high as the vault of heaven, my club would level them to the ground."

So they rode together to the gate of the fort, and Gurdafurd, wounded and wearied, dragged herself within. Her father received her with great joy, and said, "You have done well, my daughter. We have no cause to be ashamed of your courage and address. Thanks be to God, who has not suffered this stranger to kill you."

After this the girl mounted on the wall, and seeing Sohrab waiting beneath, said to him, "Why do you weary yourself with waiting, lord of the Tartars? Return to the place whence you came."

Sohrab said: "Treacherous one! I swear by heaven and earth that you will repent of this falsehood. Where is the treaty that you made with me, that you would deliver up the fort, with all its garrison and its treasure?"

The girl laughed, and said: "Take care; the great Rustem will soon be here, and not a man of your army will be left alive. But what a pity that such arms and such a breast as yours should be a prey for jackals! Pride yourself as you will on your strength, but yet the stupid cow will eat the grass upon your grave."

Sohrab was covered with shame to hear these mocking words. But he said, "It is too late to give battle to-day; but with dawn to-morrow we will lay the fort level with the dust." Then he shook the reins of his horse, and galloped back to the camp.

At dawn he marched against the fort with his army.
But there was no one to be seen upon the walls. He rode
up to the gate, and it was opened to him. But there was
not a single armed man in the whole place. In fact, the
governor and the garrison had departed in the night by
a passage under the earth, of which no one was aware,
and with them was gone the beautiful Gurdafurd. This
troubled Sohrab more than anything else, for his heart
was full of love for the girl, so beautiful and so brave.

Meanwhile the governor of the fort had sent a letter
to King Kaoüs, telling him how there had appeared
among the Tartars a mighty champion, against whom,
such was the strength of his arms, no one could stand;
how he had overthrown and taken prisoner their champion, and now threatened to overrun and conquer the
whole land of Persia. When the king had received and
read this letter he was greatly troubled, and, calling a
scribe, said to him, "Sit down and write a letter to Rustem." So the scribe sat down and wrote. The letter was
this: "There has appeared among the Tartars a great
champion, strong as an elephant and fierce as a lion. No
one can stand against him. We look to you for help. It
is of your doing that our warriors hold their heads so
high. Come, then, with all the speed that you can use, so
soon as you shall have read this letter. Be it night or day,
come at once; do not open your mouth to speak; if you
have a bunch of roses in your hand do not stop to smell
it, but come; for the warrior of whom I write is such that
you only can meet him."

King Kaoüs sealed the letter and gave it to a warrior
named Giv. At the same time he said, "Haste to Rus-

tem. Tarry not on the way; and when you are come, do not rest there for an hour. If you arrive in the night, depart again the next morning." So Giv departed, and traveled with all his speed, allowing himself neither sleep nor food. When he approached Zabulistan, the watchman said, "A warrior comes from Persia, riding like the wind." So Rustem, with his chiefs, went out to meet him. When they had greeted each other, they returned together to Rustem's palace. Giv delivered his message, and handed the king's letter, telling himself much more that he had heard about the strength and courage of this Tartar warrior. Rustem heard him with astonishment, and said, "This champion is like, you say, to the great San, my grandfather. That such a man should come from the free Persians is possible; but that he should be among those slaves the Tartars, is past belief. I have myself a child, whom the daughter of a Tartar king bore to me; but the child is a girl. This, then, that you tell me is passing strange; but for the present let us make merry."

So they made merry with the chiefs that were assembled in Rustem's palace. But after a while Giv said again: "King Kaoüs commanded me, saying, 'You must not sleep in Zabulistan; if you arrive in the night, set out again the next morning. It will go ill with us if we have to fight before Rustem comes.' It is necessary, then, great hero, that we set out in all haste for Persia."

Rustem said, "Do not trouble yourself about this matter. We must all die some day. Let us, therefore, enjoy the present. Our lips are dry, let us wet them with wine. As to this Tartar, fortune will not always be with him. When he sees my standard, his heart will fail him."

So they sat, drinking the red wine and singing merry songs, instead of thinking of the king and his commands. The next day Rustem passed in the same fashion, and the third also. But on the fourth Giv made preparations to depart, saying to Rustem, "If we do not make haste to set out, the king will be wroth, and his anger is terrible." Rustem said, "Do not trouble yourself; no man dares to be wroth with me." Nevertheless, he bade them saddle Raksh, and set out with his companions.

When they came near the king's palace, a great company of nobles rode out to meet them, and conducted them to the king, and they paid their homage to him. But the king turned away from them in a rage. "Who is Rustem," he cried, "that he forgets his duty to me, and disobeys my commands? If I had a sword in my hand this moment, I would cut off his head, as a man cuts an orange in half. Take him, hang him up alive on gallows, and never mention his name again in my presence."

Giv answered, "Sir, will you lay hands upon Rustem?"

The king burst out again in a rage against Giv and Rustem, crying to one of his nobles, "Take these two villains and hang them alive on gallows." And he rose up from his throne in fury. The noble to whom he had spoken laid his hand upon Rustem, wishing to lead him out of the king's presence, lest Kaoüs in his rage should do him an injury. But Rustem cried out, "What a king are you! Hang this Tartar, if you can, on your gallows. Keep such things for your enemies. All the world has bowed itself before me and Raksh, my horse. And you — you are king by my grace."

Thus speaking, he struck away the hand that the noble had laid upon him so fiercely that the man fell headlong to the ground, and he passed over his body to go from the presence of the king. And as he mounted on Raksh, he cried: "What is Kaoüs that he should deal with me in this fashion? It is God who has given me strength and victory, and not he or his army. The nobles would have given me the throne of Persia long since, but I would not receive it; I kept the right before my eyes. Verily, had I not done so, you, Kaoüs, would not be sitting upon the throne." Then he turned to the Persians that stood by, and said, "This brave Tartar will come. Look out for yourselves how you may save your lives. Me you shall see no more in the land of Persia."

The Persians were greatly troubled to hear such words; for they were sheep, and Rustem was their shepherd. So the nobles assembled, and said to each other: "The king has forgotten all gratitude and decency. Does he not remember that he owes to Rustem his throne — nay, his very life? If the gallows be Rustem's reward, what shall become of us?"

So the oldest among them came and stood before the king, and said: "O king, have you forgotten what Rustem has done for you and for this land — how he conquered Mazanderan and its king and the White Genius; how he gave you back the sight of your eyes? And now you have commanded that he should be hanged alive upon a gallows. Are these fitting words for a king?"

The king listened to the old man, and said: "You

speak well. The words of a king should be words of wisdom. Go now to Rustem, and speak good words to him, and make him forget my anger."

So the old man rode after Rustem, and many of the nobles went with him. When they had overtaken him, the old man said, "You know that the king is a wrathful man, and that in his rage he speaks hard words. But you know also that he soon repents. But now he is ashamed of what he said. And if he has offended, yet the Persians have done no wrong that you should thus desert them."

Rustem answered, "Who is the king that I should care for him? My saddle is my throne, my helmet is my crown, my corselet is my robe of state. What is the king to me but a grain of dust? Why should I fear his anger? I delivered him from prison; I gave him back his crown. And now my patience is at an end."

The old man said, "This is well. But the king and his nobles will think, 'Rustem fears this Tartar,' and they will say, 'If Rustem is afraid, what can we do but leave our country?' I pray you therefore not to turn your back upon the king, when things are in such a plight. Is it well that the Persians should become the slaves of the infidel Tartars?"

Rustem stood confounded to hear such words. "If there were fear in my heart, then I would tear my soul from my body. But you know that it is not; only the king has treated me with scorn."

But he perceived that he must yield to the old man's advice. So he went back with the nobles.

As soon as the king saw him, he leaped upon his feet, and said, "I am hard of soul, but a man must grow as

God has made him. My heart was troubled by the fear of this new enemy. I looked to you for safety, and you delayed your coming. Then I spoke in my wrath; but I have repented, and my mouth is full of dust."

Rustem said, "It is yours to command, O king, and ours to obey. You are the master, and we are your slaves. I am but as one of those who open the door for you, if indeed I am worthy to be reckoned among them. And now I come to execute your commands."

Kaoüs said, "It is well. Now let us feast. To-morrow we will prepare for war."

So Kaoüs, and Rustem, and the nobles feasted till the night had passed and the morning came.

The next day King Kaoüs and Rustem, with a great army, began their march. Now Sohrab was still at the fort from which the beautiful Gurdafurd had escaped. When the army of the Persians came in sight, the Tartars that were in the fort set up a great shout; and Sohrab hearing it, came and stood on the rampart, with Hedjir, the champion whom he had conquered and taken prisoner, by his side. "You do not see," he said, "in this great army a man with a great club who would be able to meet me in battle. There are many men, it is true; but not a single man of war. Verily I will cover the plain with their blood, as the waters cover the sea."

So saying he went down from the rampart, and called for a cup of wine. He had not a thought of fear in his heart. On the other side, the king's army pitched their tents on the plain, which they covered from side to side with their encampment.

That night Rustem went to the king, and said, "Will

the king suffer me to go out to-night without helmet or belt that I may see for myself who this champion is, and who are the warriors that follow him?"

The king said, "It is well thought of. Only be prudent, and may God have you in His keeping."

So Rustem put on the dress of a Tartar, and set out for the fort. He made his way into it, like a lion which steals on a herd of antelopes, and saw Sohrab and the chief sitting at the feast.

Now Sohrab's mother had said to Zendeh her brother, when her son was setting out for the war, "Go with Sohrab, for you know the face of Rustem; and when the time is come, you will show my son his father." So Sohrab sat at the feast, and Zendeh his uncle sat by him.

Rustem stood by the door watching the feasters, and it so chanced that Zendeh, leaving the room, saw him standing there. "Who are you?" he said; for there was not a man in the whole army of the Tartars that was his like in strength and stature.

Rustem answered him not a word, but struck him on the nape of the neck so fierce a blow that he fell down and died. There was no more feasting or fighting for Zendeh.

When Sohrab saw that Zendeh's place remained empty, he asked where he was. Some of the guests went to look for him, and found him lying dead by the door. They came and told Sohrab, who called the nobles and said to them, "We must not sleep to-night, but must spend the time in sharpening the points of our lances. The wolf has come into the fold, and, in spite of shepherds and dogs, has taken the best of our flock.

With God for my helper, I will avenge on the Persian the death of Zendeh."

When he had thus spoken he came back to his place, and cried, "Zendeh will be wanting by my side in the battle; but I am not weary of the feast."

Meanwhile Rustem went back to King Kaoüs, and told him what he had seen and done. "As for Sohrab," said he, "he has not his equal in Persia, or among the Tartars. He might have been the great warrior San, and what can I say more?"

The next day Sohrab put on his armor, and, going out of the fort, chose a steep place from which he could see the army of the Persians, and bade Hedjir come and stand by him. "Deal fairly with me," said he, "answer me true, and it shall go well with you. You shall have rewards to your heart's content. But if you deceive me, you shall lie in prison for the rest of your days."

Hedjir said, "I will tell you truly all that I can about the army of the Persians. And, indeed, why should I lie unto my lord?"

Sohrab went on, "I am going to ask you questions about the great men of the Persian army. Tell me now who they are. And first I see a tent of leopard skin, surrounded with brocade of many colors, and guarded by a hundred war-elephants. Over the tent there floats a violet flag, on which are figured the sun and the moon in gold. Whose is this tent?"

"That," said Hedjir, "is the tent of the Persian king."

"I see another tent," said Sohrab, "and the flag that flies over it has the figure of an elephant. Whose is it?"

"That is the tent of Thotis, son of King Nereder."

"And now," Sohrab went on, "tell me whose is that tent of green? I see, sitting on a chair, a stalwart hero, with such an air, such shoulders, and such a frame as I have never seen before. Though he is sitting, yet he overtops all the warriors that are near him. And in front of him there stands a great charger, as high as the hero himself; and from the saddle there hangs a lasso. Nowhere have I seen such a man or such a horse. See his standard; it has the figure of a dragon, and on the spear-head is a lion's head."

Hedjir said to himself, "If I were to tell this young lion that this great warrior is Rustem, he would do his best to slay him. No; I will keep his name secret." So he said: "This is one of the king's allies that is newly come from China."

"But what is his name?" said Sohrab.

"I do not know," answered the other, "for I was in the fort when he came to the king."

Sohrab was greatly grieved to find no trace of Rustem. His mother had told him certain signs by which he should know the hero. He saw them all, but he could not believe his eyes. Again he asked Hedjir about the green tent, and the mighty horse, and the lasso hanging from the saddle. But Hedjir answered: "Why should I hide the truth from you? If I do not tell you the name of this warrior from China, it is because I do not know it."

"But," said Sohrab, "where is Rustem? Not a word have you said of him; and yet so great a hero could not remain concealed in the middle of a camp. You told me that he is the chief of the army and the guardian of the provinces. Why, then, is he nowhere to be seen?"

Hedjir answered: "Perhaps he is gone to Zabulistan. It is now that they hold their feasts in the rose gardens of that land."

"This is idle," said Sohrab. "Rustem is one who will always be found in the front of the battle. Now, listen to me. If you will tell me which is Rustem, I will put you above all the people and load you with treasure. But if you hide from me what I want to know, I will cut your head from your body. Now choose between the two."

"Prince," said the other, "when you are tired of life, go out and fight with Rustem, who can kill two hundred men with one blow of his club."

Nevertheless, he thought to himself: "If I show Rustem to this young lion he will rush on him and slay him, for all his strength and vigor. After this there is not a Persian who will dare to fight with him, and he will become king of Persia. No; I will hide the truth, and if I die, I die." Then, turning to Sohrab, he said: "Why are you so angry, and why do you threaten to kill me because I do not point out Rustem to you? But after all, are you not hiding your real thought? You want to meet Rustem in battle; but I say to you, Avoid him, for surely he will bring you to naught."

Sohrab, in a rage, struck him from his horse to the ground. Then, going back to the fort, he armed himself for battle, and went out. First he charged the king's tent, and not one of the warriors of Persia dared to stand before him. He cried out to the king and said:

466

"Noble king, what are you doing here on the field of battle? How dare you take the lance of Kaoüs, you who never dare to fight among the warriors in the battle. Listen to me. The night that Zendeh was slain I swore a great oath that I would not leave a man, little or great, alive in Persia, and that I would hang the king of Persia alive on a gallows. Come, now, if you have a champion who dares to meet me, let him come forth!"

Not a man among the Persians took up this challenge; and the king, in great trouble, sent to Rustem, saying: "The faces of my warriors grow pale before this young Tartar, and there is not one who dares meet him in battle."

Rustem said to the messenger: "When other kings have called me, it has been sometimes to the battle and sometimes to the banquet; but King Kaoüs never calls me except to fight for him."

Nevertheless, he bade his people saddle his horse Raksh, and he put on his circlet of leopard skin and his royal girdle, and mounted, and set out for the battle, with his standard carried before him.

When he saw Sohrab, and observed how tall and stalwart he was, he cried out to him: " Come out from the line of your army, and I will come out from mine."

Sohrab rubbed his hands in delight, and rushed out, saying: "We are warriors, you and I. Do not call to your side any of the men of Persia, and there shall be no Tartar with me. You and I will fight alone. But listen: you cannot stand against me. You are tall of stature, and you have stalwart arms; but the weight of years is on you."

Rustem looked at the young man, and said: "Young man, the earth is dry and cold, but the air is sweet and warm. I have fought in many a battle; many an army have I put to flight; many a warrior and many a Genius have I slain, and never yet have I been beaten. But I should be grieved to do you any harm. Leave these Tartars and come to us. I know not a man in the whole land of Persia who has arms and shoulders such as yours."

When Rustem thus spake, the heart of Sohrab went out to him, and he said: "Come, now; I will ask you a question, and I beseech you to answer me truly. Tell me frankly who you are. Surely you are Rustem, the son of Zal?"

Rustem answered: "It is false; I am not Rustem; I am but a common man; I have neither throne, nor palace, nor crown."

When Sohrab heard this his heart was filled with despair, and he addressed himself to the combat.

The two champions chose a narrow place, and attacked each other with short spears. And when their spears had no more iron left on them — so fierce were the blows — they drew their Indian swords, and fell to work again. And when their swords were broken they used their clubs. Terrible blows they dealt each other! The armor of their horses was broken in pieces; their coats of mail were shattered. At last neither the warriors nor their horses moved more, so fierce had been their struggle. Surely this was a strange and marvelous thing! The beasts know their own young; but man in his fury cannot distinguish between his son and his enemy!

RUSTEM AND SOHRAB

Rustem said to himself: "The battle with the White Genius was but child's play to this. Never yet have I been conquered, and now my heart fails me before this man without a name."

When the two combatants had rest awhile they renewed the battle. Rustem seized Sohrab by the belt, hoping to drag him from his saddle; but he could not move him an inch from his place. Then Sohrab took up again his great club from where it hung by the side of the saddle, and dealt Rustem a mighty blow that bruised his shoulder. The hero writhed under the agony, but was strong enough to swallow down the pain. But Sohrab saw that he had struck a timely stroke, and smiled, saying: "Warrior, you are not one who can stand against the blows of the strong. But it is your age that disables you; it is folly for the aged to match themselves with the young."

After this the two combatants parted, and Rustem chased the army of the Tartars, as a tiger rushes on his prey. When Sohrab saw this he fell, in his turn, upon the Persians, and scattered them like a flock of sheep before him.

Rustem was filled with fury at the sight, and cried: "Man of blood, why have you fallen on the Persians, like a wolf on the fold?"

Sohrab answered: "The army of the Tartars had not joined in the battle, and yet you charged it."

Rustem said: "We will fight again to-morrow, and God shall decide who of us two shall remain the conqueror."

After this they rode back each to his own army. Rustem sought the presence of the king, and told him what a mighty champion this Sohrab was. "We tried all our arms against each other," he said; "the arrow, the sword, the mace, and the lasso, but it was all in vain. At last I caught him by the girdle, hoping to lift him from his saddle, as I have done many a warrior before; but the wind might as well try to drag a mountain from its place as I drag this young warrior from his seat. Nevertheless, I will meet him again to-morrow, and then we will see what is the will of God, whether he is to prevail or I."

That night Rustem said to his brother, "If I fall to-morrow in the conflict, let all my army depart from the field of battle and return to Zabulistan, to the old man Zal. Console my mother in her sorrow. Let her not bind her heart forever to the dead. I have no cause to complain of fate. Many a lion, many a warrior, many a Genius have I slain, many a fortress have I taken, and I have never been overcome. And say to Zal, my father, 'Be faithful to the king, and obey his commands.' As for me, let him remember that old and young must die."

Sohrab passed the night feasting. He said to one of his followers: "My heart goes out to that brave warrior with whom I have fought to-day. I see in him all the signs by which my mother told me I was to recognize my father, and my heart trembles. I must not fight against my father."

The man to whom he spoke said: "I have seen Rustem in battle, and his horse Raksh also I have seen; nor is the horse of this warrior unlike him. Nevertheless, he does not strike the earth with so heavy a tread."

The next day at dawn Sohrab put on his cuirass and

his helmet and armed himself, and, mounting his horse, rode into the space between the two armies. And Rustem, on the other hand, rode out to meet him.

Sohrab spoke to Rustem with a smile upon his lips. One would have thought that they had spent the night together as friends at a feast. "How have you slept?" he said. "How do you fare to-day? Why is your heart bent on battle? Put down your club and your sword. Let us sit together on the ground, and drive away our cares with the wine-cup. Wait till some one else shall come to do battle with you, but with me make a covenant of friendship, and tell me your name and your family. Surely you are Rustem, lord of Zabulistan, son of the white-haired Zal."

Rustem answered: "Young man, we are met here to fight; I will not listen to your deceitful words. No, we will do our best, you and I; and the issue is with God."

Sohrab said: "Old man, I have spoken in vain. I would have you die in your bed when your time shall come, and when these whom you have behind you shall prepare for your burial. But since you put your life in my hands, let us accomplish the purposes of God."

The two warriors then dismounted, and tying their chargers to the rocks, rushed upon each other. Many a blow they struck, till they were both covered with blood and sweat. And so they fought, without advantage to one or the other, from morning till noonday, and from noonday till the shadows began to lengthen upon the sand. At last Sohrab, leaping like a lion, seized Rustem by the girdle, lifted him from the ground, and threw him down, his face and mouth covered with dust; and he couched upon him, as a lion couches on a wild ass that he has caught. Then he drew his dagger, and was about to cut his enemy's head from the body.

Rustem bethought him of a device by which he might save his life. "Young man," he said, " truly you know well how to manage the lasso and the club, the sword and the bow. But listen to me. Our customs of war are not as yours. If a warrior fights with another, and throws him, he does not cut his head from the body the first time; but if he throw him a second time, then he has the right to do so. This is our custom of war."

The young man believed what the old warrior said, for he was of a generous heart; and also fate would have it so. So he let Rustem go free.

After a while came one of the Tartar warriors, and asked him how he had fared in the conflict. When Sohrab told him what had happened, and what Rustem had said, the man cried: "Alas! young man, are you weary of your life? You have let the lion, whom you had caught in your snare, escape. Beware of what will happen. It was a wise man who said, 'Despise no enemy, be he ever so weak,' and think what an enemy is this!"

Sohrab was sorry to hear these words, but said: "Trouble not yourself, I shall fight again to-morrow, and you shall see the yoke upon his neck once more." So saying, he returned to the camp.

Rustem, on the other hand, when he rose from the ground, washed his face in a stream, and prayed to God to give him the victory, not knowing for what he prayed.

It is said that Rustem's strength had once been such that when he put his feet upon a rock they would sink into it, and that he had prayed to God that a part of this strength might be taken from him. But now that he found himself in such danger, and was full of the fear of Sohrab, he prayed once more that his strength might be restored to him as it was before. And again he did not know for what he prayed.

When he had washed off the dust in the stream, he came back to the place of combat, and Sohrab also, seeing him return, left the camp. But when they met, and, laying hold of each other's belts, wrestled as before, then it seemed as if Sohrab had in a moment lost all his strength. Rustem seized him by the head and arm and bent him back, and so threw him on the ground. No thought had he of waiting till he should have thrown the young man a second time; but, knowing that he would not long remain where he lay, drew his sword from its scabbard, and plunged it into his breast.

Sohrab knew that he had received his death-blow. He said to Rustem: "This is my own doing, and it is chance that has put in your hand the key of my fate. My mother told me the signs by which I should know my father, and my love for him has led me to my death. I sought to see his face, and I have sought in vain. I shall never see it; and now I die. But as for you, were you to become a fish in the sea, or a star in the sky, my father will take vengeance on you when he shall hear that I am dead."

Rustem's heart sank in him when he heard these words. "Tell me," he cried, "what marks you have of

Rustem. If this that you say be true, may his name perish forever!" And he threw himself on the ground, and tore his hair with loud cries.

Sohrab said: "If it be so, if indeed you are Rustem, then it is of your own evil soul that you have killed me. Did I not seek by every means to make peace between us? And did I find one movement of tenderness in you? But open my cuirass, and look at what you will see. When my mother heard the sound of my trumpets at the gate, she ran to meet me, her cheeks red with weeping, and fastened a bracelet of onyx to my arm, and said, 'Keep this, it is a remembrance of your father; and use it when the time is come.' But alas! the time is come too late. We have fought together, and the son is dying before the father's eyes."

When Rustem had opened the cuirass, and saw the bracelet of onyx, he tore his garments and cried out in despair, and threw dust upon his head.

But Sohrab said: "There is no remedy. It was to be and it is. What profits this grief?"

After a while he said again: "Now that I am about to die, the Tartars are in an evil case. Show, I pray you, your love for me, by hindering the king from marching against them. It was because they trusted in me, that they have invaded the land of Persia. Let them, therefore, return to their own country in peace. And there is a prisoner in the camp; I asked him about you, and he lied to me, denying the signs which I knew in my heart to be yours. Nevertheless, see that he comes to no harm. And as for me, I came like the thunder, and I go as the wind; perhaps I shall meet you in heaven."

RUSTEM AND SOHRAB

Rustem rode back to the army. The Persians were glad to see him return alive; but when they perceived that his garments were torn and his head covered with dust, they asked him the cause. "I have slain," he said, "the noblest of sons."

Thus Sohrab died by the hand of his father.

END OF VOLUME IV

THE CHILDREN'S HOUR

IN FIFTEEN VOLUMES

ILLUSTRATED

VOLUME II

THE CHILDREN'S HOUR

IN FIFTEEN VOLUMES

ILLUSTRATED

VOLUME II

18 T166c v.2
ppan, Eva March, 1854-
930.
e Children's hour

W9-CDB-542

REF

R01167 39414

prostrate form of Antæus. With every step he looked less like a blue mountain, and more like an immensely large man. He was soon so nigh, that there could be no possible mistake about the matter. There he was, with the sun flaming on his golden helmet, and flashing from his polished breastplate; he had a sword by his side, and a lion's skin over his back, and on his right shoulder he carried a club, which looked bulkier and heavier than the pine-tree walking-stick of Antæus.

By this time, the whole nation of Pygmies had seen the new wonder, and a million of them set up a shout, all together; so that it really made quite an audible squeak.

"Get up, Antæus! Bestir yourself, you lazy old Giant! Here comes another Giant, as strong as you are, to fight with you."

"Nonsense, nonsense!" growled the sleepy Giant. "I'll have my nap out, come who may."

Still the stranger drew nearer; and now the Pygmies could plainly discern that, if his stature were less lofty than the Giant's, yet his shoulders were even broader. And, in truth, what a pair of shoulders they must have been! As I told you, a long while ago, they once upheld the sky. The Pygmies, being ten times as vivacious as their great numskull of a brother, could not abide the Giant's slow movements, and were determined to have him on his feet. So they kept shouting to him, and even went so far as to prick him with their swords.

"Get up, get up, get up!" they cried. "Up with

13

you, lazy bones! The strange Giant's club is bigger than your own, his shoulders are the broadest, and we think him the stronger of the two."

Antæus could not endure to have it said that any mortal was half so mighty as himself. This latter remark of the Pygmies pricked him deeper than their swords; and, sitting up, in rather a sulky humor, he gave a gape of several yards wide, rubbed his eye, and finally turned his stupid head in the direction whither his little friends were eagerly pointing.

No sooner did he set eyes on the stranger than, leaping on his feet, and seizing his walking-stick, he strode a mile or two to meet him; all the while brandishing the sturdy pine-tree, so that it whistled through the air.

"Who are you?" thundered the Giant. "And what do you want in my dominions?"

There was one strange thing about Antæus, of which I have not yet told you, lest, hearing of so many wonders all in a lump, you might not believe much more than half of them. You are to know, then, that whenever this redoubtable Giant touched the ground, either with his hand, his foot, or any other part of his body, he grew stronger than ever he had been before. The Earth, you remember, was his mother, and was very fond of him, as being almost the biggest of her children; and so she took this method of keeping him always in full vigor. Some persons affirm that he grew ten times stronger at every touch; others say that it was only twice as strong. But only think of it! Whenever Antæus took a walk, supposing it were but ten

14

"WHO ARE YOU," THUNDERED THE GIANT

miles, and that he stepped a hundred yards at a stride, you may try to cipher out how much mightier he was, on sitting down again, than when he first started. And whenever he flung himself on the earth to take a little repose, even if he got up the very next instant, he would be as strong as exactly ten just such giants as his former self. It was well for the world that Antæus happened to be of a sluggish disposition, and liked ease better than exercise; for, if he had frisked about like the Pygmies, and touched the earth as often as they did, he would long ago have been strong enough to pull down the sky about people's ears. But these great lubberly fellows resemble mountains, not only in bulk, but in their disinclination to move.

Any other mortal man, except the very one whom Antæus had now encountered, would have been half frightened to death by the Giant's ferocious aspect and terrible voice. But the stranger did not seem at all disturbed. He carelessly lifted his club, and balanced it in his hand, measuring Antæus with his eye from head to foot, not as if wonder-smitten at his stature, but as if he had seen a great many Giants before, and this was by no means the biggest of them. In fact, if the Giant had been no bigger than the Pygmies (who stood pricking up their ears, and looking and listening to what was going forward), the stranger could not have been less afraid of him.

"Who are you, I say?" roared Antæus again. "What's your name? Why do you come hither? Speak, you vagabond, or I'll try the thickness of your skull with my walking-stick."

"You are a very discourteous Giant," answered the stranger, quietly, "and I shall probably have to teach you a little civility, before we part. As for my name, it is Hercules. I have come hither because this is my most convenient road to the garden of the Hesperides, whither I am going to get three of the golden apples for King Eurystheus."

"Caitiff, you shall go no farther!" bellowed Antæus, putting on a grimmer look than before; for he had heard of the mighty Hercules, and hated him because he was said to be so strong. "Neither shall you go back whence you came!"

"How will you prevent me," asked Hercules, "from going whither I please?"

"By hitting you a rap with this pine-tree here," shouted Antæus, scowling so that he made himself the ugliest monster in Africa. "I am fifty times stronger than you; and, now that I stamp my foot upon the ground, I am five hundred times stronger! I am ashamed to kill such a puny little dwarf as you seem to be. I will make a slave of you, and you shall likewise be the slave of my brethren, here, the Pygmies. So throw down your club and your other weapons; and as for that lion's skin, I intend to have a pair of gloves made of it."

"Come and take it off my shoulders, then," answered Hercules, lifting his club.

Then the Giant, grinning with rage, strode tower-like towards the stranger (ten times strengthened at every step), and fetched a monstrous blow at him with his pine-tree, which Hercules caught upon his club;

and being more skilful than Antæus, he paid him back such a rap upon the sconce, that down tumbled the great lumbering man-mountain, flat upon the ground. The poor little Pygmies (who really never dreamed that anybody in the world was half so strong as their brother Antæus) were a good deal dismayed at this. But no sooner was the Giant down, than up he bounced again, with tenfold might, and such a furious visage as was horrible to behold. He aimed another blow at Hercules, but struck awry, being blinded with wrath, and only hit his poor, innocent Mother Earth, who groaned and trembled at the stroke. His pine-tree went so deep into the ground, and stuck there so fast, that before Antæus could get it out, Hercules brought down his club across his shoulders with a mighty thwack, which made the Giant roar as if all sorts of intolerable noises had come screeching and rumbling out of his immeasurable lungs in that one cry. Away it went over mountains and valleys, and, for aught I know, was heard on the other side of the African deserts.

As for the Pygmies, their capital city was laid in ruins by the concussion and vibration of the air; and, though there was uproar enough without their help, they all set up a shriek out of three millions of little throats, fancying, no doubt, that they swelled the Giant's bellow by at least ten times as much. Meanwhile, Antæus had scrambled upon his feet again, and pulled his pine-tree out of the earth; and, all a-flame with fury, and more outrageously strong than ever, he ran at Hercules, and brought down another blow.

"This time, rascal," shouted he, "you shall not escape me."

But once more Hercules warded off the stroke with his club, and the Giant's pine-tree was shattered into a thousand splinters, most of which flew among the Pygmies, and did them more mischief than I like to think about. Before Antæus could get out of the way, Hercules let drive again, and gave him another knockdown blow, which sent him heels over head, but served only to increase his already enormous and insufferable strength. As for his rage, there is no telling what a fiery furnace it had now got to be. His one eye was nothing but a circle of red flame. Having now no weapons but his fists, he doubled them up (each bigger than a hogshead), smote one against the other, and danced up and down with absolute frenzy, flourishing his immense arms about, as if he meant not merely to kill Hercules, but to smash the whole world to pieces.

"Come on!" roared this thundering Giant. "Let me hit you but one box on the ear, and you'll never have the headache again."

Now Hercules (though strong enough, as you already know, to hold the sky up) began to be sensible that he should never win the victory, if he kept on knocking Antæus down; for, by and by, if he hit him such hard blows, the Giant would inevitably, by the help of his Mother Earth, become stronger than the mighty Hercules himself. So, throwing down his club, with which he had fought so many dreadful battles, the hero stood ready to receive his antagonist with naked arms.

"Step forward," cried he. "Since I've broken your pine-tree, we'll try which is the better man at a wrestling-match."

"Aha! then I'll soon satisfy you," shouted the Giant; for, if there was one thing on which he prided himself more than another, it was his skill in wrestling. "Villain, I'll fling you where you can never pick yourself up again."

On came Antæus, hopping and capering with the scorching heat of his rage, and getting new vigor wherewith to wreak his passion, every time he hopped. But Hercules, you must understand, was wiser than this numskull of a Giant, and had thought of a way to fight him, — huge, earth-born monster that he was, — and to conquer him too, in spite of all that his Mother Earth could do for him. Watching his opportunity, as the mad Giant made a rush at him, Hercules caught him round the middle with both hands, lifted him high into the air, and held him aloft overhead.

Just imagine it, my dear little friends! What a spectacle it must have been, to see this monstrous fellow sprawling in the air, face downward, kicking out his long legs and wriggling his whole vast body, like a baby when its father holds it at arm's-length towards the ceiling.

But the most wonderful thing was, that, as soon as Antæus was fairly off the earth, he began to lose the vigor which he had gained by touching it. Hercules very soon perceived that his troublesome enemy was growing weaker, both because he struggled and kicked with less violence, and because the thunder of his big voice subsided into a grumble. The truth was, that, unless the Giant touched Mother Earth as often as once in five minutes, not only his overgrown strength, but the very breath of his life, would depart from him. Hercules had guessed this secret; and it may be well for us all to remember it, in case we should ever have to fight a battle with a fellow like Antæus. For these earth-born creatures are only difficult to conquer on their own ground, but may easily be managed if we can contrive to lift them into a loftier and purer region. So it proved with the poor Giant, whom I am really a little sorry for, notwithstanding his uncivil way of treating strangers who came to visit him.

When his strength and breath were quite gone Hercules gave his huge body a toss, and flung it about a mile off, where it fell heavily, and lay with no more motion than a sand-hill. It was too late for the Giant's Mother Earth to help him now; and I should not wonder if his ponderous bones were lying on the same spot to this very day, and were mistaken for those of an uncommonly large elephant.

But, alas me! What a wailing did the poor little Pygmies set up when they saw their enormous brother treated in this terrible manner! If Hercules heard their shrieks, however, he took no notice, and perhaps fancied them only the shrill, plaintive twittering of small birds that had been frightened from their nests by the uproar of the battle between himself and Antæus. Indeed, his thoughts had been so much taken up with the Giant, that he had never once looked at the Pygmies, nor even knew that there was such a

20

funny little nation in the world. And now, as he had travelled a good way, and was also rather weary with his exertions in the fight, he spread out his lion's skin on the ground, and reclining himself upon it, fell fast asleep.

As soon as the Pygmies saw Hercules preparing for a nap, they nodded their little heads at one another, and winked with their little eyes. And when his deep, regular breathing gave them notice that he was asleep, they assembled together in an immense crowd, spreading over a space of about twenty-seven feet square. One of their most eloquent orators (and a valiant warrior enough, besides, though hardly so good at any other weapon as he was with his tongue) climbed upon a toadstool, and, from that elevated position, addressed the multitude. His sentiments were pretty much as follows; or, at all events, something like this was probably the upshot of his speech: —

"Tall Pygmies and mighty little men! You and all of us have seen what a public calamity has been brought to pass, and what an insult has here been offered to the majesty of our nation. Yonder lies Antæus, our great friend and brother, slain, within our territory, by a miscreant who took him at disadvantage, and fought him (if fighting it can be called) in a way that neither man, nor Giant, nor Pygmy ever dreamed of fighting until this hour. And, adding a grievous contumely to the wrong already done us, the miscreant has now fallen asleep as quietly as if nothing were to be dreaded from our wrath! It behooves you, fellow-countrymen, to consider in what aspect we shall stand before the world, and what will be the verdict of impartial history, should we suffer these accumulated outrages to go unavenged.

"Antæus was our brother, born of that same beloved parent to whom we owe the thews and sinews, as well as the courageous hearts, which made him proud of our relationship. He was our faithful ally, and fell fighting as much for our national rights and immunities as for his own personal ones. We and our forefathers have dwelt in friendship with him, and held affectionate intercourse, as man to man, through immemorial generations. You remember how often our entire people have reposed in his great shadow, and how our little ones have played at hide-and-seek in the tangles of his hair, and how his mighty footsteps have familiarly gone to and fro among us, and never trodden upon any of our toes. And there lies this dear brother, — this sweet and amiable friend, — this brave and faithful ally, — this virtuous Giant, — this blameless and excellent Antæus, — dead! Dead! Silent! Powerless! A mere mountain of clay! Forgive my tears! Nay, I behold your own! Were we to drown the world with them, could the world blame us?

"But to resume: Shall we, my countrymen, suffer this wicked stranger to depart unharmed, and triumph in his treacherous victory, among distant communities of the earth? Shall we not rather compel him to leave his bones here on our soil, by the side of our slain brother's bones, so that, while one skeleton shall remain as the everlasting monument of our sorrow, the other shall endure as long, exhibiting to the whole human race a terrible example of Pygmy vengeance? Such is the question. I put it to you in full confidence of a response that shall be worthy of our national character, and calculated to increase, rather than diminish, the glory which our ancestors have transmitted to us, and which we ourselves have proudly vindicated in our warfare with the cranes."

The orator was here interrupted by a burst of irrepressible enthusiasm; every individual Pygmy crying out that the national honor must be preserved at all hazards. He bowed, and making a gesture for silence, wound up his harangue in the following admirable manner: —

"It only remains for us, then, to decide whether we shall carry on the war in our national capacity, — one united people against a common enemy, — or whether some champion, famous in former fights, shall be selected to defy the slayer of our brother Antæus to single combat. In the latter case, though not unconscious that there may be taller men among you, I hereby offer myself for that enviable duty. And, believe me, dear countrymen, whether I live or die, the honor of this great country, and the fame bequeathed us by our heroic progenitors, shall suffer no diminution in my hands. Never, while I can wield this sword, of which I now fling away the scabbard, — never, never, never, even if the crimson hand that slew the great Antæus shall lay me prostrate, like him, on the soil which I give my life to defend."

So saying, this valiant Pygmy drew out his weapon (which was terrible to behold, being as long as the blade of a penknife), and sent the scabbard whirling over the heads of the multitude. His speech was followed by an uproar of applause, as its patriotism and self-devotion unquestionably deserved; and the shouts and clapping of hands would have been greatly prolonged had they not been rendered quite inaudible by a deep respiration, vulgarly called a snore, from the sleeping Hercules.

It was finally decided that the whole nation of Pygmies should set to work to destroy Hercules; not, be it understood, from any doubt that a single champion would be capable of putting him to the sword, but because he was a public enemy, and all were desirous of sharing in the glory of his defeat. There was a debate whether the national honor did not demand that a herald should be sent with a trumpet, to stand over the ear of Hercules, and, after blowing a blast right into it, to defy him to the combat by formal proclamation. But two or three venerable and sagacious Pygmies, well versed in state affairs, gave it as their opinion that war already existed, and that it was their rightful privilege to take the enemy by surprise. Moreover, if awakened, and allowed to get upon his feet, Hercules might happen to do them a mischief before he could be beaten down again. For, as these sage counsellors remarked, the stranger's club was really very big, and had rattled like a thunderbolt against the skull of Antæus. So the Pygmies resolved to set aside all foolish punctilios, and assail their antagonist at once.

Accordingly, all the fighting men of the nation took

their weapons, and went boldly up to Hercules, who still lay fast asleep, little dreaming of the harm which the Pygmies meant to do him. A body of twenty thousand archers marched in front, with their little bows all ready, and the arrows on the string. The same number were ordered to clamber upon Hercules, some with spades to dig his eyes out, and others with bundles of hay, and all manner of rubbish, with which they intended to plug up his mouth and nostrils, so that he might perish for lack of breath. These last, however, could by no means perform their appointed duty; inasmuch as the enemy's breath rushed out of his nose in an obstreperous hurricane and whirlwind, which blew the Pygmies away as fast as they came nigh. It was found necessary, therefore, to hit upon some other method of carrying on the war.

After holding a council, the captains ordered their troops to collect sticks, straws, dry weeds, and whatever combustible stuff they could find, and make a pile of it, heaping it high around the head of Hercules. As a great many thousand Pygmies were employed in this task, they soon brought together several bushels of inflammatory matter, and raised so tall a heap, that, mounting on its summit, they were quite upon a level with the sleeper's face. The archers, meanwhile, were stationed within bow-shot, with orders to let fly at Hercules the instant that he stirred. Everything being in readiness, a torch was applied to the pile, which immediately burst into flames, and soon waxed hot enough to roast the enemy, had he but chosen to lie still. A Pygmy, you know, though so very small, might set the world on fire, just as easily as a Giant could; so that this was certainly the very best way of dealing with their foe, provided they could have kept him quiet while the conflagration was going forward.

But no sooner did Hercules begin to be scorched, than up he started, with his hair in a red blaze.

"What's all this?" he cried, bewildered with sleep, and staring about him as if he expected to see another Giant.

At that moment the twenty thousand archers twanged their bowstrings, and the arrows came whizzing, like so many winged mosquitoes, right into the face of Hercules. But I doubt whether more than half a dozen of them punctured the skin, which was remarkably tough, as you know the skin of a hero has good need to be.

"Villain!" shouted all the Pygmies at once. "You have killed the Giant Antæus, our great brother, and the ally of our nation. We declare bloody war against you and will slay you on the spot."

Surprised at the shrill piping of so many little voices, Hercules, after putting out the conflagration of his hair, gazed all round about, but could see nothing. At last, however, looking narrowly on the ground, he espied the innumerable assemblage of Pygmies at his feet. He stooped down, and taking up the nearest one between his thumb and finger, set him on the palm of his left hand, and held him at a proper distance for examination. It chanced to be the very identical Pygmy who had spoken from the top of the toadstool, and had offered himself as a champion to meet Hercules in single combat.

"What in the world, my little fellow," ejaculated Hercules, "may you be?"

"I am your enemy," answered the valiant Pygmy, in his mightiest squeak. "You have slain the enormous Antæus, our brother by the mother's side, and for ages the faithful ally of our illustrious nation. We are determined to put you to death; and for my own part, I challenge you to instant battle, on equal ground."

Hercules was so tickled with the Pygmy's big words and warlike gestures, that he burst into a great explosion of laughter, and almost dropped the poor little mite of a creature off the palm of his hand, through the ecstasy and convulsion of his merriment.

"Upon my word," cried he, "I thought I had seen wonders before to-day, — hydras with nine heads, stags with golden horns, six-legged men, three-headed dogs, giants with furnaces in their stomachs, and nobody knows what besides. But here, on the palm of my hand, stands a wonder that outdoes them all! Your body, my little friend, is about the size of an ordinary man's finger. Pray, how big may your soul be?"

"As big as your own!" said the Pygmy.

Hercules was touched with the little man's dauntless courage, and could not help acknowledging such a brotherhood with him as one hero feels for another.

"My good little people," said he, making a low obeisance to the grand nation, "not for all the world would I do an intentional injury to such brave fellows as you! Your hearts seem to me so exceedingly great, that, upon my honor, I marvel how your small bodies can contain them. I sue for peace, and, as a condition of it, will take five strides and be out of your kingdom at the sixth. Good-by. I shall pick my steps carefully, for fear of treading upon some fifty of you, without knowing it. Ha, ha, ha! Ho, ho, ho! For once, Hercules acknowledges himself vanquished."

Some writers say, that Hercules gathered up the whole race of Pygmies in his lion's skin, and carried them home to Greece, for the children of King Eurystheus to play with. But this is a mistake. He left them, one and all, within their own territory, where, for aught I can tell, their descendants are alive to the present day, building their little houses, cultivating their little fields, spanking their little children, waging their little warfare with the cranes, doing their little business, whatever it may be, and reading their little histories of ancient times. In those histories, perhaps, it stands recorded, that, a great many centuries ago, the valiant Pygmies avenged the death of the Giant Antæus by scaring away the mighty Hercules.

THE GORGON'S HEAD

By Nathaniel Hawthorne

PERSEUS was the son of Danaë, who was the daughter of a king. And when Perseus was a very little boy, some wicked people put his mother and himself into a chest, and set them afloat upon the sea. The wind blew freshly, and drove the chest away from the shore, and the uneasy billows tossed it up and down; while Danaë clasped her child closely to her bosom, and dreaded that some big wave would dash its foamy crest over them both. The chest sailed on, however, and neither sank nor was upset; until, when night was coming, it floated so near an island that it got entangled in a fisherman's nets, and was drawn out high and dry upon the sand. The island was called Seriphus, and it was reigned over by King Polydectes, who happened to be the fisherman's brother.

This fisherman, I am glad to tell you, was an exceedingly humane and upright man. He showed great kindness to Danaë and her little boy; and continued to befriend them, until Perseus had grown to be a handsome youth, very strong and active, and skilful in the use of arms. Long before this time, King Polydectes had seen the two strangers — the mother and her child — who had come to his dominions in a floating chest. As he was not good and kind, like his brother

29

the fisherman, but extremely wicked, he resolved to send Perseus on a dangerous enterprise, in which he would probably be killed, and then to do some great mischief to Danaë herself. So this bad-hearted king spent a long while in considering what was the most dangerous thing that a young man could possibly undertake to perform. At last, having hit upon an enterprise that promised to turn out as fatally as he desired, he sent for the youthful Perseus.

The young man came to the palace, and found the king sitting upon his throne.

"Perseus," said King Polydectes, smiling craftily upon him, "you are grown up a fine young man. You and your good mother have received a great deal of kindness from myself, as well as from my worthy brother the fisherman, and I suppose you would not be sorry to repay some of it."

"Please your Majesty," answered Perseus, "I would willingly risk my life to do so."

"Well, then," continued the king, still with a cunning smile on his lips, "I have a little adventure to propose to you; and, as you are a brave and enterprising youth, you will doubtless look upon it as a great piece of good luck to have so rare an opportunity of distinguishing yourself. You must know, my good Perseus, I think of getting married to the beautiful Princess Hippodamia; and it is customary, on these occasions, to make the bride a present of some farfetched and elegant curiosity. I have been a little perplexed, I must honestly confess, where to obtain anything likely to please a princess of her exquisite

taste. But, this morning, I flatter myself, I have thought
of precisely the article."

"And can I assist your Majesty in obtaining it?"
cried Perseus eagerly.

"You can, if you are as brave a youth as I believe
you to be," replied King Polydectes, with the utmost
graciousness of manner. "The bridal gift which I have
set my heart on presenting to the beautiful Hippodamia is the head of the Gorgon Medusa with the snaky
locks; and I depend on you, my dear Perseus, to bring
it to me. So, as I am anxious to settle affairs with the
princess, the sooner you go in quest of the Gorgon,
the better I shall be pleased."

"I will set out to-morrow morning," answered Perseus.

"Pray do so, my gallant youth," rejoined the king.
"And, Perseus, in cutting off the Gorgon's head, be
careful to make a clean stroke, so as not to injure its
appearance. You must bring it home in the very best
condition, in order to suit the exquisite taste of the
beautiful Princess Hippodamia."

Perseus left the palace, but was scarcely out of hearing before Polydectes burst into a laugh; being greatly
amused, wicked king that he was, to find how readily
the young man fell into the snare. The news quickly
spread abroad that Perseus had undertaken to cut off
the head of Medusa with the snaky locks. Everybody
was rejoiced; for most of the inhabitants of the island
were as wicked as the king himself, and would have
liked nothing better than to see some enormous mischief happen to Danaë and her son. The only good

31

man in this unfortunate island of Seriphus appears to have been the fisherman. As Perseus walked along, therefore, the people pointed after him, and made mouths, and winked to one another, and ridiculed him as loudly as they dared.

"Ho, ho!" cried they; "Medusa's snakes will sting him soundly!"

Now, there were three Gorgons alive at that period; and they were the most strange and terrible monsters that had ever been since the world was made, or that have been seen in after days, or that are likely to be seen in all time to come. I hardly know what sort of creature or hobgoblin to call them. They were three sisters, and seem to have borne some distant resemblance to women, but were really a very frightful and mischievous species of dragon. It is, indeed, difficult to imagine what hideous beings these three sisters were. Why, instead of locks of hair, if you can believe me, they had each of them a hundred enormous snakes growing on their heads, all alive, twisting, wriggling, curling, and thrusting out their venomous tongues, with forked stings at the end! The teeth of the Gorgons were terribly long tusks; their hands were made of brass; and their bodies were all over scales, which, if not iron, were something as hard and impenetrable. They had wings, too, and exceedingly splendid ones, I can assure you; for every feather in them was pure, bright, glittering, burnished gold, and they looked very dazzlingly, no doubt, when the Gorgons were flying about in the sunshine.

But when people happened to catch a glimpse of

their glittering brightness, aloft in the air, they seldom stopped to gaze, but ran and hid themselves as speedily as they could. You will think, perhaps, that they were afraid of being stung by the serpents that served the Gorgons instead of hair, — or of having their heads bitten off by their ugly tusks, — or of being torn all to pieces by their brazen claws. Well, to be sure, these were some of the dangers, but by no means the greatest, nor the most difficult to avoid. For the worst thing about these abominable Gorgons was, that, if once a poor mortal fixed his eyes full upon one of their faces, he was certain, that very instant, to be changed from warm flesh and blood into cold and lifeless stone!

Thus, as you will easily perceive, it was a very dangerous adventure that the wicked King Polydectes had contrived for this innocent young man. Perseus himself, when he had thought over the matter, could not help seeing that he had very little chance of coming safely through it, and that he was far more likely to become a stone image than to bring back the head of Medusa with the snaky locks. For, not to speak of other difficulties, there was one which it would have puzzled an older man than Perseus to get over. Not only must he fight with and slay this golden-winged, iron-scaled, long-tusked, brazen-clawed, snaky-haired monster, but he must do it with his eyes shut, or, at least, without so much as a glance at the enemy with whom he was contending. Else, while his arm was lifted to strike, he would stiffen into stone, and stand with that uplifted arm for centuries, until time, and the wind and weather, should crumble him quite away. This would be a very sad thing to befall a young man who wanted to perform a great many brave deeds, and to enjoy a great deal of happiness, in this bright and beautiful world.

So disconsolate did these thoughts make him, that Perseus could not bear to tell his mother what he had undertaken to do. He therefore took his shield, girded on his sword, and crossed over from the island to the mainland, where he sat down in a solitary place, and hardly refrained from shedding tears.

But, while he was in this sorrowful mood, he heard a voice close beside him.

"Perseus," said the voice, "why are you sad?"

He lifted his head from his hands, in which he had hidden it, and, behold! all alone as Perseus had supposed himself to be, there was a stranger in the solitary place. It was a brisk, intelligent, and remarkably shrewd-looking young man, with a cloak over his shoulders, an odd sort of cap on his head, a strangely twisted staff in his hand, and a short and very crooked sword hanging by his side. He was exceedingly light and active in his figure, like a person much accustomed to gymnastic exercises, and well able to leap or run. Above all, the stranger had such a cheerful, knowing, and helpful aspect (though it was certainly a little mischievous, into the bargain), that Perseus could not help feeling his spirits grow livelier as he gazed at him. Besides, being really a courageous youth, he felt greatly ashamed that anybody should have found him with tears in his eyes, like a timid little school-boy.

34

when, after all, there might be no occasion for despair. So Perseus wiped his eyes, and answered the stranger pretty briskly, putting on as brave a look as he could.

"I am not so very sad," said he, "only thoughtful about an adventure that I have undertaken."

"Oho!" answered the stranger. "Well, tell me all about it, and possibly I may be of service to you. I have helped a good many young men through adventures that looked difficult enough beforehand. Perhaps you may have heard of me. I have more names than one; but the name of Quicksilver suits me as well as any other. Tell me what the trouble is, and we will talk the matter over, and see what can be done."

The stranger's words and manner put Perseus into quite a different mood from his former one. He resolved to tell Quicksilver all his difficulties, since he could not easily be worse off than he already was, and, very possibly, his new friend might give him some advice that would turn out well in the end. So he let the stranger know, in few words, precisely what the case was, — how that King Polydectes wanted the head of Medusa with the snaky locks as a bridal gift for the beautiful Princess Hippodamia, and how that he had undertaken to get it for him, but was afraid of being turned to stone.

"And that would be a great pity," said Quicksilver, with his mischievous smile. "You would make a very handsome marble statue, it is true, and it would be a considerable number of centuries before you crumbled away; but, on the whole, one would rather be a young man for a few years, than a stone image for a great many."

"Oh, far rather!" exclaimed Perseus, with the tears again standing in his eyes. "And, besides, what would my dear mother do, if her beloved son were turned into a stone?"

"Well, well, let us hope that the affair will not turn out so very badly," replied Quicksilver, in an encouraging tone. "I am the very person to help you, if anybody can. My sister and myself will do our utmost to bring you safe through the adventure, ugly as it now looks."

"Your sister?" repeated Perseus.

"Yes, my sister," said the stranger. "She is very wise, I promise you; and as for myself, I generally have all my wits about me, such as they are. If you show yourself bold and cautious, and follow our advice, you need not fear being a stone image yet awhile. But, first of all, you must polish your shield, till you can see your face in it as distinctly as in a mirror."

This seemed to Perseus rather an odd beginning of the adventure; for he thought it of far more consequence that the shield should be strong enough to defend him from the Gorgon's brazen claws, than that it should be bright enough to show him the reflection of his face. However, concluding that Quicksilver knew better than himself, he immediately set to work, and scrubbed the shield with so much diligence and good-will, that it very quickly shone like the moon in harvest-time. Quicksilver looked at it with a smile, and nodded his approbation. Then, taking off his own short and crooked sword, he girded it about Perseus, instead of the one which he had before worn.

"No sword but mine will answer your purpose," observed he; "the blade has a most excellent temper, and will cut through iron and brass as easily as through the slenderest twig. And now we will set out. The next thing is to find the Three Gray Women, who will tell us where to find the Nymphs."

"The Three Gray Women!" cried Perseus, to whom this seemed only a new difficulty in the path of his adventure; "pray who may the Three Gray Women be? I never heard of them before."

"They are three very strange old ladies," said Quicksilver, laughing. "They have but one eye among them, and only one tooth. Moreover, you must find them out by starlight, or in the dusk of the evening; for they never show themselves by the light either of the sun or moon."

"But," said Perseus, "why should I waste my time with these Three Gray Women? Would it not be better to set out at once in search of the terrible Gorgons?"

"No, no," answered his friend. "There are other things to be done, before you can find your way to the Gorgons. There is nothing for it but to hunt up these old ladies; and when we meet with them, you may be sure that the Gorgons are not a great way off. Come, let us be stirring!"

Perseus, by this time, felt so much confidence in his companion's sagacity, that he made no more objections, and professed himself ready to begin the adventure immediately. They accordingly set out, and walked at a pretty brisk pace; so brisk, indeed, that Perseus found it rather difficult to keep up with his nimble friend

Quicksilver. To say the truth, he had a singular idea
that Quicksilver was furnished with a pair of winged
shoes, which, of course, helped him along marvelously. And then, too, when Perseus looked sideways
at him, out of the corner of his eye, he seemed to see
wings on the side of his head; although, if he turned
a full gaze, there were no such things to be perceived,
but only an odd kind of cap. But, at all events, the
twisted staff was evidently a great convenience to
Quicksilver, and enabled him to proceed so fast, that
Perseus, though a remarkably active young man, began to be out of breath.

"Here!" cried Quicksilver, at last, — for he knew
well enough, rogue that he was, how hard Perseus
found it to keep pace with him, — "take you the staff,
for you need it a great deal more than I. Are there
no better walkers than yourself in the island of Seriphus?"

"I could walk pretty well," said Perseus, glancing
slyly at his companion's feet, "if I had only a pair of
winged shoes."

"We must see about getting you a pair," answered
Quicksilver.

But the staff helped Perseus along so bravely, that
he no longer felt the slightest weariness. In fact, the
stick seemed to be alive in his hand, and to lend some
of its life to Perseus. He and Quicksilver now walked
onward at their ease, talking very sociably together;
and Quicksilver told so many pleasant stories about
his former adventures, and how well his wits had served
him on various occasions, that Perseus began to think

him a very wonderful person. He evidently knew the world; and nobody is so charming to a young man as a friend who has that kind of knowledge. Perseus listened the more eagerly, in the hope of brightening his own wits by what he heard.

At last, he happened to recollect that Quicksilver had spoken of a sister, who was to lend her assistance in the adventure which they were now bound upon.

"Where is she?" he inquired. "Shall we not meet her soon?"

"All at the proper time," said his companion. "But this sister of mine, you must understand, is quite a different sort of character from myself. She is very grave and prudent, seldom smiles, never laughs, and makes it a rule not to utter a word unless she has something particularly profound to say. Neither will she listen to any but the wisest conversation."

"Dear me!" ejaculated Perseus; "I shall be afraid to say a syllable."

"She is a very accomplished person, I assure you," continued Quicksilver, "and has all the arts and sciences at her fingers' ends. In short, she is so immoderately wise, that many people call her wisdom personified. But, to tell you the truth, she has hardly vivacity enough for my taste; and I think you would scarcely find her so pleasant a traveling companion as myself. She has her good points, nevertheless; and you will find the benefit of them, in your encounter with the Gorgons."

By this time it had grown quite dusk. They were now come to a very wild and desert place, overgrown with shaggy bushes, and so silent and solitary that nobody seemed ever to have dwelt or journeyed there. All was waste and desolate, in the gray twilight, which grew every moment more obscure. Perseus looked about him, rather disconsolately, and asked Quicksilver whether they had a great deal farther to go.

"Hist! hist!" whispered his companion. "Make no noise! This is just the time and place to meet the Three Gray Women. Be careful that they do not see you before you see them; for, though they have but a single eye among the three, it is as sharp-sighted as half a dozen common eyes."

"But what must I do," asked Perseus, "when we meet them?"

Quicksilver explained to Perseus how the Three Gray Women managed with their one eye. They were in the habit, it seems, of changing it from one to another, as if it had been a pair of spectacles, or — which would have suited them better — a quizzing-glass. When one of the three had kept the eye a certain time, she took it out of the socket and passed it to one of her sisters, whose turn it might happen to be, and who immediately clapped it into her own head, and enjoyed a peep at the visible world. Thus it will easily be understood that only one of the Three Gray Women could see, while the other two were in utter darkness; and, moreover, at the instant when the eye was passing from hand to hand, neither of the poor old ladies was able to see a wink. I have heard of a great many strange things, in my day, and have witnessed not a few; but none, it seems to me, that can compare with the oddity of these Three Gray Women, all peeping through a single eye.

So thought Perseus, likewise, and was so astonished that he almost fancied his companion was joking with him, and that there were no such old women in the world.

"You will soon find whether I tell the truth or no," observed Quicksilver. "Hark! hush! hist! hist! There they come, now!"

Perseus looked earnestly through the dusk of the evening, and there, sure enough, at no great distance off, he descried the Three Gray Women. The light being so faint he could not well make out what sort of figures they were; only he discovered that they had long gray hair; and, as they came nearer, he saw that two of them had but the empty socket of an eye, in the middle of their foreheads. But, in the middle of the third sister's forehead, there was a very large, bright, and piercing eye, which sparkled like a great diamond in a ring; and so penetrating did it seem to be, that Perseus could not help thinking it must possess the gift of seeing in the darkest midnight just as perfectly as at noonday. The sight of three persons' eyes was melted and collected into that single one.

Thus the three old dames got along about as comfortably, upon the whole, as if they could all see at once. She who chanced to have the eye in her forehead led the other two by the hands, peeping sharply about her, all the while; insomuch that Perseus dreaded lest she should see right through the thick clump of bushes behind which he and Quicksilver had hidden themselves. My stars! it was positively terrible to be within reach of so very sharp an eye!

But, before they reached the clump of bushes, one of the Three Gray Women spoke.

"Sister! Sister Scarecrow!" cried she, "you have had the eye long enough. It is my turn now!"

"Let me keep it a moment longer, Sister Nightmare," answered Scarecrow. "I thought I had a glimpse of something behind that thick bush."

"Well, and what of that?" retorted Nightmare, peevishly. "Can't I see into a thick bush as easily as yourself? The eye is mine as well as yours; and I know the use of it as well as you, or may be a little better. I insist upon taking a peep immediately!"

But here the third sister, whose name was Shakejoint, began to complain, and said that it was her turn to have the eye, and that Scarecrow and Nightmare wanted to keep it all to themselves. To end the dispute, old Dame Scarecrow took the eye out of her forehead, and held it forth in her hand.

"Take it, one of you," cried she, "and quit this foolish quarreling. For my part, I shall be glad of a little thick darkness. Take it quickly, however, or I must clap it into my own head again!"

Accordingly, both Nightmare and Shakejoint put out their hands, groping eagerly to snatch the eye out of the hand of Scarecrow. But, being both alike blind, they could not easily find where Scarecrow's hand was; and Scarecrow, being now just as much in the dark as Shakejoint and Nightmare, could not at once meet either of their hands, in order to put the eye into it. Thus (as you will see, with half an eye, my wise little auditors) these good old dames had fallen into a strange perplexity. For, though the eye shone and glistened like a star, as Scarecrow held it out, yet the Gray Women caught not the least glimpse of its light, and were all three in utter darkness, from too impatient a desire to see.

Quicksilver was so much tickled at beholding Shakejoint and Nightmare both groping for the eye, and each finding fault with Scarecrow and one another, that he could scarcely help laughing aloud.

"Now is your time!" he whispered to Perseus. "Quick, quick! before they can clap the eye into either of their heads. Rush out upon the old ladies, and snatch it from Scarecrow's hand!"

In an instant, while the Three Gray Women were still scolding each other, Perseus leaped from behind the clump of bushes, and made himself master of the prize. The marvelous eye, as he held it in his hand, shone very brightly, and seemed to look up into his face with a knowing air, and an expression as if it would have winked, had it been provided with a pair of eyelids for that purpose. But the Gray Women knew nothing of what had happened; and, each supposing that one of her sisters was in possession of the eye, they began their quarrel anew. At last, as Perseus did not wish to put these respectable dames to greater inconvenience than was really necessary, he thought it right to explain the matter.

"My good ladies," said he, "pray do not be angry with one another. If anybody is in fault, it is myself:

for I have the honor to hold your very brilliant and excellent eye in my own hand!"

"You! you have our eye! And who are you?" screamed the Three Gray Women, all in a breath; for they were terribly frightened, of course, at hearing a strange voice, and discovering that their eyesight had got into the hands of they could not guess whom. "Oh, what shall we do, sisters? what shall we do? We are all in the dark! Give us our eye! Give us our one, precious, solitary eye! You have two of your own! Give us our eye!"

"Tell them," whispered Quicksilver to Perseus, "that they shall have back the eye as soon as they direct you where to find the Nymphs who have the flying slippers, the magic wallet, and the helmet of darkness."

"My dear, good, admirable old ladies," said Perseus, addressing the Gray Women, "there is no occasion for putting yourselves into such a fright. I am by no means a bad young man. You shall have back your eye, safe and sound, and as bright as ever, the moment you tell me where to find the Nymphs."

"The Nymphs! Goodness me! sisters, what Nymphs does he mean?" screamed Scarecrow. "There are a great many Nymphs, people say; some that go a-hunting in the woods, and some that live inside of trees, and some that have a comfortable home in fountains of water. We know nothing at all about them. We are three unfortunate old souls, that go wandering about in the dusk, and never had but one eye amongst us, and that one you have stolen away. Oh, give it back, good stranger! — whoever you are, give it back!"

All this while the Three Gray Women were groping with their outstretched hands, and trying their utmost to get hold of Perseus. But he took good care to keep out of their reach.

"My respectable dames," said he, — for his mother had taught him always to use the greatest civility, — "I hold your eye fast in my hand, and shall keep it safely for you, until you please to tell me where to find these Nymphs. The Nymphs, I mean, who keep the enchanted wallet, the flying slippers, and the what is it? — the helmet of invisibility."

"Mercy on us, sisters! what is the young man talking about?" exclaimed Scarecrow, Nightmare, and Shakejoint, one to another, with great appearance of astonishment. "A pair of flying slippers, quoth he! His heels would quickly fly higher than his head, if he were silly enough to put them on. And a helmet of invisibility! How could a helmet make him invisible, unless it were big enough for him to hide under it? And an enchanted wallet! What sort of a contrivance may that be, I wonder? No, no, good stranger! we can tell you nothing of these marvelous things. You have two eyes of your own, and we have but a single one amongst us three. You can find out such wonders better than three blind old creatures, like us."

Perseus, hearing them talk in this way, began really to think that the Gray Women knew nothing of the matter; and, as it grieved him to have put them to so much trouble, he was just on the point of restoring their eye and asking pardon for his rudeness in snatching it away. But Quicksilver caught his hand.

"Don't let them make a fool of you!" said he. "These Three Gray Women are the only persons in the world that can tell you where to find the Nymphs; and, unless you get that information, you will never succeed in cutting off the head of Medusa with the snaky locks. Keep fast hold of the eye, and all will go well."

As it turned out, Quicksilver was in the right. There are but few things that people prize so much as they do their eyesight; and the Gray Women valued their single eye as highly as if it had been half a dozen, which was the number they ought to have had. Finding that there was no other way of recovering it, they at last told Perseus what he wanted to know. No sooner had they done so, than he immediately, and with the utmost respect, clapped the eye into the vacant socket in one of their foreheads, thanked them for their kindness, and bade them farewell. Before the young man was out of hearing, however, they had got into a new dispute, because he happened to have given the eye to Scarecrow, who had already taken her turn of it when their trouble with Perseus commenced.

It is greatly to be feared that the Three Gray Women were very much in the habit of disturbing their mutual harmony by bickerings of this sort; which was the more pity, as they could not conveniently do without one another, and were evidently intended to be inseparable companions. As a general rule, I would advise all people, whether sisters or brothers, old or young, who chance to have but one eye amongst them, to cultivate forbearance, and not all insist upon peeping through it at once.

Quicksilver and Perseus, in the mean time, were making the best of their way in quest of the Nymphs. The old dames had given them such particular directions, that they were not long in finding them out. They proved to be very different persons from Nightmare, Shakejoint, and Scarecrow; for, instead of being old, they were young and beautiful; and instead of one eye amongst the sisterhood, each Nymph had two exceedingly bright eyes of her own, with which she looked very kindly at Perseus. They seemed to be acquainted with Quicksilver; and, when he told them the adventure which Perseus had undertaken, they made no difficulty about giving him the valuable articles that were in their custody. In the first place, they brought out what appeared to be a small purse, made of deer skin, and curiously embroidered, and bade him be sure and keep it safe. This was the magic wallet. The Nymphs next produced a pair of shoes, or slippers, or sandals, with a nice little pair of wings at the heel of each.

"Put them on, Perseus," said Quicksilver. "You will find yourself as light-heeled as you can desire for the remainder of our journey."

So Perseus proceeded to put one of the slippers on, while he laid the other on the ground by his side. Unexpectedly, however, this other slipper spread its wings, fluttered up off the ground, and would probably have flown away, if Quicksilver had not made a leap, and luckily caught it in the air.

"Be more careful," said he, as he gave it back to Perseus. "It would frighten the birds, up aloft, if they should see a flying slipper amongst them."

When Perseus had got on both of these wonderful slippers, he was altogether too buoyant to tread on earth. Making a step or two, lo and behold! upward he popped into the air, high above the heads of Quicksilver and the Nymphs, and found it very difficult to clamber down again. Winged slippers, and all such high-flying contrivances, are seldom quite easy to manage until one grows a little accustomed to them. Quicksilver laughed at his companion's involuntary activity, and told him that he must not be in so desperate a hurry, but must wait for the invisible helmet.

The good-natured Nymphs had the helmet, with its dark tuft of waving plumes, all in readiness to put upon his head. And now there happened about as wonderful an incident as anything that I have yet told you. The instant before the helmet was put on, there stood Perseus, a beautiful young man, with golden ringlets and rosy cheeks, the crooked sword by his side, and the brightly polished shield upon his arm, — a figure that seemed all made up of courage, sprightliness, and glorious light. But when the helmet had descended over his white brow, there was no longer any Perseus to be seen! Nothing but empty air! Even the helmet, that covered him with its invisibility, had vanished!

"Where are you, Perseus?" asked Quicksilver.

"Why, here, to be sure!" answered Perseus, very quietly, although his voice seemed to come out of the transparent atmosphere. "Just where I was a moment ago. Don't you see me?"

"No, indeed!" answered his friend. "You are hidden under the helmet. But, if I cannot see you, neither can the Gorgons. Follow me, therefore, and we will try your dexterity in using the winged slippers."

With these words, Quicksilver's cap spread its wings, as if his head were about to fly away from his shoulders; but his whole figure rose lightly into the air, and Perseus followed. By the time they had ascended a few hundred feet, the young man began to feel what a delightful thing it was to leave the dull earth so far beneath him, and to be able to flit about like a bird.

It was now deep night. Perseus looked upward, and saw the round, bright, silvery moon, and thought that he should desire nothing better than to soar up thither, and spend his life there. Then he looked downward again, and saw the earth, with its seas and lakes, and the silver courses of its rivers, and its snowy mountain-peaks, and the breadth of its fields, and the dark cluster of its woods, and its cities of white marble; and, with the moonshine sleeping over the whole scene, it was as beautiful as the moon or any star could be. And, among other objects, he saw the island of Seriphus, where his dear mother was. Sometimes he and Quicksilver approached a cloud, that, at a distance, looked as if it were made of fleecy silver;

although, when they plunged into it, they found themselves chilled and moistened with gray mist. So swift was their flight, however, that, in an instant, they emerged from the cloud into the moonlight again. Once, a high-soaring eagle flew right against the invisible Perseus. The bravest sights were the meteors, that gleamed suddenly out, as if a bonfire had been kindled in the sky, and made the moonshine pale for as much as a hundred miles around them.

As the two companions flew onward, Perseus fancied that he could hear the rustle of a garment close by his side; and it was on the side opposite to the one where he beheld Quicksilver, yet only Quicksilver was visible.

"Whose garment is this," inquired Perseus, "that keeps rustling close beside me in the breeze?"

"Oh, it is my sister's!" answered Quicksilver. "She is coming along with us, as I told you she would. We could do nothing without the help of my sister. You have no idea how wise she is. She has such eyes, too! Why, she can see you, at this moment, just as distinctly as if you were not invisible; and I'll venture to say, she will be the first to discover the Gorgons."

By this time, in their swift voyage through the air, they had come within sight of the great ocean, and were soon flying over it. Far beneath them, the waves tossed themselves tumultuously in mid-sea, or rolled a white surf-line upon the long beaches, or foamed against the rocky cliffs, with a roar that was thunderous, in the lower world; although it became a gentle murmur, like the voice of a baby half asleep, before it reached the ears of Perseus. Just then a voice spoke in the air close by him. It seemed to be a woman's voice, and was melodious, though not exactly what might be called sweet, but grave and mild.

"Perseus," said the voice, "there are the Gorgons."

"Where?" exclaimed Perseus. "I cannot see them."

"On the shore of that island beneath you," replied the voice. "A pebble, dropped from your hand, would strike in the midst of them."

"I told you she would be the first to discover them," said Quicksilver to Perseus. "And there they are!"

Straight downward, two or three thousand feet below him, Perseus perceived a small island, with the sea breaking into white foam all around its rocky shore, except on one side, where there was a beach of snowy sand. He descended towards it, and, looking earnestly at a cluster or heap of brightness, at the foot of a precipice of black rocks, behold, there were the terrible Gorgons! They lay fast asleep, soothed by the thunder of the sea; for it required a tumult that would have deafened everybody else to lull such fierce creatures into slumber. The moonlight glistened on their steely scales, and on their golden wings, which drooped idly over the sand. Their brazen claws, horrible to look at, were thrust out, and clutched the wave-beaten fragments of rock, while the sleeping Gorgons dreamed of tearing some poor mortal all to pieces. The snakes that served them instead of hair seemed likewise to be asleep; although, now and then, one would writhe, and lift its head, and thrust out its forked tongue, emitting a drowsy hiss, and then let itself subside among its sister snakes.

The Gorgons were more like an awful, gigantic kind of insect, — immense, golden-winged beetles, or dragon-flies, or things of that sort, — at once ugly and beautiful, — than like anything else; only that they were a thousand and a million times as big. And, with all this, there was something partly human about them, too. Luckily for Perseus, their faces were completely hidden from him by the posture in which they lay; for, had he but looked one instant at them, he would have fallen heavily out of the air, an image of senseless stone.

"Now," whispered Quicksilver, as he hovered by the side of Perseus, — "now is your time to do the deed! Be quick; for, if one of the Gorgons should awake, you are too late!"

"Which shall I strike at?" asked Perseus, drawing his sword and descending a little lower. "They all three look alike. All three have snaky locks. Which of the three is Medusa?"

It must be understood that Medusa was the only one of these dragon-monsters whose head Perseus could possibly cut off. As for the other two, let him have the sharpest sword that ever was forged, and he might have hacked away by the hour together, without doing them the least harm.

"Be cautious," said the calm voice which had before spoken to him. "One of the Gorgons is stirring in her sleep, and is just about to turn over. That is Medusa. Do not look at her! The sight would turn you to stone! Look at the reflection of her face and figure in the bright mirror of your shield."

Perseus now understood Quicksilver's motive for so
earnestly exhorting him to polish his shield. In its
surface he could safely look at the reflection of the Gorgon's face. And there it was, — that terrible countenance, — mirrored in the brightness of the shield, with
the moonlight falling over it, and displaying all its
horror. The snakes, whose venomous natures could
not altogether sleep, kept twisting themselves over the
forehead. It was the fiercest and most horrible face
that ever was seen or imagined, and yet with a strange,
fearful, and savage kind of beauty in it. The eyes
were closed, and the Gorgon was still in a deep slumber; but there was an unquiet expression disturbing
her features, as if the monster was troubled with an
ugly dream. She gnashed her white tusks, and dug
into the sand with her brazen claws.

The snakes, too, seemed to feel Medusa's dream, and
to be made more restless by it. They twined themselves into tumultuous knots, writhed fiercely, and uplifted a hundred hissing heads, without opening their
eyes.

"Now, now!" whispered Quicksilver, who was growing impatient. "Make a dash at the monster!"

"But be calm," said the grave, melodious voice, at
the young man's side. "Look in your shield, as you
fly downward, and take care that you do not miss your
first stroke."

Perseus flew cautiously downward, still keeping his
eyes on Medusa's face, as reflected in his shield. The
nearer he came, the more terrible did the snaky visage
and metallic body of the monster grow. At last, when

he found himself hovering over her within arm's length, Perseus uplifted his sword, while, at the same instant, each separate snake upon the Gorgon's head stretched threateningly upward, and Medusa unclosed her eyes. But she awoke too late. The sword was sharp; the stroke fell like a lightning-flash; and the head of the wicked Medusa tumbled from her body!

"Admirably done!" cried Quicksilver. "Make haste, and clap the head into your magic wallet."

To the astonishment of Perseus, the small, embroidered wallet, which he had hung about his neck, and which had hitherto been no bigger than a purse, grew all at once large enough to contain Medusa's head. As quick as thought, he snatched it up, with the snakes still writhing upon it, and thrust it in.

"Your task is done," said the calm voice. "Now fly; for the other Gorgons will do their utmost to take vengeance for Medusa's death."

It was, indeed, necessary to take flight; for Perseus had not done the deed so quietly but that the clash of his sword, and the hissing of the snakes, and the thump of Medusa's head as it tumbled upon the sea-beaten sand, awoke the other two monsters. There they sat, for an instant, sleepily rubbing their eyes with their brazen fingers, while all the snakes on their heads reared themselves on end with surprise, and with venomous malice against they knew not what. But when the Gorgons saw the scaly carcass of Medusa, headless, and her golden wings all ruffled, and half spread out on the sand, it was really awful to hear what yells and screeches they set up. And then the snakes!

They sent forth a hundred-fold hiss, with one consent, and Medusa's snakes answered them out of the magic wallet.

No sooner were the Gorgons broad awake than they hurtled upward into the air, brandishing their brass talons, gnashing their horrible tusks, and flapping their huge wings so wildly, that some of the golden feathers were shaken out, and floated down upon the shore. And there, perhaps, those very feathers lie scattered till this day. Up rose the Gorgons, as I tell you, staring horribly about, in hopes of turning somebody to stone. Had Perseus looked them in the face, or had he fallen into their clutches, his poor mother would never have kissed her boy again! But he took good care to turn his eyes another way; and, as he wore the helmet of invisibility, the Gorgons knew not in what direction to follow him; nor did he fail to make the best use of the winged slippers, by soaring upward a perpendicular mile or so. At that height, when the screams of those abominable creatures sounded faintly beneath him, he made a straight course for the island of Seriphus, in order to carry Medusa's head to King Polydectes.

I have no time to tell you of several marvelous things that befell Perseus, on his way homeward; such as his killing a hideous sea-monster, just as it was on the point of devouring a beautiful maiden; nor how he changed an enormous giant into a mountain of stone, merely by showing him the head of the Gorgon. If you doubt this latter story, you may make a voyage to Africa, some day or other, and see the very mountain, which is still known by the ancient giant's name.

Finally, our brave Perseus arrived at the island, where he expected to see his dear mother. But, during his absence, the wicked king had treated Danaë so very ill that she was compelled to make her escape, and had taken refuge in a temple, where some good old priests were extremely kind to her. These praiseworthy priests, and the kind-hearted fisherman who had first shown hospitality to Danaë and little Perseus when he found them afloat in the chest, seem to have been the only persons on the island who cared about doing right. All the rest of the people, as well as King Polydectes himself, were remarkably ill-behaved, and deserved no better destiny than that which was now to happen.

Not finding his mother at home, Perseus went straight to the palace, and was immediately ushered into the presence of the king. Polydectes was by no means rejoiced to see him; for he had felt almost certain, in his own evil mind, that the Gorgons would have torn the poor young man to pieces, and have eaten him up, out of the way. However, seeing him safely returned, he put the best face he could upon the matter and asked Perseus how he had succeeded.

"Have you performed your promise?" inquired he. "Have you brought me the head of Medusa with the snaky locks? If not, young man, it will cost you dear; for I must have a bridal present for the beautiful Princess Hippodamia, and there is nothing else that she would admire so much."

"Yes, please your Majesty," answered Perseus, in a quiet way, as if it were no very wonderful deed for such a young man as he to perform. "I have brought you the Gorgon's head, snaky locks and all!"

"Indeed! Pray let me see it," quoth King Polydectes. "It must be a very curious spectacle, if all that travelers tell about it be true!"

"Your Majesty is in the right," replied Perseus. "It is really an object that will be pretty certain to fix the regards of all who look at it. And, if your Majesty think fit, I would suggest that a holiday be proclaimed, and that all your Majesty's subjects be summoned to behold this wonderful curiosity. Few of them, I imagine, have seen a Gorgon's head before, and perhaps never may again!"

The king well knew that his subjects were an idle set of reprobates, and very fond of sight-seeing, as idle persons usually are. So he took the young man's advice, and sent out heralds and messengers, in all directions, to blow the trumpet at the street-corners, and in the market-places, and wherever two roads met, and summon everybody to court. Thither, accordingly, came a great multitude of good-for-nothing vagabonds, all of whom, out of pure love of mischief, would have been glad if Perseus had met with some ill-hap in his encounter with the Gorgons. If there were any better people in the island (as I really hope there may have been, although the story tells nothing about any such), they stayed quietly at home, minding their business, and taking care of their little children. Most of the inhabitants, at all events, ran as fast as they could to the palace, and shoved, and pushed, and elbowed one another, in their eagerness to get near a balcony, on which Perseus showed himself, holding the embroidered wallet in his hand.

On a platform, within full view of the balcony, sat the mighty King Polydectes, amid his evil counselors, and with his flattering courtiers in a semicircle round about him. Monarch, counselors, courtiers, and subjects all gazed eagerly towards Perseus.

"Show us the head! Show us the head!" shouted the people; and there was a fierceness in their cry, as if they would tear Perseus to pieces, unless he should satisfy them with what he had to show. "Show us the head of Medusa with the snaky locks!"

A feeling of sorrow and pity came over the youthful Perseus.

"O King Polydectes," cried he, "and ye many people, I am very loath to show you the Gorgon's head!"

"Ah, the villain and coward!" yelled the people, more fiercely than before. "He is making game of us! He has no Gorgon's head! Show us the head, if you have it, or we will take your own head for a football!"

The evil counselors whispered bad advice in the king's ear; the courtiers murmured, with one consent, that Perseus had shown disrespect to their royal lord and master; and the great King Polydectes himself waved his hand, and ordered him, with the stern, deep voice of authority, on his peril, to produce the head.

"Show me the Gorgon's head, or I will cut off your own!"

And Perseus sighed.

"BEHOLD IT, THEN!" CRIED PERSEUS

"This instant," repeated Polydectes, "or you die!"

"Behold it, then!" cried Perseus, in a voice like the blast of a trumpet.

And, suddenly holding up the head, not an eyelid had time to wink before the wicked King Polydectes, his evil counselors, and all his fierce subjects were no longer anything but the mere images of a monarch and his people. They were all fixed, forever, in the look and attitude of that moment! At the first glimpse of the terrible head of Medusa, they whitened into marble! And Perseus thrust the head back into his wallet, and went to tell his dear mother that she need no longer be afraid of the wicked King Polydectes.

THE GOLDEN FLEECE

By Nathaniel Hawthorne

WHEN Jason, the son of the dethroned king of
Iolchos, was a little boy, he was sent away from
his parents, and placed under the queerest schoolmaster that ever you heard of. This learned person was one
of the people, or quadrupeds, called Centaurs. He
lived in a cavern, and had the body and legs of a white
horse, with the head and shoulders of a man. His
name was Chiron; and, in spite of his odd appearance, he was a very excellent teacher, and had several
scholars, who afterwards did him credit by making
a great figure in the world. The famous Hercules
was one, and so was Achilles, and Philoctetes, likewise, and Æsculapius, who acquired immense repute
as a doctor. The good Chiron taught his pupils how
to play upon the harp, and how to cure diseases, and
how to use the sword and shield, together with various other branches of education, in which the lads of
those days used to be instructed, instead of writing and
arithmetic.

I have sometimes suspected that Master Chiron was
not really very different from other people, but that,
being a kind-hearted and merry old fellow, he was in
the habit of making believe that he was a horse, and
acrambling about the school-room on all fours, and let-

ting the little boys ride upon his back. And so, when his scholars had grown up, and grown old, and were trotting their grandchildren on their knees, they told them about the sports of their school-days; and these young folks took the idea that their grandfathers had been taught their letters by a Centaur, half man and half horse. Little children, not quite understanding what is said to them, often get such absurd notions into their heads, you know.

Be that as it may, it has always been told for a fact (and always will be told, as long as the world lasts) that Chiron, with the head of a schoolmaster, had the body and legs of a horse. Just imagine the grave old gentleman clattering and stamping into the school-room on his four hoofs, perhaps treading on some little fellow's toes, flourishing his switch tail instead of a rod, and, now and then, trotting out of doors to eat a mouthful of grass! I wonder what the blacksmith charged him for a set of iron shoes.

So Jason dwelt in a cave, with this four-footed Chiron, from the time that he was an infant, only a few months old, until he had grown to the full height of a man. He became a very good harper, I suppose, and skillful in the use of weapons, and tolerably acquainted with herbs and other doctor's stuff, and, above all, an admirable horseman; for, in teaching young people to ride, the good Chiron must have been without a rival among schoolmasters. At length, being now a tall and athletic youth, Jason resolved to seek his fortune in the world, without asking Chiron's advice, or telling him anything about the matter. This was very unwise, to be sure; and I hope none of you, my little hearers, will ever follow Jason's example. But, you are to understand, he had heard how that he himself was a prince royal, and how his father, King Æson, had been deprived of the kingdom of Iolchos by a certain Pelias, who would also have killed Jason, had he not been hidden in the Centaur's cave. And, being come to the strength of a man, Jason determined to set all this business to rights, and to punish the wicked Pelias for wronging his dear father, and to cast him down from the throne, and seat himself there instead.

With this intention, he took a spear in each hand, and threw a leopard's skin over his shoulders, to keep off the rain, and set forth on his travels, with his long yellow ringlets waving in the wind. The part of his dress on which he most prided himself was a pair of sandals that had been his father's. They were handsomely embroidered, and were tied upon his feet with strings of gold. But his whole attire was such as people did not very often see; and as he passed along, the women and children ran to the doors and windows, wondering whither this beautiful youth was journeying, with his leopard's skin and his golden-tied sandals, and what heroic deeds he meant to perform, with a spear in his right hand and another in his left.

I know not how far Jason had traveled, when he came to a turbulent river, which rushed right across his pathway, with specks of white foam among its black eddies, hurrying tumultuously onward, and roaring angrily as it went. Though not a very broad river in the dry seasons of the year, it was now swollen by

heavy rains and by the melting of the snow on the
sides of Mount Olympus; and it thundered so loudly,
and looked so wild and dangerous, that Jason, bold as
he was, thought it prudent to pause upon the brink.
The bed of the stream seemed to be strewn with sharp
and rugged rocks, some of which thrust themselves
above the water. By and by, an uprooted tree, with
shattered branches, came drifting along the current,
and got entangled among the rocks. Now and then
a drowned sheep, and once the carcass of a cow, floated
past.

In short, the swollen river had already done a great
deal of mischief. It was evidently too deep for Jason
to wade, and too boisterous for him to swim; he could
see no bridge; and as for a boat, had there been any,
the rocks would have broken it to pieces in an instant.

"See the poor lad," said a cracked voice close to
his side. "He must have had but a poor education,
since he does not know how to cross a little stream
like this. Or is he afraid of wetting his fine golden-
stringed sandals? It is a pity his four-footed schoolmaster is not here to carry him safely across on his
back!"

Jason looked round greatly surprised, for he did
not know that anybody was near. But beside him stood
an old woman, with a ragged mantle over her head,
leaning on a staff, the top of which was carved into
the shape of a cuckoo. She looked very aged, and
wrinkled, and infirm; and yet her eyes, which were
as brown as those of an ox, were so extremely large
and beautiful, that, when they were fixed on Jason's

eyes, he could see nothing else but them. The old woman had a pomegranate in her hand, although the fruit was then quite out of season.

"Whither are you going, Jason?" she now asked.

She seemed to know his name, you will observe; and, indeed, those great brown eyes looked as if they had a knowledge of everything, whether past or to come. While Jason was gazing at her, a peacock strutted forward and took his stand at the old woman's side.

"I am going to Iolchos," answered the young man, "to bid the wicked king Pelias come down from my father's throne, and let me reign in his stead."

"Ah, well, then," said the old woman, still with the same cracked voice, "if that is all your business, you need not be in a very great hurry. Just take me on your back, there's a good youth, and carry me across the river. I and my peacock have something to do on the other side, as well as yourself."

"Good mother," replied Jason, "your business can hardly be so important as the pulling down a king from his throne. Besides, as you may see for yourself, the river is very boisterous; and if I should chance to stumble, it would sweep both of us away more easily than it has carried off yonder uprooted tree. I would gladly help you if I could; but I doubt whether I am strong enough to carry you across."

"Then," said she, very scornfully, "neither are you strong enough to pull King Pelias off his throne. And, Jason, unless you will help an old woman at her need, you ought not to be a king. What are kings made for, save to succor the feeble and distressed? But do as you please. Either take me on your back, or with my poor old limbs I shall try my best to struggle across the stream."

Saying this, the old woman poked with her staff in the river, as if to find the safest place in its rocky bed where she might make the first step. But Jason, by this time, had grown ashamed of his reluctance to help her. He felt that he could never forgive himself, if this poor feeble creature should come to any harm in attempting to wrestle against the headlong current. The good Chiron, whether half horse or no, had taught him that the noblest use of his strength was to assist the weak; and also that he must treat every young woman as if she were his sister, and every old one like a mother. Remembering these maxims, the vigorous and beautiful young man knelt down, and requested the good dame to mount upon his back.

"The passage seems to me not very safe," he remarked. "But as your business is so urgent, I will try to carry you across. If the river sweeps you away, it shall take me too."

"That, no doubt, will be a great comfort to both of us," quoth the old woman. "But never fear. We shall get safely across."

So she threw her arms around Jason's neck; and lifting her from the ground, he stepped boldly into the raging and foamy current, and began to stagger away from the shore. As for the peacock, it alighted on the old dame's shoulder. Jason's two spears, one in each hand, kept him from stumbling, and enabled him to feel his way among the hidden rocks; although, every instant, he expected that his companion and himself would go down the stream, together with the drift-wood of shattered trees, and the carcasses of the sheep and cow. Down came the cold, snowy torrent from the steep side of Olympus, raging and thundering as if it had a real spite against Jason, or, at all events, were determined to snatch off his living burden from his shoulders. When he was half-way across, the uprooted tree (which I have already told you about) broke loose from among the rocks, and bore down upon him, with all its splintered branches sticking out like the hundred arms of the giant Briareus. It rushed past, however, without touching him. But the next moment, his foot was caught in a crevice between two rocks, and stuck there so fast, that, in the effort to get free, he lost one of his golden-stringed sandals.

At this accident Jason could not help uttering a cry of vexation.

"What is the matter, Jason?" asked the old woman.

"Matter enough," said the young man. "I have lost a sandal here among the rocks. And what sort of a figure shall I cut at the court of King Pelias, with a golden-stringed sandal on one foot, and the other foot bare!"

"Do not take it to heart," answered his companion, cheerily. "You never met with better fortune than in losing that sandal. It satisfies me that you are the very person whom the Speaking Oak has been talking about."

There was no time, just then, to inquire what the Speaking Oak had said. But the briskness of her tone encouraged the young man; and besides, he had never in his life felt so vigorous and mighty as since taking this old woman on his back. Instead of being exhausted, he gathered strength as he went on; and, struggling up against the torrent, he at last gained the opposite shore, clambered up the bank, and set down the old dame and her peacock safely on the grass. As soon as this was done, however, he could not help looking rather despondently at his bare foot, with only a remnant of the golden string of the sandal clinging round his ankle.

"You will get a handsomer pair of sandals by and by," said the old woman, with a kindly look out of her beautiful brown eyes. "Only let King Pelias get a glimpse of that bare foot, and you shall see him turn as pale as ashes, I promise you. There is your path. Go along, my good Jason, and my blessing go with you. And when you sit on your throne, remember the old woman whom you helped over the river."

With these words, she hobbled away, giving him a smile over her shoulder as she departed. Whether the light of her beautiful brown eyes threw a glory round about her, or whatever the cause might be, Jason fancied that there was something very noble and majestic in her figure, after all, and that, though her gait seemed to be a rheumatic hobble, yet she moved with as much grace and dignity as any queen on earth. Her peacock, which had now fluttered down from her shoulder, strutted behind her in prodigious pomp, and spread out its magnificent tail on purpose for Jason to admire it.

When the old dame and her peacock were out of sight, Jason set forward on his journey. After traveling a pretty long distance, he came to a town situated at the foot of a mountain, and not a great way from the shore of the sea. On the outside of the town there was an immense crowd of people, not only men and women, but children, too, all in their best clothes, and evidently enjoying a holiday. The crowd was thickest towards the sea-shore; and in that direction, over the people's heads, Jason saw a wreath of smoke curling upward to the blue sky. He inquired of one of the multitude what town it was, near by, and why so many persons were here assembled together.

"This is the kingdom of Iolchos," answered the man, "and we are the subjects of King Pelias. Our monarch has summoned us together, that we may see him sacrifice a black bull to Neptune, who, they say, is his Majesty's father. Yonder is the king, where you see the smoke going up from the altar."

While the man spoke he eyed Jason with great curiosity; for his garb was quite unlike that of the Iolchians, and it looked very odd to see a youth with a leopard's skin over his shoulders, and each hand grasping a spear. Jason perceived, too, that the man stared particularly at his feet, one of which, you remember, was bare, while the other was decorated with his father's golden-stringed sandal.

"Look at him! only look at him!" said the man to his next neighbor. "Do you see? He wears but one sandal!"

Upon this, first one person, and then another, began

68

to stare at Jason, and everybody seemed to be greatly struck with something in his aspect; though they turned their eyes much oftener towards his feet than to any other part of his figure. Besides, he could hear them whispering to one another.

"One sandal! One sandal!" they kept saying. "The man with one sandal! Here he is at last! Whence has he come? What does he mean to do? What will the king say to the one-sandaled man?"

Poor Jason was greatly abashed, and made up his mind that the people of Iolchos were exceedingly ill bred, to take such public notice of an accidental deficiency in his dress. Meanwhile, whether it were that they hustled him forward, or that Jason, of his own accord, thrust a passage through the crowd, it so happened that he soon found himself close to the smoking altar, where King Pelias was sacrificing the black bull. The murmur and hum of the multitude, in their surprise at the spectacle of Jason with his one bare foot, grew so loud that it disturbed the ceremonies; and the king, holding the great knife with which he was just going to cut the bull's throat, turned angrily about, and fixed his eyes on Jason. The people had now withdrawn from around him, so that the youth stood in an open space near the smoking altar, front to front with the angry King Pelias.

"Who are you?" cried the king, with a terrible frown. "And how dare you make this disturbance, while I am sacrificing a black bull to my father Neptune?"

"It is no fault of mine," answered Jason. "Your

Majesty must blame the rudeness of your subjects, who have raised all this tumult because one of my feet happens to be bare."

When Jason said this, the king gave a quick, startled glance down at his feet.

"Ha!" muttered he, "here is the one-sandaled fellow, sure enough! What can I do with him?"

And he clutched more closely the great knife in his hand, as if he were half a mind to slay Jason instead of the black bull. The people round about caught up the king's words indistinctly as they were uttered; and first there was a murmur among them, and then a loud shout.

"The one-sandaled man has come! The prophecy must be fulfilled!"

For you are to know that, many years before, King Pelias had been told by the Speaking Oak of Dodona, that a man with one sandal should cast him down from his throne. On this account, he had given strict orders that nobody should ever come into his presence, unless both sandals were securely tied upon his feet; and he kept an officer in his palace, whose sole business it was to examine people's sandals, and to supply them with a new pair, at the expense of the royal treasury, as soon as the old ones began to wear out. In the whole course of the king's reign, he had never been thrown into such a fright and agitation as by the spectacle of poor Jason's bare foot. But, as he was naturally a bold and hard-hearted man, he soon took courage, and began to consider in what way he might rid himself of this terrible one-sandaled stranger.

"My good young man," said King Pelias, taking the softest tone imaginable, in order to throw Jason off his guard, "you are excessively welcome to my kingdom. Judging by your dress, you must have traveled a long distance; for it is not the fashion to wear leopard-skins in this part of the world. Pray what may I call your name? and where did you receive your education?"

"My name is Jason," answered the young stranger. "Ever since my infancy, I have dwelt in the cave of Chiron the Centaur. He was my instructor, and taught me music, and horsemanship, and how to cure wounds, and likewise how to inflict wounds with my weapons!"

"I have heard of Chiron the schoolmaster," replied King Pelias, "and how that there is an immense deal of learning and wisdom in his head, although it happens to be set on a horse's body. It gives me great delight to see one of his scholars at my court. But, to test how much you have profited under so excellent a teacher, will you allow me to ask you a single question?"

"I do not pretend to be very wise," said Jason. "But ask me what you please, and I will answer to the best of my ability."

Now King Pelias meant cunningly to entrap the young man, and to make him say something that should be the cause of mischief and destruction to himself. So with a crafty and evil smile upon his face, he spoke as follows.

"What would you do, brave Jason," asked he, "if there were a man in the world by whom, as you had reason to believe, you were doomed to be ruined and slain, — what would you do, I say, if that man stood before you, and in your power?"

When Jason saw the malice and wickedness which King Pelias could not prevent from gleaming out of his eyes, he probably guessed that the king had discovered what he came for, and that he intended to turn his own words against himself. Still he scorned to tell a falsehood. Like an upright and honorable prince, as he was, he determined to speak out the real truth. Since the king had chosen to ask him the question, and since Jason had promised him an answer, there was no right way, save to tell him precisely what would be the most prudent thing to do, if he had his worst enemy in his power.

Therefore, after a moment's consideration, he spoke up, with a firm and manly voice.

"I would send such a man," said he, "in quest of the Golden Fleece!"

This enterprise, you will understand, was, of all others, the most difficult and dangerous in the world. In the first place, it would be necessary to make a long voyage through unknown seas. There was hardly a hope, or a possibility, that any young man who should undertake this voyage would either succeed in obtaining the Golden Fleece, or would survive to return home and tell of the perils he had run. The eyes of King Pelias sparkled with joy, therefore, when he heard Jason's reply.

"Well said, wise man with the one sandal!" cried he. "Go, then, and, at the peril of your life, bring me back the Golden Fleece."

"I go," answered Jason, composedly. "If I fail, you need not fear that I will ever come back to trouble you again. But if I return to Iolchos with the prize, then, King Pelias, you must hasten down from your lofty throne, and give me your crown and sceptre."

"That I will," said the king, with a sneer. "Meantime, I will keep them very safely for you."

The first thing that Jason thought of doing, after he left the king's presence, was to go to Dodona, and inquire of the Talking Oak what course it was best to pursue. This wonderful tree stood in the centre of an ancient wood. Its stately trunk rose up a hundred feet into the air, and threw a broad and dense shadow over more than an acre of ground. Standing beneath it, Jason looked up among the knotted branches and green leaves, and into the mysterious heart of the old tree, and spoke aloud, as if he were addressing some person who was hidden in the depths of the foliage.

"What shall I do," said he, "in order to win the Golden Fleece?"

At first there was a deep silence, not only within the shadow of the Talking Oak, but all through the solitary wood. In a moment or two, however, the leaves of the oak began to stir and rustle, as if a gentle breeze were wandering amongst them, although the other trees of the wood were perfectly still. The sound grew louder, and became like the roar of a high wind. By and by, Jason imagined that he could distinguish words, but very confusedly, because each separate leaf of the tree seemed to be a tongue, and the whole myriad of tongues were babbling at once. But the noise

MYTHS OF GREECE AND ROME

waxed broader and deeper, until it resembled a tornado sweeping through the oak, and making one great utterance out of the thousand and thousand of little murmurs which each leafy tongue had caused by its rustling. And now, though it still had the tone of mighty wind roaring among the branches, it was also like a deep bass voice, speaking, as distinctly as a tree could be expected to speak, the following words:—

"Go to Argus, the ship-builder, and bid him build a galley with fifty oars."

Then the voice melted again into the indistinct murmur of the rustling leaves, and died gradually away. When it was quite gone, Jason felt inclined to doubt whether he had actually heard the words, or whether his fancy had not shaped them out of the ordinary sound made by a breeze, while passing through the thick foliage of the tree.

But on inquiry among the people of Iolchos, he found that there was really a man in the city, by the name of Argus, who was a very skillful builder of vessels. This showed some intelligence in the oak; else how should it have known that any such person existed? At Jason's request, Argus readily consented to build him a galley so big that it should require fifty strong men to row it; although no vessel of such a size and burden had heretofore been seen in the world. So the head carpenter, and all his journeymen and apprentices, began their work; and for a good while afterwards, there they were, busily employed, hewing out the timbers, and making a great clatter with their hammers; until the new ship, which was called the

74

Argo, seemed to be quite ready for sea. And, as the Talking Oak had already given him such good advice, Jason thought that it would not be amiss to ask for a little more. He visited it again, therefore, and standing beside its huge, rough trunk, inquired what he should do next.

This time, there was no such universal quivering of the leaves, throughout the whole tree, as there had been before. But after a while, Jason observed that the foliage of a great branch which stretched above his head had begun to rustle, as if the wind were stirring that one bough, while all the other boughs of the oak were at rest.

"Cut me off!" said the branch, as soon as it could speak distinctly, — "cut me off! cut me off! and carve me into a figure-head for your galley."

Accordingly, Jason took the branch at its word, and lopped it off the tree. A carver in the neighborhood engaged to make the figure-head. He was a tolerably good workman, and had already carved several figure-heads, in what he intended for feminine shapes, and looking pretty much like those which we see nowadays stuck up under a vessel's bowsprit, with great staring eyes, that never wink at the dash of the spray. But (what was very strange) the carver found that his hand was guided by some unseen power, and by a skill beyond his own, and that his tools shaped out an image which he had never dreamed of. When the work was finished, it turned out to be the figure of a beautiful woman with a helmet on her head, from beneath which the long ringlets fell down upon her shoulders. On the left arm was a shield, and in its centre appeared a lifelike representation of the head of Medusa with the snaky locks. The right arm was extended, as if pointing onward. The face of this wonderful statue, though not angry or forbidding, was so grave and majestic, that perhaps you might call it severe; and as for the mouth, it seemed just ready to unclose its lips, and utter words of the deepest wisdom.

Jason was delighted with the oaken image, and gave the carver no rest until it was completed, and set up where a figure-head has always stood, from that time to this, in the vessel's prow.

"And now," cried he, as he stood gazing at the calm, majestic face of the statue, "I must go to the Talking Oak, and inquire what next to do."

"There is no need of that, Jason," said a voice which, though it was far lower, reminded him of the mighty tones of the great oak. "When you desire good advice, you can seek it of me."

Jason had been looking straight into the face of the image when these words were spoken. But he could hardly believe either his ears or his eyes. The truth was, however, that the oaken lips had moved, and, to all appearance, the voice had proceeded from the statue's mouth. Recovering a little from his surprise, Jason bethought himself that the image had been carved out of the wood of the Talking Oak, and that, therefore, it was really no great wonder, but on the contrary, the most natural thing in the world, that it should possess the faculty of speech. It would have been very odd, indeed, if it had not. But certainly it was a great piece of good fortune that he should be able to carry so wise a block of wood along with him in his perilous voyage.

"Tell me, wondrous image," exclaimed Jason, — "since you inherit the wisdom of the Speaking Oak of Dodona, whose daughter you are, — tell me, where shall I find fifty bold youths, who will take each of them an oar of my galley? They must have sturdy arms to row, and brave hearts to encounter perils, or we shall never win the Golden Fleece."

"Go," replied the oaken image, — "go, summon all the heroes of Greece."

And, in fact, considering what a great deed was to be done, could any advice be wiser than this which Jason received from the figure-head of his vessel? He lost no time in sending messengers to all the cities, and making known to the whole people of Greece that Prince Jason, the son of King Æson, was going in quest of the Fleece of Gold, and that he desired the help of forty-nine of the bravest and strongest young men alive, to row his vessel and share his dangers. And Jason himself would be the fiftieth.

At this news, the adventurous youths, all over the country, began to bestir themselves. Some of them had already fought with giants, and slain dragons; and the younger ones, who had not yet met with such good fortune, thought it a shame to have lived so long without getting astride of a flying serpent, or sticking their spears into a Chimæra, or, at least, thrusting their right arms down a monstrous lion's throat.

There was a fair prospect that they would meet with plenty of such adventures before finding the Golden Fleece. As soon as they could furbish up their helmets and shields, therefore, and gird on their trusty swords, they came thronging to Iolchos, and clambered on board the new galley. Shaking hands with Jason, they assured him that they did not care a pin for their lives, but would help row the vessel to the remotest edge of the world, and as much farther as he might think it best to go.

Many of these brave fellows had been educated by Chiron, the four-footed pedagogue, and were therefore old schoolmates of Jason, and knew him to be a lad of spirit. The mighty Hercules, whose shoulders afterwards held up the sky, was one of them. And there were Castor and Pollux, the twin brothers, who were never accused of being chicken-hearted, although they had been hatched out of an egg; and Theseus, who was so renowned for killing the Minotaur; and Lynceus, with his wonderfully sharp eyes, which could see through a millstone, or look right down into the depths of the earth, and discover the treasures that were there; and Orpheus, the very best of harpers, who sang and played upon his lyre so sweetly, that the brute beasts stood upon their hind legs, and capered merrily to the music. Yes, and at some of his more moving tunes, the rocks bestirred their moss-grown bulk out of the ground, and a grove of forest trees uprooted themselves, and, nodding their tops to one another, performed a country dance.

One of the rowers was a beautiful young woman,

named Atalanta, who had been nursed among the mountains by a bear. So light of foot was this fair damsel that she could step from one foamy crest of a wave to the foamy crest of another, without wetting more than the sole of her sandal. She had grown up in a very wild way, and talked much about the rights of women, and loved hunting and war far better than her needle. But, in my opinion, the most remarkable of this famous company were two sons of the North Wind (airy youngsters, and of rather a blustering disposition), who had wings on their shoulders, and, in case of a calm, could puff out their cheeks, and blow almost as fresh a breeze as their father. I ought not to forget the prophets and conjurers, of whom there were several in the crew, and who could foretell what would happen to-morrow, or the next day, or a hundred years hence, but were generally quite unconscious of what was passing at the moment.

Jason appointed Tiphys to be helmsman, because he was a star-gazer, and knew the points of the compass. Lynceus, on account of his sharp sight, was stationed as a lookout in the prow, where he saw a whole day's sail ahead, but was rather apt to overlook things that lay directly under his nose. If the sea only happened to be deep enough, however, Lynceus could tell you exactly what kind of rocks or sands were at the bottom of it; and he often cried out to his companions, that they were sailing over heaps of sunken treasure, which yet he was none the richer for beholding. To confess the truth, few people believed him when he said it.

Well! But when the Argonauts, as these fifty brave adventurers were called, had prepared everything for the voyage, an unforeseen difficulty threatened to end it before it was begun. The vessel, you must understand, was so long, and broad, and ponderous, that the united force of all the fifty was insufficient to shove her into the water. Hercules, I suppose, had not grown to his full strength, else he might have set her afloat as easily as a little boy launches his boat upon a puddle. But here were these fifty heroes pushing, and straining, and growing red in the face, without making the Argo start an inch. At last, quite wearied out, they sat themselves down on the shore, exceedingly disconsolate, and thinking that the vessel must be left to rot and fall in pieces, and that they must either swim across the sea or lose the Golden Fleece.

All at once, Jason bethought himself of the galley's miraculous figure-head.

"O daughter of the Talking Oak," cried he, "how shall we set to work to get our vessel into the water?"

"Seat yourselves," answered the image (for it had known what ought to be done from the very first, and was only waiting for the question to be put), — "seat yourselves, and handle your oars, and let Orpheus play upon his harp."

Immediately the fifty heroes got on board, and seizing their oars, held them perpendicularly in the air, while Orpheus (who liked such a task far better than rowing) swept his fingers across the harp. At the first ringing note of the music, they felt the vessel stir, Orpheus thrummed away briskly, and the galley slid

80

at once into the sea, dipping her prow so deeply that the figure-head drank the wave with its marvelous lips, and rose again as buoyant as a swan. The rowers plied their fifty oars; the white foam boiled up before the prow; the water gurgled and bubbled in their wake; while Orpheus continued to play so lively a strain of music, that the vessel seemed to dance over the billows by way of keeping time to it. Thus triumphantly did the Argo sail out of the harbor, amidst the huzzas and good wishes of everybody except the wicked old Pelias, who stood on a promontory, scowling at her, and wishing that he could blow out of his lungs the tempest of wrath that was in his heart, and so sink the galley with all on board. When they had sailed above fifty miles over the sea, Lynceus happened to cast his sharp eyes behind, and said that there was this bad-hearted king, still perched upon the promontory, and scowling so gloomily that it looked like a black thunder-cloud in that quarter of the horizon.

In order to make the time pass away more pleasantly during the voyage, the heroes talked about the Golden Fleece. It originally belonged, it appears, to a Bœotian ram, who had taken on his back two children, when in danger of their lives, and fled with them over land and sea, as far as Colchis. One of the children, whose name was Helle, fell into the sea and was drowned. But the other (a little boy, named Phrixus) was brought safe ashore by the faithful ram, who, however, was so exhausted that he immediately lay down and died. In memory of this good deed, and as a token of his true heart, the fleece of the poor dead ram was miraculously changed to gold, and became one of the most beautiful objects ever seen on earth. It was hung upon a tree in a sacred grove, where it had now been kept I know not how many years, and was the envy of mighty kings, who had nothing so magnificent in any of their palaces.

If I were to tell you all the adventures of the Argonauts, it would take me till nightfall, and perhaps a great deal longer. There was no lack of wonderful events, as you may judge from what you may have already heard. At a certain island they were hospitably received by King Cyzicus, its sovereign, who made a feast for them, and treated them like brothers. But the Argonauts saw that this good king looked downcast and very much troubled, and they therefore inquired of him what was the matter. King Cyzicus hereupon informed them that he and his subjects were greatly abused and incommoded by the inhabitants of a neighboring mountain, who made war upon them, and killed many people, and ravaged the country. And while they were talking about it, Cyzicus pointed to the mountain, and asked Jason and his companions what they saw there.

"I see some very tall objects," answered Jason; "but they are at such a distance that I cannot distinctly make out what they are. To tell your Majesty the truth, they look so very strangely that I am inclined to think them clouds, which have chanced to take something like human shapes."

"I see them very plainly," remarked Lynceus, whose eyes, you know, were as far-sighted as a telescope.

"They are a band of enormous giants, all of whom have six arms apiece, and a club, a sword, or some other weapon in each of their hands."

"You have excellent eyes," said King Cyzicus. "Yes; they are six-armed giants, as you say, and these are the enemies whom I and my subjects have to contend with."

The next day, when the Argonauts were about setting sail, down came these terrible giants, stepping a hundred yards at a stride, brandishing their six arms apiece, and looking very formidable, so far aloft in the air. Each of these monsters was able to carry on a whole war by himself, for with one of his arms he could fling immense stones, and wield a club with another, and a sword with a third, while the fourth was poking a long spear at the enemy, and the fifth and sixth were shooting him with a bow and arrow. But, luckily, though the giants were so huge, and had so many arms, they had each but one heart, and that no bigger nor braver than the heart of an ordinary man. Besides, if they had been like the hundred-armed Briareus, the brave Argonauts would have given them their hands full of fight. Jason and his friends went boldly to meet them, slew a great many, and made the rest take to their heels, so that, if the giants had had six legs apiece instead of six arms, it would have served them better to run away with.

Another strange adventure happened when the voyagers came to Thrace, where they found a poor blind king, named Phineus, deserted by his subjects, and living in a very sorrowful way, all by himself. On

Jason's inquiring whether they could do him any service, the king answered that he was terribly tormented by three great winged creatures, called Harpies, which had the faces of women, and the wings, bodies, and claws of vultures. These ugly wretches were in the habit of snatching away his dinner, and allowed him no peace of his life. Upon hearing this, the Argonauts spread a plentiful feast on the seashore, well knowing, from what the blind king said of their greediness, that the Harpies would snuff up the scent of the victuals, and quickly come to steal them away. And so it turned out; for, hardly was the table set, before the three hideous vulture women came flapping their wings, seized the food in their talons, and flew off as fast as they could. But the two sons of the North Wind drew their swords, spread their pinions, and set off through the air in pursuit of the thieves, whom they at last overtook among some islands, after a chase of hundreds of miles. The two winged youths blustered terribly at the Harpies (for they had the rough temper of their father), and so frightened them with their drawn swords, that they solemnly promised never to trouble King Phineus again.

Then the Argonauts sailed onward, and met with many other marvelous incidents, any one of which would make a story by itself. At one time, they landed on an island, and were reposing on the grass, when they suddenly found themselves assailed by what seemed a shower of steel-headed arrows. Some of them stuck in the ground, while others hit against their shields, and several penetrated their flesh. The fifty heroes started up, and looked about them for the hidden enemy, but could find none, nor see any spot, on the whole island, where even a single archer could lie concealed. Still, however, the steel-headed arrows came whizzing among them; and, at last, happening to look upward, they beheld a large flock of birds, hovering and wheeling aloft, and shooting their feathers down upon the Argonauts. These feathers were the steel-headed arrows that had so tormented them. There was no possibility of making any resistance; and the fifty heroic Argonauts might all have been killed or wounded by a flock of troublesome birds, without ever setting eyes on the Golden Fleece, if Jason had not thought of asking the advice of the oaken image.

So he ran to the galley as fast as his legs would carry him.

"O daughter of the Speaking Oak," cried he, all out of breath, "we need your wisdom more than ever before! We are in great peril from a flock of birds, who are shooting us with their steel-pointed feathers. What can we do to drive them away?"

"Make a clatter on your shields," said the image.

On receiving this excellent counsel, Jason hurried back to his companions (who were far more dismayed than when they fought with the six-armed giants), and bade them strike with their swords upon their brazen shields. Forthwith the fifty heroes set heartily to work, banging with might and main, and raised such a terrible clatter that the birds made what haste they could to get away; and though they had shot half the feathers out of their wings, they were soon seen skimming among the clouds, a long distance off, and looking like a flock of wild geese. Orpheus celebrated this victory by playing a triumphant anthem on his harp, and sang so melodiously that Jason begged him to desist, lest, as the steel-feathered birds had been driven away by an ugly sound, they might be enticed back again by a sweet one.

While the Argonauts remained on this island, they saw a small vessel approaching the shore, in which were two young men of princely demeanor, and exceedingly handsome, as young princes generally were in those days. Now, who do you imagine these two voyagers turned out to be? Why, if you will believe me, they were the sons of that very Phrixus, who, in his childhood, had been carried to Colchis on the back of the golden-fleeced ram. Since that time, Phrixus had married the king's daughter; and the two young princes had been born and brought up at Colchis, and had spent their play-days in the outskirts of the grove, in the centre of which the Golden Fleece was hanging upon a tree. They were now on their way to Greece, in hopes of getting back a kingdom that had been wrongfully taken from their father.

When the princes understood whither the Argonauts were going, they offered to turn back and guide them to Colchis. At the same time, however, they spoke as if it were very doubtful whether Jason would succeed in getting the Golden Fleece. According to their account, the tree on which it hung was guarded by a terrible dragon, who never failed to devour, at one mouthful, every person who might venture within his reach.

"There are other difficulties in the way," continued the young princes. "But is not this enough? Ah, brave Jason, turn back before it is too late. It would grieve us to the heart, if you and your nine-and-forty brave companions should be eaten up, at fifty mouthfuls, by this execrable dragon."

"My young friends," quietly replied Jason, "I do not wonder that you think the dragon very terrible. You have grown up from infancy in the fear of this monster, and therefore still regard him with the awe that children feel for the bugbears and hobgoblins which their nurses have talked to them about. But, in my view of the matter, the dragon is merely a pretty large serpent, who is not half so likely to snap me up at one mouthful as I am to cut off his ugly head, and strip the skin from his body. At all events, turn back who may, I will never see Greece again unless I carry with me the Golden Fleece."

"We will none of us turn back!" cried his nine-and-forty brave comrades. "Let us get on board the galley this instant; and if the dragon is to make a breakfast of us, much good may it do him."

And Orpheus (whose custom it was to set everything to music) began to harp and sing most gloriously, and made every mother's son of them feel as if nothing in this world were so delectable as to fight dragons, and nothing so truly honorable as to be eaten up at one mouthful, in case of the worst.

After this (being now under the guidance of the

two princes, who were well acquainted with the way), they quickly sailed to Colchis. When the king of the country, whose name was Æetes, heard of their arrival, he instantly summoned Jason to court. The king was a stern and cruel-looking potentate; and though he put on as polite and hospitable an expression as he could, Jason did not like his face a whit better than that of the wicked King Pelias, who dethroned his father.

"You are welcome, brave Jason," said King Æetes. "Pray, are you on a pleasure voyage? — or do you meditate the discovery of unknown islands? — or what other cause has procured me the happiness of seeing you at my court?"

"Great sir," replied Jason, with an obeisance, — for Chiron had taught him how to behave with propriety, whether to kings or beggars, — "I have come hither with a purpose which I now beg your Majesty's permission to execute. King Pelias, who sits on my father's throne (to which he has no more right than to the one on which your excellent Majesty is now seated), has engaged to come down from it, and to give me his crown and sceptre, provided I bring him the Golden Fleece. This, as your Majesty is aware, is now hanging on a tree here at Colchis; and I humbly solicit your gracious leave to take it away."

In spite of himself, the king's face twisted itself into an angry frown; for, above all things else in the world, he prized the Golden Fleece, and was even suspected of having done a very wicked act, in order to get it into his own possession. It put him into the worst possible humor, therefore, to hear that the gallant Prince Jason, and forty-nine of the bravest young warriors of Greece, had come to Colchis with the sole purpose of taking away his chief treasure.

"Do you know," asked King Æetes, eying Jason very sternly, "what are the conditions which you must fulfill before getting possession of the Golden Fleece?"

"I have heard," rejoined the youth, "that a dragon lies beneath the tree on which the prize hangs, and that whoever approaches him runs the risk of being devoured at a mouthful."

"True," said the king, with a smile that did not look particularly good-natured. "Very true, young man. But there are other things as hard, or perhaps a little harder, to be done, before you can even have the privilege of being devoured by the dragon. For example, you must first tame my two brazen-footed and brazen-lunged bulls, which Vulcan, the wonderful blacksmith, made for me. There is a furnace in each of their stomachs; and they breathe such hot fire out of their mouths and nostrils, that nobody has hitherto gone nigh them without being instantly burned to a small, black cinder. What do you think of this, my brave Jason?"

"I must encounter the peril," answered Jason, composedly, "since it stands in the way of my purpose."

"After taming the fiery bulls," continued King Æetes, who was determined to scare Jason if possible, "you must yoke them to a plough, and must plough the sacred earth in the grove of Mars, and sow some of the same dragon's teeth from which Cadmus raised a crop of armed men. They are an unruly set of reprobates, those sons of the dragon's teeth; and unless you treat them suitably, they will fall upon you sword in hand. You and your nine-and-forty Argonauts, my bold Jason, are hardly numerous or strong enough to fight with such a host as will spring up."

"My master Chiron," replied Jason, "taught me, long ago, the story of Cadmus. Perhaps I can manage the quarrelsome sons of the dragon's teeth as well as Cadmus did."

"I wish the dragon had him," muttered King Æetes to himself, "and the four-footed pedant, his schoolmaster, into the bargain. Why, what a fool-hardy, self-conceited coxcomb he is! We'll see what my fire-breathing bulls will do for him. Well, Prince Jason," he continued, aloud, and as complaisantly as he could, "make yourself comfortable for to-day, and to-morrow morning, since you insist upon it, you shall try your skill at the plough."

While the king talked with Jason, a beautiful young woman was standing behind the throne. She fixed her eyes earnestly upon the youthful stranger, and listened attentively to every word that was spoken; and when Jason withdrew from the king's presence, this young woman followed him out of the room.

"I am the king's daughter," she said to him, "and my name is Medea. I know a great deal of which other young princesses are ignorant, and can do many things which they would be afraid so much as to dream of. If you will trust to me, I can instruct you how to tame the fiery bulls, and sow the dragon's teeth, and get the Golden Fleece."

"Indeed, beautiful princess," answered Jason, "if you will do me this service, I promise to be grateful to you my whole life long."

Gazing at Medea, he beheld a wonderful intelligence in her face. She was one of those persons whose eyes are full of mystery; so that, while looking into them, you seem to see a very great way, as into a deep well, yet can never be certain whether you see into the farthest depths, or whether there be not something else hidden at the bottom. If Jason had been capable of fearing anything, he would have been afraid of making this young princess his enemy; for, beautiful as she now looked, she might, the very next instant, become as terrible as the dragon that kept watch over the Golden Fleece.

"Princess," he exclaimed, "you seem indeed very wise and very powerful. But how can you help me to do the things of which you speak? Are you an enchantress?"

"Yes, Prince Jason," answered Medea, with a smile, "you have hit upon the truth. I am an enchantress. Circe, my father's sister, taught me to be one, and I could tell you, if I pleased, who was the old woman with the peacock, the pomegranate, and the cuckoo staff, whom you carried over the river; and, likewise, who it is that speaks through the lips of the oaken image that stands in the prow of your galley. I am acquainted with some of your secrets, you perceive. It is well for you that I am favorably inclined; for, otherwise, you would hardly escape being snapped up by the dragon."

"I should not so much care for the dragon," replied Jason, "if I only knew how to manage the brazen-footed and fiery-lunged bulls."

"If you are as brave as I think you, and as you have need to be," said Medea, "your own bold heart will teach you that there is but one way of dealing with a mad bull. What it is I leave you to find out in the moment of peril. As for the fiery breath of these animals, I have a charmed ointment here, which will prevent you from being burned up, and cure you if you chance to be a little scorched."

So she put a golden box into his hand, and directed him how to apply the perfumed unguent which it contained, and where to meet her at midnight.

"Only be brave," added she, "and before daybreak the brazen bulls shall be tamed."

The young man assured her that his heart would not fail him. He then rejoined his comrades, and told them what had passed between the princess and himself, and warned them to be in readiness in case there might be need of their help.

At the appointed hour he met the beautiful Medea on the marble steps of the king's palace. She gave him a basket, in which were the dragon's teeth, just as they had been pulled out of the monster's jaws by Cadmus, long ago. Medea then led Jason down the palace steps, and through the silent streets of the city, and into the royal pasture-ground, where the two brazen-footed bulls were kept. It was a starry night, with a bright gleam along the eastern edge of the sky, where the moon was soon going to show herself. After entering the pasture, the princess paused and looked around.

"There they are," said she, "reposing themselves and chewing their fiery cuds in that farthest corner of the field. It will be excellent sport, I assure you, when they catch a glimpse of your figure. My father and all his court delight in nothing so much as to see a stranger trying to yoke them, in order to come at the Golden Fleece. It makes a holiday in Colchis whenever such a thing happens. For my part, I enjoy it immensely. You cannot imagine in what a mere twinkling of an eye their hot breath shrivels a young man into a black cinder."

"Are you sure, beautiful Medea," asked Jason, "quite sure, that the unguent in the gold box will prove a remedy against those terrible burns?"

"If you doubt, if you are in the least afraid," said the princess, looking him in the face by the dim starlight, "you had better never have been born than go a step nigher to the bulls."

But Jason had set his heart steadfastly on getting the Golden Fleece; and I positively doubt whether he would have gone back without it, even had he been certain of finding himself turned into a red-hot cinder, or a handful of white ashes, the instant he made a step farther. He therefore let go Medea's hand, and walked boldly forward in the direction whither she had pointed. At some distance before him he perceived four streams of fiery vapor, regularly appearing, and again vanishing, after dimly lighting up the surrounding obscurity. These, you will understand, were caused by the breath of the brazen bulls, which was quietly stealing out of their four nostrils, as they lay chewing their cuds.

At the first two or three steps which Jason made, the four fiery streams appeared to gush out somewhat more plentifully; for the two brazen bulls had heard his foot-tramp, and were lifting up their hot noses to snuff the air. He went a little farther, and by the way in which the red vapor now spouted forth, he judged that the creatures had got upon their feet. Now he could see glowing sparks, and vivid jets of flame. At the next step, each of the bulls made the pasture echo with a terrible roar, while the burning breath, which they thus belched forth, lit up the whole field with a momentary flash. One other stride did bold Jason make; and, suddenly as a streak of lightning, on came these fiery animals, roaring like thunder, and sending out sheets of white flame, which so kindled up the scene that the young man could discern every object more distinctly than by daylight. Most distinctly of all he saw the two horrible creatures galloping right down upon him, their brazen hoofs rattling and ringing over the ground, and their tails sticking up stiffly into the air, as has always been the fashion with angry bulls. Their breath scorched the herbage before them. So intensely hot it was, indeed, that it caught a dry tree, under which Jason was now standing, and set it all in a light blaze. But as for Jason himself (thanks to Medea's enchanted ointment), the white flame curled around his body, without injuring him a jot more than if he had been made of asbestos.

Greatly encouraged at finding himself not yet turned into a cinder, the young man awaited the attack of the bulls. Just as the brazen brutes fancied themselves sure of tossing him into the air, he caught one of them by the horn, and the other by his screwed-up tail, and held them in a gripe like that of an iron vise, one with his right hand, the other with his left. Well, he must have been wonderfully strong in his arms, to be sure. But the secret of the matter was, that the brazen bulls were enchanted creatures, and that Jason had broken the spell of their fiery fierceness by his bold way of handling them. And, ever since that time, it has been the favorite method of brave men, when danger assails them, to do what they call "taking the bull by the horns;" and to gripe him by the tail is pretty much the same thing, — that is, to throw aside fear, and overcome the peril by despising it.

It was now easy to yoke the bulls, and to harness them to the plough, which had lain rusting on the ground for a great many years gone by; so long was it before anybody could be found capable of plough-ing that piece of land. Jason, I suppose, had been taught how to draw a furrow by the good old Chiron, who, perhaps, used to allow himself to be harnessed to the plough. At any rate, our hero succeeded perfectly well in breaking up the greensward; and, by the time that the moon was a quarter of her journey up the sky, the ploughed field lay before him, a large tract of black earth, ready to be sown with the dragon's teeth. So Jason scattered them broadcast, and harrowed them into the soil with a brush-harrow, and took his stand on the edge of the field, anxious to see what would happen next.

"Must we wait long for harvest-time?" he inquired of Medea, who was now standing by his side.

"Whether sooner or later, it will be sure to come," answered the princess. "A crop of armed men never fails to spring up, when the dragon's teeth have been sown."

The moon was now high aloft in the heavens, and threw its bright beams over the ploughed field, where as yet there was nothing to be seen. Any farmer, on viewing it, would have said that Jason must wait weeks before the green blades would peep from among the clods, and whole months before the yellow grain would be ripened for the sickle. But by and by, all over the field, there was something that glistened in the moonbeams, like sparkling drops of dew. These bright objects sprouted higher, and proved to be the steel heads of spears. Then there was a dazzling gleam from a vast number of polished brass helmets, beneath which, as they grew farther out of the soil, appeared the dark and bearded visages of warriors, struggling to free themselves from the imprisoning earth. The first look that they gave at the upper world was a glare of wrath and defiance. Next were seen their bright breastplates; in every right hand there was a sword or a spear, and on each left arm a shield; and when this strange crop of warriors had but half grown out of the earth, they struggled, — such was their impatience of restraint, — and, as it were, tore themselves up by the roots. Wherever a dragon's tooth had fallen, there stood a man armed for battle. They made a clangor with their swords against their shields, and eyed one another fiercely; for they had come into this beautiful world, and into the peaceful moonlight, full of rage and stormy passions, and ready to take the life of every human brother, in recompense of the boon of their own existence.

There have been many other armies in the world that seemed to possess the same fierce nature with the one which had now sprouted from the dragon's teeth; but these, in the moonlit field, were the more excusable, because they never had women for their mothers. And how it would have rejoiced any great captain, who was bent on conquering the world, like Alexander or Napoleon, to raise a crop of armed soldiers as easily as Jason did!

For a while, the warriors stood flourishing their weapons, clashing their swords against their shields, and boiling over with the red-hot thirst for battle. Then they began to shout, "Show us the enemy! Lead us to the charge! Death or victory! Come on, brave comrades! Conquer or die!" and a hundred other outcries, such as men always bellow forth on a battle-field, and which these dragon people seemed to have at their tongues' ends. At last, the front rank caught sight of Jason, who, beholding the flash of so many weapons in the moonlight, had thought it best to draw his sword. In a moment all the sons of the dragon's teeth appeared to take Jason for an enemy; and crying with one voice, "Guard the Golden Fleece!" they ran at him with uplifted swords and protruded spears. Jason knew that it would be impossible to withstand this bloodthirsty battalion with his single arm, but determined, since there was nothing better to be done, to die as valiantly as if he himself had sprung from a dragon's tooth.

Medea, however, bade him snatch up a stone from the ground.

"Throw it among them quickly!" cried she. "It is the only way to save yourself."

The armed men were now so nigh that Jason could discern the fire flashing out of their enraged eyes, when he let fly the stone, and saw it strike the helmet of a tall warrior, who was rushing upon him with his blade aloft. The stone glanced from this man's helmet to the shield of his nearest comrade, and thence flew right into the angry face of another, hitting him smartly between the eyes. Each of the three who had been struck by the stone took it for granted that his next neighbor had given him a blow; and instead of running any farther towards Jason, they began a fight among themselves. The confusion spread through the host, so that it seemed scarcely a moment before they were all hacking, hewing, and stabbing at one another, lopping off arms, heads, and legs, and doing such memorable deeds that Jason was filled with immense admiration; although, at the same time, he could not help laughing to behold these mighty men punishing each other for an offense which he himself had committed. In an incredibly short space of time (almost as short, indeed, as it had taken them to grow up), all but one of the heroes of the dragon's teeth were stretched lifeless on the field. The last survivor, the bravest and strongest of the whole, had just force enough to wave his crimson sword over his head, and give a shout of exultation, crying, "Victory! Victory! Immortal fame!" when he himself fell down, and lay quietly among his slain brethren.

And there was the end of the army that had sprouted from the dragon's teeth. That fierce and feverish fight was the only enjoyment which they had tasted on this beautiful earth.

"Let them sleep in the bed of honor," said the Princess Medea, with a sly smile at Jason. "The world will always have simpletons enough, just like them, fighting and dying for they know not what, and fancying that posterity will take the trouble to put laurel wreaths on their rusty and battered helmets. Could you help smiling, Prince Jason, to see the self-conceit of that last fellow, just as he tumbled down?"

"It made me very sad," answered Jason, gravely. "And, to tell you the truth, princess, the Golden Fleece does not appear so well worth the winning, after what I have here beheld."

"You will think differently in the morning," said Medea. "True, the Golden Fleece may not be so valuable as you have thought it; but then there is nothing better in the world, and one must needs have an object, you know. Come! Your night's work has been well performed; and to-morrow you can inform King Æetes that the first part of your allotted task is fulfilled."

Agreeably to Medea's advice, Jason went betimes in the morning to the palace of King Æetes. Entering the presence-chamber, he stood at the foot of the throne, and made a low obeisance.

"Your eyes look heavy, Prince Jason," observed the king; "you appear to have spent a sleepless night. I hope you have been considering the matter a little more wisely, and have concluded not to get yourself scorched to a cinder, in attempting to tame my brazen-lunged bulls."

"That is already accomplished, may it please your Majesty," replied Jason. "The bulls have been tamed and yoked; the field has been ploughed; the dragon's teeth have been sown broadcast, and harrowed into the soil; the crop of armed warriors has sprung up, and they have slain one another, to the last man. And now I solicit your Majesty's permission to encounter the dragon, that I may take down the Golden Fleece from the tree, and depart, with my nine-and-forty comrades."

King Æetes scowled, and looked very angry and excessively disturbed; for he knew that, in accordance with his kingly promise, he ought now to permit Jason to win the fleece, if his courage and skill should enable him to do so. But, since the young man had met with such good luck in the matter of the brazen bulls and the dragon's teeth, the king feared that he would be equally successful in slaying the dragon. And therefore, though he would gladly have seen Jason snapped up at a mouthful, he was resolved (and it was a very wrong thing of this wicked potentate) not to run any further risk of losing his beloved fleece.

"You never would have succeeded in this business,

young man," said he, "if my undutiful daughter Medea had not helped you with her enchantments. Had you acted fairly, you would have been, at this instant, a black cinder or a handful of white ashes. I forbid you, on pain of death, to make any more attempts to get the Golden Fleece. To speak my mind plainly, you shall never set eyes on so much as one of its glistening locks."

Jason left the king's presence in great sorrow and anger. He could think of nothing better to be done than to summon together his forty-nine brave Argonauts, march at once to the grove of Mars, slay the dragon, take possession of the Golden Fleece, get on board the Argo, and spread all sail for Iolchos. The success of the scheme depended, it is true, on the doubtful point whether all the fifty heroes might not be snapped up, at so many mouthfuls, by the dragon. But, as Jason was hastening down the palace steps, the Princess Medea called after him, and beckoned him to return. Her black eyes shone upon him with such a keen intelligence, that he felt as if there were a serpent peeping out of them; and although she had done him so much service only the night before, he was by no means very certain that she would not do him an equally great mischief before sunset. These enchantresses, you must know, are never to be depended upon.

"What says King Æetes, my royal and upright father?" inquired Medea, slightly smiling. "Will he give you the Golden Fleece, without any further risk or trouble?"

"On the contrary," answered Jason, "he is very angry with me for taming the brazen bulls and sowing the dragon's teeth. And he forbids me to make any more attempts, and positively refuses to give up the Golden Fleece, whether I slay the dragon or no."

"Yes, Jason," said the princess, "and I can tell you more. Unless you set sail from Colchis before to-morrow's sunrise, the king means to burn your fifty-oared galley, and put yourself and your forty-nine brave comrades to the sword. But be of good courage. The Golden Fleece you shall have, if it lies within the power of my enchantments to get it for you. Wait for me here an hour before midnight."

At the appointed hour, you might again have seen Prince Jason and the Princess Medea, side by side, stealing through the streets of Colchis, on their way to the sacred grove, in the centre of which the Golden Fleece was suspended to a tree. While they were crossing the pasture-ground, the brazen bulls came towards Jason, lowing, nodding their heads, and thrusting forth their snouts, which, as other cattle do, they loved to have rubbed and caressed by a friendly hand. Their fierce nature was thoroughly tamed; and, with their fierceness, the two furnaces in their stomachs had likewise been extinguished, insomuch that they probably enjoyed far more comfort in grazing and chewing their cuds than ever before. Indeed, it had heretofore been a great inconvenience to these poor animals, that, whenever they wished to eat a mouthful of grass, the fire out of their nostrils had shriveled it up, before they could manage to crop it

How they contrived to keep themselves alive is more than I can imagine. But now, instead of emitting jets of flame and streams of sulphurous vapor, they breathed the very sweetest of cow breath.

After kindly patting the bulls, Jason followed Medea's guidance into the grove of Mars, where the great oak-trees, that had been growing for centuries, threw so thick a shade that the moonbeams struggled vainly to find their way through it. Only here and there a glimmer fell upon the leaf-strewn earth, or now and then a breeze stirred the boughs aside, and gave Jason a glimpse of the sky, lest, in that deep obscurity, he might forget that there was one, overhead. At length, when they had gone farther and farther into the heart of the duskiness, Medea squeezed Jason's hand.

"Look yonder," she whispered. "Do you see it?"

Gleaming among the venerable oaks, there was a radiance, not like the moonbeams, but rather resembling the golden glory of the setting sun. It proceeded from an object, which appeared to be suspended at about a man's height from the ground, a little farther within the wood.

"What is it?" asked Jason.

"Have you come so far to seek it," exclaimed Medea, "and do you not recognize the meed of all your toils and perils, when it glitters before your eyes? It is the Golden Fleece."

Jason went onward a few steps farther, and then stopped to gaze. Oh, how beautiful it looked, shining with a marvelous light of its own, that inestimable prize, which so many heroes had longed to behold, but had perished in the quest of it, either by the perils of their voyage, or by the fiery breath of the brazen-lunged bulls.

"How gloriously it shines!" cried Jason, in a rapture. "It has surely been dipped in the richest gold of sunset. Let me hasten onward, and take it to my bosom."

"Stay," said Medea, holding him back. "Have you forgotten what guards it?"

To say the truth, in the joy of beholding the object of his desires, the terrible dragon had quite slipped out of Jason's memory. Soon, however, something came to pass that reminded him what perils were still to be encountered. An antelope, that probably mistook the yellow radiance for sunrise, came bounding fleetly through the grove. He was rushing straight towards the Golden Fleece, when suddenly there was a frightful hiss, and the immense head and half the scaly body of the dragon was thrust forth (for he was twisted round the trunk of the tree on which the fleece hung), and seizing the poor antelope, swallowed him with one snap of his jaws.

After this feat, the dragon seemed sensible that some other living creature was within reach on which he felt inclined to finish his meal. In various directions he kept poking his ugly snout among the trees, stretching out his neck a terrible long way, now here, now there, and now close to the spot where Jason and the princess were hiding behind an oak. Upon my word, as the head came waving and undulating through the air, and reaching almost within arm's length of Prince Jason, it was a very hideous and uncomfortable sight. The gape of his enormous jaws was nearly as wide as the gateway of the king's palace.

"Well, Jason," whispered Medea (for she was ill-natured, as all enchantresses are, and wanted to make the bold youth tremble), "what do you think now of your prospect of winning the Golden Fleece?"

Jason answered only by drawing his sword and making a step forward.

"Stay, foolish youth," said Medea, grasping his arm. "Do not you see you are lost, without me as your good angel? In this gold box I have a magic potion, which will do the dragon's business far more effectually than your sword."

The dragon had probably heard the voices; for, swift as lightning, his black head and forked tongue came hissing among the trees again, darting full forty feet at a stretch. As it approached, Medea tossed the contents of the gold box right down the monster's wide-open throat. Immediately, with an outrageous hiss and a tremendous wriggle, — flinging his tail up to the tip-top of the tallest tree, and shattering all its branches as it crashed heavily down again, — the dragon fell at full length upon the ground, and lay quite motionless.

"It is only a sleeping potion," said the enchantress to Prince Jason. "One always finds a use for these mischievous creatures, sooner or later; so I did not wish to kill him outright. Quick! Snatch the prize, and let us be gone. You have won the Golden Fleece."

Jason caught the Fleece from the tree, and hurried through the grove, the deep shadows of which were illuminated as he passed by the golden glory of the precious object that he bore along. A little way before him, he beheld the old woman whom he had helped over the stream, with her peacock beside her. She clapped her hands for joy, and beckoning him to make haste, disappeared among the duskiness of the trees. Espying the two winged sons of the North Wind (who were disporting themselves in the moonlight, a few hundred feet aloft), Jason bade them tell the rest of the Argonauts to embark as speedily as possible. But Lynceus, with his sharp eyes, had already caught a glimpse of him, bringing the Golden Fleece, although several stone-walls, a hill, and the black shadows of the grove of Mars intervened between. By his advice, the heroes had seated themselves on the benches of the galley, with their oars held perpendicularly, ready to let fall into the water.

As Jason drew near, he heard the Talking Image calling to him with more than ordinary eagerness, in its grave, sweet voice: —

"Make haste, Prince Jason! For your life, make haste!"

With one bound he leaped aboard. At sight of the glorious radiance of the Golden Fleece, the nine-and-forty heroes gave a mighty shout, and Orpheus, striking his harp, sang a song of triumph, to the cadence of which the galley flew over the water, homeward bound, as if careering along with wings!

THE PARADISE OF CHILDREN

By Nathaniel Hawthorne

LONG, long ago, when this old world was in its tender infancy, there was a child, named Epimetheus, who never had either father or mother; and, that he might not be lonely, another child, fatherless and motherless like himself, was sent from a far country, to live with him, and be his playfellow and helpmate. Her name was Pandora.

The first thing that Pandora saw, when she entered the cottage where Epimetheus dwelt, was a great box. And almost the first question which she put to him, after crossing the threshold, was this, —

"Epimetheus, what have you in that box?"

"My dear little Pandora," answered Epimetheus, "that is a secret, and you must be kind enough not to ask any questions about it. The box was left here to be kept safely, and I do not myself know what it contains."

"But who gave it to you?" asked Pandora. "And where did it come from?"

"That is a secret, too," replied Epimetheus.

"How provoking!" exclaimed Pandora, pouting her lip. "I wish the great ugly box were out of the way!"

"Oh, come, don't think of it any more," cried Epimetheus. "Let us run out of doors, and have some nice play with the other children."

It is thousands of years since Epimetheus and Pandora were alive; and the world, nowadays, is a very different sort of thing from what it was in their time. Then, everybody was a child. There needed no fathers and mothers to take care of the children; because there was no danger, nor trouble of any kind, and no clothes to be mended, and there was always plenty to eat and drink. Whenever a child wanted his dinner, he found it growing on a tree; and, if he looked at the tree in the morning, he could see the expanding blossom of that night's supper; or, at eventide, he saw the tender bud of to-morrow's breakfast. It was a very pleasant life indeed. No labor to be done, no tasks to be studied; nothing but sports and dances, and sweet voices of children talking, or caroling like birds, or gushing out in merry laughter, throughout the livelong day.

What was most wonderful of all, the children never quarreled among themselves; neither had they any crying fits; nor, since time first began, had a single one of these little mortals ever gone apart into a corner, and sulked. Oh, what a good time was that to be alive in! The truth is, those ugly little winged monsters, called Troubles, which are now almost as numerous as mosquitoes, had never yet been seen on the earth. It is probable that the very greatest disquietude which a child had ever experienced was Pandora's vexation at not being able to discover the secret of the mysterious box.

This was at first only the faint shadow of a Trouble;

but every day it grew more and more substantial, until, before a great while, the cottage of Epimetheus and Pandora was less sunshiny than those of the other children.

"Whence can the box have come?" Pandora continually kept saying to herself and to Epimetheus. "And what in the world can be inside of it?"

"Always talking about this box!" said Epimetheus, at last; for he had grown extremely tired of the subject. "I wish, dear Pandora, you would try to talk of something else. Come, let us go and gather some ripe figs, and eat them under the trees, for our supper. And I know a vine that has the sweetest and juiciest grapes you ever tasted."

"Always talking about grapes and figs!" cried Pandora, pettishly.

"Well, then," said Epimetheus, who was a very good-tempered child, like a multitude of children in those days, "let us run out and have a merry time with our playmates."

"I am tired of merry times, and don't care if I never have any more!" answered our pettish little Pandora. "And, besides, I never do have any. This ugly box! I am so taken up with thinking about it all the time. I insist upon your telling me what is inside of it."

"As I have already said, fifty times over, I do not know!" replied Epimetheus, getting a little vexed. "How, then, can I tell you what is inside?"

"You might open it," said Pandora, looking sideways at Epimetheus, "and then we could see for ourselves."

"Pandora, what are you thinking of?" exclaimed Epimetheus.

And his face expressed so much horror at the idea of looking into a box which had been confided to him on the condition of his never opening it, that Pandora thought it best not to suggest it any more. Still, however, she could not help thinking and talking about the box.

"At least," said she, "you can tell me how it came here."

"It was left at the door," replied Epimetheus, "just before you came, by a person who looked very smiling and intelligent, and who could hardly forbear laughing as he put it down. He was dressed in an odd kind of a cloak, and had on a cap that seemed to be made partly of feathers, so that it looked almost as if it had wings."

"What sort of a staff had he?" asked Pandora.

"Oh, the most curious staff you ever saw!" cried Epimetheus. "It was like two serpents twisting around a stick, and was carved so naturally that I, at first, thought the serpents were alive."

"I know him," said Pandora, thoughtfully. "Nobody else has such a staff. It was Quicksilver; and he brought me hither, as well as the box. No doubt he intended it for me; and, most probably, it contains pretty dresses for me to wear, or toys for you and me to play with, or something very nice for us both to eat!"

"Perhaps so," answered Epimetheus, turning away. "But until Quicksilver comes back and tells us so, we have neither of us any right to lift the lid of the box."

"What a dull boy he is!" muttered Pandora, as
Epimetheus left the cottage. "I do wish he had a little
more enterprise!"

For the first time since her arrival, Epimetheus had
gone out without asking Pandora to accompany him.
He went to gather figs and grapes by himself, or to
seek whatever amusement he could find, in other society than his little playfellow's. He was tired to death
of hearing about the box, and heartily wished that
Quicksilver, or whatever was the messenger's name,
had left it at some other child's door, where Pandora
would never have set eyes on it. So perseveringly as
she did babble about this one thing! The box, the
box, and nothing but the box! It seemed as if the box
were bewitched, and as if the cottage were not big
enough to hold it, without Pandora's continually stumbling over it, and making Epimetheus stumble over it
likewise, and bruising all four of their shins.

Well, it was really hard that poor Epimetheus
should have a box in his ears from morning till night;
especially as the little people of the earth were so
unaccustomed to vexations, in those happy days, that
they knew not how to deal with them. Thus, a small
vexation made as much disturbance then, as a far bigger one would in our own times.

After Epimetheus was gone, Pandora stood gazing
at the box. She had called it ugly, above a hundred
times; but, in spite of all that she had said against it,
it was positively a very handsome article of furniture,
and would have been quite an ornament to any room
in which it should be placed. It was made of a beau-

tiful kind of wood, with dark and rich veins spreading over its surface, which was so highly polished that little Pandora could see her face in it. As the child had no other looking-glass, it is odd that she did not value the box, merely on this account.

The edges and corners of the box were carved with most wonderful skill. Around the margin there were figures of graceful men and women, and the prettiest children ever seen, reclining or sporting amid a profusion of flowers and foliage; and these various objects were so exquisitely represented, and were wrought together in such harmony, that flowers, foliage, and human beings seemed to combine into a wreath of mingled beauty. But here and there, peeping forth from behind the carved foliage, Pandora once or twice fancied that she saw a face not so lovely, or something or other that was disagreeable, and which stole the beauty out of all the rest. Nevertheless, on looking more closely, and touching the spot with her finger, she could discover nothing of the kind. Some face, that was really beautiful, had been made to look ugly by her catching a sideway glimpse at it.

The most beautiful face of all was done in what is called high relief, in the centre of the lid. There was nothing else, save the dark, smooth richness of the polished wood, and this one face in the centre, with a garland of flowers about its brow. Pandora had looked at this face a great many times, and imagined that the mouth could smile if it liked, or be grave when it chose, the same as any living mouth. The features, indeed, all wore a very lively and rather mischievous expression, which looked almost as if it needs must burst out of the carved lips, and utter itself in words.

Had the mouth spoken, it would probably have been something like this:

"Do not be afraid, Pandora! What harm can there be in opening the box? Never mind that poor, simple Epimetheus! You are wiser than he, and have ten times as much spirit. Open the box, and see if you do not find something very pretty!"

The box, I had almost forgotten to say, was fastened; not by a lock, nor by any other such contrivance, but by a very intricate knot of gold cord. There appeared to be no end to this knot, and no beginning. Never was a knot so cunningly twisted, nor with so many ins and outs, which roguishly defied the skillfulest fingers to distangle them. And yet, by the very difficulty that there was in it, Pandora was the more tempted to examine the knot, and just see how it was made. Two or three times, already, she had stooped over the box, and taken the knot between her thumb and forefinger, but without positively trying to undo it.

"I really believe," said she to herself, "that I begin to see how it was done. Nay, perhaps I could tie it up again, after undoing it. There would be no harm in that, surely. Even Epimetheus would not blame me for that. I need not open the box, and should not, of course, without the foolish boy's consent, even if the knot were untied."

It might have been better for Pandora if she had had a little work to do, or anything to employ her mind upon, so as not to be so constantly thinking of this one subject. But children led so easy a life, before any Troubles came into the world, that they had really a great deal too much leisure. They could not be forever playing at hide-and-seek among the flower-shrubs, or at blind-man's-buff with garlands over their eyes, or at whatever other games had been found out, while Mother Earth was in her babyhood. When life is all sport, toil is the real play. There was absolutely nothing to do. A little sweeping and dusting about the cottage, I suppose, and the gathering of fresh flowers (which were only too abundant everywhere), and arranging them in vases, — and poor little Pandora's day's work was over. And then, for the rest of the day, there was the box!

After all, I am not quite sure that the box was not a blessing to her in its way. It supplied her with such a variety of ideas to think of, and to talk about, whenever she had anybody to listen! When she was in good-humor, she could admire the bright polish of its sides, and the rich border of beautiful faces and foliage that ran all around it. Or, if she chanced to be ill-tempered, she could give it a push, or kick it with her naughty little foot. And many a kick did the box — (but it was a mischievous box, as we shall see, and deserved all it got) — many a kick did it receive. But, certain it is, if it had not been for the box, our active-minded little Pandora would not have known half so well how to spend her time as she now did.

For it was really an endless employment to guess what was inside. What could it be, indeed? Just imagine, my little hearers, how busy your wits would be, if there were a great box in the house, which, as you might have reason to suppose, contained something new and pretty for your Christmas or New Year's gifts. Do you think that you should be less curious than Pandora? If you were left alone with the box, might you not feel a little tempted to lift the lid? But you would not do it. Oh, fie! No, no! Only, if you thought there were toys in it, it would be so very hard to let slip an opportunity of taking just one peep! I know not whether Pandora expected any toys; for none had yet begun to be made, probably, in those days, when the world itself was one great plaything for the children that dwelt upon it. But Pandora was convinced that there was something very beautiful and valuable in the box; and therefore she felt just as anxious to take a peep as any of these little girls, here around me, would have felt. And, possibly, a little more so; but of that I am not quite so certain.

On this particular day, however, which we have so long been talking about, her curiosity grew so much greater than it usually was, that, at last, she approached the box. She was more than half determined to open it, if she could. Ah, naughty Pandora!

First, however, she tried to lift it. It was heavy; quite too heavy for the slender strength of a child, like Pandora. She raised one end of the box a few inches from the floor, and let it fall again, with a pretty loud thump. A moment afterwards, she almost fancied that she heard something stir inside of the box. She applied her ear as closely as possible, and listened.

Positively, there did seem to be a kind of stifled murmur, within! Or was it merely the singing in Pandora's ears? Or could it be the beating of her heart? The child could not quite satisfy herself whether she had heard anything or no. But, at all events, her curiosity was stronger than ever.

As she drew back her head, her eyes fell upon the knot of gold cord.

"It must have been a very ingenious person who tied this knot," said Pandora to herself. "But I think I could untie it, nevertheless. I am resolved, at least, to find the two ends of the cord."

So she took the golden knot in her fingers, and pried into its intricacies as sharply as she could. Almost without intending it, or quite knowing what she was about, she was soon busily engaged in attempting to undo it. Meanwhile, the bright sunshine came through the open window; as did likewise the merry voices of the children, playing at a distance, and perhaps the voice of Epimetheus among them. Pandora stopped to listen. What a beautiful day it was! Would it not be wiser if she were to let the troublesome knot alone, and think no more about the box, but run and join her little playfellows, and be happy?

All this time, however, her fingers were half unconsciously busy with the knot; and happening to glance at the flower-wreathed face on the lid of the enchanted box, she seemed to perceive it slyly grinning at her.

"That face looks very mischievous," thought Pandora. "I wonder whether it smiles because I am doing wrong! I have the greatest mind in the world to run away!"

But just then, by the merest accident, she gave the knot a kind of a twist, which produced a wonderful result. The gold cord untwined itself, as if by magic, and left the box without a fastening.

"This is the strangest thing I ever knew!" said Pandora. "What will Epimetheus say? And how can I possibly tie it up again?"

She made one or two attempts to restore the knot, but soon found it quite beyond her skill. It had disentangled itself so suddenly that she could not in the least remember how the strings had been doubled into one another; and when she tried to recollect the shape and appearance of the knot, it seemed to have gone entirely out of her mind. Nothing was to be done, therefore, but to let the box remain as it was until Epimetheus should come in.

"But," said Pandora, "when he finds the knot untied, he will know that I have done it. How shall I make him believe that I have not looked into the box?"

And then the thought came into her naughty little heart, that, since she would be suspected of having looked into the box, she might just as well do so at once. Oh, very naughty and very foolish Pandora! You should have thought only of doing what was right, and of leaving undone what was wrong, and not of what your playfellow Epimetheus would have said or believed. And so perhaps she might, if the enchanted face on the lid of the box had not looked so bewitchingly persuasive at her, and if she had not seemed to hear, more distinctly than before, the murmur of small voices within. She could not tell whether it was fancy or no; but there was quite a little tumult of whispers in her ear, — or else it was her curiosity that whispered, —

"Let us out, dear Pandora, — pray let us out! We will be such nice pretty playfellows for you! Only let us out!"

"What can it be?" thought Pandora. "Is there something alive in the box? Well! — yes! — I am resolved to take just one peep! Only one peep; and then the lid shall be shut down as safely as ever! There cannot possibly be any harm in just one little peep!"

But it is now time for us to see what Epimetheus was doing.

This was the first time, since his little playmate had come to dwell with him, that he had attempted to enjoy any pleasure in which she did not partake. But nothing went right; nor was he nearly so happy as on other days. He could not find a sweet grape or a ripe fig (if Epimetheus had a fault, it was a little too much fondness for figs); or, if ripe at all, they were over-ripe, and so sweet as to be cloying. There was no mirth in his heart, such as usually made his voice gush out, of its own accord, and swell the merriment of his companions. In short, he grew so uneasy and discontented, that the other children could not imagine what was the matter with Epimetheus. Neither did he himself know what ailed him, any better than they did. For you must recollect that, at the time we are speaking of, it was everybody's nature, and con-

slant habit, to be happy. The world had not yet learned
to be otherwise. Not a single soul or body, since these
children were first sent to enjoy themselves on the
beautiful earth, had ever been sick or out of sorts.

At length, discovering that, somehow or other, he
put a stop to all the play, Epimetheus judged it best
to go back to Pandora, who was in a humor better
suited to his own. But, with a hope of giving her
pleasure, he gathered some flowers, and made them
into a wreath, which he meant to put upon her head.
The flowers were very lovely, — roses, and lilies, and
orange-blossoms, and a great many more, which left a
trail of fragrance behind, as Epimetheus carried them
along; and the wreath was put together with as much
skill as could reasonably be expected of a boy. The
fingers of little girls, it has always appeared to me,
are the fittest to twine flower-wreaths; but boys could
do it, in those days, rather better than they can now.

And here I must mention that a great black cloud
had been gathering in the sky, for some time past, although it had not yet overspread the sun. But, just
as Epimetheus reached the cottage door, this cloud
began to intercept the sunshine, and thus to make a
sudden and sad obscurity.

He entered softly; for he meant, if possible, to steal
behind Pandora, and fling the wreath of flowers over
her head, before she should be aware of his approach.
But, as it happened, there was no need of his treading
so very lightly. He might have trod as heavily as he
pleased, — as heavily as a grown man, — as heavily,
I was going to say, as an elephant, — without much

probability of Pandora's hearing his footsteps. She was too intent upon her purpose. At the moment of his entering the cottage, the naughty child had put her hand to the lid, and was on the point of opening the mysterious box. Epimetheus beheld her. If he had cried out, Pandora would probably have withdrawn her hand, and the fatal mystery of the box might never have been known.

But Epimetheus himself, although he said very little about it, had his own share of curiosity to know what was inside. Perceiving that Pandora was resolved to find out the secret, he determined that his playfellow should not be the only wise person in the cottage. And if there were anything pretty or valuable in the box, he meant to take half of it to himself. Thus, after all his sage speeches to Pandora about restraining her curiosity, Epimetheus turned out to be quite as foolish, and nearly as much in fault, as she. So, whenever we blame Pandora for what happened, we must not forget to shake our heads at Epimetheus likewise.

As Pandora raised the lid, the cottage grew very dark and dismal; for the black cloud had now swept quite over the sun, and seemed to have buried it alive. There had, for a little while past, been a low growling and muttering, which all at once broke into a heavy peal of thunder. But Pandora, heeding nothing of all this, lifted the lid nearly upright, and looked inside. It seemed as if a sudden swarm of winged creatures brushed past her, taking flight out of the box, while, at the same instant, she heard the voice of Epimetheus, with a lamentable tone, as if he were in pain.

"Oh, I am stung!" cried he. "I am stung! Naughty Pandora! why have you opened this wicked box?"

Pandora let fall the lid, and, starting up, looked about her, to see what had befallen Epimetheus. The thunder-cloud had so darkened the room that she could not very clearly discern what was in it. But she heard a disagreeable buzzing, as if a great many huge flies, or gigantic mosquitoes, or those insects which we call dor-bugs, and pinching-dogs, were darting about. And, as her eyes grew more accustomed to the imperfect light, she saw a crowd of ugly little shapes, with bats' wings, looking abominably spiteful, and armed with terribly long stings in their tails. It was one of these that had stung Epimetheus. Nor was it a great while before Pandora herself began to scream, in no less pain and affright than her playfellow, and making a vast deal more hubbub about it. An odious little monster had settled on her forehead, and would have stung her I know not how deeply, if Epimetheus had not run and brushed it away.

Now, if you wish to know what these ugly things might be, which had made their escape out of the box, I must tell you that they were the whole family of earthly Troubles. There were evil Passions; there were a great many species of Cares; there were more than a hundred and fifty Sorrows; there were Diseases, in a vast number of miserable and painful shapes; there were more kinds of Naughtiness than it would be of any use to talk about. In short, everything that has since afflicted the souls and bodies of mankind had been shut up in the mysterious box, and given to Epimetheus and Pandora to be kept safely, in order that the happy children of the world might never be molested by them. Had they been faithful to their trust, all would have gone well. No grown person would ever have been sad, nor any child have had cause to shed a single tear, from that hour until this moment.

But — and you may see by this how a wrong act of any one mortal is a calamity to the whole world — by Pandora's lifting the lid of that miserable box, and by the fault of Epimetheus, too, in not preventing her, these Troubles have obtained a foothold among us, and do not seem very likely to be driven away in a hurry. For it was impossible, as you will easily guess, that the two children should keep the ugly swarm in their own little cottage. On the contrary, the first thing that they did was to fling open the doors and windows, in hopes of getting rid of them; and, sure enough, away flew the winged Troubles all abroad, and so pestered and tormented the small people, everywhere about, that none of them so much as smiled for many days afterwards. And, what was very singular, all the flowers and dewy blossoms on earth, not one of which had hitherto faded, now began to droop and shed their leaves, after a day or two. The children, moreover, who before seemed immortal in their childhood, now grew older, day by day, and came soon to be youths and maidens, and men and women by and by, and aged people, before they dreamed of such a thing.

Meanwhile, the naughty Pandora, and hardly less naughty Epimetheus, remained in their cottage. Both of them had been grievously stung, and were in a good deal of pain, which seemed the more intolerable to them, because it was the very first pain that had ever been felt since the world began. Of course, they were entirely unaccustomed to it, and could have no idea what it meant. Besides all this, they were in exceedingly bad humor, both with themselves and with one another. In order to indulge it to the utmost, Epimetheus sat down sullenly in a corner with his back towards Pandora; while Pandora flung herself upon the floor and rested her head on the fatal and abominable box. She was crying bitterly, and sobbing as if her heart would break.

Suddenly there was a gentle little tap on the inside of the lid.

"What can that be?" cried Pandora, lifting her head.

But either Epimetheus had not heard the tap, or was too much out of humor to notice it. At any rate, he made no answer.

"You are very unkind," said Pandora, sobbing anew, "not to speak to me!"

Again the tap! It sounded like the tiny knuckles of a fairy's hand, knocking lightly and playfully on the inside of the box.

"Who are you?" asked Pandora, with a little of her former curiosity. "Who are you, inside of this naughty box?"

A sweet little voice spoke from within, —

"Only lift the lid, and you shall see."

"No, no," answered Pandora, again beginning to sob, "I have had enough of lifting the lid! You are inside of the box, naughty creature, and there you shall stay! There are plenty of your ugly brothers and sisters already flying about the world. You need never think that I shall be so foolish as to let you out!"

She looked towards Epimetheus, as she spoke, perhaps expecting that he would commend her for her wisdom. But the sullen boy only muttered that she was wise a little too late.

"Ah," said the sweet little voice again, "you had much better let me out. I am not like those naughty creatures that have stings in their tails. They are no brothers and sisters of mine, as you would see at once, if you were only to get a glimpse of me. Come, come, my pretty Pandora! I am sure you will let me out!"

And, indeed, there was a kind of cheerful witchery in the tone, that made it almost impossible to refuse anything which this little voice asked. Pandora's heart had insensibly grown lighter, at every word that came from within the box. Epimetheus, too, though still in the corner, had turned half round, and seemed to be in rather better spirits than before.

"My dear Epimetheus," cried Pandora, "have you heard this little voice?"

"Yes, to be sure I have," answered he, but in no very good humor as yet. "And what of it?"

"Shall I lift the lid again?" asked Pandora.

"Just as you please," said Epimetheus. "You have done so much mischief already, that perhaps you may as well do a little more. One other Trouble, in such a swarm as you have set adrift about the world, can make no very great difference."

"You might speak a little more kindly!" murmured Pandora, wiping her eyes.

"Ah, naughty boy!" cried the little voice within the box, in an arch and laughing tone. "He knows he is longing to see me. Come, my dear Pandora, lift up the lid. I am in a great hurry to comfort you. Only let me have some fresh air, and you shall soon see that matters are not quite so dismal as you think them!"

"Epimetheus," exclaimed Pandora, "come what may, I am resolved to open the box!"

"And, as the lid seems very heavy," cried Epimetheus, running across the room, "I will help you!"

So, with one consent, the two children again lifted the lid. Out flew a sunny and smiling little personage, and hovered about the room, throwing a light wherever she went. Have you never made the sunshine dance into dark corners, by reflecting it from a bit of looking-glass? Well, so looked the winged cheerfulness of this fairy-like stranger, amid the gloom of the cottage. She flew to Epimetheus, and laid the least touch of her finger on the inflamed spot where the Trouble had stung him, and immediately the anguish of it was gone. Then she kissed Pandora on the forehead, and her hurt was cured likewise.

After performing these good offices, the bright stranger fluttered sportively over the children's heads, and looked so sweetly at them, that they both began to think it not so very much amiss to have opened the box, since, otherwise, their cheery guest must have been kept a prisoner among those naughty imps with stings in their tails.

"Pray, who are you, beautiful creature?" inquired Pandora.

"I am to be called Hope!" answered the sunshiny figure. "And because I am such a cheery little body, I was packed into the box, to make amends to the human race for that swarm of ugly Troubles, which was destined to be let loose among them. Never fear! we shall do pretty well in spite of them all."

"Your wings are colored like the rainbow!" exclaimed Pandora. "How very beautiful!"

"Yes, they are like the rainbow," said Hope, "because, glad as my nature is, I am partly made of tears as well as smiles."

"And will you stay with us," asked Epimetheus, "forever and ever?"

"As long as you need me," said Hope, with her pleasant smile, — "and that will be as long as you live in the world, — I promise never to desert you. There may come times and seasons, now and then, when you will think that I have utterly vanished. But again, and again, and again, when perhaps you least dream of it, you shall see the glimmer of my wings on the ceiling of your cottage. Yes, my dear children, and I know something very good and beautiful that is to be given you hereafter!"

"Oh tell us," they exclaimed, — "tell us what it is!"

"Do not ask me," replied Hope, putting her finger on her rosy mouth. "But do not despair, even if it should never happen while you live on this earth. Trust in my promise, for it is true."

THE PARADISE OF CHILDREN

"We do trust you!" cried Epimetheus and Pandora, both in one breath.

And so they did; and not only they, but so has everybody trusted Hope, that has since been alive. And to tell you the truth, I cannot help being glad — (though, to be sure, it was an uncommonly naughty thing for her to do) — but I cannot help being glad that our foolish Pandora peeped into the box. No doubt — no doubt — the Troubles are still flying about the world, and have increased in multitude, rather than lessened, and are a very ugly set of imps, and carry most venomous stings in their tails. I have felt them already, and expect to feel them more, as I grow older. But then that lovely and lightsome little figure of Hope! What in the world could we do without her? Hope spiritualizes the earth; Hope makes it always new; and, even in the earth's best and brightest aspect, Hope shows it to be only the shadow of an infinite bliss hereafter!

THE DRAGON'S TEETH

By Nathaniel Hawthorne

CADMUS, Phœnix, and Cilix, the three sons of King Agenor, and their little sister Europa (who was a very beautiful child) were at play together, near the seashore, in their father's kingdom of Phœnicia. They had rambled to some distance from the palace where their parents dwelt, and were now in a verdant meadow, on one side of which lay the sea, all sparkling and dimpling in the sunshine, and murmuring gently against the beach. The three boys were very happy, gathering flowers, and twining them into garlands, with which they adorned the little Europa. Seated on the grass, the child was almost hidden under an abundance of buds and blossoms, whence her rosy face peeped merrily out, and, as Cadmus said, was the prettiest of all the flowers.

Just then, there came a splendid butterfly, fluttering along the meadow; and Cadmus, Phœnix, and Cilix set off in pursuit of it, crying out that it was a flower with wings. Europa, who was a little wearied with playing all day long, did not chase the butterfly with her brothers, but sat still where they had left her, and closed her eyes. For a while, she listened to the pleasant murmur of the sea, which was like a voice saying "Hush!" and bidding her go to sleep. But the

128

pretty child, if she slept at all, could not have slept more than a moment, when she heard something trample on the grass, not far from her, and peeping out from the heap of flowers, beheld a snow-white bull.

And whence could this bull have come? Europa and her brothers had been a long time playing in the meadow, and had seen no cattle, nor other living thing, either there or on the neighboring hills.

"Brother Cadmus!" cried Europa, starting up out of the midst of the roses and lilies. "Phœnix! Cilix! Where are you all? Help! Help! Come and drive away this bull!"

But her brothers were too far off to hear; especially as the fright took away Europa's voice, and hindered her from calling very loudly. So there she stood, with her pretty mouth wide open, as pale as the white lilies that were twisted among the other flowers in her garlands.

Nevertheless, it was the suddenness with which she had perceived the bull, rather than anything frightful in his appearance, that caused Europa so much alarm. On looking at him more attentively, she began to see that he was a beautiful animal, and even fancied a particularly amiable expression in his face. As for his breath, — the breath of cattle, you know, is always sweet, — it was as fragrant as if he had been grazing on no other food than rosebuds, or, at least, the most delicate of clover-blossoms. Never before did a bull have such bright and tender eyes, and such smooth horns of ivory, as this one. And the bull ran little races, and capered sportively around the child; so that she quite forgot how big and strong he was, and, from the gentleness and playfulness of his actions, soon came to consider him as innocent a creature as a pet lamb.

Thus, frightened as she at first was, you might by and by have seen Europa stroking the bull's forehead with her small white hand, and taking the garlands off her own head to hang them on his neck and ivory horns. Then she pulled up some blades of grass, and he ate them out of her hand, not as if he were hungry, but because he wanted to be friends with the child, and took pleasure in eating what she had touched. Well, my stars! was there ever such a gentle, sweet, pretty, and amiable creature as this bull, and ever such a nice playmate for a little girl?

When the animal saw (for the bull had so much intelligence that it is really wonderful to think of), when he saw that Europa was no longer afraid of him, he grew overjoyed, and could hardly contain himself for delight. He frisked about the meadow, now here, now there, making sprightly leaps, with as little effort as a bird expends in hopping from twig to twig. Indeed, his motion was as light as if he were flying through the air, and his hoofs seemed hardly to leave their print in the grassy soil over which he trod. With his spotless hue, he resembled a snow-drift, wafted along by the wind. Once he galloped so far away that Europa feared lest she might never see him again; so, setting up her childish voice, she called him back.

"Come back, pretty creature!" she cried. "Here is a nice clover-blossom."

And then it was delightful to witness the gratitude of this amiable bull, and how he was so full of joy and thankfulness that he capered higher than ever. He came running, and bowed his head before Europa, as if he knew her to be a king's daughter, or else recognized the important truth that a little girl is everybody's queen. And not only did the bull bend his neck, he absolutely knelt down at her feet, and made such intelligent nods, and other inviting gestures, that Europa understood what he meant just as well as if he had put it in so many words.

"Come, dear child," was what he wanted to say, "let me give you a ride on my back."

At the first thought of such a thing, Europa drew back. But then she considered in her wise little head that there could be no possible harm in taking just one gallop on the back of this docile and friendly animal, who would certainly set her down the very instant she desired it. And how it would surprise her brothers to see her riding across the green meadow! And what merry times they might have, either taking turns for a gallop, or clambering on the gentle creature, all four children together, and careering round the field with shouts of laughter that would be heard as far off as King Agenor's palace!

"I think I will do it," said the child to herself.

And, indeed, why not? She cast a glance around, and caught a glimpse of Cadmus, Phœnix, and Cilix, who were still in pursuit of the butterfly, almost at the other end of the meadow. It would be the quickest way of rejoining them, to get upon the white bull's back. She came a step nearer to him, therefore; and — sociable creature that he was — he showed so much joy at this mark of her confidence, that the child could not find it in her heart to hesitate any longer. Making one bound (for this little princess was as active as a squirrel), there sat Europa on the beautiful bull, holding an ivory horn in each hand, lest she should fall off.

"Softly, pretty bull, softly!" she said, rather frightened at what she had done. "Do not gallop too fast."

Having got the child on his back, the animal gave a leap into the air, and came down so like a feather that Europa did not know when his hoofs touched the ground. He then began a race to that part of the flowery plain where her three brothers were, and where they had just caught their splendid butterfly. Europa screamed with delight; and Phœnix, Cilix, and Cadmus stood gaping at the spectacle of their sister mounted on a white bull, not knowing whether to be frightened or to wish the same good luck for themselves. The gentle and innocent creature (for who could possibly doubt that he was so?) pranced round among the children as sportively as a kitten. Europa all the while looked down upon her brothers, nodding and laughing, but yet with a sort of stateliness in her rosy little face. As the bull wheeled about to take another gallop across the meadow, the child waved her hand, and said, "Good-by," playfully pretending that she was now bound on a distant journey, and might not see her brothers again for nobody could tell how long.

"Good-by," shouted Cadmus, Phœnix, and Cilix, all in one breath.

But, together with her enjoyment of the sport, there was still a little remnant of fear in the child's heart; so that her last look at the three boys was a troubled one, and made them feel as if their dear sister were really leaving them forever. And what do you think the snowy bull did next? Why, he set off, as swift as the wind, straight down to the sea-shore, scampered across the sand, took an airy leap, and plunged right in among the foaming billows. The white spray rose in a shower over him and the little Europa, and fell spattering down upon the water.

Then what a scream of terror did the poor child send forth! The three brothers screamed manfully, likewise, and ran to the shore as fast as their legs would carry them, with Cadmus at their head. But it was too late. When they reached the margin of the sand, the treacherous animal was already far away in the wide blue sea, with only his snowy head and tail emerging, and poor little Europa between them, stretching out one hand towards her dear brothers, while she grasped the bull's ivory horn with the other. And there stood Cadmus, Phœnix, and Cilix, gazing at this sad spectacle, through their tears, until they could no longer distinguish the bull's snowy head from the white-capped billows that seemed to boil up out of the sea's depths around him. Nothing more was ever seen of the white bull, — nothing more of the beautiful child.

This was a mournful story, as you may well think, for the three boys to carry home to their parents. King Agenor, their father, was the ruler of the whole country; but he loved his little daughter Europa better than his kingdom, or than all his other children, or than anything else in the world. Therefore, when Cadmus and his two brothers came crying home, and told him how that a white bull had carried off their sister, and swam with her over the sea, the king was quite beside himself with grief and rage. Although it was now twilight, and fast growing dark, he bade them set out instantly in search of her.

"Never shall you see my face again," he cried, "unless you bring me back my little Europa, to gladden me with her smiles and her pretty ways. Begone, and enter my presence no more, till you come leading her by the hand."

As King Agenor said this, his eyes flashed fire (for he was a very passionate king), and he looked so terribly angry that the poor boys did not even venture to ask for their suppers, but slunk away out of the palace, and only paused on the steps a moment to consult whither they should go first. While they were standing there, all in dismay, their mother, Queen Telephassa (who happened not to be by when they told the story to the king), came hurrying after them, and said that she too would go in quest of her daughter.

"Oh no, mother!" cried the boys. "The night is dark, and there is no knowing what troubles and perils we may meet with."

"Alas! my dear children," answered poor Queen Telephassa, weeping bitterly, "that is only another reason why I should go with you. If I should lose you, too, as well as my little Europa, what would become of me?"

"And let me go likewise!" said their playfellow Thasus, who came running to join them.

Thasus was the son of a seafaring person in the neighborhood; he had been brought up with the young princes, and was their intimate friend, and loved Europa very much; so they consented that he should accompany them. The whole party, therefore, set forth together; Cadmus, Phœnix, Cilix, and Thasus clustered round Queen Telephassa, grasping her skirts, and begging her to lean upon their shoulders whenever she felt weary. In this manner they went down the palace steps, and began a journey which turned out to be a great deal longer than they dreamed of. The last that they saw of King Agenor, he came to the door, with a servant holding a torch beside him, and called after them into the gathering darkness: —

"Remember! Never ascend these steps again without the child!"

"Never!" sobbed Queen Telephassa; and the three brothers and Thasus answered, "Never! Never! Never! Never!"

And they kept their word. Year after year King Agenor sat in the solitude of his beautiful palace, listening in vain for their returning footsteps, hoping to hear the familiar voice of the queen, and the cheerful talk of his sons and their playfellow Thasus, entering the door together, and the sweet, childish accents of little Europa in the midst of them. But so long a time went by, that, at last, if they had really come, the king would not have known that this was the voice of Telephassa, and these the younger voices that used to make

such joyful echoes when the children were playing about
the palace. We must now leave King Agenor to sit on his
throne, and must go along with Queen Telephassa
and her four youthful companions.

They went on and on, and traveled a long way, and
passed over mountains and rivers, and sailed over seas.
Here, and there, and everywhere, they made continual
inquiry if any person could tell them what had become
of Europa. The rustic people, of whom they asked
this question, paused a little while from their labors
in the field, and looked very much surprised. They
thought it strange to behold a woman in the garb of a
queen (for Telephassa, in her haste, had forgotten to
take off her crown and her royal robes), roaming about
the country, with four lads around her, on such an
errand as this seemed to be. But nobody could give
them any tidings of Europa; nobody had seen a little
girl dressed like a princess, and mounted on a snow-
white bull, which galloped as swiftly as the wind.

I cannot tell you how long Queen Telephassa, and
Cadmus, Phœnix, and Cilix, her three sons, and Thasus,
their playfellow, went wandering along the highways
and bypaths, or through the pathless wildernesses of
the earth, in this manner. But certain it is, that, before
they reached any place of rest, their splendid garments
were quite worn out. They all looked very much travel-
stained, and would have had the dust of many countries
on their shoes, if the streams, through which they waded,
had not washed it all away. When they had been gone
a year, Telephassa threw away her crown, because it
chafed her forehead.

"It has given me many a headache," said the poor queen, "and it cannot cure my heartache."

As fast as their princely robes got torn and tattered, they exchanged them for such mean attire as ordinary people wore. By and by they came to have a wild and homeless aspect; so that you would much sooner have taken them for a gypsy family than a queen and three princes, and a young nobleman, who had once a palace for their home, and a train of servants to do their bidding. The four boys grew up to be tall young men, with sunburnt faces. Each of them girded on a sword, to defend themselves against the perils of the way. When the husbandmen at whose farm-houses they sought hospitality needed their assistance in the harvest-field, they gave it willingly; and Queen Telephassa (who had done no work in her palace, save to braid silk threads with golden ones) came behind them to bind the sheaves. If payment was offered, they shook their heads, and only asked for tidings of Europa.

"There are bulls enough in my pasture," the old farmers would reply; "but I never heard of one like this you tell me of. A snow-white bull with a little princess on his back! Ho! ho! I ask your pardon, good folks; but there never was such a sight seen hereabouts."

At last, when his upper lip began to have the down on it, Phœnix grew weary of rambling hither and thither to no purpose. So, one day, when they happened to be passing through a pleasant and solitary tract of country, he sat himself down on a heap of moss.

"I can go no farther," said Phœnix. "It is a mere

137

foolish waste of life to spend it, as we do, in always wandering up and down, and never coming to any home at nightfall. Our sister is lost, and never will be found. She probably perished in the sea; or, to whatever shore the white bull may have carried her, it is now so many years ago, that there would be neither love nor acquaintance between us should we meet again. My father has forbidden us to return to his palace; so I shall build me a hut of branches, and dwell here."

"Well, son Phœnix," said Telephassa, sorrowfully, "you have grown to be a man, and must do as you judge best. But, for my part, I will still go in quest of my poor child."

"And we three will go along with you!" cried Cadmus and Cilix and their faithful friend Thasus.

But, before setting out, they all helped Phœnix to build a habitation. When completed, it was a sweet rural bower, roofed overhead with an arch of living boughs. Inside there were two pleasant rooms, one of which had a soft heap of moss for a bed, while the other was furnished with a rustic seat or two, curiously fashioned out of the crooked roots of trees. So comfortable and homelike did it seem, that Telephassa and her three companions could not help sighing, to think that they must still roam about the world, instead of spending the remainder of their lives in some such cheerful abode as they had here built for Phœnix. But, when they bade him farewell, Phœnix shed tears, and probably regretted that he was no longer to keep them company.

However, he had fixed upon an admirable place to dwell in. And by and by there came other people, who chanced to have no homes; and, seeing how pleasant a spot it was, they built themselves huts in the neighborhood of Phœnix's habitation. Thus, before many years went by, a city had grown up there, in the centre of which was seen a stately palace of marble, wherein dwelt Phœnix, clothed in a purple robe, and wearing a golden crown upon his head. For the inhabitants of the new city, finding that he had royal blood in his veins, had chosen him to be their king. The very first decree of state which King Phœnix issued was, that if a maiden happened to arrive in the kingdom, mounted on a snow-white bull, and calling herself Europa, his subjects should treat her with the greatest kindness and respect, and immediately bring her to the palace. You may see, by this, that Phœnix's conscience never quite ceased to trouble him for giving up the quest of his dear sister, and sitting himself down to be comfortable, while his mother and her companions went onward.

But often and often, at the close of a weary day's journey, did Telephassa and Cadmus, Cilix and Thasus, remember the pleasant spot in which they had left Phœnix. It was a sorrowful prospect for these wanderers, that on the morrow they must again set forth, and that, after many nightfalls, they would perhaps be no nearer the close of their toilsome pilgrimage than now. These thoughts made them all melancholy at times, but appeared to torment Cilix more than the rest of the party. At length, one morning, when they were taking their staffs in hand to set out, he thus addressed them: —

"My dear mother, and you good brother Cadmus, and my friend Thasus, methinks we are like people in a dream. There is no substance in the life which we are leading. It is such a dreary length of time since the white bull carried off my sister Europa, that I have quite forgotten how she looked, and the tones of her voice, and, indeed, almost doubt whether such a little girl ever lived in the world. And whether she once lived or no, I am convinced that she no longer survives, and that therefore it is the merest folly to waste our own lives and happiness in seeking her. Were we to find her, she would now be a woman grown, and would look upon us all as strangers. So, to tell you the truth, I have resolved to take up my abode here; and I entreat you, mother, brother, and friend, to follow my example."

"Not I, for one," said Telephassa, although the poor queen, firmly as she spoke, was so travel-worn that she could hardly put her foot to the ground, — "not I, for one! In the depths of my heart, little Europa is still the rosy child who ran to gather flowers so many years ago. She has not grown to womanhood, nor forgotten me. At noon, at night, journeying onward, sitting down to rest, her childish voice is always in my ears, calling, 'Mother! mother!' Stop here who may, there is no repose for me."

"Nor for me," said Cadmus, "while my dear mother pleases to go onward."

And the faithful Thasus, too, was resolved to bear

them company. They remained with Cilix a few days,
however, and helped him to build a rustic bower, resembling the one which they had formerly built for
Phœnix.

When they were bidding him farewell, Cilix burst
into tears, and told his mother that it seemed just as
melancholy a dream to stay there, in solitude, as to go
onward. If she really believed that they would ever
find Europa, he was willing to continue the search with
them, even now. But Telephassa bade him remain
there, and be happy, if his own heart would let him.
So the pilgrims took their leave of him, and departed,
and were hardly out of sight before some other wandering people came along that way, and saw Cilix's
habitation, and were greatly delighted with the appearance of the place. There being abundance of un-
occupied ground in the neighborhood, these strangers
built huts for themselves, and were soon joined by a
multitude of new settlers, who quickly formed a city.
In the middle of it was seen a magnificent palace of
colored marble, on the balcony of which, every noon-
tide, appeared Cilix, in a long purple robe, and with
a jeweled crown upon his head; for the inhabitants,
when they found out that he was a king's son, had considered him the fittest of all men to be a king himself.

One of the first acts of King Cilix's government
was to send out an expedition, consisting of a grave
ambassador and an escort of bold and hardy young
men, with orders to visit the principal kingdoms of
the earth, and inquire whether a young maiden had
passed through those regions, galloping swiftly on a

white bull. It is, therefore, plain to my mind, that Cilix secretly blamed himself for giving up the search for Europa, as long as he was able to put one foot before the other.

As for Telephassa, and Cadmus, and the good Thasus, it grieves me to think of them, still keeping up that weary pilgrimage. The two young men did their best for the poor queen, helping her over the rough places, often carrying her across rivulets in their faithful arms, and seeking to shelter her at nightfall, even when they themselves lay on the ground. Sad, sad it was to hear them asking of every passer-by if he had seen Europa, so long after the white bull had carried her away. But, though the gray years thrust themselves between, and made the child's figure dim in their remembrance, neither of these true-hearted three ever dreamed of giving up the search.

One morning, however, poor Thasus found that he had sprained his ankle, and could not possibly go a step farther.

"After a few days, to be sure," said he, mournfully, "I might make shift to hobble along with a stick. But that would only delay you, and perhaps hinder you from finding dear little Europa, after all your pains and trouble. Do you go forward, therefore, my beloved companions, and leave me to follow as I may."

"Thou hast been a true friend, dear Thasus," said Queen Telephassa, kissing his forehead. "Being neither my son nor the brother of our lost Europa, thou hast shown thyself truer to me and her than Phœnix and Cilix did, whom we have left behind us. Without thy loving help, and that of my son Cadmus, my limbs could not have borne me half so far as this. Now, take thy rest, and be at peace. For — and it is the first time I have owned it to myself — I begin to question whether we shall ever find my beloved daughter in this world."

Saying this, the poor queen shed tears, because it was a grievous trial to the mother's heart to confess that her hopes were growing faint. From that day forward, Cadmus noticed that she never traveled with the same alacrity of spirit that had heretofore supported her. Her weight was heavier upon his arm.

Before setting out, Cadmus helped Thasus build a bower; while Telephassa, being too infirm to give any great assistance, advised them how to fit it up and furnish it, so that it might be as comfortable as a hut of branches could. Thasus, however, did not spend all his days in this green bower. For it happened to him, as to Phœnix and Cilix, that other homeless people visited the spot and liked it, and built themselves habitations in the neighborhood. So here, in the course of a few years, was another thriving city with a red freestone palace in the centre of it, where Thasus sat upon a throne, doing justice to the people, with a purple robe over his shoulders, a sceptre in his hand, and a crown upon his head. The inhabitants had made him king, not for the sake of any royal blood (for none was in his veins), but because Thasus was an upright, true-hearted, and courageous man, and therefore fit to rule.

But, when the affairs of his kingdom were all settled,

King Thasus laid aside his purple robe, and crown, and sceptre, and bade his worthiest subject distribute justice to the people in his stead. Then, grasping the pilgrim's staff that had supported him so long, he set forth again, hoping still to discover some hoofmark of the snow-white bull, some trace of the vanished child. He returned, after a lengthened absence, and sat down wearily upon his throne. To his latest hour, nevertheless, King Thasus showed his truehearted remembrance of Europa, by ordering that a fire should always be kept burning in his palace, and a bath steaming hot, and food ready to be served up, and a bed with snow-white sheets, in case the maiden should arrive, and require immediate refreshment. And though Europa never came, the good Thasus had the blessings of many a poor traveler, who profited by the food and lodging which were meant for the little playmate of the king's boyhood.

Telephassa and Cadmus were now pursuing their weary way, with no companion but each other. The queen leaned heavily upon her son's arm, and could walk only a few miles a day. But for all her weakness and weariness, she would not be persuaded to give up the search. It was enough to bring tears into the eyes of bearded men to hear the melancholy tone with which she inquired of every stranger whether he could tell her any news of the lost child.

"Have you seen a little girl — no, no, I mean a young maiden of full growth — passing by this way, mounted on a snow-white bull, which gallops as swiftly as the wind?"

"We have seen no such wondrous sight," the people would reply; and very often, taking Cadmus aside, they whispered to him, "Is this stately and sad-looking woman your mother? Surely she is not in her right mind; and you ought to take her home, and make her comfortable, and do your best to get this dream out of her fancy."

"It is no dream," said Cadmus. "Everything else is a dream, save that."

But, one day, Telephassa seemed feebler than usual, and leaned almost her whole weight on the arm of Cadmus, and walked more slowly than ever before. At last they reached a solitary spot, where she told her son that she must needs lie down, and take a good, long rest.

"A good, long rest!" she repeated, looking Cadmus tenderly in the face, — "a good, long rest, thou dearest one!"

"As long as you please, dear mother," answered Cadmus.

Telephassa bade him sit down on the turf beside her, and then she took his hand.

"My son," said she, fixing her dim eyes most lovingly upon him, "this rest that I speak of will be very long indeed! You must not wait till it is finished. Dear Cadmus, you do not comprehend me. You must make a grave here, and lay your mother's weary frame into it. My pilgrimage is over."

Cadmus burst into tears, and, for a long time, refused to believe that his dear mother was now to be taken from him. But Telephassa reasoned with him, and kissed him, and at length made him discern that it was better for her spirit to pass away out of the toil, the weariness, the grief, and disappointment which had burdened her on earth, ever since the child was lost. He therefore repressed his sorrow, and listened to her last words.

"Dearest Cadmus," said she, "thou hast been the truest son that ever mother had, and faithful to the very last. Who else would have borne with my infirmities as thou hast! It is owing to thy care, thou tenderest child, that my grave was not dug long years ago, in some valley or on some hillside that lies far, far behind us. It is enough. Thou shalt wander no more on this hopeless search. But when thou hast laid thy mother in the earth, then go, my son, to Delphi, and inquire of the oracle what thou shalt do next."

"O mother, mother," cried Cadmus, "couldst thou but have seen my sister before this hour!"

"It matters little now," answered Telephassa, and there was a smile upon her face. "I go now to the better world, and, sooner or later, shall find my daughter there."

I will not sadden you, my little hearers, with telling how Telephassa died and was buried, but will only say, that her dying smile grew brighter, instead of vanishing from her dead face; so that Cadmus felt convinced that, at her very first step into the better world, she had caught Europa in her arms. He planted some flowers on his mother's grave, and left them to grow there, and make the place beautiful, when he should be far away.

After performing this last sorrowful duty, he set forth alone, and took the road towards the famous oracle of Delphi, as Telephassa had advised him. On his way thither, he still inquired of most people whom he met whether they had seen Europa; for, to say the truth, Cadmus had grown so accustomed to ask the question, that it came to his lips as readily as a remark about the weather. He received various answers. Some told him one thing, and some another. Among the rest, a mariner affirmed that, many years before, in a distant country, he had heard a rumor about a white bull, which came swimming across the sea with a child on his back, dressed up in flowers that were blighted by the sea-water. He did not know what had become of the child or the bull; and Cadmus suspected, indeed, by a queer twinkle in the mariner's eyes, that he was putting a joke upon him, and had never really heard anything about the matter.

Poor Cadmus found it more wearisome to travel alone than to bear all his dear mother's weight while she had kept him company. His heart, you will understand, was now so heavy that it seemed impossible, sometimes, to carry it any farther. But his limbs were strong and active, and well accustomed to exercise. He walked swiftly along, thinking of King Agenor and Queen Telephassa, and his brothers, and the friendly Thasus, all of whom he had left behind him, at one point of his pilgrimage or another, and never expected to see them any more. Full of these remembrances, he came within sight of a lofty mountain, which the people thereabouts told him was called

Parnassus. On the slope of Mount Parnassus was the famous Delphi, whither Cadmus was going.

This Delphi was supposed to be the very midmost spot of the whole world. The place of the oracle was a certain cavity in the mountain-side, over which, when Cadmus came thither, he found a rude bower of branches. It reminded him of those which he had helped to build for Phœnix and Cilix, and afterwards for Thasus. In later times, when multitudes of people came from great distances to put questions to the oracle, a spacious temple of marble was erected over the spot. But in the days of Cadmus, as I have told you, there was only this rustic bower, with its abundance of green foliage, and a tuft of shrubbery, that ran wild over the mysterious hole in the hill-side.

When Cadmus had thrust a passage through the tangled boughs, and made his way into the bower, he did not at first discern the half-hidden cavity. But soon he felt a cold stream of air rushing out of it, with so much force that it shook the ringlets on his cheek. Pulling away the shrubbery which clustered over the hole, he bent forward, and spoke in a distinct but reverential tone, as if addressing some unseen personage inside of the mountain.

"Sacred oracle of Delphi," said he, "whither shall I go next in quest of my dear sister Europa?"

There was at first a deep silence, and then a rushing sound, or a noise like a long sigh, proceeding out of the interior of the earth. This cavity, you must know, was looked upon as a sort of fountain of truth, which sometimes gushed out in audible words; although, for

148

the most part, these words were such a riddle that they might just as well have stayed at the bottom of the hole. But Cadmus was more fortunate than many others who went to Delphi in search of truth. By and by, the rushing noise began to sound like articulate language. It repeated, over and over again, the following sentence, which, after all, was so like the vague whistle of a blast of air, that Cadmus really did not quite know whether it meant anything or not: —

"Seek her no more! Seek her no more! Seek her no more!"

"What, then, shall I do?" asked Cadmus.

For, ever since he was a child, you know, it had been the great object of his life to find his sister. From the very hour that he left following the butterfly in the meadow, near his father's palace, he had done his best to follow Europa, over land and sea. And now, if he must give up the search, he seemed to have no more business in the world.

But again the sighing gust of air grew into something like a hoarse voice.

"Follow the cow!" it said. "Follow the cow! Follow the cow!"

And when these words had been repeated until Cadmus was tired of hearing them (especially as he could not imagine what cow it was, or why he was to follow her), the gusty hole gave vent to another sentence.

"Where the stray cow lies down, there is your home."

These words were pronounced but a single time, and died away into a whisper before Cadmus was fully satisfied that he had caught the meaning. He put other questions, but received no answer; only the gust of wind sighed continually out of the cavity, and blew the withered leaves rustling along the ground before it.

"Did there really come any words out of the hole?" thought Cadmus; "or have I been dreaming all this while?"

He turned away from the oracle, and thought himself no wiser than when he came thither. Caring little what might happen to him, he took the first path that offered itself, and went along at a sluggish pace; for, having no object in view, nor any reason to go one way more than another, it would certainly have been foolish to make haste. Whenever he met anybody, the old question was at his tongue's end: —

"Have you seen a beautiful maiden, dressed like a king's daughter, and mounted on a snow-white bull that gallops as swiftly as the wind?"

But, remembering what the oracle had said, he only half uttered the words, and then mumbled the rest indistinctly; and from his confusion, people must have imagined that this handsome young man had lost his wits.

I know not how far Cadmus had gone, nor could he himself have told you, when, at no great distance before him, he beheld a brindled cow. She was lying down by the wayside, and quietly chewing her cud; nor did she take any notice of the young man until he had approached pretty nigh. Then, getting leisurely upon her feet, and giving her head a gentle toss, she began to move along at a moderate pace, often pausing just long enough to crop a mouthful of grass. Cadmus loitered behind, whistling idly to himself, and scarcely noticing the cow; until the thought occurred to him, whether this could possibly be the animal which, according to the oracle's response, was to serve him for a guide. But he smiled at himself for fancying such a thing. He could not seriously think that this was the cow, because she went along so quietly, behaving just like any other cow. Evidently she neither knew nor cared so much as a wisp of hay about Cadmus, and was only thinking how to get her living along the wayside, where the herbage was green and fresh. Perhaps she was going home to be milked.

"Cow, cow, cow!" cried Cadmus. "Hey, Brindle, hey! Stop, my good cow."

He wanted to come up with the cow, so as to examine her, and see if she would appear to know him, or whether there were any peculiarities to distinguish her from a thousand other cows, whose only business is to fill the milk-pail, and sometimes kick it over. But still the brindled cow trudged on, whisking her tail to keep the flies away, and taking as little notice of Cadmus as she well could. If he walked slowly, so did the cow, and seized the opportunity to graze. If he quickened his pace, the cow went just so much the faster; and once, when Cadmus tried to catch her by running, she threw out her heels, stuck her tail straight on end, and set off at a gallop, looking as queerly as cows generally do while putting themselves to their speed.

When Cadmus saw that it was impossible to come up with her, he walked on moderately, as before. The cow, too, went leisurely on, without looking behind. Wherever the grass was greenest, there she nibbled a mouthful or two. Where a brook glistened brightly across the path, there the cow drank, and breathed a comfortable sigh, and drank again, and trudged onward at the pace that best suited herself and Cadmus.

"I do believe," thought Cadmus, "that this may be the cow that was foretold me. If it be the one, I suppose she will lie down somewhere hereabouts."

Whether it were the oracular cow or some other one, it did not seem reasonable that she should travel a great way farther. So, whenever they reached a particularly pleasant spot on a breezy hillside, or in a sheltered vale, or flowery meadow, on the shore of a calm lake, or along the bank of a clear stream, Cadmus looked eagerly around to see if the situation would suit him for a home. But still, whether he liked the place or no, the brindled cow never offered to lie down. On she went at the quiet pace of a cow going homeward to the barn-yard; and, every moment, Cadmus expected to see a milkmaid approaching with a pail, or a herdsman running to head the stray animal, and turn her back towards the pasture. But no milkmaid came; no herdsman drove her back; and Cadmus followed the stray Brindle till he was almost ready to drop down with fatigue.

"O brindled cow," cried he, in a tone of despair, "do you never mean to stop?"

He had now grown too intent on following her to think of lagging behind, however long the way, and whatever might be his fatigue. Indeed, it seemed as if there were something about the animal that bewitched people. Several persons who happened to see the brindled cow, and Cadmus following behind, began to trudge after her, precisely as he did. Cadmus was glad of somebody to converse with, and therefore talked very freely to these good people. He told them all his adventures, and how he had left King Agenor in his palace, and Phœnix at one place, and Cilix at another, and Thasus at a third, and his dear mother, Queen Telephassa, under a flowery sod; so that now he was quite alone, both friendless and homeless. He mentioned, likewise, that the oracle had bidden him be guided by a cow, and inquired of the strangers whether they supposed that this brindled animal could be the one.

"Why, 't is a very wonderful affair," answered one of his new companions. "I am pretty well acquainted with the ways of cattle, and I never knew a cow, of her own accord, to go so far without stopping. If my legs will let me, I'll never leave following the beast till she lies down."

"Nor I!" said a second.

"Nor I!" cried a third. "If she goes a hundred miles farther, I'm determined to see the end of it."

The secret of it was, you must know, that the cow was an enchanted cow, and that, without their being conscious of it, she threw some of her enchantment over everybody that took so much as half a dozen steps behind her. They could not possibly help following her, though, all the time, they fancied themselves doing it of their own accord. The cow was by no means very nice in choosing her path; so that sometimes they had to scramble over rocks, or wade through mud and mire, and were all in a terribly bedraggled condition, and tired to death, and very hungry, into the bargain. What a weary business it was!

But still they kept trudging stoutly forward, and talking as they went. The strangers grew very fond of Cadmus, and resolved never to leave him, but to help him build a city wherever the cow might lie down. In the centre of it there should be a noble palace, in which Cadmus might dwell, and be their king, with a throne, a crown and sceptre, a purple robe, and everything else that a king ought to have; for in him there was the royal blood, and the royal heart, and the head that knew how to rule.

While they were talking of these schemes, and beguiling the tediousness of the way with laying out the plan of the new city, one of the company happened to look at the cow.

"Joy! joy!" cried he, clapping his hands. "Brindle is going to lie down."

They all looked; and, sure enough, the cow had stopped, and was staring leisurely about her, as other cows do when on the point of lying down. And slowly, slowly did she recline herself on the soft grass, first bending her fore legs, and then crouching her hind ones. When Cadmus and his companions came up with her, there was the brindled cow taking her ease, chewing her cud, and looking them quietly in the face; as if this was just the spot she had been seeking for, and as if it were all a matter of course.

"This, then," said Cadmus, gazing around him, "this is to be my home."

It was a fertile and lovely plain, with great trees flinging their sun-speckled shadows over it, and hills fencing it in from the rough weather. At no great distance, they beheld a river gleaming in the sunshine. A home feeling stole into the heart of poor Cadmus. He was very glad to know that here he might awake in the morning, without the necessity of putting on his dusty sandals to travel farther and farther. The days and the years would pass over him, and find him still in this pleasant spot. If he could have had his brothers with him, and his friend Thasus, and could have seen his dear mother under a roof of his own, he might here have been happy, after all their disappointments. Some day or other, too, his sister Europa might have come quietly to the door of his home, and smiled round upon the familiar faces. But, indeed, since there was no hope of regaining the friends of his boyhood, or ever seeing his dear sister again, Cadmus resolved to make himself happy with these new companions, who had grown so fond of him while following the cow.

"Yes, my friends," said he to them, "this is to be our home. Here we will build our habitations. The brindled cow, which has led us hither, will supply us with milk. We will cultivate the neighboring soil, and lead an innocent and happy life."

His companions joyfully assented to this plan; and, in the first place, being very hungry and thirsty, they looked about them for the means of providing a comfortable meal. Not far off, they saw a tuft of trees, which appeared as if there might be a spring of water beneath them. They went thither to fetch some, leaving Cadmus stretched on the ground along with the brindled cow; for, now that he had found a place of rest, it seemed as if all the weariness of his pilgrimage, ever since he left King Agenor's palace, had fallen upon him at once. But his new friends had not long been gone, when he was suddenly startled by cries, shouts, and screams, and the noise of a terrible struggle, and in the midst of it all, a most awful hissing, which went right through his ears like a rough saw.

Running towards the tuft of trees, he beheld the head and fiery eyes of an immense serpent or dragon, with the widest jaws that ever a dragon had, and a vast many rows of horribly sharp teeth. Before Cadmus could reach the spot, this pitiless reptile had killed his poor companions, and was busily devouring them, making but a mouthful of each man.

It appears that the fountain of water was enchanted, and that the dragon had been set to guard it, so that no mortal might ever quench his thirst there. As the neighboring inhabitants carefully avoided the spot, it was now a long time (not less than a hundred years, or thereabouts) since the monster had broken his fast; and, as was natural enough, his appetite had grown to be enormous, and was not half satisfied by the poor people whom he had just eaten up. When he caught sight of Cadmus, therefore, he set up another abominable hiss, and flung back his immense jaws, until his mouth looked like a great red cavern, at the farther end of which were seen the legs of his last victim, whom he had hardly had time to swallow.

But Cadmus was so enraged at the destruction of his friends, that he cared neither for the size of the dragon's jaws nor for his hundreds of sharp teeth. Drawing his sword, he rushed at the monster, and flung himself right into his cavernous mouth. This bold method of attacking him took the dragon by surprise; for, in fact, Cadmus had leaped so far down into his throat that the rows of terrible teeth could not close upon him, nor do him the least harm in the world. Thus, though the struggle was a tremendous one, and though the dragon shattered the tuft of trees into small splinters by the lashing of his tail, yet, as Cadmus was all the while slashing and stabbing at his very vitals, it was not long before the scaly wretch bethought himself of slipping away. He had not gone his length, however, when the brave Cadmus gave him a sword-thrust that finished the battle; and, creeping out of the gateway of the creature's jaws, there he beheld him still wriggling his vast bulk, although there was no longer life enough in him to harm a little child.

But do not you suppose that it made Cadmus sorrowful to think of the melancholy fate which had befallen those poor, friendly people, who had followed the cow along with him? It seemed as if he were doomed to lose everybody whom he loved, or to see them perish in one way or another. And here he was, after all his toils and troubles, in a solitary place, with not a single human being to help him build a hut.

"What shall I do?" cried he aloud. "It were better

for me to have been devoured by the dragon, as my poor companions were."

"Cadmus," said a voice, — but whether it came from above or below him, or whether it spoke within his own breast, the young man could not tell, — "Cadmus, pluck out the dragon's teeth, and plant them in the earth."

This was a strange thing to do; nor was it very easy, I should imagine, to dig out all those deep-rooted fangs from the dead dragon's jaws. But Cadmus toiled and tugged, and after pounding the monstrous head almost to pieces with a great stone, he at last collected as many teeth as might have filled a bushel or two. The next thing was to plant them. This, likewise, was a tedious piece of work, especially as Cadmus was already exhausted with killing the dragon and knocking his head to pieces, and had nothing to dig the earth with, that I know of, unless it were his sword-blade. Finally, however, a sufficiently large tract of ground was turned up, and sown with this new kind of seed; although half of the dragon's teeth still remained to be planted some other day.

Cadmus, quite out of breath, stood leaning upon his sword, and wondering what was to happen next. He had waited but a few moments, when he began to see a sight which was as great a marvel as the most marvelous thing I ever told you about.

The sun was shining slantwise over the field, and showed all the moist, dark soil just like any other newly planted piece of ground. All at once, Cadmus fancied he saw something glisten very brightly, first at one spot, then at another, and then at a hundred and a thousand spots together. Soon he perceived them to be the steel heads of spears, sprouting up everywhere like so many stalks of grain, and continually growing taller and taller. Next appeared a vast number of bright sword-blades, thrusting themselves up in the same way. A moment afterwards, the whole surface of the ground was broken up by a multitude of polished brass helmets, coming up like a crop of enormous beans. So rapidly did they grow, that Cadmus now discerned the fierce countenance of a man beneath every one. In short, before he had time to think what a wonderful affair it was, he beheld an abundant harvest of what looked like human beings armed with helmets and breastplates, shields, swords and spears; and before they were well out of the earth, they brandished their weapons, and clashed them one against another, seeming to think, little while as they had yet lived, that they had wasted too much of life without a battle. Every tooth of the dragon had produced one of these sons of deadly mischief.

Up sprouted, also, a great many trumpeters; and with the first breath that they drew, they put their brazen trumpets to their lips, and sounded a tremendous and ear-shattering blast; so that the whole space, just now so quiet and solitary, reverberated with the clash and clang of arms, the bray of warlike music, and the shouts of angry men. So enraged did they all look, that Cadmus fully expected them to put the whole world to the sword. How fortunate would it be for a great conqueror, if he could get a bushel of the dragon's teeth to sow!

"Cadmus," said the same voice which he had before heard, "throw a stone into the midst of the armed men."

So Cadmus seized a large stone, and, flinging it into the middle of the earth army, saw it strike the breast-plate of a gigantic and fierce-looking warrior. Immediately on feeling the blow, he seemed to take it for granted that somebody had struck him; and, uplifting his weapon, he smote his next neighbor a blow that cleft his helmet asunder, and stretched him on the ground. In an instant, those nearest the fallen warrior began to strike at one another with their swords and stab with their spears. The confusion spread wider and wider. Each man smote down his brother, and was himself smitten down before he had time to exult in his victory. The trumpeters, all the while, blew their blasts shriller and shriller; each soldier shouted a battle-cry and often fell with it on his lips. It was the strangest spectacle of causeless wrath, and of mischief for no good end, that had ever been witnessed; but, after all, it was neither more foolish nor more wicked than a thousand battles that have since been fought, in which men have slain their brothers with just as little reason as these children of the dragon's teeth. It ought to be considered, too, that the dragon people were made for nothing else; whereas other mortals were born to love and help one another.

Well, this memorable battle continued to rage until the ground was strewn with helmeted heads that had been cut off. Of all the thousands that began the fight, there were only five left standing. These now rushed from different parts of the field, and, meeting in the middle of it, clashed their swords, and struck at each other's hearts as fiercely as ever.

"Cadmus," said the voice again, "bid those five warriors sheathe their swords. They will help you to build the city."

Without hesitating an instant, Cadmus stepped forward, with the aspect of a king and a leader, and extending his drawn sword amongst them, spoke to the warriors in a stern and commanding voice.

"Sheathe your weapons!" said he.

And forthwith, feeling themselves bound to obey him, the five remaining sons of the dragon's teeth made him a military salute with their swords, returned them to the scabbards, and stood before Cadmus in a rank, eyeing him as soldiers eye their captain, while awaiting the word of command.

These five men had probably sprung from the biggest of the dragon's teeth, and were the boldest and strongest of the whole army. They were almost giants, indeed, and had good need to be so, else they never could have lived through so terrible a fight. They still had a very furious look, and, if Cadmus happened to glance aside, would glare at one another, with fire flashing out of their eyes. It was strange, too, to observe how the earth, out of which they had so lately grown, was incrusted, here and there, on their bright breastplates, and even begrimed their faces, just as you may have seen it clinging to beets and carrots when pulled out of their native soil. Cadmus hardly knew whether to consider them as men, or some odd kind of vegetable;

although, on the whole, he concluded that there was human nature in them, because they were so fond of trumpets and weapons, and so ready to shed blood.

They looked him earnestly in the face, waiting for his next order, and evidently desiring no other employment than to follow him from one battle-field to another, all over the wide world. But Cadmus was wiser than these earth-born creatures, with the dragon's fierceness in them, and knew better how to use their strength and hardihood.

"Come!" said he. "You are sturdy fellows. Make yourselves useful! Quarry some stones with those great swords of yours, and help me to build a city."

The five soldiers grumbled a little, and muttered that it was their business to overthrow cities, not to build them up. But Cadmus looked at them with a stern eye, and spoke to them in a tone of authority, so that they knew him for their master, and never again thought of disobeying his commands. They set to work in good earnest, and toiled so diligently, that, in a very short time, a city began to make its appearance. At first, to be sure, the workmen showed a quarrelsome disposition. Like savage beasts, they would doubtless have done one another a mischief, if Cadmus had not kept watch over them and quelled the fierce old serpent that lurked in their hearts, when he saw it gleaming out of their wild eyes. But, in course of time, they got accustomed to honest labor, and had sense enough to feel that there was more true enjoyment in living at peace, and doing good to one's neighbor, than in striking at him with a two-edged

162

sword. It may not be too much to hope that the rest of mankind will by and by grow as wise and peaceable as these five earth-begrimed warriors, who sprang from the dragon's teeth.

And now the city was built, and there was a home in it for each of the workmen. But the palace of Cadmus was not yet erected, because they had left it till the last, meaning to introduce all the new improvements of architecture, and make it very commodious, as well as stately and beautiful. After finishing the rest of their labors, they all went to bed betimes, in order to rise in the gray of the morning, and get at least the foundation of the edifice laid before nightfall. But, when Cadmus arose, and took his way towards the site where the palace was to be built, followed by his five sturdy workmen marching all in a row, what do you think he saw?

What should it be but the most magnificent palace that had ever been seen in the world? It was built of marble and other beautiful kinds of stone, and rose high into the air, with a splendid dome and a portico along the front, and carved pillars, and everything else that befitted the habitation of a mighty king. It had grown up out of the earth in almost as short a time as it had taken the armed host to spring from the dragon's teeth; and what made the matter more strange, no seed of this stately edifice had ever been planted.

When the five workmen beheld the dome, with the morning sunshine making it look golden and glorious, they gave a great shout.

"Long live King Cadmus," they cried, "in his beautiful palace!"

And the new king, with his five faithful followers at his heels, shouldering their pickaxes and marching in a rank (for they still had a soldier-like sort of behavior, as their nature was), ascended the palace steps. Halting at the entrance, they gazed through a long vista of lofty pillars that were ranged from end to end of a great hall. At the farther extremity of this hall, approaching slowly towards him, Cadmus beheld a female figure, wonderfully beautiful, and adorned with a royal robe, and a crown of diamonds over her golden ringlets, and the richest necklace that ever a queen wore. His heart thrilled with delight. He fancied it his long-lost sister Europa, now grown to womanhood, coming to make him happy, and to repay him, with her sweet sisterly affection, for all those weary wanderings in quest of her since he left King Agenor's palace, — for the tears that he had shed, on parting with Phœnix, and Cilix, and Thasus, — for the heart-breakings that had made the whole world seem dismal to him over his dear mother's grave.

But, as Cadmus advanced to meet the beautiful stranger, he saw that her features were unknown to him, although, in the little time that it required to tread along the hall, he had already felt a sympathy betwixt himself and her.

"No, Cadmus," said the same voice that had spoken to him in the field of the armed men, "this is not that dear sister Europa whom you have sought so faithfully all over the wide world. This is Harmonia, a daughter of the sky, who is given you instead of sister, and brothers, and friend, and mother. You will find all those dear ones in her alone."

So King Cadmus dwelt in the palace, with his new friend Harmonia, and found a great deal of comfort in his magnificent abode, but would doubtless have found as much, if not more, in the humblest cottage by the wayside. Before many years went by, there was a group of rosy little children (but how they came thither has always been a mystery to me) sporting in the great hall, and on the marble steps of the palace, and running joyfully to meet King Cadmus when affairs of state left him at leisure to play with them. They called him father, and Queen Harmonia mother. The five old soldiers of the dragon's teeth grew very fond of these small urchins, and were never weary of showing them how to shoulder sticks, flourish wooden swords, and march in military order, blowing a penny trumpet, or beating an abominable rub-a-dub upon a little drum.

But King Cadmus, lest there should be too much of the dragon's tooth in his children's disposition, used to find time from his kingly duties to teach them their A B C, — which he invented for their benefit, and for which many little people, I am afraid, are not half so grateful to him as they ought to be.

THE MINOTAUR

By *Nathaniel Hawthorne*

IN the old city of Trœzene, at the foot of a lofty mountain, there lived, a very long time ago, a little boy named Theseus. His grandfather, King Pittheus, was the sovereign of that country, and was reckoned a very wise man; so that Theseus, being brought up in the royal palace, and being naturally a bright lad, could hardly fail of profiting by the old king's instructions. His mother's name was Æthra. As for his father, the boy had never seen him. But, from his earliest remembrance, Æthra used to go with little Theseus into a wood, and sit down upon a moss-grown rock, which was deeply sunken into the earth. Here she often talked with her son about his father, and said that he was called Ægeus, and that he was a great king, and ruled over Attica, and dwelt at Athens, which was as famous a city as any in the world. Theseus was very fond of hearing about King Ægeus, and often asked his good mother Æthra why he did not come and live with them at Trœzene.

"Ah, my dear son," answered Æthra, with a sigh, "a monarch has his people to take care of. The men and women over whom he rules are in the place of children to him; and he can seldom spare time to love his own children as other parents do. Your father will never be able to leave his kingdom for the sake of seeing his little boy."

"Well, but, dear mother," asked the boy, "why cannot I go to this famous city of Athens, and tell King Ægeus that I am his son?"

"That may happen by and by," said Æthra. "Be patient, and we shall see. You are not yet big and strong enough to set out on such an errand."

"And how soon shall I be strong enough?" Theseus persisted in inquiring.

"You are but a tiny boy as yet," replied his mother. "See if you can lift this rock on which we are sitting."

The little fellow had a great opinion of his own strength. So, grasping the rough protuberances of the rock, he tugged and toiled amain, and got himself quite out of breath, without being able to stir the heavy stone. It seemed to be rooted into the ground. No wonder he could not move it; for it would have taken all the force of a very strong man to lift it out of its earthy bed.

His mother stood looking on, with a sad kind of a smile on her lips and in her eyes, to see the zealous and yet puny efforts of her little boy. She could not help being sorrowful at finding him already so impatient to begin his adventures in the world.

"You see how it is, my dear Theseus," said she. "You must possess far more strength than now before I can trust you to go to Athens, and tell King Ægeus that you are his son. But when you can lift this rock, and show me what is hidden beneath it, I promise you my permission to depart."

Often and often, after this, did Theseus ask his mother whether it was yet time for him to go to Athens; and still his mother pointed to the rock, and told him that, for years to come, he could not be strong enough to move it. And again and again the rosy-cheeked and curly-headed boy would tug and strain at the huge mass of stone, striving, child as he was, to do what a giant could hardly have done without taking both of his great hands to the task. Meanwhile the rock seemed to be sinking farther and farther into the ground. The moss grew over it thicker and thicker, until at last it looked almost like a soft green seat, with only a few gray knobs of granite peeping out. The overhanging trees, also, shed their brown leaves upon it, as often as the autumn came; and at its base grew ferns and wild flowers, some of which crept quite over its surface. To all appearance, the rock was as firmly fastened as any other portion of the earth's substance.

But, difficult as the matter looked, Theseus was now growing up to be such a vigorous youth, that, in his own opinion, the time would quickly come when he might hope to get the upper hand of this ponderous lump of stone.

"Mother, I do believe it has started!" cried he, after one of his attempts. "The earth around it is certainly a little cracked!"

"No, no, child!" his mother hastily answered. "It is not possible you can have moved it, such a boy as you still are!"

Nor would she be convinced, although Theseus showed her the place where he fancied that the stem of a flower had been partly uprooted by the movement of the rock. But Æthra sighed and looked disquieted; for, no doubt, she began to be conscious that her son was no longer a child, and that, in a little while hence, she must send him forth among the perils and troubles of the world.

It was not more than a year afterwards when they were again sitting on the moss-covered stone. Æthra had once more told him the oft-repeated story of his father, and how gladly he would receive Theseus at his stately palace, and how he would present him to his courtiers and the people, and tell them that here was the heir of his dominions. The eyes of Theseus glowed with enthusiasm, and he would hardly sit still to hear his mother speak.

"Dear mother Æthra," he exclaimed, "I never felt half so strong as now! I am no longer a child, nor a boy, nor a mere youth! I feel myself a man! It is now time to make one earnest trial to remove the stone."

"Ah, my dearest Theseus," replied his mother, "not yet! not yet!"

"Yes, mother," said he, resolutely "the time has come."

Then Theseus bent himself in good earnest to the task, and strained every sinew, with manly strength and resolution. He put his whole brave heart into the effort. He wrestled with the big and sluggish stone, as if it had been a living enemy. He heaved, he lifted, he resolved now to succeed, or else to perish there, and let the rock be his monument forever! Æthra stood gazing at him, and clasped her hands, partly with a mother's pride, and partly with a mother's sorrow. The great rock stirred! Yes, it was raised slowly from the bedded moss and earth, uprooting the shrubs and flowers along with it, and was turned upon its side. Theseus had conquered!

While taking breath, he looked joyfully at his mother, and she smiled upon him through her tears.

"Yes, Theseus," she said, "the time has come, and you must stay no longer at my side! See what King Ægeus, your royal father, left for you, beneath the stone, when he lifted it in his mighty arms, and laid it on the spot whence you have now removed it."

Theseus looked, and saw that the rock had been placed over another slab of stone, containing a cavity within it; so that it somewhat resembled a roughly made chest or coffer, of which the upper mass had served as the lid. Within the cavity lay a sword, with a golden hilt, and a pair of sandals.

"This was your father's sword," said Æthra, "and those were his sandals. When he went to be king of Athens, he bade me treat you as a child until you should prove yourself a man by lifting this heavy stone. That task being accomplished, you are to put on his sandals, in order to follow in your father's footsteps, and to gird on his sword, so that you may fight giants and dragons, as King Ægeus did in his youth."

"I will set out for Athens this very day!" cried Theseus.

But his mother persuaded him to stay a day or two longer, while she got ready some necessary articles for his journey. When his grandfather, the wise King

Pittheus, heard that Theseus intended to present himself at his father's palace, he earnestly advised him to get on board of a vessel and go by sea; because he might thus arrive within fifteen miles of Athens, without either fatigue or danger.

"The roads are very bad by land," quoth the venerable king; "and they are terribly infested with robbers and monsters. A mere lad, like Theseus, is not fit to be trusted on such a perilous journey, all by himself. No, no; let him go by sea!"

But when Theseus heard of robbers and monsters, he pricked up his ears, and was so much the more eager to take the road along which they were to be met with. On the third day, therefore, he bade a respectful farewell to his grandfather, thanking him for all his kindness, and, after affectionately embracing his mother he set forth, with a good many of her tears glistening on his cheeks, and some, if the truth must be told, that had gushed out of his own eyes. But he let the sun and wind dry them, and walked stoutly on, playing with the golden hilt of his sword and taking very manly strides in his father's sandals.

I cannot stop to tell you hardly any of the adventures that befell Theseus on the road to Athens. It is enough to say, that he quite cleared that part of the country of the robbers, about whom King Pittheus had been so much alarmed. One of these bad people was named Procrustes; and he was indeed a terrible fellow, and had an ugly way of making fun of the poor travelers who happened to fall into his clutches. In his cavern he had a bed, on which, with great pretence of hospitality, he invited his guests to lie down; but if they happened to be shorter than the bed, this wicked villain stretched them out by main force; or, if they were too long, he lopped off their heads or feet, and laughed at what he had done, as an excellent joke. Thus, however weary a man might be, he never liked to lie in the bed of Procrustes. Another of these robbers, named Scinis, must likewise have been a very great scoundrel. He was in the habit of flinging his victims off a high cliff into the sea; and, in order to give him exactly his deserts, Theseus tossed him off the very same place. But if you will believe me, the sea would not pollute itself by receiving such a bad person into its bosom, neither would the earth, having once got rid of him, consent to take him back; so that, between the cliff and the sea, Scinis stuck fast in the air, which was forced to bear the burden of his naughtiness.

After these memorable deeds, Theseus heard of an enormous sow, which ran wild, and was the terror of all the farmers round about; and, as he did not consider himself above doing any good thing that came in his way, he killed this monstrous creature, and gave the carcass to the poor people for bacon. The great sow had been an awful beast, while ramping about the woods and fields, but was a pleasant object enough when cut up into joints, and smoking on I know not how many dinner tables.

Thus, by the time he reached his journey's end, Theseus had done many valiant feats with his father's golden-hilted sword, and had gained the renown of being one of the bravest young men of the day. His fame

traveled faster than he did, and reached Athens before
him. As he entered the city, he heard the inhabitants
talking at the street-corners, and saying that Hercules
was brave, and Jason too, and Castor and Pollux likewise, but that Theseus, the son of their own king, would
turn out as great a hero as the best of them. Theseus took
longer strides on hearing this, and fancied himself sure
of a magnificent reception at his father's court, since
he came thither with Fame to blow her trumpet before
him, and cry to King Ægeus, "Behold your son!"

He little suspected, innocent youth that he was, that
here, in this very Athens, where his father reigned, a
greater danger awaited him than any which he had
encountered on the road. Yet this was the truth. You
must understand that the father of Theseus, though
not very old in years, was almost worn out with the
cares of government, and had thus grown aged before
his time. His nephews, not expecting him to live a
very great while, intended to get all the power of the
kingdom into their own hands. But when they heard
that Theseus had arrived in Athens, and learned what
a gallant young man he was, they saw that he would
not be at all the kind of person to let them steal away
his father's crown and sceptre, which ought to be his
own by right of inheritance. Thus these bad-hearted
nephews of King Ægeus, who were the own cousins of
Theseus, at once became his enemies. A still more
dangerous enemy was Medea, the wicked enchantress;
for she was now the king's wife, and wanted to give
the kingdom to her son Medus, instead of letting it be
given to the son of Æthra, whom she hated.

It so happened that the king's nephews met Theseus, and found out who he was, just as he reached the entrance of the royal palace. With all their evil designs against him, they pretended to be their cousin's best friends, and expressed great joy at making his acquaintance. They proposed to him that he should come into the king's presence as a stranger, in order to try whether Ægeus would discover in the young man's features any likeness either to himself or his mother Æthra, and thus recognize him for a son. Theseus consented; for he fancied that his father would know him in a moment, by the love that was in his heart. But, while he waited at the door, the nephews ran and told King Ægeus that a young man had arrived in Athens, who, to their certain knowledge, intended to put him to death, and get possession of his royal crown.

"And he is now waiting for admission to your Majesty's presence," added they.

"Aha!" cried the old king, on hearing this. "Why, he must be a very wicked young fellow indeed! Pray, what would you advise me to do with him?"

In reply to this question, the wicked Medea put in her word. As I have already told you, she was a famous enchantress. According to some stories, she was in the habit of boiling old people in a large caldron, under pretence of making them young again; but King Ægeus, I suppose, did not fancy such an uncomfortable way of growing young, or perhaps was contented to be old, and therefore would never let himself be popped into the caldron. If there were time to spare from more important matters, I should be glad to tell you of Medea's fiery chariot, drawn by winged dragons, in which the enchantress used often to take an airing among the clouds. This chariot, in fact, was the vehicle that first brought her to Athens, where she had done nothing but mischief ever since her arrival. But these and many other wonders must be left untold; and it is enough to say, that Medea, amongst a thousand other bad things, knew how to prepare a poison that was instantly fatal to whomsoever might so much as touch it with his lips.

So, when the king asked what he should do with Theseus, this naughty woman had an answer ready at her tongue's end.

"Leave that to me, please your Majesty," she replied. "Only admit this evil-minded young man to your presence, treat him civilly, and invite him to drink a goblet of wine. Your Majesty is well aware that I sometimes amuse myself with distilling very powerful medicines. Here is one of them in this small phial. As to what it is made of, that is one of my secrets of state. Do but let me put a single drop into the goblet, and let the young man taste it; and I will answer for it, he shall quite lay aside the bad designs with which he comes hither."

As she said this, Medea smiled; but, for all her smiling face, she meant nothing less than to poison the poor innocent Theseus, before his father's eyes. And King Ægeus, like most other kings, thought any punishment mild enough for a person who was accused of plotting against his life. He therefore made little or no objection to Medea's scheme, and as soon as the poisonous wine was ready, gave orders that the young stranger should be admitted into his presence. The goblet was set on a table beside the king's throne; and a fly, meaning just to sip a little from the brim, immediately tumbled into it, dead. Observing this, Medea looked round at the nephews, and smiled again.

When Theseus was ushered into the royal apartment, the only object that he seemed to behold was the white-bearded old king. There he sat on his magnificent throne, a dazzling crown on his head, and a sceptre in his hand. His aspect was stately and majestic, although his years and infirmities weighed heavily upon him, as if each year were a lump of lead, and each infirmity a ponderous stone, and all were bundled up together, and laid upon his weary shoulders. The tears both of joy and sorrow sprang into the young man's eyes; for he thought how sad it was to see his dear father so infirm, and how sweet it would be to support him with his own youthful strength, and to cheer him up with the alacrity of his loving spirit. When a son takes his father into his warm heart, it renews the old man's youth in a better way than by the heat of Medea's magic caldron. And this was what Theseus resolved to do. He could scarcely wait to see whether King Ægeus would recognize him, so eager was he to throw himself into his arms.

Advancing to the foot of the throne, he attempted to make a little speech, which he had been thinking about as he came up the stairs. But he was almost choked by a great many tender feelings that gushed out of his heart and swelled into his throat, all struggling to find utterance together. And therefore, unless he could have laid his full, over-brimming heart into the king's hand, poor Theseus knew not what to do or say. The cunning Medea observed what was passing in the young man's mind. She was more wicked at that moment than ever she had been before; for (and it makes me tremble to tell you of it) she did her worst to turn all this unspeakable love with which Theseus was agitated, to his own ruin and destruction.

"Does your Majesty see his confusion?" she whispered in the king's ear. "He is so conscious of guilt that he trembles and cannot speak. The wretch lives too long! Quick! offer him the wine!"

Now King Ægeus had been gazing earnestly at the young stranger, as he drew near the throne. There was something, he knew not what, either in his white brow, or in the fine expression of his mouth, or in his beautiful and tender eyes, that made him indistinctly feel as if he had seen this youth before; as if, indeed, he had trotted him on his knee when a baby, and had beheld him growing to be a stalwart man, while he himself grew old. But Medea guessed how the king felt, and would not suffer him to yield to these natural sensibilities; although they were the voice of his deepest heart, telling him, as plainly as it could speak, that here was his dear son, and Æthra's son, coming to claim him for a father. The enchantress again whispered in the king's ear, and compelled him, by her witchcraft, to see everything under a false aspect.

He made up his mind, therefore, to let Theseus drink off the poisoned wine.

"Young man," said he, "you are welcome! I am proud to show hospitality to so heroic a youth. Do me the favor to drink the contents of this goblet. It is brimming over, as you see, with delicious wine, such as I bestow only on those who are worthy of it! None is more worthy to quaff it than yourself!"

So saying, King Ægeus took the golden goblet from the table, and was about to offer it to Theseus. But, partly through his infirmities, and partly because it seemed so sad a thing to take away this young man's life, however wicked he might be, and partly, no doubt, because his heart was wiser than his head, and quaked within him at the thought of what he was going to do, — for all these reasons, the king's hand trembled so much that a great deal of the wine slopped over. In order to strengthen his purpose, and fearing lest the whole of the precious poison should be wasted, one of his nephews now whispered to him, —

"Has your Majesty any doubt of this stranger's guilt? There is the very sword with which he meant to slay you. How sharp, and bright, and terrible it is! Quick! — let him taste the wine; or perhaps he may do the deed even yet."

At these words, Ægeus drove every thought and feeling out of his breast, except the one idea of how justly the young man deserved to be put to death. He sat erect on his throne, and held out the goblet of wine with a steady hand, and bent on Theseus a frown of kingly severity; for, after all, he had too noble a spirit to murder even a treacherous enemy with a deceitful smile upon his face.

"Drink!" said he, in the stern tone with which he was wont to condemn a criminal to be beheaded. "You have well deserved of me such wine as this!"

Theseus held out his hand to take the wine. But, before he touched it, King Ægeus trembled again. His eyes had fallen on the gold-hilted sword that hung at the young man's side. He drew back the goblet.

"That sword!" he cried; "how came you by it?"

"It was my father's sword," replied Theseus, with a tremulous voice. "These were his sandals. My dear mother (her name is Æthra) told me his story while I was yet a little child. But it is only a month since I grew strong enough to lift the heavy stone, and take the sword and sandals from beneath it, and come to Athens to seek my father."

"My son! my son!" cried King Ægeus, flinging away the fatal goblet, and tottering down from the throne to fall into the arms of Theseus. "Yes, these are Æthra's eyes. It is my son."

I have quite forgotten what became of the king's nephews. But when the wicked Medea saw this new turn of affairs, she hurried out of the room, and going to her private chamber, lost no time in setting her enchantments at work. In a few moments, she heard a great noise of hissing snakes outside of the chamber window; and, behold! there was her fiery chariot, and four huge winged serpents, wriggling and twisting in the air, flourishing their tails higher than the top of the palace, and all ready to set off on an aerial journey. Medea stayed only long enough to take her son with her, and to steal the crown jewels, together with the king's best robes, and whatever other valuable things she could lay hands on; and getting into the chariot, she whipped up the snakes, and ascended high over the city.

The king, hearing the hiss of the serpents, scrambled as fast as he could to the window, and bawled out to the abominable enchantress never to come back. The whole people of Athens, too, who had run out of doors to see this wonderful spectacle, set up a shout of joy at the prospect of getting rid of her. Medea, almost bursting with rage, uttered precisely such a hiss as one of her own snakes, only ten times more venomous and spiteful; and glaring fiercely out of the blaze of the chariot, she shook her hands over the multitude below, as if she were scattering a million of curses among them. In so doing, however, she unintentionally let fall about five hundred diamonds of the first water, together with a thousand great pearls, and two thousand emeralds, rubies, sapphires, opals, and topazes, to which she had helped herself out of the king's strong-box. All these came pelting down, like a shower of many-colored hailstones, upon the heads of grown people and children, who forthwith gathered them up and carried them back to the palace. But King Ægeus told them that they were welcome to the whole, and to twice as many more, if he had them, for the sake of his delight at finding his son, and losing the wicked Medea. And, indeed, if you had seen how hateful was her last look, as the flaming chariot flew upward, you would not have wondered that both king and people should think her departure a good riddance.

And now Prince Theseus was taken into great favor by his royal father. The old king was never weary of having him sit beside him on his throne (which was quite wide enough for two), and of hearing him tell about his dear mother, and his childhood, and his many boyish efforts to lift the ponderous stone. Theseus, however, was much too brave and active a young man to be willing to spend all his time in relating things which had already happened. His ambition was to perform other and more heroic deeds, which should be better worth telling in prose and verse. Nor had he been long in Athens before he caught and chained a terrible mad bull, and made a public show of him, greatly to the wonder and admiration of good King Ægeus and his subjects. But pretty soon, he undertook an affair that made all his foregone adventures seem like mere boy's play. The occasion of it was as follows: —

One morning, when Prince Theseus awoke, he fancied that he must have had a very sorrowful dream, and that it was still running in his mind, even now that his eyes were open. For it appeared as if the air was full of a melancholy wail; and when he listened more attentively, he could hear sobs and groans, and screams of woe, mingled with deep, quiet sighs, which came from the king's palace, and from the streets, and from the temples, and from every habitation in the city. And all these mournful noises, issuing out of thousands of separate hearts, united themselves into the one great sound of affliction, which had startled Theseus from slumber. He put on his clothes as quickly as he could (not forgetting his sandals and gold-hilted sword), and hastening to the king, inquired what it all meant.

"Alas! my son," quoth King Ægeus, heaving a long sigh, "here is a very lamentable matter in hand! This is the wofullest anniversary in the whole year. It is the day when we annually draw lots to see which of the youths and maidens of Athens shall go to be devoured by the horrible Minotaur!"

"The Minotaur!" exclaimed Prince Theseus; and, like a brave young prince as he was, he put his hand to the hilt of his sword. "What kind of a monster may that be? Is it not possible, at the risk of one's life, to slay him?"

But King Ægeus shook his venerable head, and to convince Theseus that it was quite a hopeless case, he gave him an explanation of the whole affair. It seems that in the island of Crete there lived a certain dreadful monster, called a Minotaur, which was shaped partly like a man and partly like a bull, and was altogether such a hideous sort of a creature that it is really disagreeable to think of him. If he were suffered to exist at all, it should have been on some desert island, or in the duskiness of some deep cavern, where nobody would ever be tormented by his abominable aspect. But King Minos, who reigned over Crete, laid out a vast deal of money in building a habitation for the Minotaur, and took great care of his health and comfort, merely for mischief's sake. A few years before this time, there had been a war between the city of Athens and the island of Crete, in which the Athenians were beaten, and compelled to beg for peace. No peace could they obtain, however, except on condition that they should send seven young men and seven maidens, every year, to be devoured by the pet monster of the cruel King Minos. For three years past, this grievous calamity had been borne. And the sobs, and groans, and shrieks with which the city was now filled, were caused by the people's woe, because the fatal day had come again, when the fourteen victims were to be chosen by lot; and the old people feared lest their sons or daughters might be taken, and the youths and damsels dreaded lest they themselves might be destined to glut the ravenous maw of that detestable man-brute.

But when Theseus heard the story, he straightened himself up, so that he seemed taller than ever before; and as for his face, it was indignant, despiteful, bold, tender, and compassionate, all in one look.

"Let the people of Athens, this year, draw lots for only six young men, instead of seven," said he. "I will myself be the seventh; and let the Minotaur devour me, if he can!"

"Oh, my dear son," cried King Ægeus, "why should you expose yourself to this horrible fate? You are a royal prince, and have a right to hold yourself above the destinies of common men."

"It is because I am a prince, your son, and the rightful heir of your kingdom, that I freely take upon me the calamity of your subjects," answered Theseus. "And you, my father, being king over this people, and answerable to Heaven for their welfare, are bound to sacrifice what is dearest to you, rather than that the

183

son or daughter of the poorest citizen should come to any harm."

The old king shed tears, and besought Theseus not to leave him desolate in his old age, more especially as he had but just begun to know the happiness of possessing a good and valiant son. Theseus, however, felt that he was in the right, and therefore would not give up his resolution. But he assured his father that he did not intend to be eaten up, unresistingly, like a sheep, and that, if the Minotaur devoured him, it should not be without a battle for his dinner. And finally, since he could not help it, King Ægeus consented to let him go. So a vessel was got ready, and rigged with black sails; and Theseus, with six other young men, and seven tender and beautiful damsels, came down to the harbor to embark. A sorrowful multitude accompanied them to the shore. There was the poor old king, too, leaning on his son's arm, and looking as if his single heart held all the grief of Athens.

Just as Prince Theseus was going on board, his father bethought himself of one last word to say.

"My beloved son," said he, grasping the prince's hand, "you observe that the sails of this vessel are black; as indeed they ought to be, since it goes upon a voyage of sorrow and despair. Now, being weighed down with infirmities, I know not whether I can survive till the vessel shall return. But, as long as I do live, I shall creep daily to the top of yonder cliff, to watch if there be a sail upon the sea. And, dearest Theseus, if by some happy chance you should escape the jaws of the Minotaur, then tear down those dismal sails, and hoist others that shall be bright as the sunshine. Beholding them on the horizon, myself and all the people will know that you are coming back victorious, and will welcome you with such a festal uproar as Athens never heard before."

Theseus promised that he would do so. Then, going on board, the mariners trimmed the vessel's black sails to the wind, which blew faintly off the shore, being pretty much made up of the sighs that everybody kept pouring forth on this melancholy occasion. But by and by, when they had got fairly out to sea, there came a stiff breeze from the northwest, and drove them along as merrily over the white-capped waves as if they had been going on the most delightful errand imaginable. And though it was a sad business enough, I rather question whether fourteen young people, without any old persons to keep them in order, could continue to spend the whole time of the voyage in being miserable. There had been some few dances upon the undulating deck, I suspect, and some hearty bursts of laughter, and other such unseasonable merriment among the victims, before the high, blue mountains of Crete began to show themselves among the far-off clouds. That sight, to be sure, made them all very grave again.

Theseus stood among the sailors, gazing eagerly towards the land; although, as yet, it seemed hardly more substantial than the clouds, amidst which the mountains were looming up. Once or twice, he fancied that he saw a glare of some bright object, a long way off, flinging a gleam across the waves.

"Did you see that flash of light?" he inquired of the master of the vessel.

"No, prince; but I have seen it before," answered the master. "It came from Talus, I suppose."

As the breeze came fresher just then, the master was busy with trimming his sails, and had no more time to answer questions. But while the vessel flew faster and faster towards Crete, Theseus was astonished to behold a human figure, gigantic in size, which appeared to be striding with a measured movement, along the margin of the island. It stepped from cliff to cliff, and sometimes from one headland to another, while the sea foamed and thundered on the shore beneath, and dashed its jets of spray over the giant's feet. What was still more remarkable, whenever the sun shone on this huge figure, it flickered and glimmered; its vast countenance, too, had a metallic lustre, and threw great flashes of splendor through the air. The folds of its garments, moreover, instead of waving in the wind, fell heavily over its limbs, as if woven of some kind of metal.

The nigher the vessel came, the more Theseus wondered what this immense giant could be, and whether it actually had life or no. For though it walked, and made other lifelike motions, there yet was a kind of jerk in its gait, which, together with its brazen aspect, caused the young prince to suspect that it was no true giant, but only a wonderful piece of machinery. The figure looked all the more terrible because it carried an enormous brass club on its shoulder.

"What is this wonder?" Theseus asked of the

master of the vessel, who was now at leisure to answer him.

"It is Talus, the Man of Brass," said the master.

"And is he a live giant, or a brazen image?" asked Theseus.

"That, truly," replied the master, "is the point which has always perplexed me. Some say, indeed, that this Talus was hammered out for King Minos by Vulcan himself, the skillfulest of all workers in metal. But who ever saw a brazen image that had sense enough to walk round an island three times a day, as this giant walks round the island of Crete, challenging every vessel that comes nigh the shore? And, on the other hand, what living thing, unless his sinews were made of brass, would not be weary of marching eighteen hundred miles in the twenty-four hours, as Talus does, without ever sitting down to rest? He is a puzzler, take him how you will."

Still the vessel went bounding onward; and now Theseus could hear the brazen clangor of the giant's footsteps, as he trod heavily upon the sea-beaten rocks, some of which were seen to crack and crumble into the foamy waves beneath his weight. As they approached the entrance of the port, the giant straddled clear across it, with a foot firmly planted on each headland, and uplifting his club to such a height that its but-end was hidden in a cloud, he stood in that formidable posture, with the sun gleaming all over his metallic surface. There seemed nothing else to be expected but that, the next moment, he would fetch his great club down, slam bang, and smash the vessel into a thousand pieces, without heeding how many innocent people he might destroy; for there is seldom any mercy in a giant, you know, and quite as little in a piece of brass clock-work. But just when Theseus and his companions thought the blow was coming, the brazen lips unclosed themselves, and the figure spoke.

"Whence come you, strangers?"

And when the ringing voice ceased, there was just such a reverberation as you may have heard within a great church bell, for a moment or two after the stroke of the hammer.

"From Athens!" shouted the master in reply.

"On what errand?" thundered the Man of Brass.

And he whirled his club aloft more threateningly than ever, as if he were about to smite them with a thunder-stroke right amidships, because Athens, so little while ago, had been at war with Crete.

"We bring the seven youths and the seven maidens," answered the master, "to be devoured by the Minotaur!"

"Pass!" cried the brazen giant.

That one loud word rolled all about the sky, while again there was a booming reverberation within the figure's breast. The vessel glided between the head-lands of the port, and the giant resumed his march. In a few moments, this wondrous sentinel was far away, flashing in the distant sunshine, and revolving with immense strides around the island of Crete, as it was his never-ceasing task to do.

No sooner had they entered the harbor than a party of the guards of King Minos came down to the water-

side, and took charge of the fourteen young men and
damsels. Surrounded by these armed warriors, Prince
Theseus and his companions were led to the king's
palace, and ushered into his presence. Now, Minos
was a stern and pitiless king. If the figure that guarded
Crete was made of brass, then the monarch who ruled
over it might be thought to have a still harder metal in
his breast, and might have been called a man of iron.
He bent his shaggy brows upon the poor Athenian
victims. Any other mortal, beholding their fresh and
tender beauty, and their innocent looks, would have
felt himself sitting on thorns until he had made every
soul of them happy, by bidding them go free as the
summer wind. But this immitigable Minos cared only
to examine whether they were plump enough to satisfy
the Minotaur's appetite. For my part, I wish he himself had been the only victim; and the monster would
have found him a pretty tough one.

One after another, King Minos called these pale,
frightened youths and sobbing maidens to his foot-
stool, gave them each a poke in the ribs with his sceptre
(to try whether they were in good flesh or no), and dismissed them with a nod to his guards. But when his
eyes rested on Theseus, the king looked at him more
attentively, because his face was calm and brave.

"Young man," asked he, with his stern voice, "are
you not appalled at the certainty of being devoured by
this terrible Minotaur?"

"I have offered my life in a good cause," answered
Theseus, "and therefore I give it freely and gladly.
But thou, King Minos, art thou not thyself appalled,

who, year after year, hast perpetrated this dreadful wrong, by giving seven innocent youths and as many maidens to be devoured by a monster? Dost thou not tremble, wicked king, to turn thine eyes inward on thine own heart? Sitting there on thy golden throne, and in thy robes of majesty, I tell thee to thy face, King Minos, thou art a more hideous monster than the Minotaur himself!"

"Aha! do you think me so?" cried the king, laughing in his cruel way. "To-morrow, at breakfast-time, you shall have an opportunity of judging which is the greater monster, the Minotaur or the king! Take them away, guards; and let this free-spoken youth be the Minotaur's first morsel!"

Near the king's throne (though I had no time to tell you so before) stood his daughter Ariadne. She was a beautiful and tender-hearted maiden, and looked at these poor doomed captives with very different feelings from those of the iron-breasted King Minos. She really wept, indeed, at the idea of how much human happiness would be needlessly thrown away, by giving so many young people, in the first bloom and rose blossom of their lives, to be eaten up by a creature who, no doubt, would have preferred a fat ox, or even a large pig, to the plumpest of them. And when she beheld the brave, spirited figure of Prince Theseus bearing himself so calmly in his terrible peril, she grew a hundred times more pitiful than before. As the guards were taking him away, she flung herself at the king's feet, and besought him to set all the captives free, and especially this one young man.

"Peace, foolish girl!" answered King Minos. "What hast thou to do with an affair like this? It is a matter of state policy, and therefore quite beyond thy weak comprehension. Go water thy flowers, and think no more of these Athenian caitiffs, whom the Minotaur shall as certainly eat up for breakfast as I will eat a partridge for my supper."

So saying, the king looked cruel enough to devour Theseus and all the rest of the captives, himself, had there been no Minotaur to save him the trouble. As he would hear not another word in their favor, the prisoners were now led away, and clapped into a dungeon, where the jailer advised them to go to sleep as soon as possible, because the Minotaur was in the habit of calling for breakfast early. The seven maidens and six of the young men soon sobbed themselves to slumber! But Theseus was not like them. He felt conscious that he was wiser and braver and stronger than his companions, and that therefore he had the responsibility of all their lives upon him, and must consider whether there was no way to save them, even in this last extremity. So he kept himself awake, and paced to and fro across the gloomy dungeon in which they were shut up.

Just before midnight, the door was softly unbarred, and the gentle Ariadne showed herself, with a torch in her hand.

"Are you awake, Prince Theseus?" she whispered.

"Yes," answered Theseus. "With so little time to live, I do not choose to waste any of it in sleep."

"Then follow me," said Ariadne, "and tread softly."

191

What had become of the jailer and the guards, Theseus never knew. But however that might be, Ariadne opened all the doors, and led him forth from the darksome prison into the pleasant moonlight.

"Theseus," said the maiden, "you can now get on board your vessel, and sail away for Athens."

"No," answered the young man; "I will never leave Crete unless I can first slay the Minotaur, and save my poor companions, and deliver Athens from this cruel tribute."

"I knew that this would be your resolution," said Ariadne. "Come, then, with me, brave Theseus. Here is your own sword, which the guards deprived you of. You will need it; and pray Heaven you may use it well."

Then she led Theseus along by the hand until they came to a dark, shadowy grove, where the moonlight wasted itself on the tops of the trees, without shedding hardly so much as a glimmering beam upon their pathway. After going a good way through this obscurity, they reached a high marble wall, which was overgrown with creeping plants, that made it shaggy with their verdure. The wall seemed to have no door, nor any windows, but rose up, lofty, and massive, and mysterious, and was neither to be clambered over, nor, so far as Theseus could perceive, to be passed through. Nevertheless, Ariadne did but press one of her soft little fingers against a particular block of marble, and, though it looked as solid as any other part of the wall, it yielded to her touch, disclosing an entrance just wide enough to admit them. They crept through, and the marble stone swung back into its place.

"We are now," said Ariadne, "in the famous labyrinth which Dædalus built before he made himself a pair of wings, and flew away from our island like a bird. That Dædalus was a very cunning workman; but of all his artful contrivances, this labyrinth is the most wondrous. Were we to take but a few steps from the doorway, we might wander about all our lifetime, and never find it again. Yet in the very centre of this labyrinth is the Minotaur; and, Theseus, you must go thither to seek him."

"But how shall I ever find him," asked Theseus, "if the labyrinth so bewilders me as you say it will?"

Just as he spoke they heard a rough and very disagreeable roar, which greatly resembled the lowing of a fierce bull, but yet had some sort of sound like the human voice. Theseus even fancied a rude articulation in it, as if the creature that uttered it were trying to shape his hoarse breath into words. It was at some distance, however, and he really could not tell whether it sounded most like a bull's roar or a man's harsh voice.

"That is the Minotaur's noise," whispered Ariadne, closely grasping the hand of Theseus, and pressing one of her own hands to her heart, which was all in a tremble. "You must follow that sound through the windings of the labyrinth, and, by and by, you will find him. Stay! take the end of this silken string; I will hold the other end; and then, if you win the victory, it will lead you again to this spot. Farewell, brave Theseus."

So the young man took the end of the silken string in his left hand, and his gold-hilted sword, ready drawn from its scabbard, in the other, and trod boldly into the inscrutable labyrinth. How this labyrinth was built is more than I can tell you. But so cunningly contrived a mizmaze was never seen in the world, before nor since. There can be nothing else so intricate, unless it were the brain of a man like Dædalus, who planned it, or the heart of any ordinary man; which last, to be sure, is ten times as great a mystery as the labyrinth of Crete. Theseus had not taken five steps before he lost sight of Ariadne; and in five more his head was growing dizzy. But still he went on, now creeping through a low arch, now ascending a flight of steps, now in one crooked passage and now in another, with here a door opening before him, and there one banging behind, until it really seemed as if the walls spun round, and whirled him round along with them. And all the while, through these hollow avenues, now nearer, now farther off again, resounded the cry of the Minotaur; and the sound was so fierce, so cruel, so ugly, so like a bull's roar, and withal so like a human voice, and yet like neither of them, that the brave heart of Theseus grew sterner and angrier at every step; for he felt it an insult to the moon and sky, and to our affectionate and simple Mother Earth, that such a monster should have the audacity to exist.

As he passed onward, the clouds gathered over the moon, and the labyrinth grew so dusky that Theseus could no longer discern the bewilderment through which he was passing. He would have felt quite lost, and utterly hopeless of ever again walking in a straight path, if, every little while, he had not been conscious of a gentle twitch at the silken cord. Then he knew that the tender-hearted Ariadne was still holding the other end, and that she was fearing for him, and hoping for him, and giving him just as much of her sympathy as if she were close by his side. Oh, indeed, I can assure you, there was a vast deal of human sympathy running along that slender thread of silk. But still he followed the dreadful roar of the Minotaur, which now grew louder and louder, and finally so very loud that Theseus fully expected to come close upon him, at every new zigzag and wriggle of the path. And at last, in an open space, at the very centre of the labyrinth, he did discern the hideous creature.

Sure enough, what an ugly monster it was! Only his horned head belonged to a bull; and yet, somehow or other, he looked like a bull all over, preposterously waddling on his hind legs; or, if you happened to view him in another way, he seemed wholly a man, and all the more monstrous for being so. And there he was, the wretched thing, with no society, no companion, no kind of a mate, living only to do mischief, and incapable of knowing what affection means. Theseus hated him, and shuddered at him, and yet could not but be sensible of some sort of pity; and all the more, the uglier and more detestable the creature was. For he kept striding to and fro in a solitary frenzy of rage, continually emitting a hoarse roar, which was oddly mixed up with half-shaped words; and, after listening awhile, Theseus understood that the Minotaur was saying to himself how miserable he was, and how hungry, and how he hated everybody, and how he longed to eat up the human race alive.

Ah, the bull-headed villain! And oh, my good little people, you will perhaps see, one of these days, as I do now, that every human being who suffers anything evil to get into his nature, or to remain there, is a kind of Minotaur, an enemy of his fellow-creatures, and separated from all good companionship, as this poor monster was.

Was Theseus afraid? By no means, my dear auditors. What! a hero like Theseus afraid! Not had the Minotaur had twenty bull heads instead of one. Bold as he was, however, I rather fancy that it strengthened his valiant heart, just at this crisis, to feel a tremulous twitch at the silken cord, which he was still holding in his left hand. It was as if Ariadne were giving him all her might and courage; and, much as he already had, and little as she had to give, it made his own seem twice as much. And to confess the honest truth, he needed the whole; for now the Minotaur, turning suddenly about, caught sight of Theseus, and instantly lowered his horribly sharp horns, exactly as a mad bull does when he means to rush against an enemy. At the same time, he belched forth a tremendous roar, in which there was something like the words of human language, but all disjointed and shaken to pieces by passing through the gullet of a miserably enraged brute.

Theseus could only guess what the creature intended to say, and that rather by his gestures than his words; for the Minotaur's horns were sharper than his wits, and of a great deal more service to him than his tongue. But probably this was the sense of what he uttered: —

"Ah, wretch of a human being! I'll stick my horns

196

THE AWFUL FIGHT BETWEEN THESEUS AND THE MINOTAUR

through you, and toss you fifty feet high, and eat you up the moment you come down."

"Come on, then, and try it!" was all that Theseus deigned to reply; for he was far too magnanimous to assault his enemy with insolent language.

Without more words on either side, there ensued the most awful fight between Theseus and the Minotaur that ever happened beneath the sun or moon. I really know not how it might have turned out, if the monster, in his first headlong rush against Theseus, had not missed him, by a hair's-breadth, and broken one of his horns short off against the stone wall. On this mishap, he bellowed so intolerably that a part of the labyrinth tumbled down, and all the inhabitants of Crete mistook the noise for an uncommonly heavy thunder-storm. Smarting with the pain, he galloped around the open space in so ridiculous a way that Theseus laughed at it, long afterwards, though not precisely at the moment. After this, the two antagonists stood valiantly up to one another, and fought sword to horn, for a long while. At last, the Minotaur made a run at Theseus, grazed his left side with his horn, and flung him down; and thinking that he had stabbed him to the heart, he cut a great caper in the air, opened his bull mouth from ear to ear, and prepared to snap his head off. But Theseus by this time had leaped up, and caught the monster off his guard. Fetching a sword-stroke at him with all his force, he hit him fair upon the neck, and made his bull head skip six yards from his human body, which fell down flat upon the ground.

So now the battle was ended. Immediately the moon

shone out as brightly as if all the troubles of the world, and all the wickedness and the ugliness that infest human life, were past and gone forever. And Theseus, as he leaned on his sword, taking breath, felt another twitch of the silken cord; for all through the terrible encounter he had held it fast in his left hand. Eager to let Ariadne know of his success, he followed the guidance of the thread, and soon found himself at the entrance of the labyrinth.

"Thou hast slain the monster," cried Ariadne, clasping her hands.

"Thanks to thee, dear Ariadne," answered Theseus, "I return victorious."

"Then," said Ariadne, "we must quickly summon thy friends, and get them and thyself on board the vessel before dawn. If morning finds thee here, my father will avenge the Minotaur."

To make my story short, the poor captives were awakened, and, hardly knowing whether it was not a joyful dream, were told of what Theseus had done, and that they must set sail for Athens before daybreak. Hastening down to the vessel, they all clambered on board, except Prince Theseus, who lingered behind them, on the strand, holding Ariadne's hand clasped in his own.

"Dear maiden," said he, "thou wilt surely go with us. Thou art too gentle and sweet a child for such an iron-hearted father as King Minos. He cares no more for thee than a granite rock cares for the little flower that grows in one of its crevices. But my father, King Ægeus, and my dear mother, Æthra, and all the fathers and mothers in Athens, and all the sons and daughters too, will love and honor thee as their benefactress. Come with us, then; for King Minos will be very angry when he knows what thou hast done."

Now, some low-minded people, who pretend to tell the story of Theseus and Ariadne, have the face to say that this royal and honorable maiden did really flee away, under cover of the night, with the young stranger whose life she had preserved. They say, too, that Prince Theseus (who would have died sooner than wrong the meanest creature in the world) ungratefully deserted Ariadne, on a solitary island, where the vessel touched on its voyage to Athens. But, had the noble Theseus heard these falsehoods, he would have served their slanderous authors as he served the Minotaur! Here is what Ariadne answered, when the brave Prince of Athens besought her to accompany him: —

"No, Theseus," the maiden said, pressing his hand, and then drawing back a step or two, "I cannot go with you. My father is old, and has nobody but myself to love him. Hard as you think his heart is, it would break to lose me. At first King Minos will be angry; but he will soon forgive his only child; and by and by he will rejoice, I know, that no more youths and maidens must come from Athens to be devoured by the Minotaur. I have saved you, Theseus, as much for my father's sake as for your own. Farewell! Heaven bless you!"

All this was so true, and so maiden-like, and was spoken with so sweet a dignity, that Theseus would have blushed to urge her any longer. Nothing remained for him, therefore, but to bid Ariadne an affectionate farewell, and go on board the vessel, and set sail.

In a few moments the white foam was boiling up before their prow, as Prince Theseus and his companions sailed out of the harbor with a whistling breeze behind them. Talus, the brazen giant, on his never-ceasing sentinel's march, happened to be approaching that part of the coast; and they saw him, by the glimmering of the moonbeams on his polished surface, while he was yet a great way off. As the figure moved like clock-work, however, and could neither hasten his enormous strides nor retard them, he arrived at the port when they were just beyond the reach of his club. Nevertheless, straddling from headland to headland, as his custom was, Talus attempted to strike a blow at the vessel, and, overreaching himself, tumbled at full length into the sea, which splashed high over his gigantic shape, as when an iceberg turns a somerset. There he lies yet; and whoever desires to enrich himself by means of brass had better go thither with a diving-bell, and fish up Talus.

On the homeward voyage, the fourteen youths and damsels were in excellent spirits, as you will easily suppose. They spent most of their time in dancing, unless when the sidelong breeze made the deck slope too much. In due season, they came within sight of the coast of Attica, which was their native country. But here, I am grieved to tell you, happened a sad misfortune.

You will remember (what Theseus unfortunately forgot) that his father, King Ægeus, had enjoined it upon him to hoist sunshine sails, instead of black ones, in case he should overcome the Minotaur, and return victorious. In the joy of their success, however, and amidst the sports, dancing, and other merriment with which these young folks wore away the time, they never once thought whether their sails were black, white, or rainbow colored, and, indeed, left it entirely to the mariners whether they had any sails at all. Thus the vessel returned, like a raven, with the same sable wings that had wafted her away. But poor King Ægeus, day after day, infirm as he was, had clambered to the summit of a cliff that overhung the sea, and there sat watching for Prince Theseus, homeward bound; and no sooner did he behold the fatal blackness of the sails, than he concluded that his dear son, whom he loved so much, and felt so proud of, had been eaten by the Minotaur. He could not bear the thought of living any longer; so, first flinging his crown and sceptre into the sea (useless baubles that they were to him now!), King Ægeus merely stooped forward, and fell headlong over the cliff, and was drowned, poor soul, in the waves that foamed at its base!

This was melancholy news for Prince Theseus, who, when he stepped ashore, found himself king of all the country, whether he would or no; and such a turn of fortune was enough to make any young man feel very much out of spirits. However, he sent for his dear mother to Athens, and, by taking her advice in matters of state, became a very excellent monarch, and was greatly beloved by his people.

THE CHIMÆRA

By Nathaniel Hawthorne

ONCE, in the old, old times (for all the strange things which I tell you about happened long before anybody can remember), a fountain gushed out of a hillside, in the marvelous land of Greece. And, for aught I know, after so many thousand years, it is still gushing out of the very selfsame spot. At any rate, there was the pleasant fountain, welling freshly forth and sparkling adown the hillside, in the golden sunset, when a handsome young man named Bellerophon drew near its margin. In his hand he held a bridle, studded with brilliant gems, and adorned with a golden bit. Seeing an old man, and another of middle age, and a little boy, near the fountain, and likewise a maiden, who was dipping up some of the water in a pitcher, he paused, and begged that he might refresh himself with a draught.

"This is very delicious water," he said to the maiden as he rinsed and filled her pitcher, after drinking out of it. "Will you be kind enough to tell me whether the fountain has any name?"

"Yes; it is called the Fountain of Pirene," answered the maiden; and then she added, "My grandmother has told me that this clear fountain was once a beautiful woman; and when her son was killed by the arrows of the huntress Diana, she melted all away into tears. And so the water, which you find so cool and sweet, is the sorrow of that poor mother's heart!"

"I should not have dreamed," observed the young stranger, "that so clear a well-spring, with its gush and gurgle, and its cheery dance out of the shade into the sunlight, had so much as one tear-drop in its bosom! And this, then, is Pirene? I thank you, pretty maiden, for telling me its name. I have come from a far-away country to find this very spot."

A middle-aged country fellow (he had driven his cow to drink out of the spring) stared hard at young Bellerophon, and at the handsome bridle which he carried in his hand.

"The water-courses must be getting low, friend, in your part of the world," remarked he, "if you come so far only to find the Fountain of Pirene. But, pray, have you lost a horse? I see you carry the bridle in your hand; and a very pretty one it is, with that double row of bright stones upon it. If the horse was as fine as the bridle, you are much to be pitied for losing him."

"I have lost no horse," said Bellerophon, with a smile. "But I happen to be seeking a very famous one, which, as wise people have informed me, must be found hereabouts, if anywhere. Do you know whether the winged horse Pegasus still haunts the Fountain of Pirene, as he used to do in your forefathers' days?"

But then the country fellow laughed.

Some of you, my little friends, have probably heard that this Pegasus was a snow-white steed, with beautiful silvery wings, who spent most of his time on the summit of Mount Helicon. He was as wild, and as swift, and as buoyant, in his flight through the air, as any eagle that ever soared into the clouds. There was nothing else like him in the world. He had no mate; he never had been backed or bridled by a master; and, for many a long year, he led a solitary and a happy life.

Oh, how fine a thing it is to be a winged horse! Sleeping at night, as he did, on a lofty mountain-top, and passing the greater part of the day in the air, Pegasus seemed hardly to be a creature of the earth. Whenever he was seen, up very high above people's heads, with the sunshine on his silvery wings, you would have thought that he belonged to the sky, and that, skimming a little too low, he had got astray among our mists and vapors, and was seeking his way back again. It was very pretty to behold him plunge into the fleecy bosom of a bright cloud, and be lost in it, for a moment or two, and then break forth from the other side. Or, in a sullen rain-storm, when there was a gray pavement of clouds over the whole sky, it would sometimes happen that the winged horse descended right through it, and the glad light of the upper region would gleam after him. In another instant, it is true, both Pegasus and the pleasant light would be gone away together. But any one that was fortunate enough to see this wondrous spectacle felt cheerful the whole day afterwards, and as much longer as the storm lasted.

In the summer-time, and in the beautifulest of weather, Pegasus often alighted on the solid earth, and, closing his silvery wings, would gallop over hill and dale for pastime, as fleetly as the wind. Oftener than in any other place, he had been seen near the Fountain of Pirene, drinking the delicious water, or rolling himself upon the soft grass of the margin. Sometimes, too (but Pegasus was very dainty in his food), he would crop a few of the clover-blossoms that happened to be sweetest.

To the Fountain of Pirene, therefore, people's great-grandfathers had been in the habit of going (as long as they were youthful, and retained their faith in winged horses), in hopes of getting a glimpse at the beautiful Pegasus. But of late years he had been very seldom seen. Indeed, there were many of the country folks, dwelling within half an hour's walk of the fountain, who had never beheld Pegasus, and did not believe that there was any such creature in existence. The country fellow to whom Bellerophon was speaking chanced to be one of those incredulous persons.

And that was the reason why he laughed.

"Pegasus, indeed!" cried he, turning up his nose as high as such a flat nose could be turned up, — "Pegasus, indeed! A winged horse, truly! Why, friend, are you in your senses? Of what use would wings be to a horse? Could he drag the plough so well, think you? To be sure, there might be a little saving in the expense of shoes; but then, how would a man like to see his horse flying out of the stable window? — yes, or whisking him up above the clouds, when he only wanted to ride to mill? No, no! I don't believe in Pegasus. There never was such a ridiculous kind of a horse-fowl made!"

"I have some reason to think otherwise," said Bellerophon, quietly.

And then he turned to an old, gray man, who was leaning on a staff, and listening very attentively, with his head stretched forward, and one hand at his ear, because, for the last twenty years, he had been getting rather deaf.

"And what say you, venerable sir?" inquired he. "In your younger days, I should imagine, you must frequently have seen the winged steed!"

"Ah, young stranger, my memory is very poor!" said the aged man. "When I was a lad, if I remember rightly, I used to believe there was such a horse, and so did everybody else. But nowadays I hardly know what to think, and very seldom think about the winged horse at all. If I ever saw the creature, it was a long, long while ago; and, to tell you the truth, I doubt whether I ever did see him. One day, to be sure, when I was quite a youth, I remember seeing some hoof-tramps round about the brink of the fountain. Pegasus might have made those hoof-marks; and so might some other horse."

"And have you never seen him, my fair maiden?" asked Bellerophon of the girl, who stood with the pitcher on her head, while this talk went on. "You certainly could see Pegasus, if anybody can, for your eyes are very bright."

"Once I thought I saw him," replied the maiden, with a smile and a blush. "It was either Pegasus, or a large white bird, a very great way up in the air. And one other time, as I was coming to the fountain with my pitcher, I heard a neigh. Oh, such a brisk and melodious neigh as that was! My very heart leaped with delight at the sound. But it startled me, nevertheless; so that I ran home without filling my pitcher."

"That was truly a pity!" said Bellerophon.

And he turned to the child, whom I mentioned at the beginning of the story, and who was gazing at him, as children are apt to gaze at strangers, with his rosy mouth wide open.

"Well, my little fellow," cried Bellerophon, playfully pulling one of his curls, "I suppose you have often seen the winged horse."

"That I have," answered the child, very readily, "I saw him yesterday, and many times before."

"You are a fine little man!" said Bellerophon, drawing the child closer to him. "Come, tell me all about it."

"Why," replied the child, "I often come here to sail little boats in the fountain, and to gather pretty pebbles out of its basin. And sometimes, when I look down into the water, I see the image of the winged horse, in the picture of the sky that is there. I wish he would come down, and take me on his back, and let me ride him up to the moon! But, if I so much as stir to look at him, he flies far away out of sight."

And Bellerophon put his faith in the child, who had seen the image of Pegasus in the water, and in the maiden, who had heard him neigh so melodiously, rather than in the middle-aged clown, who believed only in cart-horses, or in the old man, who had forgotten the beautiful things of his youth.

Therefore, he haunted about the Fountain of Pirene

for a great many days afterwards. He kept continually on the watch, looking upward at the sky, or else down into the water, hoping forever that he should see either the reflected image of the winged horse, or the marvelous reality. He held the bridle, with its bright gems and golden bit, always ready in his hand. The rustic people who dwelt in the neighborhood, and drove their cattle to the fountain to drink, would often laugh at poor Bellerophon, and sometimes take him pretty severely to task. They told him that an able-bodied young man, like himself, ought to have better business than to be wasting his time in such an idle pursuit. They offered to sell him a horse, if he wanted one; and when Bellerophon declined the purchase, they tried to drive a bargain with him for his fine bridle.

Even the country boys thought him so very foolish, that they used to have a great deal of sport about him, and were rude enough not to care a fig, although Bellerophon saw and heard it. One little urchin, for example, would play Pegasus, and cut the oddest imaginable capers, by way of flying; while one of his schoolfellows would scamper after him, holding forth a twist of bulrushes, which was intended to represent Bellerophon's ornamental bridle. But the gentle child who had seen the picture of Pegasus in the water, comforted the young stranger more than all the naughty boys could torment him. The dear little fellow, in his play-hours, often sat down beside him, and, without speaking a word, would look down into the fountain and up towards the sky, with so innocent a faith, that Bellerophon could not help feeling encouraged.

Now you will, perhaps, wish to be told why it was that Bellerophon had undertaken to catch the winged horse. And we shall find no better opportunity to speak about this matter than while he is waiting for Pegasus to appear.

If I were to relate the whole of Bellerophon's previous adventures, they might easily grow into a very long story. It will be quite enough to say, that, in a certain country of Asia, a terrible monster, called a Chimæra, had made its appearance, and was doing more mischief than could be talked about between now and sunset. According to the best accounts which I have been able to obtain, this Chimæra was nearly, if not quite, the ugliest and most poisonous creature, and the strangest and unaccountablest, and the hardest to fight with, and the most difficult to run away from, that ever came out of the earth's inside. It had a tail like a boa-constrictor: its body was like I do not care what; and it had three separate heads, one of which was a lion's, the second a goat's, and the third an abominably great snake's. And a hot blast of fire came flaming out of each of its three mouths! Being an earthly monster, I doubt whether it had any wings; but, wings or no, it ran like a goat and a lion, and wriggled along like a serpent, and thus contrived to make about as much speed as all the three together.

Oh, the mischief, and mischief, and mischief that this naughty creature did! With its flaming breath, it could set a forest on fire, or burn up a field of grain, or, for that matter, a village, with all its fences and houses. It laid waste the whole country round about, and used to eat up people and animals alive, and cook them afterwards in the burning oven of its stomach. Mercy on us, little children, I hope neither you nor I will ever happen to meet a Chimæra!

While the hateful beast (if a beast we can anywise call it) was doing all these horrible things, it so chanced that Bellerophon came to that part of the world, on a visit to the king. The king's name was Iobates, and Lycia was the country which he ruled over. Bellerophon was one of the bravest youths in the world, and desired nothing so much as to do some valiant and beneficent deed, such as would make all mankind admire and love him. In those days, the only way for a young man to distinguish himself was by fighting battles, either with the enemies of his country, or with wicked giants, or with troublesome dragons, or with wild beasts, when he could find nothing more dangerous to encounter. King Iobates, perceiving the courage of his youthful visitor, proposed to him to go and fight the Chimæra, which everybody else was afraid of, and which, unless it should be soon killed, was likely to convert Lycia into a desert. Bellerophon hesitated not a moment, but assured the king that he would either slay this dreaded Chimæra, or perish in the attempt.

But, in the first place, as the monster was so prodigiously swift, he bethought himself that he should never win the victory by fighting on foot. The wisest thing he could do, therefore, was to get the very best and fleetest horse that could anywhere be found. And what other horse, in all the world, was half so fleet as the marvelous horse Pegasus, who had wings as well as legs, and was even more active in the air than on the earth? To be sure, a great many people denied that there was any such horse with wings, and said that the stories about him were all poetry and nonsense. But, wonderful as it appeared, Bellerophon believed that Pegasus was a real steed, and hoped that he himself might be fortunate enough to find him; and, once fairly mounted on his back, he would be able to fight the Chimæra at better advantage.

And this was the purpose with which he had traveled from Lycia to Greece, and had brought the beautifully ornamented bridle in his hand. It was an enchanted bridle. If he could only succeed in putting the golden bit into the mouth of Pegasus, the winged horse would be submissive, and would own Bellerophon for his master, and fly whithersoever he might choose to turn the rein.

But, indeed, it was a weary and anxious time, while Bellerophon waited and waited for Pegasus, in hopes that he would come and drink at the Fountain of Pirene. He was afraid lest King Iobates should imagine that he had fled from the Chimæra. It pained him, too, to think how much mischief the monster was doing, while he himself, instead of fighting with it, was compelled to sit idly poring over the bright waters of Pirene, as they gushed out of the sparkling sand. And as Pegasus came thither so seldom in these latter years, and scarcely alighted there more than once in a lifetime, Bellerophon feared that he might grow an old man, and have no strength left in his arms nor courage in his heart, before the winged horse would appear. Oh, how heavily passes the time, while an adventurous youth is yearning to do his part in life, and to gather in the harvest of his renown! How hard a lesson it is to wait! Our life is brief, and how much of it is spent in teaching us only this!

Well was it for Bellerophon that the gentle child had grown so fond of him, and was never weary of keeping him company. Every morning the child gave him a new hope to put in his bosom, instead of yesterday's withered one.

"Dear Bellerophon," he would cry, looking up hopefully into his face, "I think we shall see Pegasus to-day!"

And, at length, if it had not been for the little boy's unwavering faith, Bellerophon would have given up all hope, and would have gone back to Lycia, and have done his best to slay the Chimæra without the help of the winged horse. And in that case poor Bellerophon would at least have been terribly scorched by the creature's breath, and would most probably have been killed and devoured. Nobody should ever try to fight an earth-born Chimæra, unless he can first get upon the back of an aerial steed.

One morning the child spoke to Bellerophon even more hopefully than usual.

"Dear, dear Bellerophon," cried he, "I know not why it is, but I feel as if we should certainly see Pegasus to-day!"

And all that day he would not stir a step from Bellerophon's side; so they ate a crust of bread together, and drank some of the water of the fountain. In the afternoon, there they sat, and Bellerophon had thrown his arm around the child, who likewise had put one of his little hands into Bellerophon's. The latter was lost in his own thoughts, and was fixing his eyes vacantly on the trunks of the trees that overshadowed the fountain, and on the grapevines that clambered up among their branches. But the gentle child was gazing down into the water; he was grieved, for Bellerophon's sake, that the hope of another day should be deceived, like so many before it; and two or three quiet tear-drops fell from his eyes, and mingled with what were said to be the many tears of Pirene, when she wept for her slain children.

But, when he least thought of it, Bellerophon felt the pressure of the child's little hand, and heard a soft, almost breathless, whisper.

"See there, dear Bellerophon! There is an image in the water!"

The young man looked down into the dimpling mirror of the fountain, and saw what he took to be the reflection of a bird which seemed to be flying at a great height in the air, with a gleam of sunshine on its snowy or silvery wings.

"What a splendid bird it must be!" said he. "And how very large it looks, though it must really be flying higher than the clouds!"

"It makes me tremble!" whispered the child. "I am afraid to look up into the air! It is very beautiful, and yet I dare only look at its image in the water. Dear Bellerophon, do you not see that it is no bird? It is the winged horse Pegasus!"

Bellerophon's heart began to throb! He gazed keenly upward, but could not see the winged creature, whether bird or horse; because, just then, it had plunged into the fleecy depths of a summer cloud. It was but a moment, however, before the object reappeared, sinking lightly down out of the cloud, although still at a vast distance from the earth. Bellerophon caught the child in his arms, and shrank back with him, so that they were both hidden among the thick shrubbery, which grew all around the fountain. Not that he was afraid of any harm, but he dreaded lest, if Pegasus caught a glimpse of them, he would fly far away, and alight in some inaccessible mountain-top. For it was really the winged horse. After they had expected him so long, he was coming to quench his thirst with the water of Pirene.

Nearer and nearer came the aerial wonder, flying in great circles, as you may have seen a dove when about to alight. Downward came Pegasus, in those wide, sweeping circles, which grew narrower, and narrower still, as he gradually approached the earth. The nigher the view of him, the more beautiful he was, and the more marvelous the sweep of his silvery wings. At last, with so light a pressure as hardly to bend the grass about the fountain, or imprint a hoof-tramp in the sand of its margin, he alighted, and, stooping his wild head, began to drink. He drew in the water, with long and pleasant sighs, and tranquil pauses of enjoyment; and then another draught, and another, and another. For nowhere in the world, or up among the clouds, did Pegasus love any water as he loved this of Pirene. And when his thirst was slaked, he cropped a

few of the honey-blossoms of the clover, delicately
tasting them, but not caring to make a hearty meal,
because the herbage just beneath the clouds, on the
lofty sides of Mount Helicon, suited his palate better
than this ordinary grass.

After thus drinking to his heart's content, and in
his dainty fashion condescending to take a little food,
the winged horse began to caper to and fro, and dance
as it were, out of mere idleness and sport. There never
was a more playful creature made than this very Pegasus. So there he frisked, in a way that it delights me
to think about, fluttering his great wings as lightly as
ever did a linnet, and running little races, half on earth
and half in air, and which I know not whether to call
a flight or a gallop. When a creature is perfectly able to
fly, he sometimes chooses to run, just for the pastime
of the thing; and so did Pegasus, although it cost him
some little trouble to keep his hoofs so near the ground.
Bellerophon, meanwhile, holding the child's hand,
peeped forth from the shrubbery, and thought that
never was any sight so beautiful as this, nor ever a
horse's eyes so wild and spirited as those of Pegasus.
It seemed a sin to think of bridling him and riding on
his back.

Once or twice, Pegasus stopped, and snuffed the
air, pricking up his ears, tossing his head, and turning
it on all sides, as if he partly suspected some mischief
or other. Seeing nothing, however, and hearing no
sound, he soon began his antics again.

At length, — not that he was weary, but only idle
and luxurious, — Pegasus folded his wings, and lay

down on the soft green turf. But, being too full of
aerial life to remain quiet for many moments together,
he soon rolled over on his back, with his four slender
legs in the air. It was beautiful to see him, this one
solitary creature, whose mate had never been created,
but who needed no companion, and, living a great
many hundred years, was as happy as the centuries
were long. The more he did such things as mortal
horses are accustomed to do, the less earthly and the
more wonderful he seemed. Bellerophon and the child
almost held their breath, partly from a delightful awe,
but still more because they dreaded lest the slightest
stir or murmur should send him up, with the speed of
an arrow-flight, into the farthest blue of the sky.

Finally, when he had had enough of rolling over
and over, Pegasus turned himself about, and, indo-
lently, like any other horse, put out his fore legs, in
order to rise from the ground; and Bellerophon, who
had guessed that he would do so, darted suddenly
from the thicket, and leaped astride of his back.

Yes, there he sat, on the back of the winged horse!

But what a bound did Pegasus make, when, for the
first time, he felt the weight of a mortal man upon his
loins! A bound, indeed! Before he had time to draw
a breath, Bellerophon found himself five hundred feet
aloft, and still shooting upward, while the winged horse
snorted and trembled with terror and anger. Upward
he went, up, up, up, until he plunged into the cold
misty bosom of a cloud, at which, only a little while
before, Bellerophon had been gazing, and fancying it
a very pleasant spot. Then again, out of the heart of

the cloud, Pegasus shot down like a thunderbolt, as if he meant to dash both himself and his rider headlong against a rock. Then he went through about a thousand of the wildest caprioles that had ever been performed either by a bird or a horse.

I cannot tell you half that he did. He skimmed straight forward, and sideways, and backward. He reared himself erect, with his fore legs on a wreath of mist, and his hind legs on nothing at all. He flung out his heels behind, and put down his head between his legs, with his wings pointing right upward. At about two miles' height above the earth, he turned a somerset, so that Bellerophon's heels were where his head should have been, and he seemed to look down into the sky, instead of up. He twisted his head about, and, looking Bellerophon in the face, with fire flashing from his eyes, made a terrible attempt to bite him. He fluttered his pinions so wildly that one of the silver feathers was shaken out, and floating earthward, was picked up by the child, who kept it as long as he lived, in memory of Pegasus and Bellerophon.

But the latter (who, as you may judge, was as good a horseman as ever galloped) had been watching his opportunity, and at last clapped the golden bit of the enchanted bridle between the winged steed's jaws. No sooner was this done, than Pegasus became as manageable as if he had taken food, all his life, out of Bellerophon's hand. To speak what I really feel, it was almost a sadness to see so wild a creature grow suddenly so tame. And Pegasus seemed to feel it so, likewise. He looked round to Bellerophon, with the tears in his beautiful eyes, instead of the fire that so recently flashed from them. But when Bellerophon patted his head, and spoke a few authoritative, yet kind and soothing words, another look came into the eyes of Pegasus; for he was glad at heart, after so many lonely centuries, to have found a companion and a master.

Thus it always is with winged horses, and with all such wild and solitary creatures. If you can catch and overcome them, it is the surest way to win their love.

While Pegasus had been doing his utmost to shake Bellerophon off his back, he had flown a very long distance; and they had come within sight of a lofty mountain by the time the bit was in his mouth. Bellerophon had seen this mountain before, and knew it to be Helicon, on the summit of which was the winged horse's abode. Thither (after looking gently into his rider's face, as if to ask leave) Pegasus now flew, and, alighting, waited patiently until Bellerophon should please to dismount. The young man, accordingly, leaped from his steed's back, but still held him fast by the bridle. Meeting his eyes, however, he was so affected by the gentleness of his aspect, and by the thought of the free life which Pegasus had heretofore lived, that he could not bear to keep him a prisoner, if he really desired his liberty.

Obeying this generous impulse, he slipped the enchanted bridle off the head of Pegasus, and took the bit from his mouth.

"Leave me, Pegasus!" said he. "Either leave me, or love me."

A THOUSAND MILES A DAY WAS AN EASY SPACE

In an instant, the winged horse shot almost out of sight, soaring straight upward from the summit of Mount Helicon. Being long after sunset, it was now twilight on the mountain-top, and dusky evening over all the country round about. But Pegasus flew so high that he overtook the departed day, and was bathed in the upper radiance of the sun. Ascending higher and higher, he looked like a bright speck, and, at last, could no longer be seen in the hollow waste of the sky. And Bellerophon was afraid that he should never behold him more. But, while he was lamenting his own folly, the bright speck reappeared, and drew nearer and nearer, until it descended lower than the sunshine; and, behold, Pegasus had come back! After this trial there was no more fear of the winged horse's making his escape. He and Bellerophon were friends, and put loving faith in one another.

That night they lay down and slept together, with Bellerophon's arm about the neck of Pegasus, not as a caution, but for kindness. And they awoke at peep of day, and bade one another good morning, each in his own language.

In this manner, Bellerophon and the wondrous steed spent several days, and grew better acquainted and fonder of each other all the time. They went on long aerial journeys, and sometimes ascended so high that the earth looked hardly bigger than — the moon. They visited distant countries, and amazed the inhabitants, who thought that the beautiful young man, on the back of the winged horse, must have come down out of the sky. A thousand miles a day was no more than an easy space for the fleet Pegasus to pass over. Bellerophon was delighted with this kind of life, and would have liked nothing better than to live always in the same way, aloft in the clear atmosphere; for it was always sunny weather up there, however cheerless and rainy it might be in the lower region. But he could not forget the horrible Chimæra, which he had promised King Iobates to slay. So, at last, when he had become well accustomed to feats of horsemanship in the air, and could manage Pegasus with the least motion of his hand, and had taught him to obey his voice, he determined to attempt the performance of this perilous adventure.

At daybreak, therefore, as soon as he unclosed his eyes, he gently pinched the winged horse's ear, in order to arouse him. Pegasus immediately started from the ground, and pranced about a quarter of a mile aloft, and made a grand sweep around the mountain-top, by way of showing that he was wide awake, and ready for any kind of an excursion. During the whole of this little flight, he uttered a loud, brisk, and melodious neigh, and finally came down at Bellerophon's side, as lightly as ever you saw a sparrow hop upon a twig.

"Well done, dear Pegasus! well done, my sky-skimmer!" cried Bellerophon, fondly stroking the horse's neck. "And now, my fleet and beautiful friend, we must break our fast. To-day we are to fight the terrible Chimæra."

As soon as they had eaten their morning meal, and drank some sparkling water from a spring called Hippocrene, Pegasus held out his head, of his own accord so that his master might put on the bridle. Then, with a great many playful leaps and airy caperings, he showed his impatience to be gone; while Bellerophon was girding on his sword, and hanging his shield about his neck, and preparing himself for battle. When everything was ready, the rider mounted, and (as was his custom, when going a long distance) ascended five miles perpendicularly, so as the better to see whither he was directing his course. He then turned the head of Pegasus towards the east, and set out for Lycia. In their flight they overtook an eagle, and came so nigh him, before he could get out of their way, that Bellerophon might easily have caught him by the leg. Hastening onward at this rate, it was still early in the forenoon when they beheld the lofty mountains of Lycia, with their deep and shaggy valleys. If Bellerophon had been told truly, it was in one of those dismal valleys that the hideous Chimæra had taken up its abode.

Being now so near their journey's end, the winged horse gradually descended with his rider; and they took advantage of some clouds that were floating over the mountain-tops, in order to conceal themselves. Hovering on the upper surface of a cloud, and peeping over its edge, Bellerophon had a pretty distinct view of the mountainous part of Lycia, and could look into all its shadowy vales at once. At first there appeared to be nothing remarkable. It was a wild, savage, and rocky tract of high and precipitous hills. In the more level part of the country, there were the ruins of houses that had been burnt, and, here and there, the carcasses of dead cattle, strewn about the pastures where they had been feeding.

"The Chimæra must have done this mischief," thought Bellerophon. "But where can the monster be?"

As I have already said, there was nothing remarkable to be detected, at first sight, in any of the valleys and dells that lay among the precipitous heights of the mountains. Nothing at all; unless, indeed, it were three spires of black smoke, which issued from what seemed to be the mouth of a cavern, and clambered sullenly into the atmosphere. Before reaching the mountain-top, these three black smoke-wreaths mingled themselves into one. The cavern was almost directly beneath the winged horse and his rider, at the distance of about a thousand feet. The smoke, as it crept heavily upward, had an ugly, sulphurous, stifling scent, which caused Pegasus to snort and Bellerophon to sneeze. So disagreeable was it to the marvelous steed (who was accustomed to breathe only the purest air), that he waved his wings, and shot half a mile out of the range of this offensive vapor.

But, on looking behind him, Bellerophon saw something that induced him first to draw the bridle, and then to turn Pegasus about. He made a sign, which the winged horse understood, and sunk slowly through the air, until his hoofs were scarcely more than a man's height above the rocky bottom of the valley. In front, as far off as you could throw a stone, was the cavern's mouth, with the three smoke-wreaths oozing out of it. And what else did Bellerophon behold there?

There seemed to be a heap of strange and terrible creatures curled up within the cavern. Their bodies lay so close together, that Bellerophon could not distinguish them apart; but, judging by their heads, one of these creatures was a huge snake, the second a fierce lion, and the third an ugly goat. The lion and the goat were asleep; the snake was broad awake, and kept staring around him with a great pair of fiery eyes. But — and this was the most wonderful part of the matter — the three spires of smoke evidently issued from the nostrils of these three heads! So strange was the spectacle, that, though Bellerophon had been all along expecting it, the truth did not immediately occur to him, that here was the terrible three-headed Chimæra. He had found out the Chimæra's cavern. The snake, the lion, and the goat, as he supposed them to be, were not three separate creatures, but one monster!

The wicked, hateful thing! Slumbering as two thirds of it were, it still held, in its abominable claws, the remnant of an unfortunate lamb, — or possibly (but I hate to think so) it was a dear little boy, — which its three mouths had been gnawing, before two of them fell asleep!

All at once, Bellerophon started as from a dream, and knew it to be the Chimæra. Pegasus seemed to know it, at the same instant, and sent forth a neigh, that sounded like the call of a trumpet to battle. At this sound the three heads reared themselves erect, and belched out great flashes of flame. Before Bellerophon had time to consider what to do next, the monster flung itself out of the cavern and sprung straight towards him, with its immense claws extended, and its snaky tail twisting itself venomously behind. If Pegasus had not been as nimble as a bird, both he and his rider would have been overthrown by the Chimæra's headlong rush, and thus the battle have been ended before it was well begun. But the winged horse was not to be caught so. In the twinkling of an eye he was up aloft, half-way to the clouds, snorting with anger. He shuddered, too, not with affright, but with utter disgust at the loathsomeness of this poisonous thing with three heads.

The Chimæra, on the other hand, raised itself up so as to stand absolutely on the tip-end of its tail, with its talons pawing fiercely in the air, and its three heads spluttering fire at Pegasus and his rider. My stars, how it roared, and hissed, and bellowed! Bellerophon, meanwhile, was fitting his shield on his arm, and drawing his sword.

"Now, my beloved Pegasus," he whispered in the winged horse's ear, "thou must help me to slay this insufferable monster; or else thou shalt fly back to thy solitary mountain-peak without thy friend Bellerophon. For either the Chimæra dies, or its three mouths shall gnaw this head of mine, which has slumbered upon thy neck!"

Pegasus whinnied, and, turning back his head, rubbed his nose tenderly against his rider's cheek. It was his way of telling him that, though he had wings and was an immortal horse, yet he would perish, if it were possible for immortality to perish, rather than leave Bellerophon behind.

"I thank you, Pegasus," answered Bellerophon. "Now, then, let us make a dash at the monster!"

Uttering these words, he shook the bridle; and Pegasus darted down aslant, as swift as the flight of an arrow, right towards the Chimæra's threefold head, which, all this time, was poking itself as high as it could into the air. As he came within arm's length, Bellerophon made a cut at the monster, but was carried onward by his steed, before he could see whether the blow had been successful. Pegasus continued his course, but soon wheeled round, at about the same distance from the Chimæra as before. Bellerophon then perceived that he had cut the goat's head of the monster almost off, so that it dangled downward by the skin, and seemed quite dead.

But, to make amends, the snake's head and the lion's head had taken all the fierceness of the dead one into themselves, and spit flame, and hissed, and roared, with a vast deal more fury than before.

"Never mind, my brave Pegasus!" cried Bellerophon. "With another stroke like that, we will stop either its hissing or its roaring."

And again he shook the bridle. Dashing aslantwise, as before, the winged horse made another arrow-flight towards the Chimæra, and Bellerophon aimed another downright stroke at one of the two remaining heads, as he shot by. But this time, neither he nor Pegasus escaped so well as at first. With one of its claws, the Chimæra had given the young man a deep scratch in his shoulder, and had slightly damaged the left wing of the flying steed with the other. On his part, Bellerophon had mortally wounded the lion's head of the monster, insomuch that it now hung downward, with its fire almost extinguished, and sending out gasps of thick black smoke. The snake's head, however (which was the only one now left), was twice as fierce and venomous as ever before. It belched forth shoots of fire five hundred yards long, and emitted hisses so loud, so harsh, and so ear-piercing, that King Iobates heard them, fifty miles off, and trembled till the throne shook under him.

"Well-a-day!" thought the poor king; "the Chimæra is certainly coming to devour me!"

Meanwhile Pegasus had again paused in the air, and neighed angrily, while sparkles of a pure crystal flame darted out of his eyes. How unlike the lurid fire of the Chimæra! The aerial steed's spirit was all aroused, and so was that of Bellerophon.

"Dost thou bleed, my immortal horse?" cried the young man, caring less for his own hurt than for the anguish of this glorious creature, that ought never to have tasted pain. "The execrable Chimæra shall pay for this mischief with his last head!"

Then he shook the bridle, shouted loudly, and guided Pegasus, not aslantwise as before, but straight at the monster's hideous front. So rapid was the onset, that it seemed but a dazzle and a flash before Bellerophon was at close gripes with his enemy.

The Chimæra, by this time, after losing its second head, had got into a red-hot passion of pain and rampant rage. It so flounced about, half on earth and partly in the air, that it was impossible to say which element it rested upon. It opened its snake-jaws to such an abominable width, that Pegasus might almost, I was going to say, have flown right down its throat.

wings outspread, rider and all! At their approach it shot out a tremendous blast of its fiery breath, and enveloped Bellerophon and his steed in a perfect atmosphere of flame, singeing the wings of Pegasus, scorching off one whole side of the young man's golden ringlets, and making them both far hotter than was comfortable, from head to foot.

But this was nothing to what followed.

When the airy rush of the winged horse had brought him within the distance of a hundred yards, the Chimæra gave a spring, and flung its huge, awkward, venomous, and utterly detestable carcass right upon poor Pegasus, clung round him with might and main, and tied up its snaky tail into a knot! Up flew the aerial steed, higher, higher, higher, above the mountain-peaks, above the clouds, and almost out of sight of the solid earth. But still the earth-born monster kept its hold, and was borne upward, along with the creature of light and air. Bellerophon, meanwhile, turning about, found himself face to face with the ugly grimness of the Chimæra's visage, and could only avoid being scorched to death or bitten right in twain by holding up his shield. Over the upper edge of the shield, he looked sternly into the savage eyes of the monster.

But the Chimæra was so mad and wild with pain, that it did not guard itself so well as might else have been the case. Perhaps, after all, the best way to fight a Chimæra is by getting as close to it as you can. In its efforts to stick its horrible iron claws into its enemy, the creature left its own breast quite exposed; and perceiving this, Bellerophon thrust his sword up to the hilt into its cruel heart. Immediately the snaky tail untied its knot. The monster let go its hold of Pegasus, and fell from that vast height, downward; while the fire within its bosom, instead of being put out, burned fiercer than ever, and quickly began to consume the dead carcass. Thus it fell out of the sky, all aflame, and (it being nightfall before it reached the earth) was mistaken for a shooting star or a comet. But, at early sunrise, some cottagers were going to their day's labor, and saw, to their astonishment, that several acres of ground were strewn with black ashes. In the middle of a field, there was a heap of whitened bones, a great deal higher than a haystack. Nothing else was ever seen of the dreadful Chimæra!

And when Bellerophon had won the victory, he bent forward and kissed Pegasus, while the tears stood in his eyes.

"Back now, my beloved steed!" said he. "Back to the Fountain of Pirene!"

Pegasus skimmed through the air, quicker than ever he did before, and reached the fountain in a very short time. And there he found the old man leaning on his staff, and the country fellow watering his cow, and the pretty maiden filling her pitcher.

"I remember now," quoth the old man, "I saw this winged horse once before, when I was quite a lad. But he was ten times handsomer in those days."

"I own a cart-horse, worth three of him!" said the country fellow. "If this pony were mine, the first thing I should do would be to clip his wings!"

But the poor maiden said nothing, for she had always the luck to be afraid at the wrong time. So she ran away, and let her pitcher tumble down, and broke it.

"Where is the gentle child," asked Bellerophon, "who used to keep me company, and never lost his faith, and never was weary of gazing into the fountain?"

"Here am I, dear Bellerophon!" said the child, softly.

For the little boy had spent day after day on the margin of Pirene, waiting for his friend to come back; but when he perceived Bellerophon descending through the clouds, mounted on the winged horse, he had shrunk back into the shrubbery. He was a delicate and tender child, and dreaded lest the old man and the country fellow should see the tears gushing from his eyes.

"Thou hast won the victory," said he, joyfully, running to the knee of Bellerophon, who still sat on the back of Pegasus. "I knew thou wouldst."

"Yes, dear child!" replied Bellerophon, alighting from the winged horse. "But if thy faith had not helped me, I should never have waited for Pegasus, and never have gone up above the clouds, and never have conquered the terrible Chimæra. Thou, my beloved little friend, hast done it all. And now let us give Pegasus his liberty."

So he slipped off the enchanted bridle from the head of the marvelous steed.

"Be free, forevermore, my Pegasus!" cried he, with a shade of sadness in his tone. "Be as free as thou art fleet!"

But Pegasus rested his head on Bellerophon's shoulder, and would not be persuaded to take flight.

"Well then," said Bellerophon, caressing the airy horse, "thou shalt be with me, as long as thou wilt; and we will go together, forthwith, and tell King Iobates that the Chimæra is destroyed."

Then Bellerophon embraced the gentle child, and promised to come to him again, and departed. But, in after years, that child took higher flights upon the aerial steed than ever did Bellerophon, and achieved more honorable deeds than his friend's victory over the Chimæra. For, gentle and tender as he was, he grew to be a mighty poet!

ARACHNE

By Josephine Preston Peabody

NOT among mortals alone were there contests of skill, nor yet among the gods, like Pan and Apollo. Many sorrows befell men because they grew arrogant in their own devices and coveted divine honors. There was once a great hunter, Orion, who outvied the gods themselves, till they took him away from his hunting-grounds and set him in the heavens, with his sword and belt, and his hound at his heels. But at length jealousy invaded even the peaceful arts, and disaster came of spinning!

There was a certain maiden of Lydia, Arachne by name, renowned throughout the country for her skill as a weaver. She was as nimble with her fingers as Calypso, that nymph who kept Odysseus for seven years in her enchanted island. She was as untiring as Penelope, the hero's wife, who wove day after day while she watched for his return. Day in and day out, Arachne wove too. The very nymphs would gather about her loom, naiads from the water and dryads from the trees.

"Maiden," they would say, shaking the leaves or the foam from their hair, in wonder, "Pallas Athena must have taught you!"

But this did not please Arachne. She would not acknowledge herself a debtor, even to that goddess

231

who protected all household arts, and by whose grace alone one had any skill in them.

"I learned not of Athena," said she. "If she can weave better, let her come and try."

The nymphs shivered at this, and an aged woman, who was looking on, turned to Arachne.

"Be more heedful of your words, my daughter," said she. "The goddess may pardon you if you ask forgiveness, but do not strive for honors with the immortals."

Arachne broke her thread, and the shuttle stopped humming.

"Keep your counsel," she said. "I fear not Athena; no, nor any one else."

As she frowned at the old woman, she was amazed to see her change suddenly into one tall, majestic, beautiful, — a maiden of gray eyes and golden hair, crowned with a golden helmet. It was Athena herself.

The bystanders shrank in fear and reverence; only Arachne was unawed and held to her foolish boast.

In silence the two began to weave, and the nymphs stole nearer, coaxed by the sound of the shuttles, that seemed to be humming with delight over the two webs, — back and forth like bees.

They gazed upon the loom where the goddess stood plying her task, and they saw shapes and images come to bloom out of the wondrous colors, as sunset clouds grow to be living creatures when we watch them. And they saw that the goddess, still merciful, was spinning, as a warning for Arachne, the pictures of her own triumph over reckless gods and mortals.

In one corner of the web she made a story of her

conquest over the sea-god Poseidon. For the first king of Athens had promised to dedicate the city to that god who should bestow upon it the most useful gift. Poseidon gave the horse. But Athena gave the olive, — means of livelihood, — symbol of peace and prosperity, and the city was called after her name. Again she pictured a vain woman of Troy, who had been turned into a crane for disputing the palm of beauty with a goddess. Other corners of the web held similar images, and the whole shone like a rainbow.

Meanwhile Arachne, whose head was quite turned with vanity, embroidered her web with stories against the gods, making light of Zeus himself and of Apollo, and portraying them as birds and beasts. But she wove with marvelous skill; the creatures seemed to breathe and speak, yet it was all as fine as the gossamer that you find on the grass before rain.

Athena herself was amazed. Not even her wrath at the girl's insolence could wholly overcome her wonder. For an instant she stood entranced; then she tore the web across, and three times she touched Arachne's forehead with her spindle.

"Live on, Arachne," she said. "And since it is your glory to weave, you and yours must weave forever." So saying, she sprinkled upon the maiden a certain magical potion.

Away went Arachne's beauty; then her very human form shrank to that of a spider, and so remained. As a spider she spent all her days weaving and weaving; and you may see something like her handiwork any day among the rafters.

PYGMALION AND GALATEA

By Josephine Preston Peabody

THE island of Cyprus was dear to the heart of Venus.
There her temples were kept with honor, and
there, some say, she watched with the Loves and Graces
over the long enchanted sleep of Adonis. This youth,
a hunter whom she had dearly loved, had died of a
wound from the tusk of a wild boar; but the bitter grief
of Venus had won over even the powers of Hades. For
six months of every year, Adonis had to live as a Shade
in the world of the dead; but for the rest of time he was
free to breathe the upper air. Here in Cyprus the people came to worship him as a god, for the sake of Venus
who loved him; and here, if any called upon her, she
was like to listen.

Now there once lived in Cyprus a young sculptor,
Pygmalion by name, who thought nothing on earth so
beautiful as the white marble folk that live without
faults and never grow old. Indeed, he said that he would
never marry a mortal woman, and people began to think
that his daily life among marble creatures was hardening his heart altogether.

But it chanced that Pygmalion fell to work upon an
ivory statue of a maiden, so lovely that it must have
moved to envy every breathing creature that came to
look upon it. With a happy heart the sculptor wrought

day by day, giving it all the beauty of his dreams, until, when the work was completed, he felt powerless to leave it. He was bound to it by the tie of his highest aspiration, his most perfect ideal, his most patient work.

Day after day the ivory maiden looked down at him silently, and he looked back at her until he felt that he loved her more than anything else in the world. He thought of her no longer as a statue, but as the dear companion of his life; and the whim grew upon him like an enchantment. He named her Galatea, and arrayed her like a princess; he hung jewels about her neck, and made all his home beautiful and fit for such a presence.

Now the festival of Venus was at hand, and Pygmalion, like all who loved Beauty, joined the worshipers. In the temple victims were offered, solemn rites were held, and votaries from many lands came to pray the favor of the goddess. At length Pygmalion himself approached the altar and made his prayer.

"Goddess," he said, "who hast vouchsafed to me this gift of beauty, give me a perfect love, likewise, and let me have for bride, one like my ivory maiden." And Venus heard.

Home to his house of dreams went the sculptor, loath to be parted for a day from his statue, Galatea. There she stood, looking down upon him silently, and he looked back at her. Surely the sunset had shed a flush of life upon her whiteness.

He drew near in wonder and delight, and felt, instead of the chill air that was wont to wake him out of his spell, a gentle warmth around her, like the breath of a plant. He touched her hand, and it yielded like the hand of one living! Doubting his senses, yet fearing to reassure himself, Pygmalion kissed the statue.

In an instant the maiden's face bloomed like a waking rose, her hair shone golden as returning sunlight; she lifted her ivory eyelids and smiled at him. The statue herself had awakened, and she stepped down from the pedestal, into the arms of her creator, alive! There was a dream that came true.

ATALANTA'S RACE

By Josephine Preston Peabody

EVEN if Prince Meleager had lived, it is doubtful if he could ever have won Atalanta to be his wife. The maiden was resolved to live unwed, and at last she devised a plan to be rid of all her suitors. She was known far and wide as the swiftest runner of her time; and so she said that she would only marry that man who could outstrip her in the race, but that all who dared to try and failed must be put to death.

This threat did not dishearten all of the suitors, however, and to her grief, for she was not cruel, they held her to her promise. On a certain day the few bold men who were to try their fortune made ready, and chose young Hippomenes as judge. He sat watching them before the word was given, and sadly wondered that any brave man should risk his life merely to win a bride. But when Atalanta stood ready for the contest, he was amazed by her beauty. She looked like Hebe, goddess of young health, who is a glad serving-maiden to the gods when they sit at feast.

The signal was given, and, as she and the suitors darted away, flight made her more enchanting than ever. Just as a wind brings sparkles to the water and laughter to the trees, haste fanned her loveliness to a glow.

Alas for the suitors! She ran as if Hermes had lent her his winged sandals. The young men, skilled as they were, grew heavy with weariness and despair. For all their efforts, they seemed to lag like ships in a calm, while Atalanta flew before them in some favoring breeze — and reached the goal!

To the sorrow of all on-lookers, the suitors were led away; but the judge himself, Hippomenes, rose and begged leave to try his fortune. As Atalanta listened, and looked at him, her heart was filled with pity, and she would willingly have let him win the race to save him from defeat and death; for he was comely and younger than the others. But her friends urged her to rest and make ready, and she consented, with an unwilling heart.

Meanwhile Hippomenes prayed within himself to Venus: "Goddess of Love, give ear, and send me good speed. Let me be swift to win as I have been swift to love her."

Now Venus, who was not far off, — for she had already moved the heart of Hippomenes to love, — came to his side invisibly, slipped into his hand three wondrous golden apples, and whispered a word of counsel in his ear.

The signal was given; youth and maiden started over the course. They went so like the wind that they left not a footprint. The people cheered on Hippomenes, eager that such valor should win. But the course was long, and soon fatigue seemed to clutch at his throat, the light shook before his eyes, and, even as he pressed on, the maiden passed him by.

THE SIGNAL WAS GIVEN, AND AS SHE AND THE SUITORS DARTED
AWAY FLIGHT MADE HER MORE ENCHANTING THAN EVER. JUST
AS A WIND BRINGS SPARKLES TO THE WATER AND LAUGHTER
TO THE TREES, HASTE FANNED HER LOVELINESS TO A GLOW

At that instant Hippomenes tossed ahead one of the golden apples. The rolling bright thing caught Atalanta's eye, and full of wonder she stooped to pick it up. Hippomenes ran on. As he heard the flutter of her tunic close behind him, he flung aside another golden apple, and another moment was lost to the girl. Who could pass by such a marvel? The goal was near and Hippomenes was ahead, but once again Atalanta caught up with him, and they sped side by side like two dragonflies. For an instant his heart failed him; then, with a last prayer to Venus, he flung down the last apple. The maiden glanced at it, wavered, and would have left it where it had fallen, had not Venus turned her head for a second and given her a sudden wish to possess it. Against her will she turned to pick up the golden apple, and Hippomenes touched the goal.

So he won that perilous maiden; and as for Atalanta, she was glad to marry such a valorous man. By this time she understood so well what it was like to be pursued, that she had lost a little of her pleasure in hunting.

CUPID AND PSYCHE

By Josephine Preston Peabody

ONCE upon a time, through that Destiny that overrules the gods, Love himself gave up his immortal heart to a mortal maiden. And thus it came to pass.

There was a certain king who had three beautiful daughters. The two elder married princes of great renown; but Psyche, the youngest, was so radiantly fair that no suitor seemed worthy of her. People thronged to see her pass through the city, and sang hymns in her praise, while strangers took her for the very goddess of beauty herself.

This angered Venus, and she resolved to cast down her earthly rival. One day, therefore, she called hither her son Love (Cupid, some name him), and bade him sharpen his weapons. He is an archer more to be dreaded than Apollo, for Apollo's arrows take life, but Love's bring joy or sorrow for a whole life long.

"Come, Love," said Venus. "There is a mortal maid who robs me of my honors in yonder city. Avenge your mother. Wound this precious Psyche, and let her fall in love with some churlish creature mean in the eyes of all men."

Cupid made ready his weapons, and flew down to earth invisibly. At that moment Psyche was asleep in her chamber; but he touched her heart with his golden arrow of love, and she opened her eyes so suddenly that he started (forgetting that he was invisible), and wounded himself with his own shaft. Heedless of the hurt, moved only by the loveliness of the maiden, he hastened to pour over her locks the healing joy that he ever kept by him, undoing all his work. Back to her dream the princess went, unshadowed by any thought of love. But Cupid, not so light of heart, returned to the heavens, saying not a word of what had passed.

Venus waited long; then, seeing that Psyche's heart had somehow escaped love, she sent a spell upon the maiden. From that time, lovely as she was, not a suitor came to woo; and her parents, who desired to see her a queen at least, made a journey to the Oracle, and asked counsel.

Said the voice: "The princess Psyche shall never wed a mortal. She shall be given to one who waits for her on yonder mountain; he overcomes gods and men."

At this terrible sentence the poor parents were half distraught, and the people gave themselves up to grief at the fate in store for their beloved princess. Psyche alone bowed to her destiny. "We have angered Venus unwittingly," she said, "and all for sake of me, heedless maiden that I am! Give me up, therefore, dear father and mother. If I atone, it may be that the city will prosper once more."

So she besought them, until, after many unavailing denials, the parents consented; and with a great company of people they led Psyche up the mountain,— as an offering to the monster of whom the Oracle had spoken, — and left her there alone.

Full of courage, yet in a secret agony of grief, she watched her kindred and her people wind down the mountain-path, too sad to look back, until they were lost to sight. Then, indeed, she wept, but a sudden breeze drew near, dried her tears, and caressed her hair, seeming to murmur comfort. In truth, it was Zephyr, the kindly West Wind, come to befriend her; and as she took heart, feeling some benignant presence, he lifted her in his arms, and carried her on wings as even as a sea-gull's, over the crest of the fateful mountain and into a valley below. There he left her, resting on a bank of hospitable grass, and there the princess fell asleep.

When she awoke, it was near sunset. She looked about her for some sign of the monster's approach; she wondered, then, if her grievous trial had been but a dream. Near by she saw a sheltering forest, whose young trees seemed to beckon as one maid beckons to another; and eager for the protection of the dryads, she went thither.

The call of running waters drew her farther and farther, till she came out upon an open place, where there was a wide pool. A fountain fluttered gladly in the midst of it, and beyond there stretched a white palace wonderful to see. Coaxed by the bright promise of the place, she drew near, and, seeing no one, entered softly. It was all kinglier than her father's home, and as she stood in wonder and awe, soft airs stirred about her. Little by little the silence grew murmurous like the woods, and one voice, sweeter than the rest, took words. "All that you see is yours, gentle high princess," it said. "Fear nothing; only command us, for we are here to serve you."

Full of amazement and delight, Psyche followed the voice from hall to hall, and through the lordly rooms, beautiful with everything that could delight a young princess. No pleasant thing was lacking. There was even a pool, brightly tiled and fed with running waters, where she bathed her weary limbs; and after she had put on the new and beautiful raiment that lay ready for her, she sat down to break her fast, waited upon and sung to by the unseen spirits.

Surely he whom the Oracle had called her husband was no monster, but some beneficent power, invisible like all the rest. When daylight waned he came, and his voice, the beautiful voice of a god, inspired her to trust her strange destiny and to look and long for his return. Often she begged him to stay with her through the day, that she might see his face; but this he would not grant.

"Never doubt me, dearest Psyche," said he. "Perhaps you would fear if you saw me, and love is all I ask. There is a necessity that keeps me hidden now. Only believe."

So for many days Psyche was content; but when she grew used to happiness, she thought once more of her parents mourning her as lost, and of her sisters, who shared the lot of mortals while she lived as a goddess. One night she told her husband of these regrets, and begged that her sisters at least might come to see her. He sighed, but did not refuse.

"Zephyr shall bring them hither," said he. And

on the following morning, swift as a bird, the West Wind came over the crest of the high mountain and down into the enchanted valley, bearing her two sisters.

They greeted Psyche with joy and amazement, hardly knowing how they had come hither. But when this fairest of the sisters led them through her palace and showed them all the treasures that were hers, envy grew in their hearts and choked their old love. Even while they sat at feast with her, they grew more and more bitter; and hoping to find some little flaw in her good fortune, they asked a thousand questions.

"Where is your husband?" said they. "And why is he not here with you?"

"Ah," stammered Psyche. "All the day long — he is gone, hunting upon the mountains."

"But what does he look like?" they asked; and Psyche could find no answer.

When they learned that she had never seen him, they laughed her faith to scorn.

"Poor Psyche," they said. "You are walking in a dream. Wake, before it is too late. Have you forgotten what the Oracle decreed, — that you were destined for a dreadful creature, the fear of gods and men? And are you deceived by this show of kindliness? We have come to warn you. The people told us, as we came over the mountain, that your husband is a dragon, who feeds you well for the present, that he may feast the better, some day soon. What is it that you trust? Good words! But only take a dagger some night, and when the monster is asleep go, light a lamp, and look at him.

You can put him to death easily, and all his riches will be yours — and ours."

Psyche heard this wicked plan with horror. Nevertheless, after her sisters were gone, she brooded over what they had said, not seeing their evil intent; and she came to find some wisdom in their words. Little by little, suspicion ate, like a moth, into her lovely mind; and at nightfall, in shame and fear, she hid a lamp and a dagger in her chamber. Towards midnight, when her husband was fast asleep, up she rose, hardly daring to breathe; and coming softly to his side, she uncovered the lamp to see some horror.

But there the youngest of the gods lay sleeping, — most beautiful, most irresistible of all immortals. His hair shone golden as the sun, his face was radiant as dear Springtime, and from his shoulders sprang two rainbow wings.

Poor Psyche was overcome with self-reproach. As she leaned towards him, filled with worship, her trembling hands held the lamp ill, and some burning oil fell upon Love's shoulder and awakened him.

He opened his eyes, to see at once his bride and the dark suspicion in her heart.

"O doubting Psyche!" he exclaimed with sudden grief, — and then he flew away, out of the window.

Wild with sorrow, Psyche tried to follow, but she fell to the ground instead. When she recovered her senses, she stared about her. She was alone, and the place was beautiful no longer. Garden and palace had vanished with Love.

THE TRIAL OF PSYCHE

By Josephine Preston Peabody

OVER mountains and valleys Psyche journeyed alone until she came to the city where her two envious sisters lived with the princes whom they had married. She stayed with them only long enough to tell the story of her unbelief and its penalty. Then she set out again to search for Love.

As she wandered one day, travel-worn but not hopeless, she saw a lofty palace on a hill near by, and she turned her steps thither. The place seemed deserted. Within the hall she saw no human being, — only heaps of grain, loose ears of corn half torn from the husk, wheat and barley, alike scattered in confusion on the floor. Without delay, she set to work binding the sheaves together and gathering the scattered ears of corn in seemly wise, as a princess would wish to see them. While she was in the midst of her task, a voice startled her, and she looked up to behold Demeter herself, the goddess of the harvest, smiling upon her with good will.

"Dear Psyche," said Demeter, "you are worthy of happiness, and you may find it yet. But since you have displeased Venus, go to her and ask her favor. Perhaps your patience will win her pardon."

These motherly words gave Psyche heart, and she

reverently took leave of the goddess and set out for the temple of Venus. Most humbly she offered up her prayer, but Venus could not look at her earthly beauty without anger.

"Vain girl," said she, "perhaps you have come to make amends for the wound you dealt your husband; you shall do so. Such clever people can always find work!"

Then she led Psyche into a great chamber heaped high with mingled grain, beans, and lintels (the food of her doves), and bade her separate them all and have them ready in seemly fashion by night. Heracles would have been helpless before such a vexatious task; and poor Psyche, left alone in this desert of grain, had not courage to begin. But even as she sat there, a moving thread of black crawled across the floor from a crevice in the wall; and bending nearer, she saw that a great army of ants in columns had come to her aid. The zealous little creatures worked in swarms, with such industry over the work they like best, that, when Venus came at night, she found the task completed.

"Deceitful girl," she cried, shaking the roses out of her hair with impatience, "this is my son's work, not yours. But he will soon forget you. Eat this black bread if you are hungry, and refresh your dull mind with sleep. To-morrow you will need more wit."

Psyche wondered what new misfortune could be in store for her. But when morning came, Venus led her to the brink of a river, and, pointing to the wood across the water, said, "Go now to yonder grove, where the sheep with the golden fleece are wont to browse.

Bring me a golden lock from every one of them, or you must go your way and never come back again."

This seemed not difficult, and Psyche obediently bade the goddess farewell, and stepped into the water, ready to wade across. But as Venus disappeared, the reeds sang louder and the nymphs of the river, looking up sweetly, blew bubbles to the surface and murmured: "Nay, nay, have a care, Psyche. This flock has not the gentle ways of sheep. While the sun burns aloft, they are themselves as fierce as flame; but when the shadows are long, they go to rest and sleep, under the trees; and you may cross the river without fear and pick the golden fleece off the briers in the pasture."

Thanking the water-creatures, Psyche sat down to rest near them, and when the time came, she crossed in safety and followed their counsel. By twilight she returned to Venus with her arms full of shining fleece.

"No mortal wit did this," said Venus angrily. "But if you care to prove your readiness, go now, with this little box, down to Proserpina and ask her to enclose in it some of her beauty, for I have grown pale in caring for my wounded son."

It needed not the last taunt to sadden Psyche. She knew that it was not for mortals to go into Hades and return alive; and feeling that Love had forsaken her, she was minded to accept her doom as soon as might be.

But even as she hastened towards the descent, another friendly voice detained her. "Stay, Psyche, I know your grief. Only give ear and you shall learn a safe way through all these trials." And the voice went on to tell her how one might avoid all the dangers of

Hades and come out unscathed. (But such a secret could not pass from mouth to mouth, with the rest of the story.)

"And be sure," added the voice, "when Proserpina has returned the box, not to open it, however much you may long to do so."

Psyche gave heed, and by this device, whatever it was, she found her way into Hades safely, and made her errand known to Proserpina, and was soon in the upper world again, wearied but hopeful.

"Surely Love has not forgotten me," she said. "But humbled as I am and worn with toil, how shall I ever please him? Venus can never need all the beauty in this casket; and since I use it for Love's sake, it must be right to take some." So saying, she opened the box, heedless as Pandora! The spells and potions of Hades are not for mortal maids, and no sooner had she inhaled the strange aroma than she fell down like one dead, quite overcome.

But it happened that Love himself was recovered from his wound, and he had secretly fled from his chamber to seek out and rescue Psyche. He found her lying by the wayside; he gathered into the casket what remained of the philter, and awoke his beloved.

"Take comfort," he said, smiling. "Return to our mother and do her bidding till I come again."

Away he flew; and while Psyche went cheerily homeward, he hastened up to Olympus, where all the gods sat feasting, and begged them to intercede for him with his angry mother.

They heard his story and their hearts were touched.

Zeus himself coaxed Venus with kind words till at last she relented, and remembered that anger hurt her beauty, and smiled once more. All the younger gods were for welcoming Psyche at once, and Hermes was sent to bring her hither. The maiden came, a shy new-comer among those bright creatures. She took the cup that Hebe held out to her, drank the divine ambrosia, and became immortal.

Light came to her face like moonrise, two radiant wings sprang from her shoulders; and even as a butterfly bursts from its dull cocoon, so the human Psyche blossomed into immortality.

Love took her by the hand, and they were never parted any more.

MYTHS OF SCANDINAVIA

THE GIANT BUILDER

By Abbie Farwell Brown

AGES and ages ago, when the world was first made, the gods decided to build a beautiful city high above the heavens, the most glorious and wonderful city that ever was known. Asgard was to be its name, and it was to stand on Ida Plain under the shade of Yggdrasil, the great tree whose roots were underneath the earth.

First of all they built a house with a silver roof, where there were seats for all the twelve chiefs. In the midst, and high above the rest, was the wonder-throne of Odin the All-Father, whence he could see everything that happened in the sky or on the earth or in the sea. Next they made a fair house for Queen Frigg and her lovely daughters. Then they built a smithy, with its great hammers, tongs, anvils, and bellows, where the gods could work at their favorite trade, the making of beautiful things out of gold; which they did so well that folk name that time the Golden Age. Afterwards, as they had more leisure, they built separate houses for all the Æsir, each more beautiful than the preceding, for of course they were continually growing more skillful. They saved Father Odin's palace until the last, for they meant this to be the largest and the most splendid of all.

Gladsheim, the home of joy, was the name of Odin's

253

house, and it was built all of gold, set in the midst of a wood whereof the trees had leaves of ruddy gold,—like an autumn-gilded forest. For the safety of All-Father it was surrounded by a roaring river and by a high picket fence; and there was a great courtyard within.

The glory of Gladsheim was its wondrous hall, radiant with gold, the most lovely room that time has ever seen. Valhalla, the Hall of Heroes, was the name of it, and it was roofed with the mighty shields of warriors. The ceiling was made of interlacing spears, and there was a portal at the west end before which hung a great gray wolf, while over him a fierce eagle hovered. The hall was so huge that it had 540 gates, through each of which 800 men could march abreast. Indeed, there needed to be room, for this was the hall where every morning Odin received all the brave warriors who had died in battle on the earth below; and there were many heroes in those days.

This was the reward which the gods gave to courage. When a hero had gloriously lost his life, the Valkyries, the nine warrior daughters of Odin, brought his body up to Valhalla on their white horses that gallop the clouds. There they lived forever after in happiness, enjoying the things that they had most loved upon earth. Every morning they armed themselves and went out to fight with one another in the great courtyard. It was a wondrous game, wondrously played. No matter how often a hero was killed, he became alive again in time to return perfectly well to Valhalla, where he ate a delicious breakfast with the Æsir; while the beautiful Valkyries who had first brought him thither waited at table and poured the blessed mead, which only the immortal taste. A happy life it was for the heroes, and a happy life for all who dwelt in Asgard; for this was before trouble had come among the gods, following the mischief of Loki.

This is how the trouble began. From the beginning of time, the giants had been unfriendly to the Æsir, because the giants were older and huger and more wicked; besides, they were jealous because the good Æsir were fast gaining more wisdom and power than the giants had ever known. It was the Æsir who set the fair brother and sister, Sun and Moon, in the sky to give light to men; and it was they also who made the jeweled stars out of sparks from the place of fire. The giants hated the Æsir, and tried all in their power to injure them and the men of the earth below, whom the Æsir loved and cared for. The gods had already built a wall around Midgard, the world of men, to keep the giants out; built it of the bushy eyebrows of Ymir, the oldest and hugest of giants. Between Asgard and the giants flowed Ifing, the great river on which ice never formed, and which the gods crossed on the rainbow bridge. But this was not protection enough. Their beautiful new city needed a fortress.

So the word went forth in Asgard, "We must build us a fortress against the giants; the hugest, strongest, finest fortress that ever was built."

Now one day, soon after they had announced this decision, there came a mighty man stalking up the rainbow bridge that led to Asgard city.

"Who goes there!" cried Heimdal, the watchman,

whose eyes were so keen that he could see for a hundred miles around, and whose ears were so sharp that he could hear the grass growing in the meadow and the wool on the backs of the sheep. "Who goes there! No one can enter Asgard if I say no."

"I am a builder," said the stranger, who was a huge fellow with sleeves rolled up to show the iron muscles of his arms. "I am a builder of strong towers, and I have heard that the folk of Asgard need one to help them raise a fair fortress in their city."

Heimdal looked at the stranger narrowly, for there was that about him which his sharp eyes did not like. But he made no answer, only blew on his golden horn, which was so loud that it sounded through all the world. At this signal all the Æsir came running to the rainbow bridge, from wherever they happened to be, to find out who was coming to Asgard. For it was Heimdal's duty ever to warn them of the approach of the unknown.

"This fellow says he is a builder," quoth Heimdal. "And he would fain build us a fortress in the city."

"Ay, that I would," nodded the stranger. "Look at my iron arm; look at my broad back; look at my shoulders. Am I not the workman you need?"

"Truly, he is a mighty figure," vowed Odin, looking at him approvingly. "How long will it take you alone to build our fortress? We can allow but one stranger at a time within our city, for safety's sake."

"In three half-years," replied the stranger, "I will undertake to build for you a castle so strong that not even the giants, should they swarm hither over Midgard, — not even they could enter without your leave."

"Aha!" cried Father Odin, well pleased at this offer. "And what reward do you ask, friend, for help so timely?"

The stranger hummed and hawed and pulled his long beard while he thought. Then he spoke suddenly, as if the idea had just come into his mind. "I will name my price, friends," he said; "a small price for so great a deed. I ask you to give me Freia for my wife, and those two sparkling jewels, the Sun and Moon."

At this demand the gods looked grave, for Freia was their dearest treasure. She was the most beautiful maid who ever lived, the light and life of heaven, and if she should leave Asgard, joy would go with her; while the Sun and Moon were the light and life of the Æsir's children, men, who lived in the little world below. But Loki the sly whispered that they would be safe enough if they made another condition on their part, so hard that the builder could not fulfill it. After thinking cautiously, he spoke for them all.

"Mighty man," quoth he, "we are willing to agree to your price — upon one condition. It is too long a time that you ask; we cannot wait three half-years for our castle; that is equal to three centuries when one is in a hurry. See that you finish the fort without help in one winter, one short winter, and you shall have fair Freia with the Sun and Moon. But if, on the first day of summer, one stone is wanting to the walls, or if any one has given you aid in the building, then your reward is lost, and you shall depart without payment." So spoke Loki, in the name of all the gods; but the plan was his own.

At first the stranger shook his head and frowned, saying that in so short a time no one unaided could complete the undertaking. At last he made another offer. "Let me have but my good horse to help me, and I will try," he urged. "Let me bring the useful Svadilföri with me to the task, and I will finish the work in one winter of short days, or lose my reward. Surely, you will not deny me this little help, from one four-footed friend."

Then again the Æsir consulted, and the wiser of them were doubtful whether it were best to accept the stranger's offer so strangely made. But again Loki urged them to accept. "Surely, there is no harm," he said. "Even with his old horse to help him, he cannot build the castle in the promised time. We shall gain a fortress without trouble and with never a price to pay."

Loki was so eager that, although the other Æsir did not like this crafty way of making bargains, they finally consented. Then in the presence of the heroes, with the Valkyries and Mimer's head for witnesses, the stranger and the Æsir gave solemn promise that the bargain should be kept.

On the first day of winter the strange builder began his work, and wondrous was the way he set about it. His strength seemed as the strength of a hundred men. As for his horse Svadilföri, he did more work by half than even the mighty builder. In the night he dragged the enormous rocks that were to be used in building the castle, rocks as big as mountains of the earth; while in the daytime the stranger piled them into place with his iron arms. The Æsir watched him with amazement;

never was seen such strength in Asgard. Neither Tyr the stout nor Thor the strong could match the power of the stranger. The gods began to look at one another uneasily. Who was this mighty one who had come among them, and what if after all he should win his reward? Freia trembled in her palace, and the Sun and Moon grew dim with fear.

Still the work went on, and the fort was piling higher and higher, by day and by night. There were but three days left before the end of winter, and already the building was so tall and so strong that it was safe from the attacks of any giant. The Æsir were delighted with their fine new castle; but their pride was dimmed by the fear that it must be paid for at all too costly a price. For only the gateway remained to be completed, and unless the stranger should fail to finish that in the next three days, they must give him Freia with the Sun and Moon.

The Æsir held a meeting upon Ida Plain, a meeting full of fear and anger. At last they realized what they had done, — they had made a bargain with one of the giants, their enemies; and if he won the prize, it would mean sorrow and darkness in heaven and upon earth. "How did we happen to agree to so mad a bargain?" they asked one another. "Who suggested the wicked plan which bids fair to cost us all that we most cherish?" Then they remembered that it was Loki who had made the plan; it was he who had insisted that it be carried out; and they blamed him for all the trouble.

"It is your counsels, Loki, that have brought this danger upon us," quoth Father Odin, frowning. "You chose the way of guile, which is not our way. It now remains for you to help us by guile, if you can. But if you cannot save for us Freia and the Sun and Moon, you shall die. This is my word." All the other Æsir agreed that this was just. Thor alone was away hunting evil demons at the other end of the world, so he did not know what was going on, and what dangers were threatening Asgard.

Loki was much frightened at the word of All-Father. "It was my fault," he cried, "but how was I to know that he was a giant? He had disguised himself so that he seemed but a strong man. And as for his horse,— it looks much like that of other folk. If it were not for the horse, he could not finish the work. Ha! I have a thought! The builder shall not finish the gate; the giant shall not receive his payment. I will cheat the fellow."

Now it was the last night of winter, and there remained but a few stones to put in place on the top of the wondrous gateway. The giant was sure of his prize, and chuckled to himself as he went out with his horse to drag the remaining stones; for he did not know that the Æsir had guessed at last who he was, and that Loki was plotting to outwit him. Hardly had he gone to work when out of the wood came running a pretty little mare, who neighed to Svadilföri as if inviting the tired horse to leave his work and come to the green fields for a holiday.

Svadilföri, you must remember, had been working hard all winter, with never a sight of four-footed creature of his kind, and he was very lonesome and tired of dragging stones. Giving a snort of disobedience, off he ran after this new friend towards the grassy meadows. Off went the giant after him, howling with rage, and running for dear life, as he saw not only his horse but his chance of success slipping out of reach. It was a mad chase, and all Asgard thundered with the noise of galloping hoofs and the giant's mighty tread. The mare who raced ahead was Loki in disguise, and he led Svadilföri far out of reach, to a hidden meadow that he knew; so that the giant howled and panted up and down all night long, without catching even a sight of his horse.

Now when the morning came the gateway was still unfinished, and night and winter had ended at the same hour. The giant's time was over, and he had forfeited his reward. The Æsir came flocking to the gateway, and how they laughed and triumphed when they found three stones wanting to complete the gate!

"You have failed, fellow," judged Father Odin sternly, "and no price shall we pay for work that is still undone. You have failed. Leave Asgard quickly; we have seen all we want of you and of your race."

Then the giant knew that he was discovered, and he was mad with rage. "It was a trick!" he bellowed, assuming his own proper form, which was huge as a mountain, and towered high beside the fortress that he had built. "It was a wicked trick. You shall pay for this in one way or another. I cannot tear down the castle which, ungrateful ones, I have built you, stronger than the strength of any giant. But I will demolish the rest of your shining city!" Indeed, he would have done so in his mighty rage; but at this moment Thor, whom Heimdal had called from the end of the earth by one blast of the golden horn, came rushing to the rescue, drawn in his chariot of goats. Thor jumped to the ground close beside the giant, and before that huge fellow knew what had happened, his head was rolling upon the ground at Father Odin's feet; for with one blow Thor had put an end to the giant's wickedness and had saved Asgard.

"This is the reward you deserve!" Thor cried. "Not Freia nor the Sun and Moon, but the death that I have in store for all the enemies of the Æsir."

In this extraordinary way the noble city of Asgard was made safe and complete by the addition of a fortress which no one, not even the giant who built it, could injure, it was so wonder-strong. But always at the top of the gate were lacking three great stones that no one was mighty enough to lift. This was a reminder to the Æsir that now they had the race of giants for their everlasting enemies. And though Loki's trick had saved them Freia, and for the world the Sun and Moon, it was the beginning of trouble in Asgard which lasted as long as Loki lived to make mischief with his guile.

THOR'S ADVENTURES AMONG THE JÖTUNS

By Julia Goddard

ONCE upon a time Thor set out upon his travels, taking Loki with him, for despite Loki's spirit of mischief he often aided Thor, who doubtless, in the present expedition, felt that Loki might be of use to him.

So they set off together in Thor's chariot, drawn by the two strong he-goats, and as night drew nigh, stopped at the hut of a peasant, where they asked food and shelter.

"Food I have none to give you," said the peasant. "I am a poor man and not able even to give supper to my children, but if you like to rest under my roof you are welcome to do so."

"Never mind the food; I can manage that," said Thor, dismounting from the chariot and entering the hut.

It was a poor place, and not at all fitted to receive one of the Asi, but Thor was glad enough to meet with it, wretched as it was.

"You can kill the goats," said he; "they will make us an excellent meal."

The peasant could not help thinking that it was a pity to kill two such fine animals; but wisely thinking that this was no affair of his, and that the stranger had a right to do as he pleased with his own, he set himself to obey Thor's orders, and with the help of his daughter Raska soon spread a savory repast before the hungry god and his attendant.

"Sit down, all of you," said Thor; "there is enough and to spare."

So they all sat down, and the peasant and his children shared a more plentiful meal than had fallen to their lot lately. Thor and Loki also did ample justice to the food, and when supper was over the thunder-god bade the peasant gather the bones and place them in the goatskins, and making them into a bundle he left them on the floor until the next morning.

When the morning came and the early sun shone in through the crevices, Thor raised his hammer, and instead of the bundle of bones the peasant and his son and daughter saw the two goats standing as fresh and lively as if nothing had happened to them, saving that one of them halted a little in his walk.

When they sought to learn why this should be, it was found that Thialfe, the boy, in getting the marrow out of one of the bones, had broken it, and it was this that caused the goat to go lame.

Thor was very angry, and was very near killing not only Thialfe but also the peasant and his daughter Raska, but they begged so hard for their lives that he consented to spare them on condition that the boy and girl should follow him in his travels.

To this they agreed, and Thor, leaving the chariot and goats in the peasant's care, went on his journey, giving Thialfe, who was a very swift runner, his wallet to carry.

On and on they journeyed until they came to a great sea.

"How are we to get over this?" asked Loki.

"Swim across it," replied Thor.

And in they all plunged, for Thialfe and Raska were used to a hardy life, and so were able to swim with scarcely more weariness than Thor and Loki, and were not long in reaching the opposite shore.

"The country does not improve," said Loki, looking round upon the desolate plain that lay outstretched between them and the borders of a dark forest, which they could just see in the far distance. One or two huge rocks thrust their jagged points high into the air, and great blocks of stone were scattered about, but there was no sign of herbage and not a tree to be seen nearer than the forest belt bounding the horizon. Heavy gray clouds were drawing nearer and nearer to the dreary earth, and twilight was fast approaching. "It looks not well, in good sooth," answered Thor, "but we must push on and perhaps may find it better as we go onward. Besides, night is drawing nigh, and as there are no dwellings to be seen we must try to gain the shelter of the forest before it is too dark to see where we are going."

So they pushed on, and though they looked to the right hand and to the left, soon found that they were in a land where no men lived. There was, therefore, nothing to be done but to quicken their speed, in order to reach the shelter of the forest. But though they strove to the utmost, the twilight deepened into darkness and the darkness became so deep by the time they reached the forest, that they only knew they had arrived there by Loki's striking his head against a low branch, and soon after this Thor cried out, —

"Good luck! I have found a house. Follow close after me and we will make ourselves comfortable for the night."

For Thor in groping along had come to what he supposed to be a wall of solid masonry.

"Where are you?" asked Loki, "for it is so dark that I cannot see you."

"Here," answered Thor, stretching out his hand; "take hold and follow me."

So Loki clutched Thor's arm, and Thialfe in turn seized the arm of Loki, whilst Raska clung to her brother and wished herself safe at home in her father's hut.

And thus they groped their way along the wall, seeking to find an entrance to the house.

At last Thor found a huge entrance opening into a wide hall, and passing through this they turned to the left into a large room which was quite empty, and here, after eating some food, they stretched themselves upon the hard floor and wearied out with the day's march, soon fell asleep.

But they did not sleep long. Their slumbers were broken by a rumbling sound as of a coming earthquake; the walls of the house shook, and peals of thunder echoed through the lofty chamber.

Thor sprang up. "We are scarcely safe here," he

said; "let us seek some other room." Loki jumpe
up speedily, as did also Thialfe and Raska, who were
in a great fright, wondering what dreadful thing was
going to happen to them. They willingly followed
Thor, hoping to find a safer place.

To the right they saw another room like a long gallery with a huge doorway, and into this Loki, Thialfe,
and Raska crept, choosing the farthest corner of it; but
Thor took his stand at the doorway to be on the watch
if any fresh danger should threaten them.

After a somewhat uncomfortable rest, Loki, Thialfe,
and Raska were not sorry to find that the day had
dawned, though as there were no windows in the
house, they only knew it by hearing the cock crow.

Thor was better off, for the doorway was so wide that
the sunlight came pouring in without hindrance. Indeed the huge size of the doorway made Thor think
that the builder must have given up all hope of ever
finding a door large enough to fit into it.

He strolled away from the house, and the first thing
that he saw was a huge giant fast asleep upon the greensward; and now he knew that the thunder that had
so frightened them in the night had been nothing more
or less than the loud snoring of the giant.

So wroth was Thor at the thought that such a thing
should have made him afraid, that he fastened on his
belt of strength and drew his sword and made towards
the giant as though he would kill him on the spot.

But the giant, opening his great round eyes, stared
so steadily at Thor that the god became mazed and could
do nothing but stare in return.

At last, however, he found voice to ask, "What is your name?"

"My name," said the giant, raising himself on one elbow, thereby causing his head to rise so high into the air that Thor thought it was taking flight altogether, "is Skrymner; you, I believe, are the god Thor?"

"I am," answered the god.

"Do you happen to have picked up my glove?" asked the giant carelessly.

Then Thor knew that what he and his companions had taken for a large house was only the giant's glove, and from this we may judge how huge a giant Skrymner must have been.

Thor made no answer, and Skrymner next asked whither Thor was traveling; and when he found that he was journeying to Utgard, offered to bear him company, as he too was going to the same place.

Thor accepted the giant's offer, and after eating a hearty meal, all were ready for another day's march.

Skrymner showed himself a kindly giant, and insisted upon carrying Thor's bag of meal, putting it into his own wallet, which he slung across his broad shoulders.

It must have been a strange sight, indeed, to see the great giant stalking along with his smaller companions at his heels; and we may well marvel how they managed to keep pace with him, or how Thor was able to raise his voice to such a pitch as to reach the giant's ears.

Nevertheless all went well, and they trudged cheerfully along, never flagging in their talk.

Once Skrymner took Raska on his shoulder, but

the height made her so giddy that she was glad to come down again and walk quietly by the side of Thialfe.

When night overtook them they encamped under one of the great oak-trees, for they were not yet out of the bounds of the forest. Skrymner, to judge by his loud snoring, fell asleep the moment he lay down upon the ground, but Thor and his comrades were not so tired as to forget that they had tasted nothing since breakfast time. Accordingly they set to work to open the wallet that Skrymner had given into their hands before closing his eyes.

But it was no easy task, and with all their efforts they failed to open it. Not a knot could they untie, and their fingers were chafed and aching.

Neither were they more able to awaken Skrymner, and Thor's anger waxed exceeding fierce. "You shall pay for this," said he, flinging his hammer at the giant.

Skrymner half opened the eye nearest to Thor, and said in a very sleepy voice, "Why will the leaves drop off the trees?" And then he snored as loudly as before.

Thor picked up his hammer, and approaching nearer drove it into the hinder part of the giant's head, who again, half waking up, muttered, "How troublesome the dust is!"

Thor was exceedingly astonished at this, but thought nevertheless that he would once more make trial of his power; so coming up close to Skrymner he struck with such force as to drive the hammer up to the handle in the giant's cheek.

Then Skrymner opened both eyes, and lazily lifting

his finger to his face said, "I suppose there are birds about, for I fancied I felt a feather fall."

Now was Thor fairly disconcerted; and the next morning, when the giant told him that they must now part, as his road led him another way, he was by no means ill-pleased, and he let Skrymner go without so much as bidding him "good speed." Skrymner, however, seemed not to notice that Thor was glad to be quit of his company, and gave him some very friendly advice before he left him.

"If you will take my advice," said the giant, "you will give up this thought of visiting Utgard. The people there are all giants of greater stature even than I, and they make nothing of little men, such as you are. Nay, more, you yourself are likely to fare but badly amongst them, for I see that you are rather apt to think too much of yourself and to take too much upon you. Be wise whilst there is time, think of what I say, and don't go near the city."

"But I will go there," shouted Thor, almost choked with rage; "I will go in spite of all the Jötuns of Jötunheim. None shall hinder me, and the giants shall see and wonder at the mighty power of the god Thor."

And as he spoke the rising sun fell full upon the city of Utgard, whose huge brazen gates glittered in the sunlight. Even though they were so far away, Thor could see how high they were; and as he drew nearer, their vast size filled him with amazement; but when he reached them his wonder was beyond all words, for he and his companions seemed no larger than grasshoppers, in comparison with their height.

The gates were not open, for it was yet early; so Thor and his comrades crept through the bars, and entered the city. As they passed along the streets the houses were so tall that it was only by crossing to the opposite side of the broad road that they were able to see the windows in the topmost stories. And the streets were so wide that it was quite a journey across them.

Once a mouse darted out of a hole, and Raska screamed, for she thought it was a grisly bear. The mouse also shrieked and made much more noise than Raska, as well it might, for a cat so huge that Thialfe half thought it must be the monster of Midgard seized it, and giving it a pat with one of its paws laid it dead on the pavement.

As for the horses, their hoofs were terrible to look at, and Thialfe and Raska must have climbed up ladders if they wished to see their heads.

The people were quite as large as Skrymner had described, and Thor and his companions were obliged to be very careful lest they should get trodden upon, as it was very doubtful if the people even saw them.

Still Thor walked along with the proud consciousness that he was the god Thor; and feeling that though he was so small he was yet a person of some importance, made his way to the palace, and desired to see the king.

After some little time he and his fellow travelers were ushered into the presence of Utgarda Loke, the king of the country. And Utgarda Loke, hearing the door open, raised his eyes, thinking to see some great courtier enter, but he knew nothing of the bows and greetings of Thor, until happening to cast his eyes to the ground, he saw a little man with his companions saluting him with much ceremony.

The king had never seen such small men before, and there was something so absurd to him in the sight, that he burst out laughing.

And then all the courtiers laughed also, pretending that they had not seen the little creatures before.

It was some time before they all left off laughing, but at length there was a pause, and Thor essayed to make himself heard.

"Though we are but small in comparison with the Jötuns," said he angrily, "we are by no means to be despised, but are gifted with powers that may surprise you."

"Really!" answered Utgarda Loke, raising his eyebrows. And then he and his courtiers laughed louder than before.

At last there was another pause in their merriment, and the king added: "However, we are willing to give the strangers a fair trial in order to prove the truth of what their spokesman, whom I take to be the god Thor, says. How say you? What can this one do?" And he pointed to Loki.

"Please your majesty, I am very great at eating," returned Loki.

"Nay," answered Utgarda Loke, "you must grow a little before you are great at anything."

At which speech the courtiers again shouted with laughter; but Utgarda Loke, turning to his servants, bade them make trial of Loki's powers. So they brought a great trough full of food, and Loki was placed at one end, and a courtier named Loge at the other. They both fell to work to devour what was before them, and met at the middle of the trough. But it was found that whilst Loki had eaten the flesh of his portion, Loge had eaten, not only the flesh, but the bones also. Therefore Loki was, of course, vanquished.

Then Utgarda Loke turned to Thialfe. "And pray, in what may this youth be specially skilled?" he asked.

"I am a swift skater," answered Thialfe.

"Try him," said the king.

And Thialfe was led to a plain of ice, as smooth as glass, and one named Hugr was set to run against him. But though Thialfe was the swiftest skater ever known in the world, yet Hugr glided past him so fleetly that he had returned to the starting-post before Thialfe had done more than a quarter of the distance.

Three times did Thialfe match his speed against Hugr, and, three times beaten, withdrew from the contest as disconsolate as Loki.

"And now may I ask what you can do yourself?" said the king to Thor.

"I can drain a wine-cup with any one," replied the god.

"Try him," said Utgarda Loke.

And forthwith the royal cupbearer presented a drinking-horn to Thor.

"If you are as great as you pretend to be," said the king, "you will drain it at one draught. Some people take two pulls at it, but the weakest among us can manage it in three."

Thor took up the horn, and, being very thirsty, took

a steady pull at it. He thought he had done very well, but on removing it from his lips he marveled to see how little had gone.

A second time he took a draught, but the horn was far from being emptied.

Again a third time he essayed to drain it, but it was full almost to the brim.

Therefore he set it down in despair, and confessed himself unable to drain it.

"I am disappointed in you," said Utgarda Loke; "you are not half the man I took you for. I see it is no use asking you to do warrior's feats; I must try you in a simpler way, in a child's play that we have amongst us. You shall try to lift my cat from the ground."

Thor turned quite scarlet, and then became white with rage.

"Are you afraid?" asked Utgarda Loke; "you look so pale."

And a large gray cat came leaping along, and planted itself firmly before Thor, showing its sharp claws, and glaring upon him with its fiery eyes.

Thor seized it, but in spite of all his efforts he was only able to raise one of the cat's paws from the ground.

"Pooh! pooh!" exclaimed Utgarda Loke, "you are a mere baby, fit only for the nursery. I believe that my old nurse Hela would be more than a match for you. Here, Hela, come and wrestle with the mighty god Thor."

And Utgarda Loke laughed disdainfully.

Forth stepped a decrepit old woman, with lank cheeks and toothless jaws. Her eyes were sunken, her brow furrowed, and her scanty locks were white as snow.

274

She advanced towards Thor, and tried to throw him to the ground; but though he put forth his whole strength to withstand her, he was surprised to find how powerful she was, and that it needed all his efforts to keep his feet. For a long time he was successful, but at length she brought him down upon one knee, and Thor was obliged to acknowledge himself conquered.

Ashamed and mortified, he and his companions withdrew to a lodging for the night, and in the morning were making ready to leave the city quietly, when Utgarda Loke sent for them.

He made them a splendid feast, and afterwards went with them beyond the city gates.

"Now tell me honestly," said he to Thor, "what do you think of your success?"

"I am beyond measure astounded and ashamed," replied the god.

"Ha! ha!" laughed Utgarda Loke. "I knew that you were. However, as we are well out of the city I don't mind telling you a secret or two. Doubtless you will receive a little comfort from my doing so, as you confess that your coming hither has been to no purpose.

"In the first place, you have been deceived by enchantments ever since you came within the borders of Jötunhelm. I am the giant you met with on your way hither, and if I had known as much of your power then as I do now, you would never have found your way within the walls of Utgard.

"Certainly I had had some slight experience of it, for the three blows you gave me would have killed me had they fallen upon me. But it was not I, but a huge mountain that you struck at; and if you visit it again, you will find three valleys cleft in the rocks by the strokes of your hammer.

"As for the wallet, I had fastened it with a magic chain, so that you need not wonder that you could not open it.

"Loge, with whom Loki strove, was no courtier, but a subtle devouring flame that consumed all before it —"

Here Loki uttered an exclamation of delight, but Thor bade him be silent, and Utgarda Loke went on:

"Thialfe's enemy was Hugr, or Thought, and let man work away as hard as he pleases, Thought will still outrun him.

"As for yourself, the end of the drinking-horn, though you did not see it, reached the sea, and as fast as you emptied it, it filled again, so that you never could have drained it dry. But the next time that you stand upon the seashore, you will find how much less the ocean is by your draughts.

"The gray cat was no cat, but the great Serpent of Midgard, that twines round the world, and you lifted him so high that we were all quite frightened.

"But your last feat was the most wonderful of all, for Hela was none other than Death. And never did I see any one before over whom Death had so little power.

"And now, my friend, go your way, and don't come near my city again, for I tell you plainly I do not want you there, and I shall use all kinds of enchantment to keep you out of it."

As he ended his speech, Thor raised his hammer, but Utgarda Loke had vanished.

THOR AMONG THE JÖTUNS

"I will return to the city, and be avenged," said Thor.

But lo! the giant city was nowhere to be seen. A fair pasture-land spread itself out around him, and through its midst a broad river flowed peacefully along.

So Thor and his companions, musing upon their wonderful adventures, turned their steps homeward.

THE QUEST OF THE HAMMER

By Abbie Farwell Brown

ONE morning Thor the Thunderer awoke with a
yawn, and stretching out his knotted arm, felt for
his precious hammer, which he kept always under his
pillow of clouds. But he started up with a roar of rage,
so that all the palace trembled. The hammer was gone!

Now this was a very serious matter, for Thor was
the protector of Asgard, and Miölnir, the magic hammer which the dwarf had made, was his mighty weapon,
of which the enemies of the Æsir stood so much in dread
that they dared not venture near. But if they should
learn that Miölnir was gone, who could tell what danger might not threaten the palaces of heaven?

Thor darted his flashing eye into every corner of
Cloud Land in search of the hammer. He called his
fair wife, Sif of the golden hair, to aid in the search,
and his two lovely daughters, Thrude and Lora. They
hunted and they hunted; they turned Thrudheim upside down, and set the clouds to rolling wonderfully, as
they peeped and pried behind and around and under
each billowy mass. But Miölnir was not to be found.
Certainly, some one had stolen it.

Thor's yellow beard quivered with rage, and his hair
bristled on end like the golden rays of a star, while all
his household trembled.

"It is Loki again!" he cried. "I am sure Loki is at the bottom of this mischief!" For since the time when Thor had captured Loki for the dwarf Brock and had given him over to have his bragging lips sewed up, Loki had looked at him with evil eyes; and Thor knew that the red rascal hated him most of all the gods.

But this time Thor was mistaken. It was not Loki who had stolen the hammer, — he was too great a coward for that. And though he meant, before the end, to be revenged upon Thor, he was waiting until a safe chance should come, when Thor himself might stumble into danger, and Loki need only to help the evil by a malicious word or two; and this chance came later, as you shall hear in another tale.

Meanwhile Loki was on his best behavior, trying to appear very kind and obliging; so when Thor came rumbling and roaring up to him, demanding, "What have you done with my hammer, you thief?" Loki looked surprised, but did not lose his temper nor answer rudely.

"Have you indeed missed your hammer, brother Thor?" he said, mumbling, for his mouth was still sore where Brock had sewed the stitches. "That is a pity; for if the giants hear of this, they will be coming to try their might against Asgard."

"Hush!" muttered Thor, grasping him by the shoulder with his iron fingers. "That is what I fear. But look you, Loki: I suspect your hand in the mischief. Come, confess."

Then Loki protested that he had nothing to do with so wicked a deed. "But," he added wheedlingly, "I think I can guess the thief; and because I love you, Thor, I will help you to find him."

"Humph!" growled Thor. "Much love you bear to me! However, you are a wise rascal, the nimblest wit of all the Æsir, and it is better to have you on my side than on the other, when giants are in the game. Tell me, then: who has robbed the Thunder-Lord of his bolt of power?"

Loki drew near and whispered in Thor's ear. "Look, how the storms rage and the winds howl in the world below! Some one is wielding your thunder-hammer all unskillfully. Can you not guess the thief? Who but Thrym, the mighty giant who has ever been your enemy and your imitator, and whose fingers have long itched to grasp the short handle of mighty Miölnir, that the world may name him Thunder-Lord instead of you. But look! What a tempest! The world will be shattered into fragments unless we soon get the hammer back."

Then Thor roared with rage. "I will seek this impudent Thrym!" he cried. "I will crush him into bits, and teach him to meddle with the weapon of the Æsir!"

"Softly, softly," said Loki, smiling maliciously. "He is a shrewd giant, and a mighty. Even you, great Thor, cannot go to him and pluck the hammer from his hand as one would slip the rattle from a baby's pink fist. Nay, you must use craft, Thor; and it is I who will teach you, if you will be patient."

Thor was a brave, blunt fellow, and he hated the ways of Loki, his lies and his deceit. He liked best the way of warriors, — the thundering charge, the flash of weapons, and the heavy blow; but without the hammer he could not fight the giants hand to hand. Loki's advice seemed wise, and he decided to leave the matter to the Red One.

Loki was now all eagerness, for he loved difficulties which would set his wit in play and bring other folk into danger. "Look, now," he said. "We must go to Freia and borrow her falcon dress. But you must ask; for she loves me so little that she would scarce listen to me."

So first they made their way to Folkvang, the house of maidens, where Freia dwelt, the loveliest of all in Asgard. She was fairer than fair, and sweeter than sweet, and the tears from her flower-eyes made the dew which blessed the earth-flowers night and morning. Of her Thor borrowed the magic dress of feathers in which Freia was wont to clothe herself and flit like a great beautiful bird all about the world. She was willing enough to lend it to Thor when he told her that by its aid he hoped to win back the hammer which he had lost; for she well knew the danger threatening herself and all the Æsir until Miölnir should be found.

"Now will I fetch the hammer for you," said Loki. So he put on the falcon plumage, and, spreading his brown wings, flapped away up, up, over the world, down, down, across the great ocean which lies beyond all things that men know. And he came to the dark country where there was no sunshine nor spring, but it was always dreary winter; where mountains were piled up like blocks of ice, and where great caverns yawned hungrily in blackness. And this was Jötunheim, the land of the Frost Giants.

And lo! when Loki came thereto he found Thrym the Giant King sitting outside his palace cave, playing with his dogs and horses. The dogs were as big as elephants, and the horses were as big as houses, but Thrym himself was as huge as a mountain; and Loki trembled, but he tried to seem brave.

"Good-day, Loki," said Thrym, with the terrible voice of which he was so proud, for he fancied it was as loud as Thor's. "How fares it, feathered one, with your little brothers, the Æsir, in Asgard halls? And how dare you venture alone in this guise to Giant Land?"

"It is an ill day in Asgard," sighed Loki, keeping his eye warily upon the giant, "and a stormy one in the world of men. I heard the winds howling and the storms rushing on the earth as I passed by. Some mighty one has stolen the hammer of our Thor. Is it you, Thrym, greatest of all giants, — greater than Thor himself?"

This the crafty one said to flatter Thrym, for Loki well knew the weakness of those who love to be thought greater than they are.

Then Thrym bridled and swelled with pride, and tried to put on the majesty and awe of noble Thor; but he only succeeded in becoming an ugly, puffy monster.

"Well, yes," he admitted. "I have the hammer that belonged to your little Thor; and now how much of a lord is he?"

"Alack!" sighed Loki again, "weak enough he is without his magic weapon. But you, O Thrym, — surely your mightiness needs no such aid. Give me the hammer, that Asgard may no longer be shaken by Thor's grief for his precious toy."

But Thrym was not so easily to be flattered into parting with his stolen treasure. He grinned a dreadful grin, several yards in width, which his teeth barred like jagged boulders across the entrance to a mountain cavern.

"Miölnir the hammer is mine," he said, "and I am Thunder-Lord, mightiest of the mighty. I have hidden it where Thor can never find it, twelve leagues below the sea-caves, where Queen Ran lives with her daughters, the white-capped Waves. But listen, Loki. Go tell the Æsir that I will give back Thor's hammer. I will give it back upon one condition, — that they send Freia the beautiful to be my wife."

"Freia the beautiful!" Loki had to stifle a laugh. Fancy the Æsir giving their fairest flower to such an ugly fellow as this! But he only said politely, "Ah, yes; you demand our Freia in exchange for the little hammer? It is a costly price, great Thrym. But I will be your friend in Asgard. If I have my way, you shall soon see the fairest bride in all the world knocking at your door. Farewell!"

So Loki whizzed back to Asgard on his falcon wings; and as he went he chuckled to think of the evils which were likely to happen because of his words with Thrym. First he gave the message to Thor, — not sparing of Thrym's insolence, to make Thor angry; and then he went to Freia with the word for her, — not sparing of Thrym's ugliness, to make her shudder. The spiteful fellow!

Now you can imagine the horror that was in Asgard as the Æsir listened to Loki's words. "My hammer!"

roared Thor. "The villain confesses that he has stolen my hammer, and boasts that he is Thunder-Lord! Gr-r-r!"

"The ugly giant!" wailed Freia. "Must I be the bride of that hideous old monster, and live in his gloomy mountain prison all my life?"

"Yes; put on your bridal veil, sweet Freia," said Loki maliciously, "and come with me to Jötunheim. Hang your famous starry necklace about your neck, and don your bravest robe; for in eight days there will be a wedding, and Thor's hammer is to pay."

Then Freia fell to weeping. "I cannot go! I will not go!" she cried. "I will not leave the home of gladness and Father Odin's table to dwell in the land of horrors! Thor's hammer is mighty, but mightier the love of the kind Æsir for their little Freia! Good Odin, dear brother Frey, speak for me! You will not make me go?"

The Æsir looked at her and thought how lonely and bare would Asgard be without her loveliness; for she was fairer than fair, and sweeter than sweet.

"She shall not go!" shouted Frey, putting his arms about his sister's neck.

"No, she shall not go!" cried all the Æsir with one voice.

"But my hammer!" insisted Thor. "I must have Miölnir back again."

"And my word to Thrym," said Loki, "that must be made good."

"You are too generous with your words," said Father Odin sternly, for he knew his brother well.

"Your word is not a gem of great price, for you have made it cheap."

Then spoke Heimdal, the sleepless watchman who sits on guard at the entrance to the rainbow bridge which leads to Asgard; and Heimdal was the wisest of the Æsir, for he could see into the future, and knew how things would come to pass. Through his golden teeth he spoke, for his teeth were all of gold.

"I have a plan," he said. "Let us dress Thor himself like a bride in Freia's robes, and send him to Jötunheim to talk with Thrym and to win back his hammer."

But at this word Thor grew very angry. "What! dress me like a girl!" he roared. "I should never hear the last of it! The Æsir will mock me, and call me 'maiden'! The giants, and even the puny dwarfs, will have a lasting jest upon me! I will not go! I will fight! I will die, if need be! But dressed as a woman I will not go!"

But Loki answered him with sharp words, for this was a scheme after his own heart. "What, Thor!" he said. "Would you lose your hammer and keep Asgard in danger for so small a whim? Look, now: if you go not, Thrym with his giants will come in a mighty army and drive us from Asgard; then he will indeed make Freia his bride, and moreover he will have you for his slave under the power of his hammer. How like you this picture, brother of the thunder? Nay, Heimdal's plan is a good one, and I myself will help to carry it out."

Still Thor hesitated; but Freia came and laid her white hand on his arm, and looked up into his scowling face pleadingly.

"To save me, Thor," she begged. And Thor said he
would go.

Then there was great sport among the Æsir, while
they dressed Thor like a beautiful maiden. Brunhilde
and her sisters, the nine Valkyrie, daughters of Odin,
had the task in hand. How they laughed as they brushed
and curled his yellow hair, and set upon it the wondrous
headdress of silk and pearls! They let out seams, and
they let down hems, and set on extra pieces, to make
it larger, and so they hid his great limbs and knotted
arms under Freia's fairest robe of scarlet; but beneath
it all he would wear his shirt of mail and his belt of
power that gave him double strength. Freia herself
twisted about his neck her famous necklace of starry
jewels, and Queen Frigg, his mother, hung at his girdle
a jingling bunch of keys, such as was the custom for
the bride to wear at Norse weddings. Last of all, that
Thrym might not see Thor's fierce eyes and the yellow
beard, that ill became a maiden, they threw over him
a long veil of silver white which covered him to the
feet. And there he stood, as stately and tall a bride as
even a giant might wish to see; but on his hands he
wore his iron gloves, and they ached for but one thing,
— to grasp the handle of the stolen hammer.

"Ah, what a lovely maid it is!" chuckled Loki; "and
how glad will Thrym be to see this Freia come! Bride
Thor, I will go with you as your handmaiden, for I would
fain see the fun."

"Come, then," said Thor sulkily, for he was ill
pleased, and wore his maiden robes with no good grace.
"It is fitting that you go; for I like not these lies and

maskings, and I may spoil the mummery without you at my elbow."

There was loud laughter above the clouds when Thor, all veiled and dainty seeming, drove away from Asgard to his wedding, with maid Loki by his side. Thor cracked his whip and chirruped fiercely to his twin goats with golden hoofs, for he wanted to escape the sounds of mirth that echoed from the rainbow bridge, where all the Æsir stood watching. Loki, sitting with his hands meekly folded like a girl, chuckled as he glanced up at Thor's angry face; but he said nothing, for he knew it was not good to joke too far with Thor, even when Miölnir was hidden twelve leagues below the sea in Ran's kingdom.

So off they dashed to Jötunheim, where Thrym was waiting and longing for his beautiful bride. Thor's goats thundered along above the sea and land and people far below, who looked up wondering as the noise rolled overhead. "Hear how the thunder rumbles!" they said. "Thor is on a long journey to-night." And a long journey it was, as the tired goats found before they reached the end.

Thrym heard the sound of their approach, for his ear was eager. "Hola!" he cried. "Some one is coming from Asgard, — only one of Odin's children could make a din so fearful. Hasten, men, and see if they are bringing Freia to be my wife."

Then the lookout giant stepped down from the top of his mountain, and said that a chariot was bringing two maidens to the door.

"Run, giants, run!" shouted Thrym, in a fever at

this news. "My bride is coming! Put silken cushions on the benches for a great banquet, and make the house beautiful for the fairest maid in all space! Bring in all my golden-horned cows and my coal-black oxen, that she may see how rich I am, and heap all my gold and jewels about to dazzle her sweet eyes! She shall find me richest of the rich; and when I have her,— fairest of the fair,— there will be no treasure that I lack,— not one!"

The chariot stopped at the gate, and out stepped the tall bride, hidden from head to foot, and her hand-maiden muffled to the chin. "How afraid of catching cold they must be!" whispered the giant ladies, who were peering over one another's shoulders to catch a glimpse of the bride, just as the crowd outside the awning does at a wedding nowadays.

Thrym had sent six splendid servants to escort the maidens: these were the Metal Kings, who served him as lord of them all. There was the Gold King, all in cloth of gold, with fringes of yellow bullion, most glittering to see; and there was the Silver King, almost as gorgeous in a suit of spangled white; and side by side bowed the dark Kings of Iron and Lead, the one mighty in black, the other sullen in blue; and after them were the Copper King, gleaming ruddy and brave, and the Tin King, strutting in his trimmings of gaudy tinsel which looked nearly as well as silver but were more economical. And this fine troop of lackey kings most politely led Thor and Loki into the palace, and gave them of the best, for they never suspected who these seeming maidens really were.

And when evening came there was a wonderful banquet to celebrate the wedding. On a golden throne sat Thrym, uglier than ever in his finery of purple and gold. Beside him was the bride, of whose face no one had yet caught even a glimpse; and at Thrym's other hand stood Loki, the waiting-maid, for he wanted to be near to mend the mistakes which Thor might make.

Now the dishes at the feast were served in a huge way, as befitted the table of giants: great beeves roasted whole, on platters as wide across as a ship's deck; plum puddings as fat as feather-beds, with plums as big as footballs; and a wedding cake like a snow-capped haymow. The giants ate enormously. But to Thor, because they thought him a dainty maiden, they served small bits of everything on a tiny gold dish. Now Thor's long journey had made him very hungry, and through his veil he whispered to Loki, "I shall starve, Loki! I cannot fare on these nibbles. I must eat a goodly meal as I do at home." And forthwith he helped himself to such morsels as might satisfy his hunger for a little time. You should have seen the giants stare at the meal which the dainty bride devoured!

For first under the silver veil disappeared by pieces a whole roast ox. Then Thor made eight mouthfuls of eight pink salmon, a dish of which he was very fond. And next he looked about and reached for a platter of cakes and sweetmeats that was set aside at one end of the table for the lady guests, and the bride ate them all. You can fancy how the damsels drew down their mouths and looked at one another when they saw their dessert disappear; and they whispered about the table,

"Alack! if our future mistress is to sup like this day by day, there will be poor cheer for the rest of us!" And to crown it all, Thor was thirsty, as well he might be; and one after another he raised to his lips and emptied three great barrels of mead, the foamy drink of the giants. Then indeed Thrym was amazed, for Thor's giant appetite had beaten that of the giants themselves.

"Never before saw I a bride so hungry," he cried, "and never before one half so thirsty!"

But Loki, the waiting-maid, whispered to him softly, "The truth is, great Thrym, that my dear mistress was almost starved. For eight days Freia has eaten nothing at all, so eager was she for Jötunheim."

Then Thrym was delighted, you may be sure. He forgave his hungry bride, and loved her with all his heart. He leaned forward to give her a kiss, raising a corner of her veil; but his hand dropped suddenly, and he started up in terror, for he had caught the angry flash of Thor's eye, which was glaring at him through the bridal veil. Thor was longing for his hammer.

"Why has Freia so sharp a look?" Thrym cried. "It pierces like lightning and burns like fire."

But again the sly waiting-maid whispered timidly, "O Thrym, be not amazed! The truth is, my poor mistress's eyes are red with wakefulness and bright with longing. For eight nights Freia has not known a wink of sleep, so eager was she for Jötunheim."

Then again Thrym was doubly delighted, and he longed to call her his very own dear wife. "Bring in the wedding gift!" he cried. "Bring in Thor's hammer, Miölnir, and give it to Freia, as I promised; for when I have kept my word she will be mine, — all mine!"

Then Thor's big heart laughed under his woman's dress, and his fierce eyes swept eagerly down the hall to meet the servant who was bringing in the hammer on a velvet cushion. Thor's fingers could hardly wait to clutch the stubby handle which they knew so well; but he sat quite still on the throne beside ugly old Thrym, with his hands meekly folded and his head bowed like a bashful bride.

The giant servant drew nearer, nearer, puffing and blowing, strong though he was, beneath the mighty weight. He was about to lay it at Thor's feet (for he thought it so heavy that no maiden could lift it or hold it in her lap), when suddenly Thor's heart swelled, and he gave a most unmaidenly shout of rage and triumph. With one swoop he grasped the hammer in his iron fingers; with the other arm he tore off the veil that hid his terrible face, and trampled it under foot; then he turned to the frightened king, who cowered beside him on the throne.

"Thief!" he cried. "Freia sends you *this* as a wedding gift!" And he whirled the hammer about his head, then hurled it once, twice, thrice, as it rebounded to his hand; and in the first stroke, as of lightning, Thrym rolled dead from his throne; in the second stroke perished the whole giant household, — these ugly enemies of the Æsir; and in the third stroke the palace itself tumbled together and fell to the ground like a toppling play-house of blocks.

But Loki and Thor stood safe among the ruins,

dressed in their tattered maiden robes, a quaint and curious sight; and Loki, full of mischief now as ever, burst out laughing.

"Oh, Thor! if you could see —" he began; but Thor held up his hammer and shook it gently as he said, —

"Look now, Loki: it was an excellent joke, and so far you have done well, — after your crafty fashion, which likes me not. But now I have my hammer again, and the joke is done. From you, nor from another, I brook no laughter at my expense. Henceforth we will have no mention of this masquerade, nor of these rags, which now I throw away. Do you hear, red laugher?"

And Loki heard, with a look of hate, and stifled his laughter as best he could; for it is not good to laugh at him who holds the hammer.

Not once after that was there mention in Asgard of the time when Thor dressed him as a girl and won his bridal gift from Thrym the giant.

But Miölnir was safe once more in Asgard, and you and I know how it came there; so some one must have told. I wonder if red Loki whispered the tale to some outsider, after all? Perhaps it may be so, for now he knew how best to make Thor angry; and from that day when Thor forbade his laughing, Loki hated him with the mean little hatred of a mean little soul.

HOW THE WOLF FENRIS WAS CHAINED

By Julia Goddard

IN the times when Odin and Thor ruled in Asgard there were giants and monsters of all sorts, and some of the evil gods had monsters for children.

So it was with Loki, who had married Signe, the daughter of one of the Jötuns, or giants. Two of his children were Jormungand, the great serpent, and the wolf Fenris; the third was a daughter, named Hela, who, though she was not a monster, was nevertheless very terrible to look upon. They were all born in Jötunheim, where they lived for some time before the Asi heard anything about them.

When at length the tidings that they lived reached the ears of Odin, he felt very uneasy, as did the Asi generally, for they called to mind certain old prophecies, which said that these monsters should arise, and in due time bring great evils upon gods and men. Nay, it was even said that the wolf Fenris should devour Odin himself. Well, therefore, might Odin wish that something should at once be done to curb the growing power of Loki's offspring. At the same time he feared to offend Loki, who was his foster-brother. He had never forgotten the days of their childhood, and would never hold a feast unless Loki were present

However, he called together a council of the Asi, and at length it was agreed that the three children should be brought from Jötunheim to some place where they might be more within his power.

If Odin could have slain them at once, he would doubtless have been well pleased to do so; but this was not in his power. He was only able to command them, and they were bound to obey him as the greatest of the gods.

So the summons went forth, and on a given day Loki, with Hela, Fenris, and Jormungand, arrived at the palace, where Odin awaited them, seated upon his throne and surrounded by the Asi in their glittering array.

Loki certainly was not dazzled by the splendor of the gods; he was used to such displays among them. Neither did it seem in any way to move his offspring, who drew near to the steps of the throne without looking either to the right or to the left.

Hela was a little in front. Her face was grim and fierce; half her body was black, half flesh-color. So terrible was she to look at, that a shudder ran through the whole assembly as they gazed upon her awful form.

"It is clear that she belongs not to us," said one of the Asi.

And Hela at the words half drew the knife out of her belt, as though she would strike at the speaker.

But Odin said, "Nay, over the Asi thou shalt have no power. In Midgard, where men dwell, shalt thou be feared, and thy rule shall be over those of human race. Sorrowfully shall they own thee as a sovereign from whose commands there is no appeal. Over them shalt thou be queen, and the greatest of kings shall stand in awe of thee. Go forth, and from the kingdom I will give thee send forth thy decrees to the children of men."

Then Odin gave Hela a dreary kingdom in Niflheim, the world of mist that is older than heaven and earth; and there she had charge over nine worlds, and had a spacious palace with many halls, but all of them were dark and gloomy.

"The dish that thou shalt eat of shall be hunger," continued Odin; "thy bed shall be the bed of sickness, and its hangings splendid woe. Only the dead shall people thy kingdom, and the light of day shall be shut out from it forever."

And Hela, having heard her sentence, turned away with a stony countenance. It mattered little to her where she reigned, so long as she could smite and slay.

Then Jormungand drew near. The slimy monster wound and twisted his huge body towards the throne, and a dull lustre shimmered round his heavy scales. The gods shrank back, for malice flashed from his cruel eyes, and the sound of his hissing was fearful to hear.

But Odin bade him be silent, and the great serpent lowered his head and crouched at the king's feet.

And lo, the palace walls suddenly opened, and over the fair gardens of Asgard came a deep, low murmur, and then a mist appeared in the distance, which, as the Asi gazed, shaped itself into the likeness of a troubled sea. Louder yet grew the murmur, until it changed into a deep roar, and the gods all wondered what was coming to pass, for it seemed as though the great ocean that surrounds all lands were rushing onward and would

overwhelm the palace. The waves reared their crest,
higher and higher, and nearer and nearer rolled the
waters.

"It is a miracle!" exclaimed the Asi.

But Odin rose and seized the huge serpent and flung
him into the advancing tide.

One heavy plunge, one blinding sheet of mist that
hid the sunlight and the bright blue sky, one hideous
cry, and then a sudden hush, — and as the white mist
cleared away, behold the waters had vanished, and
naught was to be seen but the fair land of Asgard.

The ocean had seized its prey, and in its depths the
serpent was to grow and grow until at length he should
stretch all round the world, and lie there harmless, with
his tail in his mouth, until the day of Ragnaröck should
dawn.

Then only Fenris was left to receive the sentence of
Odin.

The palace walls had closed again, and the king of
heaven bid the giant-wolf draw near.

Never had the Asi seen so huge a beast of the kind;
he was, moreover, sleek and well shaped, but his look
was full of craft and cunning, and he came stealthily
along as though he would beg a milder fate than had
befallen his brother Jormungand.

The gods pressed forward to gain a better view of the
well-formed animal, and praised his shining coat and
lithe limbs. What would be his doom? And they
waited anxiously to hear what Odin would say.

"What say you to our looking after Fenris ourselves?"
asked the king.

HOW THE WOLF FENRIS WAS CHAINED

Then several of the gods stepped forward, and stroked his sleek sides, and patted his comely head, and the wolf seemed so tame that Odin thought that now at least there was nothing to be feared from him. And in the end it was agreed that Fenris should be brought up among the Asi.

So Fenris was lodged in Asgard; and whilst he was quite young all went on well, though sometimes he showed signs of such fierceness that none but Tyr, who was a son of Odin, and one of the boldest and most stout-hearted among the gods, dared to feed him.

As he grew older his strength increased so greatly that the gods began to fear that in the end he might prove too much for them. They also called to mind the sayings concerning the evil that he was to bring upon them, and they pondered whether they should not bind him fast before he became any stronger.

Now Fenris, although he knew not what the gods were thinking of, began to fear something when he saw that they never came to him singly, but always many together, and were, moreover, well armed, and more than once brought chains with them, as if they would use them if they might be able to do so. He resolved, therefore, to keep watch.

"If they want to bind me," said he to himself, "they must find stronger chains than any that have been forged in Asgard." Still he pretended not to see what they were doing.

"I wonder if you are as strong as I am," said Thor to the wolf. "See, I can break this chain asunder easily. If you were bound with it, could you do the same?"

297

"Try me," answered Fenris, who saw at a glance that the chain was not too strong for him. And he allowed it to be wound round and round his body, and fastened to a great iron staple that ran many feet into the earth. Then he shook himself three times, and the third time the fetters fell to the ground, and he was free.

"I can break a stronger chain than that," said Fenris.

And the gods went away, and made another chain, heavier and thicker than the last, and called it Dromi.

Then again they came to Fenris, and asked him if he were willing to try his strength once more.

Fenris eyed the chain narrowly, but feeling that he had strength enough to break it, suffered himself again to be bound; and, as before, he broke the chain in pieces, and the splinters flew far and near. And the gods were filled with dismay, for Fenris was already beyond their power to bind. What were they to do?

Bragi, the eloquent god, stepped forward, and in a long speech, in which he taught them that iron and base metal could not overcome such strength as that of Fenris, he told them that from more subtle elements a magic cord might be woven that would resist the wolf's most vigorous efforts.

"But where may we get such a cord?" asked Tyr. "We have forged to the best of our power, and are unable to make a chain that can hold the monster."

"The gods are not blacksmiths," returned Bragi; "send to those who are. The dwarfs of Black-Elfland understand the secrets of the craft better than we do."

HOW THE WOLF FENRIS WAS CHAINED

Now the region of Black-Elfland, where the dwarfs and dark elves dwell, is deep below the earth. There they work in metals, and are skillful in all smith's work.

So Ull, the god who runs swiftly on snowshoes, was sent to see what the dwarfs could do. And when the dwarfs had heard his story, they told him that they could make a cord so strong that not even the Asi themselves could break it, and yet to outward seeming so slender that Fenris would not be afraid of trying it. It was to be wrought of six things, the sound of a cat's footsteps, the roots of a mountain, and a fish's breath being amongst them.

And the dwarfs set to work, and twined and twisted the materials so deftly, that none could see the joining, or guess of what woof they were woven. And when the cord was finished, they gave it to Ull, who quickly departed with it for Asgard.

The gods were a little disappointed when they saw so slender a bond, which looked as if it might be easily snapped; but when they had tried their utmost strength upon it, they found that even Thor could do no more than strain it slightly. And in very good spirits, they went to Fenris, and took him with them to the island of Syngvi, in the lake Amsvartnir.

There they feasted, and made merry, and at last began to try feats of strength. One after another broke mighty bars of iron, and rent huge chains in pieces, or hurled stones of prodigious weight.

Fenris followed their example. One crunch of his jaws shivered the strongest iron, and a stroke of his paw sundered the heaviest chains. And when the gods thought he must be somewhat tired, they showed him the rope.

"It is so late in the day," said Bragi, "that we will give you no hard task. We have kept the most slender cord until the last. You shall have the first try at it."

Certainly the cord was very fragile to look at; but Fenris was wary, he suspected treachery, and at first refused to be bound with it. But the gods laughed at his fears and said that he was becoming a coward.

"No coward am I," replied Fenris, "but I fear that ye are playing me false. Let Tyr put his hand into my mouth as a pledge of your good faith, then will I submit to be bound."

So Tyr put his hand into Fenris's mouth, and the gods wound the rope Gleipner round and round the wolf's body, and fastened his legs in such a manner that if the rope were as strong as the dwarfs had promised, there would be no doubt of his being their prisoner.

Fenris lay quite still whilst the rope was being tied, for he had Tyr in his power, and he trusted to that in case there should be any treachery.

Tyr, finding that Fenris was fast bound, attempted gently to withdraw his hand; but the wolf kept a firm hold, nor did he loose it even in the midst of his struggles to break the rope.

The Asi gave a shout. "Long live the dwarfs of the Black Elfland! Their work is to be trusted."

And again Fenris strove with all his might to free himself from his bonds, but in vain, and he lay on the ground panting and well-nigh exhausted with his efforts. Tyr's hand was still between his teeth, and he glared savagely as much as to say, "We are captives together."

Then Tyr began to try what force might do, and with the hand that was free he sought to open the wolf's jaws so as to free the other. He had half succeeded when Fenris, in fear lest he might lose it, made a sudden snap and bit it off, and Tyr stood clear of the wolf, but with only one hand.

Fenris was captive now.

And the Asi raised a shout of joy.

Tyr, however, was silent, sorrowing over his loss, and yet, perhaps, he felt that it was well to get rid of the monster even at such a cost.

Then the Asi bound Fenris to a huge rock, and to fasten him the better they drove a sword through his jaws and pinned him fast.

He howled dreadfully, and foam issued from his nostrils. And there he must lie until the day of Ragnaröck, when he, as well as Jormungand, shall once more be free. Then terrible things shall come to pass. But the gods hope that that day is far off, for when it comes they must die.

Three winters without a summer shall go before it, and on the plains of Vigrid, a hundred miles square, a fearful battle shall be fought in which all shall perish.

The gods, the giants, the living, and the dead shall all be present at it. The heroes who are dwelling in Odin's halls shall issue forth when they hear the gold-combed cock. The dead who inhabit Hela's dreary dwellings shall come forth when the red cock crows in hell. Jormungand the serpent and Fenris will be unloosed, and Odin and Thor meet their death as it had been foretold.

The gods care not to think of Ragnaröck. Though it must come, they put all thoughts of it away; and perchance they look beyond to the new earth that is promised them, when the world in which they now dwell shall have been destroyed, and to the time when the gods shall wake up after their death-sleep and live forever in joy and gladness.

THE DWARF'S GIFTS

By Abbie Farwell Brown

RED Loki had been up to mischief again! Loki, who made quarrels and brought trouble wherever he went. He had a wicked heart, and he loved no one. He envied Father Odin his wisdom and his throne above the world. He envied Balder his beauty, and Tyr his courage, and Thor his strength. He envied all the good Æsir, who were happy; but he would not take the trouble to be good himself. So he was always unhappy, spiteful, and sour. And if anything went wrong in Asgard, the kingdom of the gods, one was almost sure to find Loki at the bottom of the trouble.

Now Thor, the strongest of all the gods, was very proud of his wife's beautiful hair, which fell in golden waves to her feet, and covered her like a veil. He loved it better than anything, except Sif herself. One day, while Thor was away from home, Loki stole into Thrudheim, the realm of clouds, and cut off all Sif's golden hair, till her head was as round and fuzzy as a yellow dandelion. Fancy how angry Thor was when he came rattling home that night in his thunder-chariot and found Sif so ugly to look at! He stamped up and down till the five hundred and forty floors of his cloud palace shook like an earthquake, and lightning flashed from his blue eyes. The people down in the world below cried, "Dear, dear! What a terrible thunderstorm! Thor must be very angry about something. Loki has been up to mischief, it is likely." You see, they also knew Loki and his tricks.

At last Thor calmed himself a little. "Sif, my love," he said, "you shall be beautiful again. Red Loki shall make you so, since his was the unmaking. The villain! He shall pay for this!"

Then, without more ado, off set Thor to find red Loki. He went in his thunder-chariot, drawn by two goats, and the clouds rumbled and the lightning flashed wherever he went; for Thor was the mighty god of thunder. At last he came upon the sly rascal, who was trying to hide. Big Thor seized him by the throat.

"You scoundrel!" he cried, "I will break every bone in your body if you do not put back Sif's beautiful hair upon her head."

"Ow—ow! You hurt me!" howled Loki. "Take off your big hand, Thor. What is done, is done. I cannot put back Sif's hair. You know that very well."

"Then you must get her another head of hair," growled Thor. "That you can do. You must find for her hair of real gold, and it must grow upon her head as if it were her own. Do this, or you shall die."

"Where shall I get this famous hair?" whined Loki, though he knew well enough.

"Get it of the black elves," said Thor; "they are cunning jewelers, and they are your friends. Go, Loki, and go quickly, for I long to see Sif as beautiful as ever."

Then Loki of the burning beard slunk away to the hills, where, far under ground, the dwarfs have their furnaces and their workshops. Among great heaps of gold and silver and shining jewels, which they have dug up out of the earth, the little crooked men in brown blink and chatter and scold one another; for they are ugly fellows — the dwarfs. *Tink-tank! tink-tank!* go their little hammers all day long and all night long, while they make wonderful things such as no man has ever seen, though you shall hear about them.

They had no trouble to make a head of hair for Sif. It was for them a simple matter, indeed. The dwarfs work fast for such a customer as Loki, and in a little while the golden wires were beaten out, and drawn out, made smooth and soft and curly, and braided into a thick golden braid. But when Loki came away, he carried with him also two other treasures which the clever dwarfs had made. One was a golden spear, and the other was a ship.

Now these do not sound so very wonderful. But wait until you hear! The spear, which was named Gungnir, was bewitched, so that it made no difference if the person who held it was clumsy and careless. For it had this amazing quality, that no matter how badly it was aimed, or how unskillfully it was thrown, it was sure to go straight to the mark — which is a very obliging and convenient thing in one's weapon, as you will readily see.

And Skidbladnir — this was the harsh name of the ship — was even more wonderful. It could be taken to pieces and folded up so small that it would go into one's pocket. But when it was unfolded and put together, it would hold all the gods of Asgard for a sea journey. Besides all this, when the sails were set, the ship was sure always to have a fair wind, which would make it skim along like a great bird, which was the best part of the charm, as any sailor will tell you.

Now Loki felt very proud of these three treasures, and left the hill cave stretching his neck and strutting like a great red turkey cock. Outside the gate, however, he met Brock, the black dwarf, who was the brother of Sindri, the best workman in all the underworld.

"Hello! what have you there?" asked Brock of the big head, pointing at the bundles which Loki was carrying.

"The three finest gifts in the world," boasted Loki, hugging his treasures tight.

"Pooh!" said Brock, "I don't believe it. Did my brother Sindri make them?"

"No," answered Loki; "they were made by the black elves, the sons of Ivaldi. And they are the most precious gifts that ever were seen."

"Pooh!" again puffed Brock, wagging his long beard crossly. "Nonsense! Whatever they be, my brother Sindri can make three other gifts more precious; that I know."

"Can he, though?" laughed Loki. "I will give him my head if he can."

"Done!" shouted the dwarf. "Let me see your famous gifts." So Loki showed him the three wonders: the gold hair for Sif, the spear, and the ship. But again the dwarf said, "Pooh! These are nothing. I will show you what the master-smith can do, and you shall lose your bragging red head, my Loki."

Now Loki began to be a little uneasy. He followed Brock back to the smithy in the mountain, where they found Sindri at his forge. Oh, yes! He could beat the poor gifts of which Loki was so proud. But he would not tell what his own three gifts were to be.

First Sindri took a pig's skin and laid it on the fire. Then he went away for a little time; but he set Brock at the bellows and bade him blow — blow — blow the fire until Sindri should return. Now when Sindri was gone, Loki also stole away; for, as usual, he was up to mischief. He had the power of changing his shape and of becoming any creature he chose, which was often very convenient. Thus he turned himself into a huge biting fly. Then he flew back into the smithy where Brock was blow — blow — blowing. Loki buzzed about the dwarf's head, and finally lighted on his hand and stung him, hoping to make him let go the bellows. But no! Brock only cried out, "Oh-ee!" and kept on blowing for dear life. Now soon back came Sindri to the forge and took the pigskin from the fire. Wonder of wonders! It had turned into a hog with golden bristles; a live hog that shone like the sun. Brock was not satisfied, however.

"Well! I don't think much of that," he grumbled.

"Wait a little," said Sindri mysteriously. "Wait and see." Then he went on to make the second gift.

This time he put a lump of gold into the fire. And when he went away, as before, he bade Brock stand at the bellows to blow — blow — blow without stopping. Again, as before, in buzzed Loki the gadfly as soon as the master-smith had gone out. This time he settled

on Brock's swarthy neck, and stung him so sorely that
the blood came and the dwarf roared till the mountain
trembled. Still Brock did not let go the handle of the
bellows, but blew and howled — blew and howled with
pain till Sindri returned. And this time the dwarf took
from the fire a fine gold ring, round as roundness.

"Um! I don't think so much of that," said Brock,
again disappointed, for he had expected some wonderful jewel. But Sindri wagged his head wisely.

"Wait a little," he said. "We shall see what we shall
see." He heaved a great lump of iron into the fire to
make the third gift. But this time when he went away,
leaving Brock at the bellows, he charged him to blow
— blow — blow without a minute's rest, or everything
would be spoiled. For this was to be the best gift of
all.

Brock planted himself wide-legged at the forge and
blew — blew — blew. But for the third time Loki,
winged as a fly, came buzzing into the smithy. This
time he fastened viciously below Brock's bushy eye-
brow, and stung him so cruelly that the blood trickled
down, a red river, into his eyes, and the poor dwarf was
blinded. With a howl Brock raised his hand to wipe
away the blood, and of course in that minute the bellows stood still. Then Loki buzzed away with a sound
that seemed like a mocking laugh. At the same moment in rushed Sindri, panting with fright, for he had
heard that sound and guessed what it meant.

"What have you done?" he cried. "You have let
the bellows rest! You have spoiled everything!"

"Only a little moment, but one little moment,"

pleaded Brock, in a panic. "It has done no harm, has it?"

Sindri leaned anxiously over the fire, and out of the flames he drew the third gift — an enormous hammer.

"Oh!" said Brock, much disappointed, "only an old iron hammer! I don't think anything of *that*. Look how short the handle is, too."

"That is your fault, brother," returned the smith crossly. "If you had not let the bellows stand still, the handle would have been long enough. Yet as it is — we shall see, we shall see. I think it will at least win for you red Loki's head. Take the three gifts, brother, such as they are, and bear them to Asgard. Let all the gods be judges between you and Loki, which gifts are best, his or yours. But stay — I may as well tell you the secrets of your three treasures, or you will not know how to make them work. Your toy that is not wound up is of no use at all." Which is very true, as we all know. Then he bent over and whispered in Brock's ear. And what he said pleased Brock so much that he jumped straight up into the air and capered like one of Thor's goats.

"What a clever brother you are, to be sure!" he cried.

At that moment Loki, who had ceased to be a gadfly, came in grinning, with his three gifts. "Well, are you ready?" he asked. Then he caught sight of the three gifts which Brock was putting into his sack.

"Ho! A pig, a ring, and a stub-handled hammer!" he shouted. "Is that all you have? Fine gifts, indeed! I was really growing uneasy, but now I see that my head is safe. Let us start for Asgard immediately, where

I promise you that I with my three treasures shall be thrice more welcome than you with your stupid pig, your ugly ring, and your half-made hammer."

So together they climbed to Asgard, and there they found the Æsir sitting in the great judgment hall on Ida Plain. There was Father Odin on his high throne, with his two ravens at his head and his two wolves at his feet. There was Queen Frigg by his side; and about them were Balder the beautiful, Frey and Freia, the fair brother and sister; the mighty Thor, with Sif, his crop-haired wife, and all the rest of the great Æsir who lived in the upper world above the homes of men.

"Brother Æsir," said Loki, bowing politely, for he was a smooth rascal, "we have come each with three gifts, the dwarf and I; and you shall judge which be the most worthy of praise. But if I lose, — I, your brother, — I lose my head to this crooked little dwarf." So he spoke, hoping to put the Æsir on his side from the first. For his head was a very handsome one, and the dwarf was indeed an ill-looking fellow. The gods, however, nodded gravely, and bade the two show what their gifts might be.

Then Loki stepped forward to the foot of Odin's throne. And first he pulled from his great wallet the spear Gungnir, which could not miss aim. This he gave to Odin, the all-wise. And Odin was vastly pleased, as you may imagine, to find himself thenceforth an unequaled marksman. So he smiled upon Loki kindly and said: "Well done, brother."

Next Loki took out the promised hair for Sif, which he handed Thor with a grimace. Now when the golden

THE THIRD GIFT — AN ENORMOUS HAMMER

locks were set upon her head, they grew there like real hair, long and soft and curling — but still real gold. So that Sif was more beautiful than ever before, and more precious, too. You can fancy how pleased Thor was with Loki's gift. He kissed lovely Sif before all the gods and goddesses, and vowed that he forgave Loki for the mischief which he had done in the first place, since he had so nobly made reparation.

Then Loki took out the third gift, all folded up like a paper boat; and it was the ship Skidbladnir, — I am sorry they did not give it a prettier name. This he presented to Frey the peaceful. And you can guess whether or not Frey's blue eyes laughed with pleasure at such a gift.

Now when Loki stepped back, all the Æsir clapped their hands and vowed that he had done wondrous well.

"You will have to show us fine things, you dwarf," quoth Father Odin, "to better the gifts of red Loki. Come, what have you in the sack you bear upon your shoulders?"

Then the crooked little Brock hobbled forward, bent almost double under the great load which he carried. "I have what I have," he said.

First, out he pulled the ring Draupnir, round as roundness and shining of gold. This the dwarf gave to Odin, and though it seemed but little, yet it was much. For every ninth night out of this ring, he said, would drop eight other rings of gold, as large and as fair. Then Odin clapped his hands and cried: "Oh, wondrous gift! I like it even better than the magic spear which Loki gave." And all the other Æsir agreed with him.

Then out of the sack came grunting Goldbristle, the hog, all of gold. Brock gave him to Frey, to match the magic ship of Loki. This Goldbristle was so marvelously forged that he could run more swiftly than any horse, on air or water. Moreover, he was a living lantern. For on the darkest night he bristled with light like a million-pointed star, so that one riding on his back would light the air and the sea like a firefly, wherever he went. This idea pleased Frey mightily, for he was the merriest of the gods, and he laughed aloud.

"'T is a wondrous fine gift," he said. "I like old Goldbristle even better than the compressible boat. For on this lusty steed I can ride about the world when I am tending the crops and the cattle of men and scattering the rain upon them. Master dwarf, I give my vote to you." And all the other Æsir agreed with him.

Then out of the sack Brock drew the third gift. It was the short-handled hammer named Miölnir. And this was the gift which Sindri had made for Thor, the mightiest of the gods; and it was the best gift of all. For with it Thor could burst the hardest metal and shatter the thickest mountain, and nothing could withstand its power. But it never could hurt Thor himself; and no matter how far or how hard it was thrown, it would always fly back into Thor's own hand. Last of all, whenever he so wished, the great hammer would become so small that he could put it in his pocket, quite out of sight. But Brock was sorry that the handle was so short — all owing to his fault, because he had let the bellows rest for that one moment.

When Thor had this gift in his hand, he jumped up

with a shout of joy. "'T is a wondrous fine gift," he cried, "with short handle or with long. And I prize it even more than I prize the golden hair of Sif which Loki gave. For with it I shall fight our enemies, the Frost Giants and the mischievous Trolls and the other monsters — Loki's friends. And all the Æsir will be glad of my gift when they see what deeds I shall do therewith. Now, if I may have my say, I judge that the three gifts made by Sindri the dwarf are the most precious that may be. So Brock has gained the prize of Loki's red head, — a sorry recompense indeed for gifts so masterly." Then Thor sat down. And all the other Æsir shouted that he had spoken well, and that they agreed with him.

So Loki was like to lose his head. He offered to pay instead a huge price, if Brock would let him go. But Brock refused. "The red head of Loki for my gift," he insisted, and the gods nodded that it must be so, since he had earned his wish.

But when Loki saw that the count was all against him, his eyes grew crafty. "Well, take me, then — if you can!" he shouted. And off he shot like an arrow from a bow. For Loki had on magic shoes, with which he could run over sea or land or sky; and the dwarf could never catch him in the world. Then Brock was furious. He stood stamping and chattering, tearing his long beard with rage.

"I am cheated!" he cried. "I have won — but I have lost." Then he turned to Thor, who was playing with his hammer, bursting a mountain or two and splitting a tree here and there. "Mighty Thor," begged the dwarf, "catch me the fellow who has broken his word. I have given you the best gift, — your wonderful hammer. Catch me, then, the boasting red head which I have fairly bought."

Then Thor stopped his game and set out in pursuit of Loki, for he was ever on the side of fairness. No one, however fleet, can escape when Thor follows, for his is the swiftness of a lightning flash. So he soon brought Loki back to Ida Plain, and gave him up a prisoner to the dwarf.

"I have you now, boaster," said Brock fiercely, "and I will cut off your red head in the twinkling of an eye." But just as he was about to do as he said, Loki had another sly idea.

"Hold, sirrah dwarf," he said. "It is true that you have won my head, but not the neck, not an inch of the neck." And all the gods agreed that this was so. Then Brock was puzzled indeed, for how could he cut off Loki's head without taking an inch of the neck, too? But this he must not do, or he knew the just Æsir would punish him with death. So he was forced to be content with stopping Loki's boasting in another way. He would sew up the bragging lips.

He brought a stout, strong thread and an awl to bore the holes. And in a twinkling he had stitched up the lips of the sly one, firm and fast. So for a time, at least, he put an end to Loki's boasting and his taunts and lies.

It is a pity that those mischief-making lips were not fastened up forever, for that would have saved much of the trouble and sorrow which came after. But at last, after a long time, Loki got his lips free, and they made great sorrow in Asgard for the gods, and on earth for men.

Now this is the end of the tale which tells of the dwarf's gifts, and especially of Thor's hammer, which was afterwards to be of such service to him and such bane to the enemies of the Æsir.

BALDER AND THE MISTLETOE

By Abbie Farwell Brown

LOKI had given up trying to revenge himself upon Thor. The Thunder Lord seemed proof against his tricks. And indeed nowadays Loki hated him no more than he did the other gods. He hated some because they always frowned at him; he hated others because they only laughed and jeered. Some he hated for their distrust and some for their fear. But he hated them all because they were happy and good and mighty, while he was wretched, bad, and of little might. Yet it was all his own fault that this was so. He might have been an equal with the best of them, if he had not chosen to set himself against everything that was good. He had made them all his enemies, and the more he did to injure them, the more he hated them, — which is always the way with evil-doers. Loki longed to see them all unhappy. He slunk about in Asgard with a glum face and wrinkled forehead. He dared not meet the eyes of any one, lest they should read his heart. For he was plotting evil, the greatest of evils, which should bring sorrow to all his enemies at once and turn Asgard into a land of mourning. The Æsir did not guess the whole truth, yet they felt the bitterness of the thoughts which Loki bore; and whenever in the dark he passed unseen, the gods shuddered as if a breath of evil had blown upon them, and even the flowers drooped before his steps.

Now at this time Balder the beautiful had a strange dream. He dreamed that a cloud came before the sun, and all Asgard was dark. He waited for the cloud to drift away, and for the sun to smile again. But no; the sun was gone forever, he thought; and Balder awoke feeling very sad. The next night Balder had another dream. This time he dreamed that it was still dark as before; the flowers were withered and the gods were growing old; even Idun's magic apples could not make them young again. And all were weeping and wringing their hands as though some dreadful thing had happened. Balder awoke feeling strangely frightened, yet he said no word to Nanna his wife, for he did not want to trouble her.

When it came night again Balder slept and dreamed a third dream, a still more terrible one than the other two had been. He thought that in the dark, lonely world there was nothing but a sad voice, which cried, "The sun is gone! The spring is gone! Joy is gone! For Balder the beautiful is dead, dead, dead!"

This time Balder awoke with a cry, and Nanna asked him what was the matter. So he had to tell her of his dream, and she was sadly frightened; for in those days dreams were often sent to folk as messages, and what the gods dreamed usually came true. Nanna ran sobbing to Queen Frigg, who was Balder's mother, and told her all the dreadful dream, asking what could be done to prevent it from coming true.

Now Balder was Queen Frigg's dearest son. Thor

was older and stronger, and more famous for his great deeds; but Frigg loved far better gold-haired Balder. And indeed he was the best-beloved of all the Æsir; for he was gentle, fair, and wise, and wherever he went folk grew happy and light-hearted at the very sight of him, just as we do when we first catch a glimpse of spring peeping over the hilltop into Winterland. So when Frigg heard of Balder's woeful dream, she was frightened almost out of her wits.

"He must not die! He shall not die!" she cried. "He is so dear to all the world, how could there be anything which would hurt him?"

And then a wonderful thought came to Frigg. "I will travel over the world and make all things promise not to injure my boy," she said. "Nothing shall pass my notice. I will get the word of everything."

So first she went to the gods themselves, gathered on Ida Plain for their morning exercise; and telling them of Balder's dream, she begged them to give the promise. Oh, what a shout arose when they heard her words!

"Hurt Balder! — our Balder! Not for the world, we promise! The dream is wrong, — there is nothing so cruel as to wish harm to Balder the beautiful!" they cried. But deep in their hearts they felt a secret fear which would linger until they should hear that all things had given their promise. What if harm were indeed to come to Balder! The thought was too dreadful.

Then Frigg went to see all the beasts who live in field or forest or rocky den. Willingly they gave their promise never to harm hair of gentle Balder. "For he is ever kind to us," they said, "and we love him as if he were one of ourselves. Not with claws or teeth or hoofs or horns will any beast hurt Balder."

Next Frigg spoke to the birds and fishes, reptiles and insects. And all — even the venomous serpents — cried that Balder was their friend, and that they would never do aught to hurt his dear body. "Not with beak or talon, bite or sting or poison fang, will one of us hurt Balder," they promised.

After doing this, the anxious mother traveled over the whole round world, step by step; and from all the things that are she got the same ready promise never to harm Balder the beautiful. All the trees and plants promised; all the stones and metals; earth, air, fire, and water; sun, snow, wind, and rain, and all diseases that men know, — each gave to Frigg the word of promise which she wanted. So at last, footsore and weary, she came back to Asgard with the joyful news that Balder must be safe, for that there was nothing in the world but had promised to be his harmless friend.

Then there was rejoicing in Asgard, as if the gods had won one of their great victories over the giants. The noble Æsir and the heroes who had died in battle upon the earth, and who had come to Valhalla to live happily ever after, gathered on Ida Plain to celebrate the love of all nature for Balder.

There they invented a famous game, which was to prove how safe he was from the bite of death. They stationed Balder in the midst of them, his face glowing like the sun with the bright light which ever shone from him. And as he stood there all unarmed and smiling, by turns they tried all sorts of weapons against him; they made as if to beat him with sticks, they stoned him with stones, they shot at him with arrows and hurled mighty spears straight at his heart.

It was a merry game, and a shout of laughter went up as each stone fell harmless at Balder's feet, each stick broke before it touched his shoulders, each arrow overshot his head, and each spear turned aside. For neither stone nor wood nor flinty arrow-point nor bar of iron would break the promise which each had given. Balder was safe with them, just as if he were bewitched. He remained unhurt among the missiles which whizzed about his head, and which piled up in a great heap around the charmed spot whereon he stood.

Now among the crowd that watched these games with such enthusiasm, there was one face that did not smile, one voice that did not rasp itself hoarse with cheering. Loki saw how every one and every thing loved Balder, and he was jealous. He was the only creature in all the world that hated Balder and wished for his death. Yet Balder had never done harm to him. But the wicked plan that Loki had been cherishing was almost ripe, and in this poison fruit was the seed of the greatest sorrow that Asgard had ever known.

While the others were enjoying their game of love, Loki stole away unperceived from Ida Plain, and with a wig of gray hair, a long gown, and a staff, disguised himself as an old woman. Then he hobbled down Asgard streets till he came to the palace of Queen Frigg, the mother of Balder.

"Good-day, my lady," quoth the old woman, in a

EACH ARROW OVERSHOT HIS HEAD

cracked voice. "What is that noisy crowd doing yonder in the green meadow? I am so deafened by their shouts that I can hardly hear myself think."

"Who are you, good mother, that you have not heard?" said Queen Frigg in surprise. "They are shooting at my son Balder. They are proving the word which all things have given me, — the promise not to injure my dear son. And that promise will be kept."

The old crone pretended to be full of wonder. "So, now!" she cried. "Do you mean to say that *every single thing* in the whole world has promised not to hurt your son? I can scarce believe it; though, to be sure, he is as fine a fellow as I ever saw." Of course this flattery pleased Frigg.

"You say true, mother," she answered proudly, "he is a noble son. Yes, everything has promised, — that is, everything except one tiny little plant that is not worth mentioning."

The old woman's eyes twinkled wickedly. "And what is that foolish little plant, my dear?" she asked coaxingly.

"It is the mistletoe that grows in the meadow west of Valhalla. It was too young to promise, and too harmless to bother with," answered Frigg carelessly.

After this her questioner hobbled painfully away. But as soon as she was out of sight from the Queen's palace, she picked up the skirts of her gown and ran as fast as she could to the meadow west of Valhalla. And there, sure enough, as Frigg had said, was a tiny sprig of mistletoe growing on a gnarled oak-tree. The false Loki took out a knife which she carried in some hidden pocket and cut off the mistletoe very carefully. Then she trimmed and shaped it so that it was like a little green arrow, pointed at one end, but very slender.

"Ho, ho!" chuckled the old woman. "So you are the only thing in all the world that is too young to make a promise, my little mistletoe. Well, young as you are, you must go on an errand for me to-day. And maybe you shall bear a message of my love to Balder the beautiful."

Then she hobbled back to Ida Plain, where the merry game was still going on around Balder. Loki quietly passed unnoticed through the crowd, and came close to the elbow of a big dark fellow who was standing lonely outside the circle of weapon-throwers. He seemed sad and forgotten, and he hung his head in a pitiful way. It was Höd, the blind brother of Balder.

The old woman touched his arm. "Why do you not join the game with the others?" she asked, in her cracked voice. "Are you the only one to do your brother no honor? Surely, you are big and strong enough to toss a spear with the best of them yonder."

Höd touched his sightless eyes madly. "I am blind," he said. "Strength I have, greater than belongs to most of the Æsir. But I cannot see to aim a weapon. Besides, I have no spear to test upon him. Yet how gladly would I do honor to dear Balder!" and he sighed deeply.

"It were a pity if I could not find you at least a little stick to throw," said Loki sympathetically. "I am only a poor old woman, and of course I have no weapon. But ah, — here is a green twig which you can use as an arrow, and I will guide your arm, poor fellow."

BALDER AND THE MISTLETOE

Höd's dark face lighted up, for he was eager to take his turn in the game. So he thanked her, and grasped eagerly the little arrow which she put into his hand. Loki held him by the arm, and together they stepped into the circle which surrounded Balder. And when it was Höd's turn to throw his weapon, the old woman stood at his elbow and guided his big arm as it hurled the twig of mistletoe towards where Balder stood.

Oh, the sad thing that befell! Straight through the air flew the little arrow, straight as magic and Loki's arm could direct it. Straight to Balder's heart it sped, piercing through jerkin and shirt and all, to give its bitter message of "Loki's love," as he had said. With a cry Balder fell forward on the grass. And that was the end of sunshine and spring and joy in Asgard, for the dream had come true, and Balder the beautiful was dead.

When the Æsir saw what had happened, there was a great shout of fear and horror, and they rushed upon Höd, who had thrown the fatal arrow.

"What is it? What have I done?" asked the poor blind brother, trembling at the tumult which had followed his shot.

"You have slain Balder!" cried the Æsir. "Wretched Höd, how could you do it?"

"It was the old woman — the evil old woman, who stood at my elbow and gave me a little twig to throw," gasped Höd. "She must be a witch."

Then the Æsir scattered over Ida Plain to look for the old woman who had done the evil deed; but she had mysteriously disappeared.

"It must be Loki," said wise Heimdal. "It is Loki's last and vilest trick."

"Oh, my Balder, my beautiful Balder!" wailed Queen Frigg, throwing herself on the body of her son. "If I had only made the mistletoe give me the promise, you would have been saved. It was I who told Loki of the mistletoe, — so it is I who have killed you. Oh, my son, my son!"

But Father Odin was speechless with grief. His sorrow was greater than that of all the others, for he best understood the dreadful misfortune which had befallen Asgard. Already a cloud had come before the sun, so that it would never be bright day again. Already the flowers had begun to fade and the birds had ceased to sing. And already the Æsir had begun to grow old and joyless, — all because the little misletoe had been too young to give a promise to Queen Frigg.

"Balder the beautiful is dead!" the cry went echoing through all the world, and everything that was sorrowed at the sound of the Æsir's weeping.

Balder's brothers lifted up his beautiful body upon their great war shields and bore him on their shoulders down to the seashore. For, as was the custom in those days, they were going to send him to Hela, the Queen of Death, with all the things he best had loved in Asgard. And these were, — after Nanna his wife, — his beautiful horse, and his ship Hringhorni. So that they would place Balder's body upon the ship with his horse beside him, and set fire to this wonderful funeral pile. For by fire was the quickest passage to Hela's kingdom.

But when they reached the shore, they found that

all the strength of all the Æsir was unable to move Hringhorni, Balder's ship, into the water. For it was the largest ship in the world, and it was stranded far up the beach.

"Even the giants bore no ill-will to Balder," said Father Odin. "I heard the thunder of their grief but now shaking the hills. Let us for this once bury our hatred of that race and send to Jötunheim for help to move the ship."

So they sent a messenger to the giantess Hyrrockin, the hugest of all the Frost People. She was weeping for Balder when the message came.

"I will go, for Balder's sake," she said. Soon she came riding fast upon a giant wolf, with a serpent for the bridle; and mighty she was, with the strength of forty Æsir. She dismounted from her wolf-steed, and tossed the wriggling reins to one of the men-heroes who had followed Balder and the Æsir from Valhalla. But he could not hold the beast, and it took four heroes to keep him quiet, which they could only do by throwing him upon the ground and sitting upon him in a row. And this mortified them greatly.

Then Hyrrockin the giantess strode up to the great ship and seized it by the prow. Easily she gave a little pull, and presto! it leaped forward on its rollers with such force that sparks flew from the flint stones underneath and the whole earth trembled. The boat shot into the waves and out toward open sea so swiftly that the Æsir were likely to have lost it entirely, had not Hyrrockin waded out up to her waist and caught it by the stern just in time.

Thor was angry at her clumsiness, and raised his hammer to punish her. But the other Æsir held his arm.

"She cannot help being so strong," they whispered. "She meant to do well. She did not realize how hard she was pulling. This is no time for anger, brother Thor." So Thor spared her life, as indeed he ought, for her kindness.

Then Balder's body was borne out to the ship and laid upon a pile of beautiful silks, and furs, and cloth-of-gold, and woven sunbeams, which the dwarfs had wrought. So that his funeral pyre was more grand than anything which had ever been seen. But when Nanna, Balder's gentle wife, saw them ready to kindle the flames under this gorgeous bed, she could bear her grief no longer. Her loving heart broke, and they laid her beside him, that they might comfort each other on their journey to Hela. Thor touched the pile gently with his hammer that makes the lightning, and the flames burst forth, lighting up the faces of Balder and Nanna with a glory. Then they cast upon the fire Balder's war-horse, to serve his master in the dark country to which he was about to go. The horse was decked with a harness all of gold, with jewels studding the bridle and headstall. Last of all Odin laid upon the pyre his gift to Balder, Draupnir, the precious ring of gold which the dwarf had made, from which every ninth night there dropped eight other rings as large and brightly golden.

"Take this with you, dear son, to Hela's palace," said Odin. "And do not forget the friends you leave behind in the now lonely halls of Asgard."

BALDER AND THE MISTLETOE

Then Hyrrockin pushed the great boat out to sea, with its bonfire of precious things. And on the beach stood all the Æsir watching it out of sight, all the Æsir and many besides. For there came to Balder's funeral great crowds of little dwarfs and multitudes of huge frost giants, all mourning for Balder the beautiful. For this one time they were all friends together, forgetting their quarrels of so many centuries. All of them loved Balder, and were united to do him honor.

The great ship moved slowly out to sea, sending up a red fire to color all the heavens. At last it slid below the horizon softly, as you have often seen the sun set upon the water, leaving a brightness behind to lighten the dark world for a little while.

This indeed was the sunset for Asgard. The darkness of sorrow came in earnest after the passing of Balder the beautiful.

IDUNA'S APPLES

By A. and E. Keary

I

REFLECTIONS IN THE WATER

OF all the groves and gardens round the city of
Asgard — and they were many and beautiful —
there was none so beautiful as the one where Iduna, the
wife of Bragi, lived. It stood on the south side of the
hill, not far from Gladsheim, and it was called "Always
Young," because nothing that grew there could ever
decay, or become the least bit older than it was on the
day when Iduna entered it. The trees wore always a
tender, light green color, as the hedges do in spring.
The flowers were mostly half-opened, and every blade
of grass bore always a trembling, glittering drop of early
dew. Brisk little winds wandered about the grove,
making the leaves dance from morning till night and
swaying backwards and forwards the heads of the
flowers.

"Blow away!" said the leaves to the wind, "for we
shall never be tired."

"And you will never be old," said the winds in answer.
And then the birds took up the chorus and sang, —

"Never tired and never old."

Iduna, the mistress of the grove, was fit to live among

young birds, and tender leaves, and spring flowers. She was so fair that when she bent over the river to entice her swans to come to her, even the stupid fish stood still in the water, afraid to destroy so beautiful an image by swimming over it; and when she held out her hand with bread for the swans to eat, you would not have known it from a water-lily, — it was so wonderfully white.

Iduna never left her grove even to pay a visit to her nearest neighbor, and yet she did not lead by any means a dull life; for, besides having the company of her husband, Bragi, — who must have been an entertaining person to live with, for he is said to have known a story which never came to an end, and yet which never grew wearisome, — all the heroes of Asgard made a point of coming to call upon her every day. It was natural enough that they should like to visit so beautiful a grove and so fair a lady; and yet, to confess the truth, it was not quite to see either the grove or Iduna that they came.

Iduna herself was well aware of this, and when her visitors had chatted a short time with her, she never failed to bring out from the innermost recess of her bower a certain golden casket, and to request, as a favor, that her guests would not think of going away till they had tasted her apples, which, she flattered herself, had a better flavor than any other fruit in the world.

It would have been quite unlike a hero of Asgard to have refused such courtesy; and, besides, Iduna was not as far wrong about her apples as hostesses generally are, when they boast of the good things on their tables.

There is no doubt her apples *had* a peculiar flavor; and if any one of the heroes happened to be a little tired, or a little out of spirits, or a little cross, when he came into the bower, it always followed that, as soon as he had eaten one apple, he found himself as fresh and vigorous and happy as he had ever been in his life.

So fond were the heroes of these apples, and so necessary did they think them to their daily comfort, that they never went on a journey without requesting Iduna to give them one or two, to fortify them against the fatigues of the way.

Iduna had no difficulty in complying with this request; she had no fear of her store ever failing, for as surely as she took an apple from her casket another fell in; but where it came from Iduna could never discover. She never saw it till it was close to the bottom of the casket; but she always heard the sweet tinkling sound it made when it touched the golden rim. It was as good as play to Iduna to stand by her casket, taking the apples out, and watching the fresh rosy ones come tumbling in, without knowing who threw them.

One spring morning Iduna was very busy taking apples out of her casket; for several of the heroes were taking advantage of the fine weather to journey out into the world. Bragi was going from home for a time; perhaps he was tired of telling his story only to Iduna, and perhaps she was beginning to know it by heart; and Odin, Loki, and Hœnir had agreed to take a little tour in the direction of Jötunheim, just to see if any entertaining adventure would befall them. When they had all received their apples and taken a tender farewell of Iduna, the grove — green and fair as it was — looked, perhaps, a little solitary.

Iduna stood by her fountain, watching the bright water as it danced up into the air and quivered, and turned, and fell back, making a hundred little flashing circles in the river; and then she grew tired, for once, of the light and the noise, and wandered down to a still place, where the river was shaded by low bushes on each side, and reflected clearly the blue sky overhead.

Iduna sat down and looked into the deep water. Besides her own fair face there were little wandering white clouds to be seen reflected there. She counted them as they sailed past. At length a strange form was reflected up to her from the water — large, dark, lowering wings, pointed claws, a head with fierce eyes — looking at her.

Iduna started and raised her head. It was above as well as below; the same wings — the same eyes — the same head — looking down from the blue sky, as well as up from the water. Such a sight had never been seen near Asgard before; and, while Iduna looked, the thing waved its wings, and went up, up, up, till it lessened to a dark spot in the clouds and on the river.

It was no longer terrible to look at; but, as it shook its wings a number of little black feathers fell from them, and flew down towards the grove. As they neared the trees, they no longer looked like feathers — each had two independent wings and a head of its own; they were, in fact, a swarm of Nervous Apprehensions, — troublesome little insects enough, and well known elsewhere, but which now, for the first time, found their way into the grove.

Iduna ran away from them; she shook them off; she fought quite bravely against them; but they are by no means easy to get rid of; and when, at last, one crept within the folds of her dress, and twisted itself down to her heart, a new, strange feeling thrilled there — a feeling never yet known to any dweller in Asgard. Iduna did not know what to make of it.

II

THE WINGED GIANT

In the mean time Odin, Loki, and Hœnir proceeded on their journey. They were not bound on any particular quest. They strayed hither and thither, that Odin might see that things were going on well in the world, and his subjects comporting themselves in a becoming manner. Every now and then they halted while Odin inspected the thatching of a barn, or stood at the smithy to see how the smith wielded his hammer, or in a furrow to observe if the ploughman guided his ploughshare evenly through the soil. "Well done," he said if the workman was working with all his might; and he turned away, leaving something behind him, a straw in the barn, a piece of old iron at the forge-door, a grain in the furrow, — nothing to look at, but ever after the barn was always full, the forge-fire never went out, the field yielded bountifully.

Towards noon the Æsir reached a shady valley,

and, feeling tired and hungry, Odin proposed to sit down under a tree, and while he rested and studied a book of runes which he had with him, he requested Loki and Hœnir to prepare some dinner.

"I will undertake the meat and the fire," said Hœnir; "you, Loki, will like nothing better than foraging about for what good things you can pick up."

"That is precisely what I mean to do," said Loki. "There is a farmhouse near here, from which I can perceive a savory smell. It will be strange, with my cunning, if I do not contrive to have the best of all the dishes under this tree before your fire is burnt up."

As Loki spoke he turned a stone in his hand, and immediately he assumed the shape of a large black cat. In this form he stole in at the kitchen window of a farmhouse, where a busy housewife was intent on taking pies and cakes from a deep oven, and ranging them on a dresser under the window. Loki watched his opportunity, and whenever the mistress's back was turned he whisked a cake or a pie out of the window.

"One, two, three. Why, there are fewer every time I bring a fresh one from the oven!" cried the bewildered housewife. "It's that thieving cat. I see the end of her tail on the window-sill." Out of the window leant the housewife to throw a stone at the cat, but she could see nothing but a thin cow trespassing in her garden; and when she ran out with a stick to drive away the cow, it, too, had vanished, and an old raven, with six young ones, was flying over the garden hedge.

The raven was Loki, the little ones were the pies; and when he reached the valley, and changed himself and them into their proper shapes, he had a hearty laugh at his own cleverness, and at the old woman's dismay.

"Well done, Loki, king of thieves," said a chorus of foxes, who peeped out of their holes to see the only one of the Æsir whose conduct they could appreciate; but Odin, when he heard of it, was very far from thinking it well done. He was extremely displeased with Loki for having disgraced himself by such mean tricks.

"It is true," he said, "that my subjects may well be glad to furnish me with all I require, but it should be done knowingly. Return to the farmhouse, and place these three black stones on the table from whence you stole the provisions."

Loki — unwilling as he was to do anything he believed likely to bring good to others — was obliged to obey. He made himself into the shape of a white owl, flew once more through the window, and dropped the stones out of his beak; they sank deep into the table, and looked like three black stains on the white deal board.

From that time the housewife led an easy life; there was no need for her to grind corn, or mix dough, or prepare meat. Let her enter her kitchen at what time of day she would, stores of provisions stood smoking hot on the table. She kept her own counsel about it, and enjoyed the reputation of being the most economical housekeeper in the whole country-side; but one thing disturbed her mind, and prevented her thoroughly enjoying the envy and wonder of the neighboring wives. All the rubbing, and brushing, and cleaning in the world would not remove the three black stains from her kitchen table, and as she had no cooking to do, she spent the greater part of her time in looking at them.

"If they were but gone," she said, a hundred times every day, "I should be content; but how is one to enjoy one's life when one cannot rub the stains off one's own table?"

Perhaps Loki foresaw how the good wife would use her gift; for he came back from the farmhouse in the best spirits. "We will now, with Father Odin's permission, sit down to dinner," he said; "for surely, brother Hœnir, while I have been making so many journeys to and fro, you have been doing something with that fire which I see blazing so fiercely, and with that old iron pot smoking over it."

"The meat will be ready by this time, no doubt," said Hœnir. "I killed a wild ox while you were away, and part of it has been now for some time stewing in the pot."

The Æsir now seated themselves near the fire, and Hœnir lifted up the lid of the pot. A thick steam rose up from it; but when he took out the meat it was as red and uncooked as when he first put it into the pot.

"Patience," said Hœnir; and Odin again took out his book of Runes. Another hour passed, and Hœnir again took off the lid, and looked at the meat; but it was in precisely the same state as before. This happened several times, and even the cunning Loki was puzzled; when, suddenly, a strange noise was heard coming from a tree near, and looking up, they saw an enormous human-headed eagle seated on one of the branches, and looking at them with two fierce eyes. While they looked it spoke.

"Give me my share of the feast," it said, "and the meat shall presently be done."

"Come down and take it — it lies before you," said Loki, while Odin looked on with thoughtful eyes; for he saw plainly that it was no mortal bird who had the boldness to claim a share in the Æsir's food.

Undaunted by Odin's majestic looks, the eagle flew down, and, seizing a large piece of meat, was going to fly away with it, when Loki, thinking he had now got the bird in his power, took up a stick that lay near, and struck a hard blow on the eagle's back. The stick made a ringing sound as it fell; but, when Loki tried to draw it back, he found that it stuck with extraordinary force to the eagle's back; neither could he withdraw his own hands from the other end.

Something like a laugh came from the creature's half human, half bird-like mouth; and then it spread its dark wings and rose up into the air, dragging Loki after.

"It is as I thought," said Odin, as he saw the eagle's enormous bulk brought out against the sky; "it is Thiassi, the strongest giant in Jötunheim, who has presumed to show himself in our presence. Loki has only received the reward of his treachery, and it would ill become us to interfere in his behalf; but, as the monster is near, it will be well for us to return to Asgard, lest any misfortune should befall the city in our absence."

While Odin spoke, the winged creature had risen up so high as to be invisible even to the eyes of the Æsir:

and, during their return to Asgard, he did not again appear before them; but, as they approached the gates of the city, they were surprised to see Loki coming to meet them. He had a crest-fallen and bewildered look; and when they questioned him as to what had happened to him since they parted in such a strange way, he declared himself to be quite unable to give any further account of his adventures than that he had been carried rapidly through the air by the giant, and at last thrown down from a great height near the place where the Æsir met him.

Odin looked steadfastly at him as he spoke, but he forbore to question him further; for he knew well that there was no hope of hearing the truth from Loki, and he kept within his own mind the conviction he felt that some disastrous result must follow a meeting between two such evil-doers as Loki and the giant Thiassi.

That evening, when the Æsir were all feasting and telling stories to one another in the great hall of Valhalla, Loki stole out from Gladsheim, and went alone to visit Iduna in her grove. It was a still, bright evening. The leaves of the trees moved softly up and down, whispering sweet words to each other; the flowers, with half-shut eyes, nodded sleepily to their own reflections in the water, and Iduna sat by the fountain, with her head resting in one hand, thinking of pleasant things.

"It is all very well," thought Loki; "but I am not the happier because people can here live such pleasant lives. It does not do me any good, or cure the pain I have had so long in my heart."

Loki's long shadow — for the sun was setting — fell on the water as he approached, and made Iduna start. She remembered the sight that had disturbed her so much in the morning; but when she saw only Loki, she looked up and smiled kindly; for he had often accompanied the other Æsir in their visits to her grove.

"I am wearied with a long journey," said Loki abruptly, "and I would eat one of your apples to refresh me after my fatigue." The casket stood by Iduna's side, and she immediately put in her hand and gave Loki an apple. To her surprise, instead of thanking her warmly or beginning to eat it, he turned it round and round in his hand with a contemptuous air.

"It is true then," he said, after looking intently at the apple for some time, "your apples are but small and withered in comparison. I was unwilling to believe it at first, but now I can doubt no longer."

"Small and withered!" said Iduna, rising hastily. "Nay, Asa Odin himself, who has traversed the whole world, assures me that he has never seen any to be compared to them."

"That will never be said again," returned Loki; "for this very afternoon I have discovered a tree, in a grove not far from Asgard, on which grow apples so beautiful that no one who has seen them will ever care again for yours."

"I do not wish to see or hear of them," said Iduna, trying to turn away with an indifferent air; but Loki followed her, and continued to speak more and more strongly of the beauty of this new fruit, hinting that Iduna would be sorry that she had refused to listen when

she found all her guests deserting her for the new grove,
and when even Bragi began to think lightly of her and
of her gifts. At this Iduna sighed, and Loki came up
close to her, and whispered in her ear, —

"It is but a short way from Asgard, and the sun has
not yet set. Come out with me, and, before any one
else has seen the apples, you shall gather them, and
put them in your casket, and no woman shall ever have
it in her power to boast that she can feast the Æsir more
sumptuously than Iduna."

Now Iduna had often been cautioned by her husband
never to let anything tempt her to leave the grove, and
she had always been so happy here that she thought
there was no use in his telling her the same thing so
often over; but now her mind was so full of the wonderfully beautiful fruit, and she felt such a burning wish to
get it for herself, that she quite forgot her husband's
commands.

"It is only a little way," she said to herself; "there
can be no harm in going out just this once; " and, as
Loki went on urging her, she took up her casket from
the ground hastily, and begged him to show her the
way to this other grove. Loki walked very quickly, and
Iduna had not time to collect her thoughts before she
found herself at the entrance of Always Young. At the
gate she would gladly have stopped a minute to take
breath; but Loki took hold of her hand, and forced
her to pass through, though, at the very moment of
passing, she half drew back; for it seemed to her as if
all the trees in the grove suddenly called out in alarm,
"Come back, come back, oh, come back, Iduna!" She

half drew back her hand, but it was too late; the gate
fell behind her, and she and Loki stood together without
the grove.

The trees rose up between them and the setting sun,
and cast a deep shadow on the place where they stood;
a cold night air blew on Iduna's cheek, and made her
shiver.

"Let us hasten on," she said to Loki; "let us hasten
on, and soon come back again."

But Loki was not looking on, he was looking up.
Iduna raised her eyes in the direction of his, and her
heart died within her; for there, high up over her
head, just as she had seen it in the morning, hung the
lowering, dark wings — the sharp talons — the fierce
head, looking at her. For one moment it stood still
above her head, and then lower, lower, lower, the huge
shadow fell; and, before Iduna found breath to speak,
the dark wings were folded round her, and she was
borne high up in the air, northwards, towards the gray
mist that hangs over Jötunheim. Loki watched till she
was out of sight, and then returned to Asgard. The presence of the giant was no wonder to him; for he had,
in truth, purchased his own release by promising to
deliver up Iduna and her casket into his power; but,
as he returned alone through the grove, a foreboding
fear pressed on his mind.

"If it should be true," he thought, "that Iduna's
apples have the wonderful power Odin attributes to
them! if I among the rest should suffer from the loss!"

Occupied with these thoughts, he passed quickly
among the trees, keeping his eyes resolutely fixed on

the ground. He dared not trust himself to look round; for once, when he had raised his head, he fancied that, gliding through the brushwood, he had seen the dark robes and pale face of his daughter Hela.

III

HELA

When it was known that Iduna had disappeared from her grove, there were many sorrowful faces in Asgard, and anxious voices were heard inquiring for her. Loki walked about with as grave a face, and asked as many questions, as any one else; but he had a secret fear that became stronger every day, that now, at last, the consequence of his evil ways would find him out.

Days passed on, and the looks of care, instead of wearing away, deepened on the faces of the Æsir. They met, and looked at each other, and turned away sighing; each saw that some strange change was creeping over all the others, and none liked to be the first to speak of it. It came on very gradually — a little change every day, and no day ever passing without the change. The leaves of the trees in Iduna's grove deepened in color. They first became a sombre green, then a glowing red, and, at last a pale brown; and when the brisk winds came and blew them about, they moved every day more languidly.

"Let us alone," they said at length. "We are tired, tired, tired."

The winds, surprised, carried the new sound to Gladsheim, and whispered it all round the banquet-hall where the Æsir sat, and then they rushed back again, and blew all through the grove.

"We are tired," said the leaves again; "we are tired, we are old; we are going to die;" and at the word they broke from the trees one by one, and fluttered to the ground, glad to rest anywhere; and the winds, having nothing else to do, went back to Gladsheim with the last strange word they had learned.

The Æsir were all assembled in Valhalla; but there were no stories told, and no songs sung. No one spoke much but Loki, and he was that day in a talking humor. He moved from one to another, whispering an unwelcome word in every ear.

"Have you noticed your mother Frigga?" he said to Baldur. "Do you see how white her hair is growing, and what a number of deep lines are printed on her face?"

Then he turned to Frey. "Look at your sister Freyja and your friend Baldur," he said, "as they sit opposite to us. What a change has come over them lately! Who would think that that pale man and that faded woman were Baldur the beautiful and Freyja the fair?"

"You are tired — you are old — you are going to die," moaned the winds, wandering all round the great halls, and coming in and out of the hundred doorways; and all the Æsir looked up at the sad sound. Then they saw, for the first time, that a new guest had seated herself that day at the table of the Æsir. There could be no question of her fitness on the score of royalty, for a crown rested on her brow, and in her hand she held a sceptre; but the fingers that grasped the sceptre were white and fleshless, and under the crown looked the threatening face of Hela, half corpse, half queen.

A great fear fell on all the Æsir as they looked, and only Odin found voice to speak to her. "Dreadful daughter of Loki!" he said, "by what warrant do you dare to leave the kingdom where I permit you to reign, and come to take your place among the Æsir, who are no mates for such as you?"

Then Hela raised her bony finger, and pointed, one by one, to the guests that sat round. "White hair," she said, "wrinkled faces, weary limbs, dull eyes — these are the warrants which have summoned me from the land of shadows to sit among the Æsir. I have come to claim you, by these signs, as my future guests, and to tell you that I am preparing a place for you in my kingdom."

At every word she spoke a gust of icy wind came from her mouth and froze the blood in the listeners' veins. If she had stayed a moment longer they would have stiffened into stone; but when she had spoken thus, she rose and left the hall, and the sighing winds went out with her.

Then, after a long silence, Bragi stood up and spoke. "Æsir," he said, "we are to blame. It is now many months since Iduna was carried away from us; we have mourned for her, but we have not yet avenged her loss. Since she left us a strange weariness and despair have come over us, and we sit looking on each other as if we had ceased to be warriors and Æsir. It is plain that, unless Iduna returns, we are lost. Let two of us journey to the Urda fount, which we have so long neglected to visit, and inquire of her from the Norns — for they know all things — and then, when we have learnt where she is, we will fight for her liberty, if need be, till we die; for that will be an end more fitting for us then to sit here and wither away under the breath of Hela."

At these words of Bragi, the Æsir felt a revival of their old strength and courage. Odin approved of Bragi's proposal, and decreed that he and Baldur should undertake the journey to the dwelling-place of the Norns. That very evening they set forth; for Hela's visit showed them that they had no time to lose.

It was a weary time to the dwellers in Asgard while they were absent. Two new citizens had taken up their abode in the city, Age and Pain. They walked the streets hand-in-hand, and there was no use in shutting the doors against them; for however closely the entrance was barred, the dwellers in the houses felt them as they passed.

IV

THROUGH FLOOD AND FIRE

At length Baldur and Bragi returned with the answer of the Norns, couched in mystic words, which Odin alone could understand. It revealed Loki's treacherous conduct to the Æsir, and declared that Iduna could only be brought back by Loki, who must go in search of her, clothed in Freyja's garments of falcon feathers.

Loki was very unwilling to venture on such a search;

but Thor threatened him with instant death if he refused to obey Odin's commands, or failed to bring back Iduna; and for his own safety he was obliged to allow Freyja to fasten the falcon wings to his shoulders, and to set off towards Thiassi's castle in Jötunheim, where he well knew that Iduna was imprisoned.

It was called a castle; but it was, in reality, a hollow in a dark rock; the sea broke against two sides of it; and, above, the sea-birds clamored day and night.

There the giant had taken Iduna on the night on which she had left her grove; and, fearing lest Odin should spy her from Air Throne, he had shut her up in a gloomy chamber, and strictly forbidden her ever to come out. It was hard to be shut up from the fresh air and sunshine; and yet, perhaps, it was safer for Iduna than if she had been allowed to wander about Jötunheim, and see the monstrous sights that would have met her there.

She saw nothing but Thiassi himself and his servants, whom he had commanded to attend upon her; and they, being curious to see a stranger from a distant land, came in and out many times every day.

They were fair, Iduna saw — fair and smiling; and at first it relieved her to see such pleasant faces round her, when she had expected something horrible.

"Pity me!" she used to say to them; "pity me! I have been torn away from my home and my husband, and I see no hope of ever getting back." And she looked earnestly at them; but their pleasant faces never changed, and there was always — however bitterly Iduna might be weeping — the same smile on their lips.

At length Iduna, looking more narrowly at them, saw, when they turned their backs to her, that they were hollow behind; they were, in truth, Ellewomen, who have no hearts, and can never pity any one.

After Iduna saw this she looked no more at their smiling faces, but turned away her head and wept silently. It is very sad to live among Ellewomen when one is in trouble.

Every day the giant came and thundered at Iduna's door. "Have you made up your mind yet," he used to say, "to give me the apples? Something dreadful will happen to you if you take much longer to think of it." Iduna trembled very much every day, but still she had strength to say, "No;" for she knew that the *most* dreadful thing would be for her to give to a wicked giant the gifts that had been entrusted to her for the use of the Æsir. The giant would have taken the apples by force if he could; but, whenever he put his hand into the casket, the fruit slipped from beneath his fingers, shriveled into the size of a pea, and hid itself in crevices of the casket where his great fingers could not come — only when Iduna's little white hand touched it, it swelled again to its own size, and this she would never do while the giant was with her. So the days passed on, and Iduna would have died of grief among the smiling Ellewomen if it had not been for the moaning sound of the sea and the wild cry of the birds; "for, however others may smile, these pity me," she used to say, and it was like music to her.

One morning when she knew that the giant had gone out, and when the Ellewomen had left her alone, she

stood for a long time at her window by the sea, watching
the mermaids floating up and down on the waves, and
looking at heaven with their sad blue eyes. She knew
that they were mourning because they had no souls,
and she thought within herself that even in prison it was
better to belong to the Æsir than to be a mermaid or an
Ellewoman, were they ever so free or happy.

While she was still occupied with these thoughts she
heard her name spoken, and a bird with large wings
flew in at the window, and, smoothing its feathers, stood
upright before her. It was Loki in Freyja's garment
of feathers, and he made her understand in a moment
that he had come to set her free, and that there was no
time to lose. He told her to conceal her casket carefully
in her bosom, and then he said a few words over her,
and she found herself changed into a sparrow, with the
casket fastened among the feathers of her breast.

Then Loki spread his wings once more, and flew out
of the window, and Iduna followed him. The sea-wind
blew cold and rough, and her little wings fluttered with
fear; but she struck them bravely out into the air and
flew like an arrow over the water.

"This way lies Asgard," cried Loki, and the word
gave her strength. But they had not gone far when a
sound was heard above the sea, and the wind, and the
call of the sea-birds. Thiassi had put on his eagle
plumage, and was flying after them. For five days and
five nights the three flew over the water that divides
Jötunheim from Asgard, and at the end of every day
they were closer together, for the giant was gaining on
the other two.

All the five days the dwellers in Asgard stood on the walls of the city, watching. On the sixth evening they saw a falcon and a sparrow, closely pursued by an eagle, flying towards Asgard.

"There will not be time," said Bragi, who had been calculating the speed at which they flew. "The eagle will reach them before they can get into the city."

But Odin desired a fire to be lighted upon the walls; and Thor and Tyr, with what strength remained to them, tore up the trees from the groves and gardens, and made a rampart of fire all round the city. The light of the fire showed Iduna her husband and her friends waiting for her. She made one last effort, and, rising high up in the air above the flames and smoke, she passed the walls, and dropped down safely at the foot of Odin's throne. The giant tried to follow; but, wearied with his long flight, he was unable to raise his enormous bulk sufficiently high in the air. The flames scorched his wings as he flew through them, and he fell among the flaming piles of wood, and was burnt to death.

How Iduna feasted the Æsir on her apples, how they grew young and beautiful again, and how spring and green leaves and music came back to the grove, I must leave you to imagine, for I have made my story long enough already; and if I say any more you will fancy that it is Bragi who has come among you, and that he has entered on his endless story.

Iduna has a connection with the underworld, carried away by a giant and kept captive in his frozen regions, the earth meanwhile becoming winterly, old; death threatening all things. Her story is curiously hinted at in the Elder Edda, where Iduna is represented as falling down from Yggdrasil's Ash into the nether world. Odin sends Heimdall and Bragi to bring her up again, and to ascertain from her if she has been able to discover anything about the destruction and duration of the world and heaven. Instead of answering she bursts into tears — the bright, tearful return of spring — or may this mean the impossibility of wringing from Nature answers to the questions and longings that fill the heart; even the tender year with its messages of hope and hints of immortality is unable to give the full assurance for which we yearn.

Iduna is supposed to typify the Spring, and her falling into captivity for a time to the giant Thiassi corresponds to the falling of the leaf in autumn. The union of Poetry with Spring seems very appropriate, and we must not forget to mention that Bragi's name calls to mind the old story of the Bragarfull. At feasts, in old times, it was the custom to drink four cups of mead: one to Odin for victory, one to Frey, and one to Niörd for a good year and peace, and the fourth to Bragi. This was called the "Cup of Vows," and the drinker vowed over it to perform some great deed worthy of the song of a skald.

In connection with the story of Iduna — being, indeed, almost a sequel to it — we find the myth of Skadi, which is as follows: —

The giant Thiassi had a very tall daughter, called Skadi. When she found that her father never returned from his pursuit of Iduna, she put on her armor and set off to Asgard to avenge his death. The heroes, however, were not inclined to allow her the honor of a combat. They suggested to her that, perhaps, it would answer her purpose as well if, instead of fighting them, she were to content herself with marrying one of their number, and it appeared to Skadi that this might possibly be revenge enough. The Æsir, however, could not make up their minds who should be the victim. It was agreed, at last, that they should all stand in some place of concealment where only their feet could be seen, and that Skadi should walk before them, and, by looking at the feet, choose her husband. Now, Skadi had privately made up her mind to marry Baldur; so, after looking carefully at all the feet, she stopped before a pair, which, from their beautiful shape, she thought could only belong to the handsome Sun-god. When, however, the figure belonging to the feet emerged from the hiding-place, it was discovered that she had chosen the bluff, gusty old Niörd instead of the beautiful young Baldur; and she was not particularly well pleased with her choice, though she was obliged to abide by it.

When Skadi and Niörd were married they found, as persons do find who marry each other for the shape of their feet, and other such wise reasons, that it was not at all an easy thing to live happily together. They could not even agree about the place where they should live. Skadi was never happy out of Thrymheim, the home of noise in misty Jötunheim, and Niörd could not forget pleasant Nöatun, and the clear, sunny seas where he had dwelt in his youth. At last they agreed that they would spend three days in Nöatun, and nine days in Thrymheim; but one day, when Niörd was returning to Nöatun, he could not help breaking out into the following song: —

> "Of mountains I am weary,
> Nine nights long and dreary,
> All up the misty hill,
> The wolf's long howl I heard.
> Methought it sounded strangely —
> Methought it sounded ill
> To the song of the swan bird."

And Skadi immediately answered: —

> "Never can I sleep
> In my couch by the strand,
> For the wild, restless waves
> Rolling over the sand,
> For the scream of the seagulls,
> For the mew as he cries,
> These sounds chase forever
> Sweet sleep from mine eyes."

Then, putting on a pair of snow-skates, she set off more swiftly than the wind, and Niörd never saw more of her. Ever afterwards, with her bow in her hand, she spent her time in chasing wild animals over the snow, and she is the queen and patroness of all skaters.

THE WONDERFUL QUERN STONES

By Julia Goddard

ONCE upon a time there was a king of Denmark, or Gotland, as it was then called, whose name was Frothi. He was a great-grandson of the god Thor, and a very mighty king, and wherever the Danish language was spoken there was Frothi's name honored and respected.

Among his treasures were two quern stones; nothing much to look at, simply two common millstones in appearance, and no one who did not know what they could do would think of taking any notice of them. Nevertheless, these quern stones were of more worth than anything that King Frothi had, for they could produce anything that the grinder of the quern or hand-mill wished for. They would bring gold, silver, precious stones, anything and everything; and besides this they could grind love, joy, peace; therefore it is not too much to say that these stones were worth more than all the treasures of the king put together.

At least they would have been if he could have made use of them, but they were so heavy that few could be found to turn the quern, and just at the time of which I am speaking there was no one at all in the land of Gotland able to work away at the quern handle.

Now the more King Frothi pondered over his won-

352

derful quern stones, the greater became his desire to use them, and he sought throughout the land from north to south, from east to west, if perchance he might find some one strong enough to help him in his need. But all to no purpose, and he was utterly in despair when, by good luck, he happened to go on a visit to Fiölnir, king of Sweden, and to hear of two slave-women of great size and strength. Surely, thought Frothi, these are just the women to grind at my quern Grotti (for so it was called), and he asked King Fiölnir to be allowed to see them.

So King Fiölnir ordered the slaves to be brought before Frothi, and when Frothi saw them his spirits rose, for certainly Menia and Fenia were strong-looking women. They were eight feet in height, and broader across the shoulders than any of Frothi's warriors, and the muscles of their arms stood out like cords. And they lifted heavy weights, threw heavy javelins, and did so many feats of strength that Frothi felt quite sure that they would be able to turn the quern handle.

"I will buy these slaves," said he, "and take them with me to Gotland."

Menia and Fenia stood with their arms folded and their proud heads bowed down, whilst Frothi counted out the gold to the seller. They were slaves; with money had they been bought, with money were they sold again. What cared Frothi who was their father, or how they had come into the land of Sweden?

And he took them home with him and bade them grind at the quern. Now he should be able to test the power of the wonderful stones.

"Grind, grind, Menia and Fenia, let me see whether ye have strength for the work."

So spake King Frothi, and the huge women lifted the heavy stones as though they had been pebbles.

"What shall we grind?" asked the slaves.

"Gold, gold, peace and wealth for Frothi."

Gold! gold! the land was filled with riches. Treasure in the king's palace, treasure in the coffers of his subjects — gold! gold! There were no poor in the land, no beggars in the streets, no children crying for bread. All honor to the quern stones!

Peace! peace! no more war in the land; Frothi is at peace with every one. And more than that, there was peace in all countries where Frothi's name was known, even to the far south; and every one talked of Frothi's peace. Praise be to the quern stones!

Wealth! yes, everything went well. Not one of the counsels of King Frothi failed. There was not a green field that did not yield a rich crop; not a tree but bent beneath its weight of fruit; not a stream that ran dry; not a vessel that sailed from the harbors of Gotland that came not back, after a fair voyage, in safety to its haven. There was good luck everywhere.

"Grind on, grind on, Menia and Fenia! good fortune is mine," said King Frothi.

And the slaves ground on.

"When shall we rest, when may we rest, King Frothi? It is weary work toiling day and night."

"No longer than whilst the cuckoo is silent in the spring."

"Never ceasing is the cry of the cuckoo in the groves; may we not rest longer?"

"Not longer," answered King Frothi, "than whilst the verse of a song is sung."

"That is but little!" sighed Menia and Fenia, and they toiled on. Their arms were weary and their eyes heavy, they would fain have slept; but Frothi would not let them have any sleep. They were but slaves who must obey their master, so they toiled on, still grinding peace and wealth to Frothi: —

> "To Frothi and his queen
>   Joy and peace —
> May plenty in the land
>   Still increase.
> Frothi and his queen
>   From dangers keep;
> May they on beds of down
>   Sweetly sleep.
> No sword be drawn
>   In Gotland old,
> By murderer bold.
> No harm befall
>   The high or low —
> To none be woe,
> Good luck to all.
> Good luck to all,
>   We grind, we grind.
> No rest we find,
> For rest we call."

Thus sang the two giant women; then they begged again, "Give us rest, O Frothi!"

But still Frothi answered, "Rest whilst the verse of a song is sung, or as long as the cuckoo is silent in the spring."

No longer would the king give them.

Yet Frothi was deemed a good king, but gold and good luck were hardening his heart.

Menia and Fenia went on grinding, and their wrath grew deeper and deeper, and thus at last they spoke.

First said Fenia, "Thou wert not wise, O Frothi. Thou didst buy us because like giants we towered above the other slaves, because we were strong and hardy and could lift heavy burdens."

And Menia took up the wail: "Are we not of the race of the mountain giants? Are not our kindred greater than thine, O Frothi? The quern had never left the gray fell but for the giants' daughters. Never, never should we have ground as we have done, had it not been that we remembered from what race we sprang."

Then answered Menia: "Nine long winters saw us training to feats of strength, nine long winters of wearisome labor. Deep down in the earth we toiled and toiled until we could move the high mountain from its foundations. We are weird women, O Frothi. We can see far into the future. Our eyes have looked upon the quern before. In the giants' house we whirled it until the earth shook, and hoarse thunder resounded through the caverns. Thou art not wise, O Frothi. O Frothi, thou art not wise!"

But Frothi heard them not; he was sleeping the sweet sleep that the quern stones had ground for him.

"Strong are we indeed," laughed Fenia sorrowfully, "strong to contend with the puny men, — we whose pastime in Sweden was to tame the fiercest bears, so that they ate from our hands; we who fought with mighty warriors and came off conquerors; we who helped one prince and put down another. Well we fought, and many were the wounds we received from sharp spears and flashing swords. Frothi knows not our power, or he would scarce have brought us to his palace to treat us thus. Here no one has compassion upon us. Cold are the skies above us, and the pitiless wind beats upon our breasts. Cold is the ground on which we stand, and the keen frost bites our feet. Ah, there are none to pity us. No one cares for the slaves. We grind forever an enemy's quern, and he gives us no rest. Grind, grind; I am weary of grinding; I must have rest."

"Nay," returned Menia, "talk not of rest until Frothi is content with what we bring him."

Then Fenia started: "If he gives us no rest, let us take it ourselves. Why should we any longer grind good for him who only gives us evil? We can grind what we please. Let us revenge ourselves."

Then Menia turned the handle quicker than ever, and in a wild voice she sang:—

> " I see a ship come sailing
>   With warriors bold aboard,
> There's many a one that in Danish blood
> Would be glad to dip his sword.
> Say, shall we grind them hither?
> Say, shall they land to-night?
> Say, shall they set the palace afire?
> Say, shall they win the fight?"

Then called Fenia in a voice of thunder through the midnight air: "Frothi, Frothi, awake, awake! Wilt thou not listen to us? Have mercy and let us rest our weary limbs."

But all was still, and Frothi gave no answer to the cry.

"Nay," answered Menia, "he will not hearken. Little he cares for the worn-out slaves. Revenge, revenge!"

And Frothi slept, not dreaming of the evil that was coming upon him.

And again Fenia shouted: "Frothi, Frothi, awake! The beacon is blazing. Danger is nigh. Wilt thou not spare?"

But Frothi gave no answer, and the giant women toiled on.

"O Frothi, Frothi, we cannot bear our weariness."

And still no answer came.

"Frothi, Frothi, danger is nigh thee. Well-manned ships are gliding over the sea. It is Mysingr who comes: his white sail flutters in the wind; his flag is unfurled. Frothi, Frothi, awake, awake! thou shalt be king no longer."

And as the giant women ground, the words they spake came to pass, — they were grinding revenge for themselves, and brought the enemy nearer and nearer.

"Ho! hearken to the herald! Frothi, Frothi, the town is on fire. The palaces will soon be ruined heaps. Grind, Menia, ever more swiftly, until we grind death to Frothi."

And Menia and Fenia ground and ground till Mysingr and his followers landed from the ships. They ground until they had reached the palace.

"To arms, to arms!" shouted the warders, but it

was too late. The Gotlanders armed themselves; but who could stand against the army that the slave women were grinding against them?

Not long did the struggle last. Frothi and his Gotlanders fought bravely, but the sea-king and his allies were mightier, for the giantesses were in giant mood, and turned the handle faster and faster, until down fell the quern stones. Then sank Frothi pierced with wounds, and the fight was over. The army that Menia and Fenia had ground to help Mysingr vanished; and Mysingr and his men alone were left conquerors on the bloody field.

They loaded their ships with treasure, and Mysingr took with him Menia, Fenia, and the quern stones.

But, alas! Mysingr was no wiser than King Frothi had been.

Gold, however, was not his first thought; he had enough of that, but he wanted something else that just then was more to him than gold.

There was no salt on board the sea-king's vessels; so he said, "Grind salt."

And Menia and Fenia ground salt for Mysingr.

At midnight they asked if they had ground enough.

And Mysingr bade them grind on.

And so they ground and ground until the ship was so heavy with salt that it sank, and the sea-king and all his men were drowned.

Where the quern stones went down there is to this day a great whirlpool, and the waters of the sea have been salt ever since.

MYTHS OF JAPAN

THE ASHES THAT MADE TREES BLOOM

By William Elliot Griffis

IN the good old days of the daimios, there lived an
old couple whose only pet was a little dog. Having
no children, they loved it as though it were a baby. The
old dame made it a cushion of blue crape, and at meal-
time Muko — for that was its name — would sit on it
as demure as any cat. The kind people fed the pet with
tidbits of fish from their own chopsticks, and it was
allowed to have all the boiled rice it wanted. Whenever
the old woman took the animal out with her on holi-
days, she put a bright-red silk crape ribbon around its
neck. Thus treated, the dumb creature loved its pro-
tectors like a being with a soul.

Now the old man, being a rice-farmer, went daily
with hoe or spade into the fields, working hard from the
first croak of the raven until O Tento Sama (as the
sun is called) had gone down behind the hills. Every
day the dog followed him to work, and kept near by,
never once harming the white heron that walked in the
footsteps of the old man to pick up the worms. For
the old fellow was kind to everything that had life,
and often turned up a sod on purpose to give food to
the sacred birds.

One day doggy came running to him, putting his

paws against his straw leggings, and motioning with his head to some spot behind. The old man at first thought his pet was only playing, and did not mind it. But the dog kept on whining and running to and fro for some minutes. Then the old man followed the dog a few yards to a place where the animal began a lively scratching. Thinking it only a buried bone or bit of fish, but wishing to humor his pet, the old man struck his iron-shod hoe in the earth, when, lo! a pile of gold gleamed before him.

He rubbed his old eyes, stooped down to look, and there was at least a half peck of *kobans*, or oval gold coins. He gathered them and hied home at once.

Thus in an hour the old couple were made rich. The good souls bought a piece of land, made a feast to their friends, and gave plentifully to their poor neighbors. As for doggy, they petted him till they nearly smothered him with kindness.

Now in the same village there lived a wicked old man and his wife, who had always kicked and scolded all dogs whenever any passed their house. Hearing of their neighbors' good luck, they coaxed the dog into their garden and set before him bits of fish and other dainties, hoping he would find treasure for them. But the dog, being afraid of the cruel pair, would neither eat nor move.

Then they dragged him out of doors, taking a spade and hoe with them. No sooner had doggy got near a pine-tree growing in the garden than he began to paw and scratch the ground, as if a mighty treasure lay beneath.

"Quick, wife, hand me the spade and hoe!" cried the greedy old fool, as he danced with joy.

Then the covetous old fellow, with a spade, and the old crone, with a hoe, began to dig; but there was nothing but a dead kitten, the smell of which made them drop their tools and shut their noses. Furious at the dog, the old man kicked and beat him to death, and the old woman finished the work by nearly chopping off his head with the sharp hoe. They then flung him into the hole, and stamped down the earth over his carcass.

The owner of the dog heard of the death of his pet, and, mourning for him as if it had been his own child, went at night under the pine-tree. He set up some bamboo tubes in the ground, such as are used before tombs, in which he put fresh camellia flowers. Then he laid a cup of water and a tray of food on the grave, and burned several costly sticks of incense. He mourned a great while over his pet, calling him many dear names, as if he were alive.

That night the spirit of the dog appeared to him in a dream and said, —

"Cut down the pine-tree which is over my grave, and make from it a mortar for your rice pastry, and a mill for your bean sauce."

So the old man chopped down the tree, and cut out of the middle of the trunk a section about two feet long. With great labor, partly by fire, partly by the chisel, he scraped out a hollow place as big as a half-bushel. He then made a great, long-handled hammer of wood, such as is used for pounding rice. When New Year's time drew near, he wished to make some rice pastry. So the white rice in the basket, and the fire and pot to boil the rice dumplings, and the pretty red lacquered boxes, were got ready. The old man knotted his blue kerchief round his head, the old lady tucked up her sleeves, and all was ready for cake-making.

When the rice was all boiled, granny put it into the mortar, the old man lifted his hammer to pound the mass into dough, and the blows fell heavy and fast till the pastry was all ready for baking. Suddenly the whole mass turned into a heap of gold coins. When, too, the old woman took the hand-mill, and, filling it with bean sauce, began to grind, the gold dropped like rain.

Meanwhile the envious neighbor peeped in at the window when the boiled beans were being ground.

"Goody me!" cried the old hag, as she saw each dripping of sauce turning into yellow gold, until in a few minutes the tub under the mill was full of a shining mass of *kobans* (oval gold pieces). "I'll borrow that mill, I will."

So the old couple were rich again. The next day the stingy and wicked neighbor, having boiled a mess of beans, came and borrowed the mortar and magic mill. They filled one with boiled rice and the other with beans. Then the old man began to pound and the woman to grind. But at the first blow and turn, the pastry and sauce turned into a foul mass of worms. Still more angry at this, they chopped the mill into pieces, to use as firewood.

Not long after that, the good old man dreamed again,

and the spirit of the dog spoke to him, telling him how the wicked people had burned the mill made from the pine-tree.

"Take the ashes of the mill, sprinkle them on the withered trees, and they will bloom again," said the dog-spirit.

The old man awoke, and went at once to his wicked neighbor's house, where he found the miserable old pair sitting at the edge of their square fireplace, in the middle of the floor, smoking and spinning. From time to time they warmed their hands and feet with the blaze from some bits of the mill, while behind them lay a pile of the broken pieces.

The good old man humbly begged the ashes, and though the covetous couple turned up their noses at him, and scolded him as if he were a thief, they let him fill his basket with the ashes.

On coming home, the old man took his wife into the garden. It being winter, their favorite cherry-tree was bare. He sprinkled a pinch of ashes on it, and, lo! it sprouted blossoms until it became a cloud of pink blooms which perfumed the air. The news of this filled the village, and every one ran out to see the wonder.

The covetous couple also heard the story, and, gathering up the remaining ashes of the mill, kept them to make withered trees blossom.

The kind old man, hearing that his lord the daimio was to pass along the high road near the village, set out to see him, taking his basket of ashes. As the train approached, he climbed up into an old withered cherry-tree that stood by the wayside.

Now, in the days of the daimios, it was the custom, when their lord passed by, for all the loyal people to shut up their second-story windows. They even pasted them fast with a slip of paper, so as not to commit the impertinence of looking down on his lordship. All the people along the road would fall upon their hands and knees, and remain prostrate until the procession passed by. Hence it seemed very impolite, at first, for the old man to climb the tree and be higher than his master's head.

The train drew near, with all its pomp of gay banners, covered spears, state umbrellas, and princely crests. One tall man marched ahead, crying out to the people by the way, "Get down on your knees! Get down on your knees!" And every one kneeled down while the procession was passing.

Suddenly the leader of the van caught sight of the aged man up in the tree. He was about to call out to him in an angry tone, but, seeing he was such an old fellow, he pretended not to notice him and passed him by. So, when the daimio's palanquin drew near, the old man, taking a pinch of ashes from his basket, scattered it over the tree. In a moment it burst into blossom.

The delighted daimio ordered the train to be stopped, and got out to see the wonder. Calling the old man to him, he thanked him, and ordered presents of silk robes, sponge-cake, fans, a *nétsŭké* (ivory carving), and other rewards to be given him. He even invited him to visit him in his castle.

So the old man went gleefully home to share his joy with his dear old wife.

But when the greedy neighbor heard of it, he took some of the magic ashes and went out on the highway. There he waited until a daimio's train came along, and, instead of kneeling down like the crowd, he climbed a withered cherry-tree.

When the daimio himself was almost directly under him, he threw a handful of ashes over the tree, which did not change a particle. The wind blew the fine dust in the noses and eyes of the daimio and his Samurai. Such a sneezing and choking! It spoiled all the pomp and dignity of the procession. The man whose business it was to cry, "Get down on your knees," seized the old fool by the topknot, dragged him from the tree, and tumbled him and his ash-basket into the ditch by the road. Then, beating him soundly, he left him for dead.

Thus the wicked old man died in the mud, but the kind friend of the dog dwelt in peace and plenty, and both he and his wife lived to a green old age.

THE ELVES AND THE ENVIOUS NEIGHBOR

By A. B. Mitford

ONCE upon a time there was a certain man, who, being overtaken by darkness among the mountains, was driven to seek shelter in the trunk of a hollow tree. In the middle of the night, a large company of elves assembled at the place; and the man, peeping out from his hiding-place, was frightened out of his wits. After a while, however, the elves began to feast and drink wine, and to amuse themselves by singing and dancing, until at last the man, caught by the infection of the fun, forgot all about his fright, and crept out of his hollow tree to join in the revels. When the day was about to dawn, the elves said to the man, "You're a very jolly companion, and must come out and have a dance with us again. You must make us a promise, and keep it." So the elves, thinking to bind the man over to return, took a large wen that grew on his forehead and kept it in pawn; upon this they all left the place, and went home. The man walked off to his own house in high glee at having passed a jovial night, and got rid of his wen into the bargain. So he told the story to all his friends, who congratulated him warmly on being cured of his wen. But there was a neighbor of his who was also troubled with a wen of long standing, and, when he

370

heard of his friend's luck, he was smitten with envy, and went off to hunt for the hollow tree, in which, when he had found it, he passed the night.

Towards midnight the elves came, as he had expected, and began feasting and drinking, with songs and dances as before. As soon as he saw this, he came out of his hollow tree, and began dancing and singing as his neighbor had done. The elves, mistaking him for their former boon-companion, were delighted to see him, and said, —

"You're a good fellow to recollect your promise, and we'll give you back your pledge;" so one of the elves, pulling the pawned wen out of his pocket, stuck it on to the man's forehead, on the top of the other wen which he already had. So the envious neighbor went home weeping, with two wens instead of one. This is a good lesson to people who cannot see the good luck of others, without coveting it for themselves.

NEDZUMI

By Frank Rinder

IN the Central Land of Reed-Plains dwelt two rats.
Their home was in a lonely farmstead surrounded
by rice fields. Here they lived happily for so many years
that the other rats in the district, who had constantly
to change their quarters, believed that their neighbors
were under the special protection of Fukoruku Jin, one
of the Seven Gods of Happiness, and the Patron of
Long Life.

These rats had a large family of children. Every summer day they led the little ones into the rice fields,
where, under shelter of the waving stalks, the young
rats learned the history and cunning of their people.
When work was done, they would scamper away and
play with their friends until it was time to return home.

The most beautiful of these children was Nedzumi,
the pride of her parents' hearts. She was truly a lovely
little creature, with sleek silvery skin, bright intelligent
eyes, tiny upstanding ears, and pearly white teeth. It
seemed to the fond father and mother that no one was
great enough to marry their daughter; but, after much
pondering, they decided that the most powerful being
in the whole universe should be their son-in-law.

The parents discussed the weighty question with a
trusted neighbor, who said, "If you would wed your

daughter to the most powerful being in the universe, you must ask the sun to marry her, for his empire knows no bounds."

How they mounted through the skies, no rat can tell. The sun gave them audience and listened graciously as they said, "We would give you our daughter to wife." He smiled and rejoined, "Your daughter is indeed beautiful, and I thank you for coming so far to offer her to me. But, tell me, why have you chosen me out of all the world?" The rats made answer, "We would marry our Nedzumi to the mightiest being, and you alone wield world-wide sway." Then the sun replied, "Truly my kingdom is vast, but oftentimes, when I would illumine the world, a cloud floats by and covers me. I cannot pierce the cloud; therefore you must go to him if your wish is to be attained."

In no way discouraged, the rats left the sun and came to a cloud as he rested after a flight through the air. The cloud received them less cordially than the sun, and replied to their offer, with a look of mischief in his dusky eyes, "You are mistaken if you think that I am the most powerful being. It is true that I sometimes hide the sun, but I cannot withstand the force of the wind. When he begins to blow I am driven away, and torn in pieces. My strength is not equal to the power of the wind."

A little saddened, the rats, intent on their daughter's future prosperity, waylaid the wind as he swept through a pine forest. He was about to awaken the plain beyond, to stir the grass and the flowers into motion. The two anxious parents made known their mission. This was the whispered reply of the wind: "It is true that I have strength to drive away the clouds, but I am powerless against the wall which men build to keep me back. You must go to him if you would have the mightiest being in the world for your son-in-law. Indeed I am not so mighty as the wall."

The rats, still persistent in their quest, came to the wall and told their story. The wall answered, "True, I can withstand the wind, but the rat undermines me and makes holes through my very heart. To him you must go if you would wed your daughter to the most powerful being in the world. I cannot overcome the rat."

And now the parent rats returned to their home in the farmstead. Nedzumi, their beautiful daughter with the silken coat and sparkling eyes, rejoiced when she heard that she was to marry one of her own people, for her heart had already been given to a playfellow of the rice fields. They were married, and lived for many years as king and queen of the rat world.

THE PALACE OF THE OCEAN–BED

By Frank Rinder

HO–WORI, Prince Fire-Fade, the son of Ninigi, was a great hunter. He caught "things rough of hair and things soft of hair." His elder brother, Ho-deri, Prince Fire-Flash, was a fisher who caught "things broad of fin and things narrow of fin." But often, when the wind blew and the waves ran high, he would spend hours on the sea and catch no fish. When the Storm God was abroad, Ho-deri had to stay at home, while at night-fall Ho-wori returned laden with spoil from the mountains. Ho-deri spoke to his brother, and said, "I would have your bow and arrows and become a hunter. You shall have my fish-hook." At first Ho-wori would not consent, but finally the exchange was made.

Now Prince Fire-Flash was no hunter. He could not track the game, nor run swiftly, nor take good aim. Day after day Prince Fire-Fade went out to sea. In vain he threw his line; he caught no fish. Moreover, one day, he lost his brother's fish-hook. Then Ho-deri came to Ho-wori, and said, "There is the luck of the mountain and there is the luck of the sea. Let each restore to the other his luck." Ho-wori replied, "I did not catch a single fish with your hook, and now it is lost in the sea."

The elder brother was very angry, and with many hard words demanded the return of his treasure. Prince

375

Fire-Fade was unhappy. He broke in pieces his good sword and made five hundred fish-hooks, which he offered to his brother. But this did not appease the wrath of Prince Fire-Flash, who still raged and asked for his own hook.

Ho-wori could find neither comfort nor help. He sat one day by the shore and heaved a deep sigh. The old Man of the Sea heard the sigh, and asked the cause of his sorrow. Ho-wori told him of the loss of the fish-hook, and of his brother's displeasure. Thereupon the wise man promised to give his help. He plaited strips of bamboo so tightly together that the water could not pass through, and fashioned therewith a stout little boat. Into this boat Ho-wori jumped, and was carried far out to sea.

After a time, as the old man had foretold, his boat began to sink. Deeper and deeper it sank, until at last he came to a glittering palace of fishes' scales. In front of it was a well, shaded by a great cassia-tree. Prince Fire-Fade sat among the wide-spreading branches. He looked down, and saw a maiden approach the well; in her hand she carried a jeweled bowl. She was the lovely Toyo-tama, Peerless Jewel, the daughter of Wata-tsu-mi, the Sea-King. Ho-wori was spell-bound by her strange wave-like beauty, her long flowing hair, her soft deep-blue eyes. The maiden stooped to fill her bowl. Suddenly, she saw the reflection of Prince Fire-Fade in the water; she dropped the precious bowl, and it fell in a thousand pieces. Toyo-tama hastened to her father, and exclaimed, "A man, with the grace and beauty of a god, sits in the branches of the cassia-tree. I have seen his

THE REFLECTION OF PRINCE FIRE-FADE IN THE WATER

picture in the waters of the well." The Sea-King knew
that it must be the great hunter, Prince Fire-Fade.

Then Wata-tsu-mi went forth and stood under the
cassia-tree. He looked up to Ho-wori, and said: "Come
down, O Son of the Gods, and enter my Palace of the
Ocean-Bed." Ho-wori obeyed, and was led into the
palace and seated on a throne of sea-asses' skins. A
banquet was prepared in his honor. The *hashi* were
delicate branches of coral, and the plates were of silvery
mother-of-pearl. The clear-rock wine was sipped from
cup-shaped ocean blooms with long, slender stalks.
Ho-wori thought that never before had there been such a
banquet. When it was ended he went with Toyo-tama
to the roof of the palace. Dimly, through the blue
waters that moved above, he could discern the Sun-
Goddess. He saw the mountains and valleys of ocean,
the waving forests of tall sea-plants, the homes of the
shaké and the *kani.*

Ho-wori told Wata-tsu-mi of the loss of the fish-hook.
Then the Sea-King called all his subjects together and
questioned them. No fish knew aught of the hook, but,
said the lobster, "As I sat one day in my crevice among
the rocks, the *tai* passed near me. His mouth was swollen, and he went by without giving me greeting." Wata-
tsu-mi then noticed that the *tai* had not answered his
summons. A messenger, fleet of fin, was sent to fetch
him. When the *tai* appeared, the lost fish-hook was
found in his poor wounded mouth. It was restored to
Ho-wori, and he was happy. Toyo-tama became his
bride, and they lived together in the cool fish-scale
palace.

Prince Fire-Fade came to understand the secrets of the ocean, the cause of its anger, the cause of its joy. The Storm-Spirit of the upper sea did not rule in the ocean-bed, and night after night Ho-wori was rocked to sleep by the gentle motion of the waters.

Many tides had ebbed and flowed, when, in the quiet of the night, Ho-wori heaved a deep sigh. Toyo-tama was troubled, and told her father that, as Ho-wori dreamt of his home on the earth, a great longing had come over him to visit it once more. Then Wata-tsu-mi gave into Ho-wori's hands two great jewels, the one to rule the flow, the other to rule the ebb of the tide. He spoke thus: "Return to earth on the head of my trusted sea-dragon. Restore the lost fish-hook to Ho-deri. If he is still wroth with you, bring forth the tide-flowing jewel, and the waters shall cover him. If he asks your forgiveness, bring forth the tide-ebbing jewel, and it shall be well with him."

Ho-wori left the Palace of the Ocean-Bed, and was carried swiftly to his own land. As he set foot on the shore, he ungirded his sword, and tied it round the neck of the sea-dragon. Then he said, "Take this to the Sea-King as a token of my love and gratitude."

AUTUMN AND SPRING

By Frank Rinder

A FAIR maiden lay asleep in a rice field. The sun was at its height, and she was weary. Now a god looked down upon the rice field. He knew that the beauty of the maiden came from within, that it mirrored the beauty of heavenly dreams. He knew that even now, as she smiled, she held converse with the spirit of the wind or the flowers.

The god descended and asked the dream-maiden to be his bride. She rejoiced, and they were wed. A wonderful red jewel came of their happiness.

Long, long afterwards, the stone was found by a farmer, who saw that it was a very rare jewel. He prized it highly, and always carried it about with him. Sometimes, as he looked at it in the pale light of the moon, it seemed to him that he could discern two sparkling eyes in its depths. Again, in the stillness of the night, he would awaken and think that a clear soft voice called him by name.

One day, the farmer had to carry the midday meal to his workers in the field. The sun was very hot, so he loaded a cow with the bowls of rice, the millet dumplings, and the beans. Suddenly, Prince Ama-boko stood in the path. He was angry, for he thought that the farmer was about to kill the cow. The Prince would hear no word of denial; his wrath increased. The farmer became more and more terrified, and, finally, took the precious stone from his pocket and presented it as a peace-offering to the powerful Prince. Ama-boko marveled at the brilliancy of the jewel, and allowed the man to continue his journey.

The Prince returned to his home. He drew forth the treasure, and it was immediately transformed into a goddess of surpassing beauty. Even as she rose before him, he loved her, and ere the moon waned they were wed. The goddess ministered to his every want. She prepared delicate dishes, the secret of which is known only to the gods. She made wine from the juice of a myriad herbs, wine such as mortals never taste.

But, after a time, the Prince became proud and overbearing. He began to treat his faithful wife with cruel contempt. The goddess was sad, and said: "You are not worthy of my love. I will leave you and go to my father." Ama-boko paid no heed to these words, for he did not believe that the threat would be fulfilled. But the beautiful goddess was in earnest. She escaped from the palace and fled to Naniwa, where she is still honored as Akaru-hime, the Goddess of Light.

Now the Prince was wroth when he heard that the goddess had left him, and set out in pursuit of her. But when he neared Naniwa, the gods would not allow his vessel to enter the haven. Then he knew that his priceless red jewel was lost to him forever. He steered his ship towards the north coast of Japan, and landed at Tajima. Here he was well received, and highly esteemed on account of the treasures which he brought with him.

He had costly strings of pearls, girdles of precious stones, and a mirror which the wind and the waves obeyed. Prince Ama-boko remained at Tajima, and was the father of a mighty race.

Among his children's children was a princess so renowned for her beauty that eighty suitors sought her hand. One after the other returned sorrowfully home, for none found favor in her eyes. At last, two brothers came before her, the young God of the Autumn, and the young God of the Spring. The elder of the two, the God of Autumn, first urged his suit. But the princess refused him. He went to his younger brother and said, "The princess does not love me, neither will you be able to win her heart."

But the Spring God was full of hope, and replied, "I will give you a cask of rice wine if I do not win her, but if she consents to be my bride, you shall give a cask of *saké* to me."

Now the God of Spring went to his mother, and told her all. She promised to aid him. Thereupon she wove, in a single night, a robe and sandals from the unopened buds of the lilac and white wistaria. Out of the same delicate flowers she fashioned a bow and arrows. Thus clad, the God of Spring made his way to the beautiful princess.

As he stepped before the maiden, every bud unfolded, and from the heart of each blossom came a fragrance that filled the air. The princess was overjoyed, and gave her hand to the God of the Spring.

The elder brother, the God of Autumn, was filled with rage when he heard how his brother had obtained the wondrous robe. He refused to give the promised cask of *saké*. When the mother learned that the god had broken his word, she placed stones and salt in the hollow of a bamboo cane, wrapped it round with bamboo leaves, and hung it in the smoke. Then she uttered a curse upon her first-born son: "As the leaves wither and fade, so must you. As the salt sea ebbs, so must you. As the stone sinks, so must you."

The terrible curse fell upon her son. While the God of Spring remains ever young, ever fragrant, ever full of mirth, the God of Autumn is old, and withered, and sad.

THE VISION OF TSUNU

By Frank Rinder

WHEN the five tall pine-trees on the windy heights of Mionoseki were but tiny shoots, there lived in the Kingdom of the Islands a pious man. His home was in a remote hamlet surrounded by mountains and great forests of pine. Tsunu had a wife and sons and daughters. He was a woodman, and his days were spent in the forest and on the hillsides. In summer he was up at cock-crow, and worked patiently, in the soft light under the pines, until nightfall. Then, with his burden of logs and branches, he went slowly homeward. After the evening meal, he would tell some old story or legend. Tsunu was never weary of relating the wondrous tales of the Land of the Gods. Best of all he loved to speak of Fuji-yama, the mountain that stood so near his home.

In times gone by, there was no mountain where now the sacred peak reaches up to the sky; only a far-stretching plain bathed in sunlight all day. The peasants in the district were astonished, one morning, to behold a mighty hill where before had been the open plain. It had sprung up in a single night, while they slept. Flames and huge stones were hurled from its summit; the peasants feared that the demons from the under-world had come to wreak vengeance upon them.

383

But for many generations there have been peace and silence on the heights. The good Sun-Goddess loves Fuji-yama. Every evening she lingers on his summit, and when at last she leaves him, his lofty crest is bathed in soft purple light. In the evening the Matchless Mountain seems to rise higher and higher into the skies, until no mortal can tell the place of his rest. Golden clouds enfold Fuji-yama in the early morning. Pilgrims come from far and near, to gain blessing and health for themselves and their families from the sacred mountain.

On the self-same night that Fuji-yama rose out of the earth, a strange thing happened in the mountainous district near Kyōto. The inhabitants were awakened by a terrible roar, which continued throughout the night. In the morning every mountain had disappeared; not one of the hills that they loved was to be seen. A blue lake lay before them. It was none other than the lute-shaped Lake Biwa. The mountains had, in truth, traveled under the earth for more than a hundred miles, and now form the sacred Fuji-yama.

As Tsunu stepped out of his hut in the morning, his eyes sought the Mountain of the Gods. He saw the golden clouds, and the beautiful story was in his mind as he went to his work.

One day the woodman wandered farther than usual into the forest. At noon he was in a very lonely spot. The air was soft and sweet, the sky so blue that he looked long at it, and then took a deep breath. Tsunu was happy.

Now his eye fell on a little fox who watched him

curiously from the bushes. The creature ran away
when it saw that the man's attention had been attracted.
Tsunu thought, "I will follow the little fox and see
where she goes." Off he started in pursuit. He soon
came to a bamboo thicket. The smooth, slender stems
waved dreamily, the pale green leaves still sparkled
with the morning dew. But it was not this which
caused the woodman to stand spellbound. On a plot of
mossy grass beyond the thicket, sat two maidens of
surpassing beauty. They were partly shaded by the
waving bamboos, but their faces were lit up by the
sunlight. Not a word came from their lips, yet Tsunu
knew that the voices of both must be sweet as the
cooing of the wild dove. The maidens were graceful as
the slender willow, they were fair as the blossom of the
cherry-tree. Slowly they moved the chessmen which
lay before them on the grass. Tsunu hardly dared to
breathe, lest he should disturb them. The breeze caught
their long hair, the sunlight played upon it. . . . The
sun still shone. . . . The chessmen were still slowly
moved to and fro. . . . The woodman gazed enrap-
tured.

"But now," thought Tsunu, "I must return, and tell
those at home of the beautiful maidens." Alas, his
knees were stiff and weak. "Surely I have stood here
for many hours," he said. He leaned for support upon
his axe; it crumbled into dust. Looking down he saw
that a flowing white beard hung from his chin.

For many hours the poor woodman tried in vain to
reach his home. Fatigued and wearied, he came at last

to a hut. But all was changed. Strange faces peered curiously at him. The speech of the people was unfamiliar. "Where are my wife and my children?" he cried. But no one knew his name.

Finally, the poor woodman came to understand that seven generations had passed since he bade farewell to his dear ones in the early morning. While he had gazed at the beautiful maidens his wife, his children, and his children's children had lived and died.

The few remaining years of Tsunu's life were spent as a pious pilgrim to Fuji-yama, his well-loved mountain.

Since his death he has been honored as a saint who brings prosperity to the people of his native country.

RAI–TARO, THE SON OF THE THUNDER–GOD

By Frank Rinder

AT the foot of the snowy mountain of Haku-san,
in the province of Echizen, lived a peasant and
his wife. They were very poor, for their little strip of
barren mountain land yielded but one scanty crop a
year, while their neighbors in the valley gathered two
rich harvests. With unceasing patience Bimbo worked
from cock-crow until the barking of the foxes warned
him that night had fallen. He laid out his plot of ground
in terraces, surrounding them with dams, and diverted
the course of the mountain stream that it might flood
his fields. But when no rain came to swell the brook,
Bimbo's harvest failed. Often as he sat in his hut with
his wife, after a long day of hard work, he would speak
of their troubles. The peasants were filled with grief
that a child had not been given to them. They longed
to adopt a son, but, as they had barely enough for their
own simple wants, the dream could not be realized.

An evil day came when the land of Echizen was
parched. No rain fell. The brook was dried up. The
young rice-sprouts withered. Bimbo sighed heavily
over his work. He looked up to the sky and entreated
the gods to take pity on him.

After many weeks of sunshine, the sky was overcast. Single clouds came up rapidly from the west, and gathered in angry masses. A strange silence filled the air. Even the voice of the cicadas, who had chirped in the trees during the heat of the day, was stilled. Only the cry of the mountain hawk was audible. A murmur passed over valley and hill, a faint rustling of leaves, a whispering sigh in the needles of the fir. Fu-ten, the Storm-Spirit, and Rai-den, the Thunder-God, were abroad. Deeper and deeper sank the clouds under the weight of the thunder dragon. The rain came at first in large cool drops, then in torrents.

Bimbo rejoiced, and worked steadily to strengthen the dams and open the conduits of his farm.

A vivid flash of lightning, a mighty roar of thunder! Terrified, almost blinded, Bimbo fell on his knees. He thought that the claws of the thunder-dragon were about him. But he was unharmed, and he offered thanks to Kwan-non, the Goddess of Pity, who protects mortals from the wrath of the Thunder-God. On the spot where the lightning struck the ground, lay a little rosy boy full of life, who held out his arms and lisped. Bimbo was greatly amazed, and his heart was glad, for he knew that the gods had heard and answered his never-uttered prayer. The happy peasant took the child up, and carried him under his rice-straw coat to the hut. He called to his wife, "Rejoice, our wish is fulfilled. The gods have sent us a child. We will call him Rai-taro, the Son of the Thunder-God, and bring him up as our own."

The good woman fondly tended the boy. Rai-taro loved his foster-parents, and grew up dutiful and obedient. He did not care to play with other children, but was always happy to work in the fields with Bimbo, where he would watch the flight of the birds, and listen to the sound of the wind. Long before Bimbo could discern any sign of an approaching storm, Rai-taro knew that it was at hand. When it drew near, he fixed his eyes intently on the gathering clouds, he listened eagerly to the roll of the thunder, the rush of the rain, and he greeted each flash of lightning with a shout of joy.

Rai-taro had come as a ray of sunshine into the lives of the poor peasants. Good fortune followed the farmer from the day that he carried the little boy home in his rain-coat. The mountain stream was never dry. The land was fertile, and he gathered rich harvests of rice and abundant crops of millet. Year by year, his prosperity increased, until from Bimbo, "the poor," he became Kanemochi, "the prosperous."

About eighteen summers passed, and Rai-taro still lived with his foster-parents. Suddenly, they knew not why, he became thoughtful and sad. Nothing would rouse him. The peasants determined to hold a feast in honor of his birthday. They called together the neighbors, and there was much rejoicing. Bimbo told many tales of other days, and, finally, of how Rai-taro came to him out of the storm. As he ceased, a strange far-off look was in the eyes of the Son of the Thunder-God. He stood before his foster-parents, and said: "You have loved me well. You have been faithful and kind. But the time has come for me to leave you. Farewell."

In a moment Rai-taro was gone. A white cloud floated

upward towards the heights of Haku-san. As it neared the summit of the mountain, it took the form of a white dragon. Higher still the dragon soared, until, at last, it vanished into a castle of clouds.

The peasants looked wistfully up to the sky. They hoped that Rai-taro might return, but he had joined his father, Rai-den, the Thunder-God, and was seen no more.

THE STAR–LOVERS

By Frank Rinder

SHOKUJO, daughter of the Sun, dwelt with her
father on the banks of the Silver River of Heaven,
which we call the Milky Way. She was a lovely maiden,
graceful and winsome, and her eyes were tender as
the eyes of a dove. Her loving father, the Sun, was
much troubled because Shokujo did not share in the
youthful pleasures of the daughters of the air. A soft
melancholy seemed to brood over her, but she never
wearied of working for the good of others, and especially did she busy herself at her loom; indeed she came
to be called the Weaving Princess.

The Sun bethought him that if he could give his
daughter in marriage, all would be well; her dormant
love would be kindled into a flame that would illumine
her whole being and drive out the pensive spirit which
oppressed her. Now there lived, hard by, one Kingen,
a right honest herdsman, who tended his cows on the
borders of the Heavenly Stream. The Sun-King proposed to bestow his daughter on Kingen, thinking in
this way to provide for her happiness and at the same
time keep her near him. Every star beamed approval,
and there was joy in the heavens.

The love that bound Shokujo and Kingen to one
another was a great love. With its awakening, Shokujo forsook her former occupations, nor did she any

longer labor industriously at the loom, but laughed, and danced, and sang, and made merry from morn till night. The Sun-King was sorely grieved, for he had not foreseen so great a change. Anger was in his eyes, and he said, "Kingen is surely the cause of this, therefore I will banish him to the other side of the River of Stars."

When Shokujo and Kingen heard that they were to be parted, and could thenceforth, in accordance with the King's decree, meet but once a year, and that upon the seventh night of the seventh month, their hearts were heavy. The leave-taking between them was a sad one, and great tears stood in Shokujo's eyes as she bade farewell to her lover-husband. In answer to the behest of the Sun-King, myriads of magpies flocked together, and, outspreading their wings, formed a bridge on which Kingen crossed the River of Heaven. The moment that his foot touched the opposite bank, the birds dispersed with noisy chatter, leaving poor Kingen a solitary exile. He looked wistfully towards the weeping figure of Shokujo, who stood on the threshold of her now desolate home.

Long and weary were the succeeding days, spent as they were by Kingen in guiding his oxen and by Shokujo in plying her shuttle. The Sun-King was gladdened by his daughter's industry. When night fell and the heavens were bright with countless lights, the lovers were wont, standing on the banks of the celestial stream, to waft across it sweet and tender messages, while each uttered a prayer for the speedy coming of the wondrous night.

THE STAR-LOVERS

The long-hoped-for month and day drew nigh, and the hearts of the lovers were troubled lest rain should fall; for the Silver River, full at all times, is at that season often in flood, and the bird-bridge might be swept away.

The day broke cloudlessly bright. It waxed and waned, and one by one the lamps of heaven were lighted. At nightfall the magpies assembled, and Shokujo, quivering with delight, crossed the slender bridge and fell into the arms of her lover. Their transport of joy was as the joy of the parched flower, when the raindrop falls upon it; but the moment of parting soon came, and Shokujo sorrowfully retraced her steps.

Year follows year, and the lovers still meet in that far-off starry land on the seventh night of the seventh month, save when rain has swelled the Silver River and rendered the crossing impossible. The hope of a permanent reunion still fills the hearts of the Star-Lovers, and is to them as a sweet fragrance and a beautiful vision.

THE CHILD OF THE FOREST

By Frank Rinder

SAKATO–NO–TOKI–YUKI was a brave warrior at the court of Kyōto. He fought for the Minamoto against the Taira, but the Minamoto were defeated, and Sakato's last days were spent as a wandering exile. He died of a broken heart. His widow, the daughter of a noble house, escaped from Kyōto, and fled eastward to the rugged Ashigara Mountains. No one knew of her hiding-place, and she had no enemies to fear save the wild beasts who lived in the forest. At night she found shelter in a rocky cave.

A son was born to her whom she named Kintaro, the Golden Boy. He was a sturdy little fellow, with ruddy cheeks and merry, laughing eyes. Even as he lay crowing in his bed among the fern, the birds that alighted on his shoulder peeped trustfully into his eyes, and he smiled. Thus early the child and the birds were comrades. The butterfly and the downy moth would settle upon his breast, and tread softly over his little brown body.

Kintaro was not as other children, — there was something strange about him. When he fell, he would laugh cheerily; if he wandered far into the wood, he could always find his way home; and, when little more than a chubby babe, he could swing a heavy axe in circles round his head. In the remote hills he had no human companions, but the animals were his constant playfellows. He was gentle and kind-hearted and would not willingly hurt any living creature; therefore it was that the birds and all the forest people looked upon Kintaro as one of themselves.

Among Kintaro's truest friends were the bears who dwelt in the woods. A mother bear often carried him on her back to her home. The cubs ran out and greeted him joyfully, and they romped and played together for hours. They wrestled and strove in friendly rivalry. Sometimes Kintaro would clamber up the smooth-barked monkey-tree, sit on the topmost branch, and laugh at the vain attempts of the shaggy little fellows to follow him. Then came supper-time and the feast of liquid honey.

But the Golden Boy loved best of all to fly through the air with his arms round the neck of a gentle-eyed stag. Soon after dawn, the deer came to awaken the sleeper, and, with a farewell kiss to his mother and a morning caress to the stag, Kintaro sprang on his back and was carried, with swift bounds, up mountain-side, through valley and thicket, until the sun was high in the heavens. When they came to a leafy spot in the woods and heard the sound of falling water, the stag grazed among the high fern while Kintaro bathed in the foaming torrent.

Thus mother and son lived securely in their home among the mountains. They saw no human being save the few woodcutters who penetrated thus far into the forest, and these simple peasants did not guess their noble birth. The mother was known as Yama-uba-San, "The Wild Nurse of the Mountain," and her son as "Little Wonder."

Kintaro reigned as prince of the forest, beloved of every living creature. When he held his court, the bear and the wolf, the fox and the badger, the marten and the squirrel, and many other courtiers were seated around him. The birds, too, flocked at his call. The eagle and the hawk flew down from the distant heights; the crane and the heron swept over the plain, and feathered friends without number thronged the branches of the cedars. He listened as they told of their joys and their sorrows, and spoke graciously to all, for Kintaro had learned the language and lore of the beasts, and the birds, and the flowers from the Tengus, the wood-elves.

The Tengus, who live in the rocky heights of the mountains and in the topmost branches of lofty trees, befriended Kintaro and became his teachers. As he was truthful and good, he had nothing to fear from them; but the Tengus are dreaded by deceitful boys, whose tongues they pull out by their roots and carry away.

These elves are strange beings, with the body of a man, the head of a hawk, long, long noses, and two powerful claws on their hairy hands and feet. They are hatched from eggs, and in their youth have feathers and wings; later they molt and wear the garb of men. On their feet are stilt-like clogs about twelve inches high. They stalk proudly along with crossed arms, head thrown back, and long nose held high in the air; hence the proverb, "He has become a Tengu."

The headquarters of the tribe are in the Ōyama

KINTARO REIGNED AS PRINCE OF THE FOREST

Mountain, where lives the Dai-Tengu, their leader, whom all obey. He is even more proud and overbearing than his followers, and his nose is so long that one of his ministers always precedes him that it may not be injured. A long gray beard reaches to his girdle, and mustaches hang from his mouth to his chin. His sceptre is a fan of seven feathers, which he carries in his left hand. He rarely speaks, and is thus accounted wondrous wise. The Raven-Tengu is his chief minister; instead of a nose and mouth, he has a long beak. Over the left shoulder is slung an executioner's axe, and in his hand he bears the book of Tengu wisdom.

The Tengus are fond of games, and their long noses are useful in many ways. They serve as swords for fencing, and as poles on the point of which to balance bowls of water with gold-fish Two noses joined together form a tight-rope on which a young Tengu, sheltered by a paper umbrella and leading a little dog, dances and jumps through hoops; the while an old Tengu sings a dance-tune and another beats time with a fan. Some among the older Tengus are very wise. The most famous of all is he who dwells on the Kurama Mountain, but hardly less wise is the Tengu who undertook the education of Kintaro. At nightfall he carried the boy to the nest in the high rocks. Here he was taught the wisdom of the elves, and the speech of all the forest tribes.

One day, Little Wonder was at play with some young Tengus, but they grew tired and flew up to their nest, leaving Kintaro alone. He was angry with them, and shook the tree with all his strength, so that the nest fell to the ground. The mother soon returned, and was in great distress at the loss of her children. Kintaro's kind heart was touched, and, with the little ones in his arms, he swarmed up the tree and asked pardon. Happily they were unhurt, and soon recovered from their fright. Kintaro helped to rebuild the nest, and brought presents to his playfellows.

Now it happened that, as the hero Raiko, who had fought so bravely against the *oni*, passed through the forest, he came upon Little Wonder wrestling with a powerful bear. An admiring circle of friends stood around. Raiko, as he looked, was amazed at the strength and courage of the boy. The combat over, he asked Kintaro his name and his story, but the child could only lead him to his mother. When she learned that the man before her was indeed Raiko, the mighty warrior, she told him of her flight from Kyōto, of the birth of Kintaro, and of their secluded life among the mountains. Raiko wished to take the boy away and train him in arms, but Kintaro loved the forest. When, however, his mother spoke, he was ready to obey. He called together his friends, the beasts and the birds, and, in words that are remembered to this day, bade them all farewell.

The mother would not follow her son to the land of men, but Kintaro, when he became a great hero, often came to see her in the home of his childhood.

The peasants of the Ashigara still tell of The Wild Nurse of the Mountains and Little Wonder.

MYTHS OF THE SLAVS

THE PRINCE WITH THE GOLDEN HAND

By *Alex. Chodsko*

(Translated by Emily J. Harding.)

THERE once lived a king and queen who had an only daughter. And the beauty of this princess surpassed everything seen or heard of. Her forehead was brilliant as the moon, her lips like the rose, her complexion had the delicacy of the lily, and her breath the sweetness of jessamine. Her hair was golden, and in her voice and glance there was something so enchanting that none could help listening to her or looking at her.

The princess lived for seventeen years in her own rooms, rejoicing the heart of her parents, teachers, and servants. No one else ever saw her, for the sons of the king and all other princes were forbidden to enter her rooms. She never went anywhere, never looked upon the outside world, and never breathed the outer air, but she was perfectly happy.

When she was eighteen it happened, either by chance or by the will of fate, that she heard the cry of the cuckoo. This sound made her strangely uneasy; her golden head drooped, and covering her eyes with her hands, she fell into thought so deep as not to hear her mother enter. The queen looked at her anxiously, and after comforting her went to tell the king about it.

For many years past the sons of kings and neighboring princes had, either personally or by their ambassadors, presented themselves at court to ask the king for the hand of his daughter in marriage. But he had always bidden them wait until another time. Now, after a long consultation with the queen, he sent messengers to foreign courts and elsewhere to proclaim that the princess, in accordance with the wishes of her parents, was about to choose a husband, and that the man of her choice would also have the right of succession to the throne.

When the princess heard of this decision her joy was very great, and for days she would dream about it. Then she looked out into the garden through the golden lattice of her window, and longed with an irresistible longing to walk in the open air upon the smooth lawn. With great difficulty she at last persuaded her governesses to allow her to do so, they agreeing on condition that she should keep with them. So the crystal doors were thrown open, the oaken gates that shut in the orchard turned on their hinges, and the princess found herself on the green grass. She ran about, picking the sweet-scented flowers and chasing the many-colored butterflies. But she could not have been a very prudent maiden, for she wandered away from her governesses, with her face uncovered.

Just at that moment a raging hurricane, such as had never been seen or heard before, passed by and fell upon the garden. It roared and whistled round and round, then seizing the princess carried her far away. The terrified governesses wrung their hands, and were for a time speechless with grief. At last they rushed into the palace, and throwing themselves on their knees before the king and queen, told them with sobs and tears what had happened. They were overwhelmed with sorrow and knew not what to do.

By this time quite a crowd of princes had arrived at the palace, and seeing the king in such bitter grief, inquired the reason of it.

"Sorrow has touched my white hairs," said the king. "The hurricane has carried off my dearly beloved child, the sweet Princess with the Golden Hair, and I know not where it has taken her. Whoever finds this out, and brings her back to me, shall have her for his wife, and with her half my kingdom for a wedding present, and the remainder of my wealth and titles after my death."

After hearing these words, princes and knights mounted their horses and set off to search throughout the world for the beautiful Princess with the Golden Hair, who had been carried away by Vikher.

Now among the seekers were two brothers, sons of a king, and they traveled together through many countries asking for news of the princess, but no one knew anything about her. But they continued their search, and at the end of two years arrived in a country that lies in the centre of the earth, and has summer and winter at the same time.

The princes determined to find out whether this was the place where the hurricane had hidden the Princess

with the Golden Hair. So they began to ascend one
of the mountains on foot, leaving their horses behind
them to feed on the grass. On reaching the top, they
came in sight of a silver palace supported on a cock's
foot, while at one of the windows the sun's rays shone
upon a head of golden hair; surely it could only belong
to the princess. Suddenly the north wind blew so violently, and the cold became so intense, that the leaves
of the trees withered and the breath froze. The two
princes tried to keep their footing, and battled manfully against the storm, but they were overcome by its
fierceness and fell together, frozen to death.

Their broken-hearted parents waited for them in
vain. Masses were said, charities distributed, and
prayers sent up to God to pity them in their sorrow.

One day when the queen, the mother of the princes,
was giving a poor old man some money, she said to
him, "My good old friend, pray God to guard our sons
and soon bring them back in good health."

"Ah, noble lady," answered he, "that prayer would
be useless. Everlasting rest is all one may ask for the
dead, but in return for the love you have shown and the
money you have given the poor and needy, I am charged
with this message — that God has taken pity on your
sorrow, and that ere long you will be the mother of a
son, the like of whom has never yet been seen."

The old man, having spoken thus, vanished.

The queen, whose tears were falling, felt a strange
joy enter her heart, and a feeling of happiness steal
over her, as she went to the king and repeated the old
man's words. And so it came to pass, for a week or

two later God sent her a son, and he was in no way like an ordinary child. His eyes resembled those of a falcon, and his eyebrows the sable's fur. His right hand was of pure gold, and his manner and appearance were so full of an indescribable majesty, that he was looked upon by every one with a feeling of awe.

His growth, too, was not like that of other children. When but three days old, he stepped out of his swaddling-clothes and left his cradle. And he was so strong that when his parents entered the room he ran towards them, crying out, "Good-morning, dear parents, why are you so sad? Are you not happy at the sight of me?"

"We are indeed happy, dear child, and we thank God for having sent us you in our great grief. But we cannot forget your two brothers; they were so handsome and brave, and worthy of a great destiny. And our sadness is increased when we remember that, instead of resting in their own country in the tomb of their forefathers, they sleep in an unknown land, perhaps without burial. Alas! it is three years since we had news of them."

At these words the child's tears fell, and he embraced his parents and said, "Weep no more, dear parents, —you shall soon be comforted; for before next spring I shall be a strong young man, and will look for my brothers all over the world. And I will bring them back to you, if not alive, yet dead; ay, though I have to seek them in the very centre of the earth."

At these words and at that which followed the king and queen were amazed. For the strange child, guided as it were by an invisible hand, rushed into the garden, and in spite of the cold, for it was not yet daylight, bathed in the early dew. When the sun had risen he threw himself down near a little wood on the fine sand, rubbed and rolled himself in it, and returned home, no longer a child but a youth.

It was pleasant to the king to see his son thrive in this way, and indeed the young prince was the handsomest in the whole land. He grew from hour to hour. At the end of a month he could wield a sword, in two months he rode on horseback, in three months he had grown a beautiful mustache of pure gold. Then he put on a helmet, and presenting himself before the king and queen, said, "My much honored parents, your son asks your blessing. I am no longer a child, and now go to seek my brothers. In order to find them I will, if necessary, go to the farthest ends of the world."

"Ah, do not venture. Stay rather with us, dear son; you are still too young to be exposed to the risks of such an undertaking."

"Adventures have no terrors for me," replied the young hero. "I trust in God. Why should I for a moment hesitate to face these dangers? Whatever Destiny has in store for us will happen, whatever we may do to try to prevent it."

So they agreed to let him go. Weeping they bade him farewell, blessing him and the road he was to travel.

A pleasant tale is soon told, but events do not pass so quickly.

The young prince crossed deep rivers and climbed high mountains, till he came to a dark forest. In the distance he saw a cottage supported on a cock's foot, and standing in the midst of a field full of poppies. As he made his way towards it he was suddenly seized by an overpowering longing to sleep, but he urged on his horse, and breaking off the poppy heads as he galloped through the field, came up close to the house. Then he called out: —

> "Little cot, turn around, on thy foot turn thou free;
> To the forest set thy back, let the door be wide to me."

The cottage turned round with a great creaking noise, the door facing the prince. He entered, and found an old woman with thin white hair and a face covered with wrinkles, truly frightful to look upon. She was sitting at a table, her head resting on her hands, her eyes fixed on the ceiling, lost in deep thought. Near her were two beautiful girls, their complexions like lilies and roses, and in every way sweet to the eye.

"Ah, how do you do, Prince with Mustache of Gold, Hero with the Golden Fist?" said old Yaga, "What has brought you here?"

Having told her the object of his journey, she replied, "Your elder brothers perished on the mountain that touches the clouds, while in search of the Princess with the Golden Hair, who was carried off by Vikher, the hurricane."

"And how is this thief Vikher to be got at?" asked the prince.

"Ah, my dear child, he would swallow you like a fly. It is now a hundred years since I went outside this cottage, for fear Vikher should seize me and carry me off to his palace near the sky."

"I am not afraid of his carrying me off, — I am not handsome enough for that; and he will not swallow me either, for my golden hand can smash anything."

"Then if you are not afraid, my dove, I will help you to the best of my power. But give me your word of honor that you will bring me some of the Water of Youth, for it restores even to the most aged the beauty and freshness of youth."

"I give you my word of honor that I will bring you some."

"This, then, is what you must do. I will give you a pin-cushion for a guide; this you throw in front of you, and follow whithersoever it goes. It will lead you to the mountain that touches the clouds, and which is guarded in Vikher's absence by his father and mother, the northern blast and the south wind. On no account lose sight of the pin-cushion. If attacked by the father, the northern blast, and suddenly seized with cold, then put on this heat-giving hood; if overpowered by burning heat of the south wind, then drink from this cooling flagon. Thus by means of the pin-cushion, the hood, and the flagon you will reach the top of the mountain where the Princess with the Golden Hair is imprisoned. Deal with Vikher as you will, only remember to bring me some of the Water of Youth."

Our young hero took the heat-giving hood, the cooling flagon, and the pin-cushion, and, after bidding farewell to old Yaga and her two pretty daughters, mounted his steed and rode off, following the pin-cushion, which rolled before him at a great rate.

Now a beautiful story is soon told, but the events

of which it consists do not in real life take place so rapidly.

When the prince had traveled through two kingdoms, he came to a land in which lay a very beautiful valley that stretched into the far distance, and above it towered the mountain that touches the sky. The summit was so high above the earth you might almost fancy it reached the moon.

The prince dismounted, left his horse to graze, and having crossed himself began to follow the pin-cushion up steep and rocky paths. When he had got half-way there the north wind began to blow, and the cold was so intense that the wood of the trees split up and the breath froze; he felt chilled to the heart. But he quickly put on the heat-giving hood, and cried: —

> "O Heat-Giving Hood, see I fly now to thee,
>   Lend me quickly thine aid;
> O hasten to warm ere the cold has killed me;
>   With thee I'm not afraid."

The northern blast blew with redoubled fury, but to no purpose. For the prince was so hot that he streamed with perspiration, and indeed was obliged to unbutton his coat and fan himself.

Here the pin-cushion stopped upon a small snow-covered mound. The prince cleared away the snow, beneath which lay the frozen bodies of two young men, and he knew them to be those of his lost brothers. Having knelt beside them and prayed, he turned to follow the pin-cushion, which had already started, and was rolling ever higher and higher. On reaching the top of the mountain he saw a silver palace sup-

ported on a cock's foot, and at one of the windows,
shining in the sun's rays, a head of golden hair which
could belong to no one but the princess. Suddenly a
hot wind began to blow from the south, and the heat
became so intense that leaves withered and dropped
from the trees, the grass dried up, and large cracks
appeared in several places of the earth's surface.
Thirst, heat, and weariness began to tell upon the
young prince, so he took the cooling flagon from his
pocket and cried: —

> "Flagon, bring me quick relief
> From this parching heat;
> In thy draught I have belief,
> Coolness it will mete."

After drinking deeply he felt stronger than ever,
and so continued to ascend. Not only was he relieved
from the great heat, but was even obliged to button
up his coat to keep himself warm.

The pin-cushion still led the way, ever climbing
higher and higher, while the prince followed close
behind. After crossing the region of clouds they came
to the topmost peak of the mountain. Here the prince
came close to the palace, which can only be likened
to a dream of perfect beauty. It was supported on a
cock's foot, and was built entirely of silver, except
for its steel gates and roof of solid gold. Before the
entrance was a deep precipice over which none but
the birds could pass. As the prince gazed upon the
splendid building, the princess leaned out of one of
the windows, and, seeing him, light shone from her
sparkling eyes, her lovely hair floated in the wind,

and the scent of her sweet breath filled the air. The prince sprang forward and cried out: —

> "Silver Palace, oh turn, on thy foot turn thou free,
> To the steep rocks thy back, but thy doors wide to me."

At these words it revolved, creaking, the doorway facing the prince. As he entered, it returned to its original position. The prince went through the palace till he came to a room bright as the sun itself, and the walls, floor, and ceiling of which consisted of mirrors. He was filled with wonder, for instead of one princess he saw twelve, all equally beautiful, with the same graceful movements and golden hair. But eleven were only reflections of the one real princess. She gave a cry of joy on seeing him, and running to meet him said: "Ah, noble sir, you look like a delivering angel. Surely you bring me good news. From what family, city, or country have you come? Perhaps my dear father and mother sent you in search of me?"

"No one has sent me. I have come of my own free will to rescue you and restore you to your parents."

When he had told her all that had passed, she said, "Your devotion, prince, is very great; may God bless your attempt. But Vikher the hurricane is unconquerable, so, if life be dear to you, fly. Leave this place before his return, which I expect every minute; he will kill you with one glance of his eyes."

"If I should not succeed in saving you, sweet princess, life can be no longer dear to me. But I am full of hope, and I beg you first to give me some of the Strength-Giving Water from the Heroic Well, for this is drunk by the hurricane."

411

The princess drew a bucketful of water, which the young man emptied at one draught and then asked for another. This astonished her somewhat, but she gave it to him, and when he had drunk it he said, "Allow me, princess, to sit down for a moment to take breath."

She gave him an iron chair, but as soon as he sat down it broke into a thousand pieces. She then brought him the chair used by Vikher himself; but although it was made of the strongest steel, it bent and creaked beneath the prince's weight.

"Now you see," said he, "that I have grown heavier than your unconquerable hurricane: so take courage, with God's help and your good wishes I shall overcome him. In the mean time tell me how you pass your time here."

"Alas! in bitter tears and sad reflections. My only consolation is that I have been able to keep my persecutor at a distance, for he vainly implores me to marry him. Two years have now passed away, and yet none of his efforts to win my consent have been successful. Last time he went away he told me that if on his return he had not guessed the riddles I set him (the correct explanation of these being the condition I have made for his marrying me), he would set them aside, and marry me in spite of my objections."

"Ah, then I am just in time. I will be the priest on that occasion, and give him Death for a bride."

At that moment a horrible whistling was heard.

"Be on your guard, prince," cried she, "here comes the hurricane."

The palace spun rapidly round, fearful sounds filled the building, thousands of ravens and birds of ill omen croaked loudly and flapped their wings, and all the doors opened with a tremendous noise.

Vikher, mounted on his winged horse that breathed fire, leapt into the mirrored room, then stopped amazed at the sight before him. He was indeed the hurricane, with the body of a giant and the head of a dragon, and as he gazed his horse pranced and beat his wings.

"What is your business here, stranger?" he shouted, and the sound of his voice was like unto a lion's roar.

"I am your enemy, and I want your blood," replied the prince calmly.

"Your boldness amuses me. At the same time, if you do not depart at once I will take you in my left hand and crush every bone in your body with my right."

"Try, if you dare, woman-stealer!" he answered.

Vikher roared, breathing fire in his rage, and with his mouth wide open threw himself upon the prince, intending to swallow him. But the latter stepped lightly aside, and putting his golden hand down his enemy's throat, seized him by the tongue and dashed him against the wall with such force that the monster bounded against it like a ball, and died within a few moments, shedding torrents of blood.

The prince then drew from different springs the water that *restores*, that *revives*, and that *makes young*, and taking the unconscious girl in his arms he led the winged horse to the door and said: —

> "Silver Palace, oh, turn, on thy foot turn thou free,
> To the steep rocks thy back, but thy doors wide to me."

Whereupon the palace creaked round on the cock's foot, and the door opened on the courtyard. Mounting the horse, he placed the princess before him, for she had by this time recovered from her swoon, and cried:

> "Fiery Horse with strength of wing,
> I am now your lord;
> Do my will in everything,
> Be your law my word.
> Where I point there you must go
> At once, at once. The way you know."

And he pointed to the place where his brothers lay frozen in death. The horse rose, pranced, beat the air with his wings, then, lifting himself high in the air, came down gently where the two princes were lying. The Prince with the Golden Hand sprinkled their bodies with the Life-Restoring Water, and instantly the pallor of death disappeared, leaving in its place the natural color. He then sprinkled them with the Water that Revives, after which they opened their eyes, got up, and looking round said, "How well we have slept! But what has happened? And how is it we see the lovely princess we sought in the society of a young man, a perfect stranger to us?"

The Prince with the Golden Hand explained everything, embraced his brothers tenderly, and taking them with him on his horse, showed the latter that he wished to go in the direction of Yaga's cottage. The horse rose up, pranced, lifted himself in the air, then, beating his wings far above the highest forests, descended close by the cottage. The prince said:—

> "Little cot, turn around, on thy foot turn thou free,
> To the forest thy back, but thy door wide to me."

414

THE PRINCE WITH THE GOLDEN HAND

The cottage began to creak without delay, and turned round with the door facing the travelers. Old Yaga was on the lookout, and came to meet them. As soon as she got the Water of Youth she sprinkled herself with it, and instantly everything about her that was old and ugly became young and charming. So pleased was she to be young again that she kissed the prince's hands and said, "Ask of me anything you like, I will refuse you nothing."

At that moment her two beautiful young daughters happened to look out of the window; upon which the two elder princes, who were admiring them, said, "Will you give us your daughters for wives?"

"That I will, with pleasure," said she, and beckoned them to her. Then courtesying to her future sons-in-law, she laughed merrily and vanished. They placed their brides before them on the same horse, while the Prince with the Golden Hand, pointing to where he wished to go, said:—

> "Fiery Horse with strength of wing,
>   I am now your lord;
>   Do my will in everything,
>   Be your law my word.
> Where I point there you must go
>   At once, at once. The way you know."

The horse rose up, pranced, flapped his wings, and flew far above the forest. An hour or two later he descended before the palace of the Golden-Haired Princess's parents. When the king and queen saw their only daughter who had so long been lost to them, they ran to meet her with exclamations of joy and kissed her gratefully and lovingly, at the same time thanking the prince who had restored her to them. And when they heard the story of his adventures they said, "You, Prince with the Golden Hand, shall receive our beloved daughter in marriage, with the half of our kingdom, and the right of succession to the remainder after us. Let us, too, add to the joy of this day by celebrating the weddings of your two brothers."

The Princess with the Golden Hair kissed her father lovingly and said, "My much honored and noble sire and lord, the prince my bridegroom knows of the vow I made when carried off by the hurricane, that I would only give my hand to him who could answer aright my six enigmas: it would be impossible for the Princess with the Golden Hair to break her word."

The king was silent, but the prince said, "Speak, sweet princess, I am listening."

"This is my first riddle: 'Two of my extremities form a sharp point, the two others a ring; in my centre is a screw.'"

"A pair of scissors," answered he.

"Well guessed. This is the second: 'I make the round of the table on only one foot, but if I am wounded the evil is beyond repair.'"

"A glass of wine."

"Right. This is the third: 'I have no tongue, and yet I answer faithfully; I am not seen, yet every one hears me.'"

"An echo."

"True. This is the fourth: 'Fire cannot light me; brush cannot sweep me; no painter can paint me; no hiding-place secure me.'"

"Sunshine."

"The very thing. This is the fifth: 'I existed before the creation of Adam. I am always changing in succession the two colors of my dress. Thousands of years have gone by, but I have remained unaltered both in color and form.'"

"It must be time, including day and night."

"You have succeeded in guessing the five most difficult; the last is the easiest of all. 'By day a ring, by night a serpent; he who guesses this shall be my bridegroom.'"

"It is a girdle."

"Now they are all guessed," said she, and gave her hand to the young prince.

They knelt before the king and queen to receive their blessing. The three weddings were celebrated that same evening, and a messenger mounted the winged horse to carry the good news to the parents of the young princes and to bring them back as guests. Meanwhile a magnificent feast was prepared, and invitations were sent to all their friends and acquaintances. And from that evening until the next morning they ceased not to feast and drink and dance. I, too, was a guest, and feasted with the rest; but though I ate and drank, the wine only ran down my beard, and my throat remained dry.

THE DWARF WITH THE LONG BEARD

By Alex. Chodsko

IN a far distant land there reigned a king, and he
had an only daughter who was so very beautiful
that no one in the whole kingdom could be compared
to her. She was known as Princess Pietnotka, and
the fame of her beauty spread far and wide. There
were many princes among her suitors, but her choice
fell upon Prince Dobrotek. She obtained her father's
consent to their marriage, and then, attended by a
numerous suite, set off with her lover for the church,
having first, as was the custom, received her royal
parent's blessing. Most of the princes who had been
unsuccessful in their wooing of Pietnotka returned
disappointed to their own kingdoms; but one of them,
a dwarf only seven inches high, with an enormous
hump on his back and a beard seven feet long, who was
a powerful prince and magician, was so enraged that
he determined to have his revenge. So he changed himself into a whirlwind and lay in wait to receive the princess. When the wedding procession was about to enter
the church, the air was suddenly filled with a blinding cloud of dust, and Pietnotka was borne up high
as the highest clouds, and then right down to an underground palace. There the dwarf, for it was he who had

worked this spell, disappeared, leaving her in a lifeless condition.

When she opened her eyes she found herself in such a magnificent apartment that she imagined some king must have run away with her. She got up and began to walk about, when lo! as if by some unseen hand, the table was laden with gold and silver dishes, filled with cakes of every kind. They looked so tempting that in spite of her grief she could not resist tasting, and she continued to eat until she was more than satisfied. She returned to the sofa and lay down to rest, but being unable to sleep, she looked first at the door, and then at the lamp burning on the table, then at the door again, and then back to the lamp. Suddenly the door opened of itself, giving entrance to four negroes fully armed, and bearing a golden throne, upon which was seated the Dwarf with the Long Beard. He came close up to the sofa and attempted to kiss the princess, but she struck him such a blow in the face that a thousand stars swam before his eyes, and a thousand bells rang in his ears; upon which he gave such a shout that the palace walls trembled. Yet his love for her was so great that he did his best not to show his anger, and turned away as if to leave her. But his feet became entangled in his long beard, and he fell down, dropping a cap he was carrying in his hand. Now this cap had the power of making its wearer invisible. The negroes hastened up to their master, and placing him on his throne bore him out.

As soon as the princess found herself alone, she jumped off the sofa, locked the door, and, picking up the cap, ran to a mirror to try it on and see how it suited her. Imagine her amazement when looking in the glass she saw — nothing at all! She took off the cap, and behold, she was there again as large as life. She soon found out what sort of cap it was, and rejoicing in the possession of such a marvel, put it on her head again and began to walk about the room. Soon the door was burst violently open, and the dwarf entered with his beard tied up. But he found neither the princess nor the cap, and so came to the conclusion that she had taken it. In a great rage he began to search high and low; he looked under all the furniture, behind the curtains, and even beneath the carpets, but it was all in vain. Meanwhile the princess, still invisible, had left the palace and run into the garden, which was very large and beautiful. There she lived at her ease, eating the delicious fruit, drinking water from the fountain, and enjoying the helpless fury of the dwarf, who sought her untiringly. Sometimes she would throw the fruit-stones in his face, or take off the cap and show herself for an instant: then she would put it on again, and laugh merrily at his rage.

One day, while playing this game, the cap caught in the branches of a gooseberry bush. The dwarf, seeing this, at once ran up, seized the princess in one hand and the cap in the other, and was about to carry both off when the sound of a war-trumpet was heard.

The dwarf trembled with rage and muttered a thousand curses. He breathed on the princess to send her to sleep, covered her with the invisible cap, and seizing a double-bladed sword, rose up in the air as high as the clouds, so that he might fall upon his assailant and kill him at one stroke. We shall now see with whom he had to deal.

After the hurricane had upset the wedding procession and carried off the princess, there arose a great tumult among those at court. The king, the princess's attendants, and Prince Dobrotek sought her in every direction, calling her by name, and making inquiries of every one they met. At last, the king in despair declared that if Prince Dobrotek did not bring back his daughter, he would destroy his kingdom and have him killed. And to the other princes present he promised that whosoever among them should bring Pietnotka back to him should have her for his wife and receive half of the kingdom. Whereupon they all mounted their horses without loss of time and dispersed in every direction.

Prince Dobrotek, overpowered with grief and dismay, traveled three days without eating, drinking, or sleeping. On the evening of the third day he was quite worn out with fatigue, and stopping his horse in a field, got down to rest for a short time. Suddenly he heard cries, as of something in pain, and looking round saw an enormous owl tearing a hare with its claws. The prince laid hold of the first hard thing that came to his hand, — he imagined it to be a stone, but it was really a skull, — and aiming it at the owl, killed the bird with the first blow. The rescued hare ran up to him and gratefully licked his hands, after which it ran away; but the human skull spoke to him and said, "Prince Dobrotek, accept my grateful thanks for the good turn you have done me. I belonged to an unhappy man who took his own life, and for this crime of suicide I have been condemned to roll in the mud until I was the means of saving the life of one of God's creatures. I have been kicked about for seven hundred and seventy years, crumbling miserably on the earth, and without exciting the compassion of a single individual. You have been the means of setting me free by making use of me to save the life of that poor hare. In return for this kindness I will teach you how to call to your aid a most marvelous horse, who during my life belonged to me. He will be able to help you in a thousand ways, and when in need of him you have only to walk out on the moorland without once looking behind you, and to say: —

> 'Dappled Horse with Mane of Gold,
> Horse of Wonder, come to me!
> Walk not the earth, for I am told
> You fly like birds o'er land and sea.

Finish your work of mercy by burying me here, so that I may be at rest until the day of judgment. Then depart in peace and be of good cheer."

The prince dug a hole at the foot of a tree, and reverently buried the skull, repeating over it the prayers for the dead. Just as he finished he saw a small blue flame come out of the skull and fly towards heaven: it was the soul of the dead man on its way to the angels.

The prince made the sign of the cross and resumed his journey. When he had gone some way along the moorland he stopped, and without looking back tried the effect of the magic words, saying: —

THE DWARF WITH THE LONG BEARD

"Dappled Horse with Mane of Gold,
Horse of Wonder, come to me!
Walk not the earth, for I am told
You fly like birds o'er land and sea."

Then amid flash of lightning and roll of thunder appeared the horse. A horse, do I say? Why, he was a miracle of wonder. He was light as air, with dappled coat and golden mane. Flames came from his nostrils and sparks from his eyes. Volumes of steam rolled from his mouth, and clouds of smoke issued from his ears. He stopped before the prince, and said in a human voice, "What are your orders, Prince Dobrotek?"

"I am in great trouble," answered the prince, "and shall be glad if you can help me." Then he told all that had happened.

And the horse said, "Enter in at my left ear, and come out at my right."

The prince obeyed, and came out at the right ear clad in a suit of splendid armor. His gilded cuirass, his steel helmet inlaid with gold, and his sword and club made of him a complete warrior. Still more, he felt himself endowed with superhuman strength and bravery. When he stamped his foot and shouted, the earth trembled and gave forth a sound like thunder; the very leaves fell from the trees.

"What must we do? Where are we to go?" he asked.

The horse replied, "Your bride, Princess Pietnotka, has been carried off by the Dwarf with the Long Beard, whose hump weighs two hundred and eighty pounds. This powerful magician must be defeated, but he lives a long way from here, and nothing can touch or wound him except the sharp smiting sword that belongs to his own brother, a monster with the head and eyes of a basilisk. We must first attack the brother."

Prince Dobrotek leaped on to the dappled horse, which was covered with golden trappings, and they set off immediately, clearing mountains, penetrating forests, crossing rivers; and so light was the steed's step that he galloped over the grass without bending a single blade, and along sandy roads without raising a grain of dust. At last they reached a vast plain, strewn with human bones. They stopped in front of a huge moving mountain, and the horse said:—

"Prince, this moving mountain that you see before you is the head of the Monster with Basilisk Eyes, and the bones that whiten the ground are the skeletons of his victims; so beware of the eyes that deal death. The heat of the midday sun has made the giant sleep, and the sword with the never-failing blade lies there before him. Bend down and lie along my neck until we are near enough, then seize the sword and you have nothing more to fear. For, without the sword, not only will the monster be unable to harm you, but he himself will be completely at your mercy."

The horse then noiselessly approached the huge creature, upon which the prince bent down, and quickly picked up the sword. Then, raising himself on his steed's back, he gave a "Hurrah!" loud enough to wake the dead. The giant lifted his head, yawned, and turned his bloodthirsty eyes upon the prince; but seeing the sword in his hand he became quiet, and said, "Knight, is it weariness of life that brings you here?"

"Boast not," replied the prince, "you are in my power. Your glance has already lost its magic charm, and you will soon have to die by this sword. But first tell me who you are."

"It is true, prince, I am in your hands, but be generous; I deserve your pity. I am a knight of the race of giants, and if it were not for the wickedness of my brother I should have lived in peace. He is the horrible dwarf with the great hump and the beard seven feet long. He was jealous of my fine figure, and tried to do me an injury. You must know that all his strength, which is extraordinary, lies in his beard, and it can only be cut off by the sword you hold in your hand. One day he came to me and said, 'Dear brother, I pray you help me to discover the sharp smiting sword that has been hidden in the earth by a magician. He is our enemy, and he alone can destroy us both.' Fool that I was, I believed him, and by means of a large oak-tree, raked up the mountain and found the sword. Then we disputed as to which of us should have it, and at last my brother suggested that we should cease quarreling and decide by lot. 'Let us each put an ear to the ground, and the sword shall belong to him who first hears the bells of yonder church,' said he. I placed my ear to the ground at once, and my brother treacherously cut off my head with the sword. My body, left unburied, became a great mountain, which is now overgrown with forests. As for my head, it is full of a life and strength proof against all dangers, and has remained here ever since to frighten all who attempt to take away the sword. Now, prince, I beg of you, use the sword to cut off the beard of my wicked brother; kill him, and return here to put an end to me: I shall die happy if I die avenged."

"That you shall be, and very soon, I promise you," replied his listener.

The prince bade the Dappled Horse with Golden Mane carry him to the kingdom of the Dwarf with the Long Beard. They reached the garden gate at the very moment when the dwarf had caught sight of Princess Pietnotka and was running after her. The war-trumpet, challenging him to fight, had obliged him to leave her, which he did, having first put on her head the invisible cap.

While the prince was awaiting the answer to his challenge, he heard a great noise in the clouds, and looking up saw the dwarf preparing to aim at him from a great height. But he missed his aim and fell to the ground so heavily that his body was half buried in the earth. The prince seized him by the beard, which he at once cut off with the sharp smiting sword.

Then he fastened the dwarf to the saddle, put the beard in his helmet, and entered the palace. When the servants saw that he had really got possession of the terrible beard, they opened all the doors to give him entrance. Without losing a moment he began his search for Princess Pietnotka. For a long time he was unsuccessful, and was almost in despair when he came across her accidentally, and, without knowing it, knocked off the invisible cap. He saw his lovely bride sound asleep, and being unable to wake her he put the cap in his pocket, took her in his arms, and, mounting his steed, set off to return to the Monster with the Basilisk Eyes.

426

The giant swallowed the dwarf at one mouthful, and the prince cut the monster's head up into a thousand pieces, which he scattered all over the plain.

He then resumed his journey, and on coming to the moorland the dappled horse stopped short and said, "Prince, here for the present we must take leave of each other. You are not far from home, — your own horse awaits you; but before leaving, enter in at my right ear and come out at my left."

The prince did so, and came out without his armor, and clad as when Pietnotka left him.

The dappled horse vanished, and Dobrotek whistled to his own horse, who ran up, quite pleased to see him again. They immediately set off for the king's palace.

But night came on before they reached the end of their journey.

The prince laid the sleeping maiden on the grass, and, covering her up carefully to keep her warm, he himself fell fast asleep. By chance, a knight, one of her suitors, passed that way. Seeing Dobrotek asleep, he drew his sword and stabbed him; then he lifted the princess on his horse and soon reached the king's palace, where he addressed Pietnotka's father in these words: "Here is your daughter, whom I now claim as my wife, for it is I who have restored her to you. She was carried off by a terrible sorcerer who fought with me three days and three nights. But I conquered him, and I have brought you the princess safely back."

The king was overjoyed at seeing her again, but finding that his tenderest efforts were powerless to awake her, he wanted to know the reason of it.

"That I cannot tell you," replied the impostor; "you see her as I found her myself."

Meanwhile, poor Prince Dobrotek, seriously wounded, was slowly recovering consciousness, but he felt so weak that he could hardly utter these words:—

> "Come, Magic Horse with Mane of Gold,
> Come, Dappled Horse, O come to me.
> Fly like the birds as you did of old,
> As flashes of lightning o'er land and sea."

Instantly a bright cloud appeared, and from the midst thereof stepped the magic horse. As he already knew all that had happened, he dashed off immediately to the Mountain of Eternal Life. Thence he drew the three kinds of water: the Water that gives Life, the Water that Cures, and the Water that Strengthens. Returning to the prince, he sprinkled him first with the Life-giving Water, and instantly the body, which had become cold, was warm again, and the blood began to circulate. The Water that Cures healed the wound, and the Strength-giving Water had such an effect upon him that he opened his eyes and cried out, "Oh, how well I have slept!"

"You were already sleeping the eternal sleep," replied the dappled horse. "One of your rivals stabbed you mortally, and carried off Pietnotka, whom he pretends to have rescued. But do not worry yourself; she still sleeps, and none can arouse her but you, and this you must do by touching her with the dwarf's beard. Go now, and be happy."

The brave steed disappeared in a whirlwind, and Prince Dobrotek proceeded on his way. On drawing near the capital he saw it surrounded by a large foreign army; part of it was already taken, and the inhabitants seemed to be begging for mercy. The prince put on his invisible cap, and began to strike right and left with the sharp smiting sword. With such fury did he attack the enemy that they fell dead on all sides, like felled trees. When he had thus destroyed the whole army, he went, still invisible, into the palace, where he heard the king express the utmost astonishment that the enemy had retired without fighting.

"Where, then, is the brave warrior who has saved us?" said his majesty aloud.

Every one was silent, when Dobrotek took off his magic cap, and falling on his knees before the monarch, said, "It is I, my king and father, who have routed and destroyed the enemy. It is I who saved the princess, my bride. While on my way back with her I was treacherously killed by my rival, who has represented himself to you as her rescuer, but he has deceived you. Lead me to the princess, that I may awaken her."

On hearing these words the impostor ran away as quickly as possible, and Dobrotek approached the sleeping maiden. He just touched her brow with the dwarf's beard, upon which she opened her eyes, smiled, and seemed to ask where she was.

The king, overcome with joy, kissed her fondly, and the same evening she was married to the devoted Prince Dobrotek. The king himself led her to the altar, and to his son-in-law he gave half his kingdom. So splendid was the wedding banquet that eye has never seen, nor ear ever heard, of its equal.

THE SUN; OR, THE THREE GOLDEN HAIRS OF THE OLD MAN VSÉVÈDE

By Alex. Chodsko

CAN this be a true story? It is said that once there was a king who was exceedingly fond of hunting the wild beasts in his forests. One day he followed a stag so far and so long that he lost his way. Alone and overtaken by night, he was glad to find himself near a small thatched cottage in which lived a charcoal-burner.

"Will you kindly show me the way to the high-road? You shall be handsomely rewarded."

"I would willingly," said the charcoal-burner, "but God is going to send my wife a little child, and I cannot leave her alone. Will you pass the night under our roof? There is a truss of sweet hay in the loft where you may rest, and to-morrow morning I will be your guide."

The king accepted the invitation and went to bed in the loft. Shortly after, a son was born to the charcoal-burner's wife. But the king could not sleep. At midnight he heard noises in the house, and looking through a crack in the flooring he saw the charcoal-burner asleep, his wife almost in a faint, and by the side of the newly born babe three old women dressed in white, each holding a lighted taper in her hand, and all talking together. Now these were the three Soudiché, or Fates, you must know.

430

The first said, "On this boy I bestow the gift of confronting great dangers."

The second said, "I bestow the power of happily escaping all these dangers, and living to a good old age."

The third said, "I bestow upon him for wife the princess born at the selfsame hour as he, and daughter of the very king sleeping above in the loft."

At these words the lights went out and silence reigned around.

Now the king was greatly troubled, and wondered exceedingly; he felt as if he had received a sword-thrust in the chest. He lay awake all night thinking how to prevent the words of the Fates from coming true.

With the first glimmer of morning light the baby began to cry. The charcoal-burner, on going over to it, found that his wife was dead.

"Poor little orphan," he said sadly, "what will become of thee without a mother's care?"

"Confide this child to me," said the king. "I will look after it. He shall be well provided for. You shall be given a sum of money large enough to keep you without having to burn charcoal."

The poor man gladly agreed, and the king went away promising to send some one for the child. The queen and courtiers thought it would be an agreeable surprise for the king to hear that a charming little princess had been born on the night he was away. But instead of being pleased he frowned, and calling one of his servants, said to him, "Go to the charcoal-burner's cottage in the forest, and give the man this purse in exchange for a new-born infant. On your way back drown the child. See well that he is drowned, for if he should in any way escape, you yourself shall suffer in his place."

The servant was given the child in a basket, and on reaching the centre of a narrow bridge that stretched across a wide and deep river, he threw both basket and baby into the water.

"A prosperous journey to you, Mr. Son-in-Law," said the king, on hearing the servant's story; for he fully believed the child was drowned. But it was far from being the case; the little one was floating happily along in his basket cradle, and slumbering as sweetly as if his mother had sung him to sleep. Now it happened that a fisherman, who was mending his nets before his cottage door, saw the basket floating down the river. He jumped at once into his boat, picked it up, and ran to tell his wife the good news.

"Look," said he, "you have always longed for a son; here is a beautiful little boy the river has sent us."

The woman was delighted, and took the infant and loved it as her own child. They named him Plavacek (the floater), because he had come to them floating on the water.

The river flowed on. Years passed away. The little baby grew into a handsome youth; in all the villages round there were none to compare with him. Now it happened that one summer day the king was riding unattended. And the heat being very great, he reined in his horse before the fisherman's door to ask for a drink of water. Plavacek brought the water. The king looked at him attentively, then turning to the fisherman, said, "That is a good-looking lad; is he your son?"

"He is and he is n't," replied the fisherman. "I found him, when he was quite a tiny baby, floating down the stream in a basket. So we adopted him and brought him up as our own son."

The king turned as pale as death, for he guessed that he was the same child he had ordered to be drowned. Then recovering himself he got down from his horse and said, "I want a trusty messenger to take a letter to the palace; could you send him with it?"

"With pleasure! Your majesty may be sure of its safe delivery."

Thereupon the king wrote to the queen as follows:

"The man who brings you this letter is the most dangerous of all my enemies. Have his head cut off at once; no delay, no pity, he must be executed before my return. Such is my will and pleasure."

This he carefully folded and sealed with the royal seal.

Plavacek took the letter and set off immediately. But the forest through which he had to pass was so large, and the trees so thick, that he missed the path and was overtaken by the darkness before the journey was nearly over. In the midst of his trouble he met an old woman who said, "Where are you going, Plavacek? Where are you going?"

"I am the bearer of a letter from the king to the queen, but have missed the path to the palace. Could you, good mother, put me on the right road?"

"Impossible to-day, my child; it is getting dark, and you would not have time to get there. Stay with me to-night. You will not be with strangers, for I am your godmother."

Plavacek agreed. Thereupon they entered a pretty little cottage that seemed suddenly to sink into the earth. Now while he slept the old woman changed his letter for another which ran thus: —

"Immediately upon the receipt of this letter introduce the bearer to the princess our daughter. I have chosen this young man for my son-in-law, and it is my wish they should be married before my return to the palace. Such is my pleasure."

The letter was duly delivered, and when the queen had read it, she ordered everything to be prepared for the wedding. Both she and her daughter greatly enjoyed Plavacek's society, and nothing disturbed the happiness of the newly married pair.

Within a few days the king returned, and on hearing what had taken place was very angry with the queen.

"But you expressly bade me have the wedding before your return. Come, read your letter again; here it is," said she.

He closely examined the letter; the paper, handwriting, seal — all were undoubtedly his. He then called his son-in-law, and questioned him about his journey. Plavacek hid nothing, — he told how he had lost his way, and how he had passed the night in a cottage in the forest.

"What was the old woman like?" asked the king.

From Plavacek's description the king knew it was the very same who, twenty years before, had foretold the marriage of the princess with the charcoal-burner's son. After some moments' thought the king said, "What is done is done. But you will not become my son-in-law so easily. No, i' faith! As a wedding present you must bring me three golden hairs from the head of Dède-Vsévède."

In this way he thought to get rid of his son-in-law, whose very presence was distasteful to him. The young fellow took leave of his wife and set off. "I know not which way to go," said he to himself, "but my god-mother the witch will surely help me."

But he found the way easily enough. He walked on and on and on for a long time over mountain, valley, and river, until he reached the shores of the Black Sea. There he found a boat and boatman.

"May God bless you, old boatman," said he.

"And you, too, my young traveler. Where are you going?"

"To Dède-Vsévède's castle for three of his golden hairs."

"Ah, then you are very welcome. For a long weary while I have been waiting for such a messenger as you. I have been ferrying passengers across for these twenty years, and not one of them has done anything to help me. If you will promise to ask Dède-Vsévède when I shall be released from my toil I will row you across."

Plavacek promised, and was rowed to the opposite bank. He continued his journey on foot until he came in sight of a large town half in ruins, near which was passing a funeral procession. The king of that country was following his father's coffin, and with the tears running down his cheeks.

"May God comfort you in your distress," said Plavacek.

"Thank you, good traveler. Where are you going?"

"To the house of Dède-Vsévède in quest of three of his golden hairs."

"To the house of Dède-Vsévède? Indeed! What a pity you did not come sooner; we have long been expecting such a messenger as you. Come and see me by and by."

When Plavacek presented himself at court the king said to him:—

"We understand you are on your way to the house of Dède-Vsévède? Now we have an apple-tree here that bears the fruit of everlasting youth. One of these apples eaten by a man, even though he be dying, will cure him and make him young again. For the last twenty years neither fruit nor flower has been found on this tree. Will you ask Dède-Vsévède the cause of it?"

"That I will, with pleasure."

Then Plavacek continued his journey, and as he went he came to a large and beautiful city where all was sad and silent. Near the gate was an old man who leant on a stick and walked with difficulty.

"May God bless you, good old man."

"And you, too, my handsome young traveler. Where are you going?"

"To Dède-Vsévède's palace in search of three of his golden hairs."

"Ah, you are the very messenger I have so long waited for. Allow me to take you to my master, the king."

On their arrival at the palace, the king said, "I hear you are an ambassador to Dède-Vsévède. We have

436

here a well, the water of which renews itself. So wonderful are its effects that invalids are immediately cured on drinking it, while a few drops sprinkled on a corpse will bring it to life again. For the past twenty years this well has remained dry. If you will ask old Dède-Vsévède how the flow of water may be restored, I will reward you royally."

Plavacek promised to do so, and was dismissed with good wishes. He then traveled through deep, dark forests, in the midst of which might be seen a large meadow; out of it grew lovely flowers, and in the centre stood a castle built of gold. It was the home of Dède-Vsévède. So brilliant with light was it that it seemed to be built of fire. When he entered there was no one in sight but an old woman spinning.

"Greeting, Plavacek. I am well pleased to see you."

She was his godmother, who had given him shelter in her cottage when he was the bearer of the king's letter.

"Tell me what brings you here from such a distance," she went on.

"The king would not have me for a son-in-law, unless I first got him three golden hairs from the head of Dède-Vsévède. So he sent me here to fetch them."

The Fate laughed. "Déde-Vsévède indeed! Why, I am his mother; it is the shining sun himself. He is a child at morning time, a grown man at midday, a decrepit old man, looking as if he had lived a hundred years, at eventide. But I will see that you have the three hairs from his head; I am not your godmother for nothing. All the same you must not remain here. My son is a good lad, but when he comes home he *is* hungry, and would very probably order you to be roasted for his supper. Now I will turn this empty bucket upside down, and you shall hide underneath it."

Plavacek begged the Fate to obtain from Dède-Vsévède the answers to the three questions he had been asked.

"I will do so certainly, but you must listen to what he says."

Suddenly a blast of wind howled round the palace, and the Sun entered by a western window. He was an old man with golden hair.

"I smell human flesh," cried he. "I am sure of it. Mother, you have some one here."

"Star of day," she replied, "whom could I have here that you would not see sooner than I? The fact is that in your daily journeys the scent of human flesh is always with you, so when you come home at evening it clings to you still."

The old man said nothing, and sat down to supper. When he had finished he laid his golden head on the Fate's lap and went to sleep. Then she pulled out a hair and threw it on the ground. It fell with a metallic sound like the vibration of a guitar string.

"What do you want, mother?" asked he.

"Nothing, my son; I was sleeping, and had a strange dream."

"What was it, mother?"

"I thought I was in a place where there was a well, and the well was fed from a spring, the water of which cured all diseases. Even the dying were restored to health on drinking that water, and the dead who were sprinkled with it came to life again. For the last twenty years the well has run dry. What must be done to restore the flow of water?"

"That is very simple. A frog has lodged itself in the opening of the spring; this prevents the flow of water. Kill the frog, and the water will return to the well."

He slept again, and the old woman pulled out another golden hair, and threw it on the ground.

"Mother, what do you want?"

"Nothing, my son, nothing; I was dreaming. In my dream I saw a large town, the name of which I have forgotten. And there grew an apple-tree the fruit of which had the power to make the old young again. A single apple eaten by an old man would restore to him the vigor and freshness of youth. For twenty years this tree has not borne fruit. What can be done to make it fruitful?"

"The means are not difficult. A snake hidden among the roots destroys the sap. Kill the snake, transplant the tree, and the fruit will grow as before."

He again fell asleep, and the old woman pulled out another golden hair.

"Now look here, mother, why will you not let me sleep?"

"Lie down, my darling son; do not disturb yourself. I am sorry I awoke you, but I have had a very strange dream. It seemed that I saw a boatman on the shores of the Black Sea, and he complained that he had been toiling at the ferry for twenty years without any one having come to take his place. For how much longer must this poor old man continue to row?"

"He is a silly fellow. He has but to place his oars in the hands of the first comer and jump ashore. Whoever receives the oars will replace him as ferryman. But leave me in peace now, mother, and do not wake me again. I have to rise very early, and must first dry the eyes of a princess. The poor thing spends all night weeping for her husband, who has been sent by the king to get three of my golden hairs."

Next morning the wind whistled round Dède-Vsévède's palace, and instead of an old man, a beautiful child with golden hair awoke on the old woman's lap. It was the glorious sun. He bade her good-by, and flew out of the eastern window. The old woman turned up the bucket and said to Plavacek, "Look, here are the three golden hairs. You now know the answers to your questions. May God direct you and send you a prosperous journey. You will not see me again, for you will have no further need of me."

He thanked her gratefully and left her. On arriving at the town with the dried-up well, he was questioned by the king as to what news he had brought.

"Have the well carefully cleaned out," said he, "kill the frog that obstructs the spring, and the wonderful water will flow again."

The king did as he was advised, and rejoiced to see the water return. He gave Plavacek twelve swan-white horses, and as much gold and silver as they could carry.

On reaching the second town and being asked by the king what news he had brought, he replied, "Excellent, — one could not wish for better. Dig up your apple-tree, kill the snake that lies among the roots, transplant the tree, and it will produce apples like those of former times."

And all turned out as he had said, for no sooner was the tree replanted than it was covered with blossoms that gave it the appearance of a sea of roses. The delighted king gave him twelve raven-black horses, laden with as much wealth as they could carry. He then journeyed to the shores of the Black Sea. There the boatman questioned him as to what news he had brought respecting his release. Plavacek first crossed with his twenty-four horses to the opposite bank, and then replied that the boatman might gain his freedom by placing the oars in the hands of the first traveler who wished to be ferried over.

Plavacek's royal father-in-law could not believe his eyes when he saw Dède-Vsévède's three golden hairs. As for the princess, his young wife, she wept tears, but of joy, not sadness, to see her dear one again, and she said to him, "How did you get such splendid horses and so much wealth, dear husband?"

And he answered her, "All this represents the price paid for the weariness of spirit I have felt; it is the ready money for hardships endured and services given. Thus, I showed one king how to regain possession of the Apples of Youth; to another I told the secret of reopening the spring of water that gives health and life."

"Apples of Youth! Water of Life!" interrupted the king. "I will certainly go and find these treasures for myself. Ah, what joy! having eaten of these apples

I shall become young again; having drunk of the Water
of Immortality, I shall live forever."

And he started off in search of these treasures. But
he has not yet returned from his search.

MYTHS OF INDIA

MUCHIE LAL

By M. Frere

ONCE upon a time there were a Rajah and Ranee who had no children. Long had they wished and prayed that the gods would send them a son, but it was all in vain — their prayers were not granted. One day a number of fish were brought into the royal kitchen to be cooked for the Rajah's dinner, and amongst them was one little fish that was not dead, but all the rest were dead. One of the palace maid-servants, seeing this, took the little fish and put him in a basin of water. Shortly afterward the Ranee saw him, and thinking him very pretty, kept him as a pet; and because she had no children she lavished all her affection on the fish and loved him as a son; and the people called him Muchie Rajah (the Fish Prince).

In a little while Muchie Rajah had grown too long to live in the small basin, so they put him into a larger one, and then (when he grew too long for that) into a big tub. In time, however, Muchie Rajah became too large for even the big tub to hold him; so the Ranee had a tank made for him, in which he lived very happily, and twice a day she fed him with boiled rice. Now, though the people fancied Muchie Rajah was only a fish, this was not the case. He was, in truth, a young Rajah who had angered the gods, and been

445

by them turned into a fish and thrown into the river as a punishment.

One morning, when the Ranee brought him his daily meal of boiled rice, Muchie Rajah called out to her and said, "Queen Mother, Queen Mother, I am so lonely here all by myself! Cannot you get me a wife?" The Ranee promised to try, and sent messengers to all the people she knew, to ask if they would allow one of their children to marry her son, the Fish Prince. But they all answered, "We cannot give one of our dear little daughters to be devoured by a great fish, even though he is the Muchie Rajah and so high in your Majesty's favor."

At news of this the Ranee did not know what to do. She was so foolishly fond of Muchie Rajah, however, that she resolved to get him a wife at any cost. Again she sent out messengers, but this time she gave them a great bag containing a lac of gold mohurs, and said to them, "Go into every land until you find a wife for my Muchie Rajah, and to whoever will give you a child to be the Muchie Ranee you shall give this bag of gold mohurs." The messengers started on their search, but for some time they were unsuccessful; not even the beggars were to be tempted to sell their children, fearing the great fish would devour them. At last one day the messengers came to a village where there lived a Fakeer, who had lost his first wife and married again. His first wife had had one little daughter, and his second wife also had a daughter. As it happened, the Fakeer's second wife hated her little stepdaughter, always gave her the hardest work to do and the least food to eat, and tried by every means in her power to get her out of the way, in

order that the child might not rival her own daughter.
When she heard of the errand on which the messengers
had come, she sent for them when the Fakeer was out,
and said to them, "Give me the bag of gold mohurs, and
you shall take my little daughter to marry the Muchie
Rajah." ("For," she thought to herself, "the great fish
will certainly eat the girl, and she will thus trouble us
no more.") Then, turning to her stepdaughter, she
said, "Go down to the river and wash your saree, that
you may be fit to go with these people, who will take
you to the Ranee's court." At these words the poor girl
went down to the river very sorrowful, for she saw no
hope of escape, as her father was from home. As she
knelt by the river-side, washing her saree and crying
bitterly, some of her tears fell into the hole of an old
Seven-headed Cobra, who lived on the river-bank. This
Cobra was a very wise animal, and seeing the maiden,
he put his head out of his hole, and said to her, "Little
girl, why do you cry?" "Oh, sir," she answered, "I am
very unhappy; for my father is from home, and my stepmother has sold me to the Ranee's people to be the wife
of the Muchie Rajah, that great fish, and I know he will
eat me up." "Do not be afraid, my daughter," said the
Cobra; "but take with you these three stones and tie
them up in the corner of your saree;" and so saying,
he gave her three little round pebbles. "The Muchie
Rajah, whose wife you are to be, is not really a fish, but
a Rajah who has been enchanted. Your home will be a
little room which the Ranee has had built in the tank
wall. When you are taken there, wait and be sure you
don't go to sleep, or the Muchie Rajah will certainly

come and eat you up. But as you hear him coming rushing through the water, be prepared, and as soon as you see him, throw this first stone at him; he will then sink to the bottom of the tank. The second time he comes, throw the second stone, when the same thing will happen. The third time he comes, throw this third stone, and he will immediately resume his human shape." So saying, the old Cobra dived down again into his hole. The Fakeer's daughter took the stones and determined to do as the Cobra had told her, though she hardly believed it would have the desired effect.

When she reached the palace the Ranee spoke kindly to her, and said to the messengers, "You have done your errand well; this is a dear little girl." Then she ordered that she should be let down the side of the tank in a basket to a little room which had been prepared for her. When the Fakeer's daughter got there, she thought she had never seen such a pretty place in her life (for the Ranee had caused the little room to be very nicely decorated for the wife of her favorite); and she would have felt very happy away from her cruel stepmother and all the hard work she had been made to do, had it not been for the dark water that lay black and unfathomable below the door, and the fear of the terrible Muchie Rajah.

After waiting some time she heard a rushing sound, and little waves came dashing against the threshold; faster they came and faster, and the noise got louder and louder, until she saw a great fish's head above the water — Muchie Rajah was coming toward her open-mouthed. The Fakeer's daughter seized one of the stones that the

Cobra had given her and threw it at him, and down he sank to the bottom of the tank; a second time he rose and came toward her, and she threw the second stone at him, and he again sank down; a third time he came more fiercely than before, when, seizing a third stone, she threw it with all her force. No sooner did it touch him than the spell was broken, and there, instead of a fish, stood a handsome young prince. The poor little Fakeer's daughter was so startled that she began to cry. But the prince said to her, "Pretty maiden, do not be frightened. You have rescued me from a horrible thraldom, and I can never thank you enough; but if you will be the Muchie Ranee, we will be married to-morrow." Then he sat down on the doorstep, thinking over his strange fate and watching for the dawn.

Next morning early several inquisitive people came to see if the Muchie Rajah had eaten up his poor little wife, as they feared he would; what was their astonishment, on looking over the tank wall, to see, not the Muchie Rajah, but a magnificent prince! The news soon spread to the palace. Down came the Rajah, down came the Ranee, down came all their attendants, and dragged Muchie Rajah and the Fakeer's daughter up the side of the tank in a basket; and when they heard their story there were great and unparalleled rejoicings. The Ranee said, "So I have indeed found a son at last!" And the people were so delighted, so happy and so proud of the new prince and princess, that they covered all their path with damask from the tank to the palace, and cried to their fellows, "Come and see our new prince and princess! Were ever any so divinely beautiful? Come see a right royal couple, — a pair of mortals like the gods!" And when they reached the palace the prince was married to the Fakeer's daughter.

There they lived very happily for some time. The Muchie Ranee's stepmother, hearing what had happened, came often to see her stepdaughter, and pretended to be delighted at her good fortune; and the Ranee was so good that she quite forgave all her stepmother's former cruelty, and always received her very kindly. At last, one day, the Muchie Ranee said to her husband, "It is a weary while since I saw my father. If you will give me leave, I should much like to visit my native village and see him again." "Very well," he replied, "you may go. But do not stay away long; for there can be no happiness for me till you return." So she went, and her father was delighted to see her; but her stepmother, though she pretended to be very kind, was in reality only glad to think she had got the Ranee into her power, and determined, if possible, never to allow her to return to the palace again. One day, therefore, she said to her own daughter, "It is hard that your stepsister should have become Ranee of all the land instead of being eaten up by the great fish, while we gained no more than a lac of gold mohurs. Do now as I bid you, that you may become Ranee in her stead." She then went on to instruct her that she must invite the Ranee down to the river-bank, and there beg her to let her try on her jewels, and whilst putting them on give her a push and drown her in the river.

The girl consented, and standing by the river-bank, said to her stepsister, "Sister, may I try on your jewels?

— how pretty they are!" "Yes," said the Ranee, "and we shall be able to see in the river how they look." So, undoing her necklaces, she clasped them round the other's neck. But whilst she was doing so her step-sister gave her a push, and she fell backward into the water. The girl watched to see that the body did not rise, and then, running back, said to her mother, "Mother, here are all the jewels, and she will trouble us no more." But it happened that just when her step-sister pushed the Ranee into the river her old friend the Seven-headed Cobra chanced to be swimming across it, and seeing the little Ranee like to be drowned, he carried her on his back until he reached his hole, into which he took her safely. Now this hole, in which the Cobra and his wife and all his little ones lived, had two entrances,— the one under the water and leading to the river, and the other above water, leading out into the open fields. To this upper end of his hole the Cobra took the Muchie Ranee, where he and his wife took care of her; and there she lived with them for some time. Meanwhile, the wicked Fakeer's wife, having dressed up her own daughter in all the Ranee's jewels, took her to the palace, and said to the Muchie Rajah, "See, I have brought your wife, my dear daughter, back safe and well." The Rajah looked at her, and thought, "This does not look like my wife." However, the room was dark and the girl was cleverly disguised, and he thought he might be mistaken. Next day he said again, "My wife must be sadly changed or this cannot be she, for she was always bright and cheerful. She had pretty loving ways and merry words, while this woman never opens her lips." Still, he did not like to seem to mistrust his wife, and comforted himself by saying, "Perhaps she is tired with the long journey." On the third day, however, he could bear the uncertainty no longer, and tearing off her jewels, saw, not the face of his own little wife, but another woman. Then he was very angry and turned her out of doors, saying, "Begone; since you are but the wretched tool of others, I spare your life." But of the Fakeer's wife he said to his guards, "Fetch that woman here instantly; for unless she can tell me where my wife is, I will have her hanged." It chanced, however, that the Fakeer's wife had heard of the Muchie Rajah having turned her daughter out of doors; so, fearing his anger, she hid herself, and was not to be found.

Meantime, the Muchie Ranee, not knowing how to get home, continued to live in the great Seven-headed Cobra's hole, and he and his wife and all his family were very kind to her, and loved her as if she had been one of them; and there her little son was born, and she called him Muchie Lal, after the Muchie Rajah, his father. Muchie Lal was a lovely child, merry and brave, and his playmates all day long were the young Cobras. When he was about three years old a bangle-seller came by that way, and the Muchie Ranee bought some bangles from him and put them on her boy's wrists and ankles; but by next day, in playing, he had broken them all. Then, seeing the bangle-seller, the Ranee called him again and bought some more, and so on every day until the bangle-seller got quite rich from selling so many bangles for the Muchie Lal; for the Cobra's hole was full of treasure, and he gave the Muchie Ranee as much money to spend every day as she liked. There was nothing she wished for he did not give her, only he would not let her try to get home to her husband, which she wished more than all. When she asked him he would say, "No, I will not let you go. If your husband comes here and fetches you, it is well; but I will not allow you to wander in search of him through the land alone."

And so she was obliged to stay where she was.

All this time the poor Muchie Rajah was hunting in every part of the country for his wife, but he could learn no tidings of her. For grief and sorrow at losing her he had gone well-nigh distracted, and did nothing but wander from place to place, crying, "She is gone! she is gone!" Then, when he had long inquired without avail of all the people in her native village about her, he one day met a bangle-seller and said to him, "Whence do you come?" The bangle-seller answered, "I have just been selling bangles to some people who live in a Cobra's hole in the river-bank." "People! What people?" asked the Rajah. "Why," answered the bangle-seller, "a woman and a child; the child is the most beautiful I ever saw. He is about three years old, and of course, running about, is always breaking his bangles, and his mother buys him new ones every day." "Do you know what the child's name is?" said the Rajah. "Yes," answered the bangle-seller carelessly, "for the lady always calls him her Muchie Lal." "Ah," thought the Muchie Rajah, "this must be my wife." Then he said to him again, "Good bangle-seller, I would see these strange people of whom you speak; cannot you take me there?" "Not to-night," replied the bangle-seller; "daylight has gone, and we should only frighten them; but I shall be going there again to-morrow, and then you may come too. Meanwhile, come and rest at my house for the night, for you look faint and weary." The Rajah consented. Next morning, however, very early, he woke the bangle-seller, saying, "Pray let us go now and see the people you spoke about yesterday." "Stay," said the bangle-seller; "it is much too early. I never go till after breakfast." So the Rajah had to wait till the bangle-seller was ready to go. At last they started off, and when they reached the Cobra's hole the first thing the Rajah saw was a fine little boy playing with the young Cobras.

As the bangle-seller came along, jingling his bangles, a gentle voice from inside the hole called out, "Come here, my Muchie Lal, and try on your bangles." Then the Muchie Rajah, kneeling down at the mouth of the hole, said, "Oh, lady, show your beautiful face to me." At the sound of his voice the Ranee ran out, crying, "Husband, husband! have you found me again?" And she told him how her sister had tried to drown her, and how the good Cobra had saved her life and taken care of her and her child. Then he said, "And will you now come home with me?" And she told him how the Cobra would never let her go, and said, "I will first tell him of your coming; for he has been as a father to me." So she called out, "Father Cobra, father Cobra, my husband has come to fetch me; will you let me go?" "Yes," he said, "if your husband has come to fetch you, you may go." And his wife said, "Farewell, dear lady, we are

loath to lose you, for we have loved you as a daughter."
And all the little Cobras were very sorrowful to think
that they must lose their playfellow, the young Prince.
Then the Cobra gave the Muchie Rajah and the Muchie
Ranee and Muchie Lal all the most costly gifts he could
find in his treasure-house; and so they went home,
where they lived very happy ever after.

PANCH-PHUL RANEE

By M. Frere

A CERTAIN Rajah had two wives, of whom he preferred the second to the first; the first Ranee had a son, but, because he was not the child of the second Ranee, his father took a great dislike to him, and treated him so harshly that the poor boy was very unhappy.

One day, therefore, he said to his mother: "Mother, my father does not care for me, and my presence is only a vexation to him. I should be happier anywhere than here; let me therefore go and seek my fortune in other lands."

So the Ranee asked her husband if he would allow their son to travel. He said, "The boy is free to go, but I don't see how he is to live in any other part of the world, for he is too stupid to earn his living, and I will give him no money to squander on senseless pleasures." Then the Ranee told her son that he had his father's permission to travel, and said to him, "You are going out into the world now to try your luck; take with you the food and clothes I have provided for your journey." And she gave him a bundle of clothes and several small loaves, and in each loaf she placed a gold mohur, that on opening it he might find money as well as food inside; and he started on his journey.

When the young Rajah had traveled a long way, and left his father's kingdom far behind, he one day came upon the outskirts of a great city, where (instead of taking the position due to his rank, and sending to inform the Rajah of his arrival) he went to a poor carpenter's house, and begged of him a lodging for the night. The carpenter was busy making wooden clogs in the porch of his house, but he looked up, and nodded, saying, "Young man, you are welcome to any assistance a stranger may need and we can give you. If you are in want of food, you will find my wife and daughter in the house; they will be happy to cook for you." The Rajah went inside and said to the carpenter's daughter, "I am a stranger, and have traveled a long way; I am both tired and hungry; cook me some dinner as fast as you can, and I will pay you for your trouble." She answered, "I would willingly cook you some dinner at once, but I have no wood to light the fire, and the jungle is some way off." "It matters not," said the Rajah; "this will do to light the fire, and I'll make the loss good to your father;" and taking a pair of new clogs which the carpenter had just finished making, he broke them up and lighted the fire with them.

Next morning he went into the jungle, cut wood, and, having made a pair of new clogs — better than those with which he had lighted the fire the evening before — placed them with the rest of the goods for sale in the carpenter's shop. Shortly afterward, one of the servants of the Rajah of that country came to buy a pair of clogs for his master, and seeing these new ones, said to the carpenter, "Why, man, these clogs are better than all the rest put together. I will take none other to the Rajah. I wish you would always make such clogs as these." And throwing down ten gold mohurs on the floor of the hut, he took up the clogs and went away.

The carpenter was much surprised at the whole business. In the first place, he usually received only two or three rupees for each pair of clogs; and in the second, he knew that these which the Rajah's servant had judged worth ten gold mohurs had not been made by him; and how they had come there he could not think, for he felt certain they were not with the rest of the clogs the night before. He thought and thought, but the more he thought about the matter the more puzzled he got, and he went to talk about it to his wife and daughter. Then his daughter said, "Oh, those must have been the clogs the stranger made!" And she told her father how he had lighted the fire the night before with two of the clogs which were for sale, and had afterward fetched wood from the jungle and made another pair to replace them.

The carpenter at this news was more astonished than ever, and he thought to himself, "Since this stranger seems a quiet, peaceable sort of man, and can make clogs so well, it is a great pity he should leave this place; he would make a good husband for my daughter;" and, catching hold of the young Rajah, he propounded his scheme to him. (But all this time he had no idea that his guest was a Rajah.)

Now the carpenter's daughter was a very pretty

girl — as pretty as any Rance you ever saw; she was also good-tempered, clever, and could cook extremely well. So when the carpenter asked the Rajah to be his son-in-law, he looked at the father, the mother, and the girl, and thinking to himself that many a better man had a worse fate, he said, "Yes, I will marry your daughter, and stay here and make clogs." So the Rajah married the carpenter's daughter.

This Rajah was very clever at making all sorts of things in wood. When he had made all the clogs he wished to sell next day, he would amuse himself in making toys; and in this way he made a thousand wooden parrots. They were as like real parrots as possible. They had each two wings, two legs, two eyes, and a sharp beak. And when the Rajah had finished them all, he painted and varnished them and put them one afternoon outside the house to dry.

Night came on, and with it came Parbuttee and Mahdeo, flying round the world to see the different races of men. Amongst the many places they visited was the city where the carpenter lived; and in the garden in front of the house they saw the thousand wooden parrots which the Rajah had made and painted and varnished, all placed out to dry. Then Parbuttee turned to Mahdeo, and said, "These parrots are very well made — they need nothing but life. Why should not we give them life?" Mahdeo answered, "What would be the use of that? It would be a strange freak, indeed!" "Oh," said Parbuttee, "I only meant you to do it as an amusement. It would be so funny to see the wooden parrots flying about! But do not do it if

you don't like." "You would like it, then?" answered
Mahdeo. "Very well, I will do it." And he endowed
the thousand parrots with life.

Parbuttee and Mahdeo then flew away.

Next morning the Rajah got up early to see if the
varnish he had put on the wooden parrots was dry;
but no sooner did he open the door than — marvel
of marvels! — the thousand wooden parrots all came
walking into the house, flapping their wings and chattering to each other.

Hearing the noise, the carpenter and the carpenter's
wife and daughter came running out to see what was
the matter, and were not less astonished than the
Rajah himself at the miracle which had taken place.
Then the carpenter's wife turned to her son-in-law, and
said, "It is all very well that you should have made
these wooden parrots; but I don't know where we are
to find food for them! Great, strong parrots like these
will eat not less than a pound of rice apiece every
day. Your father-in-law and I cannot afford to pro-
cure as much as that for them in this poor house. If
you wish to keep them, you must live elsewhere, for
we cannot provide for you all."

"Very well," said the Rajah; "you shall not have
cause to accuse me of ruining you, for from henceforth I will have a house of my own." So he and his
wife went to live in a house of their own, and he took
the thousand parrots with him, and his mother-in-law
gave her daughter some corn and rice and money to
begin housekeeping with. Moreover, he found that the
parrots, instead of being an expense, were the means

of increasing his fortune; for they flew away every
morning early to get food, and spent the whole day out
in the fields; and every evening, when they returned
home, each parrot brought in his beak a stalk of corn
or rice, or whatever it had found good to eat. So that
their master was regularly supplied with more food
than enough; and what with selling what he did not
require, and working at his trade, he soon became
quite a rich carpenter.

After he had been living in this way very happily
for some time, one night, when he fell asleep, the
Rajah dreamed a wonderful dream, and this was the
dream: —

He thought that very, very far away beyond the Red
Sea was a beautiful kingdom surrounded by seven
other seas; and that it belonged to a Rajah and Ranee
who had one lovely daughter, named Panch-Phul Ranee
(the Five-Flower Queen), after whom the whole kingdom was called Panch-Phul Ranee's country; and
that this princess lived in the centre of her father's
kingdom, in a little house round which were seven
wide ditches, and seven great hedges made of spears;
and that she was called Panch-Phul Ranee because
she was so light and delicate that she weighed no more
than five white lotus flowers! Moreover, he dreamed
that this princess had vowed to marry no one who could
not cross the seven seas, and jump the seven ditches,
and seven hedges made of spears.

After dreaming this the young Rajah awoke, and
feeling much puzzled, got up, and sitting with his
head in his hands, tried to think the matter over and

discover if he had ever heard anything like his dream before; but he could make nothing of it.

Whilst he was thus thinking, his wife awoke and asked him what was the matter. He told her, and she said, "That is a strange dream. If I were you, I'd ask the old parrot about it; he is a wise bird, and perhaps he knows." This parrot of which she spoke was the most wise of all the thousand wooden parrots. The Rajah took his wife's advice, and when all the birds came home that evening, he called the old parrot and told him his dream, saying, "Can this be true?" To which the parrot replied, "It is all true. The Panch-Phul Ranee's country lies beyond the Red Sea, and is surrounded by seven seas, and she dwells in a house built in the centre of her father's kingdom. Round her house are seven ditches, and seven hedges made of spears, and she has vowed not to marry any man who cannot jump these seven ditches and seven hedges; and because she is very beautiful many great and noble men have tried to do this, but in vain.

"The Rajah and Ranee, her father and mother, are very fond of her and proud of her. Every day she goes to the palace to see them, and they weigh her in a pair of scales. They put her in one scale and five lotus flowers in the other, and she's so delicate and fragile she weighs no heavier than the five little flowers, so they call her the Panch-Phul Ranee. Her father and mother are very proud of this."

"I should like to go to that country and see the Panch-Phul Ranee," said the Rajah; "but I don't know how I could cross the seven seas." "I will show you how to manage that," replied the old parrot. "I and another parrot will fly close together, I crossing my left over his right wing; so that we will move along as if we were one bird (using only our outside wings to fly with), and on the chair made of our interlaced wings you shall sit, and we will carry you safely across the seven seas. On the way we will every evening alight in some high tree and rest, and every morning we can go on again." "That sounds a good plan; I have a great desire to try it," said the Rajah. "Wife, what should you think of my going to the Panch-Phul Ranee's country, and seeing if I can jump the seven ditches, and seven hedges made of spears. Will you let me try?"

"Yes," she answered. "If you like to go and marry her, go; only take care that you do not kill yourself; and mind you come back some day." And she prepared food for him to take with him, and took off her gold and silver bangles, which she placed in a bundle of warm things, that he might be in need of neither money nor clothes on the journey. He then charged the nine hundred and ninety-eight parrots he left behind him to bring her plenty of corn and rice daily, that she might never need food while he was away, and took her to the house of her father, in whose care she was to remain during his absence; and he wished her good-by, saying, "Do not fear but that I will come back to you, even if I do win the Panch-Phul Ranee, for you will always be my first wife, though you are the carpenter's daughter."

The old parrot and another parrot then spread their wings, on which the Rajah seated himself as on a chair, and rising up in the air, they flew away with him out of sight.

Far, far, far they flew, as fast as parrots can fly, over hills, over forests, over rivers, over valleys, on, on, on, hour after hour, day after day, week after week, only staying to rest every night when it got too dark to see where they were going. At last they reached the seven seas which surrounded the Panch-Phul Ranee's country. When once they began crossing the seas they could not rest (for there was neither rock nor island on which to alight), so they were obliged to fly straight across them, night and day, until they gained the shore.

By reason of this the parrots were too exhausted on their arrival to go as far as the city where the Rajah, Panch-Phul Ranee's father, lived, but they flew down to rest on a beautiful banyan tree, which grew not far from the sea, close to a small village. The Rajah determined to go into the village and get food and shelter there. He told the parrots to stay in the banyan-tree till his return; then, leaving his bundle of clothes and most of his money in their charge, he set off on foot toward the nearest house.

After a little while he reached a Malee's cottage, and giving a gold mohur to the Malee's wife, got her to provide him with food and shelter for the night.

Next morning he rose early, and said to his hostess, "I am a stranger here, and know nothing of the place. What is the name of your country?" "This," she said, "is Panch-Phul Ranee's country."

"And what is the last news in your town?" he asked. "Very bad news indeed," she replied. "You must know our Rajah has one only daughter — a most beautiful Princess — and her name is Panch-Phul Ranee, for she is so light and delicate that she weighs no heavier than five lotus flowers. After her this whole country is called Panch-Phul Ranee's country. She lives in a small bungalow in the centre of the city you see yonder; but, unluckily for us, she has vowed to marry no man who cannot jump on foot over the seven hedges made of spears, and across the seven great ditches that surround her house. This cannot be done, Babamah! I don't know how many hundreds of thousands of rajahs have tried to do it and died in the attempt! Yet the princess will not break her vow. Daily, worse and worse tidings come from the city of fresh people having been killed in trying to jump the seven hedges and seven ditches, and I see no end to the misfortunes that will arise from it. Not only are so many brave men lost to the world, but, since the Princess will marry no one who does not succeed in this, she stands a chance of not marrying at all; and if that be so, when the Rajah dies there will be no one to protect her and claim the right to succeed to the throne. All the nobles will probably fight for the Raj, and the whole kingdom be turned topsy-turvy."

"Mahi," said the Rajah, "if that is all there is to do, I will try and win your princess, for I can jump right well."

"Baba," answered the Malee's wife, "do not think of such a thing; are you mad? I tell you, hundreds of thousands of men have said these words before, and been killed for their rashness. What power do you think you possess to succeed where all before you have failed? Give up all thought of this, for it is utter folly."

"I will not do it," answered the Rajah, "before going to consult some of my friends."

So he left the Malee's cottage, and returned to the banyan-tree to talk over the matter with the parrots; for he thought they would be able to carry him on their wings across the seven ditches and seven hedges made of spears. When he reached the tree the old parrot said to him, "It is two days since you left us; what news have you brought from the village?" The Rajah answered, "The Panch-Phul Ranee still lives in the house surrounded by the seven ditches, and seven hedges made of spears, and has vowed to marry no man who cannot jump over them; but cannot you parrots, who brought me all the way over the seven seas, carry me on your wings across these great barriers?"

"You stupid man!" answered the old parrot; "of course we could, but what would be the good of doing so? If we carried you across, it would not be at all the same thing as your jumping across, and the Princess would no more consent to marry you than she would now; for she has vowed to marry no one who has not jumped across *on foot*. If you want to do the thing, why not do it yourself, instead of talking nonsense? Have you forgotten how, when you were a little boy, you were taught to jump by conjurers and tumblers (for the parrot knew all the Rajah's history)? Now is the time to put their lessons into practice. If you can jump the seven ditches, and seven hedges made of spears, you will have done a good work, and be able to marry the Panch-Phul Ranee; but if not, this is a thing in which we cannot help you."

"You reason justly," replied the Rajah. "I will try to put in practice the lessons I learnt when a boy; meantime, do you stay here till my return."

So saying, he went away to the city, which he reached by nightfall. Next morning early he went to where the Princess's bungalow stood, to try and jump the fourteen great barriers. He was strong and agile, and he jumped the seven great ditches, and six of the seven hedges made of spears; but in running to jump the seventh hedge he hurt his foot, and, stumbling, fell upon the spears and died — run through and through with the cruel iron spikes.

When Panch-Phul Ranee's father and mother got up that morning and looked out, as their custom was, toward their daughter's bungalow, they saw something transfixed upon the seventh hedge of spears, but what it was they could not make out, for it dazzled their eyes. So the Rajah called his Wuzeer and said to him, "For some days I have seen no one attempt to jump the seven hedges and seven ditches round Panch-Phul Ranee's bungalow; but what is that which I now see upon the seventh hedge of spears?"

The Wuzeer answered, "That is a rajah's son, who has failed like all who have gone before him."

"But how is it," answered the Rajah, "that he thus dazzles our eyes?"

"It is," replied the Wuzeer, "because he is so beautiful. Of all that have died for the sake of Panch-Phul Ranee, this youth is, beyond doubt, the handsomest."

467

"Alas!" cried the Rajah, "how many and how many brave men has my daughter killed? I will have no more die for her. Let us send her and the dead man together away into the jungle."

Then he ordered the servants to fetch the young Rajah's body. There he lay, still and beautiful, with a glory shining round him as the moonlight shines round the clear bright moon, but without a spark of life.

When the Rajah saw him, he said, "Oh, pity, pity, that so brave and handsome a boy should have come dying after this girl. Yet he is but one of the thousands of thousands who have died thus to no purpose. Pull up the spears and cast them into the seven ditches, for they shall remain no longer."

Then he commanded two palanquins to be prepared and men in readiness to carry them, and said, "Let the girl be married to the young Rajah, and let both be taken far away into the jungle, that we may never see them more. Then there will be quiet in the land again."

The Ranee, Panch-Phul Ranee's mother, cried bitterly at this, for she was very fond of her daughter, and she begged her husband not to send her away so cruelly — the living with the dead; but the Rajah was inexorable. "That poor boy died," he said; "let my daughter die too. I'll have no more men killed here."

So the two palanquins were prepared. Then he placed his daughter in the one, and her dead husband in the other, and said to the palkee-bearers, "Take these palkees and go out into the jungle until you have reached a place so desolate that not so much as a sparrow is to be seen, and there leave them both."

And so they did. Deep down in the jungle, where no bright sun could pierce the darkness, nor human voice be heard, far from any habitation of man or means of supporting life, on the edge of a dank, stagnant morass that was shunned by all but noisome reptiles and wandering beasts of prey, they set them down and left them, the dead husband and the living wife, alone to meet the horrors of the coming night, — alone, without a chance of rescue.

Panch-Phul Ranee heard the bearers' retreating footsteps, and their voices getting fainter and fainter in the distance, and felt that she had nothing to hope for but death.

Night seemed coming on apace, for though the sun had not set, the jungle was so dark that but little light pierced the gloom; and she thought she would take a last look at the husband her vow had killed, and sitting beside him wait till starvation should make her as he was, or some wild animal put a more speedy end to her sufferings.

She left her palkee and went toward his. There he lay with closed eyes and close-shut lips; black curling hair, which escaped from under his turban, concealed a ghastly wound on his temple. There was no look of pain on the face, and the long, sweeping eyelashes gave it such a tender, softened expression she could hardly believe that he was dead. He was, in truth, very beautiful; and watching him she said to herself, "Alas, what a noble being is here lost to the world!

what an earth's joy is extinguished! Was it for this that
I was cold, and proud, and stern, — to break the cup
of my own happiness and to be the death of such as
you? Must you now never know that you won your
wife? Must you never hear her ask your pardon for the
past, nor know her cruel punishment? Ah, if you had
but lived, how dearly I would have loved you! Oh, my
husband! my husband!" And sinking down on the
ground, she buried her face in her hands and cried
bitterly.

While she was sitting thus, night closed over the
jungle, and brought with it wild beasts that had left
their dens and lairs in search of prey — to roam about,
as the heat of the day was over. Tigers, lions, elephants,
and buffaloes all came by turns crushing through the
underwood which surrounded the place where the
palkees were, but they did no harm to Panch-Phul
Ranee, for she was so fair that not even the cruel
beasts of the forest would injure her. At last, about
four o'clock in the morning, all the wild animals had
gone, except two little jackals, who had been very busy
watching the rest and picking the bones left by the
tigers. Tired with running about, they lay down to
rest close to the palkees. Then one little jackal said to
the other, who was her husband, "Do tell me a little
story." "Dear me!" he exclaimed, "what people you
women are for stories! Well, look just in front of you;
do you see those two?" "Yes," she answered; "what
of them?" "That woman you see sitting on the ground,"
he said, "is the Panch-Phul Ranee." "And what son
of a Rajah is the man in the palkee?" asked she.

THE WILD ANIMALS HAD GONE EXCEPT TWO LITTLE JACKALS.

"That," he replied, "is a very sorrowful son. His father was so unkind to him that he left his own home, and went to live in another country very far from this; and there he dreamed about the Panch-Phul Ranee, and came to our land in order to marry her, but he was killed in jumping the seventh hedge of spears, and all he gained was to die for her sake."

"That is very sad," said the first little jackal; "but could he never by any chance come to life again?" "Yes," answered the other; "maybe he could, if only some one knew how to apply the proper remedies." "What are the proper remedies, and how could he be cured?" asked the lady jackal. (Now all this conversation had been heard by Panch-Phul Ranee, and when this question was asked she listened very eagerly and attentively for the answer.)

"Do you see this tree?" replied her husband. "Well, if some of its leaves were crushed, and a little of the juice put into the Rajah's two ears and upon his upper lip, and some upon his temples also, and some upon the spear-wounds in his side, he would come to life again and be as well as ever."

At this moment day dawned, and the two little jackals ran away. Panch-Phul Ranee did not forget their words. She, a princess born, who had never put her foot to the ground before (so delicately and tenderly had she been reared), walked over the rough clods of earth and the sharp stones till she reached the place where the tree grew of which the jackals had spoken. She gathered a number of its leaves, and, with hands and feet that had never before done coarse or common work, beat and crushed them down. They were so stiff and strong that it took her a long time. At last, after tearing them, and stamping on them, and pounding them between two stones, and biting the hardest parts, she thought they were sufficiently crushed; and rolling them up in a corner of her saree, she squeezed the juice through it onto her husband's temples, and put a little on his upper lip and into his ears, and some also on the spear-wound in his side. And when she had done this, he awoke as if he had been only sleeping, and sat up, wondering where he was. Before him stood Panch-Phul Ranee shining like a glorious star, and all around them was the dark jungle.

It would be hard to say which of them was the most astonished — the Rajah or the Princess. She was surprised that the remedy should have taken such speedy effect, and could hardly believe her eyes when she saw her husband get up. And if he looked beautiful when dead, much more handsome did he seem to her now, so full of life and animation and power — the picture of health and strength. And he in his turn was lost in amazement at the exquisite loveliness of the lady who stood before him. He did not know who she could be, for he had never seen her like except in a dream. Could she be really the world-renowned Panch-Phul Ranee, or was he dreaming still? He feared to move lest he should break the spell. But as he sat there wondering, she spoke, saying, "You marvel at what has taken place. You do not know me — I am Panch-Phul Ranee, your wife."

Then he said, "Ah, Princess, is it indeed you? You

have been very hard to me." "I know, I know," she answered; "I caused your death, but I brought you to life again. Let the past be forgotten; come home with me, and my father and mother will welcome you as a son."

He replied, "No, I must first return to my own home a while. Do you rather return there now with me, for it is a long time since I left it, and afterward we will come again to your father's kingdom."

To this Panch-Phul Ranee agreed. It took them, however, a long time to find their way out of the jungle. At last they succeeded in doing so, for none of the wild animals in it attempted to injure them, so beautiful and royal did they both look.

When they reached the banyan tree, where the Rajah had left the two parrots, the old parrot called out to him, "So you have come back at last! We thought you never would, you were such a long time away! There you went, leaving us here all the time, and after all doing no good, but only getting yourself killed. Why didn't you do as we advised you, and jump up nicely?"

"Well, I'm sure," said the Rajah, "yours is a hard case; but I beg your pardon for keeping you waiting so long, and now I hope you'll take me and my wife home."

"Yes, we will do that," answered the parrots; "but you had better get some dinner first, for it's a long journey over the seven seas."

So the Rajah went to the village close by and bought food for himself and the Panch-Phul Ranee. When he

473

returned with it, he said to her, "I fear the long journey before us for you: had you not better let me make it alone, and return here for you when it is over?" But she answered, "No! what could I, a poor, weak woman, do here alone? and I will not return to my father's house till you can come too. Take me with you, however far you go; only promise me you will never leave me." So he promised her, and they both, mounting the parrots, were carried up in the air across the seven seas, across the Red Sea, on, on, on, a whole year's journey, until they reached his father's kingdom, and alighted to rest at the foot of the palace garden. The Rajah, however, did not know where he was, for all had much changed since he left it some years before.

Then a little son was born to the Rajah and Panch-Phul Ranee. He was a beautiful child, but his father was grieved to think that in that bleak place there was no shelter for the mother or the baby. So he said to his wife, "I will go to fetch food for us both, and fire to cook it with, and inquire what this country is, and seek out a place of rest for you. Do not be afraid; I shall soon return." Now, far off in the distance smoke was to be seen rising from tents which belonged to some conjurers and dancing-people, and thither the Rajah bent his steps, feeling certain he should be able to get fire, and perhaps food also, from the inhabitants. When he got there, he found the place was much larger than he had expected, — quite a good-sized village in fact, the abode of nautch people and conjurers. In all the houses the people were busy, some dancing, some singing, others trying various conjuring tricks

474

or practicing beating the drum, and all seemed happy and joyful.

When the conjurers saw him, they were so much struck with his appearance (for he was very handsome) that they determined to make him, if possible, stay among them and join their band. And they said one to another, "How well he would look beating the drum for the dancers! All the world would come to see us dance, if we had such a handsome man as that to beat the drum."

The Rajah, unconscious of their intentions, went into the largest hut he saw, and said to a woman who was grinding corn, "Bai, give me a little rice, and some fire from your hearth." She immediately consented, and got up to fetch the burning sticks he asked for; but before she gave them to him, she and her companions threw upon them a certain powder, containing a very potent charm; and no sooner did the Rajah receive them than he forgot about his wife and little child, his journey, and all that had ever happened to him in his life before; such was the peculiar property of the powder. And when the conjurers said to him, "Why should you go away? stay with us, and be one of us," he willingly consented to do so.

All this time Panch-Phul Ranee waited and waited for her husband, but he never came. Night approached without his having brought her any food or news of having found a place of shelter for her and the baby. At last, faint and weary, she swooned away.

It happened that that very day the Ranee (Panch-Phul Ranee's husband's mother) lost her youngest child, a fine little boy of only a day old; and her servants took its body to the bottom of the garden to bury it. Just as they were going to do so, they heard a low cry, and, looking round, saw close by a beautiful woman lying on the ground, dead, or apparently so, and beside her a fine little baby boy. The idea immediately entered their heads of leaving the dead baby beside the dead woman, and taking her living baby back with them to the palace; and so they did.

When they returned, they said to their mistress, "Your child did not die; see, here it is — it got well again," and showed her Panch-Phul Ranee's baby; but after a time, when the Ranee questioned them about it, they told her the whole truth, but she had become meanwhile very fond of the little boy, and so he continued in the palace and was brought up as her son; being, in truth, her grandson, though she did not know it.

Meantime the palace Malee's wife went out, as her custom was every morning and evening, to gather flowers. In search of them she wandered as far as the jungle at the bottom of the garden, and there she found the Panch-Phul Ranee lying as dead, and the dead baby beside her.

The good woman felt very sorry, and rubbed the Ranee's cold hands and gave her sweet flowers to smell, in hopes that she might revive. At last she opened her eyes, and seeing the Malee's wife, said, "Where am I? has not my husband come back? and who are you?"

"My poor lady," answered the Malee's wife, "I do not know where your husband is. I am the Malee's wife, and coming here to gather flowers, I found you lying on the ground, and this your little baby, which is dead; but come home with me, I will take care of you."

Panch-Phul Ranee answered, "Kind friend, this is not my baby; he did not die; he was the image of his father, and fairer than this child. Some one must have taken him away, for but a little while ago I held him in my arms, and he was strong and well, while this one could never have been more than a puny, weakly infant. Take me away; I will go home with you."

So the Malee's wife buried the dead child and took the Panch-Phul Ranee to her house, where she lived for fourteen years; but all that time she could learn no tidings of her husband or her lost little boy. The child, meanwhile, grew up in the palace, and became a very handsome youth. One day he was wandering round the garden and chanced to pass the Malee's house. The Panch-Phul Rance was sitting within, watching the Malee's wife cook their dinner.

The young prince saw her, and calling the Malee's wife, said to her, "What beautiful lady is that in your house? and how did she come there?" She answered, "Little prince, what nonsense you talk! there is no lady here." He said again, "I know there is a beautiful lady here, for I saw her as I passed the open door." She replied, "If you come telling such tales about my house, I'll pull your tongue out." For she thought to herself, "Unless I scold him well, the boy'll go talking about what he's seen in the palace, and then perhaps some of the people from there will come and take the poor Panch-Phul Ranee away from my care." But whilst the Malee's wife was talking to the young Prince, the Panch-

Phul Ranee came from the inner room to watch and listen to him unobserved; and no sooner did she see him than she could not forbear crying out, "Oh, how like he is to my husband! The same eyes, the same shaped face, and the same king-like bearing! Can he be my son? He is just the age my son would have been had he lived."

The young prince heard her speaking and asked what she said, to which the Malee's wife replied, "The woman you saw, and who just now spoke, lost her child fourteen years ago, and she was saying to herself how like you were to that child, and thinking you must be the same; but she is wrong, for we know you are the Ranee's son." Then Panch-Phul Ranee herself came out of the house, and said to him, "Young prince, I could not, when I saw you, help exclaiming how like you are to what my lost husband was, and to what my son might have been; for it is now fourteen years since I lost them both." And she told him how she had been a great princess, and was returning with her husband to his own home (to which they had got halfway in reaching that place), and how her little baby had been born in the jungle, and her husband had gone away to seek shelter for her and the child, and fire and food, and had never returned; and also how, when she had fainted away, some one had certainly stolen her baby and left a dead child in its place; and how the good Malee's wife had befriended her, and taken her ever since to live in her house. And when she had ended her story she began to cry.

But the prince said to her, "Be of good cheer; I will endeavor to recover your husband and child for you: who knows but I may indeed be your son, beautiful lady?" And running home to the Ranee (his adopted mother), he said to her, "Are you really my mother? Tell me truly; for this I must know before the sun goes down." "Why do you ask foolish questions?" she replied; "have I not always treated you as a son?" "Yes," he said; "but tell me the very truth, am I your own child, or the child of some one else, adopted as yours? If you do not tell me, I will kill myself." And so saying, he drew his sword. She replied, "Stay, stay, and I will tell you the whole truth: the day before you were born I had a little baby, but it died; and my servants took it to the bottom of the garden to bury it, and there they found a beautiful woman lying as dead, and beside her a living infant. You were that child. They brought you to the palace, and I adopted you as my son, and left my baby in your stead." "What became of my mother?" he asked. "I cannot tell," answered the Ranee; "for two days afterward, when I sent to the same place, she and the baby had both disappeared, and I have never since heard of her."

The young Prince, on hearing this, said, "There is in the head Malee's house a beautiful lady, whom the Malee's wife found in the jungle fourteen years ago; that must be my mother. Let her be received here this very day with all honor, for that is the only reparation that can now be made to her."

The Ranee consented, and the young prince went down to the Malee's house himself to fetch his mother to the palace.

With him he took a great retinue of people, and a beautiful palanquin for her to go in, covered with rich

479

trappings; also costly things for her to wear, and many jewels and presents for the good Malee's wife.

When Panch-Phul Ranee had put on her son's gifts, and come out of the Malee's poor cottage to meet him, all the people said there had never been so royal-looking a queen. As gold and clear crystal are lovely, as mother-of-pearl is exquisitely fair and delicate-looking, so beautiful, so fair, so delicate appeared Panch-Phul Ranee.

Her son conducted her with much pomp and state to the palace, and did all in his power to honor her; and there she lived long very happily, and beloved by all.

One day the young prince begged her to tell him again, from the beginning, the story of her life, and as much as she knew of his father's life; and so she did. And after that he said to her, "Be no longer sad, dear mother, regarding my father's fate; for I will send into all lands to gather tidings of him, and maybe in the end we shall find him." And he sent people out to hunt for the Rajah all over the kingdom, and in all neighboring countries, — to the north, to the south, to the east, and to the west, — but they found him not.

At last (after four years of unsuccessful search), when there seemed no hope of ever learning what had become of him, Panch-Phul Ranee's son came to see her, and said, "Mother, I have sent into all lands seeking my father, but can hear no news of him. If there were only the slightest clue as to the direction in which he went, there would still be some chance of tracing him, but that, I fear, cannot be got. Do you not remember his having said anything of the way which he intended to go when he left you?" She answered, "When your father went away, his words to me were, 'I will go to fetch food for us both, and fire to cook it with, and inquire what this country is, and seek out a place of shelter for you. Do not be afraid — I shall soon return.' That was all he said, and then he went away, and I never saw him more."

"In what direction did he go from the foot of the garden?" asked the prince. "He went," answered the Panch-Phul Ranee, "toward that village of conjurers close by. I thought he was intending to ask some of them to give us food. But had he done so, he would certainly have returned in a very short time."

"Do you think you should know my father, mother darling, if you were to see him again?" asked the prince. "Yes," answered she, "I should know him again." "What!" he said, "even though eighteen years have gone by since you saw him last? Even though age and sickness and want had done their utmost to change him?" "Yes!" she replied; "his every feature is so impressed on my heart that I should know him again anywhere or in any disguise."

"Then let us," he said, "send for all those people in the direction of whose houses he went away. Maybe they have detained him among them to this day. It is but a chance, but we can hope for nothing more certain."

So the Panch-Phul Ranee and her son sent down orders to the conjurers' village that every one of the whole band should come up to the palace that afternoon — not a soul was to stay behind. And the dancers were to dance and the conjurers to play all their tricks for the amusement of the palace inmates.

The people came. The nautch girls began to dance — running, jumping, and flying here, there, and everywhere, some up, some down, some round and round. The conjurers conjured, and all began in different ways to amuse the company. Among the rest was one wild, ragged-looking man, whose business was to beat the drum. No sooner did the Panch-Phul Ranee set eyes on him than she said to her son, "Boy, that is your father!" "What, mother!" he said, "that wretched-looking man who is beating the drum?" "The same," she answered.

The prince said to his servants, "Fetch that man here." And the Rajah came toward them, so changed that not even his own mother knew him — no one recognized him but his wife. For eighteen years he had been among the nautch people; his hair was rough, his beard untrimmed, his face thin and worn, sunburnt and wrinkled; he wore a nose-ring and heavy ear-rings such as the nautch people have; and his dress was a rough, common cumlee. All traces of his former self seemed to have disappeared. They asked him if he did not remember he had been a Rajah once, and about his journey to Panch-Phul Ranee's country. But he said, No, he remembered nothing but how to beat the drum — Rub-a-dub! tat-tat! tom-tum! tomtum! He thought he must have beaten it all his life.

Then the young prince gave orders that all the nautch people should be put into jail until it could be discovered what part they had taken in reducing his father to so pitiable a state. And sending for the wisest doctors in the kingdom, he said to them, "Do your best and restore the health of this Rajah, who has to all appearance lost both memory and reason; and discover, if possible, what has caused these misfortunes to befall him." The doctors said, "He has certainly had some potent charm given to him, which has destroyed both his memory and reason, but we will do our best to counteract its influence."

And so they did. And their treatment succeeded so well that, after a time, the Rajah entirely recovered his former senses. And they took such good care of him that in a little while he regained his health and strength also, and looked almost as well as ever.

He then found to his surprise that he, Panch-Phul Ranee, and their son had all this time been living in his father's kingdom. His father was so delighted to see him again that he was no longer unkind to him, but treated him as a dearly beloved, long-lost son. His mother also was overjoyed at his return, and they said to him, "Since you have been restored to us again, why should you wander any more? Your wife and son are here; do you also remain here, and live among us for the rest of your days." But he replied, "I have another wife — the carpenter's daughter — who first was kind to me in my adopted country. I also have there nine hundred and ninety-eight talking wooden parrots, which I greatly prize. Let me first go and fetch them."

They said, "Very well; go quickly and then return." So he mounted the two wooden parrots which had brought him from the Panch-Phul Ranee's country (and which had for eighteen years lived in the jungle close to the palace), and returned to the land where his first wife lived, and fetched her and the nine hundred and ninety-eight remaining wooden parrots to his father's kingdom. Then his father said to him, "Don't have any quarreling with your half-brother after I am dead " (for his half-brother was son of the old Rajah's favorite wife). "I love you both dearly, and will give each of you half of my kingdom." So he divided the kingdom into two halves, and gave the one half to the Panch-Phul Ranee's husband, who was the son of his first wife, and the other half to the eldest son of his second but favorite wife.

A short time after this arrangement was made, Panch-Phul Ranee said to her husband, "I wish to see my father and mother again before I die; let me go and see them." He answered, "You shall go, and I and our son will also go." So he called four of the wooden parrots — two to carry himself and the Ranee, and two to carry their son. Each pair of parrots crossed their wings; the young prince sat upon the two wings of one pair, and on the wings of the other pair sat his father and mother. Then they all rose up in the air, and the parrots carried them (as they had before carried the Rajah alone) up, up, up, on, on, on, over the Red Sea, and across the seven seas, until they reached the Panch-Phul Ranee's country.

Panch-Phul Ranee's father saw them come flying through the air as quickly as shooting stars, and much wondering who they were, he sent out many of his nobles and chief officers to inquire.

The nobles went out to meet them, and called out, "What great Rajah is this who is dressed so royally and comes flying through the air so fast? Tell us, that we may tell our Rajah."

The Rajah answered, "Go and tell your master that this is Panch-Phul Ranee's husband, come to visit his father-in-law." So they took that answer back to the palace; but when the Rajah heard it, he said, "I cannot tell what this means, for the Panch-Phul Ranee's husband died long ago. It is twenty years since he fell upon the iron spears and died; let us, however, all go and discover who this great Rajah really is." And he and all his court went out to meet the newcomers just as the parrots had alighted close to the palace gate. The Panch-Phul Ranee took her son by the one hand and her husband by the other, and walking to meet her father, said, "Father, I have come to see you again. This is my husband who died, and this boy is my son." Then all the land was glad to see the Panch Phul Ranee back, and the people said, "Our princess is the most beautiful princess in the world, and her husband is as handsome as she is, and her son is a fair boy; we will that they should always live among us and reign over us."

When they had rested a little, the Panch-Phul Ranee told her father and mother the story of all her adventures from the time she and her husband were left in the palkees in the jungle. And when they had heard it, her father said to the Rajah, her husband, "You must never go away again; for see, I have no son but you. You and your son must reign here after me. And behold all this great kingdom will I now give you, if you will only stay with us; for I am old and weary of governing the land."

But the Rajah answered, "I must return once again to my own country, and then I will stay with you as long as I live."

So, leaving the Panch-Phul Ranee and her son with the old Rajah and Ranee, he mounted his parrots and once more returned to his father's land. And when he had reached it, he said to his mother, "Mother, my father-in-law has given me a kingdom ten thousand times larger than this. So I have but returned to bid you farewell and fetch my first wife, and then I must go back to live in that other land." She answered, "Very well; so you are happy anywhere, I am happy too."

He then said to his half-brother, "Brother, my father-in-law has given me all the Panch-Phul Ranee's country, which is very far away; therefore I give up to you the half of this kingdom that my father gave to me." Then bidding his father farewell, he took the carpenter's daughter back with him (riding through the air on two of the wooden parrots, and followed by the rest) to the Panch-Phul Ranee's country, and there he and his two wives and his son lived very happily all their mortal days.

CHANDRA'S VENGEANCE

By M. Frere

THERE was once a Sowkar's wife who had no children; one day she went crying to her husband and saying, "What an unhappy woman I am to have no children! If I had any children to amuse me I should be quite happy." He answered, "Why should you be miserable on that account; though you have no children, your sister has eight or nine; why not adopt one of hers?" The Sowkar's wife agreed, and, adopting one of her sister's little boys, who was only six months old, brought him up as her own son. Some time afterward, when the child was one day returning from school, he and one of his schoolfellows quarreled and began to fight, and the other boy (being much the older and stronger of the two) gave him a great blow on the head and knocked him down, and hurt him very much. The boy ran crying home, and the Sowkar's wife bathed his head and bandaged it up, but she did not send and punish the boy who hurt him, for she thought, "One can't keep children shut up always in the house, and they will be fighting together sometimes and hurting themselves." Then the child grumbled to himself, saying, "This is only my aunt; that is why she did not punish the other boy. If she had been my mother, she would certainly have given him a great knock on his head to punish him for knocking mine, but because she is only my aunt, I suppose she does n't care." The Sowkar's wife overheard him, and felt very much grieved, saying, "This little child, whom I have watched over from his babyhood, does not love me as if I were his mother. It is of no use; he is not my own, and he will never care for me as such." So she took him home to his own mother, saying, "Sister, I have brought you back your child." "How is this?" asked her sister. "You adopted him as yours for all his life. Why do you now bring him back?" The Sowkar's wife did not tell her sister what she had heard the boy say, but she answered, "Very well, let him be yours and mine: he shall live a while with you, and then come and visit me; we will both take care of him." And returning to her husband, she told him what she had done, saying, "All my pains are useless; you know how kind I have been to my sister's boy, yet after all I have done for him, at the end of seven years he does not love me as well as he does his mother, whom he had scarcely seen. Now, therefore, I will never rest until I have seen Mahdeo and asked him to grant that I may have a child of my own."

"What a foolish woman you are!" answered her husband; "why not be content with your lot? How do you think you will find Mahdeo? Do you know the road to heaven?" "Nay," she replied, "but I will seek for it until I find it out, and if I never find it, it cannot be helped, but I will return home no more unless my prayer is answered." So she left the house, and wandered into the jungle, and after she had traveled through it for many, many days, and left her own land very far behind, she came to the borders of another country, even the Madura Tinivelly country, where a great river rolled down toward the sea. On the river-bank sat two women — a Ranee named Coplinghee Ranee and a nautch woman.

Now, neither the Ranee, the nautch woman, nor the Sowkar's wife had ever seen each other before they met at the river-side. Then, as they sat down to rest and drink some of the water, the Ranee turned to the Sowkar's wife and said to her, "Who are you, and where are you going?" She answered, "I am a Sowkar's wife from a far country, and because I was very unhappy at having no children, I am going to find Mahdeo and ask him to grant that I may have a child of my own."

Then in her turn she said to the Ranee, "And pray who are you, and where are you going?" The Ranee answered, "I am Coplinghee Ranee, queen of all this country, but neither money nor riches can give me joy, for I have no children; I therefore am going to seek Mahdeo and ask him to grant that I may have a child." Then Coplinghee Ranee asked the nautch woman the same question, saying, "And who may you be, and where are you going?" The nautch woman answered, "I am a dancing woman and I also have no children, and am going to seek Mahdeo and pray to him for a child." At hearing this, the Sowkar's wife said, "Since we are all journeying on the same errand, why should we not go together?" To this Coplinghee Ranee and the dancing woman agreed, so they all three continued their journey together through the jungle.

On, on, on they went, every day farther and farther; they never stayed to rest nor saw another human being. Their feet ached dreadfully and their clothes wore out, and they had nothing to live on but the jungle plants, wild berries, and seeds. So weary and worn did they become that they looked like three poor old beggar women. Never had they by night-time sleep nor by day-time rest; and so, hour after hour, month after month, year after year, they traveled on.

At last one day they came to where, in the midst of the jungle, there rolled a great river of fire. It was the biggest river they had ever seen, and made of flames instead of water. There was no one on this side and no one on that, — no way of getting across but by walking through the fire.

When Coplinghee Ranee and the nautch woman saw this, they said, "Alas! here is the end of all our pains and trouble. All hope is over, for we can go no farther." But the Sowkar's wife answered, "Shall we be deterred by this after having come so far? Nay, rather seek a way across the fire." And so saying, she stepped into the fire waves; the others, however, were afraid, and would not go. When the Sowkar's wife had half crossed the river of fire, she turned, and waving her hands toward them, said, "Come on, come on, do not be afraid. The fire does not burn me. I go to find Mahdeo; perhaps he is on the other side." But they still refused, saying, "We cannot come, but we will wait here until your return; and if you find Mahdeo, pray for us also, that we may have children."

So the Sowkar's wife went on her way, and the fire-waves lapped round her feet as if they had been water, but they did not hurt her.

When she reached the other side of the river she came upon a great wilderness, full of wild elephants and buffaloes and lions and tigers and bears, that roared and growled on every side. But she did not turn back for fear of them, for she said to herself, "I can but die once, and it is better that they should kill me than that I should return without finding Mahdeo." And all the wild beasts allowed her to pass through the midst of them and did her no harm.

Now it came to pass that Mahdeo looked down from heaven and saw her, and when he saw her he pitied her greatly, for she had been twelve years wandering upon the face of the earth to find him. Then he caused a beautiful mango tree, beside a fair well, to spring up in the desert to give her rest and refreshment, and he himself, in the disguise of a Gosain fakeer, came and stood by the tree. But the Sowkar's wife would not stay to gather the fruit or drink the water; she did not so much as notice the fakeer, but walked straight on in her weary search for Mahdeo. Then he called after her, "Bai, Bai, where are you going? Come here." She answered, scarcely looking at him, "It matters not to you, fakeer, where I am going. You tell your prayer-beads and leave me alone." "Come here," he cried; "come here." But she would not, so Mahdeo went and stood in front of her, no longer disguised as a fakeer, but shining brightly, the Lord of Kylas in all his beauty; and at the sight of him the poor Sowkar's wife fell down on the ground and kissed his feet, and

he said to her, "Tell me, Bai, where are you going?"
She answered, "Sir, I seek Mahdeo, to pray him to grant
that I may have a child, but for twelve years I have
looked for him in vain." He said, "Seek no farther,
for I am Mahdeo; take this mango," and he gathered
one off the tree that grew by the well, "and eat it,
and it shall come to pass that when you return home
you shall have a child." Then she said, "Sir, three
women came seeking you, but two stayed by the river
of fire, for they were afraid; may not they also have
children?"

"If you will," he answered, "you may give them
some of your mango, and then they also will each have
a child."

So saying, he faded from her sight, and the Sowkar's
wife returned glad and joyful, through the wilderness
and the river of fire, to where the Ranee and the dancing woman were waiting for her on the other side.
When they saw her, they said, "Well, Sowkar's wife,
what news?" She answered, "I have found Mahdeo,
and he has given me this mango, of which if we eat
we shall each have a child." And she took the mango,
and squeezing it gave the juice to the Ranee, and the
skin she gave to the nautch woman, and the pulp and
the stone she ate herself.

Then these three women returned to their own homes,
— Coplinghee Ranee and the dancing woman to the
Madura Tinivelly country, and the Sowkar's wife
to very, very far beyond that, even the land where her
husband lived, and whence she had first started on her
journey.

But on their return all their friends only laughed at them, and the Sowkar said to his wife, "I cannot see much good in your mad twelve years' journey; you only come back looking like a beggar, and all the world laughs at you."

"I don't care," she answered; "I have seen Mahdeo and eaten of the mango, and I shall have a child."

And within a little while it came to pass that there was born to the Sowkar and his wife a little son, and on the very same day Coplinghee Ranee had a daughter and the nautch woman had a daughter.

Then were they all very happy, and sent everywhere to tell their friends the good news; and each gave, according to her power, a great feast to the poor as a thank-offering to Mahdeo, who had been merciful to them. And the Sowkar's wife called her son "Koila," in memory of the mango stone; and the nautch woman called her daughter "Moulee;" and the little princess was named Chandra Bai, for she was as fair and beautiful as the white moon.

Chandra Ranee was very beautiful, the most beautiful child in all that country, so pretty and delicately made that everybody who saw her loved her. She was born, moreover, with two of the most costly anklets on her ankles, that ever were seen. They were made of gold and very precious stones, dazzling to look at, like the sun. No one had ever seen any like them before. Every day, as the baby grew, these bangles grew, and round them were little bells, which tinkled when any one came near. Chandra's parents were very happy and proud, and sent for all the wise men in the kingdom to tell her fortune. But the most learned Brahmin of them all, when he saw her, said, "This child must be sent out of the country at once, for if she stays in it she will destroy all the land with fire and burn it utterly."

The Rajah, at hearing these words, was very angry, and said to the Brahmin, "I will cut off your head, for you tell lies and not the truth." The Brahmin answered, "Cut off my head if you will, but it is the truth I speak, and no lie. If you do not believe me, let a little wool be fetched, and put it upon the child, that you may know my words are true."

So they fetched some wool and laid it upon the baby, and no sooner had they done so than it all blazed up and burnt till not a bit was left, and it scorched the hands of the attendants.

Then the Brahmin said, "As this fire has burnt the wool, so will this princess one day, if she comes here, burn this whole land." And they were all very much frightened, and the Rajah said to the Ranee, "This being so, the child must be sent out of the country instantly." The poor Ranee thereat was very sad, and she did all in her power to save her little baby, but the Rajah would not hear of it, and commanded that the princess should be placed in a large box, and taken to the borders of his land, where a great river rolled down to the sea, and there thrown into the stream, that it might carry her far, far away, each minute farther from her native land. Then the Ranee caused a beautiful golden box to be made, and put her little baby in it with many tears (since all her efforts to save it were of no avail), and it was taken away and thrown into the river.

The box floated on, and on, and on, until at last it reached the country where the Sowkar and the Sowkar's wife lived. Now it chanced that, just as the box was floating by, the Sowkar, who had gone down to the river to wash his face, caught sight of it; and seeing a fisherman not far off prepared to throw his net into the water, he cried, "Run, fisherman, run, run! do not stop to fish, but cast your net over that glittering box and bring it here to me!"

"I will not, unless you promise me that the box shall be mine," said the fisherman. "Very well," answered the Sowkar, "the box shall be yours, and whatever it contains shall belong to me."

So the fisherman cast his net in that part of the river and dragged the box ashore.

I don't know which was more astonished — the merchant or the fisherman — when they saw what a prize they had found. For the box was composed entirely of gold and precious stones, and within it lay the most lovely little child that ever was seen.

She seemed a little princess, for her dress was all made of cloth of gold, and on her feet were two anklets that shone like the sun.

When the Sowkar opened the box, she smiled, and stretched out her little arms toward him. Then he was pleased, and said, "Fisherman, the box is yours, but this child must belong to me." The fisherman was content that it should be so, for he had many children of his own at home, and wanted no more.

but was glad to have the golden box; while the Sowkar, who had only his one little son and was rich, did not care for the box, but was well pleased to have the baby.

He took her home to his wife, and said, "See, wife, here is a pretty little daughter-in-law for us. Here is a wife for your little son." And when the Sowkar's wife saw the child looking so beautiful and smiling so sweetly, her heart was glad and she loved her, and from that day took the greatest care of her, just as if the baby girl had been her own daughter. And when Chandra Ranee was a year old they married her to their son, Koila.

Years wore on, and the Sowkar and his wife were in a good old age gathered to their fathers. Meantime, Koila and Chandra had grown up the handsomest couple in all the country: Koila tall and straight, with a face like a young lion, and Chandra as lithe and graceful as a palm tree, with a face calm and beautiful like the silver moonlight.

Meantime Moulee, the nautch woman's daughter (and third of the mango children), had likewise grown up in the Madura Tinivelly country, and was also very fair — fairer than any one in all the land around. Moreover, she danced and sang more beautifully than any of the other nautch girls. Her voice was clear as the voice of a quail, and it rang through the air with such power that the sound could be heard a twelve days' journey off. The nautch people used to travel about from place to place, staying one day in one town and the next in another, and so it happened

496

that in their wanderings they reached the borders of the land where Koila and Chandra lived.

One morning Koila heard the sound of singing in the distance, and it pleased him so well that he determined to try and discover who it was that possessed such an exquisite voice. For twelve days he journeyed on through the jungle, each day hearing the singing repeated louder and louder, yet still without reaching the place whence it came. At last, on the twelfth day, he got close to the nautch people's encampment, not far from a large town, and there saw the singer (who was none other than Moulee), singing and dancing in the midst of a great crowd of people who had collected around her. In her hand she held a garland of flowers, which she waved over her head as she danced.

Koila was so charmed with the sound of her voice that he felt spellbound, and stood where he was, far off on the outskirts of the jungle, listening, without going any nearer.

When the entertainment was over, all the people crowded round Moulee, saying, "Why should you, who have such a beautiful voice, go away and leave our city? Marry one of us, and then you will stay here always." Then, the number of her suitors being so great that she did not know whom to choose, she said, "Very well; he on whose neck this garland falls shall be my husband." And waving the flowers she held two or three times round her head, she threw them from her with her utmost force.

The impetus given to the garland was so great that

it swung through the air beyond the crowd and fell upon the neck of Koila as he stood by the borders of the jungle. And the people ran to see who was the fortunate possessor, and when they saw Koila they were astonished, for he looked more beautiful than any of the sons of men: it was as if an immortal had suddenly come among them. And the nautch people dragged him back to their camp, crying, "You have won the garland; you must be Moulee's husband." He answered, "I only came here to look on; I cannot stay. This is not my country; I have a wife of my own at home." "That is nothing to us," they said; "it is your destiny to marry Moulee — Moulee the beautiful one — Moulee, whose voice you heard and who dances so well. You must marry her, for the garland fell on you."

Now so it was that though Koila was very kind to his wife, he did not love her as well as she loved him (perhaps it was that, having been accustomed to her from a child, Chandra's goodness and beauty struck him less than it did other people); and instead of thinking how unhappy she would be if he did not return, and going back at once, he stopped and hesitated and debated what to do. And the nautch people gave him a drink that was a very powerful spell, insomuch that he soon totally forgot about his own home, and was married to Moulee, the nautch girl, and lived among the nautch people for many months. At last, one day, Moulee's mother (the very nautch woman who had gone with Coplinghee Ranee and the Sowkar's wife to find Mahdeo) said to Koila, "Son-in-law, you are a lazy fellow; you have been here now for a long time, but you do nothing for your support; it is we who have to pay for your food, we who have to provide your clothes. Go now and fetch us some money, or I will turn you out of the house, and you shall never see your wife Moulee again." Koila had no money to give his mother-in-law: then for the first time he bethought him of his own country and of Chandra, and he said, "My first wife, who lives in my own country, has on her feet two bangles of very great value; let me return home and fetch one of them to sell, which will more than pay whatever I owe you." The nautch people consented. So Koila returned to his own home, and told Chandra what he wanted the money for, and asked her to let him have one of her bangles; but she refused, saying, "You have been away a long, long time, and left me all alone, and chosen for your second wife one of the nautch people, and become one of them; and now you want to take one of my bangles — the bangles that I had when a little child, that have grown with my growth, and never been taken off — and to give it to your other wife. This shall not be; go back, if you will, to your new friends, but I will not give you my bangle."

He answered, "They gave me an enchanted drink which made me forget you for a time, but I am weary of them all; let me but go and pay my mother-in-law the money I owe her for food and clothes, and I will return and live in my own land, for you are my first wife."

"Very well," she said, "you may take the bangle and sell it, and give the money to your second wife's mother, but take me also with you when you go; do not leave me here all alone again." Koila agreed, and they both set off together toward the Madura Tinivelly country.

As they journeyed, Krishnaswami, who was playing at cards with his three wives, saw them, and when he saw them he laughed. Then his wives said to him, "Why do you laugh? You have not laughed for such a long time: what amuses you so much now?" He answered, "I am laughing to see Koila and his wife Chandra Ranee journeying toward the Madura Tinivelly country. He is going to sell his wife's bangle, and he will only be killed, and then she in anger will burn up all the country. O foolish people!" The goddesses answered, "This is a very dreadful thing; let us go in disguise and warn him not to enter the country." "It would be useless," said Krishnaswami; "if you do, he will only laugh at you and get angry with you." But the goddesses determined to do their best to avert the threatened calamity. So they disguised themselves as old fortune-tellers, and went out with little lamps and their sacred books to meet Koila as he came along the road, followed by his wife. Then they said to him, "Come not into the Madura Tinivelly country, for if you come you will be killed, and your wife in her fury will burn all the land with fire." At first Koila would not listen to them; then he bade them go away; and lastly, when they continued warning him, got angry and beat them out of his path, saying, "Do you think I am to be frightened out of the country by a parcel of old crones like you?"

Then Krishnaswami's three wives returned to him, much enraged at the treatment they had received; but he only said to them, "Did I not tell you not to go, warning you that it would be useless?"

On getting near the Rajah's capital, Koila and Chandra came to the house of an old milk-seller, who was very kind to them and gave them food and shelter for the night. Next morning Koila said to his wife, "You had better stay here; this good old woman will take care of you while I go into the town to sell your bangle." Chandra agreed, and remained at the old woman's house while her husband went into the town. Of course he did not know that the Rajah and his wife (the Coplinghee Ranee) were Chandra's father and mother, any more than they or Chandra herself knew it, or than the three mango children knew the story of their mothers' journey in search of Mahdeo.

Now a short time before Koila and Chandra reached the Madura Tinivelly country, Coplinghee Ranee had sent a very handsome pair of bangles to a jeweler in the town to be cleaned. It chanced that in a high tree close to the jeweler's house two eagles had built their nest, and the young eagles, who were very noisy birds, used to scream all day long and greatly disturb the jeweler's family. So one day, when the old birds were away, the jeweler's son climbed up the tree and pulled down the nest, and put the young eagles to death. When the old birds returned home and saw what was done, it grieved them very much, and they said, "These cruel people have killed our children; let us punish them." And seeing in the porch one of Coplinghee

Ranee's beautiful bangles, which the jeweler had just been cleaning, they swooped down and flew away with it.

The jeweler did not know what to do. He said to his wife, "To buy such a bangle as that would cost more than all our fortune, and to make one like it would take many, many years; I dare not say I have lost it, or they would think I had stolen it and would put me to death. The only thing I can do is to delay returning the other as long as possible, and try somehow to get one like it." So next day, when the Ranee sent to inquire if her bangles were ready, he answered, "They are not ready yet; they will be ready to-morrow." And the next day and the next he said the same thing. At last the Ranee's messengers got very angry at the continued delays; then, seeing he could no longer make excuses, the jeweler sent the one bangle by them to the palace, beautifully cleaned, with a message that the other also would shortly be ready; but all this time he was hunting for a bangle costly enough to take the Ranee as a substitute for the one the eagles had carried away. Such a bangle, however, he could not find.

When Koila reached the town, he spread out a sheet in the corner of a street near the market-place, and, placing the bangle upon it, sat down close by, waiting for customers. Now he was very, very handsome. Although dressed so plainly, he looked like a prince, and the bangle he had to sell flashed in the morning light like seven suns. Such a handsome youth and such a beautiful bangle the people had never seen before; and many passers-by, with chattees on their heads, let the chattees tumble down and break for watching him, they were so much astonished; and several men and women who were looking out of the windows of their houses, leaned too far forward and fell into the street, so giddy did they become from wonder and amazement!

But no one could be found to buy the bangle, for they all said, "We could not afford to buy such jewels; this bangle is fit only for a Ranee to wear." At last, when the day had nearly gone, who should come by but the jeweler who had been employed to clean Coplinghee Ranee's bangles, and was in search of one to replace that which the eagles had stolen. No sooner did he see the one belonging to Chandra, which Koila was trying to sell, than he said to himself, "That is the very thing I want, if I can only get it." So he called his wife, and said to her, "Go to that bangle-seller and speak kindly to him; say that the day is nearly gone, and invite him to come and lodge at our house for the night. For if we can make friends with him and get him to trust us, I shall be able to take the bangle from him and say he stole it from me. And as he is a stranger here, every one will believe my word rather than his. This bangle is exactly the very thing for me to take Coplinghee Ranee, for it is very like her own, only more beautiful."

The jeweler's wife did as she was told, and then the jeweler himself went up to Koila and said to him, "You are a bangle-seller, and I am a bangle-seller; therefore I look upon you as a brother. Come home, I pray you, with us, as my wife begs you to do, and we will give you food and shelter for the night, since you are a stranger in this country." So these cunning people coaxed Koila to go home with them, and pretended to be very kind to him, and gave him supper, and a bed to rest on for the night; but next morning early the jeweler raised a hue and cry and sent for the police, and bade them take Koila before the Rajah instantly, since he had stolen and tried to sell one of Coplinghee Ranee's bangles, which he (the jeweler) had been given to clean. It was in vain that Koila protested his innocence, and declared that the bangle he had belonged to his wife; he was a stranger — nobody would believe him. They dragged him to the palace, and the jeweler accused him to the Rajah, saying, "This man tried to steal the Ranee's bangle (which I had been given to clean) and to sell it. If he had done so, you would have thought I had stolen it, and killed me; I demand, therefore, that he in punishment shall be put to death."

Then they sent for the Ranee to show her the bangle, but as soon as she saw it she recognized it as one of the bangles which had belonged to Chandra, and burst into tears, crying, "This is not my bangle. Oh, my lord, no jeweler on earth made this bangle! See, it is different from mine; and when any one comes near it, it tinkles and all the little bells begin to ring. Have you forgotten it? This was my beauty's bangle! My diamond's! My little darling's! My lost child's! Where did it come from? How did it come here? How into this land, and into this town and bazaar, among these wicked people? For this jeweler must have kept my bangle and brought this one in its place. No human goldsmith's hands made this, for it is none other than Chandra's." Then she begged the Rajah to inquire further about it.

But they all thought her mad; and the jeweler said, "It is the Ranee's fancy, for this is the same bangle she gave me to clean." The other people also agreed that both the bangles were almost exactly alike, and must be a pair; and it being certain that Koila had had the bangle when he was seized by the police, the Rajah ordered him to be instantly executed. But the Ranee took Chandra's bangle and locked it away in a strong cupboard, apart from all her other jewels.

Then they took Koila out into the jungle and would have cut off his head, but he said to his guards, "If I must die, let me die by my own hands," and drawing his sword he fell upon it; and as the sword was very sharp it cut his body in two—one half fell on one side of the sword, and the other half on the other side — and they left his body where it fell.

When the news of what had taken place came to the town, many people who had seen Koila selling his bangle the day before began to murmur, saying, "There must be some injustice here — the Rajah has been over-hasty. Most likely the poor man did not steal the bangle. It is not likely that he would have tried to sell it openly before us all in the bazaar if it had been stolen property. How cruel of the Rajah to put such a handsome, gentle, noble-looking youth to death! — and he was a stranger, too!" And many wept at thought of his hard fate. When the Rajah heard of this

505

he was very angry, and sent and commanded that the matter should be no further discussed in the town, saying, "If any one speaks another word of what has been done, or laments or sheds tears for the dead, he shall be instantly hanged." Then the people all felt much frightened, and not a soul dared to speak of Koila, though every one thought about him.

Early the very morning that this happened the old milk-seller (at whose house, which was a little out of the town, Chandra had been sleeping) took her guest a bowl full of milk to drink; but no sooner had Chandra tasted it than she began to cry, saying, "Good mother, what have you done? my mouth is full of blood!" "No, no, my daughter," answered the old woman; "you must have been dreaming some bad dream. See, this is pure, fresh, warm milk I have brought you; drink again." But when Chandra tasted it for the second time, she answered, "Oh, no! oh no! it is not milk that I taste, but blood. All last night I had a dreadful dream, and this morning when I woke I found that my marriage necklace had snapped in two; and now this milk tastes to me as blood. Let me go! let me go! for I know my husband is dead."

The old woman tried to comfort her, saying, "Why should you fancy he is dead? he was quite well yesterday, when he went to sell your bangle; and he said he would come back to you soon; in a little while, very likely, he will be here." But she answered, "No, no; I feel sure that he is dead! Oh, let me go! for I must find him before I die." Then the old woman said, "You must not go; you are too beautiful to run

about through the streets of this strange town alone,
and your husband would be very angry if he saw you
doing so; and who knows but that you might lose
your way, and get carried off as a slave; remember,
he told you to stay here till he returned. Be patient;
remain where you are, and I will go quickly into the
town and seek your husband. If he is alive, I will
bring him back to you, and if he is dead I will bring
you word." So, taking a chattee full of milk on her
head, as if to sell, she went to the town to find Koila,
while every minute seemed an hour to Chandra until
her return.

When the old milk-seller reached the town, she
went up and down all the streets looking for Koila, or
expecting to hear some one mention the handsome
stranger who had gone to sell such a wonderful bangle
the day before. But she could not find him, nor did she
hear him spoken of, for all were afraid to say a word
about him on account of the Rajah's decree. Being
unable to trace him, the old woman got suspicious,
and began to search, more carefully than before, down
all the streets near the market-place, where she thought
he was most likely to have gone; but, lest people should
wonder at her errand, she called out each time as if
she had some different thing to sell. First, "Buy some
milk — who'll buy milk — who'll buy?" Then, on
going for a second time down the same street, "Buy
butter — butter! very fine butter!" and so on. At last
one woman, who had been watching her with some
curiosity, said, "Old woman, what nonsense you talk!
you have been half a dozen times up and down this

same street, as if you had half a dozen different things to sell in that one chattee. Any one would think you had as little sense as that pretty young bangle-seller yesterday, who spent all the day trying to sell a bangle, and got put to death for his pains."

"Of whom do you speak?" asked the old woman. "Oh," said the other, "I suppose, as you're a milk-seller from the country, you know nothing about it. But that's not to be talked about, for the Rajah has said that whoever speaks of him or mourns him shall be instantly hanged. Ah, he was very handsome."

"Where is he now?" whispered the old woman. "There," answered the other; "you can see the place where that crowd of people has collected. The Rajah's jeweler accused him of having stolen the bangle; so he was executed, many thought unjustly; but do not say I said it." And so saying, she pointed toward the jungle some way off. The old woman ran to the place, but when she there saw two halves of Koila's body lying side by side, stiff and cold, she threw her earthen chattee down on the ground and fell on her knees, crying bitterly. The noise attracted the attention of the Rajah's guards, some of whom immediately seized her, saying, "Old woman, it is against the law to lament that dead man or murmur at the Rajah's decree ; you deserve to be put to death." But she answered quickly, "The dead man! I do not cry for the dead man: can you not see that my chattee is broken and all the milk spilt? Is it not enough to make one weep?" And she began to cry again. "Hush! hush! " they answered; "don't cry! Come, the chattee wasn't worth much; it was only an earthen thing. Stop your tears, and maybe we'll give you a chattee of gold."

"I care neither for your golden chattees nor for silver," she said angrily. "Go away; go away! my earthen chattee was worth them all. My grandfather's grandfather and my grandmother's grandmother used this chattee; and to think that it should now be broken and all the milk spilt!" And picking up the broken pieces, she went home sobbing, as if the loss of her chattee was all her grief. But when she got to her own house, she ran in to where Chandra was, crying, "Alas! my pretty child! alas, my daughter! your fears are true!" and as gently as she could she told her what had happened.

No sooner did Chandra hear it than she ran away straight to the Rajah's palace in the midst of the town, and rushing into the room where he was, said, "How did you dare to kill my husband?"

Now, at the sound of her voice, her bangle, which the Ranee had locked up in the cupboard, broke through all the intervening doors and rolled to Chandra's feet.

The Rajah was unable to answer her a word. Then she fell on her knees and rent her clothes and tore her hair; and when she tore it all the land began to burn and all her hair burned too.

Then the old milk-seller, who had followed her, ran and put a lump of butter on her head, thinking to cool it, and two other women, who were by, fetched water to pour upon her hair, but by this time nineteen lines of houses were in flames. Then the old woman cried, "Oh, spare the Pruwari lines; don't burn them down, for I did all I could for you." So Chandra did not burn that part of the town near which the old woman and her friends lived. But the fire burnt on and on in the other direction; and it killed the Rajah and the Ranee and all the people in the palace, and the wicked jeweler and his wife; and as he was dying Chandra tore out his heart and gave it to the eagles who hovered overhead, saying, "Here is vengeance for the death of your little ones." And the nautch girl, Moulee, and her mother, who were watching the fire from far off, were smothered in the flames.

Then Chandra went to where Koila's dead body lay and wept over it bitterly; and as she was weeping, there fell down to her from heaven a needle and thread; and she took them, saying, "Oh, that I could by any means restore you!" and placing the two halves of his body side by side, she sewed them together.

And when she had done this, she cried to Mahdeo, saying, "Sire, I have done the best I can; I have joined the body; give it life." And as she said these words Mahdeo had pity on her, and he sent Koila's spirit back, and it returned to his body again. Then Chandra was glad, and they returned and lived in their own land.

But to this day in the Madura Tinivelly country you can trace where all the land was burnt.

END OF VOLUME II